To My Children

and

In Memory of my sister and my parents

PAMELA SERIES 13

by

Patricia Lee Strunk

PUBLISHED BY AB FILM PUBLISHING
New York USA

ISBN: 978-0-9904852-9-2

Cover Design by Thomas Romano, USA

Published by
AB Film Publishing
290 West 12 Street, Suite A
New York, New York 10014
(212) 741-1441
2015

ACKNOWLEDGEMENTS

I want to thank my children, my "raison d'être," Trevor and Vinciane, from the bottom of my heart for their continued encouragement and belief in me which made it possible for me to persevere and write this story.

I want to extend my heartfelt thanks to my sister, Pamela, who before her untimely death, left me with her impression of a better world and to my parents, Hermana and Robert, whose love and confidence in me throughout their lifetimes have remained my source of strength and determination.

I want to give special thanks to my dear friends, Gwenaëlle who inspired me to write, and Christine and Vasu who gave me praise and reassurance every step of the way. And, finally, I want to thank my brothers, John and William, and other family members and friends who over the last few years, in various ways, prompted me to finish Pamela Series 13.

I want to extend my most profound thanks to Frank Romano, a friend, colleague and author, whose brilliant editorial skills guided me in turning my rough draft into a publishable manuscript; and to the illustrator, Thomas Romano, for his magnificent visual conception of my book.

And finally, I want to extend my sincere and humble thanks to my publisher, Alan Baxter of AB Film Productions, for giving me this extraordinary opportunity to present my manuscript to the public.

Chapter 1: An Omen

That inexplicable sensation of being alive was returning to Captain Michael Hadley, as the cryogenic temperature inside his tightly bound cocoon slowly dissipated and was replaced by warmth, revitalizing him. This was not the first time that Captain Hadley had experienced the exhilarating effect of recovering his physical force and mental processes. He was an experienced astronaut who had voyaged in space for years, maybe even centuries, exploring new worlds. He had no idea how old he was simply because he spent the greater part of his life in suspended animation. He always woke up in a youthful state with his body and mind vigorous and reliable despite his age.

He breathed deeply as he waited for the outer crust of his cocoon to give way permitting him to delicately peel away this exterior and recuperate his true self. He liked to compare his rebirth to that of the metamorphosis of a caterpillar into a butterfly.

As always, his legs and feet were swollen and he had difficulty focusing his eyes through courants of tears, washing away the residue of the cryogenic substance. He moved slowly into the tiny shower where he cleansed his body. He knew the procedure well. He discarded his used cocoon and readied the next one for his return trip, whenever that might be. He sat naked, letting his skin readjust to a natural environment, while he slowly drank a special, good tasting liquid that would recharge his system so that he could accomplish his mission. He then dressed in his khaki-colored uniform. He would wear his military jacket that displayed his name and rank when he disembarked. He took two discrete laser guns, from the weapons unit that he concealed in his jacket, as a precautionary measure. The most complicated task putting on his socks and high black boots he left for last.

He took his seat behind the control panel and looked over the screen. To his dismay, the automatic pilot was still functioning. It should have been flashing yellow by now, reminding him that he would soon have to take over the controls. The guidance system indicated that he was far outside the Earth's atmosphere. "So why was I awakened so soon?" He wondered. The answer came within minutes of this thought.)

"Captain Hadley, we have worrisome news to report." The Commander of the Mother Ship, Colonel Shannon, was on the screen, her face haggard and her eyes blank. "I am going to send you the last communication we received from Captain Daniel Anderson, after he entered the Earth's atmosphere. There is every reason to believe that you should abort your mission and return to our ship."

Captain Hadley felt his heart drop. He had been looking forward to exploring the planet Earth all his life. He wanted to meet those Earthlings imbued with a superior intelligence who were immortalized in legends. The legends spoke of how their genius created a world where Humans lived together in peace and harmony with each other and with nature. A vision of a world where technological perfection brought happiness and comfort to everyone invaded his consciousness. He wanted to stroll along one of those magnificent walkways inside a dome protected city. He wanted to feel the serenity of a perfect world. He was so close to realizing his lifelong dream. He looked closely at the screen. Colonel Shannon was surrounded by her two trusted officers, Ranier and Trend. He was not going to let the three of them deprive him of it. He would not abort his mission, regardless of the risk to his life or his career. Even though anger surged inside of him, he hid his feelings and replied in a voice void of emotion. "I want your permission to continue my descent into the Earth's atmosphere."

"You may change your mind after you hear the communication." The Colonel moved closer to the screen. "Captain Anderson was the only one of many astronauts sent back to explore the planet Earth who was able to send us any message before disappearing. The others just vanished off our screen." She stopped for a second, as if paying homage to their memory. "If we had not received this communication from Captain Anderson we probably would have drawn the same conclusions we drew in the past."

"And, what were those conclusions?" Captain Hadley's voice was bold with defiance.

"We concluded that the spacecraft could not support the gravitational force and that the astronauts died in the crash." She hesitated. "That is why your spacecraft and that of Anderson were reinforced to withstand a difficult entry."

After a long pause from both sides, Captain Hadley picked up the conversation. "So...what did this communication reveal?"

Captain Hadley was definitely a person disposed to skepticism especially where a hierarchy was involved. His impatience was also mounting as he watched the group on the screen desperately trying to locate that famous communication sent off by Captain Anderson. He was ready to stand up and stretch his legs when they started to run the tape. Captain Anderson's voice came through loud and clear. "I am Captain Daniel Anderson, an astronaut of human origin, returning home to the planet Earth."

"We have no record of a human called Daniel Anderson." The receiving party stated in a strange, grating, vibrating voice.

"I am a descendant of the former Daniel Anderson, an astronaut and explorer, who left the planet Earth a long time ago and colonized a distant planet, light years away, in another solar system." The receiving party did not reply so Captain Anderson continued. "I am hovering just above a large circular building and request permission to land within a mile distance of that structure."

"What is the nature of your visit?" The receiving party asked in a resonating voice that sent chills up and down Captain Hadley's spine.

"I request permission to land on the planet that my ancestors inhabited." Captain Anderson repeated his request.

"I need to get authorization and will be back to you rapidly." The receiving party replied.

Within minutes Captain Anderson's voice broke in. "I am being pursued by an unidentified aircraft."

They heard a cryptic order emanating from the receiving party to a member of his staff to intercept and destroy the intruder. The content of this order was in part muddled by the loud, panic-ridden screams of Captain Anderson. "I am under attack. Please send backup to defend me. Are you listening? I need backup. I am coming in friendship. Send me the backup!"

There was a long pause on the tape before another grating, crackling, inhuman voice reported. "Mission accomplished. The intruder has been intercepted and all traces of the vessel destroyed."

Captain Hadley was sitting straight, very straight in his chair. He let the scene repeat itself over and over again in his mind before addressing the Commander. "Colonel Shannon, I agree that something dreadful happened to someone and that someone's vessel was destroyed."

"What are you implying?"

"Who was the intruder? Was the intruder Captain Anderson who was destroyed by another vessel that was pursuing him? Or, was he being pursued by an intruder, who was intercepted by the earthlings and destroyed?"

"We have already considered those scenarios, but that doesn't change the fact that Anderson's mission was far more dangerous than what we had expected. And I have no intention of losing another pilot."

"Perhaps Captain Anderson is alive; maybe injured or unconscious." He was not quite certain where he was going with all of this. "There are many scenarios that could be imagined."

3

"It is too dangerous, though. And there is that ominous voice that is definitely not human. I think that the mission should be aborted."

"I am going to land with or without your permission." He said audaciously. "I am too close to my dream to abandon it now on a pretext." He too shuddered at the sound of that voice but was not ready to abort the mission for that reason alone. "And I am a much better pilot than Captain Anderson was. I know how to dodge aircraft."

"But it is your life that is at stake." Colonel Shannon admonished and then gave him a few minutes to reconsider his decision. She knew that he was stubborn and that there was very little chance that she would be able to convince him to abort the mission. She also knew that he was a distinguished member of her team whose determination and military prowess were rewarded on many occasions. His stern eyes met hers. Yes, she could even understand why it was so important for him to land on the planet Earth. He had explored many celestial bodies in their solar system and returned with vital natural resources. The Earth promised something more for him, an encounter with a life form, and, not just any life form. She pondered their chances of success and determined that Captain Hadley was the right choice for this mission. So in response to his relentless silence, she acquiesced and gave him permission to enter the Earth's atmosphere. She ordered him to keep audio contact even if he left the ship.

He flipped off the autopilot and took over the controls. His enthusiasm was back and he was bursting with energy. He moved rapidly into the Earth's atmosphere. He was trained to respect protocol, like Anderson, and automatically tried to make audio contact. "I am Captain Michael Hadley and request permission to land on the planet Earth."

"Captain Hadley, you have permission to land." An uncontestably human, male voice filled with excitement replied. "Tell me more about yourself and where you will be landing?"

Captain Hadley, as well as Colonel Shannon and her protégés sighed with relief. "I am a descendant of a small community of astronauts and scientists that were sent off to explore the viability of certain planets in the next solar system. They found a planet that was suitable for life. The entire group survived the long journey and gave birth to new generations." He was proud of who he was. He then added something that he prepared years ago, if ever he came in contact with another life form. "We need supplies and equipment as well as qualified personnel willing to return with us to make our world more attractive to explorers and new world pioneers." He was happy, things were going well. "I am sending you my landing coordinates." He said as he entered them into the system.

4

"This is wonderful news. We shall have so much to talk about after you land." The human replied. "But…"

Captain Hadley safely landed the spacecraft and then verified the audio system. It was in perfect condition. "I wonder why we were cut off." He shrugged his shoulders nonchalantly, "I made it! I landed!" He screamed enthusiastically as he gathered up his vest and stepped out of the spacecraft. "Where am I?" he queried in a low, exacerbated voice, as he turned in circles hoping to see something other than the red, barren wasteland that stretched out for miles in front of him. He stopped abruptly. He had the feeling that something was wrong. The death of Anderson and others, the inhuman voice, and the lifelessness of his surroundings stripped him of his confidence and filled him with fear. For the first time in his life, he felt strangely alone and incredibly vulnerable. "Where is the welcoming committee?" He thought as his fear turned to panic giving rise to an onslaught of questions. "What has happened to this planet? It is devastated! There is nothing but barren and scarred land! Have I landed on the Earth? Answer me! Am I on the Planet Earth? Where are you and the others?" In that rapid stream of boisterous questions, Captain Hadley showed his disdain, horror, confusion and contempt for the unmitigated wrongs that befell this beloved Earth. Impelled by an image, whether real or illusory, of the Earth and its illustrious inhabitants, he emitted an anguished scream, as he charged furiously at the object in front of him, beating his fists up against the side of his ship.

And then he heard one of those grating, vibrating, ominous voices. "You will have no answers. This is no longer your world. You are an intruder."

Captain Hadley did not have the time to draw his laser gun. He only had the time for one last thought: "What kind of World is this?"

"Everything is normal. The intruder has been eliminated. Over and Out."

Chapter 2: Awakening

What is real and what is an illusion? Is our vision of life a bit of both? Is how we see ourselves in the world around us all that should ever count?

My world changed so dramatically in such a short time. I lost my focus on what was real and wondered if everything I knew before was only imagined. That world that always seemed so beautiful and euphoric just vanished, ceased to exist...in a few seconds. I was conscious of the frantic need to act quickly in my search to become a part of this new and frightening world surging dramatically inside of me, in my awakening moments. This urge to do something, even anything, regardless of the consequences, grew stronger and stronger, until finally my rational side surfaced, and I resisted and suppressed its impulsiveness, preferring to ponder my situation.

I was awake but refused to open my eyes. I heard a voice deep inside telling me to lie still, while concentrating on avoiding any gestures that would expose my pretended unconsciousness. If I didn't move, no one would know I was alive; as such, no one would try to hurt me. For the first time in my life, I encountered an instinct for survival that was protecting me and controlling my reactions.

I was uncomfortable with the impenetrable silence of my space and had difficulty thinking about something other than its ominous, distracting effect on me. I finally broke free and let my thoughts wander as I tried to put the pieces of the puzzle back in place. I looked deep within the corners of my mind for answers in an attempt to understand what happened. I remembered nothing, until finally, in a violent effort to retrieve an image, a last visual impression, I saw myself entering the cubicle I shared with Jonathan. But then all went blank.

Clearly, I didn't remember what happened to me, but I resolved that I must at least discover where I was at this moment. And yet, I quickly realized that I felt anxious and my body trembled just thinking about where I was. In fact, the more I thought about where I was the more urgent was the need to push up the barriers. Alas, I faltered in my determination; I did nothing. I reasoned that perhaps I didn't know how to proceed or what to do to change my situation; or, perhaps I felt lost and confused; easily imagining myself falling slowly and helplessly into the tight grips of despair. Suddenly I shook myself out of these nightmarish ideas and boldly reached out to recover that desire to survive that I had unwittingly abandoned. Almost immediately, I was in contact with it as it rallied strongly within me, wiping out all my dismal and anquished thoughts, leaving behind a vibrant positive energy. I wholeheartedly embraced this desire to exist that pervaded me, this time giving me the courage to continue to move on in my quest to find answers.

Tempering my movements, I embarked on a discovery of my immediate environment. I contemplated for an instance how much easier it would be if I opened my eyes. But instead, I followed my instinct and remained determined to keep them firmly closed. So, I reacted spontaneously, but cautiously. I let my outstretched hands glide slowly reaching out over the edge of the platform where I found myself. I tried to control my movements by making them as inconspicuous as possible, just in case someone was watching. While exploring the space around me, I discovered that I could easily touch both sides of the platform, the texture and form of a narrow bed, like the one I had as a child. I knew for certain that I was not in that large, spacious bed that Jonathan and I shared for years. I had been taken to a faraway place.

This thought triggered other violent reactions inside of me, as I experienced emotions that I had never known before; feelings that were at the same time exhausting and exhilarating. I discovered later that I was frightened and that I was overcome by fear. But at the time, I didn't know why my body turned so rigid and why my heart beat so rapidly that I heard a sound laboriously pounding my head. I was saturated with drops of water oozing out of every pore of my body. Ironically, I liked the feelings; like a strange excitement. Part of me wanted these feelings to end, the other part longed to discover their limits.

And then within minutes of this surreal discovery, the brutal reality was that I was losing everything. I involuntarily controlled my respiration. Deep breathing calmed me. That phenomenal surge of emotional energy disappeared and I thought that it was gone forever.

So I continued my meticulous scanning of my surroundings. My fumbling fingers_became my eyes and moved slowly over my body, as I desperately sought answers. For a brief instance I imagined with excitement that I could just get up and walk away, that I was not strapped to the bed and I could even lift my legs if I wanted to. And then, I trembled slightly as my fingers stumbled over something that protruded from the upper left hand side of my chest. I had no discomfort unless I moved it about and then a burning pain jolted my side. I gently followed it to its source, discovering the thin, flexible tube that was attached to it. I rightly surmised that this rather tiny object was keeping me rooted to the bed. The more I concentrated on that spot, the more I felt a burning liquid entering into my body; and my heart began to beat strongly and rapidly again. For the first time in my life, I wanted to cry out that I was suffering; that I didn't deserve to be punished.

This frenzied anxiety attack set off a whirlwind of emotions, swirling inside, desperately pulling me up out of the bed. I put up a windbreak to regain control of myself. I urgently grasped at anything, any idea that would calm me. I concentrated on the word punished.

Punished---a strange word, a strange concept. I didn't know much about punishment. I recalled a colleague once used that term when referring to a past experience. He was a musician, although we referred to him as "magician" because he just mesmerized everyone with his violin. He was punished, he told me, because he didn't want to participate in a concert; he did not feel comfortable with the musical score he was given. He said that no one should ever be punished for their views, their ideas, and that it was an injustice. I wasn't that interested in his remarks and never pursued the discussion with him. He was terminated shortly thereafter. I didn't even know what his previous punishment was; but now, I wished I had encouraged him to continue his discussion in more detail. I might have learned something important or useful. At the very least, I would have understood what he meant by an injustice and could prepare myself now for what might happen next.

I went in a different direction. I didn't know what happened; I didn't know where I was; but did I know who I was? I philosophized; something that could be considered a passive act in view of the potential physical gravity of my situation. Nonetheless, as I mentally clamored for a simple explanation or reason for my problem today, which I imagined was linked to my very existence, my mood changed. I realized that I was not accustomed to being unhappy or worried. Yes, I knew only the bright side of life, as laughing and joking was what suited me. Actually it suited everyone that I knew and associated with in our small musical community; living alongside others with whom we had no informal, close or intimate relationship. We were all such a happy group. With that wonderful thought in mind, I felt a calm suffusing me; everything surrounding my existence appeared to be...euphoric. I was optimistic.

I breathed slowly and deeply to evacuate my stress and retrieve my natural inner calm. Relaxed, I was now certain that the answer was so evident; less gruesome and oppressive. I surmised that I fell or cut myself and I was being cured not punished. Maybe I should open my eyes and look around just to reassure myself. I might even find humor in all this.

But, then I heard voices. Someone had arrived and my optimism disappeared. I sensed the seriousness of my situation. I could hear the voices approaching me. I reasoned wrongly imagining safety instead of danger and now I had no time to prepare the right strategy. I was relieved that I had not yet opened my eyes as my body stiffened like preparing for violent physical impact as I continued to pretend to be asleep, while listening to the voices hovering over me.

"This is number 16011305120113 that I told you about." Stated someone whose voice appeared so strange that it sounded like he or she was speaking through a tunnel.

"Oh yes, I remember," confirmed the equally distant voice of the second interlocutor. "She is the one who was running hysterically through the corridors. Apparently her visual receptor is malfunctioning. Why didn't you just repair it? What is she doing here for treatment?"

So, I was right. I had no major problem. But the treatment. . .

"No, it is more complicated than that. Her wristband is in perfect order although we have removed it for the moment. It appears that her brain refuses to accept the imagery that is communicated to it. She is no longer sensitive to the programming system. That is why we thought that she had some sort of chemical imbalance and put her on the standard treatment. It should be clear in a couple of months whether she will be able to continue or a decision to terminate will be necessary." Explained the first interlocutor.

"Ok, we shall follow her closely because she represents an enormous risk for the safety of the center. Her attitude and reaction were quite violent. We were lucky to have subdued her. I want to be advised of her progress on a daily basis. Perhaps you should try now to wake her up," warned the second interlocutor.

The first voice continued: "Yes, but I must advise you that she has always been considered a bit "different" by our group. I myself find that quite interesting and one of the principle reasons why I would like to keep her alive to study her behavior. It is doubtful that she will respond to her code number. For now, let me just say that she refuses to call friends or colleagues by their code number. She prefers a "name basis" as she says even though there is nothing clever about all that. It seems like she's playing a child's game. It is easy to make letters of the alphabet from a series of numbers. But, it is a bit in contradiction with the context of their environment. So, we should humor her and refer to her as, Pamela series 13, or just Pamela, as she puts it."

"Whatever, just get on with it and be careful about becoming a toy in her hands. I wonder if I should assign someone else to this case." Protested the second interlocutor whose linear, stern voice marked him as the person in charge.

"Pamela," came that grating and irritating voice. "Pamela, will you please try to open your eyes. We are doctors. We are here to help you. You don't have to be afraid."

But I was. I was very much afraid. I was worried, silently trembling, just hearing the word, terminate. If I were to open my eyes now, they would have the advantage. I mused: they are prepared to ask questions and I am not prepared to give answers. I will continue pretending to be asleep. I thus buy myself more time to come up with a better strategy.

"Sorry, it looks like the sedative that we gave her was a bit strong. But when people are as hysterical as her, their system is often more sensitive to sedatives. In any event, we shall try later." The first voice replied nonchalantly.

"I am not so sure that she is asleep, but I don't want to waste any more time," said her superior who had leaned so close to me that I could feel the movement of his lips on my face. His words revealed that I must be very careful when I speak to him.

Chapter 3: Introspection

I was still lying on the narrow bed, awake with my eyelids firmly glued. I didn't know how much time had passed since their visit and I had no intention of opening my eyes until I started to understand what was going on.

I continued to have difficulty remembering what happened and deciding what I should do now. I concluded that I hadn't had one single relevant thought pass through my mind since those doctors disappeared, until now. I wondered what liquid they were putting in my body. I wondered if the liquid was affecting my concentration. I knew that someone attached plastic sacks on a regular basis to feed the tube. I felt the object in my chest move as he or she pulled harshly to readjust the long tube. I was wasting precious time lying here doing nothing. It was time that I concocted a viable strategy.

Instead, I had a compulsive need to introduce myself to myself as I divulged my interior, in the way that I knew it, and with the same sincerity, to better understand how I might cope with my situation, my new reality. I was and must still be a concert pianist, I thought, as my life unraveled before my eyes. I gave piano concerts for years. I was well known for my improvisations. Unlike most of my fellow musicians, I loved improvising and the audience always rewarded me with standing ovations. From time to time, I played with the symphony. The conductor, Newton, had a harsh personality. Stubborn and overbearing, he was clearly not open to new ideas, even those that would call for a small glimmer of change, in tempo or in pitch. For him, a talented musician was one who did what he said; no more no less. Sadly, he only liked his own relatively innocuous, passionless interpretations and style. That was my opinion, anyway. No one else seemed to have an opinion about the music renditions in the Newton style. But alas, I didn't remember ever having brought up that subject. Oh well, Newton didn't feel the music; he was nothing more than a technician concentrating on the speed, the rhythm, and the tonality. But then he got all the different instruments to move together smoothly and harmoniously, which seemed to please the audience

I liked classical music. On occasion, I played a bit of jazz. That was about as far as I went with modern music. I had colleagues who played various instruments in modern and classical music groups. They could make the transition between the two periods without any problems. Not me. I preferred the classical period. I had strong feelings for certain of the composers, like Chopin and Liszt. I almost felt like I knew them. When I played one of their pieces, I entered into the magic of their time. I would have liked to have lived in that period. I wanted to believe that I played their music the best because I could feel their energy. For certain, my interpretations gave me that honorable status of "virtuoso."

But now, as I was experiencing other sensations, most of which I didn't understand, I realized that I also wanted to communicate something else to the audience. Yes, that was it; I wanted them to feel the music as well. How strange. "Why did this revelation disturb me?" I mused. I concentrated, as I struggled to return to another time to better understand when and how my musical inspirations developed. My strong relationship with Ferdinand, an extraordinary musician and musicologist, surfaced. I could almost feel his presence in a strange kind of way. He was an enigma. He called himself a statesman which meant nothing to me. I ignored his efforts to explain himself. I refused to listen to his bizarre references to a stolen glory. I thought that he was losing touch with reality, or suffering from delusions, and I avoided him when he introduced those subjects. Eventually, he accepted my indifference and changed his approach with me. He concentrated on what I liked by giving me detailed descriptions of the composers who interested me and the world in which they lived. I was fascinated by his stories, certainly the fruits of his fertile imagination that brought my hidden musical talents to life. I confronted the truth. This small, frail man with bushy greyish-black hair and heavy eyebrows inspired me to feel my music, to understand the style of the composer's period, to add my own energy to the musical compositions, and to go beyond the bland, technical approach of the Conductor Newton. I smiled as I remembered the many times that he sat listening to me practice for a concert, interrupting me with his suggestions and motivating me to go further and further with my own musical expression. He was the Maestro and I was his student. I understood now that he was my guiding light; spurring me onwards, making me great. Undoubtedly, my musical success was inextricably linked to his interest in me. What would I have been without him?

I wanted to remember more but my happy thoughts of Ferdinand were replaced by a profound sadness. I didn't know why. So I turned to other memories, as I continued to introduce myself to myself.

My partner, Jonathan, played the clarinet with the symphony. I could listen to him play for hours at a time. We were very much suited for each other. We lived together for almost five years, in a small cubicle in the musicians' wing of the center, in close vicinity with all of our friends and colleagues.

Our cubicle was our private living quarter. For the first time, I tried to picture the room. It was functional, that was what I would say, functional, which was all that anyone would need; a functional living quarter. The entrance was large and spacious. On the right of the entrance was a built in shower room, with a door for privacy. Occupying the rest was a tiny dining area, with its small wall cabinet with dishes that sat above an L-shaped counter top that framed the small square table and two straight-backed chairs. On the left side of the entrance was a very large and spacious bed. We never visited each other in our living quarters, so I didn't know if all the cubicles were identical. Everything in our room was in white, from the walls to the furniture to the towels to the bedding, to the dishes. I was disturbed today by this absence of any other color; it seemed unnatural, even though I never paid attention to the absence of color before.

I was delighted with my memory of a cubicle having its own personality, coming alive to welcome us. Yes, at our arrival, the cubicle invited us to enter with a sudden burst of luminosity, filtering down from every corner of its ceiling and with secretions of an enticing and seductive perfume - a sublime blend of flowers, herbs and spices,- meant to charm and envelope its guests.

I thought about our carefree lifestyle. Even though we actually spent very little time in our cubicle, when we were there, we never had to worry about food or clothes or any of the mundane things in life. Everything was provided for us on a daily basis. Everyone was awakened at the same time by an unpleasant wakeup call that repeated several times. The dining area was always cleared of the past evening's meals and our breakfasts were on the countertop. Breakfast was a simple meal, bread or pastry with an energy drink. In the morning, we had just enough time to change into the clean, long, white robes hanging on our personal hooks in the shower room-the same hooks that hung our sleeping robes the night before- eat our breakfast and brush our teeth. It was a routine that required strict coordination to avoid being late for work; and we were never late.

The meals were in separate containers, displaying our identification numbers. We were taught to respect food as the personal property of others. We would never eat, even taste, the food belonging to someone else; that was inappropriate. It was important, therefore, that we only put the contents of our container on our own shiny, white plates.

I could feel my mouth water just thinking about the evening meal, my favorite meal of the day. It was comprised of shapely pieces of colorful vegetables and fruits, varying from one day to the other. Jonathan sometimes had an extra something in his meal. We didn't know what it was but he told me that he liked the taste. We always ate slowly with small portions on our forks, to savor the taste. Eating slowly made it easier to linger over our evening meal, and engage in easy conversation about what we did all day. Jonathan was very entertaining. He liked to act out different scenes from his working day, mimicking voices of colleagues, and reproducing their gestures. I found his performances quite amusing and he seemed to enjoy making me laugh. How much I wished that I were living one of those wonderfully pleasant evenings right now. I sighed and moved on with my thoughts.

Over the course of the evening, the light in our cubicle slowly diminished until there was only a glimmer of light, a signal that the day was over and it was time to prepare to go to sleep. Interestingly, as if synchronized with the level of luminosity, we had already taken our separate showers and changed into our sleeping attire. As darkness descended, exhaustion overcame us and we fell into a deep sleep as our heads hit the pillows.

I was one of 30 musicians who met daily in a musicians lounge close to the auditorium. The auditorium was built to receive more than 200 visitors. The smaller instruments, the personal property of a given musician, were stored in cabinets near the classrooms, which were also situated along the corridor next to the auditorium. The pianos, drums, harps, marimbas, and other large and bulky instruments, were few in number. There were only three grand pianos and I preferred the piano in the orchestra pit because it was perfectly tuned for my ear. We practiced individually and in groups at assigned moments, in small classrooms or in the orchestra pit. My practice time was never regular, as our schedule varied from day to day. Our days were full. Concerts, recitals, rehearsals, practices, and lessons were our principle activities. We were never alone and never bored.

I smiled knowing that my revelation of my existence such as it was and this vision of my former world such as it appeared, filtered through my own subjectivity and lapses of memory was one of total harmony and blissful happiness that surfaced so strongly, in my awakening moments. But this profound memory of happiness so true to my consciousness did not help me to understand why I was here, in this hospital room today. Why was I hysterical, and what did that mean anyway? If I could only remember what happened just before I arrived here.

"Pamela, Pamela, can you please try to wake up." She, the first interlocutor, was back begging me to respond.

"She hasn't moved for hours," someone answered as she changed the IV bag. "I think that you had better wait until tomorrow morning. Anyway, it is already 7:00 P.M. and you should be off duty," she went on. Her voice,

I noticed, was not hollow and mutated. It was a soft and musical voice, soothing to the ear. I understood from her words that she was protecting me, either because of who I was or because I was her patient, by suggesting to the Doctor to return tomorrow.

"Thank you for the information. I don't come in before 2:00 in the afternoon tomorrow. She should be awake by then. Have a nice evening."

I waited a few minutes to be sure that she had left and slowly opened my right eye. When I sensed that there was no one watching me or even close to me, I opened my other eye. I was in a child's bed that was very high off the ground. I might have even fallen if I had tried to get up on my own. I stared at that long tube that was connected to a sack, attached to a metal support. I gasped as I watched the bright red liquid dripping into my body. I shuddered at the thought and was tempted to rip it out of my body. I realized that the plug in my chest was inserted so deeply that I surely could not remove the tube without dislodging the plug. I accepted that there was little else to do but to lay still.

I turned my attention to the room. I had difficulty to focus on my surroundings. I felt dizzy and my vision was blurred. Eventually, things took shape and form. The walls and the ceiling were in a shiny white color. The vast number of single beds with white metal frames and white sheets seemed to blend together. The sacks suspended from the white metal stands helped me to orient myself. I could count twenty such beds in two columns facing each other. But, there could have been more because I couldn't lift my head high enough to view the rest of the room. I had a lot of pain in my chest and arms, which might have been the reason why I couldn't lift my head. I also realized that my legs felt heavy.

I looked at the bed directly in front of me. The patient's identification number, something that meant nothing to me today, was prominently placed at the back of the bed. I couldn't see the face of the person receiving the same red chemical as me, but she appeared lifeless in that there was no movement whatsoever. She did not even appear to be breathing.

I had the wall on my left side and an immobile figure in a bed on my right side. I wanted to leave this place. If I was with other people who had the same problem as I did, it didn't seem like they were recovering. It didn't seem like they are suffering either. But I was suffering; I couldn't move, my head was heavy, and my body was burning up. What was I going to do, what could I do to change this?

I couldn't sleep now that I was fully aware of my environment. I considered abandoning my earlier idea of developing a long-term strategy. I worried where the short-term strategy of pretending I was asleep would take me as I hadn't figured out the next step. I decided that the only reasonable thing to do was to concentrate on what was happening around me. I was awake and I would stay awake, even though the room was quite dark, adding to my anxiety. Someone just entered the room and was making rounds. Perhaps, if I listened closely enough, I could get some explanation. I heard a woman's voice now asking what was going on with someone at the other end of this long room. There were two people and both of them were talking about the same patient. I couldn't hear very much of what they were saying, but I understood the last comment.

"We have no choice; we must terminate this person. There is very little chance of recovery and we should move him before the others wake up."

I saw the bed being moved out of the room and had a clear view of the person running alongside the bed. I was surprised, because even in the absence of my visual receptor, I could see someone. He, at least I believed it was a man, was so visually repulsive, bordering on grotesque that I had to put my hand over my mouth to stifle the scream that was building up inside of me. Were my eyes playing tricks on me? Was my vision real, or imagined? He was gone, in an instance, and I wondered how many disappeared like that during the night. Just a quick decision then out the door.

This scene reminded me of something that happened recently, plunging me in a deep trance, forcing me to relive a traumatic moment in my life. Its effect on me then was as violent as its effect on me today. I confronted the mystery and grasped the context, as I saw myself sitting in the string section of the orchestra that was tuning up. The conductor was insulting us because we were using this infernal pause to organize our holidays. In the middle of this mayhem, the ID number of Ferdinand, the number one cellist, my mentor and my friend, came over the loud speaker. He was being summoned. He refused to move and the conductor motioned to him to leave his seat. We all sat very still. His number was repeated over and over again without a single reaction on his part. And then they appeared, the bright ones. There were at least four of them, as far as I could tell. They spoke with that hollow, gasping, tunnel voice that I heard yesterday, asking him to follow them out of the room.

He refused to leave and started to fight back. I could see his arms and legs swinging at the bright ones who continued to advance in an attempt to subdue him. He spoke to us in a strange way. He said that he was not ready to be terminated and that this was unfair, radically unjust. He said that he had a long life still ahead of him and there was no reason for him to be replaced. He added that the bright ones never considered the value of the individual. He eventually raised his voice as he screamed that we were human beings, unlike them, and that our lives were important.

His incoherent ravings continued. None of us moved to help him. We did not understand when he bellowed out in a resounding voice that one day we would be suffering the same indignities that he was suffering that day. He got no reaction from us when he raised his voice in a thundering tone, as if he were no longer the person speaking, and directed the following warning to all of us "You must try to understand. It is so important that you start now, at this very moment to act, to fight back, because you must change the future by saving humanity." Those were his last words as his body collapsed under the force and into the arms of his assailants. Even though he disappeared from the orchestra pit and from our lives, Ferdinand would always stay inscribed in my memory.

I sighed thinking about the scene and its aftermath. None of us understood his warning. I spoke to my colleagues about his words, but they seemed to be unaffected, maybe indifferent, to what he said. But I wasn't numb to his words; they triggered something, inside me. Why did he mention human beings and humanity? I tried to find the definitions for these words, but they did not exist in any of the dictionaries. Ferdinand was considered to be a brilliant man. He often used vocabulary that we had never heard of before. No one understood how he could find these words, although most people thought that he simply invented them to give himself a greater sense of importance and superiority. I was saddened by his termination. I missed him from the moment they carried him out of the orchestra pit.

Victor arrived within minutes of Ferdinand's departure. He took Ferdinand's chair and Ferdinand's cello. But, he could not replace Ferdinand. He did not have the talent of his predecessor. He had only one thing that made him a good choice, he was enamored by the lifeless style of the conductor

I cogitated the bright ones. In all my years, I was not exactly sure of my age, my encounters with the bright ones were always pleasant. They never threatened any of us. Before Ferdinand was ignominiously dragged away from us, I never saw anyone escorted to the termination center. Did they want to make an example out of Ferdinand? Why? Normally people just disappeared. We all knew that they had been terminated, but we didn't witness their removal.

I imagined that Ferdinand was very intellectually frustrated living amongst our uninquisitive group. I regretted that I did not try to understand why Ferdinand called himself a statesman. I understood that it was certainly because of my lack of curiosity that Ferdinand never confided in me about anything other than what he believed to be the musical inspiration for classical composers. He never mentioned how he knew so much about them and their

17

period. And, I never asked him either because I was so certain that he was just a storyteller.

I felt deep sadness and remorse for the loss of this exceptional man. I vowed that Ferdinand's termination would be my incentive to survive. I wanted to understand why his last remarks remained imbedded in my consciousness and were so significant for me. I even presumptuously believed that his final remarks were directed to me and to me alone. Regardless of the truth, I wanted to follow in his footsteps and discover what it was that he found that drove him to defy the bight ones and try to change our vision of ourselves and our world.

I feel very tired now and must get some sleep. Before dosing off, let me introduce myself to you, the readers. My name is 16011305120113, Pamela Series13. You might ask what that means. It is an identity that corresponds to an individual, in my case, Pamela, reproduced and reproduced over time, over years. I am her thirteenth edition and this is my story.

It started some five years ago when I began my struggle to understand the world and to find a place for myself. Why, when, where and how did the human race change? I have found answers to those questions and shall share them with you. They are imbedded in the pages that follow. If you remember anything, though, of what I am going to tell you, remember that danger is versatile; it can take any form, can be anywhere and can arrive at any time. Beware of the destiny of the human race; it is fragile. Today, I worry about survival, the survival of an individual and of a race, and I'll still be worried about it tomorrow.

Chapter 4: Decision

"Pamela, try to wake up. I am Dr. Gordon and I am here to take care of you." I recognized the voice. She had mentioned that she would not be on duty before 2:00 P.M so I figured it was the afternoon.

I opened my eyes. Now I understood, Dr. Gordon was one of those bright lights, she was a bright one. But, was she here to help me or to terminate me?

"Oh, I am glad to see that you have recovered. I was afraid that the sedative that I administered was too strong," her voice trailed off.

"Where am I?" I asked defensively.

"You are in the hospital. You have certainly heard of hospitals, haven't you?" she asked.

I nodded with lips curled tightly to show her contempt for my situation.

"So how do you feel?" she went on.

"I want some answers," I insisted. "Why am I here? What happened?" My strategy took shape automatically: I would interrogate them while not allowing them to ask questions. And, since she seemed intent on making me feel at ease, she would certainly answer all my questions.

"Let me explain. You are sick. Oh, I can see by your expression that you don't know what that means. Quite simply put, your body is not functioning correctly. In the past, sick could have meant that you caught a virus, a germ, a disease, but today, your body is never invaded by microscopic organisms like in the past."

"I have to admit that I never heard of microscopic organisms. My vocabulary is not medically oriented. I am not a scientist; I am a musician. You are not answering my question. I thought that the only reason why someone would be in hospital was because of an accident. I have no broken bones or injury to my flesh or organs. The only injury that I have is this opening in my chest and you put it there." I answered with disgust.

"Yes, you are right. I shouldn't use medical terms." She sighed. "Your body has not been damaged by an accident and I did put that plug in your chest. We are trying to correct a chemical imbalance that affected your vision. Do you remember seeing strange things?" she asked.

"I don't remember anything. I know that you have taken off my wristband. So, everything is blurred. I can't even look at you. You are too bright for my eyes. They hurt." I continued aggressively. It was very clear now that she was my only chance to survive, even if I didn't like her.

"Your species can not see us. Nonetheless, I can see you quite clearly. And, I can assure you that you are not visibly suffering. You are a bit aggressive, however, probably because you're confused. You must calm down. I can try to understand your emotions, but others will not make the effort. If you are as intelligent as your profile indicates, you will pay very close attention to what I am about to tell you. My supervisor, Dr. Crawford, is not interested in studying you, or your race. If he finds his task complicated by emotional problems, he will turn to an easy solution---termination. He will be here in the next hour. I recommend that you smile and thank him for taking care of you, and, that you tell him how much you want to recover and return to your musical career. I shall try to see you regularly and help you through this treatment. Your future depends upon you."

She left me deep in thought and continued her visits to other patients in the same room. What did she mean by confused and aggressive? What did she mean by studying me? And, what were complicated emotional problems? Was she suggesting that I changed and that the person that I was now was not going to please this Dr. Crawford? Regardless of what the answers to these questions were, I recognized more and more that she was my only hope, and that I didn't have a choice but to follow her advice and repeat what she told me to say. I hoped that I would be convincing.

"Hello, Pamela, I am Dr. Crawford. How do you feel?" he asked.

"Hello, Dr. Crawford. I feel a bit weak, but I know that I shall recover. I appreciate your taking such good care of me." I added, with as much sincerity as I could muster.

"Excellent. We shall continue to give you chemicals for the next few months. You realize that all these sacks are not chemicals. Some of them are feeding your body and rinsing through the chemicals. You mustn't worry. We have a lot of experience with this treatment and our results are very positive." He said with his echoing, tunnel voice. He then turned and walked away.

I could hear him tell Dr. Gordon that he was quite pleased with my appreciative attitude and that he would recommend that she continue to follow my progress. He added that he would like to be kept informed on a regular basis. So, she gave me good advice and I used it well. Now I started to think for the first time that I might leave this place alive.

Chapter 5: Suspicion

The days turned into weeks and nothing much changed. Dr. Gordon came to visit me every day. Neither of us was very talkative so our conversations were short. I worried about my health. She explained to me many times that I was only receiving the chemicals every two weeks, with 10 hours on Monday and 4 hours on Friday during the same week. She confirmed Dr. Crawford's explanation that the other IV bags contain vitamins and minerals. But I didn't notice any difference between the chemicals and the nutritional products. I was nauseous all the time and had lots of pain in my stomach. When I did manage to eat something, like a protein cake, I had a terrible taste in my mouth. I wondered sometimes if it was the taste in my mouth that was the most difficult part of the treatment.

I was also feeling strange because my usual enthusiasm had vanished and was replaced by constant fatigue as if all my energy had been drained out of me. I lost weight. I knew it, although no one mentioned anything to me. I also lost all my hair.

Dr. Gordon was not surprised by that fact. For her, that was not a problem because anyone who came in contact with me would see me with hair. My ID number had not changed and so my physical description remained the same. She claimed that the bright ones were completely disinterested in the physical characteristics of my species, and they could care less if I had hair or not. She convinced me that as only the bright ones were able to see me, and the changes that I was undergoing, it didn't matter. She told me that I should just forget about the loss of my hair. She added, as a matter of fact, that my hair would grow back the moment that my treatment was finished.

I considered my situation and decided that the loss of weight, the loss of hair, the loss of appetite, the loss of energy, and the loss of motivation were becoming very heavy burdens to carry. Sometimes, I went further and fantasized that I longed for my imminent termination. I started to feel myself growing farther and farther away from life as I remembered it. I didn't care anymore what happened to me. It was almost like I was starting to look down on my life from another level. It was emotionally and mentally upsetting.

Nonetheless, I knew that I couldn't mention this to Dr. Gordon. She was completely devoid of emotions and her rational approach to problems was not what I needed. I needed someone who could understand what I was going through to give me confidence and courage to continue.

They moved me around a great deal. I left the big ward, as Dr. Gordon called it, a few weeks ago. At first I was in a semi-ward and now I am in a room with three other people.

I no longer needed my wristband to identify the people around me. Maybe the chemicals were responsible for my newfound vision. Nonetheless, the problem remained the same; there were very few people that I wanted to look at and I was quick to classify most people as physically repulsive.

"Pamela, how are you feeling today?" asked Dr. Gordon as she interrupted my thoughts.

"Quite frankly I am not my best today, although I am certain that I will be much better tomorrow," I answered positively.

"No matter. You are definitely improving. How is your vision, by the way? We haven't spoken about it for a long time." She went on in her hollow, resounding toned voice.

"Why does my vision interest you?" I queried.

"That is a silly question. You know that you were brought to the hospital because you couldn't see properly." She replied assertively.

"But I haven't got my wristband, so how could I see anybody?" I asked, refusing to fall into her trap.

"Are you sure that you need your wristband? I want you to know that you can confide completely in me. I do not tell Dr. Crawford very much about you. He seems to be less and less curious about you anyway. He hasn't forgotten though, so we must be careful."

"There is something bothering me. I have thought a lot about a friend of mine, Ferdinand. He was the brilliant cellist whose life was terminated a few months ago. Do you know anything about him and why his life was terminated?"

"Yes, his case got a lot of attention. The Board even considered cancelling his termination. It would have been bad policy for them to intervene. You see the date of each of your race's termination is fixed on the day of your birth. It is random and even we don't know that date. Our only role is to conduct you to the termination center. Strange as it might seem, we have no decision making power." She seemed apologetic.

"But why then did Ferdinand resist so violently and why did he warn us of the injustice of his and our future terminations?" I asked.

"Ferdinand was a brilliant man. At a young age the Board gave him the right to use the Research Library. This is a rare privilege accorded to your race. He spent hours and hours each day reading and absorbing as much information as he could. We were all rather impressed with his persistence and his intelligence. We enjoyed having him around. He was amusing, entertaining; yes, a nice distraction. Unfortunately, Ferdinand stopped just absorbing the information he received, he started to analyze it. He started to develop his own theories about life on this planet, life in this center, and the relationship between the bright ones and his species. His ideas were dangerous and horrifying. The Board convoked him and explained to him that he was showing signs of paranoia."

She recognized that I did not understand the word and quickly defined it as a form of irrational behavior and then went on to say: "It was more than a clash of ideas or philosophies that day in the Board Room. Ferdinand accused us of all sorts of monstrosities and threatened to destroy us. The Board punished him by taking away his rights to use the Research Library. This made him even more irrational. He started to write articles that he wanted to publish and circulate to your species. These articles called for violence. We confiscated his articles on a daily basis. You can imagine how relieved we were when his termination date was announced. You should forget everything he said. He lost all reason before his termination. Do not ever mention him to Dr. Crawford" She added firmly.

An uncomfortable silence followed and was broken by her when she said. "I am sorry I must continue my rounds but I shall try to give you more time tomorrow. Remember that you can always confide in me. I am your friend." She turned and left me to my thoughts.

"I would like to have access to the Research Library," I thought to myself. "I wonder if Dr. Gordon could help me to secure that privilege." I could feel myself coming to life again just thinking about following down the prestigious path of Ferdinand.

I decided that she might be more willing to help me realize this dream, if she thought that I trusted her. Tomorrow I shall tell her what I see, just to test her loyalty. I observed she insisted that termination dates were pre-determined; but she could have lied. I knew of two suspicious cases concerning early termination, that of Ferdinand and that of the unknown patient terminated in the beginning of my hospitalization. I assumed that she must have had a very good reason to lie.

Chapter 6: Flashbacks

Dr. Gordon arrived early that morning bringing me a special protein cake; she claimed that it would taste good. I took it reluctantly and with my usual lack of enthusiasm bit into it. I didn't know what it was made of or what exotic spice was added, but after all these weeks of injecting substances, I could finally discover taste, good taste, and from something that did not stick to the inside of my dry mouth.

"This is great. Can I have one every day?" I asked, my voice high with enthusiasm.

"Yes, if you like it. I have ordered something for your mouth disorder that will be resolved in a couple days." She said.

"I decided to confide in you today." I uttered impulsively. "After all you told me that I could trust you. Didn't you?" I hoped that she would detect the subtle sarcasm in my words. It was my way of reminding her that I was still uncertain whether I could trust her, but was ready to take the risk and test her.

This seemed to arouse her interest and she was quick to confirm her intention of keeping everything I said in the strictest confidence.

"I see other people. I don't need the wristband anymore." I announced, as if it was not a surprising revelation.

"Really." She hesitated before continuing, as if she were searching for the right words to reassure me of her trustworthiness. "You don't have to tell me more. We can stop there for today, if you are worried about my keeping your secret." Was that a sign of her intention to be discrete?

I looked at her blinding light and, even as I worried, even doubted, her sincerity, I had the overwhelming impression that I had to go forward. I concluded that my refusal to speak, a passive action on my part, was no longer my best strategy. I had to take action and make her believe I could be a useful source of information, or of study, whichever was the more important for her.

"I saw a number of the patients in the ward and other places, like here." I paused for more of an effect. "But most of them were grotesque. I could not look at them for more than a brief instance. Only a few people have the attractive physical features that I am used to seeing through the wristband."

"So what do you consider to be grotesque—the color, the hair, the weight, the height?" she asked with a lot of interest.

"The points you raised are not significant. I don't consider any of what you mentioned as being repulsive. No, grotesque is deformed," I protested.

"I am listening; please continue."

"Well there was a very strange man. I called him the saxophone man. I like trying to identify people with musical instruments. He had a strange pointed head that looked exactly like the beak of a saxophone. His long neck was attached to a large, curved body. His arms and legs were so short that they were practically unrecognizable. And, he was covered with hair. Yes, he looked exactly like a hairy, walking saxophone. I suppose that someone might find that funny, but I found it disgusting." I remarked.

"Where did you see this walking saxophone?" she asked, nonchalantly, as if bored by my revelation.

"I saw him in the ward. The bright ones took him away the first night I was there. Everyone thought that I was asleep, but I heard everything that was happening around me. And, I saw him escorted out of the room." I realized that I liked defying her with my statement. I particularly liked the fact that I had fooled her up until now with a pretended blindness of my environment. But, she did not respond in the way I anticipated.

"Would you have liked to have met him?" she asked dryly.

"Not at all. I could never have had contact with someone so ugly. Maybe he was a nice person, but I would never have gotten past his physical features. He actually scared me, he was so grotesque."

"Well, you did know him. He would be Marshall, as you like first name basis. He taught you musicology a number of years ago."

"No, it is not possible. Marshall was a tall, slim man. He had very sharp but nice features." I groped to explain myself.

She ignored my protestations by simply asking "And, abnormal, what does that mean to you?"

"Normal is what the wristband communicates to me, to all of us. I never saw Marshall described as a saxophone man by my wristband. If that is what he looked like why was he described differently?" I continued rather defensively. In fact, I was not sure which description was exact. Maybe my eyes were functioning very badly in the ward, but I did not want her to sense any doubt on my part as to what I saw. "And, perhaps his appearance would not have frightened me if I had seen him that way all along." I added just to see where the truth was.

"Doubtful." She replied dryly, bitterly, in ignoring my awkward quest for truth. "Did you see anyone else who you considered, hmm, grotesque?" she asked mockingly.

"There was a woman in the bed in front of me in the ward. I only saw her face once and that was enough for me. She had long, blond hair and large protruding eyes. Her nose was nothing special; but her mouth. . . She had excessively large lips and huge teeth. As if that was not bad enough, she had a long, thin tongue that slithered in and out of her mouth like a snake. I was glad when they moved her."

That statement produced a reaction. She made a horrible gurgling sound, as if something had gotten stuck in her throat. I wondered what she would look like now if I could see her, what would I see? Would I see beady eyes cast over me, making me squirm? We sat quietly for a long moment, before she broke the silence.

"We shall continue with this tomorrow. I need to think about all this. Don't worry. I shall tell no one." She said perfunctorily.

Deep thoughts penetrated me the rest of the day. My life seemed happy until now. There may have been big gaps in my memory, but that didn't seem to matter before or . . . now. But, simply to pass the time, I searched once again for what I did remember.

I returned to my early years. In the beginning we were children together. There were no adults. Only the bright ones were present to oversee our fun and games. Later, we started to learn how to take care of ourselves and prepare for the future.

We sat for hours with headsets watching a screen and absorbed all that passed before our eyes. Time didn't seem to matter to us, so I have no idea how long we lived as children in a communal environment. But, some of us retained more information than others and some showed particular talents that we were allowed to develop. There were the scientists, the artists and musicians, and the others. I was so happy to be assigned to the musical group that I never paid a lot of attention to what others were doing, apart from the scientists, because they were considered the superior group. As such, there could have been many categories for the vast majority of them, if that matters.

I studied with Music Professors who were in the same species as me. I had so much fun learning how to be a great pianist. The hours and hours that I practiced were all part of becoming good and I, like my colleagues and friends, was motivated and enthusiastic about my career.

Then one day I was told that I would soon leave the learning center and would start my professional career. Jonathan was selected as my partner and we moved into a small cubicle in the musicians' wing. Just like before, we were free to do what we were trained to do without any daily constraints.

"But, was that a perfect world?" I wondered to myself. "Was never having to worry about food or clothes or any of the mundane things in life a fundamental source of happiness for our species? Was a world where everything was provided for you on a daily basis the epitome of happiness? It seemed to be so perfect before, in another life. But, today… Were we actually, honestly, happy with this simplicity, because we never imagined anything else? Did we ever wonder whether our species should ask for more, or less, of that simplicity? Could we have had something different if we had asked for it? The incessant flow of questions, without answers, inspiring doubt, kept coming until I heard the word, No, No, in frantic repetition resounding in my head, as if I were addressing someone else inside of me."

"Stop! You have to stop frightening yourself with these questions," I screamed out loud, awakening myself from this nightmare. "It must be the treatment," I spoke softly now, "that has given me such a distorted thinking pattern. I must stop this incessant flow of questions. But how?" Finally, I gained control by forcing myself to turn to other memories of my life with Jonathan and to concentrate on what I liked.

I breathed easier as nice memories returned. In the morning, I took the monorail on the automated circuit. It was nice to plug in my card and sit back while I rode past all the beautiful countryside on my way to work. I loved looking at the big trees and green grass and varied and colorful flowers that were always in bloom. Once, when I went on vacation, I passed by massive rivers and crashing waterfalls. I wanted so badly to touch the water in this natural setting, but that was not possible. We didn't have the right to walk in natural areas. We might destroy the natural beauty. We could just admire it from a distance; something that was already visually fantastic."

Vacations; how I loved vacations. We went on vacation regularly. My vacations were invariably too short. Everyone in the Center went on vacation on a rotational basis to the one and only vacation club, which, of course, met all our expectations for fun and relaxation. We had to choose our activities beforehand. There were many individual sports offered, which were very much like the ones we had available to us in the exercise room, close to the music department. Physical activity and sports were encouraged; if not imposed. I liked aerobics, and was a fan of stretching and gymnastics, which I did during my free time; so I liked to delve into other activities on vacation. Wall climbing and kickboxing gave me the same healthy vibrant workout that I needed to feel good, when I was on vacation.

I closed my eyes and pretended that I was preparing for a week away and was instantly caught up in the excitement, as I relived a memorable moment. We took the monorail directly to the vacation center where we were assigned to a room, very similar to our cubicle, except that there was no dining area. Breakfast, lunch and dinner were served in the vacation center restaurant. That meant that we had more time to socialize with other members of our musical group. Our meals were specially boxed and labeled with our identification number so that we would continue to eat and drink properly. We never returned to the cubicle before the end of the day, because we were so busy having such fun. Laughter was definitely in the air. Everyone was just so happy.

Jonathan and I loved to swim and play wall tennis, so we were perfect partners for both activities. But, as there was only one swimming pool and three tennis walls, we had to find other things to fill in the day.

The swimming pool, with its water slides and inflated rafts, was one of my favorite vacation activities. Jonathan and I had such fun splashing about, just like children, playing silly hide and seek games under water or pushing each other off a mat or relaxing in the waves. Nonetheless, we did some serious swimming for exercise, as we are both excellent swimmers. And, oh yes, the artificial waterfall situated at the entrance of the swimming pool was a real treat if you liked being hit by impressive showers of heavily falling water. The screams and laughter of swimmers slipping and sliding on the ground as they tried to defend against the onslaught of running water added to the pleasure and excitement, putting you in the vacation mood. "Although this was fun, would I experience something different, even more exhilarating if I passed through or under a natural waterfall?" I mused.

When we played wall tennis, I wanted to be at the wall next to Jonathan so that I could watch him play. I was not as good a tennis player as he was. His movements were elastic, his arms and legs moving so fast in many directions without any noticeable effort on his part. He never missed the ball. He visibly had great moves and real technique.

There was also the relaxation unit with steam baths, massages, and silence chambers. I liked the hot, steam baths, for their invigorating sensation during and afterwards. Jonathan went for massages, at least once during the vacation. Most of us shuddered at the idea. We were not allowed to touch anyone else; so we cringed at the idea of being touched. Even an accidental touching, like brushing up against someone, or touching someone else's hand, was frowned upon and considered offensive. Those, like Jonathan, who went for the massages, claimed that a kind of machine gave the massage. I never wanted to find out, although Jonathan insisted that the massages made him feel good. He had lots of muscles, so maybe this was a good relaxation for him. I was never interested either in the silence chamber. There were those who liked this room with moving pictures that appeared on a circular wall;

you sat in strict silence; they found the monotonous movement of images hypnotically relaxing.

Jonathan was not fond of kickboxing and wall climbing, so I engaged in these sports when he went off cycling or pole-vaulting. Even though the bright ones encouraged us to do things together, short breaks for individual sports were permissible.

Jonathan and I both enjoyed jogging and there were two very interesting trails; one took us past the Zoo and the other, past the Botanical Garden. I preferred jogging alongside the Botanical Garden. I wanted to breath in the fragrances of the many different kinds of flowers, stroke the luscious green plants and climb high in tall trees. I dreamed of reaching out and touching as I passed by the delicate and sensual roses in their many shapes and colors, standing proud or hunched in humility, or when I stopped to admire the beautifully shaped leaves of the honorable Oak tree. But the Gardens were not open to us, and, for good reason. We would touch and damage the plants, trample over and destroy the natural undergrowth, and pick the beautiful flowers. For that reason the bright ones sealed the Botanical Gardens behind protective glass enclosures; we could not reach out and destroy.

I always took the walking tour of the Botanical Garden that was a learning experience that fueled my desire to be close to nature. Unfortunately, I never concentrated enough to register the various names, but the images, my distraction, were implanted in my mind.

I was not as fond of the Zoo trail. The zoo animals were also behind high glass enclosures, but this time for our protection. I preferred to jog rapidly along the zoo trail, catching quick glimpses of the animals. I went on a walking tour once and we were warned that all animals were very dangerous, cruel and vicious; the more beautiful the animal, the more dangerous it was. The bright one, the guide, told us stories of how, in the past, vacationers were ripped apart and eaten alive by what looked to be very inoffensive and beautiful animals, like cows and horses. I asked once why the animals never moved. The guide explained that it was part of their cunning. By staying so still, they gave the impression that they were kind and gentle, so our species would be tempted by their beauty to approach them with open hands; and then they could eat us.

Apparently, all the various types of animals, big or small, had insatiable appetites that would drive them to attack one another. We were told that the bright ones tricked these ravenous creatures into eating food that looked, smelled and tasted like other animals, even though it was comprised of pulverized vegetables.

There was one group of animals—the birds—that fascinated me. There were many different kinds of birds living together in complete harmony with each other in a very large enclosed cage at the entrance of the zoo. I enjoyed observing and admiring their delicate bodies, and the different wingspans when they prepared to fly.

Suddenly, my mood changed and my smile vanished. I was no longer living a fun vacation, I was back in my real world. I felt sad. I missed Jonathan and my life, in a certain way. We were so happy together. I wondered if everyone was so happy, if everyone had what he or she wanted and if everyone was doing what he or she wanted to do. Was I the exception or the rule? And yet, I wanted to believe that my circle of friends and colleagues were as euphoric as I was.

I once again experienced an onslaught of questions raising doubt of the authenticity of my past life. When I heard in my mind's eye questions like were the bright ones ever honest with us? I was struck for an instance by the absurdity of visiting a zoo with immobile animals, all of who detested my species. Either we were the most hideous of creatures to deserve that reaction, or these animals never existed and they were a pure fabrication of the bright ones. And then my thoughts turned to Ferdinand. I didn't believe that Dr. Gordon's evaluation of him was correct. I sensed that she just didn't like him and thus wanted to get rid of him and his ideas as fast as possible.

Chapter 7: Cooperation

I used to sleep soundly, from the moment my head hit the pillow. Not anymore. I tossed and turned before falling to sleep and then awakened three or four times during the night. In fact, sleep had become an afterthought since I was always in bed. "Hi, I have another special protein cake for you," said Dr. Gordon, whose cheerful greeting broke my trend of thought.

"Thanks. It is the only thing that tastes good. The nurses took care of me after you left yesterday. I am feeling a bit better." I replied, with a slight touch of affection in my voice.

"I have given some thought to what you had to say yesterday." She hesitated for a brief moment, as if to assure herself that she had my attention. "I am not certain what would be the appropriate action for me to take, regarding your visual perceptions of your environment. Nonetheless, it is certainly too soon for us to connect your visual receptor, the wristband. You are simply not ready. Are you frightened by the physical characteristics you are seeing? Would you like to tell me about your emotional feelings?" Dr. Gordon pursued.

"No to both of your questions. I would rather have a description of me. Could you give that to me? And not the one that I have been told." I retorted.

"Ok. That is only fair, but you might find yourself unhappy or confused afterwards. Are you ready?" she answered.

I nodded and she started her description.

"Actually you are quite pretty if the standards of your species are reliable. You must understand that we, the bright ones as you call us, accept all kinds of physical characteristics as normal. But, as I said, you are a prototype for pretty or beautiful. You are slightly more than 6 feet tall which makes you above average in women's height. You have long, well-shaped legs and a curvy upper body. Standards changed during the history of your species. The last information we have showed a preference for full- breasted women with tiny waists. You fit that standard. Your semi-oval face is strikingly aesthetic. In fact, you have again the absolute in facial features; all in perfect harmony. You have a prominent nose, full lips, large, green eyes and long, wavy auburn hair. Everything about you would have made you one of the most sought after women in the past. You have one slight defect in your overall superb and seductive femininity. Your hands are a dichotomy; long, thin sensual fingers and muscular palms. Certainly your long fingers helped you master the piano keyboard, and they distract attention away from your muscular hands." She stopped to observe my reaction to that, but I kept a straight face and she continued. "You started the piano very young and forced your fingers to reach the octaves, which could account for the development of your hands. It is understandable though if we accept that classical music was written for men to play; it was a man's world at that time. You simply had to adapt." She concluded.

I said nothing. Her description was identical to my ID. So, I confirmed that my projected image was accurate and not a visual distortion.

"Are you disappointed, Pamela? Did you expect me to describe you differently?" she ventured.

"I don't know what I expected. I am not disappointed, if I actually look like that. Why should I be? My only problem is why some people are described as being attractive or even handsome, when they are completely deformed? And, why are you playing games with me? You know that I am clever enough to understand that there are different realities? The reality that I see now, and that which you and your visual receptor communicated to me?" I felt very uncomfortable and raised my voice. I thought to myself, "She frustrates me, because she enjoys testing me."

"Let me ask you something, Pamela. Would you say that you were happier with what you were doing and seeing, a few months ago, or today?"

"I know that I was happier without this treatment. I feel you're torturing me, but I am certain that I would rather be unhappy and knowing the truth, than happy living lies." I replied.

"Well, tomorrow I shall take you to the gym. I think you need some exercise. Exercise will help you feel calmer. You must get back in shape, anyway. You lost a lot of weight and your muscles are looking flabby. I must go now. You should try not to think so much." She said.

Her hollow sounding voice irritated me more and more and I was becoming impatient with her lamentable failure to understand me. Sometimes I likened her to a machine. She had no idea what I needed and what would make me happy. She probably was destitute of all happiness. And if I had said that I preferred playing the piano rather than working out in the gym, I wonder how she would have reacted?

I started working out on the exercise machines the following day. She blindfolded me and escorted me to the gym. She explained to me that my visual distortions might create psychological problems in the future. She did not want me to continue seeing such hideous persons and my visual receptor could not be connected until the treatment was finished.

She was right about only one thing, I had no beautiful perception of the people around me. Whether they were hideous or not, I was oblivious to the truth.

My blindfolds were removed the minute I entered my private quarters in the gym. I spent at least an hour a day moving from one machine to another. In no time I noticed that my muscles were becoming firm and that I was feeling stronger and stronger. I am not certain that I actually gained back the weight I had lost, but I did feel better.

I had no real discussions with Dr. Gordon during these training sessions. She was either there to observe or to make sure that I did not leave the gym and circulate on my own. My training varied from day to day. I either lifted weights or used the exercise bike or jogging treadmill. There was not much equipment, but what was available was enough to get me back in shape. I also did something referred to, as Shadow Boxing, where I used both my arms and legs in combat exercises. It was very demanding physically and left me drained afterwards.

I noticed that Dr. Gordon spent very little time with me outside of my training sessions. I wondered if she was trying to avoid me. But then she seemed a bit worried, so maybe she had another complicated case to handle.

My chemical treatments were coming to an end. I had only two more over the next month. I did notice that the effects of the treatment were less and less tiring both physically and emotionally. In fact, my earlier aggressiveness was vanishing and I had recovered my previous calm.

I worried about my future. I had had too much time to think during this treatment and, although I wanted to return to my piano concerts, I was certain that I could not return to my former partner and my former life style. I wanted to learn more about the past. The Research Library was becoming an obsession. I had to find the right moment to talk to Dr. Gordon about my plans. Could she help me? Would she be interested in helping me?

Well, she was arriving blindfolds in hand. I asked myself how I knew that she was there. She was still nothing more than a bright light. Even though I thought that it was simply instinctive, I discerned something more than that. I could see her movements, her way of walking. In fact, I could almost make out her form, if I concentrated hard enough. I was perhaps beginning to penetrate her shield.

"Are you ready for a long work out today?"

"As always, I find my hour a day training session relaxing and intellectually stimulating." I answered hoping that this would get a reaction from her and it did.

"Intellectually stimulating?" she repeated slowly; she was concerned.

"Yes, since I have gotten my body back in shape, so to speak, my mind has also become more alert and inquisitive." I answered in a taunting way.

"Perhaps we should talk about that," she proposed.

"Not yet, but maybe during or after my work out, as you like," I replied.

We agreed that she would reserve an hour over the next few days, just for me. She explained that she was working on a paper that she had to present to the Board tomorrow; she added that it was the reason why she had had very little time for me recently. She vowed that she remained deeply interested in me and wanted to help me to recover and that she was my friend. More importantly, she assured me that she had not revealed any of my secrets to anyone.

I didn't trust her, but I needed her. I assumed, and rightly so, that if she was helping me, it was because it was in her interest. Nevertheless, I was still so naive and uninformed that I could not imagine how I could be useful for her. I knew my suspicions were warranted. If she betrayed me, I would be lost…forever.

Chapter 8: Victory

Ilearned much later that Dr. Gordon's research paper was my best ticket to freedom. She presented her ideas before the Board and was, of course, met with opposition from Dr. Crawford. Dr. Gordon's thesis was that it was necessary to study the emotional makeup of human beings, a classification that was unknown to me at the time. She insisted that the reason why the visual receptor did not function properly in certain cases had nothing to do with Dr. Crawford's conclusion. That to follow the chemical treatments, as Dr. Crawford recommended, was completely useless. That the vast majority of the patients had to be terminated because their brains refused to receive the programmed imagery and it was too risky to allow them to circulate with the rest of the population. They were considered either physically dangerous or psychologically disturbed. In any event, early termination clashed with the law. In fact, many fell into the category of exceptional cases, contrived to keep them from the jaws of the executioner.

She also argued that there were more and more incidents of visual distortions even though the standard programming was followed to the letter. The only conclusion she could draw from this was that negative emotions were the cause of the problem. In each and every case of destabilization, the patient had become angry, depressed, frightened, defensive, or shown some other such reaction. The number of cases was on the rise and it was becoming imperative that a new treatment be found.

She wanted the opportunity to study some of these cases. She specifically asked to have me assigned directly to her and she asked for complete freedom to handle my case. Dr. Gordon made it clear that I should have contact with other so called "renegades," if that were possible, and that she should have access to as much information as possible in order to enhance my emotional development. It was important to understand what stimuli cause certain negative reactions. She wanted to explore all areas, from religion to discrimination, from wars and to love, etc. Dr. Crawford said that he was both surprised and shocked by her requests prompting him to lament that he had erred by assigning 16011305120113 to Dr. Gordon. He claimed she had falsified her reports made to him and that she was dangerous to the society. He asked that Dr. Gordon be removed from her post at the hospital or at the very least assigned to another service.

Dr. Gordon defended herself well. She demonstrated that it was difficult, if not impossible, to discuss new ideas with Dr. Crawford. She raised the case of Ferdinand who, she emphasized, was erroneously terminated. Potential research with respect to him would have been unlimited. In addition, she pointed out, the fact that 16011305120113 is also a musician was an asset. Musicians were in touch with their emotions through their music. Successful musicians, particularly those who were adept at improvisations, put a lot of feeling into their music.

"As we all know," she said, "scientists have caused us problems before. In the past, scientific research often ended in discoveries that could destroy civilization. The fact that we are ourselves scientists is easier, in a way for us, because we have their sense of logic. They are less emotionally driven, so in the end, we can control them. We need to understand emotions if we are going to ensure a future for this planet." She pleaded.

Dr. Gordon went on to explain that the small renegade group she had been studying for the last two years was comprised exclusively of scientists. She deemed excellent the Board's decision to let them live on their own and that how physical attraction and what the humans refer to as love could change the entire atmosphere of a group. She also admired the protective nature of human beings and their fondness for their offspring. But even so, scientists rationalize more than other groups and they are less emotionally motivated than say musicians or artists. Nonetheless, one had to admit that they found themselves members of this group because of an emotional reaction that interfered with and ended their visual program.

As she told me later, the Board voted unanimously in her favor. They felt that her arguments, although non-conformist, were well developed and plausible. They nevertheless agreed that Dr. Crawford's treatments had produced some good results and recommended that they continue. Dr. Crawford was offended by the decision but informed her that he was determined to invalidate her findings.

"I have a strong interest in theoretically and scientifically refuting your study and I intend to do just that." he announced quite boldly and pretentiously.

But the Board did assign me to Dr. Gordon and gave her unlimited power in deciding how to study me. This was the best thing that could have happened at that moment for me, but perhaps not for them. . .

Chapter 9: Deliverance

The hour that Dr. Gordon had reserved for me went by like a blur. I began by requesting access to the Research Library. What I presented as my overwhelming interest was my fascination with the historical period of Chopin. She knew how much his music inspired me, so that seemed to be the best argument to raise. She listened quietly and attentively as I told her how much I would have liked to live at that time. It might have sounded a bit ridiculous, if not outrageous, for me to have glamorized a period that I had never studied in great detail. I brought up my impulses about an elegant and glamorous time that I felt and admired through his music. I could not divulge the real reason why I had become obsessed with the Research Library. She would certainly have taken offense, if I told her that I wanted to dig up, understand and appreciate Ferdinand.

In any event, she never contradicted me with real facts about this historical period, which she thoroughly understood and she did not try to stifle my enthusiasm. Instead, she summarized her meeting with the Board. She had won her case and I noticed she began to treat me like a friend after receiving the green light from the Board.

She told me, however, that the research center would have to wait until I finished my treatment. She added that I would have to be in top form to follow her research; I might have to read or absorb information for hours at a time.

She took my hand in hers as she spoke with a voice modified with determination and a slight trace of compassion. "Pamela, I want you to know, to understand that your life will never be the same again. I am very interested in the emotional makeup of your species. My species relies upon logic to obtain objectives. You are about to discover your species. I don't know whether or not you are strong enough to properly understand the information you will discover, but that doesn't matter that much to me. I want to see what makes you react and in what manner you react. So I am going to introduce emotionally volatile subjects. Can I count on your?"

I couldn't fathom what she was saying. And yet, I was as much intrigued by her offer as I was confused by it. I had already undergone a horrible, humiliating and physically draining treatment that did not seem properly adapted to my case. This left me weary of her intentions which was why I hesitated to say yes to her request for cooperation. I desperately needed to know more. To her surprise and my satisfaction, my questions just seemed to spill out. What was the composition and function of the Board? Why was I being treated like a laboratory animal? How much freedom would I have? What if I didn't respond emotionally? And, were they going to replace my visual receptor? And, if not, was what I was seeing the real world or an illusion?

She informed me that most of my questions would be answered over time and that it was useless for us to discuss them now. She did explain: the Board was comprised of five to nine members, depending upon the subject, and a majority vote was necessary for decisions to be made. The Governor had the decisive vote and was therefore considered the most important member. The Board had administrative and operational functions and as such, was responsible for the overall management of the center. When parties were in dispute, it acted as a judicial body. That was precisely its role with respect to her and Dr. Crawford. But, as disputes between parties were very rare, the Board spent most of its time dealing with more practical matters.

Lastly, she told me that my visual receptor would be connected temporarily over the next two weeks. I would then know the difference between reality and illusion. She preferred to wait before saying more.

Her indifference to the majority of my questions bothered me, but I knew that it would do no good to press for answers. I accepted the arrangement, knowing that I had no other choice.

I had to wait another ten days, until the final treatment was finished. During that period she asked me lots of questions about how I felt emotionally during the treatment. That was almost impossible for me to answer, because I could not ascertain the difference between an intellectual and an emotional response to the questions. So we just talked.

I revealed my fears and apprehensions. "At first, I was certain that my life would be terminated. I tried to cooperate with you and specifically with Dr. Crawford because I was not ready for my life to end, to be terminated. Why? I can't explain." The only valid argument that I had was that Ferdinand had left me with the impression that there was something to live for. As such, before his outburst, termination was just an event like anything else. I did not want to share this with her.

"The treatment made me feel more agitated," I confessed. "Sometimes, I pined for termination, even though I was opposed to the principle of it, but there seemed no end to the pain and suffering. Moreover, nobody seemed to understand. Everyone was bustling about doing their job, sometimes, in a broken half-voice, telling me it would someday be over and I'd recover completely without compassion for my feelings about what was happening to me, my body. . . I think that that lack of concern was very destructive and I found myself wishing that I would just disappear."

If she didn't understand what I meant, she hid it and showed great enthusiasm. I imagined that a smile spilled over into the slight tremble that I detected.

The last treatment was finally administered and in three short days, I would move to an annex of the Research Library. I was ready to begin my long and tedious sessions, in spite of the fact that I didn't trust Dr. Gordon. But then something unexpected happened.

The night before I was moved, another human, I can call him that now that I recognize humans from the bright ones, entered my life. I can still feel his presence, like I did that night, when he lightly stroked my arm to wake me up. When I saw him looking down at me, I was certain that I was in a better world. He was so good looking. He had big hazel-brown eyes that illuminated his intelligence. I recognized strength of character in his very manly, chiseled face. I trusted him implicitly when he revealed his beautiful, devastating smile that spread so naturally over his face, adding sparkles to his eyes. In fact, I liked everything about him from his medium-length, brownish-blond hair to his tall, muscular body. He lifted me easily from my bed. I couldn't resist him. I wanted to be with him and accepted to follow him.

He whispered, "It is dangerous for you to stay any longer in the hospital." He assured me that he was following my case closely, although indirectly. A friend of his worked in the hospital and informed him of my progress regularly.

He grabbed my hand and we ran out of the room and down a long corridor. He knew his way around the labyrinth of hallways that eventually led us to a small opening. He told me to climb through the hole. I hesitated. I didn't know what was on the other side and the opening was so small that I wasn't sure that I wouldn't get stuck. He stepped forward and entered first, pulling me through the hole along with him. Even though the hole was very small, the material was so flexible that we could slide through expanding sides.

We were now underneath the moving highway. I cringed as the cars passed above me. Then something triggered the sirens. They knew that I was no longer in my room and they were coming for me. Now, more than ever, escape was urgent; I had to leave the bizarre personnel and inhumane treatment. The idea suffused my mind, to leave my entire past behind. I could feel my heart beating faster as I ran more and more rapidly down the underground path. I clung firmly to the hand of my protector, who guided me forward.

"We are almost there. I think that we are far enough ahead of them that they will not catch us." He said between breaths.

And, within minutes he opened a hatch and we exited the Center. I closed my eyes just as I passed through the hatch because I wanted to take in all the splendor of the outside. I had dreamed of walking through tall grass and climbing big, old trees. How I had always wanted to run barefoot through a rippling stream or shower under a calm and welcoming natural waterfall. I was about to realize a dream and needed to cherish the first impression.

As I opened my eyes, I was hit by another reality. "I am now outside of the Center?" I asked, my voice revealing my deception. He nodded yes and I stood confused and horrified with what was in front of me.

He took me gently in his arms, as if to comfort me or protect me from the truth. "We have all had the same reaction as you. The world is not what we thought. This barren earth with its red, dusty soil is all there is. The trees, the grass, the flowers, the vegetation, the rivers, the streams, the many things of beauty that we saw as we passed along our route every morning from the windows of the electric cars is gone, or worse . . . never existed. The only thing that we understand is that in the Center the bright ones want us to believe that we are confined in a given space in order to protect the beauty that surrounds us. That is a lie. It is their way of controlling us. We shall talk about this in more detail later. We shall have lots of time to talk."

I told him that I needed to sit down: that I felt dizzy and nauseous. He led me to a place that was hidden from view should anyone still be following us. He stood guard while I tried to relax, but I couldn't. Instead, my mind returned to the horrible episode that led me to my initial capture and treatment.

◆

I was playing a light sonata by Chopin and the Conductor was listening. I didn't get very far before he started tapping his wand against the piano and telling me that I was destroying a beautiful work of art. We disagreed over everything from the volume to the rhythm. He insisted that I play the Sonata as he instructed me, or he would replace me. Something exploded inside me. I was livid and started to scream and say nasty, but truthful, things to him like he had no feeling for music. I accused him of being a mere technician playing notes, not communicating the passion of the composer. I was no longer seated at the piano, but rather pacing up and down on the stage. I started to perspire profusely and my hands were shaking. He was following close behind and I thought that I felt him reach for me. He was angry and responding with insults of his own.

At one point, I stopped moving about and turned to face him, but he had disappeared. I panicked and began pounding the button of my visual receptor, hoping for an image. Nothing! I rubbed my eyes so hard that they started to burn. I tried even harder to focus and then everything changed. What I saw was too frightening for me to accept. The Conductor only partially resembled himself; only one side of his body and his face were like the visual receptor had transmitted. One side of his face was normal, the other side of his face was red and scaly. One side of his body appeared normal, while the other side was twisted and warped into place. It was as if he were two different people glued together. He lunged for me, perhaps because he wanted to hit me, but I reacted too fast for him. I turned and ran. That is when I caught the glimpse of others whose appearances were ugly distortions, making me tremble even more.

I ran directly to the transport center and inserted my destination card into the monorail that appeared. I was wet with sweat and my whole body was shaking. I was breathing rapidly. I needed to calm down because I felt weak and dizzy. I stared out of the window of my car that sped slowly along the monorail hoping that the beautiful scenery would be soothing and tranquilizing. To my despair, I didn't see the rolling hills and soft meadows filled with wild flowers. I didn't see the distant mountaintops covered in snow. I didn't see the wide river rapidly moving along its curvy shoreline. I didn't see a blue sky with puffy white clouds. I didn't see anything that even resembled the external world that I thought I knew, loved and admired. Instead, I saw barren earth, red dusty dirt that seemed to extend as far as the distant horizon. There were only small rocky masses that wreaked of destruction. As I focused on the nakedness of that barren, greyish-blue sky, a desperate uncontrolled trembling suffused my body. I had to leave the car, flee this nightmare now, so I started screaming and banging on the windows. I thought of Jonathan and that I would soon see and talk to him. The trembling stopped.

When I reached my destination, I jumped out of the car, just making it to the platform. I ran to our cubicle. Everything seemed to be the same, except for a strange, eerie feeling that the corridors I strolled through were the passages of a gigantic honeycomb. Everything was open, even the entrance to our place. I never before realized that Jonathan and I had no privacy; that our cubicle had no door. I found it unnatural even though it had never bothered me before.

"Jonathan", I called out as I entered the living space. "Where are you?"

"I'm here in the kitchen laying out our dinner. It just arrived and looks great. There are all kinds of fresh vegetables. The kinds that you like and they are cooked in a wonderful smelling sauce." He answered with his usual happy self.

I rushed into the kitchen. The person before me was not Jonathan even though he had Jonathan's voice and Jonathan's expressive, gentle eyes. But the rest of his appearance had nothing to do either with the man who was standing close to me or with the man that I spent three, four or five years of my life. His normally tall torso was so hunched over that a huge bulge protruded from the middle of his back. His arms were flabby. His disfigured face cradled an oversized, flat nose and a large, protruding forehead.

He looked like a monster, a repulsive ogre. I backed up from him, his soft, musical voice trailing along. I fixed my eyes on his to avoid confronting the rest of his deformed body. I must have fainted because I remember nothing else that happened before I woke up in the hospital.

Poor Jonathan. He was such a nice companion for all those years. He was so kind and gentle by nature. Why was I afraid of him, then? If I knew that he looked like that from the beginning, would I have rushed into his arms? Would I have stayed with him? Would I ever have wanted to know him? These were the same kinds of questions that Dr. Gordon had asked me. But I didn't have answers about Jonathan or anyone else. I felt disappointed in myself because physical characteristics were becoming important to me. At this moment, I did not think that I could ignore the physical side of Jonathan long enough to know how many other beautiful and inviting qualities he might have. Maybe I will feel differently tomorrow.

So, I could finally confirm that my last real impression of the outside world was not based upon hysteria but on the truth. I wasn't ready to share my story or my thoughts with the young man who had just rescued me. He was still standing guard when I sneaked up behind him. He didn't show any signs of surprise or fear. He took my hand and led me to the living quarters of the small group of humans, those whom the bright ones referred to as the renegades, who were given permission to live outside the center and were now sitting in a circle waiting for me to arrive.

Chapter 10: Illumination

It was late when we arrived in the small cavern that was home to eleven other humans, an expression that I would get used to using over time. The term, humans, was not used by the bright ones, who simply referred to me, and others who were dependent upon a visual receptor, as a species. Species sounds unpleasant and derogatory. I was to discover our species had a more dignified, or illustrious, title- humans, human beings. I liked the name and I felt proud to say it.

I was very tired and was happy when one of the women offered me a rocky surface in a small alcove, cubicle, in the cavern and a warm cover for the night. It was not at all the kind of bed that I was used to, but I liked the independence that it offered me and I was particularly glad to be out of a hospital bed.

In the morning I met the other members. The first thing that I recognized was that they all had very normal appearances. Some were nicer to look at than others, but they were not in any way deformed like the ones I had seen before my hysteria deregulated my visual receptor, and even recently in the hospital quarters.

They had all chosen names used by someone they read about. Their adopted name had no relationship with a decoding of their identification number integrated into the visual receptor system. I had decoded my name from my identity number, by finding letters in the alphabet to replace the numbers. They tried to convince me that I should break from my past by doing the same thing they had done, just picking a name that I liked. I told them that I felt very comfortable with the name, Pamela, a name that I had ingeniously created from my numerical code name. I offered to do the same thing for them, but none of them cared to reveal their former identity number. Why? Maybe they didn't remember it, or, didn't want to be constantly reminded of it?

They were all members of the scientific community and were assigned to different departments where they worked on research projects. I understood straight away that they were in no way certain that the research that they were involved in had not already been conducted in the distant past; certainly not in the present. They seemed to think that in certain cases the bright ones wanted to confirm or disaffirm past studies. That seemed credible to me probably because Dr. Gordon gave me the impression that the bright ones were involved in conducting studies of Human Beings. It seemed logical to me, as well, that they had an interest in validating or invalidating past discoveries made by Humans.

"Who are the bright ones?" I asked convinced that one or more of them could answer my question.

"You don't know?" John, a member of the group who appeared to be either the leader or spokesperson asked, holding back his laughter.

I confirmed my near ignorance and he calmed down and explained what they knew about them.

"Actually, Pamela, I was as much in the dark for years as you are. I realized early on that they were surrounded with some sort of luminous shield, but I was never able to pierce it, even though I am supposedly a brilliant physicist. It would appear that the luminous shield is impenetrable so long as one's normal vision is controlled by the visual receptor. As you must have realized by now, very strong, aggressive emotions can neutralize the visual receptor. We humans are not devoid of what the others want to call, negative emotions, simply because the stimuli for them is rendered absent. Our lives are controlled. We are given everything to keep us happy, laughing to avoid frustration or stress. Whenever we show signs of frustration or stress, our environment automatically changes. We thus receive nothing but positive vibes in our lives. Are you following me?"

"Yes, please continue," I replied, anxious to get as much insight into myself as possible.

"In your case, if our sources are correct, you became angry and aggressive because you were being criticized for your interpretation of your favorite composer. You started to dislike the Conductor, even hate him, a very strong negative emotion. And, the result was that you entered into a new dimension. This new visual dimension, penetrated by powerful emotions, is in fact. . . reality."

"I am not yet sure that what I see is real," I interrupted. "I don't like most of what I see, in fact. I understand now that I was happier with the beautiful images of the world and the people. Who are the others, as you prefer to call them, and why are they manipulating us like this?" I asked with some trepidation. I wasn't certain I wanted to know even though logically, I had to.

"They are not human. They are androids, kinds of machines that can exist in perpetuity. We don't know what happened to the human race and the reason why these androids took over. That we hope you will discover for us. We know that you have been selected by Dr. Gordon to participate in one of her studies. She is very much interested in human creativity and accomplishment and is certain that our ability to invent new technology in every area of life is linked to our emotional structures. That indeed emotion is linked to pure intelligence, and is not just a palpitating heart, uncontrolled cries and flailing arms. She thinks that we like and need changes, spearheaded by emotions. One might almost imagine that she would like to have human emotions and that she hopes that the closer she gets to understanding how emotions rule our lives, the more human she will become. She is certainly an exception to her race." He stopped there and looked straight into my eyes. "Do you think that you can work for her and us at the same time? It might be dangerous."

How could I answer that question? I wasn't sure of anything at this moment. Why should I take the risk of communicating information to this group? And, why did they want me to return to the center. That was about the last thing that I wanted to do. I wasn't even sure I could return.

"I am sorry. I thought that I was going to join your community; to live here with you and learn how to survive outside the center. What you are saying is that you, is that all of you, expect me to go back to that center, as if nothing changed for me. Shouldn't I be given the right to decide what I want to do?" I said emphatically.

"You are our guest. I don't know what Mathieu, the young man who escorted you to us, told you, but you are an asset, a very important asset, to this group; but only if you carry out your mission, which is to gather as much information as possible to help us to understand what happened and how we, the human race, can reclaim our true heritage." He replied coldly.

"And you, what are you doing? Are you continuing your research or are you just enjoying your freedom?" I asked with disgust.

"Actually, we shall have plenty of time to talk because you will be with us for quite some time." He replied audaciously. "By the way, the chase scene in the Center was probably staged. We think that Dr. Gordon anticipated our intervention and didn't want you to be caught; which explains why the guards never left the Center confines. Dr. Gordon is hopeful that you will learn more about human emotions by living with us in an uncontrolled environment." He noticed that my body was rigid and my facial expression severe. He took on a more paternal tone. "What I mean is that you are human and will discover the human side of your emotional structure faster and easier living with us. It must be evident to you by now that we are in touch with all our emotions – the good and the bad—if that is how they should be classified. We think that certain emotions, like hatred or anger, emotions that provoke even physical reactions, are sometimes essential and can even encourage a human to become more resourceful and productive. Naturally, they can also provoke undesirable reactions, like murder, a concept that you will come in contact with during your study."

"Then the others, I shall also refer to them like that, are aware of your existence and they haven't done anything to put an end to your independence?" I queried, a bit confused by the entire arrangement and lost with some of the terms that he used, like murder.

"Yes, they are aware of our community and even provide us with food. Your breakfast came from an alcove next to the Center's kitchen. As you can see, there is nothing to eat here. The ground is infertile and nothing grows. We selected this cavern because it provides us with shelter from the cold winds that come up in the evening. We desperately searched for food in the beginning. We found nothing within a reasonable proximity and we didn't have the physical force to explore farther away. We were starving; but we refused to go back to the Center. And, I want you to understand that each of us was free to do as they wanted. And then one morning, our individual rations of food were just outside the entrance to this cave. Each subsequent meal was placed closer and closer to the Center, drawing us, like a programmed animal, to a more convenient delivery place. It is an easy place for the others to dispose of our rations. The alcove, as we call it, is closed off to everyone in the Center and is a safe place for us to go. You see, Dr. Gordon, or someone else, did not want us to die, terminate as you see it. We don't know if they are watching and studying us, but at least we can live like humans." He shook his head, I presumed, in relief or in disgust over the dependency of their situation. "As we advance and learn more we shall be able to live with dignity." He concluded, his eyes meeting mine with real determination.

I closed my eyes and said, "I don't know what my promise to play this role will bring me, but I hope for you, and others, who believe in a better future for us, that what I contribute will better serve you and all of humanity." No other response seemed appropriate. And so, I was committed as a kind of double agent—a term that I discovered through my studies and that had historical relevancy. It described me well.

I spent the rest of the day observing the others. What John had told me was already too much for one day. I sat on a rocky ledge outside the cavern to relax. My thoughts turned to John. What kind of man was he? I could easily describe his physical appearance. John was a robust, tall man who towered over me. I assumed that his thick, curly, black hair and long beard gave him the name, the wise one. He was the head of the community, if that meant anything. And, he was given this honorary position, I would discover later, only because he led the exodus of this group from the Center. He had big, dark brown, almost black eyes, that changed from kind to furious in a matter of seconds. He was not humble and his haughtiness irritated me; even though the other members of this community seemed oblivious to it and clearly respected him. He fathered two children, 2 and 4 years old, with different women, Sarah and Ruth. He had a noticeable preference for Sarah, the mother of the 2 year old, Samuel. He showed no preference, however, between his children as Samuel and Rebecca were often in his arms, laughing and hugging him. I did respect his visibly kind paternal manner.

I discretely observed the other members of this community. The first thing that I noticed was that no one was busy doing anything. They didn't even engage in much conversation with others, at least not in front of me. I was happy when Mathieu appeared late in the day and invited me to go along with him and Isabelle to retrieve the food. The alcove was very close to the cavern and we were not gone very long. I was glad, though, that I didn't have to carry back gallons of water. I ate one of my favorite meals: fresh, crunchy vegetables with pasta and garlic bread culminating with a fresh fruit dessert of alternate slices of sweet melon and ripe, sumptuous mangos, crowned with bright red, firm cherries. I had already eaten a copious lunch so I probably didn't need to eat all that food, but then there was nothing else to do. And, admittedly, I had finally recuperated my taste buds and was so glad to rediscover the flavors of my favorite dishes. I decided that I would explore the area tomorrow. A sedentary life style was anathema to me.

Chapter 11: Exploration

Mathieu was happy to accompany me on my discovery trip. I liked being with him. His shyness did not seem to disturb me. We spent hours together in blissful silence as we trudged over endless stretches of barren, dry land for hours at a time and returned tired and haggard at the end of each day. I liked climbing the small round hills that shined so brightly in the sun that they looked polished. They gave me a perspective of the area, although everything looked pretty much the same.

At night I ignored the rest of the community that simmered with uneasy anticipation. After what John told me, I imagined that everyone was waiting for me to return to the Center. I had the best contact with the children. Their laughter, even their cries, made me feel more alive. They seemed less disturbed by the emptiness of the area than the adults. The dry, red soil laced with very tiny stones provided them with an endless assortment of play treasures. Sarah and Ruth worked together to educate them the best they could. Actually, I was impressed with the close relationship between the two women. They never argued and they never fought for the attention of John. I suspected that most of the members of this community moved around from one hard, stone bed to another, except for Benjamin and Stanislas who were as inseparable as Mathieu and Isabelle seemed to be. I didn't know Isabelle. She avoided me even when we were together. Once or twice I tried to strike up a conversation with her, to no avail.

It was difficult for me at night. I found myself alone with only a big blanket to keep me warm. And, the other thing that made me feel even more forgotten was the fun some people seemed to be having during the night. I was awakened more than once every night by laughter, heavy breathing or grunts and screams. I could not imagine what they were doing. Jonathan and I slept in the same bed for years and we never made noises like that. We never touched each other or jumped into each other's arms; something that I witnessed regularly in this human community. Jonathan and I never had close physical contact and I couldn't understand why anyone would want to. Nonetheless, as the days became weeks, I longed to be accepted by the group.

I also started to feel different physically, giving me the impression that I was being physically deprived of something special. My body was longing for something.

In any event, something else happened to put my physical desires on hold for a little while. Mathieu and I left very early one morning to continue our discoveries of the outlying regions. This time we took a new direction. He started off in the direction of the Center. I was frightened at first, because I thought that he was leading me back to the Center, to complete my mission. But, no, just as we came within a few feet of the building, he turned in a southeastern direction. In fact, we passed the length of the Center and then its width, arriving on the other side of the building. It took the better part of the day to reach Mathieu's objective. The natural landscape on the other side was very different from what we had already encountered. Very low mountains, or high mounds of dirt, loomed in front of us and the soil was not as dry and dusty. We weren't very far away from where we were living, but everything had changed, at least slightly.

"I am glad you are with me," he said smiling. "I have wanted to visit this area for a long time, but John discouraged me. I didn't mention to him where we were heading; he would have tried to stop me. But I wanted to try something different and I knew that you would follow me. We explored the northwestern and southwestern sections for weeks and found nothing. I might add that other members of our community, over the years, wandered even farther in that direction and never encountered anything of interest. We might discover something new in this area. And, even if we don't, I will have satisfied my curiosity."

I nodded in agreement and followed him. We had decided, days ago, to eat less at lunch and dinner so that we could take a picnic lunch with us for a long, long trip. We had plenty of water, fruit and bread to go on for two days. Mathieu was intent on walking fast. Fortunately, I had recovered from my treatment and was able to keep up with him. I was actually in good shape. Walking every day had given me nice, solid muscles and I felt that my body looked more toned and attractive than it was before. My hair had even started to grow, if that little short bristles was the beginning of hair. I was still obsessed by my baldness, but, true or not, other members of the community assured me that I was quite beautiful like that. Well, I did want to look beautiful to Mathieu, even though I was not certain why.

I was lost in my thoughts; thoughts that were very much concentrated on me and my happiness, and not on humanity as a whole, when I heard Mathieu call out to me. Actually, I was so absorbed in my thoughts I had fallen far behind him without realizing it. I ran to catch up with him and finally reached his side. He was hovering over something on the ground.

"What is it?" he asked me.

"I don't know, but I think that it is alive." I replied and then added, "What happened to it?"

I was accustomed to seeing ugly things. The word, ugly, was not yet part of my vocabulary. I was already frightened by what I now imagined were ugly people. I found repulsive the physical appearance of many of my colleagues and former friends. But, whatever was lying on the ground was outrageously deformed. And, it was wrinkled, maybe shriveled, and pale. I guessed that "it" was probably human.

We poked at the object with a stick and eventually, it moved. We forced it to sit up so that we could have a better impression of what had happened to it. Its skin was all wrinkled and dried out and its bones stretched the skin in crooked bumps. Nonetheless, its eyes were friendly and kind and it smiled back at us.

"Don't be afraid", he said; it definitely had a male voice. "I can understand. You have never seen an old person before. I am right aren't I?" he asked.

Without giving us a chance to answer, he continued, "My name is Jason and I am an old man. I think around 75, if the birth date I was given is correct. I could even be older. I have been wandering around this miserable planet for years, making contact with other humans. But, now I am getting tired, and this might very well be my last visit to a human community."

"How did you get to be so old? I thought that we could only live to be around 30. Termination is automatic at that time." I replied, very much in awe of the situation.

"Termination is automatic if one lives in the Center," he corrected me. "They will tell you that the date is fixed and that no one leaves before their time, but don't believe it. Termination is imposed when the others think that someone is too sick or too dangerous. I escaped their claws when I was very young, around 13 years old. I was on a day visit to a park. I left my group for a couple minutes and found myself next to an evacuation tunnel. I climbed through it and was on the outside. I ran and ran until I could run no more. I was lucky because I was taken in and cared for by others who had escaped from the center. I don't remember where they were living. It has been so long. I remember that when they disconnected my visual receptor I started a new life." He explained.

Ferdinand popped into my mind. So he was terminated before his time because he was considered dangerous. I was right all along which meant Dr.

Gordon had lied to me. I knew that from now on she could not be trusted and that made me sad.

Mathieu offered water and food to the old man and in a short time, he was able to get up and walk. He was not very tall and looked like a mixture of bones tightly wrapped up in old, dry skin. I stared with dismay at his crooked bones that seemed to protrude in every direction giving him a comic appearance. His leathery, wrinkled skin intrigued me and disgusted me at the same time. I promised myself that I would never let myself get old. Age was cruel, unattractive and frightening. He must have sensed my rejection of him, because he moved closer to me, eventually grabbing my hand as we walked, because he needed to lean on someone. This first physical contact with an old human disgusted me and made me feel dirty. I wanted to wash not just the hand he held but my entire body. And yet, as I wrestled with my desire to free myself from his bound and cleanse myself to avoid being infected, something strange and unexpected happened. I felt an energy surge followed by warm serenity, as a calm flowed from his decaying body--what else could have caused such a strong, unpleasant odor, but a decaying body-- into mine. It was as if for a brief moment we were one. The effect on me was so exhilarating that I found myself smiling back at him, and happily walking, hand in hand.

We walked much slower now that Jason was with us. He tired easily which meant long and frequent stops, as well. We knew that we could never get back to the rest of the community by nightfall and were happy that we had brought supplies with us.

Jason liked to talk and could just talk about anything. He was an explorer, he announced with pride. For the last fifty or sixty years of his life, he kept on the go, walking over barren land looking for other humans and a better place to live. He had met lots of other small communities, like our own and the one that had sheltered him as a child. He always stayed long enough to learn a bit about them; often times for several years. He said that he was very disappointed with the attitude of the human race, as he knew it. He found humans rather lazy once they left the center, and, even worse than that, apathetic. They were not even interested in their environment. The casual trips that they took led them only a few miles from their home group. They rarely ventured off for long times and always returned to their community. The few people that wanted to follow him on his journeys tired early on and stayed with new communities. Only once did someone stay with him for a long time; in fact, Jason told us, that the man stayed with him until he died.

He called himself Thomas. He started. "Thomas was already up in years when I met him. He said that he was approaching fifty, but he looked a lot older to me. I myself was in my early fifties or sixties, so I had a reference point for fixing ages. Either he had forgotten his real birth date or he was hiding it, but I put his age closer to sixty." He paused for an instance, thinking about how to continue. "I should add though that none of us know what year it really is. I am not certain myself that I was given my real date of birth. Strange, we don't have a real reference point for time. We just imagine that years have passed, without being certain. Oh well, no matter, Thomas was an excellent travelling companion. He had a natural instinct for locating new communities. We were never more than 14 days walking before he started off fast and straight for new groups of humans. But our real discovery was a marvelous, spacious area full of wild life and plants. I had never seen trees and flowers up close. I was very young when I left the center and had never had the opportunity to visit the botanical garden or the zoo. Remember, I escaped the very moment when I was to visit a park. I was so taken by the magnificence of it all. We ran for weeks, maybe months, through this paradise, observing the animals and tasting the wild fruits and vegetables. As Thomas was a biologist and knew a great deal about animals and plants, it was easy for him to know what plants were edible or not. We never ate the animals and never killed one either.

I interrupted him at this point. "You said that you lived with the animals?" I didn't give him the chance to answer, but added, "The bright ones told us that all animals are very cruel and vicious and that, even those that are small and inoffensive looking are capable of devouring us."

That made him laugh, if the raucous sound that he expelled could be called laughter. "Those creations will say anything to discourage curiosity." He shook his head and sighed deeply. "No, not all animals are cruel and vicious. There are those, however, that do not instill confidence. But the ones that I saw were more afraid of me than I was of them. Admittedly I would have been afraid of the big predators, like wolves and jaguars, and would have taken refuge in the trees, if I had come in contact with them."

"Where is this place?" Mathieu inquired. "I would very much like to visit it."

"I made a map of my travels, but it is bad quality. I am not even sure that I could follow it. I tried to use landmarks as reference points, but those landmarks could change." He handed the map to Mathieu who looked in awe at the number of arrows and zigzagged lines that marked out his voyages.

"I suppose that you are right. It doesn't make a lot of sense. It would appear though that you came from the Northwest and have been heading south. So where exactly would you situate this natural paradise? Could you just point it out?" Mathieu put the map in front of Jason.

"You see this octagonal form in the middle. That is where Thomas and I discovered this hidden valley bursting with everything one needs to survive. I didn't tell you, there was a lake. The water was a deep clear blue and we swam every day. The weather was perfect most of the time, warm and sunny. But, from time to time, the clouds would burst open and spray us with warm, droplets of water... rain. Thomas told me that the area reminded him of a tropical rain forest. There was a small stream hidden deep in the forests. Thomas insisted that we capture our drinking water as it flowed over a waterfall. He explained that the waterfall acted as a natural filter for the stream and that the water at that level was safe to drink. If he hadn't been with me, I would have drunk the lake water just like the animals."

He explained to us that thirst is one of the most difficult problems he encountered on his journeys. He said that he almost died in his early years from thirst. For that reason, he carried a lot of drinking water with him and learned to use it sparingly. Then he laughed and added, "Even with all my experience you found me today dying from thirst. "

Before we could utter a word, he returned to his story, "And, the surrounding mountains were so high that they disappeared in the beautiful clouds that enveloped them. I was sure that the peaks were covered with snow, but we never climbed them. Thomas wasn't interested in climbing. He said that he was afraid of heights and I didn't want to go it alone."

"Why didn't you stay," I asked. I could not imagine myself walking away from such a wonderful place.

"Well, it is the sad part of my story. Thomas got sick. He was a biologist, as I told you, and thought that he knew what his problem was and how to cure it. He asked me to gather certain plants for him. He said that he was going to make himself a medicine that would cure him. Unfortunately, I couldn't find all the ones he described. He seemed annoyed with me and very anxious about his situation. I went off every day looking for the ones that were missing. I still feel a bit guilty about that. Maybe those plants were there and I was simply unable to recognize them as I passed by. I like to think though that those plants didn't exist or didn't look the same as he described them. In any event, he became very weak and even thinner than he was. He coughed and took gasping breaths, especially when sleeping. Things just got worse and worse. He started complaining about being too cold and having chills, as he called it. The chills made his whole body shake. Since we didn't have blankets and only the clothes on our backs, I tried covering him with leaves and, even dirt. He sometimes burst out screaming that he was cold even though he was sweating from the heat boiling up inside of him." He stopped and lowered his eyes, as if struck by a hidden emotion making him relive that moment.

"His incomprehensible babble frightened me. I felt helpless, but continued looking for his plants. I brought him fruit and lots of water in a basin we used to wash in. He got worse and worse."

He said, "I'm dying, I'm dying" as he grabbed his head in his hands and started to cry.

"I had never seen anyone cry before and I was intrigued by experiencing a new emotion. I pushed myself to cry with him, but no tears fell. . .nothing happened. I learned later that crying was linked to our proper feelings. That is probably why I couldn't cry with Thomas." He paused and then added with real sorrow and regret in his voice, "If I knew then the emotional pain that his absence, his death, would bequeath on me, I would have forced myself to cry with him."

His brow furrowed and he shook his head and closed his eyes as if confused. Then his face smoothed over as he opened his eyes, more concentrated on continuing his story. "The next morning I found him lifeless. Oh that was the worst thing I'd ever seen! I knew he was dead before I touched him. When I was just a young man I heard people talk about that lifeless state that they called death. But, no one had ever explained to me what it was. Was Thomas dead or just his body? I looked desperately for Thomas. I didn't know where he had gone, and I was angry that he had left his body for me to take care of. I dug a deep hole in the ground and covered it with dirt, just in case Thomas came back looking for it. Strange, isn't it? What else could I do?" His eyes glistened as his desperate stare pleaded with us to give him answers.

We just sat there, incredulous, and couldn't say anything. He sighed as if letting out all the sorrow that had built up inside of him over the years, "I left this green luscious area by the same passage I had entered by. It was a small opening that Thomas had found interesting enough to explore. I guess it was just a fissure in the Mountain that we passed through, but I wasn't thinking about the importance of our find when I left. I was thinking about my own solitude and the loss of a close friend. So I cannot tell you where to find this place. What I can tell you is that it took me years of walking to get from that place to where we are right now. How many years, I don't know. But no matter what, it is far, far away." With that he took a deep breath as his head drooped. After a few minutes his rhythmic breathing and half-closed eyes told us he was asleep.

Mathieu and I sat staring at him for a long time, in silence. Everything about him was strange to us from his age worn appearance, to his extraordinary discovery and to his profound sadness. Then it occurred to us that we had been so engrossed in his stories that we had not even looked for a proper place to spend the night. We had no choice now but to do as he did, fall asleep on the barren, unprotected earth.

We were lying back to back, guarding a distance between us, when I felt him turn in my direction. He pulled me close to him and I didn't resist. I liked feeling his arms around me; the warmth of his body against mine. This was the first time someone touched me, and I enjoyed it. His hands moved slowly over me and I felt an uncontrollable desire to continue and to continue on until, at last, our entangled limbs pulled us together in a burning ecstasy. I now understood why my body longed, sometimes screamed, for want of an unknown pleasure; a longing that surged more and more every day; every day since the day I left the Center. That natural desire, that pleasure, that quest for corporal balance and satisfaction, is the human side of me. It was normal for me to want emotional and physical fulfillment.

I learned later that our natural desires were suppressed by the medications that were sprinkled on our individual food, adapted in proper doses; the food that we ate every day when we lived in the Center. The very short time that I spent away from the Center, eating uncontaminated food, had eliminated the inhibitory effects of my former diet and my natural desires had dramatically surfaced, in a rapid and voracious manner. It explained why I thought that I was suffering from an unknown compulsion or desire that I could not satisfy. It was also why I had trouble sleeping and properly integrating in the group.

New feelings opened inside me and made me wonder what it would be like to make love with others. Mathieu had triggered something inside me that made me hungry to understand everything about it, to achieve the maximum of pleasure. Even though I desired to be in Mathieu's arms every night, I yearned to be with others. This tendency of mine would persist, even though love would eventually anchor me and evolve my thinking.

Chapter 12: Natural Affinity

Jason talked incessantly during the day as we walked side by side. His disappointment with humankind was more and more evident as we walked. He talked about a group of humans, who, due to their reddish-yellow, skin color, were rebuffed in their attempts to join Community groups. He explained that they were even expelled from their original community, afraid they were infected with some contagious disease. They wandered for days and days, without enough food and water to survive for any length of time, before, eventually stumbling upon a community of people like themselves. Jason spent years afterwards doing his own study of the problem. As he had lived with these humans of many colors, not just reddish-yellow, but also pale green and shocking pink, he knew that they were not infected. He decided to spread the word to other communities.

In no time, he realized that nobody believed him because they had never seen anyone that was not white. He returned to the Community of non-whites, explained his problem and asked if someone would be willing to accompany him. No one was interested. So he left and continued his long voyage. Eventually, a few years later, he met up with a community of mixed colors. No one lived in fear or discrimination based on the color of their skin. The white members of this community refused to believe his story about discrimination based on color. They were so convinced that he had dreamed up this idea of discrimination against non-whites within those other communities that he started to doubt it himself. It was clear that he had not yet come to terms with where the truth was.

Mathieu and I listened intently as he recounted his adventures. They always ended with a rhetorical question, like: Does he really expect us to believe all this? But, then, Mathieu and I had long discussions after Jason fell asleep. A gnawing question remained: Was Jason telling us the truth? It wasn't his age that raised suspicions, but rather his scanty and disjointed stories led us to believe he may be trying to hide something. Sometimes we were convinced that he was recounting one of his dreams. Other times we thought that he was deliriously imagining the events, especially those that took place during his feverish escapades into the forest after midnight.

Sometimes he appeared to consciously omit important details and his ramblings only recounted suspiciously superficial details. In time, however, I was able to visualize the jungle paradise that he discovered. I mused that if I were him, instead of incongruously rambling on and on, I would have started from the beginning and described the effort that I had made to claw my way through the thick vegetation that almost sealed off the entrance.

I would also never have forgotten my first contact with nature. The overwhelming odors of the forest from the trees to the flowers, the excitement and sensations of actually touching and fondling the plants, the pleasure of wading in an open stream and slipping and sliding over its natural stone paths. And the animals—how could I have forgotten how I reacted when I first saw animals in their natural setting?

I would learn the source of Jason's problem much later and why he and I were very different. And, even though my analysis today is not wrong, just not complete, it is important for me to reveal it. From my perspective, Jason was not living his life; he was passing through it; like an explorer who goes forward in an endless search for facts, devoid of feelings. He was not fueled by emotions because he either ignored them or refused to be in touch with them. His ultimate objective was pure factual discoveries. Like a semi-Proust, he observed and recounted. Yes, he felt sad for the loss of a friend, but, it did not prevent him from quickly picking up and moving on. He did not linger over the grave in a tropical forest, to mourn the loss of his friend whose absence might have filled him with fear for his own life and future. He left to find other communities. I believed that this lack of a clear emotional motor for his discoveries was what raised doubt as to the authenticity of his stories, which seemed incredible and sometimes disjointed.

Nonetheless, his stories stimulated us, triggering unknown yearnings still hibernating inside us leading us to ask the questions, "Did exotic, natural places exist on this planet? Was there something else out there besides dry, red earth? Were there people of different colors?"

We couldn't imagine all that, but then, why not? I thought about the strange shapes and sizes of my colleagues and those deformities seemed much more difficult to accept than a different color. Mathieu convinced me that to reject other people because of their skin color was not human. I liked his conclusion at the time and wished that he had been right. But it played out differently, much later.

It took us almost three days to get back to the safety of our Communal Cavern. No one had ever been gone for so long. As they had no idea which direction we took, the decision was made to send Benjamin and Stanislas to find us, if we did not return by the end of the third day. We arrived as our two saviors, carrying sacks laden with food, water and blankets, were preparing to leave. The entire group came running towards us with open arms; some were crying from happiness; others in relief that we were back among them safe and sound. I was touched by their real concern for me. Concern for Mathieu, an integral member of their group for a long time, was evident. But, when I saw worried eyes turned in my direction, and the tears of joy that sprung forth, I understood that they loved and cared about me as well. Mathieu and I were so taken back by their warm embraces and screams of happiness that we forgot all about our new traveling companion.

We had gotten used to Jason and forgot just how upsetting his physical appearance could be. We laughed heartily when the others ran and hid from his presence. Jason simply ignored all their screams and cuddled up before the fire.

Isabelle rushed into Mathieu's arms and clung tight to him. It was visible that she was very attached to him and must have missed him very much. The brief moment that she looked at me made me very uncomfortable. I was confused and astonished but didn't understand her feelings at the time. With time I discovered negative emotions and in retrospect believe that she was jealous because she thought that I might take Mathieu away from her or, at best, want to share him with her. Fidelity was an important part of her relationship with Mathieu and she did not want anything or anyone to compromise that fidelity.

Mathieu opened up my eyes to new worlds from the planet that we lived on to the emotions that we harbored. My relationship with Mathieu was one of discovery, nothing more. He was the teacher and I was the student. He introduced me to the technical side of making love, while bringing to life my personal, private, and sensual, physical side of human interaction with another. He helped me to feel comfortable about my body and my intimacy with another. He was patient with me, taking the time to help me to overcome my inhibitions, to relax and learn how to both give and receive pleasure. He showed me by his actions that making love was more than penetration; it was the exchange of all the special touches and caresses before and during that would eventually determine the degree of pleasure and fulfillment that our physically and emotionally charged bodies would experience. I often wondered if without his early guidance, I would have seen making love in such a positive way.

I felt sad, at this moment that Isabelle resented me, without even trying to understand. Even as I learned more and more about how jealousy can destroy by studying it in-depth when I returned to the Center, I sensed that it is the way in which people react to jealousy that makes it destructive. "Jealousy, for me," I mused, "is like a looking glace that reveals one's inner desires. Jealous because someone prefers someone else, tells you that a relationship is important to you: that your sense of happiness includes sharing your life with someone. Jealousy can be positive because it encourages you to continue to look for a perfect partner; or to strive to save an existing one. Jealousy can also be seen as a discovery that can help you make the kinds of changes in your personality or choice of a partner that will assure you the complicity that you need. Jealousy toward your rival can reveal that you want to develop a better presentation of yourself to the one you love.

If one drowns in sorrow and hates with jealousy, the very raison d'être for that emotion is fraught. That is why I accept this emotion and believe that being jealous, is not in and of itself a bad emotional state; even though refusing to explore the reasons why it arose and how it can guide you is a mistake."

Unfortunately, it rarely worked that way. Perhaps some people would think, or say, that I violated Isabelle's confidence in me by having a very brief sexual relationship with her partner. But, then I would say, that I never promised otherwise and that what happened between Mathieu and me did not in any way destroy what they had together. I never had the intention of taking him away from her. But, she never asked me why it happened and what my interest was in Mathieu. That may have been her better choice. Instead, the jealousy of Isabelle closed off any relationship between her and me for a very long time. It also affected Mathieu's relationship with me. Consequently, we never left the cavern alone together, as we had freely done before.

It was evident from that moment onwards that Mathieu and I could never grow closer. That evening I felt that Mathieu turned away from me when he took his place next to Isabelle. He never brought the subject up because we were never alone together. I also didn't look at him the same way after that. I never felt as secure in his presence and I never relied upon him for comfort or protection, even though we would continue exploring with other members of the group.

My return to the community affected me in other ways. My sleep, like so many nights before and after, was restless. My dreams were exhausting. I seemed to be racing backwards and forwards between two worlds. I wanted the security of my past and often dreamt that I was living that idyllic life where only my music mattered. I sat so comfortably in the cozy passenger seat of the electric car and reveled in the beautiful sights that I saw. The barren red earth that I trample over every day has nothing to do with the luscious green forests and magnificent floral life that dotted the countryside of yesteryear. And even though that was all artificial, I missed the beauty of it. I also missed the vibrant conversations with colleagues over different musical styles and different ways of playing an instrument, like a trumpet or a saxophone, depending upon whether we are playing jazz or classical. We spent so much time mentally preparing for our concerts and encouraging each other to reach new dimensions in musical performance.

My mind turned to the group, and I sadly admitted that my observations of the group were exactly the same. I disliked the complacency around me which was so different from the vibrant discussions I had with Mathieu and Jason. There was very little discussion within this small community and no one seemed to want to improve the situation. In fact, we were like children in our dependency upon parents, who, for us, were the bright ones, who provided us with necessities. We were cold, so we have extra covers. Our long drab garments are used, so we have new ones. We are bored, so we have little tools, tiny shovels, to dig. For what reason, to make holes, or to look for buried treasurers, like Rebecca and Samuel. We did nothing interesting or fascinating and nothing new happened.

To amuse myself, I wondered about all sorts of other things. Where does the water come from? Why can I only swim in the Center? I love water from swallowing this refreshing liquid to feeling its cooling and calming effect on my body. And to think that I need to return to the limits of the Center to find this life supporting product, surprises me. Shouldn't water be available everywhere. Jason found it in that luscious tropical forest. How did it get there? Maybe if I dig deep enough I can find it.

Ideas flowed but I was drowning in boredom. I was disappointed in myself, in everyone, in this community void of initiative and enthusiasm. These are emotions that I have come to understand, just like I now understand fear and anger. But, it was so difficult to laugh and joke here only because it seemed we had nothing to live for. Jason was still with us. If he leaves, I shall follow him. But, even as I said that to myself, I doubted that following Jason would bring any excitement into my life. I thought that he was only happy when he was actively looking for a new community. His life, as an explorer marching across unknown, and maybe dangerous, territory must have been stimulating and rewarding. It brought him in touch with other people, but he didn't stay long. He told me once that the life in other communities was equally uneventful. "Over time, some people become so sedentary, he said, "that they grow so fat, that they could barely stand up, let alone, walk short distances." I never saw a fat person, but then I never saw people as they were, before now.

Jason was good at describing people and this inspired me to test my skill. I knew that Sarah and Ruth were very kind to Jason and he appreciated the attention they showed to him and their easy-going, patient manner. I found the opportunity to observe them closely and draw my own portrait of the two of them. They were a bit like twins and sometimes one even has the impression that they looked alike. Yet, this was not true. Sarah was quite beautifully put together. She was a tall, long legged red head. Her high cheekbones and long nose went well together and her light green eyes set off the luster of her long, red hair. She had full, well-shaped lips and long, eyelashes that added the finishing touch to a sensual face. Ruth on the other hand was far from the beauty. Her short grey hair hung straight and lifeless against her round, slight featured face. Her small eyes and short up-turned nose were the perfect match for a small mouth and thin, almost invisible lips. She was also short and round; John described her as maternal. He said he remembered seeing pictures of women who had lots of children and whose hips got larger with each baby. I would have thought then that Ruth had given birth to many or more children. But, maybe she was an exception and melded with her maternal instincts after just one. Both Sarah and Ruth had full, high breasts. John loved to hide his face in one or the other's chest. Maybe, that was the only thing that excited him.

I spoke to Sarah and Ruth about childbirth. They found it to be one of the most extraordinary events in their lives, but they felt that children did not have a life, especially in terms of learning and discovering, outside of the center and thus would not consider having other children. I was so curious about how they felt when they were pregnant and whether they had a relationship with the child while in their uterus. They spoke frankly about the experience; each of them was emotionally overwhelmed with the reality of being pregnant, but happy, with the changes in their body. Sarah claimed that she had an enormous stomach and expected her baby to be gigantic when born. She was very surprised to see just how little he was. Feeling the baby move inside of them was one of the more memorable events and they were both convinced that they had established a rapport with their babies from the moment of their conception.

"I loved to feel the baby moving inside of me," Sarah started off, her voice full of energy, leaving me with the feeling that she was reliving the experience. "When I found myself sitting alone, I would press on my stomach to wake the baby up." She started laughing, something that I had never seen her do before.

"You told Pamela that you had an enormous stomach, don't you remember how big mine was, Sarah," Ruth broke in. "I was afraid to bend over, because I was certain that I would never be able to get up again."

"Now that you mention it, John and I both thought that you were carrying twins." This brought more laughter and soon, we were a rather lively group. "What a wonderful change from the silent boredom I was living," I said to myself.

"Ruth and I were supportive of each other. We were both worried about the physical well-being of the baby, weren't we?" Sarah turned to Ruth.

"That was normal, we were not receiving any regular care. What did those half-crazy androids tell us, Sarah? Didn't they tell us, something ridiculous, like they had no experience with child birth or routine pregnancy care?"

"Yes, it was that, exactly that; such a stupid remark, to cover up their indifference, that is what I would say." Sarah said in a loud voice.

"Right the only thing that they did for us was put out boiling water and ten towels when we went into labor." Ruth bit her lips in disgust.

"We managed, didn't we, Ruth?" She nodded in agreement.

"Fortunately, neither one of us had any problem, apart from the weight gain, during the pregnancy." Ruth said looking at me.

"I am glad to hear that." I answered empathetically.

"As I was the first one pregnant, we learned together how to deal with a pregnancy and then with child birth." Ruth started off. "I had a very difficult delivery, probably because I was not sure of how to deal with the contractions, when they arrived." Hearing that made Sarah laugh hysterically. Ruth sat stiff-lipped so I stifled my laughter. After a long silence, Ruth just burst out laughing as well.

"It was not funny at all," She tried to regain control. "I thought that I had to fight the contractions, which I wrongly thought were a danger for the baby. The contractions continued for almost 24 hours. I was completely exhausted. And, I was quite scared; I had excruciating pain." She screamed to Sarah to stop laughing. "John was worried and sent Mathieu to get one of those androids to help us. He was gone for a long time. We later learned that he was held captive for a few hours—someone, I think it was a Dr. Crawford, pretended that he was a spy." She shook her head in disgust and went on. "They did that only because they didn't know what to do for me, I guess. The whole absurdity of the situation ended, when my body simply went with the contractions, horrible as they were. I started to feel the baby moving down. Who screamed that they saw the baby's head presenting, was it you, Sarah?"

"Don't you remember, John and I were so stressed that we left you; we couldn't handle seeing you in such pain. We left you with Stanislas and Benjamin. They were the ones who grabbed Rebecca as she broke through the barrier?" Sarah confessed. "And, within minutes of Rebecca's birth, Mathieu showed up with medical scissors, which someone in the Center gave to him. They had explained to him how to cut the umbilical cord."

"Right! " Ruth sighed. "Benjamin and Stanislas have always been reliable in times of emergency." With a twisted expression of horror that seemed to move in waves from her forehead to her mouth, she turned to Sarah and shouted, "That was a horrible description of Rebecca's birth." They both looked at each other before they burst into another round of laughter.

"I gather that Samuel's birth was easier?" I ventured.

"Much easier, because I understood after giving birth that one has to use breathing and pushing during the delivery." She looked hard at Sarah again, "You were lucky that I went first." She sighed. "Anyway, Pamela, I trained Sarah in breathing and together we discovered the best position to take to reduce the pain."

"And, what is that, I asked?"

"Squatting." Ruth demonstrated for me what she meant by squatting. "It is important that a responsible person is present to help to catch the baby; it is a lot of effort to expect from the Mother." She looked at me as if I were going to give birth soon and needed instruction; and then turned to Sarah, who from her standpoint, was not a responsible person. "And, remember this, Pamela, don't forget to scream. Scream your lungs out, if you have to, but don't hide the pain."

"Well," I started off. "After listening to your experiences, I am not ready to have a baby." I put it point blank.

They both looked at me in surprise and then Sarah spoke for both of them. "How can you say that? Look at our children, aren't they the most wonderful and precious part of us?"

"Absolutely," I was very serious. I loved their children. "But, you are now in another stage...parenting?"

A long discuss ensued and the mood became more somber as the discussion progressed, with Ruth taking the lead, "Parenting is not a recognized profession in the center. The bright ones take care of the children. We learn to be happy with everything and everyone around us and even if we fall on the dark side emotionally for even an instance, miraculously, everything falls back into place and we are, once again, euphoric. I can't remember ever being frustrated during my childhood. When I observe our children, I recognize the contrary. They are often angry at each other. The verbal fighting over who found a stupid stone can result in a violent confrontation. I never witnessed this kind of behavior before and don't know whether it is more natural to be competitive and possessive with people and things, or whether our present environment incites this kind of unnatural behavior."

"None of us are that familiar with childhood, but even less with conception and childbirth," I jumped into the conversation with my observations. Surprisingly I had a clear memory of medical visits. "From an early age, most young men and women have regular visits with the reproduction center. I had several visits over a short two year period. These visits always lasted a few hours where I met with a number of nurses and doctors specialized in reproduction. Twice, if I remember correctly, I had consecutive visits during one month. The frequency of these visits were linked to a specific treatment that the doctor had given me. I never understood why I had this special treatment, even though the doctor indicated that it was to enhance my energy level; I wasn't feeling exhausted with my work or lifestyle. On the contrary, I was disgusted and drained from taking all the medication which made me nauseous."

We all sat in silence, reminiscing. I decided to continue with my story, "I have to conclude that those visits were very strange. I was escorted into a small room where I was asked to lie down. The doctor explained to me that the examination he had to conduct could be uncomfortable, even painful, so it was better for me to be asleep. When I woke up, I was escorted directly to the exit door of the treatment center, without any explanation. As I was young, I thought that these treatments were necessary to assure good hormonal development and normal energy levels, as the doctor had told me. But now it doesn't make any sense. My hormones were apparently never at a normal level which is why Jonathan and I never had sexual relations. I had to wait until now to discover something very natural between a man and a woman, or loving partners." It only seemed natural that I should explore this problem in more detail with Sarah and Ruth.

I asked them if they had sexual relationships with their partners before leaving the center. I listened as Ruth, the biologist, explained the use of drugs in inhibiting sexual desire. "Our natural instincts" as Ruth put it, "were in fact turned off."

"But, why, are we treated in such a way? Isn't human reproduction necessary?" I asked showing how horrified I was by this news. "And, how were we conceived then?"

"I can't tell you why. We were certainly controlled by the bright ones, those wretched androids, in all aspects of our lives." She repeated what John had already told me, but in her own words, adding a nasty comment about the androids. "You were frightened when your visual receptor stopped functioning correctly, right? " I nodded. "It was actually your anger in the beginning that created a kind of short circuit in the system. Violent emotions produce cerebral brain waves that inhibit the operation of the visual receptor or maybe even burn out the system. The first level of control is visual. Then it becomes necessary to create a life style that is pleasant and carefree, where people are happy with what they do and are surrounded with people who have the same interests," Sarah explained.

"But that doesn't explain why we are not allowed to reproduce?" I repeated. I was hoping that she had answers.

"Would you have wanted to reproduce with Jonathan?" she asked.

"Not with the Jonathan that I saw the last time; but maybe with the Jonathan I was programmed to see every day. He is a gentle, kind and caring person. And, he has wonderfully expressive eyes." I answered; pretending that what I know today should not be taken into account, even though I would rather not have reproduced with a severely deformed person.

"That is simply not true. As a biologist, I can assure you that your genetic composition in combination with Jonathan's genetic composition would not necessarily have produced good-looking, normal children; even though, mismatched people have sometimes produced very beautiful children with marvelous levels of intelligence. Between you and Jonathan there would have been a strong risk that his genetic deformities would appear in your offspring. And, even more worrisome, his genes for physical handicaps would certainly have been part of the genetic composition of your children, whether in a dominant or recessive order." She retorted, showing disgust over the results of that genetic combination.

"But, none of us here, are deformed, so there must be other perfect beings," I continued, not yet ready to abandon the subject.

"True, but we don't know statistically what the percentage is. In any event, we don't know how reproduction is carried out and why the bright ones, I am going to refer to them as Androids, if you don't mind," she stated, " are still producing deformed beings, both physically and mentally. My research in reproduction never led to an understanding of their actual reproductive procedures. I certainly recommended that the genetic composition of individuals be the overriding factor in reproduction. But, quite frankly, I was in the same situation as you. I was living with a man that had serious physical and mental handicaps. Naturally, I was unaware of that until I, like you, went beyond the control of the visual receptor."

I stopped her. "What happened to short-circuit," I picked her expression, "your visual receptor?"

"Frankly, I am not that certain." She answered pensively. "I think it was an overdose of frustration with the Android's refusal to re-evaluate their genetic choices, coupled with an accident in the lab." She did look a bit confused over what was the actual stimulus. "What I remember is waking up on the laboratory floor, with broken glass plates and overturned bottles, oozing substances of varying colors, predominantly green and yellow, all of which were moving in my direction. I was frightened and petrified with the idea of being covered with these chemicals. When I finally stood up, I felt very dizzy and had difficulty focusing on the lab table in front of me which appeared to be in a dramatically, disorganized state. I stumbled about wondering how I was going to clean up the mess around me, when my Android assistant showed up. She mentioned an explosion. I must have buried that in my sub-conscious, because I still don't remember that." She stopped again to organize her thoughts.

"My assistant was not completely visible to me because of her bright light but I noticed that she was taking on a curious form. I stayed calm. Don't ask me how or why? I don't know. Instinct protected me. Even with hazy vision, I saw that the wall clock indicated that it was time for me to return to my cubicle. I mentioned to the Android that I was hungry and tired and would like to go back to my cubicle and she agreed. She promised to clean up the lab; which is exactly what she did, as it was in perfect condition the following morning.

I took things in a slow, methodical manner. I carried on as usual with my android assistant, hiding my new found vision. Day by day I realized what the world around me looked like and stayed quiet about it. I became frightened of my partner's appearance but had to suppress those feelings. I pretended that everything was fine for me until one day I came in contact with John. We knew instantly that we were in the same situation. We were both seeing the world in its true sense. You will discover with time, Pamela, that only deprogrammed people recognize deprogrammed people. As the identity code no longer functions, your existence is not communicated to the programmed humans." She was definitely kind and caring, like Jason said; and, even more so now that we had laughter together.

"John knew others that were in the same situation—in fact the members of our community—and one day we left together. What we didn't realize was that we would be condemned by the Androids to live here forever. This outside world, the Androids warned us, had nothing to offer us and that we would become more and more dependent upon the center to survive. This dependency would eventually destroy our happiness and make us very bitter about life." She spoke with sarcasm and regret.

"But why then don't you look for that marvelous place that Jason found? Why do you act as if you are in a prison or being punished?" I asked. And then add. "Maybe abandoning, leaving the center, was the punishment. Being alive and not being able to live; or being subjectively deprived of the possibility of starting up a new life, even if objectively possible, must be a form of punishment," I philosophized.

"You are right, we should make an effort to take care of ourselves. That is where you come in. We need to know more about what happened to the human race. The way in which the Androids want to control us must be in some way related to the history of our race. They use us to invent new things; or, as John thinks, to rediscover old things. But John's position doesn't make any sense; unless they are just studying us. In this case, where does our creativity and inventiveness come from? You see," she said looking straight into my eyes, "We must learn more about what happened to our ancestors. This will help to explain so many things."

"John told me that the bright ones were androids, kind of machines. Do you mean the same thing when you use the term Android?" I asked and she nodded in agreement. I continued. "For me they are still a luminous mass. I have not had the good fortune of seeing through their protective shield, as John referred to it. Perhaps you are all right that I must find out as much as I can about them. Answers. That is what we need, answers." I replied, hoping to get more insight into how she perceived the bright ones.

"Yes, you understand now why we are relying on you. Living outside the center has not measured up to our expectations. Like you, we were aware of the bareness of the earth. We had discussed this point many times before deciding to leave. What we did not understand was that the bareness was not just a small zone encircling the Center. We were convinced that we would find food sources and water in a close proximity to the Center. We did explore great distances, actually, during the first year. As you found out, the bareness is never ending."

She stopped to rub her hands together, as if she were about to make a surprising revelation. "I would like to believe Jason; but he is old and may have been hallucinating. After all those years of wandering over dry, infertile earth, he may have imagined this paradise, like a mirage. He brought nothing with him to confirm his discovery. John looked over his map, if one can call it that. His drawings are incomprehensible; only he can understand them. And, he is too old and tired to lead an expedition."

"But there is danger: if the story about the death of his friend is true, then we must be prepared to protect ourselves against microscopic organisms." Ruth replied tight-lipped. She was also deeply disturbed by the inactivity of her life and the inevitable dependence of the community on the Center to survive.

"Microscopic organisms," I ventured even though I was familiar with this term. Dr. Gordon had used it once.

"It is not necessary for you to understand biology and the physiology of human beings and more to help us," retorted Sarah, interrupting her own silence.

"How was your visual receptor short-circuited? " I asked. I was annoyed with her last comment, which I found condescending.

"Ok, I shall start from the beginning she said. "I am a bio-chemist and geneticist like Ruth and worked closely with Ruth in the Center. When one of our experiments had gone awry, the bright ones wanted to take me off the project. Violent anger surged inside of me and I responded with loud, piercing screams. I even threw papers on the floor and overturned test tubes and different bottles of chemicals. My reaction was violent. My visual receptor shut down instantaneously. Fortunately, I gained control of myself as rapidly as I lost it, leaving my android assistant speechless. She never questioned me about what had happened and carried on working with me as if I had never lost my calm."

Like Ruth, she hid her deprogramming from the Androids. She lived alone; her partner had been terminated months before. She did not want to say more about her experience, except that she and Ruth never discussed their changes with each other.

I interrupted her that at point. "I don't understand. Ruth just mentioned deprogrammed people recognize others in the same situation. Did you both know that your visual receptors were no longer functioning?"

Ruth broke in with: "Fair enough, Pamela." She took a deep breath before proceeding. "I can only speak for myself because Sarah and I have never touched upon the subject before. My situation was very complicated. We are scientists, but not in the same field as John or Peter, or even Mathieu, whose fields of physics and math and chemistry made it easier for them to understand this new deprogrammed reality faster. Biology did not help me. Actually, I didn't realize that I was still in the same dimension." She saw that I looked confused. "I'll explain." Again, she hesitated. "The Android naturally saw me, which led me to believe that everyone would now see me. So, when I left the lab, I had no idea that I would be invisible to other, humans. I'll use the term. I was pushed and shoved in the corridors as I hurried to reach the monorail. I understood immediately how important that point was as I started to come to terms with my deprogramming. When I rushed into my cubicle, I was overcome by the horrible physical appearance of the person opening up one of our evening meals. I called out the identification number of my partner, just to scare off the intruder. The intruder turned out to be my partner."

"What did he look like?" I interrupted her.

"He had a brown, scaly exterior. On top of his tall reptilian body, with muscular arms and legs, was a large, flat reptilian head, framed in spiny picks. He didn't turn his head towards me when I called out the code, because his large reptilian eyes gave him excellent side or peripheral vision. He didn't see, couldn't see me, as I learned later. At the time, I thought that perhaps I was in another dimension, a parallel dimension, something I had read about during my studies." She shook her head as if wiping out the memory of that scene and then looked at me. "Did you ever see a picture of a lizard, Pamela?'

"No, I don't think so." I replied.

Ok, well, I guess that you cannot picture the creature that was occupying the same cubicle as me." She said with disappointment and then continued. "I stifled my scream and stood immobile close to the entrance. I ate my dinner when he went into the shower. I would continue to do the same thing the rest of the time that we were together. I showered in the dark, when he was already in bed and, as always, fell sound asleep when my head hit the pillow. I avoided my partner in the mornings by dressing before him, and gulping down my breakfast, next to the bed." She went on to explain that she understood, quickly that no one saw her. She mentally surveyed her steps when she walked in the corridors, avoiding others; and, when she went to lunch, found a place at an empty table, leaving the moment when others arrived. She was very worried that the Androids, who were everywhere, would notice that she was no longer programmed.

"When I realized that Sarah was like me, I purposely avoided her. I had enough problems of my own. I just did not want anymore." She said firmly.

"I had less difficulty than Ruth, simply because my partner was no longer around. On the other hand, as I mentioned, I was worried that the androids were watching me more closely because I was living alone. Like Ruth, I was careful in the corridors and in the restaurant at lunch time." She swallowed and twisted her mouth in thought. "Ruth and I were no longer in the same lab. We crossed in the corridor, once or twice and in a conference room. They were not the right places to communicate and it was risky to go back to her lab just to talk to her."

"And, John, how did you meet him?" I continued my investigation.

"We both met him at the same time, at one of the science meetings that we had to attend. I was so relieved to see that another member of my race, apart from Sarah, was deprogrammed." Ruth pointed out.

As I understood, it was only through their individual contacts with John that Sarah and Ruth got back in touch and shared some of their experiences with each other. As Ruth said earlier in the discussion, John arranged for the departure of all the deprogrammed humans shortly after they had deprogrammed.

We sat silent. I learned a lot. My thoughts were moving certainly in a different direction than theirs. I didn't understand their close relationship with each other and John. Loving the same man and bearing children with him seemed to bring Sarah and Ruth even closer to each other. I wondered if they might both be playing a very good game. Perhaps, they might be rivals. Even if that were the case, what did it matter? I presumed it was just easier, under the circumstances. Anyway, what else could they do? They were condemned to stay together in this barren wilderness.

I was still offended by Sarah's earlier remark, which indicated that she did not consider me to be her intellectual equal. Perhaps I was oversensitive; perhaps she didn't mean anything by it when she said I didn't have to understand human biology and physiology to do my spying job for them, or something like that. It annoyed me just the same.

I eventually moved to leave. They looked at me. I said coldly that I would do my best. I added that I thought that everything I learned about them and everything that I could learn about life would be useful for me in my mission.

I was tired anyway with the conversation which I felt had gone on too long. Laughter had brought us closer. The mood change left me anxious, sad, worried and afraid to get more involved. I stepped outside the cavern to fill my lungs with a cool stream of night air.

The sun was beginning its descent, on the distant shadowy horizon. There were evenings when the sky took on a ghastly cold gray color; no shine from either the moon or the stars.

"That sky frightens me," I mused. But tonight the sun was setting in virtual glory with reds and yellows striking up the heavens, filling me with a warm glow. It was an optimistic and promising kind of sunset and I sat watching until the red and yellow flames faded and were replaced by the full and radiant face of the moon, courted with shimmering stars. Stunning! I felt better and started to forget how frustrated I felt talking to Ruth and Sarah at the end.

"Hi, how are you feeling?" Peter asked, in a charming, friendly manner.

He stood in front looking down at me. "I am obsessed with the world beyond and the structure of the planets and the stars." He said in a deep, friendly voice. He advanced and bent low enough that he could whisper in my ear, "I want to visit them."

Peter and I rarely ran into each other. Mathieu told me that Peter was a bit of an introvert and was sometimes criticized as pretentious. I closely observed him, trying to penetrate his true nature. Actually, I liked his air of self-confidence and I found him very attractive physically, as he met my idea of a good-looking, sexy man. For me, the sex appeal of a man is in his face and Peter's face was absolutely charming. His high forehead, pronounced black eyebrows and big, mysterious dark brown eyes, were enough to draw me willingly in his direction. His features so perfectly conceived with a long, sculpted nose, high wide cheekbones and a prominent, chiseled chin revealed his inner strength and sexual power. His inviting mouth with a fuller bottom lip spread naturally into a playful, seductive smile. And his thick, dark brown wavy shoulder-length hair and unshaven look enhanced his virility.

His mysterious eyes revealed his quick, agile mind and intelligence. I sensed his sincerity and felt that I could trust him. I could easily have fallen straight into the arms of this man. He was slightly taller than John, making him close to 7 feet tall. I was infatuated with his tall, slim, yet muscular athletic body, from years of working out in the gym when he was at the center, and wanted to lean my head comfortably on one of his broad, protective shoulders.

I answered his first question, as if I hadn't heard anything else he said. "I am feeling much better now that I am sitting here, watching this spectacular sunset" I let my words fall in a rather tired way, hoping to dissimulate my strong attraction to him.

"I have seen you sitting often by yourself watching the inviting world above spread majestically its nightly wings." He replied in an attractive poetic manner to perhaps impress me. I smiled sheepishly and continued watching the stars take their place in the dark sky. He sat down next to me and cocked his head in the same upright position. We must have sat enjoying the many celestial bodies for an hour, before he broke the silence once again.

"I like looking at you, Pamela. I have been looking at you a lot recently." He spoke in a soft, breathy voice. "It is rare to see someone as beautiful as you. You are captivating."

"Strange that you should say that. I am the only woman who sleeps alone." I replied, pretending to be irritated with him.

"But, you are the only woman that every man in this group would like to have next to him every night." He winked.

"You are flattering me and I must admit that I like it, even though I know that there is no truth in what you say." I answered, trying to hide my interest and mounting desire for him. I continued, "My life is rather boring just like I am rather boring." I got no reaction from him. "You must know that I am lonesome. I spend my time trying to engage people in conversation. They are not interested in what I think. Most people don't even want to share information with me. They tolerate me because they see me as the sole means of discovering the reality of our world. I am a kind of representative of the bright ones. They sent me here to learn about life and to discover feelings." I spoke so honestly to him, revealing my deceptions and my hostility to the group, in an effort to discourage him. I was not in the mood to be placated, if that is what he was doing.

"The way you just put it, your life in this community sounds a bit sad." He flashed his eyes at me. "And, have you discovered feelings…emotions?" He teased. He interested me. I could feel the quickening of my pulse and my knees falling limp.

I held back, mustering a cool calm when I said, "Many, I imagine. I haven't put names to them. But all my feelings make me sad." I responded.

"Then it is time that we change all that." He replied, as he moved closer to me. There was no doubt that I would feel good in his arms. I sat motionless enjoying the surge of desire that arose inside of me, creeping up my loins. This momentary warmth and hiding within protected shrouds felt good as I was shielded from the sadness of the life around me.

There was tenderness and sincerity in the way that he wrapped his arms around me and buried his head in my neck, letting his warm breath flow over my shoulders, descending over my breasts. I pulled him closer to me, as his mouth moved against my throat and along my uncovered shoulder. Our hearts were beating rapidly and our breathing had quickened, when he swiftly and easily moved us from the low wall where we were sitting onto the barren earth. He so delicately took my head in his hands as he stared intensely into my eyes. I felt as if he saw and understood the fragility that I so desperately wanted others to understand. As his mouth met mine, an energy, and extraordinary energy, passed between us. My basic instincts came alive in an incredibly audacious burst of desire. "I love his tender touch and his enticing odor," resounded over and over in my mind. I knew that he felt the same way because that slight hesitation on his part that I sensed at first turned into confidence, as he lovingly caressed and fondled me until I was aflame with passion.

I wanted to know him, every part of his alluring body, and transcend his very nature. When our interlaced bodies finally came together, I didn't want the moment to end. But when it did, uncontrollable, vibrant waves passed through us and between us, leaving behind a euphoric sensation of physical and ethereal pleasure. I was drained and fulfilled at the same time. I felt the weight of his body upon me as he relaxed, waiting for nature to slowly draw us a part. I knew then, as I know now. "He is my force; my other half; the man with whom I hold a feeling of deep and natural affinity. He is the man that I love now and will love, no matter what happens, for the rest of my life."

He eventually swept me up off the ground and carried me in his strong arms to his private cubicle in the cavern. "I love you, Pamela," he said softly, as he gently lowered me onto the bed. "I have loved you from a distance from the very moment that I saw you."

I cuddled up close to him and buried my head in his chest, "I love you too, Peter." This was the first time in weeks that I slept well.

From that moment on, Peter and I were a couple, inseparable, ready to face the contempt of the community, the threat of my mission, and whatever else was out there waiting for us.

Chapter 13: A Secret

In the days that followed, Peter and I became carefree lovers, bowing to our urges whenever and wherever it pleased us. Falling in love with Peter validated my leaving the Center and gave me a fertile reason to continue living in this dry and barren land. However, loving him made me more susceptible to new emotional feelings. I became more and more possessive of him. I was afraid of losing him and finding myself alone and unhappy, particularly at night.

Something perverse was birthed by our relationship. My fascination and longing for him made him even more attractive to other female members of the community, as if our relationship gave him a new look of resurgent virility and self-confidence.

At first I imagined that my refusal to share him clashed with the standards of free sex, total promiscuity, among members of the group. I felt threatened when another female member of the community got too close to him. I would discover later that my reasoning was wrong; the life-style that I imagined just did not exist. But my irrational behavior and thinking at the time, left me depressed and worried, like the evening when Peter left me alone and joined Mat Hilda for a walk after the evening meal. I wanted to go with them, but Peter insisted that I needed to rest. I imagined Mathilda, with her sensual movements and inviting style, bewitching him and dragging him far away from me.

Peter never mentioned my behavior, but reassured me of his love and devotion for me in a more clever way. Little by little, he told me his story. A story that he had not revealed in its entirety to anyone before me. He avoided their questions or was very vague in his answers and never discussed his inner concerns, fears and anxieties with others. He explained to me that he wanted to share his past with me so that I would better understand him. He also wanted to open himself up to me, to demonstrate his vulnerability. He told me what had driven him to bypass the effects of the visual receptor and the events that led him to join this group of renegades.

Although Peter spent his time studying the movement of planets and their composition, as an astrophysicist, his other specializations were of more interest to the bright ones. His assignments were normally related to the fields of robotic engineering and bio-medical engineering. Astronomy, the whole field of astrophysics, remains his passion. He often stayed up late into the night watching the celestial bodies as they turned around him. His observations were documented and the bright ones were very happy with his results. And, interestingly, they never imposed a curfew on him, giving him access to the facilities whenever he wanted. He got along well with his colleagues who shared with him their enthusiasm about their various discoveries.

"One night, everything changed for me." He began. "I was certain that the comet I was observing and studying was transmitting sound waves. Anxious to confirm my theory, I ventured into the communication department, where I hoped to find someone who could localize and identify the sound. A bright one was at the controls homing in on a distress call. I was surprised, Pamela, because the bright ones, even when acting as assistants, never participated manually in the projects. They introduced different research projects to humans, observed the experiments, and commented on the results. They never manipulated anything in the lab and never sat down at a laboratory table. Perhaps they conducted research on their own, after hours. But, to date, I had not run into any of them when I worked at night." He shook his head in disbelief.

"That should have been my clue to leave; I didn't take it; I quietly and discretely entered the room. It was more than curiosity that overtook my normal clear sense of duty. In any event, I hid behind a large telecommunications screen, which was so conveniently in arm's reach. What I witnessed afterwards was startling even alarming. The volume was set on maximum so I heard everything that was said on both sides of the conversation. A voice, unmistakably, a human voice—a voice resembling ours in tone and amplification-- was broadcasting over the network. It was a distress call. The astronaut, as he called himself was returning from a long mission on a planet outside our solar system. He requested permission from the Control Center of Planet Earth to land. The bright one asked for his coordinates, which he communicated with precision. The bright one then put the astronaut on hold and contacted a member of his staff. He communicated the coordinates and then returned to confirm that the astronaut could proceed to a landing."

I sat wide-eyed listening intently to this extraordinary discovery. He smiled at me; satisfied with my visible interest and curiosity in what he was saying. His voice took on a serious, menacing tone. "Until that moment, there was nothing suspicious. I even had the impression that for the bright one, there was nothing unusual about receiving this kind of communication. In fact, I can go further. The bright one acted as if this was a routine operation; certainly nothing that he hadn't dealt with before. Then the astronaut broke in, repeating several times that an unidentified aircraft was pursuing him. He finally confirmed that he was under attack and asked for backup to defend him. The bright one simply acknowledged his request and then sat back and waited. The last voice that I heard was that of another bright one reporting that the mission was accomplished, 'the intruder has been intercepted and all traces of the vessel destroyed.' I stood breathless trying to make sense out of what I heard." He looked at me, his pupils dilated. "Who was the intruder? Was the intruder, the human astronaut, destroyed by another vessel behind it, sent off by the bright ones? Or, was someone else invading the planet? Were our lives in danger?"

"If Peter didn't know, how could I," was running through my mind.

"I had heard of astronauts and space travel, but never imagined it to be true," he told me. "Communication between and among different members of the scientific community is at the heart of the problem. The members of different scientific teams do not all have access to the same information. In my field of study, it was never necessary for me to know anything about intergalactic space voyages; and, yet today I find that incongruous. This information should be made available to everyone. The overriding question is why the bright ones feel threatened by these space voyagers, if that is the case. As we now know that the land is not habitable outside the center, space travel and other planets seem to be excellent solutions for our race." The enthusiasm in his voice when he said space travel gave me the strange impression that he would like to be part of that and that made me feel anxious.

"Days passed and I became more and more troubled by the nightmare of that evening. I wanted to get a copy of the communication between the astronaut and the base just to make certain that everything was not just a dream. So I made friends with one of the communications specialists just to get invited for a tour of the facility. Months passed before I conjured up the courage to re-enter the facility at night. The several times that I was alone, I tried in vain to access the records. I was unable to break through the code."

"Nonetheless, Pamela, my obsession to find the truth drove me to continue my efforts. My questions turned in a different direction, reflecting a new kind of reasoning; a disjointed reasoning that inferred culpability on the part of the bright ones. Why would the bright ones send out an aircraft to intercept and destroy a spacecraft piloted by humans? Even more, where did the bright ones house their aircraft and why were we never told about these vehicles? Were we being invaded? But why were we never warned about it?"

He got up and paced up and down the sandy soil, as if he were reliving the past and stamping out all his frustrations and disappointments. "Eventually, luck was on my side. One night, the room was empty, but the control panels were still lit up and functioning. Before I had time to do anything a voice came over the radio. The person identified himself as, I believe, Captain Michael Hadley. Regardless, the party was requesting permission to land. With all my playing around with the controls over the last few months, I had learned the basics and was able to acknowledge the request and give the party permission to land. I didn't stop there. I asked him questions. The astronaut explained that he was a descendent of a small group of astronauts from Earth that were sent off to explore the viability of certain planets in the next solar system. He was happy to report that a planet suitable for life had been discovered and that the entire group had survived the long journey and had given birth to new generations. They wanted new supplies and, equipment as well as qualified personnel to return with them, to make this new world attractive to other explorers and new world pioneers."

"My heart was racing! This was wonderful news! I wanted to know everything. I was so intent on listening to his story that I was practicably oblivious to a bright one's entry into the control room. I started to reply, telling him that we would have so much to talk about, when I sensed the presence of that bright one. I acted rapidly in cutting off the communication, hoping to protect the astronaut. I lunged underneath the control panel and slithered along until I finally found a better hiding place inside a tall cabinet used to store lab coats and the like." He acted out his escape, sliding along the sandy soil.

"I left the door slightly ajar so that I had a full view of the bright one and could hear the voices being broadcasted. To my ultimate regret the astronaut went back on and announced that he had landed the vessel." Peter held his head in his hands. This painful reality was still bothering him.

"The bright one, confused or perturbed, difficult for me to say, did not react straight away. During this slight interval, the voice of the astronaut came through so clearly that I had the impression that he was in the same room." Peter stopped in mid-stream to remind me that he was still programmed at that time. "There were strong emotions in the astronaut's voice, emotions that I had never encountered before, and that profoundly affected; undoubtedly, the reason why both his voice and his very words are indelibly inscribed in my memory." I nodded to reassure him that I understood. "Yes, Pamela, in a rapid stream of boisterous questions, the astronaut showed, what I know now to be, his profound sorrow and regret, as well as his disdain, horror, confusion, even contempt for what had happened to the planet Earth: "What has happened to this planet? It is devastated. There is nothing but barren and scarred land? Have

I landed on Earth? Answer Me! Am I on the Planet Earth? Where are you and the others?" There was a long pause, before I heard an excruciating scream.

The bright one eventually replied. "You will have no answers. This is no longer your world. You are an intruder."

The bright one contacted one of his staff and ordered the party to eradicate the intruder.

"Everything is normal. The intruder has been eliminated. Over and Out." These were the last words that Peter heard.

"I could hardly believe what happened. The entire situation, from the senseless killing of this human to my helplessness to prevent it, was horrifying. I wanted to destroy, rather rip apart, the cruel and murderous robotic machine, that took the astronaut's life without any regret, or remorse, by ordering the execution of this human in that neutral and indifferent tone." He clenched his fists and tightened his face expressing his anger; an anger, which had irrationally transformed into a kind of shame. "Instead, I had to be ignominiously content waiting in my hiding place until the bright one left the room. Then and only then could I cautiously regain my office and prepare to return to my cubicle." He sat down next to me and took my hands in his. "That is when I discovered that I was overcome by a blurry, double- vision that made me feel nauseous. I lost consciousness and fell on the office floor. Fortunately, Pamela, I woke up on my own and was able to stumble back to my cubicle before morning. I learned sometime later that violent emotions, like my unabated rage, short-circuit our systems."

He stopped for a long moment. I sat patiently, hoping that he would finish the story, but finally I needed to reassure myself. "Are you alright, Peter?" I asked. I was worried that he was painfully affected about all that he had experienced.

"Yes, don't worry, I am ok. I just needed a couple minutes to come to terms with what I just said." He pulled me close to him and I leaned back into his arms. I could identify with what he said next. "When I regained consciousness, everything was in focus. I was seeing the 'real world.' I hid my newfound vision from the bright ones. Like you, I saw many people whose physical appearances were shocking. Luckily my partner was just as beautiful as before my transformation. That was a real consolation. I longed to be with her, just to cast my eyes upon her. There were very few people who look like us." He told me. He was certain of that. I couldn't say, because I had been shuffled about and hospitalized during my traumatic stage. I was glad to hear that our small group did not represent all physically normal people at the center.

"In the end, I became more and more intolerant with everyday life. People who live in the center, under the control of their visual receptors, are not at all inquisitive about life, just pathetically accepting and submissive. Discovering visual reality made me want to know more and that made it more, more and more disturbing for him to be with people whose lives were programmed. Everyone displayed a perfunctory smile, void of emotion, at work, at lunch, in the corridors, whenever and wherever I passed by them.

"So, that is what awaits me?" I thought to myself.

"I realized instantly that I had to give my code number to programmed humans if I wanted them to recognize me. I acted aloofly, pretending that the problem with my imagery projection was temporary. I had to be careful, though, when there were bright ones hovering about. You will have to remember this, we are seen by those like us who have bypassed their own programming. And, this was more delicate because we had to hide this reality from the bright ones." He swallowed hard. "I quickly understood that I was better off without contact with the programmed humans."

"They stressed me and revolted me." He said vehemently. "I hated the idea that I had been one of them. I couldn't shake off that feeling of outrage and indignation that overcame me whenever I found myself in their presence." He turned to me and added with a strong tone of resentment in his voice. "You don't know how lucky you are that you did not have to face up to the reality of our lives. Even when you go back, it will be easier for you, because you have been informed and warned about the environment."

I was staring back at him, feeling slightly outraged and offended by what he had just said. "Should I feel guilty?"

"No, Pamela. No, of course not! You should never feel guilty." He replied as he squeezed me tightly in his arms, in a consoling and apologetic way. "I didn't mean to hurt you. I never want to hurt you again." There was sorrow in his voice and another long pause.

"Oh, there is still more." He released his arms and moved in front of me. "I was grateful that my heavy work load kept me out of circulation." He said facetiously. "The daily schedule posted on the door of our cubicle was calculated to keep us occupied every minute of the day."

We spent a few minutes exchanging opinions regarding the complacency, even the culpability, of programmed humans. In spite of the fact that we both believed that our programmed existences were, in retrospect, utterly appalling, we agreed that it was not our fault that all the information that we received about others appealed to us. It was also not our fault that we felt gratified with our programmed lives. We liked everyone we met. They were both physically and intellectually compatible. In fact, they were perfect in every respect. We were blissfully happy in this programmed environment.

"I had to develop a new strategy to survive in that environment." He said, as he picked up the conversation, "but, even more so to control, publicly, my growing intolerance of programmed humans. So, I pretended to like everyone. It helped, but it wasn't enough for me to shake myself out of the morose state of mind."

He did not give me time to answer. "I wanted to leave that Hell Hole!" He screamed. "I didn't know where I could go, what I could do. But I was certain that I could not go on living in that place much longer." It was visible on his face that he was reliving the horror of what he thought would be an interminable prison of despair. He sat playing with the red soil, letting it slide through his fingers, appreciating its calming effect. I sat patiently watching.

"Day dreaming" he finally said, "helped me. Sometimes I imagined myself living on the top of one those faraway snow-capped mountains that I saw from the monorail when my view of the world was artificially induced. Other times, I wanted to hide in fields where I would be mesmerized by the new fragrances I bathed in. Alas these beautiful places had disappeared and, like you, sorry to say, I saw the barren, ugliness of the exterior. Quite frankly, frustrated as I was with this depressing reality, the only enticing place for me was a new planet in a new solar system." I quivered over the idea of his leaving.

"There was very little real, factual information available to support the viability of space travel. Everything that I found spoke in terms of probabilities. Then something extraordinary happened, by accident. I was asked to make a basic report on lunar craters. Bored and annoyed with this busy work task, I sat far too long in front of the telescope without writing anything down, much to the dissatisfaction of the bright one who was overseeing my research." He had a silly smirk on his face. "So this unwanted guest boldly sat down on the seat right next to me. What audacity, I thought at the time. This type of behavior was, as I mentioned before, abnormal, in my sector. But this foolish bright one's inopportune move was significantly revealing. I sensed that I was being watched, closely, too closely; something that I was not aware of before. It was clear though, Pamela, that I could not have run all those risks and made the discoveries I had made without being noticed, or caught. As you know, the bright ones were, after all, controlling all our lives." He said with a sad drone.

"But, the best is to come." He was now vibrant and enthusiastic, as he jumped back up on his feet to act out the scene. "Within minutes of that thought running through my mind, the electricity went out and when it started up again, no more than seconds later, an electrical charge hit the bright one sitting next to me, cutting off its luminous glow." He let out a belly laugh as he relived the episode in his own mind. "It was so funny. I had to control myself at the time. I tell you, Pamela, he knew that I had seen him. That creation understood that I saw his android body."

"How did he know?" I asked, curious about what they looked like.

"I think it was because my mouth dropped open in total shock when I caught a glimpse of his android body." He said and then added, "He, easy to confirm on first glance, as he stood completely naked in front of me. Normally, he should have been wearing something." Then he laughed with fervor. "He knew that I recognized that he was an android. After all I am a robotic engineer." He announced with pleasure. "It was so evident, for me that he had robotic traits, as he had no visible muscles, or fingernails, and so forth, even though, admittedly, he had an extraordinary skin-like exterior." Peter's eyes were sparkling and his whole face lit up with pleasure before he laughed again. "Anyway, where was I?" He asked rhetorically. " Right, I had a feeling then, and even now, that the Android didn't report the incident because he felt responsible and did not want any trouble, assuming that he might have had any. That is the only rational explanation I can give you."

"So, tell me more about what he looked like." I begged.

"He had human characteristics, but, as I just mentioned, it was visible to me that he was manufactured; that he was inhuman. John saw one, as well, and like me identified the creation as an android, the name given to a manufactured, humanoid machine. I didn't know that it was possible to construct one. My robotics research is far behind in that field. I wondered who made these machines and when. I don't know very much about these sophisticated humanlike machines, but it does explain why they hide behind blinding lights." He bit his lower lip in reflection and then added, "You have to understand, Pamela, that they look more vulnerable when their shield is down. They need to keep us controlled and submissive. The blinding light gives them power."

"In any event, Pamela, I told you that I wanted to and needed to leave that place. I felt defenseless and anxious; conscious that I was walking on dangerous turf. If I thought too much, I felt petrified with fear. It was time for me to leave and that is exactly what I wanted. So when the opportunity presented itself to me, I went with it."

"Dangerous?" I queried.

"Danger is instinctive to all forms of life, Pamela. I was alive with panic. Everything that I didn't understand or like terrified me. So, naturally, I sensed danger approaching me from every direction."

"But, what did you imagine could happen to you?" I continued questioning him.

"That is more inexplicable. I didn't know; but I didn't dwell on the consequences. The worse that could have happened to me was to be terminated; but that didn't worry me. We are prepared for that day from the day that we start learning." That is true, we are told that we have a limited life span from a young age. "We are programmed for it. Moreover, it's an eventuality that we can't even resist. Yet, I was scared of something indefinable and atrocious, happening to me, and was being very cautious about everything." He paused to take a deep breath. "Witnessing the undressing, if you like, of a "bright one" could not be without consequence. That expression of surprise, which I knew was visible on my face, exposed me to real danger."

I felt even closer to him after hearing his story because I understood him better. Yes, he could be vulnerable, afraid, worried, just like me, but he could also be determined, persistent, brave, intelligent, clever, and more when he had to be. I hoped that I would not disappoint him. I hoped that I would have a story to tell him one day that would make him admire and respect me, as I do him. Already I understood exactly what he meant by danger. I experienced it without knowing what name to give it. We both were terrified of some horrible, impending peril, that made us tremble and shudder with fear; but neither one of us was capable of rationally defining what we were afraid of.

He interrupted my thoughts with self-criticism. He dwelt on the fact that he now realizes that he didn't give his decision to leave the center enough thought. "I was guided and fueled by naivety and hopeful thinking. Like the others, I believed that nature and its promise of a new life existed. And, I believed that this idyllic natural environment that was fed to us over and over again as we were transported throughout the Center existed and that it would be within walking distance of the Center. I was convinced that it was not a dream, but a reality. I was even certain that I could survive on my own; that I could find food and shelter; that all the rest would follow and that life would be more challenging and satisfying than it was for me in my programmed existence in the Center. So I took nothing with me when I left, not that that would have made a big difference."

"My thinking was more rational where my partner was concerned. All throughout this ordeal I was more obsessed about my partner's future than my own. I didn't want to leave her alone, but I didn't know how to explain to her what I discovered. In the end, I had to say goodbye." His voice trembled with emotion.

Strange, I thought to myself, how protective he felt towards this woman that was chosen for him. I wonder how I would have reacted if Jonathan had been more physically appealing to me. Perhaps I rejected him only because his physical appearance frightened me. I never once considered his feelings. Was Jonathan with someone else now? Did he suffer from my absence? I just assumed that he went on living like before, as if nothing had changed. And, why not? We had no particular affection for one another and were a couple in a very vague sense of the term, in that we would spend our lives living together, as if that created an inseparable bond between us.

Peter explained to me that John received written information regarding each of the members, the deprogrammed humans who would become members of the outside community, from an insider, a spy, at the Center, who left written messages on John's laboratory table. John then arranged meetings with each of the members of the small group, including Peter, to offer each of them the opportunity to join him in his adventure to move outside the Center. This invisible network of informants is still in existence. These informers apparently planned and organized the operation carried out by Mathieu.

We sat next to each other in silence. Each of us deep in thought. Even though I was not convinced about this network of informers, it would be nice if there were informers on the inside who I could turn to in time of need. That was a consoling thought.

The members of this scientific community had at least one thing in common. They were able to confront the problem of deprogramming in a rational manner. Nonetheless that did not justify that condescending remark by Sarah weeks ago. It still bothered me because it left me with the impression that the scientific community, apart from Peter, did not consider me to be at their intellectual level. Scientists considered themselves to be at the epitome of logical problem solving. They thought that musicians were illogical, flighty, or out of touch with reality. I had another impression of musicians." I think that musicians are quite logical. Music is mathematical and when the rhythm of a piece does not fit together perfectly, it is as frustrating as an irresolvable equation." I mused. "I have to stop being so sensitive and feel more secure about myself." I resolved.

What I would like to say to them is that, regardless of our professional qualifications, we can all act illogically. They all did that by blindly following John who was presumably guiding them to find something better.

There are a lot more pieces to the puzzle that don't fit. Perhaps they never will?

Chapter 14: Tension

We regularly received general reports from those presumed informers containing nothing more than affirmations of the tension between Dr. Crawford and Dr. Gordon and the fact that I was still the object of her research.

The conflict over ideas between Gordon and Crawford intensified on a daily basis and the parties prepared to defend their individual positions before the Board. Crawford was a formidable opponent whose strategy was to corner Gordon before the meeting, in the hopes of convincing her to relinquish her position. Trying to avoid Crawford was not easy for Gordon; sooner or later he was bound to catch up with her. She could feel his presence just about everywhere, even when he was miles away.

Her study of Pamela was taking up much of her time, but it was far too early for her to make her findings official. She was more convinced than ever that letting Pamela live outside the center was an excellent idea. Her subject was discovering new emotions every day and, more importantly, was reacting in that unpredictable way so characteristic of her race. This was the first time that anyone of her species had surveyed the development of human emotions. Her colleagues in this field concentrated on emotional inhibitors. The traditional premise was that human emotions must be inhibited in order to assure the perpetuation of this race.

Even though she was an ardent proponent of this position during much of her long career, her position changed radically two years ago. Human creativity was suffering, particularly in the field of scientific research. In addition, invention and discovery periods were much longer than before. The human race had not yet caught up with itself and was falling behind as well. She worked with a small group of five very influential and impressive colleagues to determine the cause. Dr. Crawford was a member of this group. She and two other members, Dr. Flanders and Dr. Miller, held the controversial position that emotions were the cause of this serious lack of creativity. Humans were no longer aggressive and determined competitors. They were no longer motivated for personal, or even humanitarian or other reasons to succeed, and, consequently, had no meaningful relationship with their work or the future of the Center. Dr. Gordon went so far as to say that human emotions, positive and negative, at all levels, must be restored if the planet were to be saved.

Other Centers carried out the same study and Dr. Gordon was pleased to see that her small group was not alone. Other acclaimed colleagues like Dr. Fleming and Dr. Jarod shared their viewpoint. Nonetheless, they were still a minority and that meant that they all had to be careful of how far they went in criticizing established procedure.

"I have scheduled a new meeting for us in two weeks' time with the Board," Dr. Crawford announced, as he jogged next to her in the hospital corridor.

"No matter, I am ready." She replied.

"You have got to stop letting yourself be so personally caught up in this problem. There are times that I think that you would like to be human, at least you would like to experience human emotions." He suggested.

Dr. Gordon had asked herself that question many times and knew that there was some truth in what he said even though there was no way that she could ever express emotions. Even where Dr. Crawford was concerned, she avoided him because she wanted to continue her work, not because she detested him, as she was incapable of experiencing emotions.

"It is important to explore all angles. My theory takes into account the true psychological structure of humans. I have never said that we should let them go off on their own and do whatever. We all know the consequences of that. However, to put them back in touch with emotions would benefit us scientifically. Even in the arts, we could only benefit. Nonetheless, the security issue is a problem and I have not had time to investigate that."

He grabbed her just as she went to enter her office and added. "Be careful, Dr. Gordon. I don't think that you realize how dangerous it would be for you, for us and for them to reinstate that which we have tried so long to eradicate."

She shut the door on him and took her seat behind her tiny desk. The Center had everything, but in small sizes. She thought about another time when she had plenty of space to arrange her things. At one time her office was ten times the size of the small cell she occupied today. She remembered well what had happened and presumably why. Cause and effect was well embedded in her memory. As she flashed back in her memory banks for answers, there were none. The world was different. Was it a better world? She didn't know. What she did know, however, was that humans had changed too much.

Chapter 15: Concerns

Knowing that she still considered me to be her research project, I wondered when Dr. Gordon would come to get me. I knew that all kinds of emotions were now alive inside of me and worried that she was also aware of that. If she was, she must also be aware of the fact that I was unprepared for the onset of emotions. My emotional levels must be more in tune than the scientists I live with because, unlike them, I operated at emotional extremes. They just took everything in stride while at the same time I could feel guilty about the way I reacted to others. I even worried about how they saw me. It seemed important to me to be accepted and liked. But Peter didn't care at all what the others thought about him. I wished that I could be like him.

Many times, like now, I would just sit back and ponder my situation. Each day brought me closer to Peter, and closer to the day when we would become parents. Months passed since I left the Center and the only thing that broke the boredom of this monotonous life was the baby that I was carrying. As my child grew inside of me, I felt stronger. The baby's dependency on me gave me more and more self-confidence. His dependency also made me more concerned about his future. I feared for his future. That was one of the reasons why I hoped that Dr. Gordon would abandon her study of me and let me live in peace.

Jason completely recovered and was ready to start off on a new expedition. I wanted to accompany him. I wanted to live the life of an adventurer. Even though he still calls himself an explorer, I have not changed my mind about how I see him in the role of an explorer. But, I wondered if he could ever become methodical enough to be rightly referred to as an explorer. Unfortunately, his maps were practically useless and the only thing he had going for him was his sense of adventure that drove him forward. Why couldn't he have been a real explorer? He could have given us the directions to find his floral paradise; the place where Peter and I and our child could spend the rest of our lives. I have given up listening to his descriptions of this paradise. He even admitted that he could never find the place again and this frustrates and angers me. Sometimes I wish that he had never mentioned this paradise.

Children were more interesting to me now. I observed them closely. I realized that they ran around and laughed a lot. They seemed to be happy doing nothing special. They had been digging the same hole for months and had not discovered anything. They just piled mounds of red, barren, dry earth around the top of a deep pit. In the beginning, I believed that they would discover something that could explain what had happened to this planet, if the contentions of the astronaut held any weight. Apart from an array of different sized stones, they hadn't dug up anything that seemed in any way important. But unlike the adults, they had not given up digging.

I started to see things differently. Was the euphoria of my childhood real or imagined? Even though the children of Ruth and Sarah were not privy to our education, they did not seem to have missed anything. Ruth and Sarah taught them how to read and write. They scratched the letters in the dirt; they did the same with mathematics. There was something sane about learning like this. Was sitting in front of a computer screen for hours at a time, absorbing the information that was fed to me, a better way to learn? Our terminals were our teachers when we were young. John explained to me that we were given aptitude tests regularly. These tests determined our future. I found that revelation sad. When I started my piano classes, I had only one objective, to master this instrument. If John is right, I scored high in music, maybe in the arts in general. But did I display a subconscious interest in the piano? That I believed was a legitimate question.

Mathilda mentioned the conscious and subconscious parts of the brain to me one day. I never delved into this subject at school and was never even aware of the fact that we had subconscious desires and needs. Probably because of my pregnancy, this subject aroused my curiosity. I wanted to offer the right environment to my unborn child. I wondered if my child was receiving messages from my subconscious self. According to Mathilda, the personnel at the Center observed and studied our conscious and subconscious behavior on a daily basis. As we were monitored to be happy—what I consider now to be complacent—our dream patterns, in particular, were an index of stability. This explained why there were sleep consoles in our bedrooms. Each bed had a head terminal, comfortably padded and restful. I hadn't thought much about this apparatus until Mathilda brought up the subject. I used to fall asleep the instant my head settled into the headrest. Everything was perfectly timed so that everyone, every human, fell asleep and woke up at the same time. Our programmed, chronometric days all ended and started at the same time. Dreams were probably induced to block out subconscious impulses according to Mathilda.

A consoling thought was that I was not an occasional insomniac all my life. Since I left the center, I have had restless nights and even nightmares, seemingly related to periods of stress. Because I am suffering from insomnia at the moment, I sought Mathilda's advice. She was a psychologist. She said that her work was particularly interesting although she never personally met with any of her subjects or patients. She was routinely given a written report. The report could be hundreds of pages. If she wasn't able to diagnose the problem, she received more written information about her subject.

"You, know, Pamela, since I left the Center and engaged in direct contact with our community members," she said, as she stared off in the distance, "I question the relevance of my previous work. I think that the subjects of the reports that I was given never existed." She sighed. "And, if they existed, it was in another time and place."

She was specialized in phobias of all sorts that include fear of closed spaces, heights, crowds, noise, animals, machines, and so on-the list seems to be never ending. In the Center, she provided curative solutions for phobia-induced disorders in different patients. She was never given the opportunity to follow up on her patients, so she just assumed that her diagnoses and recommended treatments were correct.

Like the rest of the scientists, she doubted the credibility of her work. "Sometimes, Pamela, I wonder if I repeated a study that was already conducted." She stated. "But, what would be the point in that? How could that benefit anyone?" She was plagued by these questions to the point that her only viable explanation for this repetitive, bureaucratic work and proverbial nonsense was the need to keep her occupied and thus give her the impression that she served a purpose.

Unlike Mathilda, I had access to all forms of music: from classical, folkloric to modern. We were free to compose new music, if we felt inspired to do so; and, just like those working in the arts, we invented new techniques and new forms of artistic expression. But then we were no threat to the bright ones. We were simply a form of entertainment for them, unless we let our thoughts develop which was what happened to Ferdinand.

Mathilda helped me over those nightmares, which she told me were related to my pregnancy and my fear of having a child, all of which she found completely normal under the circumstances. I told her about the discussions that I had with Sarah and Ruth, regarding pregnancy and childbirth.

"That should put you more at ease. " She suggested.

"Yes, to the extent that I know that Sarah and Ruth will be there for the child birth; and, of course to reassure me during the next few months." Admittedly, I felt good about that. "But, they weren't worried about the psychological stability of their babies growing in utero." I replied pensively. "I want to communicate the right thoughts to my baby." That was a real concern for me.

Mathilda replied like a psychologist. At least that is what I thought because her answer was rather clinical. "Your baby is certainly in touch with you. This baby hears your voice and the voices of your entourage and senses your personal likes and dislikes." She stopped to organize her thoughts. "I believe, Pamela, that this unborn baby knows which members of the community you feel the most comfortable with, simply because we humans are not capable of masking our deep seeded feelings, especially hiding them from the creature witnessing them deep inside the womb." She ended the discussion by saying, "You have nothing to worry about, Pamela, you are a very nice person and we all appreciate you. Your baby knows that. I found our discussion stimulating and hope to sit down with you again to explore your feelings."

Her analysis of my situation put me under pressure to maintain a happy, carefree approach to life and constantly stretch my lips into a smile, as I desperately wanted to convey only positive feelings to my baby.

In spite of my efforts and Mathilda's kind and supportive words, I still had doubts about the future. I had trepidations that I would not have the opportunity to raise my own child. As Dr. Gordon has not abandoned me, as her project, I might have to return to the Center for the rest of my life. Perhaps I won't ever see or interact with my child. That obligation to return to the Center hung over me like an evil force suffocating the light and happy feelings that should be blossoming inside me during my pregnancy. More worrisome than being excluded from my child's life, I was afraid that someone else in our small community would assume my maternal role. If so, who? I looked around me and wondered which of the women would replace me.

One day it became evident, as if someone slapped me in my face. The only way for me to deal with this problem was for me to choose someone right now, to act in my place. I ran down the list. Ruth and Sarah were very good to their children, but how would they treat a child that was not their own? Mathilda seemed to be a perfect choice because she was alone. Nonetheless, she had the habit of moving from one person to another on the sly. Isabelle caught her in Mathieu's arms one night and the entire community was called in to calm the scandal. As far as I knew, she never approached Peter, but that didn't mean that she wouldn't jump into bed with him the very day that Dr. Gordon came looking for me. Mathilda was out of the question. As was Isabelle, because we were not that close.

Frustrated, I focused my thoughts on what I wanted. And, as always, the same thing popped into my mind; that dream that we might never realize. I didn't want to lose or be torn away from Peter or my child. I wanted us to find an idyllic surrounding, home to us for the rest of our lives. To help me think, I stretched out on that hot, red, barren ground, closed my eyes and took a nap.

Miraculously, the answer appeared; it came to me out of nowhere. "Of course," I said out loud. "Why didn't I think about them before?" Benjamin and Stanislas were the perfect choice to replace me. I didn't know how Peter would feel about this. Maybe he would rather raise the baby alone. We never talked about it. Yet Benjamin and Stanislas would be very caring and protective; and, as they can't have a baby on their own, they might be happy to assume the maternal role, in my absence. Singularly, or in the context of a couple, they were both capable of adoring and cherishing my child. With that thought in mind, I was ready to confront Peter. If he was worried about going it on his own, maybe my idea would appeal to him.

Chapter 16: Inspiration

We tried to keep track of time by markings on the cavern wall; a primitive but relatively reliable method. Even though I was not certain of the exact date when my baby was conceived, chances were that I was near the end of my sixth month. I had a nice round and solid belly that I just loved to look at and touch. I marveled at my pregnancy and cherished every moment of it.

Peter liked to play with the baby, to get the baby to move and jump around inside of me. It made us laugh with joy. I started singing a few months back and believed that the baby responded eagerly to my melodies. Actually, I missed my piano and the other musicians. I felt sad about the end of something that brought me so much pleasure and satisfaction.

I should not have used the word singing, because there were no lyrics to our music; I hum. In fact, there were never any words to our music; the words were deleted. I learned later that there were real songs in the past, with catchy phrases, but we didn't know them. We never studied the history of music in any detail. The bright ones decided that it was inappropriate for us to understand the evolution of the human race. Anything that could communicate the past through words or pictures was systematically erased. Songs are a form of historical representation. Telling stories about a time, conveying feelings like sadness and happiness, revealing the dreams and the frustrations of a generation, and more, were therefore considered "dangerous" for the preservation of our programmed states of mind.

Even though the composers, the composers' lives and the historical period were never presented to us, the bright ones always gave us a picture of the composer's face. Curiously, the melody was enough to form a picture of the style of life, of the society, and of the time. The melody communicated more to a musician than words. The instruments themselves, whether a guitar instead of a piano or a clarinet instead of a cello, resonated the tone of a vitality, emotional energy and intellectual insight that could be reminiscent of a period in history. Right or wrong, as musicians we chose our preferred music by an innate identification with a period in human history. In my case, Ferdinand, as I mentioned, played a vital role in my musical expression. He was the one who painted the picture of the composers and their lives. Even though I was instinctively drawn to a period or a composer, Ferdinand inspired me to understand and thereby achieve perfect musical expression, if that is not too pretentious for me to say.

In my beginning years as a pianist, I played in piano concerts. I was later invited to participate in symphonies with piano solos, and occasionally, as accompaniment for string or wind instruments. I was fond of baroque music, with its spiritual aspect. I moved into other classical styles, Mozart and Beethoven. With maturity in music, I found Chopin and Liszt. I loved immersing myself in Liszt's Hungarian Rhapsody, which, bewitching and mysterious in the beginning, moves into a happy, festive ending. Today, I hummed 'Liebestraum', Love Dream, No.3 by Liszt, which has a warm and loving complexion. Nonetheless, with all the talented and impressive classical composers, I was seduced by the music of Chopin and believed that I honored him, in a certain way, when my fingers touched the keys. My favorite piece of music was Chopin's, E-flat Nocturne, op.9 no2. It was extraordinary how delicately he combined sadness, joy, violence and mystery in one piece. And, of course, his Nocturne OP.27 no. 2, with its hypnotic rippling water was ingenious.

I loved lullabies. I was told that lullabies induced sleep. Humming Brahms' masterpiece, Lullaby and Goodnight, seemed to calm my baby's movements. I had no doubt, though, that the masterpiece of lullabies must be the one and only that Chopin ever composed, his improvisation Op.57. Difficult to play, more difficult to hum, it was definitely a sublime work of art.

I liked to think about my baby's future and wondered if he would be a musician or a scientist. If someone asked me that question, I would answer that I prefer that he become a musician. I wondered if it was a human reflex to want to create our offspring in one's own image. Maybe? But was it wrong? I didn't know. What I wanted to believe was that when one loved another, he or she would naturally want that person to be as happy as possible. If someone was doing something that brought much personal happiness, then it would appear logical, inevitable, almost unavoidable, to communicate that passion and happiness as well as inspire the same feelings in their child. On the contrary, if one were miserable, it would be vicious and cruel to force their child to live that same sort. I imagined that everything was relative. Did people have choices in the past? Today, there were no choices. But, there was total bliss for those who accepted the system in the Center.

Were we making history now? We were producing a new generation. Will they return to the Center or will they stagnate on the extremities? Although I was very worried about the present, I was even more worried about the future.

Chapter 17: Confrontation

More than a few weeks, virtually months, rolled by since Dr. Crawford warned Dr. Gordon of an impending meeting with the Commission. Unlike Dr. Crawford, Dr. Gordon was not as interested in the administrative side of her unit, which could take precious time away from her research. She never even contacted Dr. Crawford to find out why the meeting had been postponed. In reality, it was postponed because Dr. Crawford requested it. He was hoping that delaying the meeting could only work in his favor, waiting for Dr. Gordon's project to melt down. What she was doing was too dangerous for everyone.

Nonetheless, the Commission had received some interesting findings from the other centers. There seemed to be some truth in what Dr. Gordon was recommending and the Commission decided to convene another meeting.

Dr. Crawford was determined to side step the problem of emotions by focusing on the group's desire to procreate and the pregnancy of "16011305120113". He felt that Dr. Gordon had not fully considered the consequences of this on the future of humankind.

"Distinguished members of the Board, I would like to examine a tangential issue that has become a real problem for the future of our race and the human race." He began. "Today we see a tendency in these isolated, exiled communities to procreate. Humans are physical creatures, as we have seen in the past. Most of their emotions are linked to experiencing physical love. Procreation and parental responsibilities are by-products of this primitive emotion. Knowing how to love, as Dr. Gordon must be aware, is not the beginning of positive emotional reactions, but rather negative consequences: jealously, fear, anger, possessiveness, frustration, paranoia, to name just a few. A simple example: We have seen that it is rare for humans to take an interest in the newborns of others in these small communities. They are more interested in their own. They are connected with this new creature simply because it is an extension of themselves. They cannot imagine that anyone other than themselves can produce a child better than their own. They are sensitive to its physical characteristics in the beginning. Later, they are certain that it is physically stronger and intellectually superior to the others. If they discover the contrary, there is competition, jealousy, resentment, and so forth. Need I say more on this subject to show you just how dangerous it is to study these renegade societies that enjoy abounding freedom in renewing life? The solution: We should put an end to their existence."

"Dr. Gordon would you like to answer Dr. Crawford on this point?" queried the Governor.

"Dr. Crawford is obsessed with the concept of love as the root of all problems. I don't see it that way. If we had wanted to avoid the natural consequences of human communities—that is reproduction—we could have continued to put the sexual inhibitors in their food. Our objective was to observe the evolution of society. Agreed, these so-called modern human beings are reacting in primitive ways. They are starting by putting together a community, enjoying a bizarre sexual intimacy, producing a new generation, and creating …a societal hierarchy. There is in every community a kind of leader, someone that others go to for advice. There is very little structure apart from that, unfortunately. But this can be explained by the fact that the members of these societies have no challenges. They still receive clothes and food from the centers. Nonetheless, in general these humans live in complete harmony. And, contrary to what Dr. Crawford would like us to believe, there are no violent disputes or physical violence."

"And, the jealousy, possessiveness, egoism, fear, anger, and more of this race? That is not evident to you?" Dr. Crawford responded.

"Yes, but we need to understand these emotions. Love is a complacent emotion in and of itself. In my estimation, if there were no other emotions to come in contact with other than that, humans would be docile and uncreative. I would like to emphasize the fact that the negative emotions are what propel the human race. Without jealously, envy, anger, fear, and others, there would be no competition and no creativity. These studies will help us to direct these negative emotions into productive performance. We are only starting to understand what triggers these negative emotions. And, as you rightly pointed out, love seems to be the first strong emotion experienced. In fact, it seems to be the emotion sought after. It seems to give a purpose to an otherwise mundane life. In any event, we need time to understand how to use them for our benefit." She replied.

"Time, Members of the Commission that is exactly what we cannot afford, if we believe that life must go forward." He said. "Sometimes I believe that you have forgotten everything that happened before. That part of your memory was accidentally, can I say, erased."

"Yes, Dr. Crawford, your warnings must be taken seriously. The

Commission is well aware of that." The Governor said. "But remember, we are in a position of strength. We are starting to catch up with the past in terms of scientific research. But we need incentives to go forward. Humans can provide that and more."

"But why don't we just stop here? Why do we have to go further?" Dr. Crawford asked showing his dismay over the reaction of the Commission.

"Because we can't. You know and understand why. We cannot change what must be. We have already delayed that, but we cannot avoid it. We are starting to share the position that emotions are necessary. In a complacent, euphoric environment, they are like our "pets." We feed them, clothe them and care for them. We must start to exploit them. And, at the same time, continue to keep them happy." The Governor retorted.

"Do I understand that Dr. Gordon is given the green light to continue her project?"

"Yes, Dr. Crawford, and you should probably think about how you might be able to help her, rather than to sabotage her mission. That will be all."

As Dr. Gordon left the Board Room, she felt good about herself. She noticed that her long and energetic stride gave her a look of dominance. She had won for the moment. She felt different, but should she? Dr. Crawford might have described her as happy. But how could she experience that emotion. . . She was not human. She couldn't have human sensations.

She stopped long enough for Dr. Crawford to catch up with her.

"Well, Dr. Gordon, I guess that I shall have to become a member of your research team if I want to have any voice in your project. But, I am not convinced. I shall certainly always be the skeptic, but maybe that is not so bad. So what do you think?"

She looked at him for moment as her thoughts wondered. In keeping with their race, he was unemotional. He wasn't hurt that the decision was not in his favor and he was not angry with her. He has his ideas but is not as attached to them as she is to hers. That must be the answer. For him there is no real right or wrong. There are just two or more versions and he must feel obliged to say "black" when she says "white." Certainly it must just be in his programming. Yet, the fact that she felt victorious when he did not feel defeated was a bit disconcerting.

"I am pleased that you are ready to join my research team. We need someone like you. Your skepticism will be an asset."

They shook hands, a human form of politeness that the androids adopted for themselves, and walked away. "Emotions," Dr. Gordon said to herself as she entered her office.

In the quiet surroundings, she let her mind go back to another period.

What had Dr. Crawford said about her memory? That it had been erased. Impossible. She was part of a limited edition that had always functioned at an optimum. Her systems had never shut down. She was intact. Nothing had been changed or modified. At least that was how she remembered it. The only way to ascertain that she had not been tampered with was to open her file. Did he have access to her file? Did he have her code?

"Dr. Gordon," someone was knocking at her door.

"Yes, Come in," she answered. It was one of the nurses.

"We have a problem in the ward. One of the patients is refusing treatment. He is very aggressive. We want your permission to sedate him."

"You have it. I'll drop by to see him later."

It was late in the day and she still had rounds to make. She could access her file another time.

Chapter 18: Moments of Melodrama

"Pamela, I would like to talk to you, if it is convenient." said John, who knew when to approach me when I had nothing pressing to do. The biggest problem that we faced was how to find enough to do each day. The only possible exceptions to that are Sarah and Ruth who filled their days teaching the children. But even they looked bored.

"What is bothering you, John," I asked nonchalantly. I had taken to avoiding him from the beginning. I felt uneasy around him because he had all the answers and if someone ventured to contradict him, he would insult them. His remarks about Jason were even cruel. For instance he condemned Jason for living in an imaginary world, that his years of wandering had destroyed his sense of reality and that he was an embarrassment to humankind, the human race. He often crowned his diatribes by blurting out that anyone who did not have the common sense to keep a record of his voyages should keep his mouth shut.

I didn't agree with John since Jason was very young when he left the center and did not receive as good an education as us. The map he gave us was certainly the best he could do. But admittedly, I also held a harsh position, principally because I was so disappointed that he was unable to show me the way to that tropical paradise. John was not just critical of Jason, he was also very critical of others. If he were so fantastic and capable, why hasn't he accomplished more? The answer was evident, because he couldn't. John impressed me as the kind of person that strives for conflict. The only way to avoid a confrontation with someone like that is to completely avoid him.

"Nothing is bothering me, Pamela. It is just that your pregnancy is coming to an end and I believe that the others will come to get you shortly after the baby is born. There is a lot that we have to talk about if you are going to help us; help our race."

"I don't know exactly what I agreed to do, though. We haven't talked about my mission since my arrival." I admit that discussion comes up from time to time; I do have supplications. I am not going to mention this to John;

I shall be a bit cagey. "You all just let me find my place in this group." I answered dryly.

"True, but I have observed you. I have gotten to know your personality and now I can help you to better accomplish your goal." He continued to play his leadership role.

"There he goes again," I thought to myself. "He has all the answers. Just because he is a scientist doesn't make him the most intelligent. He is pretentious; that is what he is. Pretentious and arrogant, those are the words that Peter used to describe him. In my mind, those attitudes do not breed respect. I shall just humor him for the moment."

"Ok, so what would you like me to do?" I queried.

"First of all, you have to give some thought to how you are going to respond to their questions on your emotional development, the single most important reason why you have been living with us. So, do you know what you might say?"

"Good question," I had to admit.

"Ok, so let's start with this: Which emotion do you feel is the most difficult to control?"

"That's easy---Anger."

"What makes you angry, Pamela?"

"I realized early on that we humans are by nature cruel. We play psychological games with our entourage. Mathilda explained to me that certain human behavior is meant to cause pain. For example, we can make a decision to target an individual and to make him or her feel inferior to us. We could isolate someone; or just simply look bored with somebody."

I was actually talking about him, but he didn't seem to be aware of that. So I went on. "I experienced that emotion when I first arrived. I couldn't understand why I did not receive a warm welcoming from certain people. In fact, that attitude towards me, in at least one case, has never changed. At first I felt sad, rejected and then I felt angry. I wanted to hurt them too, but I didn't. Why? Perhaps because I am not a vengeful person. Or, perhaps I just don't like conflict. In any event, I can't be cruel."

"Who made you angry?" John asked, completely oblivious to the target of my anger.

"It is not important to give names. I am not looking for an ally in you. I have just gone beyond my anger and tried to get to know them better. Their attitude towards me was based more on fear and insecurity, than an honest dislike of me. There is a positive side to all this. I understand how anger can be a very dangerous emotion. If I responded to my anger, at that time, I might have lashed out physically or said something extremely brutal that I would regret today. Anger is perhaps the most difficult emotion to control."

"Ok, fair enough. You might have been right to be angry. I am glad that you have gone past that." He nodded in approval and then asked, "And me, how do you feel about me?"

"I don't like you very much." I was direct. "You have one redeeming quality; you love your children. Aside from that, you are power hungry. You want to control others. You do this by belittling them and making them feel foolish. In fact I did not want this meeting with you. I don't like how you treat people and the words that you use are sometimes offensive. It is easy for you to have power here. We are a small group that you led out of the center; you organized the departure. How far would you go to maintain control?" I wanted to throw the ball back in his camp to see his weaknesses, if any.

John started to laugh with such fervor that I felt a cold shiver tingle down my spine. His grating laughter offended me; a vicious form of mockery and humiliation, that pushed me to stand up to leave. "No, don't leave, Pamela." He pleaded. "I am not laughing at you. I am laughing at the situation. In fact, I feel completely powerless in this community. I worry that we are wasting precious time because we are in fact doing nothing. I was always trying to motivate people. Before you arrived, I was more positive. I suggested different projects. At first, there were those who wanted to go ahead with them. But, we were never able to discover a new land that was fertile and habitable. It is true that we never wandered far away from the center, but for practical reasons. We need life support like water and food. We also were probably not courageous enough to take the kinds of risks that we would have had to take to find fertile land. Consequently, we returned to this cavern time and time again. Eventually, we lost interest. We abandoned our hopes of independence. Complacency, even resignation, set in. I am bitter which may account for my sarcasm. I sincerely want something different for me and for my children."

"Then why did you make fun of Jason?"

"Because he disappointed me. He came with stories of a better place. But, where was that place? In one instance he gave us hope; and, in the second instance, he took it away, like a tease. How could we find it? He said that he had walked for years before reaching us. But, does he have a notion of time? And, if this place exists, why didn't he bring any evidence as proof of its existence. If I had discovered such a place, I would have taken something with me—a flower, a leaf, a stone, the fur from a dead animal, anything other than a pocketful of this dry, red earth; the only thing that he has to offer." I was convinced and shared his well-described disappointment with Jason. His head dropped and he took a deep breath, before continuing. "The saddest part of his story, for me, Pamela, is that I want to believe that this place exists; the real source of my frustration with him. He offers only ambiguous sketches and muddled memories of how to find this paradise."

He and I have more in common than I realized, I felt very empathetic towards him, as he picked up the conversation with, "Look at our group. Who could we send on this mission? How could we be certain that they would survive? Would anyone in this group risk their life for the others? I doubt it. I wouldn't anyway. We have been dependent upon the center for four or five years; maybe less time; maybe more time. It does not matter. It is too late for us to do things differently. We need you. You are our hope. Your very presence is helping us to dream again about a better future. You bring new blood, new energy, to us. We may not be explorers. But, Pamela, I assure you that we could be Rebels; yes, rebels, ready to take back the rightful place of the human race. That is my dream. That is our dream."

Mind-boggling questions flowed and distracted me. "Why me? I am no hero and I don't want to be a hero. How did this responsibility fall on my shoulders?" I kept my eyes focused on his. I could see the sincerity in his look. How could I refuse to help? So, I asked a silly question, "What was taken away from us?"

"Everything." he answered with strong emotion. "Everything. Believe me, I did not flee right after my sight came back. I spent time observing the interaction of the others with the humans. I realized that they knew I could see everything, including them. I worked in an isolated unit in telecommunications and video surveillance equipment. I am a physicist. I recognized that the luminosity of these creations was a shield and I constructed a small device that helped me to penetrate their luminosity. They were aware of what I was doing; but that did not stop me. I didn't understand why they did not confiscate the device. They did impose restrictions on me. I was not allowed to wander off into all the other sectors to see what was going on. Nonetheless that did not prevent me from studying them, as they were studying me. What I concluded is that they are very passive and dependent upon us. And, yet they took control."

"What do you mean that they took control?"

"I had a brief encounter with Ferdinand. You knew Ferdinand?" I nodded yes. "He told me lots," he continued. "He had access to the historical records, but his research was disjointed. He was not studying things chronologically or systematically. I have the impression though that the closer he came to understanding what had happened, the more radical and dangerous he became. For me, he seemed completely out of control towards the end of his life. If he had been less emotional and more practical, he might have accomplished something and gotten a following. He also may have manipulated them better. Ferdinand was responsible for his termination."

"You have to go back for minute, there are things that I don't understand." I wanted explanations. "I realize now that only deprogrammed people can see other deprogrammed people and that the programmed humans cannot see us. If that is true, was Ferdinand deprogrammed?"

"Yes, but at the end, when he was dragged off for termination, he was in a deprogrammed state of mind." He answered firmly.

"So how could you have met with him and gotten information from him?"

"Legitimate question that deserves an answer." He pulled his lips tightly together, as if it was painful for him to extract the truth. He took his time before explaining. "Ferdinand was a pure intellectual. His discoveries of the human race were intellectual discoveries; not emotional discoveries."

"What does not that mean?" I was very confused.

"My contact with him was quite special. I overheard an android discussing Ferdinand, his exceptional intellectual ability, and his use of the library." He stopped. "I followed him, cautiously, to the library. When he was alone, I asked questions." He stopped and looked at me. "Believe it or not, Pamela, even though he could not see me, he was not afraid of me. He didn't even ask me who I was. He imagined that I was living in a parallel universe, which he referred to as a spiritual world. He seemed happy to be able to communicate with me. I didn't understand his reference then or now but I did not bother to correct his error. He seemed comfortable with that explanation, which he considered plausible." He shrugged his shoulders. "Such confusedness was as laughable as pitiable. But, as a result of this absurdity, he confided in me, told me what he knew and what he had learned. I only met with him a few hours before his termination, but, it was enough to convince me that we were different at another time in our history." He swallowed hard before saying that it was sad that Ferdinand was unable to present a clear picture of who we were and what happened.

I asked Dr. Gordon for the right to use the library. Her answer was rather vague. "Do you think that they will let me conduct research? Will they give me absolute freedom to read and study whatever I want? And, will the information be reliable?" I asked.

"Maybe I am naïve, but knowing how they got control will help us to reclaim our control. If they let you use the library, try to focus on what happened."

"And, what if we never had control, could you live with that?" We all assumed that the human race was different, but then…

"Whatever the truth may be, I want to know it. If we have always been at the mercy of the others for survival, I want to know anyway. But, even if this is about our past, I don't want it to be our future. So your research, whatever it brings, can only help us." His eyes were aflame with compassion and his face flushed with strong emotion.

"Ok, I am willing to take the risk. I am willing to pass the research on to you, but how?"

"We have people, spies if you will, in the center that report to me. We are not the only ones who can see clearly. If they are discovered, their termination would be only the beginning of our problems. Who knows what they might do to us? We are completely vulnerable and there are the children." We stared at each other, my heart beating rapidly as my hands cradled my unborn child.

He knew that he had my attention and that I would be more and more cooperative. He was calling the moves now. He picked up the conversation. "There are others in the center who have bypassed their programming. They chose to stay on to help others, like you, to escape and to send us information. They are frustrated because they have no access to historical records and are not privy to any present strategy on the part of the others. The most that they can do is to keep us informed of current events. For example, they confirmed that the Board gave a green light to Dr. Gordon to continue her research. Dr. Crawford will be less of a problem now. Nonetheless, you must be careful with him even though he is part of Dr. Gordon's team. Personally, I think that he agreed to work with her so that he could better sabotage her project. Just watch what you say to him."

"Ok, that I know how to do!" I replied emphatically.

"Our contacts in the Center will find you. Just remember that all our contacts are human. Oh yes, Jonathan, your former partner, was brought into the hospital yesterday for treatment. He was sedated because he resisted treatment. He will probably be terminated."

He said that so casually, ignoring whether I might still have feelings for Jonathan. His insensitivity, brutal indifference, reminded me of why I disliked him sometimes. So I pretended that I was not affected; "Oh, did he have an accident?"

"No, apparently his visual receptor has been malfunctioning for quite some time now. Someone got wise to that and he was admitted for treatment. People with deformities are never allowed out of the center and that is why I assume that he will be terminated. Do you care?"

"Of course I care. He and I lived very happily for years. I am sad to hear that his life will be terminated," I shocked him out of his cruel indifference.

"You could talk to Dr. Gordon about it. If she thought that you would not cooperate on her project if she did not attempt to save his life, maybe she would do something."

He spoke as if he had already given a lot of thought to the future of this man. But why should he care about him? I didn't know how to answer him. Certainly I could not put that kind of pressure on Dr. Gordon. If I did it once, I would do it again and again and I knew that she would not accept being manipulated by me. It was the wrong approach to take. Nevertheless, it was a way to find out exactly how far she would go to keep me around. How precious was I to her?

"I don't honestly know what to do. I don't even know how important Jonathan's life is to me or to us. What kind of pressure can I put on Dr. Gordon and what kinds of risks can I take if I want to protect us all?"

"Exactly. You must be careful. But, this Jonathan is confusing; he interests me. He does not seem to be depressed with his newly found reality. I would have imagined that he would have been taken back with his own appearance and yet my informants have not found that to be the case. He shows no signs of being depressed. If my information is accurate, his fight is against the system. They have heard him say that he does not want to be programmed for a second time, which might be the reason why he is resisting treatment. You know him, Pamela. How would you interpret that?"

I mused that this kind of discussion could lead me nowhere. From John's lofty position, my opinions were always categorically wrong. I almost wished that someone would just walk in on us and put an end to this discussion. There was furthermore nothing private about this space. It was a corner of the cavern, but no one had privacy here. And, where were all the others, I wondered. I could read his impatience with me in his eyes. He must be irritated with me. I am taking too much time for someone as spontaneous as John.

"Well," I hesitated, "I never knew much about Jonathan. We only ever talked about music, the up and coming concerts and how fortunate we were to be musicians. We never had in depth conversations about the life we were leading. Maybe you scientists did; we didn't. How can I comment on his reaction? We were close to each. Well, as close as we humans can get in a controlled environment." I added with disgust. "I miss him, in a certain way. He is alone, deprogrammed and developing emotional reactions. I don't want anything bad to happen to him. I know that I don't want him to be terminated; but, I don't see his mixing well with this community because of his physical appearance." I sighed. "Maybe he is worried about what happened to me. Or, maybe he found out that I escaped and would like to see me." I was not convinced myself with that explanation. It sounded absurd in reference to our superficial, programmed lifestyle in the Center. So, I retracted my statement by adding. "I am afraid that I cannot help you."

"And, if we could save him?"

That idea was alarming. I was living a new life. Why should I have to relive the past? I wanted to scream in John's face. Who did he think he was? I just agreed to risk my life by going back to the Center to get answers to help us have a better future, and that is not enough. Nothing that I do will ever be enough for him, for them. I could feel the anguish and despair that drove me back to Jonathan on that horrifying and emotionally charged day. I thought that I was going to jump into Jonathan's protective arms, but, instead, his appearance frightened and repelled me. I would like to wipe my last image of Jonathan out of mind. Why would I want to see him again?

I know that John could see the disgust and anger on my face. How can John ask me that? He knows that I love Peter; that soon our baby will be born. How could Jonathan's presence here be good for me? No, I don't want to see him. How could we be friends?

I looked up at him, my eyes filled with tears of foreboding. "Why are you doing this to me? Are you working for them? Are you plotting against me? You know that seeing Jonathan could not help me. His presence could be very destabilizing for me."

He smiled as if amused by seeing me so upset. "Ok." he snickered. "If I understand well, you would rather see his life terminated than try to arrange his transfer outside with us."

"That is unfair. Incredibly unfair." Overwhelmed now by anxiety, I screamed back at him, letting my words take off in a frenzied, rapid flow. "He would be hurt if he came here. We are all physically normal. You know that no one would accept him. You are cruel to make me the person responsible for wanting him dead." I finally used the word that Jason had taught me.

"I would have no problem looking at him," John replied in a cool, arrogant way. "Why should I reject him because of his deformities? There is more than just the physical side; there is the person. I am sorry that you are still only able to focus on what is on the outside."

What he said was true. How did this happen to me? Jonathan was kind, gentle and musically talented, and all that I could see now were his deformities. I started to cry tears of sadness for Jonathan. "Yes, do what you can for him. My attitude is completely wrong. Jason's aging body scared me at first, but I got beyond that. Don't expect me to get physically close to Jonathan. I can't. Think whatever you want. Just don't ask me to do something that would destroy us both!"

"I am glad that you want us to help, because he is already very close to our cavern." He answered. He got up and left me sitting in virtual shock.

Jonathan's arrival was less disturbing for me than I had anticipated. He was not as hideous as I had imagined. Apart from his hunched back, the rest of him was acceptable. I suppose that my own hysteria and inability to see clearly made me believe that he was extraordinarily grotesque. Everyone, including Peter, greeted him with enthusiasm. He did not put me in any awkward position with respect to Peter or my pregnancy. In fact, he did not even pretend that we had a special relationship that he wanted to preserve. We were just good friends, just like we had always been.

He was a lot more insightful than I was. Unlike me, Jonathan was not at all shocked by his own physical appearance or with that of others who were also displaying deformities. "There are those who were more pleasant to the eyes," He said "but that did not necessarily make them more interesting," a point that I had not even considered. He hid his deprogramming by giving his code to others. He used the same method that Peter used to survive in the center. He spent time talking to everyone who came into contact with him, and evaluating them more on their personalities than their physical appearances. I was startled by his remarks and embarrassed with myself. I avoided him for a few days so I could think about what he had said.

Days later I approached him sheepishly; I stuttered when I addressed him. "I…. never wanted ….to hurt you then or now. I have good memories…. of the time we shared together." I stopped to find the right words; the words that would be more comforting for him. "I don't want to be superficial with people, focusing more on the physical side than the intellectual. And, I thought about what you said-that we had personalities. But, Jonathan, we were all programmed, devoid of emotions. We were like machines in the Center. So how can you begin to talk about real personalities? It doesn't make any sense at all. We were what they wanted us to be."

"Oh, Pamela, you didn't stay in the Center long enough to discover things. You were swept off into the hospital within the first 24 hours after you had bypassed the programming. I was there longer before they discovered that I too had bypassed the system. That is why you have so much difficulty understanding what kind of environment we were part of." He replied, in his calm, easy going manner.

"Ridiculous," I felt frustrated by his virtual side, which I automatically labeled, pretentious.

I realized later on that I was quick to qualify people as pretentious. I didn't like to be contradicted and when someone did firmly contradict me, I felt threatened.

"Look at the others." I was lecturing to him. "They are scientists and they share the same position as me. They lived in the center a lot longer than I did and had plenty of time to study different subjects. No one has ever raised the idea that a basic personality existed even in spite of the programming. Really, Jonathan, you surprise me with your naivety."

"Perhaps I am naive, Pamela, but that is not necessarily a bad thing. I never ventured outside of our sector, so I cannot compare my impressions with those of our scientists, here today. Nonetheless, you know how music, the arts in general, bring to life feelings. Every time I picked up my instrument, I had a 'feeling' about how I should approach a piece of music. Even though I did not personally understand the feeling of violence, for example, I understood how to interpret violence in music. I didn't know love, but I knew how to be tender in the way I played the notes. Those feelings are visible in other aspects. I noticed them with our colleagues. I noticed that we were not objective in the way we played our instrument. I am not saying that we understood or even played with our emotions, but we did add something personal to our interpretations."

"Ok. I agree, Jonathan that when we were in touch with our music we showed feelings. But, our personal lives were controlled. I have spent almost a year outside the center discovering human emotions. They are all new to me. I don't remember being jealous, hurt, violent, in love….should I go on?"

"I completely agree with you, Pamela, in part of what you are saying, particularly, that we are discovering those emotions that we always had deep inside. But, the way that they present themselves, the order in which they arrive, is part of what our personality always was. That is, the importance that we give to certain emotions over others. It is the personality that was always there that I detected. In any event, we should pick this conversation up later as I promised the children that I would do some digging with them. Funny, they think that my body is more adapted than their own to that sort of work. Maybe they are right, although I think that I am just more adapted to living underground." He started laughing as he pulled his twisted, heavy body up off the floor and then added –"What a wasteland you are all living in. It never occurred to you to move on?"

"Of course it did," I mused, but why go into that. He will find out soon enough that we are stuck here. Dependent upon food and clothing from the center, there is no reason to wander off into the emptiness that surrounds us. Sad. All the energy I had in the beginning is gone. I no longer wonder what might be out there. It is as if time has zapped me of all my desire to live differently. And then, I thought with a big smile on my face, it is so nice to have Jonathan here; maybe he will inspire me.

I watched as he played with the children. He was like a big, teddy bear. They jumped all over him and he just laughed. He didn't do much digging; but he gave them the impression that he was very much interested in what they were doing. He encouraged them to continue. "Who knows, maybe you are going to find the remains of a big temple. You just haven't dug deep enough to discover anything." He teased.

I started to think about other things, as my baby distracted me. I could feel it moving inside me. It was getting very close to its birth date. I have almost as much difficulty as Jonathan, manipulating in close quarters and getting back up on my feet. I was impatient to hold my baby in my arms, but when I focused on the actual birth of my baby, I felt petrified. How will I react? Ruth and Sarah talked about excruciating pain. They have been working with me for months on breathing techniques. Is that going to be enough for me? Will I be a good Mother? What is a good Mother? Are Ruth and Sarah good mothers? I don't know. All I know is the children seem happier since Jonathan arrived.

Peter approached with a big smile on his face. He too has fallen under the charm of Jonathan. "He's crazy," he blurted out with eyebrows raised. "He has got those children so motivated with digging that they won't stop until they reach the center of the earth."

He looked down at me and took on another tone. "I have been staring off into the distance imagining that we might discover something better. I am a bit tired of hanging out in the cavern every day, doing nothing. Ok, I exercise, but apart from that, there is nothing interesting to do." He replied, as he sat down beside me and fondled my belly.

"Bored, that is what you are. Maybe the baby will change all that for you." I suggested.

"Everyone is bored. We repeat our stories over and over again. But those stories are about a recent past. The thing is that I don't remember much about my childhood. It is blurred; especially, the part about at what age do you do this or that. I don't remember how I got into the sciences. That I find annoying, incredibly frustrating. You would think that I could at least recall the first time I studied the universe." Peter said, showing his disdain.

"Oh, you are what your parents were." Jonathan entered into the conversation." I guess that he had enough of digging.

"What do you mean by that? We don't even know who our parents were. You realize that we were conceived in a test tube." It was evident that my pregnancy had made Peter very sensitive about his own birth. Watching our baby growing in a normal environment made him detest what happened to all of us.

"Whatever. I am not a scientist, but I did make discoveries. I was curious about why I was so physically deformed. I was obsessed with learning the reality, so I spent all my spare time, which, as we all know, was very limited, trying to access the birth records. I was unable to identify who my parents were, but I did solve the bigger problem. Who and how were these people chosen? It was all quite complicated, actually, and the story is long. Maybe we should pick this up another time?" He questioned.

"I want to know everything. I don't care how long the story is or how difficult it will be for me to accept; I just want to know," I was adamant.

"Well, everything dates back to that famous night when Pamela was taken away. It was her emotional reaction to me, more so than the sequence of events that burned out my visual receptor. I had a bad headache and blurry vision when the emergency unit arrived to take Pamela away. They didn't even give me a second look. I guess that they imagined that I would never be able to transcend their reality. I don't even remember anyone asking me if I was alright. I just remember the horror on Pamela's face."

"The following day, I went off to work as usual. My vision was blurry. I had windows of reality blocked out by the latent programming inside of me. It was as if I was fumbling around in another dimension. I didn't mention any of this to anyone. Five days after Pamela left, a Dr. Crawford came to talk to me. He explained to me that Pamela was very sick and had to undergo special treatment and that she would not be able to return for a long time. He recommended that I return to the selection committee for a new companion, emphasizing the fact that having a companion was natural and obligatory if I wanted to continue to live in the same way and . . .in the same sector."

"I asked questions. He was in a hurry to leave and wanted to finish with me; so he didn't like my asking questions. To placate me, he said that the treatment involved chemicals. From time to time, according to him, members of the community suffered chemical imbalances that caused them to hallucinate. The treatment took time and was not effective in every case. Sometimes the individuals had to be terminated in the interest of everyone else. That being the case, it was imperative that I take the necessary steps to replace you," he turned to look at me, "Pamela."

"I told him that I wanted to wait a little while to see how you reacted to the treatment before asking for someone else. That was a mistake. He showed interest in my case and was no longer in a hurry to leave. He sat down and started questioning me. He asked me how I was feeling and if I had problems with my vision. I felt anything but relaxed in his presence." He stopped to look at me and I nodded in agreement. I could not imagine anyone feeling relaxed with Dr. Crawford. "I know now," Jonathan went on, "that I didn't like Dr. Crawford and, under the influence of this emotion, my vision cleared up as well as his objectives. The more he spoke, and particularly the more questions he asked, the more other sensations aroused inside me. For the first time in my life, I felt . . . hate. I felt hate towards Dr. Crawford and the urgent need to protect myself from him. He continued to use terms like natural and necessary to have a companion and could not understand why I was reluctant to ask for someone else. He claimed that my reaction was not normal. He came so close to me at one point that I started to see beyond the blinding light. That made me even more uncomfortable because he did not appear. . .human. I wanted him to disappear, to just leave me alone. But time was not on my side. I was treading on dangerous ground and courting termination. So I had to abandon my views and accept his, if I wanted to survive. To do that I had to retreat into that automatism that we were programmed for. It wasn't easy."

"I answered in that monotone style of ours that I would go directly to the committee and that convinced him that I was still under his control."

Then Jonathan stopped cold and looked at me, saying, "What I don't understand, Pamela, is why you were so afraid of my physical appearance. How did you see me?"

I hesitated, partly because I didn't remember well enough and partly because I didn't want to hurt him. "You simply had so many deformities. Your voice and mannerisms were the same as always which is why I recognized you in the beginning. I was already terrified from what happened in the orchestra pit when I came back that night. My vision changed instantaneously because, as I understand now, my emotions were so strong and out of control that all my programming broke down. When I arrived at our cubicle I wanted to be with you, probably to be reassured or even protected. And, when I did not find the same person in front of me, I felt as if I were living a nightmare." I retorted. "Of course, I can explain my reaction today, because I have had time to understand what happened to me. I was not rational at that time and didn't know that I had, in a certain sense, awakened, from an artificial world, into reality."

"So, in fact, when we were together you saw me as I would have been if my body had not been twisted and every part of me out of proportion?"

"Yeah, right!" I answered even though he must have detected the regret in my voice.

What I said seemed rational to him, as he went forward with the rest of his story. "Well, in any event, I went before the committee and requested a new companion. They sent me one. She was quite beautiful by human standards, as I have come to understand them. In fact, she looked a lot like you and she played the flute. She was not as talented a musician as you are or you were. But, after I played around with my visual receptor, and eventually learned how our access codes were determined, I realized that she was not coded like she was. In fact, she was coded as deformed, even more than I. I wondered if this was a trick. The bright ones were curious about whether I would reject her because that would indicate a human emotion. Nonetheless, it was confusing, because no one else in the orchestra was coded as deformed. I didn't know how to react to this. She saw me as you did although I had to give her my code every time we were alone together. I asked her once what I looked like and her description of me was quite flattering."

"Dr. Crawford got back to me a few months after your replacement arrived. He asked me how it was going."

"I said that he was right that it was better to have a companion. I needed someone to talk to."

"He then asked me about how she looked. I suspected a trap, so I told him that she was not pleasant to look at but pleasant to be around."

"He asked me if I wanted to change her for someone else and I said that I didn't see why I should since she was compatible with me. He left it at that. That gave me time to investigate. Actually, I was interested in you, Pamela. I was worried about what might have happened to you and I didn't want them to terminate you before your time. That was probably the reason why I wanted to continue living. Actually, I was horrified by my physical appearance. I saw others that were as bad, maybe even worse than me, but it didn't help. I couldn't understand what happened to me and to them. That was another driving force. I wanted to understand why I was born like that."

"It is amazing how you dealt all alone with this situation and controlled the outcome. Dr. Crawford is a vicious creation as you rightly suspected. I would say that you were very courageous, Jonathan." The truth was there even though I also wanted to flatter him. "I regretted that I was so weak and that I lost all my sense of reasoning in the beginning."

"Our circumstances were different, Pamela. I had goals, namely to save you and discover my roots. That changes everything."

His slight pause gave me time to imagine a different scenario. "Should I have tried to communicate with him? Was I just a high-strung emotional person, unable to maintain the minimum of control under pressuring circumstances? Would we be better off today if I had confronted him with my problem, by telling him that I saw the world differently? How would he have reacted to me then, if I had told him the truth?

Peter broke the silence by asking, "How are we coded?"

"I have no scientific or mathematical training so much of what I am going to say is conjecture. My wristband was still in place and functioning. I just didn't see the reasoning behind it and the codes in the beginning. Then I realized that there were those of us that looked similar. Certain characteristics were dominant. For example, Pamela calls herself Pamela 13. In her case, she is probably right. She is probably the 13th product of a genetic mix. That is probably why her replacement looked so much the same. They must come from the same parentage and Dr. Crawford was hoping to confuse me with a close duplicate. Imagine, I found some other people who resembled me. They were even more deformed than I am, if you can believe that. And, even though I don't like to say it, their facial features, like my own, were completely out of proportion. I realized that we had access codes that were very similar. I was actually fascinated with the access code descriptions that were always excessively complementary. Why, I don't know. But, most of what the bright ones are doing is placating us; giving us the false impression that we like each other and are happy." He hung on the word happy—letting it come across like a long note." And then added, "Maybe they think that seeing only beautiful people will make us happy."

He stopped talking for a few minutes and let his head bob up and down. His eyelids drooped and his lips curled up under his chin as he started sobbing. I reached out, drawing myself closer to him, to calm his quivering body. Tears came streaming down his face passing warmly over my shoulder and along my arm. We never touched each other during all the time we lived together; nevertheless, it seemed the natural and right way to console him at this moment. Our lives are such a mystery. And now, how can we unravel it?

Peter finally broke the silence. "Jonathan, perhaps we should leave things at that point for the moment. You are probably tired."

"No, I'm ok. It's just that we all have found minute traces of our identities. You, Peter, told me about the astronauts. John told me that the bright ones are androids. Me, well I discovered the mixtures of human genomes. I wandered out of my sector. No one stopped me, because, as I now know, they were observing me. They let me make discoveries. They arranged for me to meet people working in the birthing center. Why they did that makes no sense, unless, of course, they wanted to register my reactions to their breeding choices?"

"And our baby, Pamela. What will our baby look like?" Peter lobbied for some input into the conversation.

I wanted to reassure him. Maybe he was concerned that we could have a child that would be physically handicapped. So I said what seemed the most natural, but turned out to be the most selfish thing to say. "Why worry? Neither one of us has any noticeable abnormalities, so why should our child be in any way deformed.' I caught a glimpse of Jonathan and felt just awful. "I am sorry, Jonathan. What does physical appearance mean, anyway? It is not everything."

He laughed, mockingly. "You know that that is not true, Pamela. It means everything on first contact and, probably for the long term."

"I think that Peter was right when he suggested that we pick up this discussion another time," I too was feeling uncomfortable with this conversation that was leading nowhere. It seemed that with every other word, I had insulted or humiliated someone who did not deserve it.

"Ok, I agree. I am tired of sitting, anyway" said Jonathan, as he lifted his heavy, awkward body. Just watching him move like that made me sad for him. Did my agility, even pregnant, and well-proportioned frame, give me a feeling of superiority? Was it automatic, involuntary, to compare my body to someone else's body? I am sad for him because he does not have a normal male body. He is not sad for the same reason as I am. He is not jealous of me, Peter or John or anyone else and has made it very clear that physical appearances are only the exterior of someone. What is inside is and should be more important. His sadness then is based on what, because it is real? He is perhaps just seeking answers, not looking for changes.

No one had much privacy in this cavern. It was, as I would come to realize, tribal living; the way different humans associated themselves in ethnic groups, or otherwise, in communal living. The sounds of others constantly invaded the space. It seemed so natural to live that way, packed together in a small space, like animals, that we got used to it. From my last impression of the cubicle in the center, after my programming broke down, we were living in the same open environment, in equally small quarters. I wondered why that bothered me here, even though the answer was so evident. WE were becoming more and more human.

Jonathan moved into his space and Peter and I laid down in ours. The enclosures were protective and gave a better feeling of privacy, if the noise could be turned off. Peter's arms curled around my bulging stomach, as he pulled me close to him. I liked feeling him next to me. I also liked feeling his breath on my shoulders and his chest rise and fall, slowing down as he drifted into sleep. I couldn't imagine falling asleep without him next to me. In spite of my increasing episodes of insomnia, linked to my apprehension over my pregnancy, I still felt rested in the morning simply because he was there next to me.

Tonight I focused on the baby, speculating on whether my baby would be normal, a blend of Peter and me. But, that assumed that Peter and I were normal. I went so far as to imagine that perhaps normal was like Jonathan and that the rest of us might be considered abnormal. I shook that thought off, because it seemed a bit ridiculous, as I had seen plenty of pictures of the faces of musicians and dancers from the past whose physical appearances resembled those common to our intimate community; and, not Jonathan's appearance. That should have been enough validation for me, but I couldn't leave it there;

I had go further. Did the human race evolve and acquire incongruous physical traits, like those of Jonathan? How do I know that what I see today is real and not imaginary? Images of all that is animate, from plants to animals to people, passed through my mind; making me dizzy. The baby was moving a great deal, pushing and pushing as if it wanted to escape. I felt a warm liquid running down my legs. I tried to get up, as my body doubled up under me. I felt like my body was being ripped apart. Undoubtedly this was the pain that Sarah and Ruth warned me about. My first experience with pain, excruciating pain, and I didn't know how to cope with it, so all I could do was scream at the top of my lungs.

Peter reached out to me. "I am here, Pamela." I shoved him away. He made me angry. It was his fault that I was in pain. He did this to me!

"Pamela," he said calmly in spite of my rejection. "Don't move, I am going to get Sarah or Ruth. I shall be right back." I think that I snarled at him and then turned away, I didn't even want to see him.

Sarah heard my screams and arrived as Peter jumped out of the bed.

"It is ok, Pamela. Everything is ok. Just breathe deeply. Don't fight the contractions." She said in a drowsy voice.

"We are all here," she continued. "You and the baby are in good hands."

I was perspiring profusely, my normal reaction in time of stress, but I tried to follow her advice. My entire body was writhing in pain. Peter's face was white with fear. I was in no mood to comfort him. Through clenched teeth I blurted out, "Peter leave, now. Just get out of here!" The pain subsided for a few minutes, at which point I worried about the baby. And, then for a slight instance I thought about Peter. I didn't have time to worry about him, even though I felt guilty for being so brusque with him a few minutes before. As I gained more control of my body, I felt more courageous and protective of my baby. "If I am suffering," I thought to myself, "what horrible pain is my baby feeling?"

Then something clicked inside of me and I started to relax and follow the rhythm of the baby. I began to writhe under the pain of the contractions that shook my body, as they got closer and closer. I clenched my teeth down harder and focused on the baby, the only person who mattered now. Peter was just an afterthought.

I heard someone say that Jonathan had run off to the outskirts of the Center where we collected our clothes and food and water, hoping to find the kinds of supplies that were left for Sarah and Ruth when their babies were born. The package complete with everything necessary for the baby's birth was there. How did they know? Was it always there and we didn't notice it before? How could they have been so sure that there would be no complications with the birth? Those were the questions I asked afterwards. But, when Jonathan returned with all the necessaries, I just felt thankful that they were taking care of my baby and me.

Ruth and Mathilda were now with Sarah. They held my hands and wiped my forehead. Sarah told me what to do – when to push and when to relax. She was very good at guiding me through the delivery. I was so glad that she was there.

The baby arrived in a final violent effort on my part. I heard him take his first breath through a long outward cry. And, then the baby was in my arms. Peter never left. He was there all the time. He wanted to be with me to watch his child slide out of my body and out of its protective womb. Our eyes met, broad smiles covering our faces. Oh, I was glad that Peter ignored my orders and stayed on. He hid in the shadows, watching and hoping that both the baby and I would make it through what he later described as both a horrifying and incredibly beautiful ordeal.

"He is beautiful, Pamela. He is just so beautiful." He said over and over again, as held his baby up in front of us.

"I have a son! We have a son. It's a boy." His happy scream resonated off the cavern walls.

"Is he like us?" I asked, not yet certain that he was without deformities. I was afraid to look.

Sarah nodded her head. "Look at him," she said. He is perfect. He is perfect in every way, with two eyes, two ears, a nice little nose, a sweet tiny mouth, two arms, two legs, two hands, two feet, and the rest that makes him a little boy." Her voice was full of excitement. Then she added, "You were amazing, Pamela. Once you got into the swing of it, you made childbirth look easy!"

I laughed, a laugh of joy. She laughed, a laugh of relief and happiness, as she lifted my head so that I could have a better view of my son. He is the most beautiful person I ever saw. I looked him over and felt reassured because every part of him was well proportioned. All his facial features were in perfect harmony. My heart was thumping against my chest. "I am so happy and proud!" I screamed and then looked at Peter and said; "We did it, Peter, we produced a masterpiece." He sat next to me looking down at his son, cradling against my chest. I saw his beaming smile and sparkling eyes; his face was alight with happiness. He tenderly stroked and moved my hair to the sides of my face, saying in a voice charged with adoration and emotion. "Oh! I love you and our baby, with all my heart!" he repeated this over and over again to be certain that we heard him. And then he smothered both of us in kisses, while the others watched on.

When he finally pulled away, I noticed that the entire group was in our little cubicle, laughing and dancing. They were celebrating the birth of our son. When Jonathan came, in his turn, to congratulate us, he bent down and kissed the baby's forehead. I saw the tears of happiness in his eyes, as he looked in admiration at my child. I was touched by Jonathan's sensitivity which contrasted so sharply with his physical appearance. What could be done about that?

I turned back to my child and was abruptly hit by the reality that Peter and I never chose a name. "Hey, Peter," I got his attention rapidly, "We need a name for our baby. Have you thought of one, Peter?" I was excited about the prospect of naming my son. I felt proud and thankful that my baby would not have a code number. He would have a name from the very beginning.

"I never thought about that." he said with a startled look on his face. "I have absolutely no idea what name to give our son," protested Peter. "You are the one that deciphered codes to make names; you must have a long list to choose from. So…start calling out names." he ordered.

"Ok, but the name we choose must be special." I said, as I contemplated. "I want it to be a name that will convey strength of character."

"What does that mean?" Peter laughed. "A future, here in the middle of a dusty, hot desert does not require strength of character." He was teasing me and I responded with a childlike grimace. "Well… Ok. If that is what you want then we shall find the right name that conveys strength of character." He conceded to my wishes.

I repeated out loud all the names that I invented, or deciphered, over the years: Oliver, William, Thomas, Michael, Alexander, Charles, Adam, Arthur, and so on and so on, the list was long. Peter was shaking his head in a definitive No, to all the names I was suggesting. He was right. None of them seemed appropriate. I found myself laughing with Peter over some of the drab and austere names, like Ray, Sweety, Horatio... that the others were enthusiastically calling out.

"How exasperating it is to name a baby." I protested, as I looked down at the tiny bundle that I was fondling in my arms. "What would you choose?" I asked my child, as my thoughts wandered in the direction of those fabulous composers that I had admired and worshipped over the years. "They inspired my music," I mused, "why not choose one of their names. Hans, Wolfgang, and Frederic. "Yes," Hey, everyone, I've got it. I found the name that fits him." I had the undivided attention of the group and they were all looking at me with bated breath. "We shall call him Frederic!" I joyfully yelled out his name, without inhibitions. .

Chapter 19: Betrayal

It was 9 o'clock in the morning, a Monday, if the day, time and place made any difference to Dr. Gordon. Her days never seemed to end and the years just kept accumulating. She continued doing the same things; hospital rounds, meetings with the Governor over the administration of hospital, and defending her position of human development. Nothing changed and would probably never change, unless her research turned more convincing. "Oh," she sighed. Nothing about me has changed either; I am just eternally young and logical, far from achieving…

This morning the Board was meeting to discuss the birth of Pamela's baby boy. The ultimate questions would be: "How and when would we recuperate our experiment? There was, of course, the matter of the child. Who would raise him?"

Dr. Gordon was, as always, worried about Dr. Crawford's reaction. There seemed to be Dr. Crawford's everywhere, drastically limiting case studies or sabotaging the results. But, then, her Dr. Crawford was showing some signs of change. He was cooperating very well with Dr. Gordon's group, just like he promised he would after the last meeting. Crawford was working well with Dr. Jarod; and the sub-committee studying human psychology seemed to interest him very much. He was not an advocate of allowing humans to discover emotions, but he did admit that in some cases, it could be useful; especially in scientific research and development, where creativity and inventiveness was paramount. He, like others, recognized that the Centers were reaching the end of an era and that the humans would have to be inventive, inquisitive and in particular, research driven in order to avoid stagnation. Thinking positively, Dr. Gordon admitted to herself that there may be hope for Dr. Crawford and thus for everyone at this Center.

She opened the door to the Board Room to find everyone present. The Governor triggered the discussion by asking Dr. Gordon what course of action she would like to pursue.

"Well, it is rather complicated. Pamela, we all agree to use her adopted name, right?" She asked looking from one to the other. No one objected, so she continued, "I do have a kind of contract with her, which assures her cooperation. I don't think that I mentioned this before; but, even if I did, I think that it is a good way to open the discussion today. She wants access to the Research Library and, in return, will make herself available to me for study. The contract is, shall we say, suspended, only because her programmed escape came a bit earlier than I expected. No doubt, that was a good thing. But, one day she will have to live up to her commitment. I hesitate to bring her back straight away. I would like to observe her maternal side for a while. And, I think that taking her away from her child later will be more traumatic. This will give us more insight into human emotions; like, in her case, how she will handle being separated from her love ones? Will she be lethargic, depressed, angry, passive, or will she become more clever, diabolical, manipulative, or resourceful?"

"Oh, this is just a waste of time." Dr. Crawford broke into the conversation. "Dr. Gordon knows exactly how this individual will respond. She has a profile of her. There will be no surprises here. This Pamela is going to dramatize her situation, refuse to cooperate and try to find her child. We know the rest. To bring her back now will simplify things a bit. She is probably expecting us to order her return now and has more or less decided on a course of action, hopefully, complete cooperation, which will be interesting for us. We can side step all the drama, which is, of course, extraneous to our study and delve more rapidly into the aspects of creativity which is our main objective."

Even though Dr. Gordon expected Dr. Crawford to disagree, she did not realize that there was still rivalry between them. His reaction took her off guard and she needed a few minutes to reflect on it before responding. "What Dr. Crawford suggests makes a great deal of sense in the short term. Perhaps we can negotiate creativity or, even better, sincere cooperation on Pamela's part by using the child as an incentive for good conduct; for example, giving her the right to visit her child in exchange for information, a system of reward for proper conduct."

"Exactly, now you are starting to make sense," he broke in.

Agitated Dr. Gordon struggled desperately to maintain her composure, hoping to restore her previous advantage and control the situation. "No, you must let me finish. I said in the short term. But, we need to take full advantage of our experiment. We must push every possible button to get the maximum number of reactions so that we understand the ones that follow. Why sabotage this experiment? The time that we invest in it is going to help us in the long term. And, the long term should be our main objective. I believe that we should use elements of surprise; lead our subject to believe that her life is stable, that she is out of danger. Also let her invest in her child and get strongly attached to him. Only then will we have better insight into maternal feelings and how they can influence the behavior of a human mother separated from her offspring," Dr. Gordon explained her cold, calculated strategy.

"What about the Father?" The Governor queried.

"Right. I have not given much thought to him. It seemed logical to leave the child with him and go from there. But, we might involve him more closely in our research."

"Then, what about the other members of the community? Why don't we study them?" Dr. Crawford asked.

"Impossible," retorted the Governor. "We have an arrangement. We promised safe passage and care in the outside world to a member of the Group. This person has remained faithful to us. We have no reason to go back on our promise. We have learned a lot already about humans. Look at how inert they are? They just pass their days doing nothing. They all have emotions now." He stopped and turned to Dr. Gordon, "Yes, Dr. Gordon, what do you I think about that? How do you explain the pathetic attitude of this human colony? Even the arrival of Jason did nothing to motivate them. Why should we imagine that in another context emotions will make them creative?"

"True, in fact our research group has considered that problem. It is not easy to diagnose. Something certainly inhibits curiosity and creativity. Maybe, fear—that has been suggested. It could be that. Then, of course, they have no incentive to move on. The food, clothing, water, and all that we provide, makes it easier for them to become complacent. That is the next question. Should we treat the group as an experiment, instead of just, Pamela? It was suggested that the center reduce the food and water supply. They would realize that almost immediately. But, it is very risky. Will the quest for survival render them curious or will it make them violent?" She looked at the Governor showing her straight, rigid posture behind folded arms, in manifest opposition. "Personally, I was not aware of your promise to any members of that group. And, I am very surprised that you find it so important to respect your promise."

Enough of that, Dr. Gordon. This is none of your business." He was showing his authority by raising himself slightly from his chair. "It is imperative that you accept and remember that the group in place before the arrival of Pamela is under my protection." We-you- can observe them, but we don't have the right to interfere." He said firmly, as if giving an order, before letting himself fall gently back into his chair.

"That doesn't make any sense," Dr. Crawford interjected. "Why would we have made such an arrangement?"

"I just said that I don't owe you an explanation. The circumstances at that time necessitated a quick and equitable decision. That is what I gave. I am programmed for those kinds of decisions and there is no reason for you to contest my ability or my authority to act properly in this context. And, as I explained, the negotiation and consequent compromise make it impossible for me to consider the group as a scientifically constituted test group. Nonetheless, simple observation is possible. That is apparently what is happening anyway," retorted the Governor and that put an end to that discussion.

"Going back to a point that was raised by Dr. Gordon," began another member of the Judicial Board, Dr. Jarod, "what kinds of extraordinary behavior do you envisage if the group is deprived of basic necessities for life?"

"This behavior is difficult to anticipate as these members of the human race have not grown up with the same values of former generations." She stopped and looked at Dr. Jarod. "Unfortunately, Dr. Jarod, your question is now irrelevant, as the Governor has made it very clear that we cannot interfere with the group as a whole." She said as she turned back to the Governor. "Does that mean that we are obliged to feed and clothe them?"

"Now, yes. In the beginning we didn't, but I saw clearly that they needed our assistance and my promise...We must continue to care for them." He said adamantly.

She sighed over the fruitlessness of her up-coming explanation. "Nonetheless I shall try to answer the question, as I can." She said apologetically. "There are a few scenarios that I can imagine. First, as I just mentioned, the values we have given these humans are different from those of humans at other periods in their history. Most importantly, survival is not a priority for these new breed humans, who have been raised to accept their termination. That being the case, they might not take extraordinary measures to survive, if they are deprived of food and water, or receive smaller rations. This scenario, however, does not seem the more plausible to me, as I believe that the instinct to survive is innate to human beings. And, the governor has just confirmed that this option is not feasible. Nonetheless, that does not prevent me from presenting my views on how these humans might react, if deprived of basic necessities to survive." She glared at the Governor.

"Accordingly that basic instinct for survival would resurge in life-threatening conditions and would replace other fundamental values. That has always been the problem for humans. For example, taking the life of another human is in complete contradiction with natural law, the fundamental value and respect of human life in society; or communal living. It would not be a natural choice within the context of this center for an individual to threaten someone's life. But then, the individual would never find himself or herself in a life-threatening situation within the center." Dr. Gordon stopped for a minute, to organize her thoughts, which were definitely going off in different and confusing directions, before continuing. "Taking someone's life is primitive behavior that, unfortunately, was a problem throughout all human history, as we all know". She let out a long, heavy sigh, underlining her contempt for this kind of behavior. "If we deprive our coveted group of renegade creatures of food and water, forcing them to fend for themselves on that wasteland, would they show primitive behavior? Or, would they live and die united by a sense of solidarity and respect? The answer to this question lies in whether the group living outside our center can or has regressed. Did we wipe out their basic instincts through our programming? Would our programming of fundamental values have a residual effect on their actions today and tomorrow? That is why our study of emotional behavior is so important today. We, that is the members of my team, have conjectured that taking another human's life to satisfy a basic standard of living, food, more than anything else, is within the realm of possibilities."

"Are you going to speak about that detestable tribal behavior—cannibalism?" Crawford interrupted, as he raised his hand in protest. No one paid any attention to him, so Dr. Gordon went on with her speech.

"Absolutely or exactly, but not from the standpoint of a quasi-religion. You must bear in mind that cannibalism was a kind of religious practice, within a broad definition of religion. Here, it would be just for survival. Cannibalism was condemned as murder around the 19th century, maybe earlier. I would have to verify that. Yet, the eating of an individual who had died a natural death in order to survive was permissible. The humans prided themselves in their intellectual qualities; nonetheless, what they considered to be civilized behavior was not always the most intelligent choice. Their decisions were most often, simply practical." Replied Dr. Gordon.

In one of her conversations with me, she would reveal her fascination with religious practices of all kinds. I imagine that she enjoyed overwhelming the Board Members with her knowledge of cannibalism. She shared the same position as Dr. Crawford, being that the human race was by its nature intellectually inferior, but, unlike him, she felt that they overcompensated for that, and thus excelled over other races, by relying upon instinct and other innate emotions that gave them the courage and capacity to go beyond pure intellect. So, Dr. Gordon believed, and I think still does, that pure intellect is insufficient for real achievement.

"Right. We can't take any risks because these creatures are quite unpredictable." The Governor was now taking charge. "As we cannot study the group then we must decide at what point we should recuperate the human subject of our experiment. How many of you agree with Dr. Gordon that we should use the element of surprise to our advantage?"

The Board members, except for Dr. Crawford, responded favorably. Dr. Crawford asked that his objections be made part of the record. Dr. Gordon thanked the Board for their understanding and promised to keep them informed by getting back to them over the next six months to fix a date to recuperate...Pamela.

The meeting ended with that strange human behavior of a quick handshake, which meant nothing to them; it was simply part of their programming.

Chapter 20: Intimacy

The days that followed the birth of Frederic were not just the beginning of a routine of feeding and gentle caring for my child, but the beginning of a new wave of emotions, a binding warmth and affection that would endure throughout our lives. Motherhood— such a lovely name for the force and desire to protect and shelter a child from invisible and unknown dangers, while giving a child the strength and confidence to confront life in its many disguises. "I am fortunate, privileged," I mused as I studied my son, a physical reflection of Peter and myself and a statement of our love, "to be one of a few to call myself, a Mother."

A few days after Frederic's arrival, John came to talk to me about maternal instinct. He was studying every move I made matching my reactions to those of Sarah and Ruth after the births of their children. He called this the maternal instinct, a desire to protect and care for the child. I found that a bit insulting, if not demeaning, to relegate everything I was doing to mere instinct, when I found motherhood to be an existentially pleasing experience. So why not humor him by playing along with him? I asked myself. And, in spite of the fact that he irritates me with his arrogance, he added a bit to the monotony of my day-to-day life and sometimes, I even learned something from him.

"So, what are you going to do with this new project on the intricacies of Motherhood, John?" I asked to keep the conversation going.

"Oh, nothing really. I am like you, Pamela, a bit bored and your newfound Motherhood gives me something to think about and analyze." He replied half-heartedly.

"Right," I threw it out with a nuanced tone of disbelief and disgust.

"You don't believe me," he mocked.

"Should I?" I queried.

"Yes. I am very serious. I think a great deal about how lethargic and boring we all are. The arrival of Frederic comes at the right time for me. I am starting to think about accomplishing something. You know I even went so far in my thoughts lately as to imagine a break-in into the Center. I would like to steal some equipment just basic things that I could use here. What do you think?"

"Better to study maternal love, John, than to talk about breaking-in. You know that if they are spying on us, just saying that in my presence puts me in danger as well. A break-in would destroy all of our comforts."

"I don't think so." He said with a half-smile on his face, as if he were testing me. "I agree that they might be observing us. How would they have known about the birth of Frederic? And yet, I am not…certain. That doesn't matter, anyway; but they must be expecting something from us. Don't you think?"

"I want to forget about the Center. They are letting me live here so that I can develop different emotions. One day they will come to get me. That was the deal."

"They didn't send you here; you escaped!" John exclaimed.

"Did I? Wasn't it all planned? You should know; you are in charge of this community; aren't you? You even told me. Don't you remember?" I replied emotionally. "You want to confuse by changing your statements. In any event, you know a lot more than you are willing to share and that has always bothered me. That is why I don't trust you. You know that and you continue to play your game. Pretend that Pamela is naive and stupid. That is how you put me in touch with my emotions from the very beginning. It was as if I were on a schedule and you had to make certain that I respected the timing."

"Wow! Revelations like that don't come every day. You know what I think? I think that your pregnancy has made you aggressive," He said.

Then he started laughing so loudly and violently, that I found myself swept up by his mocking euphoria. It felt good to laugh and the more I laughed, the more I wanted to, especially at myself. I just wished that I had been laughing so heartily with someone else.

"Ok." I finally calmed down. "I believe you. Bored like you are, studying my maternal instinct is as good a form of divergence as anything else." I said patronizingly and then added, "But motherhood has a special meaning for me at the moment, so I would rather wait awhile before broaching this subject with you. You know that I have been very cooperative in the past with discussing my emotional development; but quite frankly, your presence today is disarming. I am preoccupied with my son. So, if you don't mind, I would rather pick this up another time." As an afterthought, I added. "I have to feed the little one and I notice that he eats better when we are alone together."

"No problem, Pamela. We shall continue the conversation later?" He asked a bit hesitantly.

"If you think that there is anything to be said," I replied sardonically.

John was not the only visitor that passed by to see Frederic. Everyone stopped by at least once during the day to see and hold him. Frederic was spoiled with all the attention. The best playmates for Frederic were the other children, Samuel and Rebecca. They spent the better part of the day amusing him by dancing and jumping around in front of him. Even when he was asleep, which was most of the time, they would sit patiently and watch over him. In the end, they knew every one of his movements and would signal me before he started to cry because he was hungry or needed to be changed.

I ignored Peter's attention and particularly his advances. I was tired most of the time and I did not feel like I was very enticing physically. My breasts were swollen and sore from breastfeeding and my stomach looked flabby to me. I didn't want him to see me in this shape. The memory of Frederic's birth, with the ripping and tearing of my insides, made me wonder if I could ever have sexual relations again. I was too embarrassed to ask Ruth or Sarah about that. I was afraid of how Peter would react if I had pain.

Whether Peter was aware of my insecurities about myself or not, he was not ready to be shoved aside forever. He said only nice things to me not just about my role as a Mother, but more specifically about how beautiful and sensual I looked. He gave me the impression that bearing a child had given me a new sexuality, a new allure; that was impossible for him to resist. He didn't force himself on me, just gave me soft caresses in passing. On several occasions, when I was nursing Frederic, he enveloped us both in his strong arms, in a loving and protective way.

His persistence paid off, giving way to quick and then more intense kisses until, finally, I started to feel alive again in his presence and that burning desire to be intimate with him returned. A different intensity, or hunger for each other, marked with a certain violence or ravenous expression of love, emerged. The kisses were more penetrating, and our reactions less inhibited. I found myself squeezing, scratching, even clawing him, as if trying to break through his outer shell; he responded energetically, erotically to my advances. It turned into a game of love, where he dominated me, even as I struggled to dominate him; and I loved it; it excited me. When, with determination and vigor, he entered me for the first time since Frederic's birth, all the sensations that Frederic's passage into the world outside inscribed inside of me seemed to disappear; all that I felt was Peter's force and strength; all that I wanted was to feel Peter deeper and deeper inside of me. Our relationship moved forward to another level of expression and passion with intense love, and carnal flames enveloping our liberated bodies.

Our conversations turned around us, our love and fidelity, and our son. We frequently sought advice from Ruth and Sarah, who assured us over and over again that Frederic was in excellent health. We worried about his present, and even more about his future. Watching Samuel and Rebecca was helpful. "They seem happy in their relationship," I often said to Peter, who nodded in agreement. And yet, I pondered over what lies ahead, more boredom and intense frustration for the children, like what we are experiencing every day in the cavern. I calmed myself by saying, well, since they didn't know any other life to compare this one to, maybe they will be content forever in this bliss without problems. But was this bliss?

"Perhaps, Pamela, we should go back to exploring the outlying areas. I have changed my mind. I am beginning to think that there is hope for us. It is impossible that the entire planet is barren. The Center must be situated in a desert." Peter startled me out of my thoughts. "As I remember from my studies, deserts are vast, sandy wastelands. They have their charm, but they are hot during the day and cold at night. That is exactly what we are experiencing. And, it is difficult to find your way in a desert. One can easily lose the sense of direction." His excitement over this discovery was real.

"I thought that the ground was composed of red dirt. I didn't realize that it was sand." I said confused with what he said.

"No; you are right, it seems to be dirt and it looks like dirt. Its chemical makeup even is not that different from dirt. Nevertheless, I am convinced, by its texture that it is sand, and that this place resembles a desert. Yes, Pamela, we are walking on sand." The corners of his mouth coiled up. "Maybe it wasn't always a desert; maybe those Androids destroyed the planet." His mood was swinging from angry to excited. "Yes, that must be it. They destroyed the planet but for some weird reason they will go to great lengths to convince us it wasn't destroyed."

"That doesn't make any sense. Why convince us that the planet wasn't destroyed? There seems to be a kind of reversal of roles. Who is controlling whom? If the Androids, as you like to call them, destroyed the planet, then they control it. Why should they care what we think?" I argued.

"Exactly. Everything goes back to the same question. In fact, what is our relationship with the Androids? They are not our parents. Do we work for them or do they work for us? Who is taking care of whom?"

"That question is easy to answer, Peter. Of course, they are taking care of us; otherwise they would not be providing us with food, water and shelter." I replied with the same tone that I use with the children when I know that I am right and they are wrong.

"Think, Pamela. You had lots of conversations with Dr. Gordon. What were your impressions? You spent more time with one of those creations than anyone else here. Even though we took our orders ultimately from them and, in the experimental stages, performed under their watchful eyes, I personally, and I am sure that it is the same for most of us, never had any intimate contact with any one of the creations. What about Dr. Gordon?"

"She," I stopped to explain. "I referred to her as a "she" because Dr. Gordon told me that she is a woman. She was very kind to me. Yes, she needed me then and needs me still for her own project. Nonetheless, she listened to me and tried to make me comfortable. She reassured me. She even warned me. For example, from the very beginning I was a bit afraid of Dr. Crawford. She told me that I should be careful what I say to him. That was a risk. Why would one of these humanoid machines care about me? That is why I have trouble thinking about them like machines." I answered him the best that I could.

"Like you said, she needed you and still needs you. She was simply protecting you like we would protect a scientific project, right?" He queried.

"I can't say. But, we did speak about Ferdinand. What I understood from her reaction to his termination was that he had not kept up his side of the bargain. They had an arrangement and he didn't respect it. Did you know that he had access to all information logged in the Research Library? She promised me the same thing if I cooperated with her. She did not exactly say it that way. I am interpreting what happened. At the time, I thought that it was a good idea to cooperate and to have access to the Research Library. In any event, I thought that I was condemned to live at the Center. I never imagined the life I have now. What do you think, Peter?" I asked with enthusiasm.

He had a very strange expression on his face. He was staring at me as if he just met me. "What is the matter, Peter? What did I say?" I pleaded. I felt ashamed and worried all at the same time.

"I never believed what the others said about you. They said that you were a spy. If not that, you were planted to provide information about us. I refused to believe that and now you admit, after all this time together, that you made a deal with our enemies? That is different than being the object of an experiment. Dr. Gordon wanted to study your emotions and you wanted access to the total universe of information. And, she agreed. Who are you that she would agree to that? You are not Ferdinand!" He virtually screamed. And, this aroused a reaction from other corners of the cavern. I heard footsteps, as someone called out. I didn't want anyone else to be privy to our arguments or disagreements.

I was desperate, though, to hit the ball back in his court as his tone was beginning to sound like the inquisition. "Who was Ferdinand? For me he was a musician with a great deal of talent. He was also a very interesting person who had ideas about life and our purpose. And, what was he to you, Peter?"

He didn't answer so I kept the pressure on, "I never accepted to spy on this community. I didn't even know this community existed. The agreement, and I should probably not call it that as I really never had a choice, was between Dr. Gordon and me. In fact, she tried to seduce me into that deal by offering some kind of compensation. I could have opted for my piano, but, as I told you, I liked Ferdinand. He fascinated me because he was different even though at the time I didn't realize all that. His termination upset me and probably led to my defiance with the conductor and to the breakdown of my system. I think it is only logical that I wanted to know what he had discovered."

He remained silent for what appeared to be a long moment. When he answered, it was evident that he was not interested in pursuing my revelations any further. "I guess that I jumped to the wrong conclusion. I should have given you the chance to explain yourself before accusing you of doing something wrong." He stopped to observe my reaction and maybe to collect his thoughts. "I apologize for being so rash. " He was walking towards me. "I love you---I love you more than I can show you. And, our son, he is so precious and a big part of our love." There were tears in his eyes as he continued. "I want him to have advantages, to have a life. We both owe him that. If you go back to the center and get to use that Library, you must share the information with us. You can help us to find a better life, Pamela" he grabbed me and held me so tightly that I could hardly breathe. "I don't want to lose you." He whispered in my ear. "I don't know how I will manage in your absence. And yet, I am going to have to let you go; you are our only hope. It is painful for me to admit the truth that you, only you, can save us!"

"Oh, Peter" I felt his mouth searching mine. How much I need him; how much I love him. How right he is. I left my thoughts slide away as our bodies moved together in that warm and luscious intimacy that I crave. My last thought was the most appropriate of all. Why did those bright ones deprive us of natural human relationships and --undulating orgasms?

Chapter 21: Commitment

W eeks went by and the routine had set in. Samuel and Rebecca came by less frequently to see Frederic. The novelty had apparently worn off. All that made me just a bit sad. When I told Sarah how I felt she told me that it was normal; I was just experiencing the post-natal blues. "Don't worry, Pamela, I experienced the same feelings—sadness, fatigue and loss of sexual drive." She explained. I smiled and shook my head in agreement even though I knew that she was wrong. I had already experienced all that months ago; it had helped Peter and me to form a stronger couple.

My depression was caused by something else, fueled by something else and developed into a kind of irrational and persistent fear of everyone around me; thereby complicating my life for the weeks that followed. No doubt I was seriously paranoid.

To pamper my fallen spirit, I decided to take evening strolls that didn't lead me very far away from the others. Privacy and peace of mind accompanied me. Being at the beck and call of a newborn can be very exhausting, physically and psychologically. Just taking an hour off and investing in oneself can be so constructive, at least that is the advice Sarah gave to me. On one particular evening, I sat peacefully on the red soil and watched the sun disappear behind a beautifully orchestrated display of colors, shades of orange, red, pink and yellow in delicately structured harmony, fading into the final smoky tone of purple. I felt so at peace that I stayed to observe the rest of this visual symphony as it presented bright and flashing stars, the soloists, followed by the celestial movement and grouping of those forming the many constellations that Peter had introduced me to and that I could now identify on my own. I was feeling very good when I finally entered the cavern walls. Everyone else was gathered together in the communal dining room talking and even arguing with a great deal of enthusiasm. The moment I was in view everyone stopped. They smiled crooked smiles, pretending that nothing interesting was being discussed. Then they retired for the evening. Peter told me that I should just forget anything that I may have heard. After I assured him I had heard nothing, he drew in a heavy breath and exhaled, completely relieved. He suggested that we get some rest.

I couldn't sleep at all and was grateful that Frederic was awake to keep me company. The following day, I tried to get answers. Everyone treated me as if I had merely imagined an animated discussion. The more that I insisted, the more they denied having had a discussion, that made me feel even more excluded from the group. My relationship with Peter and our child had brought me closer to everyone over the last year. Their attitudes now were reminiscent of my arrival and I resented having to prove myself for a second time.

Sometimes I had the impression that everyone was ganging up on me. I imagined that they were following me and spying on my every move. I became very cautious, even with Peter. I was even certain that everything they said or did was against me. They all seemed to be whispering behind my back, which only intensified my suspicions and…paranoia. I wasn't able to have a real conversation with anyone, not even Peter, who always found some silly excuse to avoid talking to me.

I was obsessed with what could have provoked this change. Both John and Peter had discussed the Center with me just after the birth of Frederic. As I mentioned over and over again, I am not certain that I can trust John; he seemed to be so devious that he might be behind some diabolical plot that concerned me and my baby. At one point I was so worried that they might be planning to take my baby back to the Center. Maybe that was the reason why John wanted to sponsor a break-in, to give the bright ones my son to draw me back to the Center. I was so overcome by paranoia that I was hiding in different parts of the cavern trying to find clues as to what was going on. I was eavesdropping at every occasion and was even rummaging through the affairs of others when they were outside the cavern walls.

I rarely left Frederic alone; and, if I had to for any reason, I left him with Stanislas. I still trusted him and Benjamin more than anyone else. I could not imagine their kidnapping my child.

I stopped talking to most people and refused to confide in Peter, like I had in the past. I started to distrust him profoundly. Whenever Frederic was in his arms, I was beside him, ready to save my son from an orchestrated kidnapping or other sinister machination. Merely hearing a voice triggered sinister thoughts and made me feel more and more alienated. I was certain that the voices I heard, echoing from inside the cavern walls, were plotting against me. I could not tolerate anyone being happy in face of my desperate situation and anguish. Worse than anything else, in my irrational state of mind, their laughter signaled imminent danger for me and for my child.

It took them a while to understand that my previous cordial attitude toward the community had rapidly deteriorated to an abysmal pathological state, and that I might be…dangerous. Little by little, in view of diffusing my potentially violent temperament, they started to humor me by inviting me to sit down and talk about Frederic and about my plans. I saw these niceties as dubious attempts to cover up their schemes against my baby and me. Their efforts made me even more suspicious. I rejected their endeavors to appease me and remained in my corner of the cavern with my baby in my arms.

As time passed, I realized that I definitely had become an object of discussion and I overheard them on numerous occasions express their concern for me. I never heard any solutions proposed; but, it didn't matter, I would not have believed that their concern was genuine.

Jonathan and Peter started to avoid me. Even though Peter and I still slept in the same bed, our bodies never touched. Fortunately, Frederic liked to crawl in between us, his little body forming the dividing line between Peter and me. I felt so alone and so vulnerable. Protecting my baby and myself against this group of humans was draining me of all my energy. And, then finally, at the very moment when I was absolutely certain that I had lost my mind, John came to see me.

"Can you leave the baby for a little while?" he asked.

Even though my eyes were aflame, my nostrils flared, and my clenched teeth hidden behind straight stern lips, he stood in front of me, relaxed and flashing a big, bright smile. His composure had a calming effect on me. I felt a bit foolish even slightly embarrassed with my rigid body and angry face. I loosened up and said. "He is asleep and there is no one around to watch him. Jonathan told me that he would be by to take care of him later."

Jonathan had not been around very much lately because of my behavior, but the day before he suggested that I give him a chance to play Uncle. He was so convincing that I agreed to give him a chance. Actually, I was glad to know that he was still concerned about me. I took another look at John and said, "I guess that I can take the chance to leave for a few minutes, when Jonathan gets here. Why do you want to see me?"

"There is Jonathan," he said as he waved and called out to Jonathan to hurry up.

"Hi, what's up?" Jonathan asked as he bent down to kiss my forehead.

"We just wondered if you could keep an eye on the baby for a few minutes starting now." John winked to him.

"No problem. I thought that you were expecting me anyway, Pamela?" I nodded and he continued. "I left the other children rummaging around in the dirt. I could use a few minutes of calm; that is if Frederic lets me sit and stare at the walls."

The winks and smiles that passed between John and Jonathan were too obvious to go unnoticed. "Wait, a minute!" I screamed at them. "What are you two up to? You have something planned? Don't you? You are going to kidnap Frederic or get rid of me?" I ran towards John and started hitting him in his chest with all my force. He grabbed my hands and held them tightly. He was robust, and strong. I couldn't release myself from his grip, as he pulled me close up against him and spoke softly in my face.

"Stop it, Pamela, You have to stop this perverse comedy." I could hear the emotion in his voice. "No one is going to hurt you or Frederic, but if you don't stop acting the way you are acting, they –the creations—will put an end to you, us and your child."

His warning shocked me back into reality. I tried to pull away, but he held me tight. I looked up at him and saw his serious eyes staring back at me. I was terrified, but intrigued, so I nodded yes. He released his grip of my body, gently taking my hand in his. We walked slowly. When we got to the large doorway leading to the cubicles, he asked me to wait for his signal.

He looked around to see if anyone was watching and then put his finger to his lips with one hand, while waving me in his direction with the other. When we were outside of the cubicles, he asked me to take a walk with him and he would explain when it was the right time.

He steered us back into the cavern. We walked through the dining hall and he pointed discretely to the ceiling. I saw a couple of black boxes planted in the ceiling of the cavern, but it didn't mean anything to me and he quickly put his hand over my mouth to prevent me from asking. I was horrified by his sudden gesture and found myself stumbling over him and my own feet as he pulled me off into a corner of the room. He pushed me up against the wall and side stepped pulling me towards him as we slipped in behind the wall. Then, he let me go.

"Ok; that is fine with me," John said as he grabbed one the torches on the wall and lit it. Then he took my hand in his and slightly tugged as we ventured farther into the interior of another part of our cavern, a part unknown to me. I quickly adapted to the freshness of the inside cavern and started to feel invigorated by it. It wasn't easy to climb over the slimy rocks in smooth moccasin shoes. But, I was determined to prove my value and marched forward at his rhythm. Eventually we came to a very narrow ledge. The cavern was so dark that the flame from the torch didn't provide enough light and assurance for me as I ventured forward. At one point, he held the torch out far enough that I could see the enormous crater below sending off strange lapping sounds like small waves wafting the shore. He understood my curiosity and, in a soft, low voice confirmed that the crater was, as I thought, filled with water.

We didn't speak as we trudged along. I was getting very tired by the time we reached the end of this long tunnel. He pushed up against a part of the wall which opened into a luminous room.

"We can talk now." He said.

At this point, I was gasping for breath. He stood watching me struggle to regain a semblance of composure.

"Pamela, I noticed that you are acting a bit strangely lately," he started, like he was playing psychiatrist, as if he had any clues as to how to psychoanalyze someone.

"I don't know what you are talking about but if this is any example of how you want to reassure me, it's not working. I don't know where I am; maybe no one else knows either. Maybe you want to leave me here; lock me away. Well, if I wasn't showing signs of paranoia before, I sure am now." I was shaking all over, in part because it was definitely cold and damp in this strange place. I also shivered with trepidation, not knowing what was next. That set me out of whack again, in a whirlpool of emotions since that feeling of helplessness overwhelmed me.

He pretended that he hadn't noticed the effect all of this was having on me and just went on with the conversation.

"Yes, you do. You are hiding in places, spying on everyone. You think that we haven't noticed. You are clinging to your baby like his life is in danger and you haven't said very much to anyone over the last three weeks. So, what is going on?"

"The last two weeks," I corrected him. "You know what's going on because you are responsible for it."

"Pamela, I assure you that I have nothing against you. I was disappointed, in the beginning, when Mathieu brought you here. He has a friend who keeps him posted on new arrivals to the pre-termination Center. That is actually where you were. The majority of the people move quite rapidly into the termination module and Mathieu wanted you to be spared. Mathieu is very sensitive and when he first saw you he could not bear to have someone as beautiful as you terminated, particularly, at such a young age. We voted on the idea and I was outnumbered. The others didn't see any harm in bringing you here. Whereas, I felt that it would put us in danger. After all, I negotiated the departure of our group with the Governor. It wasn't easy to get this approval and I didn't want anything to upset our situation. And, the fact that you were being protected by one of those androids made me suspicious. I think that you can understand that?"

He stopped and looked at me. I could see in his eyes that what he was telling me was the truth, for perhaps the first time, and whether I liked it or not I could understand his concern for the other members of the group.

He continued. "What did you think about your escape? Did you think that it was life threatening?" He asked, his mouth contorting sardonically.

"My escape--in retrospect, I was afraid for a long time. In fact, the first real emotion I experienced was fear. I guess though what you want to say is that the escape was pretty easy. Maybe for you, but I didn't know whether I should follow Mathieu or stay. After all, I had done my own negotiating with Dr. Gordon. She promised me access to the Research Library if I participated in her study. Nonetheless, I never liked or trusted Dr. Crawford and he was always hanging around in the background, so to speak."

"All of us knew about that agreement, Pamela. Remember, we have spies in the Center. I am referring to the escape itself. " He sighed.

So, Peter knew about that, as well, I mused. Why did he make such a big deal of out of my agreement a month or so ago. I didn't want to discuss that with John, so I explained. "I just followed Mathieu. We ran. I never ran like that before. He knew the way out. I never had any idea where we were going. You know that sirens were blasting and we could see ourselves being tracked on the visual screens. They were following closely. I could almost feel someone behind me. And, the audio sound was excruciating. Stop them, Catch them, were repeated over and over again. We ran a long way, I think."

I stopped for a brief minute to gather my thoughts and then felt my emotions taking over. "Quite frankly, John, for me, my escape was neither easy nor a sure thing! I was perspiring profusely and my heart was beating like a drum. Mathieu was dragging me along at one point because I was too afraid to go forward. He made the decision to continue for me, because if I had gone off on my own, I would have surrendered. I hadn't had time to evaluate the rationality of an escape. It all happened so fast. How can you always undermine everything that I do?"

"I am not undermining what you did. I am just trying to point out to you that your escape seems to have fit quite nicely into Dr. Gordon's plans and that you were in a no risk situation even if you thought otherwise." He took a deep breath and added, "Mathieu told me at the time that he was surprised that there was no real threat or impediment."

"Ok, but that part is obvious now. We have gone over this part so many times that I am quite fed up with the subject. I have already agreed to go forward with Dr. Gordon's study and to help the community as much as possible. I don't know what else I can do. And, now, you told me something that I didn't know. You negotiated with the bright ones? How curious, perhaps you are working with them. Perhaps you are still working with them?" My voice rose prompting him to place his hand over my mouth.

"Just calm down. I shall explain as best I can. As you are aware we are all scientists with different specialties. The others--I prefer to identify them like that--don't care who lives out of the center. They are observing us and are certainly quite disappointed with what they see. We look like a group of unhappy humans, completely dependent upon them for food and water, and principally bored and unmotivated. That is exactly what we want them to think. You are different and, to a certain extent, we have been trying to protect you because you will eventually go back to the center. They are clever and will try to get lots of information out of you. How much pressure can you take before you will tell them everything? That is essentially why we have kept you out of our discussions. Do you think that you are capable of handling the truth and becoming a committed member of the group? You might regret knowing and participating in our projects."

I wondered why I was in such a mess. How could anyone have gotten into this type of situation where nothing made any sense? No, it was time that I took charge of my life and went forward. I needed to know, whatever the risk, what their projects were and to what extent I could be useful.

I stood sternly and then with a sudden surge of emotions spoke up, in a voice showing strong conviction, "I don't want to be the intruder any more. It is time that I became one of you."

"I that case," he smiled in a warm and reassuring way, "I shall bring you up to date. First of all let me explain why we couldn't talk earlier. Those black boxes in the ceiling of the main hall are listening devices. You probably never noticed that they are positioned throughout the cavern. There are certain things that we want them to know which is why we had conversations with you indiscriminately since your arrival. We wanted them to witness the development of your emotions; that interests them very much. And, we wanted them to know that we retained certain useful information, more particularly, that these years of presumed boredom did not render us stupid, so to speak. It is important that they continue to respect us as potentially useful resources; if not, they may decide to stop feeding and clothing us. So the various conversations with you served a double purpose."

"I feel almost offended by what you just said. In fact, I feel foolish--that is it, completely foolish. And why, why on earth was I never told about the black boxes?"

John cut me off, "That is the problem with you. You personalize everything. We would have done the same thing to anyone who came here." He purposely put the problem on me as it would be tiresome to argue over my fidelity to them today or in the future, once I was back at the center. My fidelity was something that I would have to prove to them.

"But, you didn't do the same thing to Jonathan."

"Are you listening to me?" I nodded vigorously and he continued. "Because, I thought that I was clear on one point: The difference between you and every other member, including Jonathan, is that you will be going back to the Center. We understood that from the beginning and it was confirmed by the lack of interest they showed in your escape."

"Right. I am sorry but this, can I say, "privileged" position of mine is very disconcerting." It was time to ask questions. "How did you know that these boxes were listening devices?"

"I am an engineer. I have training in many areas including communications, electricity, etc. They must have considered me a bit of a genius because I worked in so many different areas. I was working on a new type of listening device before my departure. I never gave them the details so they are still using the same faulty and inaccurate equipment. If anyone has replaced me in this area they have been very slow to arrive at the next stage. But, even assuming that they do, I would recognize it immediately, and know how to avoid the new forms of surveillance."

"Then all those so called secret conversations I had about biology, about the boredom of the group, about my promises to help you, and so forth, were heard by those Androids."

"Exactly, you got it." He said point blank and then stopped to observe or enjoy the startled expression on my face, before continuing. "But that part is necessary if I want the Governor to continue to respect our community. As our group was formed in the Center, we had to decide how to live. It was evident that it became more and more difficult to remain stoic after the visual receptors short-circuited. Some of us handled it better than others. But, the mere fact that we were able to identify those of us who were no longer being controlled meant that sooner or later the Androids were bound to do the same. So I decided to take action. We were important in our own individual areas and were all working on critical projects. Let's just say that we were able to find our way into the Governor's office to plead our case. We wanted out-- but, like you, we thought that the outside was livable, viable. The Governor warned us that we would be unable to survive on our own and our dependency on the Center was inevitable."

"You mean that, as a group, you spoke to him." I was surprised and impressed at the same time.

"Are you kidding? We threatened him." His face beamed with satisfaction. "Not every member of the group was present; just the best negotiators--yes, that is a good way to say it--just the best negotiators, Peter and myself. The others were strategically placed so as to destroy the Center. The Governor realized quite rapidly that he was not ready to take that kind of risk. Actually, he responded quite logically. He told us that there were other colonies outside the different Centers and that he could see no reason why he would not help us, especially since our ultimate objective was to live. He said that it was even a bit prestigious to set up a small colony on the outside to house the most brilliant of our species. In fact he said that living outside the Center was the prison for the intellectual elite. He agreed to provide us a place and to continue to feed and clothe us if we promised to stay outside the Center."

"But you didn't keep your agreement." I answered.

"Yes, we did, Pamela, because Mathieu was invited back to help you to escape!"

"It is not possible. You are working with them." I shook my head in disbelief. "You just told me that you voted against my joining the community. The truth, John?" I screamed and pounded his stiff chest with my clenched fists. I tried to hurt him physically like he was hurting me psychologically.

He grabbed my hands in his and pulled me under his grip. "True, I lied. Don't look so surprised, Pamela. I had no choice when the subject came up before. Now, I can tell you what really happened." He began the story. "Dr. Gordon contacted us and told us that she wanted to protect you; that she needed to give you the time to develop your personality and the Center was not the right place. She made it clear that there was no risk in our helping you. She informed us that she had the support of the Governor, who would ignore the circumstances of your escape; but that you, Pamela, would never make an attempt to leave on your own. The rest just happened as expected, although a bit sooner than planned. That was our way of telling them that we were still capable of decision making."

"Ok. Now I understand better why everyone has treated me so strangely. And all those conversations, were just theatrics."

"Not at all. We were sending our messages back to the Center. That is true; but you have been very inquisitive and sometimes it has been awkward for us. We have all tried in our own ways to give vague answers in order to protect all of us. But just imagine the contrary. If you knew the truth right after you arrived, you would not have developed your own personality." He noticed my furrowed brows and went on to explain. "Those androids wanted to see your negative emotions…at least, what they consider to be your negative emotions and study how they develop. If we had invited you to join in our game, you might have been too comfortable and looked too happy for those androids. We had to give you the opportunity to run the gamut of emotions and we decided that the best way to do that was to stay mysterious and keep you in the dark." He showed me a kind, friendly smile. "And look at you, you have developed a very interesting personality." He replied, quickly changing the subject. "So, what do you think of this place?" he queried.

"It is much better than where we lived." I answered without much emotion. I felt completely drained of all emotions. It was so strange to be told after 2 years that I was just a pawn to the others, just a pawn. . .

"Does Peter love me?" I asked.

"I believe he does. Not everything that happened was staged. You must however accept that some things happened because of who you are and who we are."

"So what should I know now; and, by the way, did those Androids hear my promises to help you?" I was a bit nervous about that thought.

"Yes, of course. We wanted them to see that aspect of human nature; that our species is capable of aligning itself and defending itself. We thought that Dr. Crawford would enjoy that revelation. He is so suspicious of everything."

"So, it is not that important?" I asked.

"Not at all. They don't pay much attention to the substance behind that because they don't feel threatened by us."

"So, how did you find this place?"

"We have been here for a long time. We saw the site on a map in the Center before we left and were able to calculate the importance of the area. These underground passages have been in place for thousands of years. It took us quite a long time to find out how to access them."

"Oh, by the way, those secret meetings you were holding."

"No relevance. We wanted to create diversion."

"And, when Peter told me that we were in a desert and you told me that you wanted to stage a break-in. Well, they heard all that." I found it risky.

"We really do have spies in the inside. Those were messages for them. Certain times of the day the Androids transfer the listening devices to "programmed people." Some of our group took the risk to stay inside. From time to time, they get a message to us -usually with the evening meals. But, in general, we let them know that they can count on us, if they need us--the real reason for those remarks. Nonetheless, we do have a plan and it is a Break-In." What we lack out here is not brains; it is basic components, materials, all those things that would help us to fight back. For example, if we could get one of those vehicles we could travel and see what is in our vicinity and farther."

"But, you laughed at Jason." I insisted. "I always thought that that was a bit cruel."

"We only laughed at him around you; part of the game." He smiled. I didn't find it funny. "He was a fantastic source of information; but we don't have the means to circulate like he does. He is just a voyager and has done nothing to confirm his discoveries. He might be dead now for all we know. He just keeps going and going. He may even be passing in the same circle. But, he was a wonderful source of hope and that revitalized our Project. Jonathan's arrival was another impetus for discovery. We may have gotten tired and bored a bit. You, Jason, Jonathan--all within the last 2 years have given us back the courage to keep going. This very room has another secret passage that will allow us to pass underneath the center. That is where you are so important. We need to have the maps. You can get them off the computers. If you do it casually enough they won't be suspicious. In the inside, you can pass us the information that we need to fight back. Are you ready for that?"

"I think that I have a lot to prove to this group and am ready to do it. I want a future for my son and I don't think that living in a dust ball is going to do it. Yes, I am ready to help you take over the Center." I said with conviction. I would prove my worth is what I thought to myself.

"Next meeting is here in this room in two days. Each person must come alone. A few of us must stay visible and close to the listening devices. You are invited. Now, as we go back along the slippery tunnel, please no talking. Even though I have no reason to believe that they can track us this far, we must be cautious. I want you to be calmer and return to mothering Frederic. The closer they think that you are to your son, the sooner they will come for you. You have to believe me when I say that Frederic will be protected and that he will know that his mother is coming back. Hopefully, we can pull things off fast enough that he is still little when we take command."

I saw the cavern in an entirely new light. I finally felt a part of this group and had a very important mission. I even realized that my former fears concerning the safety and care of my son were superfluous. I did not need to choose someone to replace me because my son would know that I would return. Peter and the group would protect him. Now I had to be careful about what I said and stop distrusting everyone. My paranoia dropped away like it never existed. I was proud. I would not only be a source of information, I would be one of the moving forces in the destiny of this human colony. I thought about Ferdinand and promised him that I would finish what he had started.

Peter was sitting with Frederic on his knees when I arrived. He told me that Jonathan had only just left. I couldn't tell him anything. If he weren't already aware of it, he would be in the next 48 hours. I took my little one in my arms and, for first time in a long time, I felt relaxed and happy to be a Mother. I would give him all the love and attention that I could while I was there so that he would never forget me. But how much time with him did I have left?

Chapter 22: Agent Provocateur

"Dr. Gordon." One of the nurses was running after her. "Dr. Gordon, I must talk to you."

This time she heard her name and turned round." Yes, number 1141417. What can I do for you?"

"I just received a message from the Commission. An emergency meeting has been called for 1 P.M. You are expected to be there."

"Thank you. Now please get on with your other work." She said nonchalantly, as she wondered about the reason for this meeting. It was 11:30. She calculated that she would have just enough time to finish her rounds and go back to her office to shut down her system for at least 30 minutes, something that she should have done two days ago.

Her last patient, Diana, was a problem and reminded her of Pamela. Yet, she was not as clever as Pamela. She sensed that Diana was even more dangerous than she was dissimulating. The treatment was not working and Dr. Gordon deduced this patient would never reintegrate successfully into the community. Dr. Gordon hesitated about seeing her because she knew the instant she saw Diana, she'd have another dilemma in her complicated life. This human would be better off on the exterior, but how could she negotiate the departure of yet another one of these creatures? First Pamela, then Jonathan, and now Diana, the 15th series of her kind. And she wondered whether this one would be emotionally stable enough?

"Hi. I hope that you are feeling fine." Dr. Gordon pleasantly greeted her new patient.

"Not at all. Leave me alone. You know that eventually I shall be terminated. Just do it and get it over with. Stop torturing me like this" And, as if that was not enough, she added, "Just hearing your voice and smelling your rusty odor is nauseating. Do I have to support your hypocritical pleasantries as well?" She turned her head away from Dr. Gordon in disgust.

"Ok. Well, I don't have time to do very much for you today. I am glad that you are still alive and fighting." Dr. Gordon turned and walked away, very tired of the routine. Nonetheless, she was motivated by this emergency meeting. The timing was good in that she might be able to plead Diana's case; maybe even get the approval from the board to give Diana freedom to live with the outside community. She meditated on what effect Diana would potentially have on the calm and complacent lifestyle of the outside group? As she labored over this, an interior signaling system reminded her she needed to recharge her energy level. She would always be functional, even without recharging; but recharging had a positive effect on heightened reasoning. Recharging was the only real inconvenience, she thought, to being an android and not a human. She definitely wanted to be fit for the up-coming meeting; so she rushed back to her office to shut down for 30 minutes.

Dr. Gordon arrived on time feeling quite up for this meeting. The Secretary started off with the minutes from the last meeting and then the Governor addressed the problem of the day.

"Everyone knows that we are listening to the conversations of our study group. I had extra time over the last few days and decided to listen to recent recordings. We have always insinuated that it is quite surprising that these rather intelligent humans have just been doing nothing for the last few years. At least that has been our impression." He stopped and looked at the other members to see what their reaction was. "I guess that what I have to say will come as a shock to all of you."

"What is this nonsense? "Dr. Crawford spoke up. "These humans are incapable of independent thinking even when they have gotten back those negative emotions, the principle concern of everyone here today."

"Well, listen to this then," the Governor said as he played out the conversation between John and Pamela ending with the suggestion that the humans take control of the Center. This met with android style laughter; a high decibel crackling reminiscent of an electrical shock. Everyone was incredulous as to how they could break-into the Center?

Apart from Dr. Gordon, who said nothing, and the Governor, who expressed his concern, the other members of the Board felt that there was no reason to believe that this discussion was important. The general opinion, expressed by Dr. Crawford, was that even if they did break-into the Center to steal equipment, it could not be used on the outside.

As Dr. Crawford said contemptuously, "A small handful of humans against the Center's staff could do nothing. Maybe they want us to worry. This may be their way of getting revenge. Just imagining that we would be adding patrols would be satisfying for them. They are incapable, I want to emphasize, incapable of collective action and to overrun this center requires coordination and commitment to a cause. They have none of that. We are providing them with everything they need to survive. We have seen how passive they are, as they want for nothing. The majority of them have been on the outside for more than 6 years and the only thing that they have been able to make are babies." His observations were applauded by the others; much to the humiliation of the Governor.

That was Dr. Gordon's cue to bring up Diana. "As we are all together perhaps I can get your impressions on one of my patients. I call her Diana--using Pamela's decoding."

"Dr. Gordon, I think that we are all getting tired of your project. And, this is the third time in a year that you are bringing up a special case." Dr. Benjamin broke in.

"Yes; you are right. But, if the project is to be successful--that is, if it is going to give us insight into the effect of negative emotions on humans, we must continue to add new elements. Diana is a special case and, as you well know, she has been very useful to us in the past." While heads nodded in agreement she continued, "At this moment, I am fascinated by her aggressiveness and hatred for me and everything around her. This human could upset the passivity of the group." All heads were pointed in her direction so she knew she had their attention.

"Go on," encouraged the Governor who needed to redeem himself.

"She is the fifteenth of this series. Considering the menial tasks the others were programmed to do, they were terminated quite young." She realized that she had to explain herself. "I thought that all of you were aware that longevity is accorded only to the intellectual class here at the center. The categories of intellectuals are limited to the scientists, artists, musicians, and writers." They all nodded their heads in agreement. "She is only 19 years old and in fact years away from her termination date. I looked into the genetic composition of this group and discovered that we exploited the violent tendency of her line. She even verbalizes very well her violent hatred. If our previous experience with humans is valid, I think that she could go so far as to commit murder. That would be wonderful, in a way, for the study, that is. We could study how the others would react to her and whether they would be able to finish with her; that is, maybe execute her."

"This study is getting out of hand." Interjected Dr. Crawford. "We know what kinds of cruelties humans are capable of. We don't need to see these horrors again." This brought general approval.

"You are right Dr. Crawford, to a certain extent; but we need a catalyst to inspire real human development in this outside community. We might have to add the worst to get the best results. I might be wrong but it's worth a try." She looked around hoping to find nods. Most sat and stared at her.

"Tell you what," the Governor interrupted, "let's take a vote. How many of you consider it a good idea to let this human--Diana--leave the center?"

By a simple majority, the decision was made to let her go. Dr. Crawford voted in favor of it reveling in the thought that perhaps this person would kill the entire group and render Dr. Gordon's emotional study a complete failure.

A decision was made to drug her and just leave her outside the Center. The other humans might consider her a spy and that would accelerate the total destruction of this worthless community, which was naturally the position of Crawford and his allies who were tired of Dr. Gordon's study.

"But her treatment?" protested Dr. Gordon. "It is not finished."

The Board voted to take the risk. Even if stopping the treatment terminated the Human. Diana's termination in the Center or outside was of no real interest or consequence to the board members.

"Before retiring from this meeting I would like to know when you plan to pick up Pamela?" the Governor asked, to the satisfaction of the group.

"I plan to let her stay on for another two months so I can observe her interaction with Diana, assuming that Diana survives with lack of treatment." She hesitated, hoping for some response to her final effort to provide proper treatment for Diana. Her remark seemed to pass unheard, so she sighed and finished with, "I also believe that Pamela is becoming more and more attached to her child and the separation in two-months-time will have the effect I am waiting for."

After the meeting, Dr. Gordon walked away grudgingly, her normal long and energetic stride was replaced with short, heavy steps, as she laboriously found her way back to her office. Even though she had the Board's approval to do what she wanted to do, it seemed like everyone except the Governor was hoping that her project would fail. And even though Dr. Crawford had to work with her, he was hoping that she would be exposed as a charlatan, swimming in complete failure and eventually ordered to shut down permanently.

Chapter 23: Trickery

Exhilarated--that was it, I was feeling exhilarated by John's revelations. Everything began to fall into place. Discovering that I was not part of a passive community of humans, wasting away in a barren land, but, the final link in a long chain of hopes and aspirations, targeting--- Freedom. I felt like I had plunged into a glassy pool of water and washed away all those haunting fears and suspicions that stifled me; that dragged me through a state of paranoia. I was alive, dynamic with a sincere desire to succeed both for myself and for the group.

I passed by John in the afternoon of this, to be famous, day. He asked about Frederic and then about Peter. He indicated that he was going off to his cubicle to relax for a few hours and I quickly grasped the meaning of what he was saying. I took my time to go through the hidden passage and to light my torch. I was not as relaxed this time compared to traveling this path with John. I slipped more than once, along the narrow, but high passage. I even hesitated at one moment about continuing. But, I persisted and made it to that spacious room to find Ruth, Sarah, John, Stanislas and Peter waiting for me. Jonathan arrived just after me and we sat on the cold damp floor to talk.

"This is the plan," began John. "I know that I am going to repeat myself a bit, for the benefit of Pamela. So, please be patient. And, I know that we cannot stay away too long or the androids will become suspicious. I'll be fast so that we return soon." He informed all of us.

"It is all rather simple. We need to know the location of one of those hover crafts that they send out to patrol the region and intercept space voyagers."

"I am sorry." I interrupted. "Peter told me what he saw and heard. Has anyone else been able to confirm this?"

"What do you mean, Pamela?" Peter seemed offended. "I don't see why you should want confirmation. Don't you trust me?"

"Of course I trust you," I responded quickly and firmly. "The only problem is that I, like you, Peter, have no idea where they are located. It would be helpful if someone else had some more information to give. That is all. You don't have to be so upset. I want to be efficient and not waste time looking in the wrong places."

"Ok. Your point is well taken, Pamela, but we have no more information, other than suppositions." John took up his speech. "Let me explain. All of us scientists have been working on projects that indicate that space travel was possible even though we didn't know that for sure. Why space travel was scrapped, we don't know either. So, Peter's experience fills in enough of the gaps for me to confirm space travel. Then there was the hovercraft pilot that the communication's officer ordered to intercept the space vessel. Even though Peter communicated with the space ship pilot, he only heard a voice. He never saw anything or anyone. He did also hear the confirmation from the android that the vessel was destroyed. Nonetheless, it all seems logical that they're keeping it secret to avoid upsetting the society as it exists." He concluded.

"Well, I just can't ask Dr. Gordon to show me the hover craft hangar, Can I?" I replied condescendingly. I felt uneasy with the non-existent, or at best, flimsy plan that was being proposed. I wondered how much I would have to improvise and how willing Dr. Gordon would be to placate my curiosity. I was ready and willing to take calculated risks based upon a concrete plan, which was not evident from the discussion underway. As I saw it, they were not only counting on me to give them information but also mastermind the strategy. I did not think that I was cut out to be a spy, let alone a hero.

"Yes." That full baron tone voice of John's shattered my thoughts and I was back with the group again. "Your mission is rather risky, but no more risky than what each of us is doing. In fact, to a certain extent, your relationship with Dr. Gordon is your veil of protection. What we are counting on is the general naivety of the androids. They are not suspicious of us because they think of us as complacent, lazy and bloated with their care packages. We'll have to reach an extreme frenzy, like becoming hysterical or violent, before they'll react. I can assure you, Pamela, I lived quite a long time with them before I negotiated our departure. If I hadn't gone to see the Governor, I would still be living in the Center interacting with those creations and they would be regarding me as one of the rest of the programmed humans. They are not that clever." He raised his voice and hands in frustration. "You can easily manipulate them and get permission to move about. You will be invited back to the center to be studied. It will be normal for you to be curious. They are expecting that from you. Looking around, investigating and even asking questions will be considered perfectly normal."

"Are you telling me that opening doors and looking in drawers will not be considered spying?"

"I don't think so. I could be wrong. In that case we will come to your rescue." He affirmed and then placated me by saying, "I know that you are not all that much at ease, but you have to be human for them. That is what they want and expect. Lying, spying, stealing are those negative human characteristics that they are just so interested in. You'll see; they will be so intent on studying the value of these emotions that they will not see your real objective."

"I wish that I could share your optimism," I said, showing my trepidation.

"I know that you will find it hard in the beginning, but trust me…you'll see…you will be in control."

"So how do I play up to Dr. Gordon?" I asked.

"It's simple, just tell her what she wants to hear." he replied rather nonchalantly.

"What do you mean?"

"She will ask the questions. Just respond exactly in the way she expects. Don't add anything else. You play naive and you insist upon using the library facilities." John showed his impatience again. "It is important that you get access to the Library. What has happened over the years is crucial. When we know our history, we will be able to rewrite it." He exclaimed.

"So, once I find the location of this hovercraft, you will break-in."

"Yes and No." He continued. "We have to finish the tunnel. We are not yet ready to access the Center from the inside. We will need some time; how long, I don't know. We don't have the right equipment here. That might be one of the first things that you could do. You could ask for some tools so that we can try to build things. That should make them laugh, if they could, but I am sure that they will comply. You should make a lot of demands in the beginning. I shall give you a list. Are you clear on everything?"

"Not at all, but I don't think that you can clarify anything much better. In fact, I realize that until I accomplish the better part of my mission inside, you won't be able to clarify anything. It doesn't matter though. Even though I have come to like everyone, and really love Peter and Frederic, I have difficulty imagining years of collective solitude in this barren wasteland as a commendable future." I stopped for a few seconds as I focused on Peter. I did not want to disappoint him, my son, and all the others. I had to stop vacillating back and forth and looking weak. "Of course, Yes, I am ready to take the necessary risks and do my best." I ended with a question, "Did those so-called informers give you any idea of whether or not those bright ones will let me go back and forth?"

"I doubt that." Stanislas spoke up. "That will make them uneasy. Avoid that. If Dr. Gordon suggests a visit, don't refuse it, but don't look too excited either. Just pretend that you are willing to cooperate as she wants."

"Excellent advice," Ruth chimed in. "Do nothing that could give them the impression that you are in need of us for any reason. Be careful."

"Time to go," Sarah announced. "We have been out of sight long enough."

One by one we returned to the interior of the main cavern and took our places as if nothing had happened. I was deep in thought. There was nothing special that happened during the meeting, other than John's offer to give me a list of priorities and my unequivocal agreement to work actively for the liberation of the group. Stanislas's comment made a very big impression on me. He was usually so passive. He rarely took part in discussions, remaining very polite and congenial. His advice on how to interact with Dr. Gordon showed good intuitive thinking and startled me. He seemed so sure of himself with his warning. It was if he had already tested the bright ones and knew how they would react. I considered that to be good advice to prepare me to be more cautious and efficient.

Within a few instances of our return, a new drama was upon us. Mathieu and Isabelle appeared, carrying someone into the cavern.

"Can you please help us?" Isabelle screamed, as John and Peter were the first to move. Isabelle and Mathieu advanced, weighted down by something; John and Peter pushed forward, side-stepping Isabelle, to get a better view. "Imagine", Isabelle continued to speak in a high, hysterical voice, "we found her lying on the ground just outside the Center."

"What is wrong with her?" I ventured.

"We have no idea. She hasn't moved since she's been in our arms. She must be unconscious or something like that."

"No doubt." Sarah replied. "Put her over here on the floor and I shall take a closer look at her." She said as she pointed to the place.

They placed her on the cold floor and Sarah immediately went about examining her. Word of her arrival spread fast and soon we were all grouped together watching and waiting impatiently for Sarah to tell us what was wrong. But, she didn't know. We had absolutely no clue why she was unconscious and no idea whether or not she would ever wake up. The news was particularly upsetting. As I looked at each of us one by one it was clear that we all had the same apprehension. What would we do with her if she just faded away--a particularly distasteful possibility?

Mathieu and Isabelle had not taken the food with them. I volunteered to go back to the delivery area, just outside the Center, with Jonathan and pick it up. It had been a very long time since I ventured out of the safety of the community and I felt like it was the right moment to move about.

Jonathan and I walked quite a while before talking. We realized that we both had bad feelings about this new arrival. He thought that he had run into her once or twice. If he was right and it was the same person that he met on the inside, he thought that her arrival was a kind of trap; but, what for? As far as he and I were concerned, there was no reason to want to destroy our little group. We hadn't done anything yet that could be considered offensive to the Androids, had we?

"Jonathan, what do you remember about her that makes you so suspicious?" I asked. Before he could answer I added. "There is something strange about her. Maybe it is her very long straight black hair." I suggested. "But, that must sound a bit ridiculous to you."

"No, it doesn't sound ridiculous. In fact that is exactly how I reacted to her. She worked with the cleaning staff and I noticed her one evening when I was still lingering in the concert hall after rehearsal. She was nervous from the instance that she entered the room, moving in all directions and doing nothing. I introduced myself after a few minutes and she gave me her code. Her code image was much more pleasant, not that she isn't pretty by human standards in reality. It is just that she has that strange air about her. She is incredibly thin, almost skeletal. You must have noticed that." I nodded. "And, her slightly slanted deep black eyes, which you have not yet witnessed, are penetrating. She acted as if I had caught her doing something wrong; I had that gut reaction that she was unpredictable, if that makes any sense?"

As Jonathan is not the kind of person to be affected by physical appearance—pleasant or unpleasant—his critical comments had a strong impact on me. I imagined that Dr. Crawford had something to do with all this. He had the kind of simmering vicious attitude towards us in general that he could have planted a kind of lunatic in our midst just to create chaos. But, there was no real evidence to support those conclusions. Our group had grown more rapidly since my arrival and maybe the bright ones just got used to the idea of sending the social and psychological rejects to us. Perhaps our group was not ready to grow so quickly, which is why the arrival of this strange woman was one person too much.

I looked up at Jonathan in silence; even hunched over, he was still tall. He reached for my hand and we continued without speaking until we arrived at the outskirts of the Center and picked up the food. This time, though, there was one more meal.

She was still unconscious when we returned. I approached her cautiously and was struck by the absolute beauty of this young woman. Yes, she was wiry thin but also muscular. Her facial features were in absolute harmony. She had high cheekbones, a small but flat nose and wonderfully full lips. Evidently, I admired this well-built young woman, with her high, firm breasts that were only partially hidden under the drab white linen robe that all of us wore. Her long, thick black hair and shrouding olive colored skin fascinated me even more. I walked away believing that I had come face to face with a different race of humans, humans of color, as Jason had called them. I found her exquisite.

There was no change in her condition during or after dinner so when we went off to bed feeling relatively certain that she would still be asleep in the morning. That assumption was a serious mistake.

How many rooms she visited before entering ours, we shall never know. I must have sensed her presence the instance she leaned over our bed. I screamed so loudly that I frightened Frederic whose persistent crying woke up everyone. To my surprise our visitor presented no immediate physical threat. She just stood staring down at me. But the anger and hatred on her face enhanced by cold gleaming eyes overwhelmed me. I shook with fear until my bones clattered. My raw unabated fear took over, causing me to violently thrust my arms forward snapping her body back as it thudded on the hard floor. I rolled over on top of her and tried to gouge her eyes and pull her hair. That provoked the others crowding around us to yell "stop" until Peter pulled me away from her.

As things calmed down, the community began to discuss how to integrate the new member. She was human and we had to find a place for her to live.

Sarah broke the silence by stating that Diana had certainly been sedated and that there was no need to worry about her recovery. At least one problem seemed to be resolved. Jonathan then took the lead welcoming her to our little community, explaining that we were dependent upon the center for food and clothing, and emphasizing that our principle objective was to live in peace and harmony.

When she finally spoke she was not very reassuring. She wanted to know why we had kidnapped her. Isabel calmly explained to her that she had been found outside the Center and we had no idea how she got there, and that she should be grateful to us for bringing her to our community.

Her behavior in face of this was particularly alarming. She stood up and then started to sleek around, rolling her back and shoulder muscles like a cat. As she approached us, one by one, we instinctively backed away. Her eyes and sadistic grin did not invite friendly contact. After this long, tense session, she seemed perfectly satisfied with herself and sat down on one of the high rocks where she could observe us. She certainly imagined herself to be the person in charge of a group of individuals ready to move at her command.

Are you alright?" I ventured, my voice trembling as I spoke, hoping to draw her from her fantasy world back to our reality.

"Quite alright," she started. "You can all see me as I am; I would imagine? Describe me." She ordered.

"Tall, thin, black hair; do you want me to go on?" My voice trembled.

"I don't know. Some of you are quite distasteful for me. Him, over there-she pointed to Jonathan--what is he? How do I know that you won't try to make me as ugly as him?"

"You know me," Jonathan replied. "We met one evening in the orchestra pit when you were cleaning up."

"You are wrong." She laughed a sinister laugh. "If I had seen you, I would never have forgotten."

Jonathan explained about the visual receptor and how the images of humans and all living things were projected into the visual center of the brain. He told her that we were programmed and always saw the beautiful side of people and of life. Now, she was seeing some of the ugly sides; but, as he stated, the physical part is just the shell. It is what is inside of someone that makes someone nice and he knew that he was nice.

She shrugged it off and stepped down from her throne. "I am not interested in staying here. I don't want to get to know any of you. In any event, I don't trust any of you. As far as I am concerned, this visual receptor story is nonsense." she made a sound like an animal and started unmercifully swinging her arms in our direction. She obviously knew how to frighten people. She walloped Peter in the mouth and he fell to the ground grasping his jaw. She laughed and then quickly grabbed Sarah by her long hair with her strong snake-like hands and in a quick second yanked her downwards to her knees. Sarah screamed with pain.

"She knows how to defend herself; how to fight" I thought to myself just as she lifted me up in the air and threw me heavily on the ground.

"Are you crazy! " I screamed at the top of my lungs. "You could have really hurt me. And look at the others. Look what you have done." She flung her head back in laughter, as I tried to gather myself up. I ached all over and felt wobbly. Peter grabbed me around my waist and pulled me close to him.

We started to back away from her. She moved fearlessly and with determination in our direction. We weren't use to this kind of violence which seemed so primitive. We stood grouped together just waiting for the next blow, and then, John, took off in a fast fury calling out to us to follow.

"We have to rush her", he yelled frantically as he clamored toward her. He grabbed her arms and at the same time tripped her. She fell as we all leaped on top of her to restrain her. In spite of our efforts, she continued to resist, squirming under the weight of several people and trying to detach John's grip by head butting him. She refused to calm down and there was no way to reason with her. Someone screamed for cords and I tore off my sash. John held onto her hands while Stanislas tied them. I quickly grabbed the remaining cord and wrapped it several times around her flailing legs. I was able to tightly cinch the cord until her legs were frozen beneath the pressure. She sat sulking surrounded by bewildered faces.

We collapsed next to her. No one screamed with delight. No one hailed a victory. Instead, we first stared at her then at each other, with sadness; we were humiliated by what was a revolting display of a basic human instinct to survive. We couldn't stop ourselves!

In the midst of this insanity, Ruth started to talk in her low, calm voice. She tried to explain to her, once again, that she had to calm down and accept what had happened. "We don't know why you have been evicted from the center, but you can probably never go back." Ruth made it very clear that we all understood the shock she was under now that her visual receptor had been shut down. We had all dealt with the same fears; but she was going to have to learn how to adjust to normal vision and to trust us, or she was going to find herself all alone.

I started to laugh convulsively and then warm stream of tears flowed, provoked by a strange mixture of fear, rage and then shame. Everyone was looking at me until I finally said what was bothering me. "This situation resembles in too many ways an experiment in human behavior, and we are the guinea pigs!" I screamed out hoping that the bright ones could hear me. The group nodded in agreement. I went on to mention just how very sad it was to see how cruel the bright ones could be. I wanted those horrible creations to hear the anger in my voice as I continued to address the group; "They knew that she was very different from the rest of us. This would give them more insight into the irrational side of human emotions that they found so interesting and detestable. According to them, we were boringly predictable and members of an inferior species who reasoned with emotions and not logic."

I wiped away my tears and approached the others who had gathered around Diana. I noticed her deep, black penetrating eyes on me. She sneered and spit at me. She was not showing any signs of remorse. We stood around her watching her struggling to free herself.

"What are we going to do with her?" Peter asked. And, then went on to answer his own question by suggesting that we simply return her to the center. "They are watching us. They will know that we have given her back. It might be the best solution. If she stays with us, we are all in danger. She isn't stable and she is very violent."

Jonathan added speaking through his teeth, out of character, "And those b_____, they knew it all along. They planted her. . ."

Mathieu stood up, shaking his fists vehemently, and screaming, "What kind of ungrateful creature are you? Isabelle and I carried your wretched body to our small sanctuary, where you tried to kill us." He moved forward and kicked her in the arms and legs and she responded with an eerie laughter.

Benjamin and Stanislas, together, pulled Mathieu away from her, as Benjamin pleaded, "We have to stop this kind of behavior. We look as crazy as she is."

"Who cares what we look like," I heard Sarah break in. "Did you see what she did to me?" She was looking at Benjamin and Stanislas. "She could have killed me. Do you realize that she could have killed me?" she repeated. "Why should we care what happens to her. Put her back where she came from."

"Let's do it. We shall get rid of her." Ruth broke in. "Did you hear me you warped and vicious androids. You can have her, for your fun or your pleasure." She swallowed hard. "Keep this Bitch. We don't want her!" She screamed in a frantic and irrational way.

Angry and teary-eyed from fear, we all nodded in agreement. Stanislas, Benjamin and Jonathan picked her up and started the march back to the center, when an epiphany… Diana asked for forgiveness.

"I was afraid to be with you; but now I am even more afraid to go back." She sounded like she was in shock. Her words were void of emotion. "They may punish me because I didn't adapt. They may terminate me simply because they don't want me. They almost did before. . ." She rambled on a bit more before she started to cry and beg to stay on. Those slanted, deep, black, penetrating eyes that frightened me earlier were overflowing with tears. She stopped struggling to free herself and let her body relax under the constraining cords. Her face took on the softness, bringing forth her exquisite beauty; the same beauty that I so admired before she awakened.

Confusion. It was total confusion. Half of us wanted to try again; the other half warned that we could not trust her. And then, the moving force in our community stepped forward and made the final decision.

"I like her." John said. "He took her from her three porters and held her like a baby in his arms. "I like you, Diana. You are a fighter. After all this time, you have helped us to find our own fighting spirit. That we need. We all need to fight to overcome the injustices of our lives that the bright ones have imposed on us. Yes, Diana, you are different; but your violence and your intimidation and your fearlessness are important for us as well. We need you as much as you need us. The others thought that we would terminate you. That we would allow those negative emotions to take control of our actions; to prevent us from thinking and reasoning like our species is capable of doing. Yes, they wanted to see us as the inferior species. But, we showed them we are not so foolish and predictable as we have done what was necessary to reassure you and to calm you down; we proved that we are a superior and not inferior race." He stopped to address the rest of us. "Yes, some of what happened was a bit dramatic, but nothing to be ashamed of in view of the situation. Let me assure you that you are welcome to live with us in peace and harmony. You are welcome to help us recover our true identity and to control our destiny. I believe, Diana, that you may be the catalyst that we have been waiting for."

He untied her cords and she cradled herself in his arms as would a baby. She cuddled up to him and fell into a sound and calm sleep. We watched in surprise and satisfaction over the simple way in which John had solved everything in just a few minutes.

With each consecutive day, Diana affirmed her desire to become an integral member of our community. In the beginning, she observed and learned how we humans respected one another and lived comfortably in this small community. She spent time talking to us in private, getting to know who we were and why we were living on the outside. Her complicity, as John had foreseen, advantaged us because she knew her way around the Center. She had worked or cleaned in almost every part of the facility and, even though she did not understand the workings of certain equipment and machinery, she knew where they were located and how to access them. By the end of the first week, she was looking healthier. Her natural beauty was more visible. The calm had given her a sensual air and her black midnight eyes revealed intelligence rather than danger. She started to develop into a trusting and faithful member of the community.

She tried so hard to be liked that it was easy to forget how frightened we had been. She got on so well with Frederic and was quick to volunteer to help and to play with him. I eventually felt comfortable with her and trusted her with my baby. She was patient and kind. In spite of all that I had imagined, I realized that she was sincere and caring, and, that her initial reaction was one of fear, rather than confrontation. But most of all, I inherently knew that she would not allow anyone with bad intentions to come close to Frederic, not for a second!

In the first few days John brought her up-to-date on all our projects. That was probably a smart move since it gave her an immediate feeling of belonging that she, like the rest of us needed so badly. She adjusted slowly to the loss of her visual receptor and expressed genuine sadness at the disastrous conditions we lived in. She however wasn't interested in exploring and didn't want to accompany anyone to get the food. One day she confided in me; crouching next to me she admitted that her real enemies were those in the Center and one day she would show them how strong she could be. But, until then, she just wanted to learn what it was like to be human.

Chapter 24: Rivalry

D r. Gordon looked up from her desk as Dr. Crawford rushed into her office. He passed her an official envelope and sat down in the chair opposite her as he stared at her face.

She knew that he was not bringing her good news. Something must have gone wrong. She had been so busy putting together certain elements related to her research that she had not paid attention recently to the outside community. Before opening the envelope, under the surveillance of the piercing eyes of Dr. Crawford, she sought to anticipate the most inopportune series of events that could have prompted the Governor to contact her. No doubt, the letter concerned Diana, who, as Dr. Gordon predicted, caused major problems for the other humans. Dr. Gordon preferred to imagine that the members of the community were up in arms, ready to punish Diana, even execute her. That would be good news for her, as that was what she was hoping for. And, if that were the case, the Governor, not Crawford, would be sitting in front of her. No, she was wrong; how could she have been so wrong about the character of Diana and the group? She shook her head, contemplating this question, and looked down at the envelope.

She picked up the envelope and opened it. She pulled the letter slowly out of the folds and placed it flat on her desk. It was marked urgent and was from the Governor who wanted to see her tomorrow. In his message, he made it clear before signing off that he was not impressed with her analysis of human characteristics.

"Well, what happened?" she asked timidly.

"Not at all what you expected." Dr. Crawford replied with conviction. "They like her." His grave voice echoed, "I told you so, imbecile," he said as he stood up in front of her and waved his hand at her in disgust.

"It is not possible." She couldn't believe it. How could she be wrong about somebody as unstable as Diana? Had she missed something in that creature's character that could account for this? Of course, she suspected something, but something else; she was sure Diana was destined to do something seriously wrong.

"Well, you were wrong and it is about time that your competence was seriously questioned." He raised his grated android voice to show his dissatisfaction with her incompetence. "You have had too much support from the Governor and have manipulated the board members with your stories of needing to study in more detail the emotional structure of humans. How could you have ever imagined that giving them back their genetic identities would help us in our quest for knowledge? Don't you remember what it was like for us living under their domination in the past? Have you completely forgotten how cruel they were to us and even to themselves? Sometimes I think that a good part of your memory bank has been deleted or you align yourself with these human creatures in defiance of your own people." he ruthlessly drove the point home, trying to hit her android heart.

"What do you know, Dr. Crawford, of my experiences?" She hesitated as some of the critical moments in the past flashed before her, in a disorderly fashion. "What do you remember?"

"What you should always remember. We saved those ungrateful humans and we serve them and, in case you haven't noticed, we are still saving and serving them." He was consistently arrogant. "Sometimes you don't act like one of us. I'm going to recommend that you be examined closely. There must be something wrong with your circuitry."

"There is nothing wrong with me." Dr. Gordon protested. "We just don't see things the same way. That doesn't mean that I am less logical than you. Granted, we were all programmed a bit differently; but we have existed together for a long time without major conflicts. You always refuse categorically to consider other opinions. Let me remind you that it is helpful for us to be receptive to other ideas."

"Let me remind you that I am not human." He spoke frankly. "I am neither hurt nor offended nor irritated by opposition. But, I know that I was constructed by one of the best and therefore my opinion should hold more weight than anyone else's. This is simply logical."

"So, you would consider me your inferior?" She questioned with contempt.

"If you like." He raised his shoulders in a programmed gesture. "I might say it a bit differently but whatever words I choose, it comes out the same. We are the products of our creators and their intellectual levels varied."

"I don't like your conclusion and I don't like your arrogance, which, by the way, is also a human trait. Perhaps you should be examined closely, as you put it." Dr. Gordon wanted to be alone. "As far as I am concerned, this conversation is over. I shall see you at the Governor's meeting tomorrow."

Once the door closed behind Dr. Crawford, Dr. Gordon contacted the unit in charge of the surveillance of the humans for some details. They suggested that she come over and listen to the conversations and watch a few of the recent tapes.

What she saw did not please her at first. The Diana that she observed for many months had changed dramatically. She was noticeably calmer and even outgoing. Nonetheless, the more Dr. Gordon observed the tapes, the more certain she was that her initial position and impressions were the right ones. She classified Diana as a survivor. In that context, yes, she had changed because it was necessary, but the change was only superficial. This, for Dr. Gordon, was not a good sign for the small community, but an excellent discovery for her, as well as a rejuvenation of her initial findings. When she viewed Diana alone, she revealed her former instability through her body language, particularly facial expressions. Her psychological instability was too subtle for the members of the community to notice it, but it was evident. Diana was just playing a game. And, she was playing it very well, but she could erupt into a violent fury at any time.

She informed the Board of her conclusions in the morning and assured them that her plan would work perfectly in the near future. She and the other Board Members, including the Governor, shrugged off the warnings of Dr. Crawford. It was decided that Dr. Gordon would be given selected parts of the tapes at the end of each day. If ever she thought that something was not working out as planned, she would notify the Governor. Dr. Crawford was reprimanded and advised to stop trying to sabotage the project. He was told that if he had a better way of stimulating creativity in humans, he should present the project as an alternative to that of Dr. Gordon. Otherwise, he should keep his distance and concentrate on his other projects.

It was also decided that Pamela would be brought back to the Center within two months according to plan. Dr. Gordon had convinced everyone, except Dr. Crawford, that she would be ready to be examined more closely. It was further decided that all the members of the Center would meet her requests, even those that considered the Pamela study rather ridiculous. It was understood that to create an effective working relationship between Pamela and them, it was important that she feel protected and appreciated by the android authorities.

After Dr. Gordon evoked her complete satisfaction and gratitude to the other members, Dr. Crawford nodded and left.

Chapter 25: The Strategy

John was and will probably always be an enigma for me. He intrigued me. I never knew if trusting him was my best offence or my best defense, for maintaining a viable, working relationship with him. I came to respect him. He was brilliant like the entire group of scientists in this compound. But, in addition, he was clever. He impressed me as a formidable strategist, who could easily turn devious if he felt threatened. He gave suggestions, in the form of orders. And, most importantly, he read the Androids better than anyone else.

On many occasions, he said to me; "They, the Androids, are not vicious and don't even know how to be. They are stuck on logic and only one of them is reaching out for a new identity. That's Dr. Gordon. You must be careful with her because she is so fascinated with the psychological, as she says, the emotional side of humans. She gives the impression that she wants to cross some vast divide between Androids and humans. I could be wrong about her personal objective. But, watch how you act with her, Pamela. You must always resist putting all your trust and confidence in her. She could easily change her research project or decide that you are not the right subject for her study. Stay alert." He warned.

"As you will see clearer with time, the other androids are cautious and wary of our emotional makeup; even the few that appear curious about it. They recognize more than Gordon that they are unprepared for a different future." After which he laughed heartily. I understood that he was addressing a future in which the Androids would no longer be in control. I was not so certain and never joined him in his folly of laughter. I did, however, take his warning about Dr. Gordon very seriously.

He was also clever and intuitive with Diana. His attitude towards Diana was positive from the beginning. Diana was with John when I ran into them. He led both of us away from the viewing screen and away from all the sound tracks. I didn't understand why he was doing this, until he said, "now we are safe and I can speak to you heart to heart, Diana." He looked at her intensely before asking. "Do you know, Diana, that you have been diagnosed by Dr. Gordon as mentally unstable." he went straight to the point.

"Doesn't surprise me. Everyone here, except you, had the same opinion of me when I arrived. I have to admit, I never quite understood why," she replied.

"It is because of your body language more than anything else. Your body movements are aggressive. I would say that you resemble a predator--like a lion, for example." He stopped for a second to study her reaction to that.

She shook her head in disbelief, which he took as a signal to continue. "I don't know what human history is, but I know now what emotions are. We can want something someone else has, we can feel rejected, we can feel excluded, we can feel hurt, and so forth. Within our small group, we finally voice our feelings and get the reassurance we need to be happy. But imagine if we couldn't get that reassurance. You hit people; you hit us, do you remember?" She nodded. "You did that to protect yourself because you were frightened. The other members hit back to calm you down but also to defend themselves. That was an interesting episode to watch and fortunately it took place within the cameras."

He continued the same dialogue filled with the same explanations that he gave to all of us, "Are you both following me for the moment?" We both nodded and he continued. "Imagine if someone felt that their life was threatened. What would that person be capable of doing? And, imagine someone very aggressive who hated someone so much, for whatever reason, that he or she wanted that person to disappear. Now, I am guessing; but maybe some people destroyed other people. That would be very illogical for the androids. They could force someone to shut down their system, but they would never eliminate or as we would put it, kill one of their own. That would be the ultimate of cruelty which is the darkest and most dreaded of all human emotions."

He scared me with his stories, which made me worry that my life and that of Peter and Frederic and all the others was in imminent danger. I trembled over the idea that our small group could be attacked or killed, by treacherous humans seeking only bloodshed. "Enough of all of this, I am going to have nightmares. I feel a creeping sensation going up and down my spine," I exclaimed, looking at the both of them. John stopped his story of humans driven by ramped emotions to kill. Diana did not look upset; she did not even look uncomfortable, as she asked, "Are you trying to tell me, John, that they sent me here to terminate some or all of you?"

"You got it." He chuckled. "They watched your body language and saw you as a predator, just as we do, and imagined that you would be capable of taking a life. That would have created an enormous outpouring of emotions on our part. They could study our vicious and vengeful sides." He chuckled again and added. "Can you imagine how disappointed they must be?"

"I don't care about them. Why should I?" She asked inquisitorially.

John continued unabashedly. "Their ultimate disappointment pleases me. It is just that we don't want them to be disappointed before it is time for us to implement our plan of action. That is why you are both here with me today. I have mentioned this point to others and was waiting for the opportunity to talk to you both about it. We believe that the best strategy for us is to give them the impression that what they want will happen."

"Wait just a minute." She said motioning him to stop. "I want to go back to your earlier remark. I should be insulted; at the least, unhappy that I was diagnosed as a raving lunatic, shouldn't I?" John and I said nothing, just stared at her hoping that she would not do anything rash. She surprised us by asking. "Are you sure that I am not?"

"Perfectly certain. You are as stable as any of us." He answered calmly.

"What am I doing that gives the impression that I am a predator?" she insisted.

"Unfortunately, I don't have your genetic profile so you can always say that my conclusion is inexact. Nonetheless, I assure you that you are normal, whatever is normal for humans. But you do have a tendency to stalk others. What I mean is, you follow someone, hiding behind stones and walls so that you won't be seen, as if you were hunting prey. You jump out from behind a barrier when your subject is off guard. And, you have the tendency to show your teeth when you aren't happy and to strain your eyes in such a way that they appear to have an eerie, red threatening-appearance like a stalking jaguar. We have gotten use to this and have accepted you as you are. But, quite frankly, that kind of behavior does seem to be excessive." He said this as if he were testing her, tempting her to show the contrary.

"Oh, that." She replied and started laughing. "That is because you don't know who and what I am?" She got our attention and then she went on to say something unexpected. "I never much liked to be with other people which is probably why I liked cleaning up after everyone had left. Whenever there were other people, I tried to hide. I didn't like having conversations." She was being honest. "But, since I have been out here with this community, with my own people, I feel much better and less like a caged animal."

"It is normal." He rubbed his mouth and continued." I think that there was always a problem with your visual receptor. It didn't function instantaneously and that a couple of seconds of wasted time must have frightened or disoriented you. Now, I want you to listen very closely. I don't want you to stop stalking and hiding. I want you to make strange faces--show your teeth as much as possible and pop your eyes out like you're mad, whenever you are alone and in camera range."

She broke into his conversation with laughter. "As I said before, you don't know who and what I am?"

"You just told us. You are a housekeeper." John and I screamed in frustration.

"That is my cover—housekeeping is my cover." She smiled. "I am a marine biologist and engineer in the field of maritime transport." We both stared in disbelief as she went on to say that that was what she did 60 or 70% of the time.

John and I stared speechlessly. "Ok," she went on. "I am trained in martial arts. Do you know what that is?"

I didn't know, but John said that he had a very vague idea of it. "Ok, let me explain. I am trained for physical combat. My job is to physically defend the androids."

"What? It is not possible. You work for them?" I over reacted to her revelation.

"Stop, control yourself, Pamela." Diana interjected. She knew very well that I was horrified with the news. "If I had wanted to kill all of you I would have done that on my arrival." She started to laugh again. "I was so touched by your commitment to each other. When I saw you group together to take me down, I decided to let you do just that. I could have gotten out of your ropes in a couple seconds and taken care of all of you. But, I didn't want to. I wanted to find out more about you."

"For the androids?" John's voice was full of disgust and dismay.

"No." She laughed again, something that was getting on my nerves. "I did it for me. I wanted to understand you. In fact, I was very disappointed when you made the decision to return me to the center, the reason why I pretended to cry and ask for help." She hesitated and then asked; "Do you want my story?" John nodded affirmatively; I hesitated looking around sheepishly.

"We are a very small group of humans that have been trained in the martial arts. As I mentioned, the androids use us for protection. In fact we are not only their protectors; but their spies."

I started to stand up and John pushed me back down. "Let her finish," he insisted his eyes flashing.

"When they get suspicious about one of the humans, one of us –I think that we are 5---gets called in to follow the suspect and report. Basically, what they are worried about is whether or not the suspect has by-passed the visual receptor, as you put it. The androids never described the problem like that. What they told me, and the others, was that a given person was not doing their job properly and was not interacting with their colleagues in a normal way. What we were able to confirm most of the time was that the colleagues were rejecting the subject in question, which was sufficient for them to ask that the subject be brought to the termination center."

"I know that you are both wondering if I stalked one of you." She had a self-satisfied smile on her face, before she said, "No. But, Pamela, I did stalk your Peter. He was a very interesting assignment for me. I took my time with him. He fascinated me with all his discoveries that meant very little to me. He was spying on them, while I was spying on him." She laughed about it; perhaps it seemed even more ridiculous now that she had her emotional configuration intact. "At the same time that I was ready to confirm that his colleagues did not identify him without his repeating his code number, Peter was officially taken off the list of suspected humans. I was asked to stop following him, so I let the assignment drop." Hearing that my mouth dropped wide open, I was speechless. I started to shudder and tremble from head to foot in disbelief.

When I calmed down, John spoke up. "I don't understand why the androids need you to use physical force, are we that much of a threat?" John asked with curiosity.

"Not all the subjects passively follow the android guards to the termination center. Sometimes they are very violent and fight back and then one of us must use physical force to subdue them." She noticed our eyes widening and the grimaces on our faces. She went on to explain that the androids were excellent at target practice. In fact, they were trained to stun or kill a human with a laser weapon, without blinking an eye. Her dark head turned in both directions, noticing our eyes were glued to her. She smiled ironically and continued. "But they are inept at hand-to-hand combat and can't take down a human. Also, weapons are not always appropriate as too many people are in the hallways; that's why we are called in."

We sat silently for a good moment. I wondered if she just dreamed up this story to impress, scare us or disgust us. But, her story, disconcerting, seemed credible. To think that the day she didn't want to be around us, she could kill all of us. Nonetheless, I could not shake off the thought that even as it sounded incredible, it was believable. I certainly didn't want to be the first one to test her skills.

She took a deep breath looking straight ahead, as if she knew she had shocked us but was happy to have our undivided attention, and went on, "I know that what I have said frightens you." We nodded vigorously. "I am very quick and effective in physical combat. I trained with the best." She looked at me and then said, "I even trained with Stuart in my early years." John's mouth dropped open. He later explained to me that Stuart was one of our contacts on the inside. "And another thing, we never worked together, we didn't need to. We are considered the ninjas, the invisible warriors, of the center. You could say we are. . .killing machines."

"How did you bypass your visual receptor?" I asked with trepidation.

"I was assigned to Jonathan. Remember, he is the one who told you that I worked for the housekeeping department." She laughed. "Just as an aside, only the androids do the housekeeping, because it is considered to be one of the most vital and secret of all the jobs in the center. That is because cleaning up is done at the end of the day when the housekeeping staff verifies the work that each person has performed to ascertain that no one, I mean no one, is conducting independent work."

She was studying us, watching our body language. I looked at John who was sitting like me with his arms folded and fists clenched. She was very relaxed with her arms resting comfortably on her knees. Her eyes glistened as she captured our defensive position. She smiled, a broad open smile, and continued. "I found Jonathan quite good looking and very kind. I was surprised he was so nice to me. You are programmed to believe that housekeepers are non-intellectuals that should be avoided, which is why just mentioning housekeeping department gets even the late night researcher out of the area. Jonathan seemed so blasé about that. I was flattered when he paid attention to me and made me feel. . ." she hesitated, "he cared." She looked down with tight lips like she was trying to control a surging emotion, or had made a mistake. Both John and I were quick to realize. She bit down on her lower lip, and then confessed that she was, as John recognized, living in a semi-programmed state. She did not see physical appearances, but she had a primitive emotional structure in place.

She passed that off as natural, because of her combat role that required strong surges of adrenaline. Up until Jonathan, she felt no regret for taking a life, in the exercise of her duty. But, Jonathan's kindness triggered other feelings.

"That is why," she went on to say, "I had so much difficulty spying on him. When I told Crawford that Jonathan was no longer acting properly, I felt an enormous guilty wave of energy pass through my body. I staggered out of Crawford's office and meandered through the corridors. My head was aching and I felt dizzy. One of the android guards approached me to help me, I guess, and I lashed out at him. I practically tore him apart with the beating that I gave him; but, with each stroke I delivered, I started to see who, what he was more clearly. . .a machine. I don't think that I passed through their luminous shield, instead I saw him because the guard was damaged, shutting off his luminous rays. I saw what he was—a humanoid machine. How horrible, I was protecting and spying for, cold metallic machines. I wanted to vomit right there on the floor."

"They sedated me over and over again but didn't want to terminate me because I was too useful for them. That is probably why, after months of sedating me and trying to convince me that what I thought I saw were just illusions, they sent me out here." She started to laugh all over again. "Can you imagine how disappointed they are?" Our nervous laughter joined hers.

"But, why did you insult Jonathan?" I probed in spite of the horror of the life she was revealing to us.

"I am probably still not completely normal, Pamela. When I see enemies, I am trained to spy and kill them. I like physical combat. I guess that I wanted to provoke him; after all he was responsible for my bypassing my programming, as you put it. And, let's be honest," above her crooked but slightly satirical smile, her black eyebrows raised, "his programmed appearance is a lot more appealing than his real life look!"

"Sounds rational, I guess." John broke in. "Now, let's get down to the real reason for this discussion. I don't want them to see any improvements in your personality."

"I don't understand. You just described me as an eerie creature that your group was getting used to, but did not feel totally comfortable with. Why don't you want me to act like you?" The tone of Diana's voice dropped with each word, showing her disappointment.

"I do want you to react like us, "John said, in a slow, gentle way. "You must, actually act like us to justify or explain your being accepted as an integral member of our community. You absolutely need to take on a more normal behavior. But within another week or so, you will be at ease, less defensive around us, and your body language will show it. The androids will see that you changed. They will know that you are no longer a threat for us. For that reason, you must continue to act irrationally for them. To make things clear, whenever you are within camera range, regardless of whether you are alone or with others, act irrationally, out of control and dangerous, exactly like you were when you were attacking us. Do you understand?"

"Ok. No Problem. I see what you are saying. If I want to stay here and help with the revolt, I must give them the impression that I am unstable, unpredictably violent and could injure someone without reason or provocation." That brought a vicious grin to her face.

"Exactly!" He screamed with enthusiasm. "Do you think that you can do it?"

"No problem. If acting like a lunatic is what they want from me; well, then, that is what they will get." She seemed to like the assignment.

Before the three of us split up, John suggested that he inform the other members of the group of our discussion, in his own way. Both Diana and I understood that he would probably not reveal the entire conversation, just the essential facts regarding her past, and her commitment to play the game for the androids.

I was convinced with what John had recommended and supported this strategy a hundred percent. On a couple of occasions I had the opportunity to observe Diana's acting skills; they were splendidly intimidating. Her happy, laughing face turned quickly into a sadistic scowl, while her relaxed walk took on the air of a ravenous animal pursuing its prey. It appeared simple and easy for her to switch roles in a split second. In spite of our laughter when we caught a glimpse of her, she was more than acting; stalking was in her blood.

Within a few days after this conversation, Diana came with a very interesting offer. She suggested that she train certain of us in self-defense and the martial arts. She felt that John, Sarah and Ruth were too old to do the required movements. She also said that Stanislas and Benjamin, although physically capable, were too nice and gentle to enter into combat. They were not psychologically strong enough for that. So they were out of the program.

After eliminating our five companions, Diana took the rest of us aside every morning and gave us exercise programs. We started with jogging and stretching exercises to build up our muscles and limber our bodies. It took us awhile to get back into good enough shape to start the combat practice. I probably needed the exercise program even more than the others, because I had not done anything special to get my body in shape after my pregnancy. It was tough physically and psychologically for all of us.

Mathilda, who was in better shape overall than either Isabel or myself, dropped out. She said that she just couldn't deal with violence. As I watched her prepare to leave our group, I studied her. Mathilda was incredibly good looking and carried herself in an alluring and seductive way. She walked gracefully in lingering strides to be certain that everyone captured a glimpse of her elegant, well-built body, in passing. She even accentuated her full firm breasts and small waist by pulling the sash of her long white robe very tightly along her waistline. Her oval face with its deep, blue eyes, aquiline nose and bow-shaped lips heightened her sex appeal. Her disheveled, long, thin, blond hair falls to the middle of her back. As I watched her leave the group, I understood why I was worried months ago when she took an evening stroll with Peter. I have been told that I am beautiful, but I didn't know how to flaunt my beauty like she did.

Diana was a good coach. She used Jonathan as her partner to demonstrate different combat techniques. It was amusing to see how easily she flipped the heavy body of Jonathan on the floor. She enjoyed his early futile efforts to resist her rapid, effective techniques. But, Jonathan liked the challenge and gradually improved his moves. Mathieu and Peter caught on fast and trained together. Isabel and I were naturally competitive, and I might add, had the necessary grit to muster up the energy and barred- teeth to attack someone.

We all followed the example of Diana and pulled our white robes up to the middle of our thighs to give us more freedom of movement. My leg movements were good because I had trained in kickboxing on vacations back at the center. Knowing the technique, though, was not enough. I lacked rapidity and skill in self-defense. It was different when there was a live person, and not a punching bag, in front of you. Both Isabelle and I worked hard on mixed martial arts where we had to resort to punching, kicking, lifting and throwing an adversary.

It was easier for me, in the beginning, to throw Isabelle, as I was taller than her. Nonetheless, she had strong muscular arms and legs and moved rapidly, which kept the pressure on me. We were frequently in face-to-face combat, which gave me the opportunity to meticulously examine her facial features. She was nervous around me and that came forth in her flickering eyes, frowning eyebrows, and shaky, unnatural smile, which I found disconcerting and unattractive. I didn't like her life-less shaggy, shoulder length, light brown hair, and her small breasts and wide hips; undermining femininity. I could not understand why Mathieu was so attached to this very unattractive woman.

With time, Isabelle got more relaxed around me. I then discovered that her deep emerald green eyes, slightly turned up nose, and thin lips gave her face a sensual look. I liked the special glowing effect of her light, brown freckles on her cheeks. Training together helped us to form a genuine friendship and as time went on I came to appreciate Isabelle and understand her relationship with Mathieu.

After two months of intensive training, Diana told us that we had made progress. "Well," She started out with a stern look on her face, "I am happy to say that the five of you form a better than average combat unit." We started to laugh. "I am serious," she said. "If we were ready today to break into the Center, I do believe that we would put up an excellent fight!" She said with fervor. That was enough for us to cheer, flaunting the image she gave us of a real combat unit.

We had reason to be happy. In addition to a combat unit in place, the tunneling in the inner cavern progressed, making it easier to believe that someday we might break-into the Center. Diana continued her lunatic behavior in front of the cameras; a splendid and talented actress who was putting the androids off guard. Unfortunately, I would not be able to admire her savage pantomimes for much longer, as my time on the outside was nearing its end.

I remember well my last evening with the group. Peter and I had gone off to get the food, leaving Frederic with Diana and Jonathan. They got along very well now. I was happy to hear Diana tell Jonathan that he was right when he pointed out that the outside shell of someone was less important than what was in the inside. I could see that he was bewitched, even obsessed, by Diana; even before he confided in me.

"Pamela, I believe that I am falling in love with Diana" he said shamefully. "I don't think that she feels the same about me." He said sadly.

"What makes you think that you are in love" I asked, not certain how else to respond.

"It can't be anything else." He replied pensively. "I could sit forever looking into her dark, black hypnotic eyes which have a kind of orgasmic effect on me!" He laughed in a giddy way, as if embarrassed by his sexual reference. "I feel alive when she is close to me." He turned his head away from me, before saying, "I am completely inexperienced in love...expressing love by words, or otherwise. But, I have such a strong and burning desire, almost compulsive desire, to hold her in my arms. I want and need to know her profoundly, if you understand what I mean."

"Well, my dear Jonathan, there is nothing else to say but, try! If you feel that strongly towards her, then you must tell her, show her and see what that leads to." I said smiling. "I believe that it will lead you to great happiness."

Nothing he said surprised me. His strong emotional attachment to Diana, coupled with the combat training, had given him a new appearance, a pleasant allure. I was not the only one to have noticed it and expressed an unabated joy over the major physical changes in Jonathan over the last few months. He was becoming quite handsome, looking more and more like the image I had of him through the visual receptor. His olive-colored skin, brown eyes, dark eyebrows, and black curly hair were always part of him, but in a disorganized way on a nonsymmetrical, mutant face, which was now dramatically different. His large forehead, distorted nose and bulging chin were remodeled, in a harmonious way. His features were smoother; with a less imposing forehead, a long roman nose, wide lips, high cheeks and a prominent chin. Even his hunched back was disappearing and being replaced by a stiff and muscular torso. Could love do this? How far would his physical changes go? What would happen to him if the magic of his relationship with Diana were to end?

Then it came. That night when we opened the food bundle, there was a letter for me from Dr. Gordon. I was ordered to return to the Center in the morning. Dr. Gordon would be there to let me in. I felt my heart drop and tears swell up in my eyes. My whole body was reacting or over reacting. I hadn't felt so frightened and confused since the day of intense epiphany, my escape, more than two years ago. I was wailing and protesting in a cold sweat.

"I don't want to go back," I said adamantly as I stood up and paced up and down the dining room.

John grabbed me and pulled me away from the video equipment to talk. The others followed.

"Please, Pamela, don't be frightened." I heard Peter's sweet, reassuring voice soothing me as his arms moved slowly around me in a protective way.

A series of questions throttled me: "How was I going to live without him? How would I fall asleep without his arms around me? How would I live without all the intimacy and pleasure that he gave to me? And most importantly, how could I ever leave my son?"

"I know that we are asking you to do something that none of us would like to do. I'm not even sure any of us could do it. But you can, my love." He was looking in my eyes as he spoke. "In spite of the monotony of our existence-ameliorated a bit with training and digging- we all prefer to be here rather than in the uncertainty of the Center. I'm speaking for all of us, and we understand your apprehensions about going back into that ambiguous and frightening environment. But, Pamela," He was pleading. "We need you to help us all. You represent hope for us; the hope that we shall all live better lives." He sighed and said in a voice quivering with emotion. "Oh, how I am going to miss you."

His words calmed me. "His emotion is untainted, undeniably real. He believes in me, but I could not shake the feeling of despair. "How can I leave?"

He felt my anxiety. "But, we-you and me and Frederic- shall be back together again very soon." He declared in a strong, persuasive voice as he pulled me even tighter up against him, reassuring me of his unconditional belief in...us!

My eyes filled with tears and my upper lip trembled with emotion, as I revealed my hidden fears to my friends and family. "I am afraid." I said in a loud, shaky voice. "I am afraid to confront the Center now that I can see what is happening. I am also afraid to disappoint all of you." Tears were spilling over my face as I stopped to think about day-to-day conversations with Dr. Gordon. "And, most of all. . .I'm, I'm worried about falling under the spell of Dr. Gordon!"

Everyone, even me, started laughing when Mathieu quickly replied. "Come on Pamela, about the last thing that you have to worry about is falling under the spell of one of those androids, mere machines."

On a more serious note, John reminded me of the confidence he had in me. "I know that you will be strong and that you will manipulate that Dr. Gordon into sticking to the former arrangement."

"Dr. Gordon had promised me access to any and all of the documents in the library," I thought pensively, feeling an inner confidence surging. I will remember my objectives. I will show curiosity by asking about the construction of the center, how it functions and where the electricity and water come from. I focused on the play -acting of Diana. I can be like her, I can pretend to be naive and get as much information as I can. If I could just be as convincing as she is…"

Over the flustered voices of the others, I heard John saying, "Trust me, Pamela. My vital contacts will be in touch with you and they will protect you." That gave me the glimmer of hope that I needed. I would not be alone.

It was well into the early morning hours when Peter and I, with Frederic asleep in my arms, dozed off. I received a lot more advice than I could cope with and a lot more encouragement than I wanted. I wanted a bit of time with my little family and there was not very much of it left. I looked down at my beautiful six-month old son nestled comfortably in my arms. Everyone said that he was a perfect mixture of the two of us. No matter, he was so gentle, loving and happy. Leaving him would be the greatest challenge and nothing seemed important enough to abandon him and yet...I unbelievably was going to do just that.

I watched my son sleep on for a few more minutes and then laid him gently in his little bed. I joined Peter who was sitting and watching me.

"I know that I was not invited, but I shall go with you tomorrow morning." He said.

"No, Peter. It is not a good idea." I protested. "Dr. Gordon will not like it very much; I am certain of that."

"I don't care what she likes, Pamela. I am going with you. What can she do about it? She will be privy to our last few minutes together for several months and might find it to be scientifically or psychologically revealing."

"Hmm, now that you put it that way, alright, but I want to bring Frederic along so that she can see with her own eyes that humans can love and be very attached to one another." I moved over close to him and felt his mouth reach mine. I stopped thinking and started feeling. I wanted to make him a part of me to soften the anticipated brutal separation. I wanted to bury somewhere deep in my mind all those sensations so intense and unique to us--the way he touches me, caresses me and enters me. I wanted to remember him, his reactions and his pleasure. We never went to sleep. I knew that expressing that love for each other over and over again in different ways, in different positions and with more and more intensity would make me desire him more and even miss him more. But, I needed him to leave his imprint on every part of my body; on the outside and on the inside so that when I would close my eyes and think about him that I would relive each minute of this evening. I would always be reminded of us. Peter and me alone in our universe seeking and achieving the ultimate physical pleasures of love. In retrospect, I do believe that this moment was the most incredibly fulfilling of all those to come.

The morning of the next day was upon us too soon. My sadness outweighed the enthusiasm that each of the other members so strongly felt but so vehemently hid behind a wall of silence. With Frederic in my arms and Peter at my side, I walked away from a place of security and love on into a place of turmoil and uncertainty.

Chapter 26: Enlightenment

She is there in all her brightness was my first impression. She left me a few quick minutes to say Good-bye. The fear of being trapped forever in the Center, or even worse, being terminated because I did not turn out to be the right subject to study and, in any event, never seeing the outside again weighed so heavily upon me that my normal steadfast walk turned into a listless wobble. Each step I took reminded me of a distant past, in which I was only half alive. It seemed an eternity before I stood in front of Dr. Gordon. She took my hand and guided me through the hidden entrance. We stepped into a large room that I recognized instantly as the concert hall.

"I have a surprise for you, Pamela. Your piano is waiting for you."

How did Dr. Gordon know that the only one possible thing that could make my return bearable was to have the opportunity, after such a long time, to play the piano? I looked at that burning light and smiled.

I felt so comfortable on the piano seat with my hands perched above the keys. I let them drop randomly, delighted with the sound. I tried a few bars of different pieces I had played, like Mozart's Piano Sonata, No. 12 in F major and Bach's Piano Concerto No.1 in D minor, just to loosen up. I felt I was almost drooling over the keys. Then I attacked my warm up exercises and after a good hour of testing and retesting my skill, I started to play the works of my favorite composer, Chopin. I started with Nocturne, op.9 no.2, and went on to play Nocturne, op.27, no.2, Op. 57, D Flat, Berceuse, and others. I had never played so well. I could feel the emotion of the composer, his sadness, his happiness and his carefree attitude. I understood love and the emotions that go with his compositions. It was like I was living my music for the first time in my life. Dr. Gordon sat listening, as I played for hours. If the conductor and other members of the orchestra had not arrived, I would have continued all day.

I heard the conductor make a comment on how badly I played as I walked past him. It made me laugh. A long time ago, I broke out of their mundane existence when I first tried to play music with compassion and not like a perfunctory robot. Today, I was doing that, playing music with compassion, so his remark was received as a veritable compliment. I felt sorry for him and the musicians.

Dr. Gordon proposed lunch and, to my pleasure, assured me that I was receiving uncontaminated food. In other words, there were no sexual inhibitors in my meal, not that that made a great deal of difference to me now that Peter was no longer there. It would even have made life in the center easier, I mused. I was grateful, though, for her gesture which indicated that my status had changed and Dr. Gordon wanted me to know that.

"We have so much to talk about, Pamela."

That horrible, grating hollow sound of Dr. Gordon's voice, irritated me; it even made it difficult for me to concentrate, which was imperative at this moment. Eventually, I replied, indifferent to what kind of effect my answer might have on her. "Yes, of course, we do have a lot to discuss, like, for example, why you let me escape and live outside the center? But," I continued, "I think that you should drop your guard if you want me to feel comfortable. I see you as a blinding light and I find it difficult to communicate with someone I can't see now that I have crossed over into another world. And, if you could temper your voice I would be grateful." I added.

"Here I am." She proclaimed in a very seductive, feminine voice. She turned off her blinding shield and I perceived an upright body standing in front of me. She didn't look like a machine. If I hadn't been told the contrary, I would have thought that she was human. She was definitely female from her physical appearance. She had a well-shaped face and excellent features. Her eyes, nose, mouth and ears were perfect from human standards. She had no hair, although it did not distract from her overall perfection.

"So what do you think?" She asked.

"You are a woman and you don't hide that?" I went straight to the point.

"Oh. Interesting. Well, you see, we do not all look the same. I know that John told you that we are androids. Some of us have slightly different outside appearances. There are those robotic-androids who have no sexual identity. Some of us have more intellectual capacity than others." She stopped to make her next statement more dramatic. "Nonetheless, regardless of where we are on the android hierarchy, we are superior intellectually to humans."

I bit down on my lips to prevent myself from jumping on her final pretentious remark that she certainly hoped would get a reaction. Instead, I stated calm. "You didn't answer my question." I persisted and repeated it. "Why did you let me escape and live with the outside community?"

She acted as if she hadn't heard me and continued with her discourse. "I have always considered myself to be very feminine because my creator was a woman. I spent all my time with her and adapted myself to her habits and ways of doing things. All of us have taken on the sex of our creators. Did I answer that question for you?"

"No." I said firmly, "You did not answer my question." She didn't answer. That gave me some time to think about what to say next. I was glad that she had taken on a form and ameliorated her voice. I knew that I would not have all my demands met so easily. Yet, as I wrongfully thought that I was in control, I pushed forward. "Am I to assume that in refusing to answer my question that you agree that you let me escape and live with the outside community?" She stared at me with her expressionless face. Her silence made me nervous, but I did not want her to know that so I continued to take the initiative. "Now I have many more questions." I knew that I was a bit aggressive, but I thought that I should take the initiative. I thought that if I could control the situation with my questions and my gestures that she would eventually bow to my dominance, and I would make her the subject of my study. I was totally wrong.

With her response, she quickly put me back in my place, "Interesting. Your behavior is very interesting indeed." She smacked her lips to convey her satisfaction. "Well, Pamela, I hope that you will find answers to all your questions in time. For now, we must talk about what I need to know." I understood that what she wants comes first and, even though I expected that, I was disappointed. My play for dominance had failed. Better for me to be naïve and innocent, I mused for a brief instance before focusing on her instructions. "We shall have to meet a few hours each day to discuss the evolution of your personality. Even though you were not aware of it, we did monitor your progress. It was interesting to see how fast your emotions developed. Nonetheless, my research team and I need to know to what extent these emotions have changed you. If you think differently, for example."

"Ok, I shall respect my part of the agreement by answering your questions the best that I can." I was not that worried about how the sessions might go, simply because I had absolutely no idea what she expected from me. "But, I would very much like to use the library, in exchange for my cooperation, if that is possible. "I added the last point to show respect. "Remember you promised me that I would be able to have access to all the information, just like Ferdinand."

"Yes I remember. We androids do not have problems with memory." That remark was not strange but what she said next was particularly alarming. "The use of the Library is very restricted and I do need to get approval from the Board. I might feel more interested in helping you if you first promised to help me to experience certain sensations and develop emotions."

I didn't know what to say. How could I promise to do something that I wasn't certain I could be done? There was an enormous divide between her world and mine. I found her request to be. . . alarming! But, in the back of my mind, I could hear John telling me that she was our only hope and that I should do everything in my power to keep her interested in me and in her study of humans in order to acquire maximum information. So, I promised to do everything in my power to help her, even though I could not promise the results. And in turn, she promised to get me into the Library; all of this being a restatement of what we had formerly agreed to.

She had arranged for me to use my former cubicle. I suppose that was intentional and somehow related to the attention she was paying to my new psychological profile. In effect, the ride back and the room itself triggered strong emotions of happiness, sadness and also ...resentment, because she knew that the last time I stepped into my cubicle was when I was in the early, dramatic stage of my deprogramming. The memory of that moment, discovering Jonathan, was very strongly implanted in my mind. I found it vicious on her part to send me back on my own to that cubicle, hoping that I would experience a strong emotional reaction that she could register in her report. "Naïve, innocent, susceptible, as I am, I am going to disappoint you, Dr. Gordon," I said in a low voice.

I retraced my former life in my mind, as I calmly and assuredly entered into the cubicle. That imaginary world that Jonathan and I had known for so many years was euphoric but insulated from reality whatever that reality was. And, apart from the euphoria of the past, there was very little to remember. The days were routine; those days seem light years away from… today filled with nuances and complications. My consolation was to derive personal satisfaction from today's obstacles and to be happy that I was one of the lucky ones who bypassed the programming.

Dr. Gordon warned me the first day that the sleeping pillow, the pillow connected with our consciousness, inducing sleep the moment that our head came in contact with it, would not work for me anymore, because I was no longer under the programming. I would have preferred the contrary as I struggled every night to fall asleep. I would lay awake thinking about the other members of the community and the hopes they had put in me to help them. I was also worried that I hadn't made much progress since my return to the battlefield; which was one week or two weeks ago? Even though I wandered about the center entering into new quarters, I had not made any genuine discoveries. And while I thought of Frederic often during the days, I thought of and definitely missed Peter at night.

The days went by fast, greatly accelerated by playing music and my frequent visits to the orchestra pit. My visits to the Library were however so short in the beginning that I barely had chance to open a document before shown the door to leave. I found that very frustrating and complained to Dr. Gordon about it regularly. As such, progress was greatly impeded. I knew no more now about the history of my kind than the day of my return to this center. I was desperate to start moving forward but it seemed I was only treading water.

I was also discouraged on other levels. Even though I had the impression that I was free and could wander off into other areas of the center, I never had the opportunity to go too far before Dr. Gordon would call me on the pocket phone she gave me, asking me to meet her at her office for a quick up-date. She inevitably contacted me the very moment when I was about to discover a new wing of the center.

Moreover, my visits with her were very brief. Her interest exclusively revolved around, among others, strong emotions like jealousy, hatred, vengeance, resentment and rejection. I was ill at ease with these discussions. She accused me of holding back, refusing to cooperate according to the deal we had which justified, she said, withholding her part of the bargain. I realized that I would have to try harder, but found it difficult to focus on a detailed description of my feelings.

I discerned that certain sensations were sometimes intense, sometimes short-lived and other emotions I wasn't even aware of. I tried to fill in the gaps in my knowledge by looking them up in the library, but found nothing. Finally, I decided to invent theories on how I felt in a given situation, notably experiences of emotions that I'd never felt before, like vengeance. It was urgent that I proceed with my research as the days were slipping by like water, without results.

I was also ill at ease with my surroundings. From time to time I felt a bizarre suffocating feeling, especially when I aimlessly walked the vacant halls by myself. On many occasions, I didn't know quite what I was searching for. I became totally alienated from my objectives and, to myself, I became a strange woman in a strange land, devoid of feelings. Sometimes I was convinced I had become a walking dead woman; other times I feared I was slipping into darkness, into the slowly turning, churning lonely whirlpool . . .of insanity.

Finally, I woke up one morning inspired. I realized I'd been going about my objective in the wrong way. I decided to take a new track, that of satisfying her interests. I needed to make her believe I was cooperating. As such, the next time we met I started with jealousy, something I had experienced. "You want to know about Jealousy, Dr. Gordon?" I took the lead in that session.

"No, not today." I had the feeling that she was purposely thwarting my efforts. "I would rather have your impressions on the people you have met at the center."

That was ridiculous. I hadn't spoken to anyone. "I don't know what to say," I began. "I haven't spoken to anyone."

"Exactly. I want to know why."

"They don't interest me." She glared at me and I knew that she wanted more. The problem was that other humans did not realize that I was there because they could not see me. Peter had warned me about that, but I did not want to disclose that to Dr. Gordon. "Ok, you want the truth, don't you? Well, quite frankly they aren't acting human. Their conversations are uninteresting. We have nothing in common."

"Even the musicians don't interest you." She queried.

"I know all of this sounds strange to you, but no, they don't interest me." I continued. "Now I remember that we were given a subject to discuss each day. There wasn't very much to say about it. We studied, more or less, the rhythm and the timing, all superficial points. We never discussed, what is now the most essential for me, the feelings that are embodied in each musical composition. For me, they play very well on a technical level, but the music lacks vitality. Quite frankly, Dr. Gordon, how can I tell them that?"

"Yes, of course, we don't want you to look for recruits." I thought that finding recruits is exactly what I should be doing and I smiled ironically to Dr. Gordon who put me back on track.

"Well, perhaps you are right. I should give them a chance." I lied without the slightest hesitation.

"And physically, do you find any of them repulsive?" I suppose that that was a question she wanted to ask for a long time.

I explained to her that I had gone far beyond the physical side of my species. I understood for whatever reason, which was still not clear to me, that some of us had major deformities. I felt sad for those who had those deformities, but, in the context of the center, the programming obviously worked to their advantage.

"And, Pamela, how do you feel about me?" She seemed quite at ease to ask that question. She waited, her eyes cloaked my every movement waiting for the response to this …added question.

"I am grateful that you protected me by making me the subject of your study of humans. Without your intervention, I probably would have been terminated," I replied without emotion. It was a cold response, which she should have appreciated and understood; but her drooping eyes suggested she expected something different.

"Gratitude. That is all that you feel for me?"

"Yes, but that's a lot. I guess that you don't understand that."

"You mean more than that to me." Her nuanced message made my heart flutter, reminding me that I should find a way to play along and that she had power of life and death over me.

"Dr. Gordon. Please, you mean as much to me as you can, but you're a machine? Right?" I tried to make it up but felt I was descending into a quagmire that I may not be able to pull myself out of.

She didn't see our relationship that way. And, as she went on to tell me, she felt that she had other things in her programming that made her different from all the others. She spoke about her creator, a genius in her time, who dedicated herself to producing a few androids that could have human reactions and feelings. The problem was that she didn't survive long enough to start up the programming that would convert them from machines into humans.

"From the very first moment that I saw you, Pamela, I started to sense changes inside of me. My programming is responding differently. I do believe that I love you."

I stood up and started to back out the room. She jumped from behind her desk and grabbed me. I managed to unravel her arms and push her away and with my voice shaking, trembling I managed to cry out, "Dr. Gordon, I find what you are saying revolting," just as emotions engulfed me and I started to choke and the words stopped. After frantically gulping, I screamed, "Let go of me and leave me alone. Please don't ever talk to me about this again!" But her bloated eyes told me she realized the danger to her and to me if anyone witnessed this. It would compromise everything. . .

I fled the office and ran down the hall, pushing people out of my way. I heard her, coming up behind me saying in a sweet voice, "Please, don't worry. I shall never mention this again." My only thought was to get away from her, to avoid her, as I turned in all different directions. My phone started ringing and I threw it in one of the open doorways. I would never be given another. I needed to leave the Center, Now, and I never wanted to see Dr. Gordon again. Suddenly I felt an arm around my waist pull me behind a barrier. My first thought was I'm gone, a ninja warrior automaton had me in her grips.

Then a calm, masculine voice surged out of nowhere. "Don't be frightened." I quickly glanced at the source; in my hysteria I saw a head attached to the arm that held me. I opened my mouth wide to let out a piercing scream. But before I could emit a sound, his hands slid quickly over my mouth.

Then he said firmly, "Don't scream, you are safe with me. We shall wait it out here and discuss the strategy." I collapsed in his arms.

He was sitting looking at me when I regained consciousness. He had a wonderful smile and reminded me of Peter. I wondered if he had the same parentage. Nonetheless, he was much taller than Peter and with his muscular body looked like a statue of Adonis. His heavy eyebrows framed his dark brown eyes and hovered delicately over his long, prominent nose. His thin lips opened in a broad, friendly smile that accentuated playful, laughing eyes. My first impression of him was right. He was a calm, easy- going person with a marvelous sense of humor. I felt safe with this man that I didn't know and I yearned to be held again in his arms.

He asked me what happened and I explained the scene with Dr. Gordon. He started laughing and then he explained. "She has more to worry about than you do. Try to forget what she said, since it could compromise her and we need her on our side."

"You are my contact?" I asked timidly and he nodded.

I let my eyes wander; they fixed on the impressive equipment in his engineering lab. I never saw such a display of metal pieces and machinery, from computers to generators and particle fusion reactors and I didn't know what else. The lab was the size of our concert hall and he was the only person in this lab. I was so curious about all that I saw. "Don't touch anything; you could hurt yourself." He warned me and then went on to tell me that it was impossible for him to contact me because I was being followed all the time. He confirmed that whenever I got too close to highly sensitive units, Dr. Gordon was informed and my return was signaled. I had already surmised that was happening. "At least now" he said, "I can explain to you how you can reach me quickly and easily."

It was evident that he didn't have as much freedom of movement within the center. He needed to be careful, act cautiously, to protect himself. The androids were not yet aware of his deprogramming, which he had been hiding from them for years. As a result, he avoided contact with other humans whenever he could. I obviously had to protect his cover, as well, and avoid, at all costs, talking to him in a public place. He suggested that I ask for a few days in the vacation center and make it clear to Dr. Gordon that I needed to relax, and, at the same time, use her confession to my advantage. He assured me that she wouldn't let anyone terminate me, especially if she believed that I was her key to developing emotions. "She is far too committed to you and to you future, to the chagrin of some more conservative androids, to deny your request." He reassured me.

"I am Pamela, series 13, did you know that?"

"Yes, I have been told." He confirmed smiling.

"And, you?

"Here is my code: 180114041512160807." He raised his eyebrows. "So what name are you going to give me?"

"Very Easy—Randolph, Series 7." I replied affirmatively.

"Wow, I like!"

"By the way, Randolph, what are you working on?" I asked hoping that he would let me see how one of those pieces of machinery that fascinated me actually functioned.

"Sorry, Pamela, it is better for me and for you that you don't know, at least for the moment." He took me by the hand and led me to a different door. "In fact, Pamela, today, I want you to exit by this way; otherwise, you use the side door that I indicated to you earlier. This passage is a direct exit into the main hall. I shall see you at the vacation spot." He said as he waved goodbye.

Within seconds of my appearance, I was escorted by two official androids to the office of Dr. Gordon, who told me how she regretted what she said. I pretended that I could forget all that if she would be willing to send some rudimentary digging and construction equipment to the outside community. I explained that everyone needed to be occupied. That boredom was our biggest enemy and if they could have equipment and materials to construct a new environment, they would be much more interesting to study. She thankfully didn't suspect anything and even liked my idea and appreciated my discretion. So within 24 hours, the community had received what they needed to accomplish their objectives. It was so easy I expected a hitch somewhere.

I followed the instructions of that mysterious man and asked for a long weekend in the vacation center. I told Dr. Gordon that I had been yearning for some sports, something that was missing on the outside. Even though I had barely started complying with my side of the bargain at the center, she agreed straight away, adding that we would have to get down to work when I got back.

"By the way, Dr. Gordon, is my visual code still operative?" It was important that I confirm this detail in order to protect Randolph.

She contacted someone right away to be certain. "Ok, you must memorize your code and communicate it so that the others will be able to recognize you." I could hear in her light-heartened voice that my revelation of my naivety and innocence amused her. "Oh, Pamela, I understand now why you have not been able to have contact with others. Your visual receptor being down, you are simply not visible to other people, unless you give your identification code." She stopped for an instance before continuing in a firmer tone. "That was a major oversight on my part which I hope that you will keep confidential." I nodded in agreement, realizing that her error might cause her problems. What kind? I had no idea.

So, within 48 hours I was sitting at poolside next to Randolph, the mysterious young man. People mingled in the vacation center. Normally they came as couples. For that reason, I would have stood out like a sore thumb if the programmed humans could see me. Randolph's partner was, from my point of view, quite unattractive. Her body, with its short legs, long arms and a broad, long torso gave her a lopsided appearance. In addition, her round face, tiny pale blue eyes, flat nose, wide cheeks and heavy lower lip were, when taken as a whole, completely unattractive. The fact that she was in no way deformed was, of course, a plus. She was still under the spell of the visual receptor and I asked Randolph if he had tried to help her to see reality. That was interesting.

"Actually, yes, Pamela. I did." He replied. "I tried to convince her that she is, like I was, under a spell and that she had to try to break out of her programming; maybe even leave the center. She responded badly to that and seemed to be uncomfortable in my presence." He languished over that thought for an instance and then picked up the conversation. "My being deprogrammed means that I have to constantly remind her of my code so that she will visually recognize me. I understood rapidly that I had to communicate my code number to the programmed humans; a logical consequence of being deprogrammed. I have to keep this practice up to protect myself against android surveillance."

He expanded more on my initial question, confiding in me that he even tried to use her disapproval of him and other upsetting things he told her as a catalyst for a violent reaction that he hoped would catapult her out of her complacent programmed self. He told me that he tried in vain with others as well.

"I have come to the conclusion that a violent, outside force is the effective stimulus, but only if the person receiving it is ready to accept that stimulus and react accordingly." I listened, but was not certain that I understood. He recognized my confusion and explained a bit more. "I believe that the basic personality of someone, hidden behind the programming, is critical. If someone is complacent and accepting by nature, whereby the programming is compatible with their natural self, the deprogramming process becomes more difficult, maybe even impossible." He noticed that my brows creased and I twisted my mouth in disbelief. He laughed. "Ok, Pamela, I could be wrong, but, I have been frustrated with my partner's inability to cross the line for years now. All my efforts to deprogram her have been futile and I have come to accept the fact that not everyone can pass into reality."

He went on to tell me that they did not work in the same scientific field. He is an experimental scientist and his partner is a theoretical scientist. They rarely discuss their projects with each other.

His visual receptor neutralized when one of his experiments went awry. There was a big explosion. The explosion damaged some of the equipment and threw him so violently across the room, that he banged his head hard up against the wall and lost consciousness. When he recovered he found himself in the care of his two android assistants whose persistent slapping him on his face finally revived him. "What I am going to say now will probably sound ridiculous to you." He said, drawing the sides of his mouth up in a silly smile. "When I saw those android creations looking at me with their expressionless faces, I burst out laughing. They looked funny to me. Oh, they didn't laugh; they backed off and waited until I stood up before asking me if I was alright."

"Weren't you scared?" I interrupted him.

"Not at all, but I was fascinated with what I saw."

"You saw through their luminous shield right after the accident?" I was surprised that he could have penetrated their outside protection so easily.

"Yes, I saw those creations, as they truly exist, instantly, when I opened my eyes. I think that I suffered from a concussion that had the double effect of deprogramming me and amplifying my visual capacity." He did not deny having problems adjusting to the new reality, but managed to stay calm, as he pretended nothing had changed.

"I was working on one of my most important experimental discoveries in the field of nuclear fusion and did not want anything to interfere with my concentration." He stretched his arms and then tapped me playfully on my face before continuing. "Losing my programming was simply a scientific fact; and I wanted it to stay, just a scientific fact. Crossing into a new reality did not frighten or disturb me. I won't deny having had certain problems adjusting to the new reality. For example, I was weaving around the room and stumbling up against the lab tables, in the beginning. Nonetheless, I stayed calm and pretended that nothing had changed because of the accident."

He stopped to gather his thoughts. "Of course, I was not aware of the potential consequences this could have on my life. I would discover its impact on me later on. But, at the very moment that I crossed into the real world, I had another objective, to complete my research." He looked at me mockingly. "I needed to stay in control. And, I have done that all along. You see, Pamela, I have hidden and have continued to hide my deprogramming from the androids who remain completely oblivious to my new found identity. They still give me projects, highly sensitive projects that are relatively dangerous for their own future like working on nuclear weapons."

"Admittedly, Pamela, it has not always been easy to continue the charades and face other reality based challenges, like dealing with my partner. This is not that easy to confront on a daily basis, but I trudge forward taking things step by step."

He expounded his belief that most scientists have a kind of mental buffer system that allowed them to approach new and even dangerous situations without becoming extremely alarmed. And their sense of curiosity worked in their favor by suppressing emotional outbursts that would signal, as in our case, deprogramming. Apparently, he was surprised that Jonathan and I were able to bypass our systems. We stood out as exceptions for him because our deprogramming was provoked by strong emotions. Even though he admitted that emotions of any kind seemed to be the key to being human, he was still convinced that deprogramming needed a violent outside force, like the explosion in his lab.

"I think that your reasoning or, if you like scientific reasoning which, of course, is very interesting, does not take into account all the variables, Randolph." I was fed up with scientists pretending that they were such a privileged class that even deprogramming was reserved for them. "I believe that strong emotional reactions can be as violent to the human psyche as an outside physical force. In my case, my strong desire to interpret my music differently from that of the conductor was such a consuming force that it precipitated a violent emotional reaction which provoked my by-passing my programming. And, Jonathan's transition was understandable, because he witnessed my hysteria, suffered my rejection of him, and then my dramatic arrest. And, like you, Jonathan stayed calm and controlled, hiding his deprogramming from the androids for a long time." I stopped. "With that in mind, can't we just say that scientists are just as human as the rest of us?"

"Touché" He laughed with delight.

I asked him about John and he explained their relationship. He had worked with John in the beginning as a junior researcher. When he accidentally ran into John not too long after he had crossed over in our human world, simple eye contact was all that was needed for the two of them to recognize that they were both operating on the same plain. John offered to take Randolph with him and the others, but Randolph refused. He wanted to stay on as an inside contact.

After this long discussion, we split up for the evening and met again early the next day to talk about how we were going to improve our own future and that of the outside community. I quickly brought him up to date, by informing him that the material and equipment that John requested had arrived. I also pointed out that I would have to count on someone else on the inside to let me know if more supplies and equipment were needed. I underlined the fact that I didn't want my stay in the Center to drag on for too long so I counted on him to keep me informed and to help me to accomplish my objectives rapidly.

"Now that I know the short cut to your office, I shall try to slip by the personnel at least once a week to get an update, if that is alright with you." He nodded in agreement. "I am not worried about our being seen together during the work days."

"Oh, are you sure?" He broke in.

"Yes. Dr. Gordon took a rather harsh, critical approach to my indifference towards the other humans. I thought that I might just mention to her that I made a few friends on vacation. I could also tell her that living with scientists on the outside for the last few years made me realize that I like being around people with scientific backgrounds, the reason why I migrated towards the scientists on vacation and away from the musicians. What do you think? Will she be convinced?" I asked with trepidation.

"It sounds convincing to me!" He exclaimed.

"I could always thank her for suggesting that I make an effort to meet people, because it is true, I do need to be with other humans." He nodded as I continued, "At least that would make it so much easier for us to exchange information."

We were ready to get up and leave when I remembered the transport vehicles. "One minute, Randolph, I have one last point." He sat back down and listened as I explained to him that Diana had given me a map of the center. She thought that she had seen where the simple train cars were stocked. However, Diana was not sure where the more sophisticated air and land craft were located.

Randolph replied. "I know where they are. The area is heavily guarded. If our friends want to enter that area, I will have to study the surveillance system--see if there are any weaknesses in it." He had a serious look on his face when he added. "This is more John's field. I shall do my best to try to get information."

When I returned from this long weekend, I felt like I had finally accomplished something. And, I felt more prepared to confront Dr. Gordon.

Chapter 27: Enigma

Ientered her office very enthusiastically and ready to work. I told her how much I appreciated the long weekend at the vacation center. I rambled on about how much I liked swimming and using different gym equipment and that I always liked working out and keeping in shape. Then I commented that everyone in the Center seemed to be in good shape. When I mentioned that point to her, she perked up and explained. "That is normal. Everyone has a diet adapted to their particular needs, hence why your number is on the food boxes. The proper amount of vitamins and minerals are in everyone's diet and no one is given anything more. Some people are given less of certain foods only because obesity is in their genes. And, as you have been informed, the sexual inhibitors are sprinkled on the food and are adapted, as well, to the hormonal levels of different individuals." When she did not get a reaction from me, she ended with. "I am so pleased with your acute sense of observation, Pamela."

I changed the subject. "I took your advice and started to interact with other members of the center." She nodded approvingly. "And, I met a young man who I call Randolph while at the vacation center and I like him a lot.

She clapped her hands in approval. "Marvelous! I am really pleased that you're getting along with others even though I understand how much you must miss Peter and Frederic."

That brought tears to my eyes and I found it rather vicious on her part. She waited patiently until I recovered and went on with the subject of the day. "You told me that you were ready to discuss jealousy. I would like you to tell me about that today."

"It is difficult to describe emotions, Dr. Gordon. I don't have a text book in front of me so you will have to bear with me." I started off like that. "You said that I was under observation, from the moment that I arrived in that small community." She nodded and I continued. "You must know then that my first sexual relationship was with Mathieu. I trusted him because he helped me to escape from the center. I felt close to him as well and he was the only one I wanted to be with. I felt uncomfortable with the others because they were not warm and welcoming from the beginning. Apart from Mathieu, the others treated me with coldness, acting like I was a spy."

"A spy; how curious." She was adapting her voice so well that she actually sounded surprised even though she had no demonstrative facial expression of surprise. "Whom would you be spying for?"

I found that question a bit ridiculous, but with time most of her questions seemed a bit naive or inept. "For you, of course." I answered indignantly.

"For me--but we didn't need you to spy for us; we are spying for ourselves." It was pointless to argue with her shielded android logic, with blinders, although I reminded her that we didn't know that they were spying on us and that she was the one who mentioned earlier that they were observing us. I insisted that I was completely oblivious to all of this while I was living on the outside. I took this position because it seemed the best for the moment. John pointed out the audio-visual equipment of the androids and asked Diana to act a certain way in front of the cameras, but I assumed, and rightly so, that I was not to divulge our knowledge of their espionage tactics and equipment.

"Ridiculous. It seems absurd to me that people like John, for instance, have not noticed our video cameras. He worked in communications."

"If he did, Dr. Gordon, he never told me about them." I replied. And, then everything got complicated. She accused me of lying, a nasty human quality and even though I denied it, she insisted I had lied to her. So, I had to use another nasty human quality, to manipulate her.

"If I had known that, Dr. Gordon, I would never have rebelled, I assure you, and I would have refused to develop human emotions in their fullest. When I escaped from this Center, I never expected to come back. If I had known that you were studying me, do you honestly think that I would have allowed myself to go so far as to have a child that you, one day in the future, would force me to abandon, even if only temporarily?"

"I don't know what to think about you, but I do know that John and the Governor know each other. His departure and the departure of the others was an arrangement between the two of them. Every one of us androids is aware of that agreement. The Governor brought us all up-to-date quite recently; not that that should be of any importance to you." I noticed that she was starting to confide in me. Interesting, I thought. "It is possible that John promised the Governor to keep certain information secret. In any event, it is quite logical for me to assume the contrary as I lived and worked in the past with humans."

"Sorry to disappoint you on that point, Dr. Gordon. But, like it or not, I was treated like a spy. It was only when Peter and I settled down together and Frederic was born that the core group-that is John, Sarah and Ruth, along with Mathilda, Mathieu and Isabelle-accepted me. Before that, Stanislas and

Benjamin, probably because of their life style, treated me kindly, but they kept their distance."

"If that is the case, everything that we observe on film is the truth. No one is hiding anything." She was not yet convinced or she needed to hear that to prove her theories or she wanted to irritate me enough that I would say things I shouldn't. My best guess was that she wanted to trap me into admitting knowledge of the audio-video surveillance, so I just shrugged it off and added that she could think whatever she wanted. I started to get ready to leave when she asked about jealousy again.

"I already touched on the subject but you interrupted me and then accused me of lying." I felt like I was under constant stress to stay one step ahead of her. "Actually, I feel like you are purposely interrupting, playing mind games with me, just to make this even more difficult." I said impatiently and then went on to be more direct. "Regardless of how you see yourself and your creator, imagine how complicated it is for me to try to explain feelings to a machine. So if you want me to continue, stop interrupting."

"Well, I would say that you are angry with me. Maybe you should tell me how you feel."

"So you'd like to analyze my anger right now. You'd like that; well, I feel like I'm in a fish bowl." I ejaculated wildly until I began to reel it in, knowing I could only hurt myself in the end. "You are right. I am a bit angry," I couldn't help a new surge of anger so I let it out, "Not angry enough to try to take you apart like a common kitchen appliance, but angry enough to want to leave this office, which is what I am going to do. Follow me if you like just to see how I am going to calm down."

"No, don't leave. I like seeing all these feelings--even anger--surging inside of you. I don't think that you have a great deal of patience though, Pamela." She said it in a nice sort of way.

That made me laugh; I couldn't help it. Here I was livid and mean and she remained tranquil. That calmed my ardor. She prodded me to talk a bit more about jealousy. I admitted that my adventure with Mathieu came to a brutal end when we returned with Jason to the group.

"I felt hurt on the inside and resented the trust that I had put in him. After having awakened in me a strong desire for physical contact, making love, if you like, he just walked away from me. I felt even more alone than before and I imagined that everyone was laughing at how naive I had been. I suffered, the same as if someone had cut off my hand. And, I wanted him to leave Isabelle and come back with me. Every time they went off together, I felt angry, stressed, sad and bitter. I realized later that I wanted him because I couldn't have him and not because I had strong enough feelings for him. We never talked about that. He never apologized to me for having put me in such a painful situation. And, I never told him how much I resented what he did and how I even hoped that Isabelle would just disappear. All that I suffered was because I was jealous. I wanted something that belonged to someone else. I realized that I had to have my own plans and objectives and did not compare my wants and desires with others. Sarah was particularly helpful in making me understand my feelings. She and Ruth share John and they don't seem to need to be possessive; something that just does not appeal to me. I hope that Peter will wait for me."

I didn't share with her my deep-rooted convictions on jealousy and I did not mention how possessive Isabelle was. I left that part out. I did not want Dr. Gordon to know that I was not as much affected by the absence of Mathieu in my life, as I was by the absence of a man in my life. I saw Mathieu, as I said earlier, as my teacher. The person who brought to life my sexual desires and showed me the intimacy that can exist between humans. I was pleased with myself for being able to deceive Dr. Gordon, even in this relatively insignificant discussion.

When I finished, she told me that she recorded all our discussions and listened to them over and over again to make certain that she understood everything. That was why it was so important that we talk. Discussion often opened other unexplored topics. "You are right to a certain extent, Pamela. Monogamous relationships were more prevalent in human society than polygamous relationship and monogamous coupling was a sign of deep emotional commitment between two humans. Although there were plenty of examples in your history where polygamy was recognized and approved which explains why Sarah and Ruth accept their situation."

I thought that she had finished and started to prepare for a second time to leave, when she went further on in her analysis. "I didn't know that preferences for monogamous or polygamous relationships could be a personal or natural choice and not exclusively imposed upon individuals." She expressed more interest in this subject than in my description of jealousy.

And, then she looked at her watch. My time was up. As I stood up she told me that she had arranged that the library would be open for me the following day and that I could arrive as early as I wanted and leave as late as I wanted as well. I was so happy I could have hugged and kissed her, but didn't-too risky. Instead I thanked her profusely for her kindness.

"Pamela," she called out to me as I was leaving. "I just want to warn you. If you are looking for the story of your species, you won't find it in its entirety. We edited your story."

I just looked at her trying not to reveal my total disgust. I thought to myself, "Why, why, why did they do a thing like that? I can't imagine what my species did to merit a complete overhaul of their history. On the contrary, I've got plenty of ideas about what the androids were doing wrong." Nonetheless, her comment triggered new thoughts about the interaction between humans and androids in the past, was it always so pathetic? This aroused my curiosity about how and why the androids acquired control, if they didn't always have it; and inspired my desire to find the truth, whatever that was, hidden between the lines in a story that was edited by cold, calculating machines. But I hid my true objective from Dr. Gordon, behind a generous smile, as I graciously thanked her for the information.

I woke up early the next morning and rushed to catch the shuttle. I had to use my time properly and not just look up the lives of my favorite composers. Actually, I didn't have to worry because the librarians brought me disks in chronological order. I, like most of the other humans, read very rapidly. We trained from the beginning to absorb the rapid flow of information we received. That might seem a strange word to describe learning or even memorizing, but it is the most accurate. We were ironically programmed to respond to information as if we were computers. Dr. Gordon mentioned to me in one of our conversations that it was the most recent evolutionary stage for my species. Our minds evolved in such a way that our capacity to understand and assimilate and use information was as rapid as the androids'. I didn't much like that comparison at the time but was pleased to know that my species was as intellectually capable as theirs.

That accounts for the fact that I could read through a considerable number of disks from the prehistoric period to the middle ages in a few hours. Her advice to me seemed completely useless in the beginning, because I couldn't identify the gaps that would have naturally existed if the history had not been edited. I noticed that certain main themes entered into the history of my species. The problems of first living together in small then expanding to bigger and even bigger communities, the many different cultures and people with physical differences and the attitudes of superiority in beliefs, physical appearance and governance. There were many conflicts--wars as they were referred to. Humans were cruel with themselves, physically and psychologically. I was surprised and sad to see how some people had food and shelter and other people didn't. There was no sharing of property, what they referred to as wealth. That was my first contact with feelings of selfishness, egocentrism, individualism, at least, that is what the commentary pointed out.

The commentary was also a very interesting point to focus on. At the end of each period, there was an analytical study, referred to as the commentary. The mere fact that this commentary existed raised questions on its historical accuracy. The commentary was always negative, underlining the bad side of humans. Even from the very beginning, the prehistoric period, the commentary failed to highlight the inventiveness, resilience, curiosity and determination of my species in face of natural obstacles. Instead, it highlighted the cruelty of humans, their insensitivity to other life forms, their need to conquer and their cruelty to one another. If I had only read the commentary I would not have had much respect for my people. Perhaps Dr. Gordon's warning was not directed towards the events themselves but rather the analysis of human events. I understood that in spite of the negative side, humans were compassionate, caring, and clever. As such, the manuscripts were clearly edited.

By the end of the middle ages, I discovered the significance of the belief in a superior being, a point which I intended to evoke with Dr. Gordon. I had skimmed past the period of tribal worshipping, as it was called. These primitive humans were in awe of nature, which certainly accounted for their believing that natural forces were superior beings in disguise. I found that rather humorous just as I did the Greek and Roman vision of a kingdom of superior beings living just above the cloud cover in a mythical kingdom called Olympiad. There were hypotheses that Egyptians and some of their contemporaries were in touch with supernatural beings, who were in reality space travelers. These extraterrestrial Gods presumably accelerated human development. The Egyptian beliefs seemed more credible to me than the tribal or Greco-Roman beliefs. Nonetheless, the beliefs of the different groups and their names for their Gods were not as important to me as the existence of Gods.

Nonetheless, true or imagined, what was intriguing to me was the idea that worshipping superior beings with superior intelligence could make the impossible become. . . possible. I was particularly interested in the one God theory advanced after the Roman period and wanted to study that in more detail. We were never taught about superior beings, the force of nature or the power of the Gods… I wasn't certain that I understood the delicate relationship between humans and their Gods and was a bit confused about how to worship those Gods, be they linked with tribal, Greco-Roman, Egyptian, or One God cultures. I did want, so desperately to understand how to contact these beings. Maybe they could or would help us to recover our freedom and help us to find new fertile land to live on. They seemed to be capable of extraordinary assistance in exchange for the simplicity of worship.

When I was asked to leave, I was happy that I had taken advantage of every minute allowed, even though there was so much more to read and understand. I knew that I wasn't going to be able to hide some of my enthusiasm from Dr. Gordon and wasn't certain why I should. She would be thrilled that I had feelings concerning the people I read about and the events. And, above all I wanted her to find my time in the library beneficial to her so that I would be able to go more regularly.

I entered my cubicle exuding with excitement and Randolph jumped out from behind the cloture the android's had constructed for my privacy; he shoved his hand over my mouth to stifle any cries; reminiscent of our first encounter. He pulled me close to him and whispered in my ear that he had received word from someone in the aircraft hangar and would try to meet with him the following day. He was breathing heavily between syllables making it almost impossible to concentrate on his words, not to mention feeling his warm body envelope mine, which pleased me and irritated me at the same time. He turned me round as I fought to regain control over myself.

"Are you frightened, Randolph?" I asked hoping that he would deny it; but he didn't.

"I knew that I was taking a big risk." He started off in a nervous, agitated tone, as he paced up and down the length of the cubicle. "In spite of the fact that I know my way around the center, there are many long, wide corridors where it will be difficult for me to pass without being seen." He was worried about this assignment. "If I am caught then you must find a way to meet 19202101182006 (Stuart 6) to get the information that he wanted me to pass on to John and the others. Do you understand?"

"Yes, I understand what you want me to do, but I prefer that you stay alive." I replied sentimentally." I heard about Stuart. How well do you know him?"

"We have been working together on information gathering for a very long time. You can trust him, Pamela." He was sincere.

"Ok, but I don't want you to be caught." I answered trying to hide my feelings in the softness of my voice. "I shall help you if you are."

"No. You mustn't get involved." He protested.

"It is too late. I already told Dr. Gordon that I know you and enjoy talking to you. Our complicity will be obvious. For that reason, you must take every precaution. Don't draw attention to yourself. Walk as slowly and act as programmed as the others and if you are stopped, pretend that you got lost." I don't know why I was giving him any advice. Certainly he had more experience than I did slinking around, staying out of view.

"Pamela. If all goes well, I shall return to see you in two days. If I don't return. . ." He continued. "Here is the key to locker 7 in the sports center. You must get the information that I have compiled to date and pass it on to John; and, you must do all this before you arrange to meet Stuart." He looked at me and added. "You will find a way."

"Don't leave;" I protested. "Stay with me. I don't like thinking that I could lose you. And, I don't think that I am cut out for dangerous missions."

"No, Pamela." He smiled. "You would be very disappointed if I stayed. Don't forget, I'm still eating the contaminated food, with its sexual inhibitors." He said teasingly. I didn't like his being so frank and besides I was not necessarily implying that. It was strange he should jump to such a conclusion and terribly embarrassing that he did. Was I giving off vibes?

"Are you ok, Pamela?" He asked, sensitive to my sudden silence. I nodded affirmatively.

" I am going to do my best to be back in two days to take back this key that I'm giving to you as a precaution," he paused, "should something happen. But don't worry!"

He slipped out of the cubicle and I stood there frozen to his shadow moving away from me holding the small key. I had never seen a key before, even though I knew that they existed. We didn't need keys because we never locked anything; only the androids locked boxes and doors. I wondered how he got a key to a box in the sports center without the guards knowing about it. I was fascinated with his sense of adventure and suspense; annoyed by his pretentiousness, and, saturated with enough adrenaline to keep me awake all night.

In spite of my sleepless night, I felt so motivated and enthusiastic in the morning that I actually enjoyed swallowing my morning shake and ran to catch the monorail as it arrived in the station. I slipped my card in place and, for the first time since my return, turned on the descriptive tape while I observed from the windows. I could almost see all the thick, green vegetation, hear the rushing streams, see the luscious pastures surrounded by high mountains and smell the perfume of blooming flowers. I said almost, because my vision was diverted to the barren, red earth of home. I missed Peter and Frederic, the main reason why I was determined to accomplish my mission as quickly as possible.

I was in the music room playing the piano when Dr. Gordon called out to me. I didn't hear her at first because I was caught up in the rhythm and sensuality of the composition. I was more and more convinced that I understood Chopin and what he wanted to communicate to others through his compositions.

She was wearing a blond wig this morning and, I didn't recognize her at first. She looked quite pretty, and I complimented her on her appearance. She made it clear that the wig might help to intensify our relationship; or, at best, to put me more at ease. What she said did not always make sense to me. I didn't care if she had hair or not; but I did not want to complicate anything, and thereby put myself at risk of being psychoanalyzed android style, so I assured her that the latter offer was the most appropriate. And, we headed off in the direction of her office, passing by all those smiling, laughing humans who radiated with happiness. From time to time, Dr. Gordon nodded at one of her kind. They wore large nametags so they could be easily recognized.

"Why do you feel the need to use names?" I asked as she unlocked the door to her office.

"I told you. We took on the names of our creators." She replied.

"Yes, but the creators must have made more than one of you. So, in effect, there must be two Dr. Gordon's out there." I ventured.

"Pamela, it is much more complicated than that. If you like, there are others that are slightly similar in their internal composition and programming, but, they did not work closely with my creator and, thus, they do not have my intellectual capacity." I sat staring at her as she grappled with words trying to make sense out of what she was saying. I found her bafflement quite amusing. "Their resemblance with me is insignificant. I am the only one with whom my creator interacted; worked with and educated to be her legitimate descendant. The other physically similar androids were constructed to carry out other, less important, tasks. So, naturally, I have the right to use her name." She added, "There is a hierarchy among us androids; just like among humans." She sat down and took on that official style. "So, how was your day in the library?"

I beamed with pleasure as I told her how helpful it was to have access to historical tapes. She nodded with satisfaction as I revealed some of what I had discovered. Then I asked her if she had the pleasure of meeting any of those superior beings that the humans worshipped. That did not seem to please her. She fidgeted a bit and tapped her long, android index finger on the desk, before pointing it in my direction.

"You should not let yourself be influenced by their beliefs. The idea of a superior being is a figment of the imagination. If you cannot read the history of your species with a critical eye, then perhaps we should stop right now." She stood up and started to pace back and forth in front of me. It was clear that I had asked the wrong question; but I didn't know how to get myself out of this one. I could feel tears swelling up in my eyes, tears of fear and frustration. Maybe, this time, she would go to the extreme and terminate me. Within seconds my face was bathed in that warm, salty water and I was having a difficult time focusing on her.

"Why are you crying?" she asked. Her voice was no longer soft and feminine.

My mind was working so fast trying to find the best strategy. She repeated herself; her voice was loud and masculine. Had she lost control—maybe?

Perhaps I had the upper hand? Perhaps I had to assert myself? Or, perhaps she was going to explode.

"I was crying for you, Dr. Gordon." Could I confuse her even more? "You seem scared and befuddled and I don't know how to help you. Perhaps you should sit down again." I wiped away my tears and tried to be more composed. She surprised me and sat down, but her body was jerking about, like she was experiencing a short circuit. I had to do something. A horrible thought crossed my mind, what would happen to me if she shut down? I panicked. I jumped up and rushed to pull her from her chair. Which I did as she threw those well shaped arms around me and hid her head on my shoulder. We stayed like that for what seemed to be hours, and then we didn't move apart. She drew my mouth up to hers and pressed softly, yet firmly, exhuming desire.

She opened her lab coat and slithered out of it rapidly. Her hands vibrated slowly down the length of my body, sliding up under my long, white robe, as they carefully lifted and moved it away from me and raised it over my head, liberating me from any constraints, any inhibitions. The effect of her vibrating hands, lingering and pressing up against my naked body was so sexually arousing that my entire body was responding licentiously. She must have studied me in incredible detail, because her vibrating hands were moving over my body, touching and pressing up against every secret spot imaginable, arousing a heightened sexual desire, to which she responded by giving me more pleasure than I ever had or could ever imagine having. I couldn't get enough and I found myself gripping and squeezing her in return as she let out sounds of joy and pleasure as I touched her. We stopped and started up over and over again. I drifted in gushes of orgasms until I was completely drained of energy. She could have continued exerting power over me. We lay naked next to her steel desk. Her wig had long since fallen from her head, but it didn't matter. She looked so beautiful to me.

How could this machine have known so well how to give me so much pleasure and love; even more startling, after all the warnings I had been given, how could I have let this happen? Now reality struck full blast as I was worried about the consequences for me, for Peter, for Frederic and, for all the others.

Chapter 28: Adversity

The relationship was beyond control. The next few times we met, we hugged as our hands moved about each other's body craving the contact and the pleasure. I was surprised that she had the body of a woman, in every detail. She was tall and thin with an hourglass shaped body; her well-defined waist gracefully curved out to her rounded hips, in perfect harmony with her full, firm breasts. Her rounded shoulders along with her round, firm bottom and proportionate long shapely legs and arms were the finishing touches to this perfectly conceived human-like body.

I would have thought that her creator would have preferred to reserve intimacy, making love, for herself and her kind, and yet Dr. Gordon was created with outer feminine organs, including other passages, resembling mine. I could not understand why she was designed in this way. Was she designed and programmed to have sex? She definitely had cognitive sexual ability because she read my body like a map filled with hot and cold zones; she knew where to touch me and for how long to linger to stimulate me beyond reason; and she knew how to stay focused until I reach extraordinary, and vibrant waves of orgasmic pleasure. Nonetheless, it was clear from her noticeable lack of sexual fulfillment that she was not designed or programmed to enjoy sex. So why does she pursue it with me? Does she want to give me pleasure or to stimulate emotions in herself?

Looking at her made me aware of my own imperfections; my body was not designed in her perfect harmony. Her skin fascinated me as well. It had a human texture-soft, supple, yet firm. If she had a defect it is the one that Peter mentioned and I discovered; she had no muscles. But, she was ageless on top of everything else, as her skin would not experience the cruel markings of time; wrinkling, folding and sagging, under pressure of age, like that of Jason. She was a machine whose exterior was designed to resist time and exist forever.

I was perplexed by my intimate relationship with her, which was strangely seductive and fulfilling, in spite of the fact that it did not seem natural. The fact that we were the same sex did not disturb me. Stanislas and Benjamin had a wonderful relationship. They were an angelic couple both in their physical appearances and in their tenderness towards each other. They also looked alike; both tall and thin with brown curly hair that framed their slightly round faces. They both had big, brown eyes, an unpretentious nose and beautiful white teeth that were hidden behind thin, yet firm, lips. I liked them very much individually and as a couple.

What disturbed me was that I left a very satisfying and loving relationship with Peter to find myself reaching waves of orgasmic pleasure with a female machine. I didn't seek this libertine lifestyle; and yet, even in face of its unabated, raw perversion, I just couldn't resist Dr. Gordon when we were together.

Fortunately, sex was not the only thing on my agenda. I did keep up with other more vital matters. Randolph's visit to the hangar was a turning point. Stuart gave him the codes to enter into the air transport hangar and but could not find the technical guides to use the machines. Nonetheless, this, coupled with what Randolph had himself gathered was going to help John to accomplish the last phase of our objective. Randolph's safe return from this secret mission gave us hope of achieving it.

The next problem was how to transfer to John this information and the different communication devices that Randolph had stolen from the Center and that were hidden in locker 7 until we came up with a solution.

Perhaps this solution would be forthcoming, because my situation was improving daily. Sex with Dr. Gordon gave me a clear advantage over my future and the crazy pleasure of it was an added perk. I thereafter got unconditional access to the library and the right to explore the center. I continued with the library, burying myself in those historical disks, hoping that the history of the human race would give me answers. Dr. Gordon came to visit me, from time to time, just to tell me how much she loved me. I would just shake my head in approval. Even though I knew that she had no idea what love entailed, I did not want to offend her by reminding her of what she is—a machine. And, it would have been cruel, as she promised to always be there to protect me, which was more important to me than her unsolicited love. Nonetheless, it sounded bizarre that a machine could experience love, but…?

My emotional attachment was different. I had strong feelings of gratitude and felt dependent upon her protection. Yes, I experienced genuine sexual pleasure with her. This strong emotional binding could lead to something more profound, like love. Nonetheless, my deep emotional ties were with Peter who I missed more and more as the days, and the months went by. I doubted that I could ever have that kind of desperate longing for Dr. Gordon, or anyone else, but Peter.

I started to have a picture, finally, of the planet Earth. I understood, as well, that different races existed because of the environment people lived in. After that, I observed more carefully, the appearances of the people living at the Center. The Center had a very large assortment of different colors and distinctive features among the humans. Sadly, a lot of the people had some kind of physical deformity; I did not know why. Yet, I started to appreciate the beauty of different races, and, tried to make contact with non-Caucasians. Again, the problem of programming made it difficult for me to have normal relationships with any of them, even after communicating my visual code to assure my visibility. They were living in that euphoric world where discussions were so superficial. In addition, as everyone they saw and met was perfectly compatible with them, they were devoid of a cognitive knowledge of differences. So, there was nothing to be gained by introducing this subject to them.

I continued to focus my attention on superior beings and found myself delving into the different religions that built up over the centuries. I couldn't understand why the different religions were so hostile to each other. Dr. Gordon told me that religion was the downfall of humanity, but refused to explain why. There were so many religious wars throughout human history that I wondered if the superior being was actually kind. Why didn't he and his fellow emissaries just reveal themselves so that everyone would know the right way to worship and contact them? Dr. Gordon returned to the original explanation she gave me that humans were always searching for this superior being because of their obsession with who created them.

"In fact "she said. "Each religion was based upon the existence of an earthly contact, the emissary for the superior being. The problem was that the representatives said different things to different cultures or ethnic groups which explained why the religions embraced different principles and practiced different rituals." She found it all particularly boring and pointed out that androids were always and will always be in a better position than humans because they know who created them. That was of course if it really mattered because she considered existence more important than the identity of the being that created them or why they were created. Of course, that is not exactly what she said to me earlier when she defended her use of the name, Dr. Gordon, the name of her creator.

She, definitely, wanted to confuse me. I conjectured that if religious practices were responsible for the world we lived in today, then, one could not dispose of the importance of religion as easily as Dr. Gordon could. Even though I didn't feel at ease with any particular religion and its practices, I was becoming more and more convinced that a creator and other superior beings existed. The leaders of the various religions seemed to be more politically than spiritually motivated, which was lamentable. Some religious leaders inculcated their followers into believing that if they didn't toe the line, they would be punished during and after their lives. The commentaries on the 11th to the 16th century addressed this problem and highlighted the tense relationship between Christians, Muslims and Jews, among others. Killing, torturing, and mutilating people in the name of their defined God was shocking. I desperately needed to talk to someone rational about all this.

My efforts to understand the impossible took a back seat to the encounter I had with Dr. Crawford, ironically right after one of my particularly sensual meetings with Dr. Gordon. She had accompanied me to my train. I had not noticed that she had changed and that she was not acting so much like an android any more. Her actions and her thinking were certainly more android than human. Dr. Crawford jumped in front of us and I had to jam my fingers between my teeth to squelch the scream building up inside of me.

He quickly made the observation, his smug smile painted on his face, "Dr. Gordon you are acting more human every day. I don't think you want to be an Android any longer." I was surprised by his comment. Her actions and thinking were certainly more android than human.

He pointed to her wig. "It's weird Dr. Gordon that you have been wearing a wig every day for the last two weeks. And, how do you explain your swinging your body in a suggestive sort of way when you are walking?" He didn't give her a chance to answer. "You are acting like those human females centuries ago, with their flirtatious, seductive moves. It is demeaning to all of us androids to see you repeat their vulgar gestures. All of this leads me to believe that there is a problem, a major problem, in your circuits and I am going to ask that you be examined by one of our technicians."

"You have gone too far with your criticisms and accusations." Dr. Gordon took offense and responded energetically. "There are other androids here at the Center who have been wearing wigs for years. I don't think that my decision to wear one is a sign of problems in my circuitry or a rejection of my android being." She stopped for a brief second and finished with. "I shall carry and move my hips however I like. There is no rule or regulation that requires androids to march in a straight, up-right, rigid way."

"Huh! Did you hear yourself? Do you realize that you raised your voice?" He retorted, provoking her.

"You are exaggerating everything, Dr. Crawford." She answered calmly. "You know that I adapted the tone of my voice to help Pamela feel more secure in my presence. Our linear, android voice is not compatible with the human auditory system. And, even though we speak in our normal voice tone to our programmed humans, I wanted Pamela to be at ease with me so that we would be able to properly work together." She looked piercingly at Crawford before continuing. "Of course, as you rightly pointed out, my switching back and forth in a few seconds did create a bit of confusion in my vocal circuits, which bothered you. As you can see, my voice rapidly readjusted. Finally, Dr. Crawford, what I have just told you is part of my experimental study; my report will appear in final form very soon and will be submitted directly to the Governor."

Dr. Gordon took offense and responded a bit more vigorously than she should have. This gave the impression that she was starting to develop an emotional base and Dr. Crawford picked up on this by warning me that if Dr. Gordon continued like this that he was going to hold me responsible and that would give him the right to read my mind.

"Nonetheless, your behavior is radically different. I believe that you should have yourself gone over." He looked at me and backed up a bit jerking his head in the direction of Dr. Gordon. "Does she see me?"

Of course I saw him. Dr. Gordon had given me a small device to block out the bright light veil. I didn't need this device later on, but, in the beginning, I was very affected by the luminosity and had difficulty piercing it. Not only was I seeing Dr. Crawford, but I was also comparing him to Dr. Gordon. Her oval face was symmetrically constructed and everything from her nose, to her eyes, ears and mouth were in exact proportion. Dr. Crawford, on the contrary, was not as well built. He had a very large, round face, with a long, flat nose. His upper lip was practically invisible and his small beady eyes were far from flattering. I would say that it gave him a severe and malicious look. He was rather short, at least in comparison to Gordon, and had short, thin arms and large fingers. I couldn't see his legs, but imagined them to be short and pudgy.

I heard Dr. Gordon answer his question with a definitive. "No!" I couldn't help but snicker to myself as I contemplated her taking on deplorable human traits like. . .lying.

He turned to me with piercing eyes. I thought I saw a sinister smile appear on his face and stepped back. He knew that I could see him and this gave him the opportunity to send me a warning. "You—you—! "He was pointing his finger at me as he raised the tone of his voice. "You are responsible for all the strange behavior of Dr. Gordon. I warn you that if her android behavior continues to deteriorate I am ready to prove that you are the one responsible." He seemed so sure of himself. "I shall ask that you be assigned to me for study and, unlike Dr. Gordon," He was now licking his lips like a predator ready to devour its prey---"I shall use more invasive psychological tactics to study you. I hope that what I said is clear."

I nodded as I moved closer to Dr. Gordon who enveloped me in her maternal arms, comforting me like a child. She spoke up showing her disapproval. "This conversation is terminated. Your efforts to intimidate me and to frighten Pamela have gone on long enough."

He was not satisfied and blocked our passage. "I am going to speak to the Governor about scheduling an emergency board meeting. This human has been with you for two months and you have not yet submitted a single report on the progress of your study. I am going to request that your human subject be summoned to appear as well."

All this time, I was studying his reactions. His behavior, pretentious for a human and shocking for a robot, was incredibly fascinating. It was clear that he did not like me and did not appreciate Dr. Gordon's study; his warning frightened me. Nonetheless, as I was so focused on his mannerisms and dialogue, unnatural and irrational, I did not register just how dangerous he could for me. I even chuckled to myself…

He left us, walking rapidly in the wrong direction, giving Dr. Gordon the opportunity to pull me back into her office. She explained that this was a very crucial moment for both of us and that she needed to be alone so that she could recuperate some of her natural poise before the meeting. She suggested that I take the time to explore the Center. I told her that I hadn't realized that I was there for two months and wondered if I couldn't return just for an instance to see my son. She reacted as if she were jealous.

"I can't let you do that. Try to be serious. You just can't move in and out of the Center when it appears convenient for you. And, your son—well, he is being taken care of. You have more important things to do at the moment, so he can't be your priority." I looked at her showing my disappointment with the tears building up in my eyes. She quickly changed her approach. "It is too dangerous, Pamela, at this moment, especially now that Dr. Crawford is going to be watching both of us very closely. However, in the event that the meeting goes badly, I shall arrange in advance for your safe passage to the outside."

"What could go wrong?" I asked, pretty much aware of the ultimate danger.

"The Governor could order me to shut down permanently." She continued. "And, your imminent termination could be ordered. One or both of those decisions could take place. I won't be able to escape my punishment but I shall assure your protection."

"I hope that it doesn't come down to that." I protested. "Dr. Crawford cannot have that much influence."

"He is dangerous, because he has a superiority complex, if you like, a bit strange for an android. Huh." She continued. "But it is part of his programming.

His creator was brilliant and transferred his view of others to Dr. Crawford. He can't resist his superiority complex. He doesn't like it, because he certainly does not want to emulate humans in any way. He obviously does not hold the human race in high esteem."

That was the first time I heard her use the expression, human race. She always referred to us as a species. I myself was using the expression, human race. As I mentioned, I liked it the first time I heard it when living with the outside community. It also appeared in the historical accounts and I found it a much nicer and flattering expression. I wondered if she was going to be able to conceal all her changes from the Board. Why did she have to be so interested in crossing that wide divide between her and us? Maybe her programming was open to her developing limited human attitudes or traits, like the programming in Dr. Crawford, which gave him a superiority complex. Of course, what did programming matter when the main problem now was, how to survive.

"I shall continue reading in the library and spend my early mornings and late evenings in the concert hall. The piano helps me to express my emotions, to get rid of my fear and my worries. And, I promise you that I shall not do anything that could in any way jeopardize either one of our futures." I sincerely believed that I could keep my promise.

I started out with good intentions, but I was unhappy being alone. It was ok when I was immersing myself in my music. My solitude gave me the unlimited freedom to bring my pain and my happiness into my improvisations. I could let the tones flow in a powerful, bold manner by using more energy in the way I touched the keys, or letting a tone ring out, vibrate, longer to show the intensity of a feeling, happy or sad. I could let my fingers dance delicately across the keys producing soft, gentle, even playful melodies. I could just relax with a calming, pleasant, soothing romantic combination of tones and cords. It didn't matter how I combined notes and touched the keys to produce my passionate display of music. I was the master of my improvisations. No one was going to criticize my performance. I would leave, anyway, when the members of the orchestra arrived and would usually go directly to the library to continue my research.

One day I didn't go to the library. I needed to talk to someone, so I sought out Randolph. He was in the middle of an experiment when I popped into the lab. He nodded and pointed to a chair where I could sit down and watch. He looked so serious and immersed in his study that I could almost feel his concentration.

One of the androids stopped by to observe his work and asked me what I was doing there. I had no reason to believe that the unfettered liberty that Dr.

Gordon had given me to circulate in the Center could until now be contested, or otherwise, restricted, and certainly not by Randolph's android assistant.

So I introduced myself. "You may have heard of me, I am Pamela, series 13 and am part of a research project conducted by Dr. Gordon." She stood expressionless so I continued. I met," gave the identification number, "Randolph, at the vacation center. I stopped by the lab because I wanted to observe an experiment." I explained, fluffing it as much as possible. "It is important that I acquaint myself with all different types of jobs and professions so that I will be better able to give my impressions about life in general for the success of Dr. Gordon's research study involving human emotions." I thought that she would be happy with my explanation, but no.

The android picked up a phone and called central. Before I had chance to understand the consequences of her call, another android appeared to escort me to the Governor's office. The Governor and I stood looking at each other for a few minutes before the questioning started. He wasn't certain that I could see him, as I pretended to be bothered by the luminosity that would normally have surrounded him. Nonetheless, he had a kind look about him. He was tall and thin and well-proportioned physically. He was wearing a short-sleeved smock that accentuated the nice shape of his upper body. He walked slowly and laboriously, as if he were carrying a heavy burden. His eyes were slightly slanted, like Diana's eyes, perhaps because his creator was Asian. He had high cheekbones and full lips, and an unusually small nose. I had the impression that whoever built him wanted to make a handsome specimen but messed up on the special blend of facial features. I was thinking about how I might have improved upon his looks when he started to speak.

"So you are Pamela." I nodded and he continued. "What were you doing in the laboratory?"

"Just watching."

He repeated back what I said as if he didn't believe the sincerity of it, "Really, Just watching."

That made me uncomfortable so I started to explain. "In fact, I am fascinated with science, because of the small community I lived with outside the center. They often discussed experiments and I just wanted to see what took place, behind the scenes, in laboratories." I apologized for my indiscretion and promised not to disturb other people again.

He didn't answer but stared at me with such intensity that I thought perhaps he could see inside of me. I continued blinking my eyes and forcing tears to convince him that I was suffering from the strong light surrounding his body.

"I am going to make this easier for you by lifting my screen." He declared.

"I know that Dr. Gordon lets you see her. There is certainly no reason why you should not be able to see all of us. I shall tell Dr. Gordon to give you a decoder so that your vision will not be disturbed."

I thanked him with the most sincere acting I could muster and started to get up to leave. "Not just yet," He motioned me to sit down. "I want to know about your relationship with Dr. Gordon. I want the real truth about that relationship and not what you think that you should tell me. I never liked the ugly human characteristic of lying."

"Dr. Gordon is nice to me and I have learned to trust her; another human characteristic that you must be aware of." I began rather sarcastically even though I was aware of the importance of this interview. "I know that you approved her experiment with me and are interested in discovering the value of emotions and the distinction between the bad and good ones and their effect on human creativity. I feel fortunate that I was given the opportunity to be a whole person and appreciate what Dr. Gordon is doing for me, as well as what you are doing for me indirectly."

"Perfect. You said all that quite well." He replied. "Your intellectual ability, due to your genetic composition, which was something of my choosing, is quite extraordinary for humans and for that reason alone I chose music as your orientation. It was my way of controlling you. Or, perhaps I should say harnessing your potential." My mouth fell open and my eyes widened in disbelief; he picked up on my shocked expression.

"I can see the idea surprises you a bit." He forced a horrifyingly grotesque grinding sound that I assumed was an android laugh. "I am by profession a geneticist and worked in that capacity before taking over the governance of this unit. Your series was one of my last accomplishments. Dr. Gordon does not know this. She, like everyone else here, has no access to my files, which are well guarded."

He patted his chest like a gorilla after a conquest and then shrugged his shoulders in a human sort of way. I thought it must have been one of those mannerisms that his creator had passed on to him. "But all that doesn't matter, does it?" He added. His rhetorical question went unanswered and so he continued. "The Board will be meeting at the end of the week. I have refused Dr. Crawford's request that you be present. I would like to see you from time to time to talk about your descendants. For example, I am very pleased with the genetic mix between you and Peter and would very much like to follow the development of Frederic."

"I don't want anyone to touch my child!" My adamant response was so automatic that I could hardly believe my own words.

"Don't be so human with your spontaneous violent emotional reactions.

I obviously have no intentions in harming your child. I have an intellectual curiosity, that's all. If he were inside the center, I would put him on the most important scientific projects when he comes of age, which means he would be very young. You'd be proud of him. But since he lives on the outside, I want to merely observe how someone with his potential will develop in a non-creative and passive environment. Of course my hypothesis is that he will vegetate like the rest of you and never realize his own potential." He tried to smile as he reached for my hand. "We shall become good friends, just like you and Dr. Gordon; I am certain."

I wasn't sure what he meant by being friends like my friendship with Dr. Gordon and hoped he didn't know just how friendly we were. His comments reminded me that the android mentality was not easy to understand. What they promised could not be interpreted literally, because behind their words resided that android logic, that android mentality. It could be dangerous to put too much trust in them. I had to constantly remind myself that I could not, even if I wanted to, trust Dr. Gordon a hundred percent. Yes, there was something cold and calculating in their reflections, which were not outright lies, but lacked a sense of morality. Yet, even though I found their enigmatic behavior despicable; I could not live under the same paranoia I experienced with the outside community. I had to act cautiously, but I had to act. Was I right then in thinking that the Governor was going to protect me for his own interests and that, in fact, I now had two relatively strong allies in the Center? As such, I expected to have unbridled freedom. To test that theory I opened the door to find that no one was following me.

The first thing that I did to benefit from my newfound freedom was to return to Randolph's laboratory.

Chapter 29: Intrigue

There was something that Randolph and I had to resolve very soon; how to get all this vital information to John. I suggested to Randolph that we put the information inside Jonathan's clarinet.

"Listen to me," I insisted, as he turned his head to hide his laughter. "I am serious. The Governor is interested in Frederic; he said so himself. What kind of child did a scientist and a musician produce? Was he preoccupied or even obsessed by this?"

Randolph's sense of humor was refreshing and uplifting when I was feeling down, but today all of his laughter was getting on my nerves. "Can't you be serious?" I pleaded.

"Ok. I'll try." He choked out as he stifled his laugher. "But," he said in a more serious tone, "I think that shipping something outside is a risk. I don't think that Stuart is going to feel comfortable with this either." He warned. And, challenging me to change his mind, he sat straight up, unfolded his arms and stared in my eyes ready to listen, but not necessarily to agree.

I told him about the Governor and his clinical interest in my son. Randolph listened attentively. It took me a long time to convince Randolph that it might be interesting for the Governor to see Frederic's reaction to music. I based my argument on what the Governor had revealed to me, concerning my own orientation. "After all, the Governor did confide in me, explaining that he was the one who decided that I should be a musician. He might be curious about whether I might have genetically passed on my musical inspiration to my son. This could easily be observed when Frederic listens to music." Randolph's facial expressions seemed more relaxed and he signaled me with his hand to continue. "I hummed music to Frederic when I was pregnant. Mathilda told me that babies are sensitive to our voices and to our emotions when they are in the uterus." I noticed that he twisted his face in surprise. "Perhaps the Governor would let me send the clarinet to Jonathan just to see how much music inspires my son. Is it in his blood, so to speak?"

"Ok. You convinced me." He bit the inside of his lip. "Even so, how are we going to get this clarinet past the inspection crew?"

That was my only concern; it certainly was an important part of the success of the operation. I suggested that I would have to get permission to take it out of the Center. I could also be allowed a couple minutes to see my child and my Peter. Why not?

"If you think that you can get him to agree then we can put the info inside the lining of the case. I can place a reader in the clarinet base so that John can decipher the chips." He shook his head in doubt. "It is a big risk, Pamela, and if something goes wrong, we are both going to be in a great deal of trouble. It could be the end. . ."

I interrupted him. "I shall drop in to see the Governor tomorrow and see how he reacts to the idea."

"Good idea. Be careful. And, of course, Good Luck!" He smiled and gave me a friendly tap on the shoulder. "Keep me informed."

The following morning I rushed up to the Governor's office and pressured his android guard to let me see him for a couple minutes. I entered enthusiastically. He liked my idea; at least that is what I thought then. He gave me a written authorization to give to the stock room so I could get Jonathan's clarinet. The case was a lot smaller than I imagined. Randolph had micro-chipped all the information and was able to slip it into the various corners of the case and the clarinet itself. Now, I needed permission to take it out of the Center and hand it to Peter.

After receiving the clarinet, I returned to the Governor's office in the late afternoon. I had to again force my way past his android guard to get the transport document signed and stamped by the Governor. The case and content were labelled…"No inspection is required" and bore the Governor's signature. He gave me a copy of his authorization for transport of the clarinet case and contents to the outside community, which I was to present to the android supervisor in charge of approving the food boxes. He told me that the android would understand that the case and contents be placed with the food boxes that would be leaving the center over the next hour. He also signed a document giving me permission to visit my family, which he informed me had to be co-signed by Dr. Gordon. Dr. Gordon would decide on my departure date.

It all went so smoothly, perhaps too smoothly. I arrived in the kitchen as the meals were being boxed. I passed the clarinet case with its contents to the android supervisor, along with the document bearing the Governor's signature. The Governor's clearance worked like a charm. No one asked any questions. I stayed long enough to verify that the package was on the food cart and watch the deliverers move the cart out of the kitchen and into the hallway leading to the tunnel and the outside community. This just meant that

Randolph, Stuart and I had succeeded in passing on very precious information to our friends outside. We knew that one of them, John or Peter, would know exactly how to use this information.

I was so relieved and proud of myself that I had remained calm during the tense moments leading up to receiving the authorization for the safe passage of the clarinet. As everything went so fast and easy, I had extra time to kill so I opted for a few hours at the library. The librarian who always looked me up and down and then waved me into the small reading room was not there. A Dr. Miller whose appearance was shocking and funny greeted me. She noticed that I could see her. I couldn't help but stare.

She had a simply gorgeous face framed with thick, straight blond hair. Her high cheekbones led you straight to the most beautiful dark blue eyes I had ever seen. I felt as if I could drown inside of them. She had an oval face, typical of female androids, a long thin sculptured nose, and a well-shaped mouth with perfectly balanced rounded lips. But, this gorgeous, stunning head was planted on top of a crude robotic structure. Her body was comprised of a large metallic box with two long, rubbery tubes, as arms. She was moving on wheels, invisible under the weight of her metallic body. There was absolutely no coherency between the face and the body.

I was definitely in shock from her appearance, because I stared, through petrified eyes, at her for a long time; how long, I don't know. Finally, I caught a glimpse of her long metal fingers that looked more like bits of wire hanging loosely from the end of those swaying tube arms, pointing in the direction of the reading room. I was frozen in front of her, as if in a trance, and this incited her to move her arms and fingers more violently, until I eventually set off in the direction of the reading room. I was seated in front of a computer terminal when she delivered the next series of historical tapes that I ordered for today.

"I am sorry," I started because I felt the need to say something, to compensate for my reaction.

She interrupted me observing that I must be the protégé of Dr. Gordon. "My colleague told me about you. It is rare for humans to be in the library." She said in a soft, musical voice, evidently she understood that nice melodies might entice humans, before giving me a warm, friendly smile. "It will be intriguing serving you." I smiled back at her and then turned to insert the tape.

"You have never seen a primitive robot before, I would imagine?" She wanted to talk. That made me nervous. I wanted to get on with my work, my reading. I also felt suspicious of her enthusiasm and interest in me. Was she spying for somebody? So, hoping to discourage her, I simply smiled again and turned back to my tape. "You probably wonder how I ended up like this, huh?" She did not want to leave me in peace.

"I am very sorry that I was shocked by your appearance. I shouldn't have been," I went on, "because I have no real standard of reference for what constitutes a well-constructed robot or android. My astonishment was based solely on the fact that you do not look like any other android I have run into. But, that doesn't mean that you are unattractive—or strange looking…" I was embarrassed with my awkwardness. "In fact, now that I have spoken to you, I find your appearance very nice. And, of course, I have no right to ask you to explain your life or why you were constructed like this. So, if you don't mind, I'll just go on with my reading." I was hoping that she would let the subject drop, but she didn't. She apparently needed to tell her story so I sat back and let her spill it out.

Her story is sad. In listening, my impulse was to believe that she was capable of feeling, pain? She was not always a librarian, but a member of a genetic research team. She worked very closely with Dr. Gordon and the Governor on a top secret project.

As she spoke, she moved around in circles, which got larger with each turn. It looked as if she had difficulty controlling the guidance system in her heavy metallic casing and that this constant circling was not an intentional action to confuse or disturb me. Yes, I got the distinct impression that she could not stand still. The cause of it was not discernable, but I felt dizzy watching her spin around and exacerbated the turning by asking her to repeat herself over and over again. Finally, I just could not handle it any longer and reached out and placed my hands on her broad iron shoulders holding her stationery, something that she did not seem to mind and something that did not interrupt her monologue. It was, of course, tiring for me to maintain her in place.

According to her, the Governor treated Dr. Gordon and Dr. Miller as rivals, playing one against the other. She explained to me that everybody knew she was more beautiful than Dr. Gordon but that should never have been an issue between them." Interesting, I mused, "Is she telling me that they have a standard for beauty?"

"I accused Dr. Gordon once of being jealous of my beauty," Dr. Miller shook her head in disbelief and continued. "Can you imagine? We are both androids and she was giving me the impression that she was displaying human emotions." Her metal casing was starting to vibrate, but this did not discourage her from continuing. "Dr. Gordon actually told me that if she was displaying a human emotion; then so was the Governor. I realized that I was misinterpreting everything. How could any of us be displaying human emotions?"

"Oh," I mused. "She reports back to Dr. Gordon, who wants someone to follow me closely while I am in the library."

"And, then," her voice shook me out of my thoughts, "there was that terrible explosion and fire in the lab and by the time I was rescued, the only part of my android body that was still intact was my head. Of course, my memory banks and creative capacity along with all other intellectual components were undamaged. There was no android body around for me, so the committee connected my head to this primitive robotic casing." That seemed to me to be a very horrible decision!

That should not have prevented her from continuing with her research, but it was decided by the Board that she should be given new assignments. Even though she had the intellectual capacity to participate, she no longer had the agility necessary to conduct experiments. She raised her metal fingers in front of my eyes, to show me that she did not have the proper means to manipulate vials of chemicals.

"This is a very sad story; and, I am very sorry that this happened to you." I thought that was the proper thing to say. But, her answer showed me just how wrong I was.

"Sad. Interesting. But how could I be sad? I am composed of pure intellect and logic. Sad is an emotion. It means nothing to me." Her response shocked me. "I am still productive and I have a place in the community. I was not shut down, something that all of us know could happen, but prefer won't happen. Not because we would be "sad", but because we would have to recognize that we had no more utility and could bring nothing to the Center."

"So why did you tell me this story?" I was irritated with her. "Why bother to waste my time with all that if you aren't looking for compassion, consolation or something." I regretted as soon as it left my mouth, but it was too late to take it back.

"Oh, right. I told you because you are here and you seemed surprised by my appearance. I just wanted to make you feel more at ease around me."

I expected this mindless robotic answer that allowed me to open up. "As far as I am concerned," I started, "you thought it was necessary to warn me about Dr. Gordon, someone who you think has developed some human emotions, right?" She just stared and I went on with a series of hypotheses. "The birth of these human emotions started long before I was created; if I can venture a guess. And, you don't like Dr. Gordon. You don't trust Dr. Gordon. And, you are not so happy in that metallic body because you were a beautiful, seductive android before. Probably even more beautiful than she."

She stared at me for a long moment until her eyes burned bright and feverishly. Then she rolled toward me and I recoiled with fear; her hatred now radiated by red burning eyes. I kept backing off as she drew even closer. And, as if her internal circuits could not handle the variations in her thinking, she stopped dead in front of me. Her facial expression returned to that of a cold, indifferent android.

"You humans, you will never understand. We are not the same and never will be. My appearance doesn't count among us. We don't have to hide behind a visual transformer like you. We have gone beyond emotions. We are the perfection, the purity. We are the intellectuals, the superior beings. You are still children in the evolutionary scale. When will you start to realize just how dependent and useless you are?"

"Egocentric, manipulative, hypocritical machine!" You can be certain that I shall never take any interest in you again." I blew off steam in her face and then stepped back, reveling in my emotions in front of her and proud to show her.

Finally, I pushed her rather violently out of my way and sat down to work. From the corner of my eye, I could see her spinning in large circles as she tried to regain control of herself and roll her way back to the entrance desk. I ignored her even though I wanted to break out with a belly laugh. . . but common sense held my tongue.

She fumbled with the disks and then brought me a stack of ones on religion; she was aware of my obsession with it. I decided this beast of a robot wasn't going to unilaterally decide what I would read today so I threw them on the floor and stormed out of the library.

I walked slowly back to the train. My mind turned automatically to the idea of the need in believing in someone or something. Maybe we humans need to believe that we can find guidance from a higher source. Apparently, though, very few people were privileged enough to communicate with those superior beings. As I saw it only a few humans were ever glorified by followers who believed or wanted to believe that they were in direct contact with a superior being. I had read about the lives of many prophets and the beginnings of many religions. I found them all very convincing and I imagined myself having difficulty choosing the one I would follow. There was no one of them that impressed me more than the others. They all had more in common than they had differences; for instance, they all taught about love and harmony with life. There was also that intriguing idea of an afterlife only for those that behaved themselves down here. I would have liked to meet all those prophets at the same time. I was certain that they would have told me that I was right; that they were all seeking the truth of our existence and meaning of human life.

For the first time, I endeavored to find out the year and century we were living in. I had shuffled through many centuries of human existence in the library and had even seen the world before humans appeared. The last series of tapes were the 21st century. I'll have to ask Dr. Gordon whether the 21st century is the present or the distant past.

"Are you going to get into that car?" The hollow, grating voice of the station guard startled me. I was so deep in thoughts I didn't realize I was standing in front of a monorail car. I quickly apologized and jumped in. I leaned my head on the headrest and closed my eyes. I didn't want to see from the windows that empty wasteland which could only make me sad. How I missed Peter and Frederic; I longed for those moments when I was with a group of people who shared the same concerns, probably the same desires and ambitions, and certainly the same destiny. I would have to take advantage of the very brief moment I would have on the outside. I could not pack all my feelings and emotions into a couple minutes. Perhaps, Dr. Gordon would give me an early departure date as she seemed to be sensitive to my requests.

All that was flowing through my mind as I scrambled out of the car and dashed into my cubicle. The last thing that I expected was to find Dr. Gordon sitting comfortably in my chair waiting for my arrival. I stopped short.

"Good evening, Pamela. How are you doing these days?" she asked so matter of fact that I felt a bit offended. After all, she was the one that decided that we should stop seeing each other and now I guess she had, on her own, decided that the time was right to start up again.

"Actually, I would like to take a nice warm shower, if you don't mind."

"Of course. I understand." And then she added. "You know, Pamela, we androids don't have problems with odor like you humans. One could say that it is another aspect of our perfection. What do you think?"

"I don't know about that." I answered as I threw off my white linen dress and jumped into the shower. "But I do think that you are missing out on something special like the perfumed scent of a clean, warm, body to caress."

"How's that?"

"Well it feels just so soothing and relaxing to have these drops of water glide over one's naked body. It is an exotic sensation that, unfortunately, you will never have the pleasure of experiencing" I was speaking very loudly now.

She entered the bathroom and watched as I sussed up with wonderful scenting soap. At that instant I remembered what John had said "Find out where the water comes from."

"By the way, Dr. Gordon, where does this delicious water come from? We drink it and bathe in it, but I never saw a source."

"We have enormous reservoirs that are filled by underground streams. When it rains, the system captures the liquid."

"When it rains? " I had never seen rain.

"Well, we are in a dry zone, but we have access to water. Let's talk about something else," she suggested.

I wasn't ready to change the subject and mentioned Jason and his story about a tropical forest. "You already told me about this demented man. I don't see why this interests you, but then I do like your curiosity. In brief, the planet is in a transitional phase and I am not aware of all the new zones."

Now, I could not let go. "Transitional stage. Wow, so we are in what century?"

"Pamela, I came to see you for a very important reason. You are now wasting my time."

"Ok, but can you just humor me for a bit, Dr. Gordon. I realized today that human history stopped in the 21st century. So I just wondered if we were still in that century; and, if not, what happened to all the records after that date?"

"Now I have had enough." Her voice took on that hollow android ring, as she blurted out her answer, or the truth. "You foolish human. Of course your history stopped centuries ago; later though than the 21st century. Your race is ancient history. It doesn't matter what century we are in today. Android history started when yours ended and our history will continue when you no longer exist."

"When we no longer exist? Are you telling me that we will all be terminated?"

"No." She was back to her seductive voice. "I didn't mean what I said. And, Pamela, you must stop looking for answers to questions that are completely irrelevant. I repeat, your species was very important up until the end of the 21st century. They were driven by emotions and they self-destructed, if you like. We were there and gave a sense back to your species existence. That is it; finished, nothing else to say."

I knew that I was not going to get any more information out of Dr. Gordon that evening and decided to let the subject drop. Nonetheless, I registered her reference to emotions and self-destruction for a future discussion. "So, then why are you here?" I asked as I stepped out of the shower. I grabbed my towel and started to dry off, pretending that I was equally bored with the course of our previous discussion and ready for something else.

She came up behind me and pulled me close to her. "It has been too long since we were together;" she whispered in my ear. "I missed you. I need you." She continued as she turned me in her direction. Her lips were warm and inviting. Even if I wanted to resist--which I am not sure I did--I could not.

Like always making love with her was intensely fulfilling, almost too much. Humans together could not generate that kind of physical energy and physical pleasure. But even so, I still missed Peter. I loved being close to him. Just thinking about being wrapped up in his arms brought a big smile to my mouth. I liked the way he smelled; his warmth, his taste; the sound of his heart beating and racing as we climaxed together. I looked over at Dr. Gordon. I pushed her aside, rather abruptly, as I covered myself with my robe. Thinking about Peter made me rather ashamed of what had just happened.

"Right. We must get on with the real purpose of my visit."

"Ok", I'm ready."

"Dr. Crawford has created certain problems for me. He managed to convince the Board that there might be a problem with my programming because I am under your influence."

"That is ridiculous", I shouted. "If anyone is under the influence of anyone, it is I."

"Perhaps. But I have no choice now but to shut down and then await the order to reactivate." She stopped and sat back in her chair in a very relaxed, slumping human kind of way. She stayed frozen in that position for a good five minutes before telling me how worried she was about going through this. "The procedure is not dangerous and all androids are expected to go through this at least once a year." Now, she fidgeted in her chair. "I had my annual visit, four months ago. Everything was fine. But, now, Dr. Crawford and other members of the Board along with the android engineer will be present. This is unusual. In all other cases, the engineer is the only one present and will give the order to reactivate the circuitry. This order has to be given within 30 minutes of the shutdown in order to allow for self-reactivation. I'm afraid that the order to reactivate will be denied by Dr. Crawford and that the others will not want to cross his authority." I unbelievably thought I heard a slight trembling trail away with her voice.

"Why would Dr. Crawford refuse to give the order?" I asked even though I suspected what the response would be.

"Even though he has opposed all my scientific projects until now, my study of human emotions has been his nemesis. All of his efforts to thwart my study have come up empty. And, to his utter dissatisfaction, the board has repeatedly refused to take his arguments seriously. I believe that he is convinced that the only way to stop my project is to shut me down, for good!"

"And the board agreed to the shutdown procedure. That was an important victory for him." I ventured.

"No, Pamela. They didn't accept his proposal to ruin me, but to prove to him that nothing was interfering with my programming. In effect, I should be happy that the members have confidence in me." She hesitated for a second. Her eyes were so focused on me that I felt I was being pulled into a magnetic field. I was happy when she spoke again. "I need you to do me a favor. I want you to be present. You watch the clock. If the time remaining falls below 3 minutes, you must give the order. It is simple. You say, "Dr. Gordon, you may now reactivate." Can you do this for me?"

"Yes, but will Dr. Crawford let me assist?"

"He can't refuse my request. I shall explain to everyone that you are there to see with your own eyes that I am an android. To see that you have been communicating with a machine and that this machine is interested in understanding human emotions. I will explain that this reality will assure even stronger emotions on your part, that I've failed to trigger, —such as disgust, hatred and denial, even vengeance. But, in any case, you will have reactions that you have not had to date. And, I shall convince them that this will help me to gain valuable time and to deliver results much sooner."

I didn't have a choice. If she were shut down, I'd lose my protector and would be vulnerable and probably immediately terminated, thanks to my nemesis, Dr. Crawford. She didn't share concerns for my own safety and I wasn't even sure she had considered the risks to me. She was acting quite selfishly and egocentrically for a machine, like she was as desperate for survival as humans are. Now, I understood why Dr. Crawford was getting so worried. He could see even better than I could that Dr. Gordon was crossing over. I still couldn't see, however, what the consequences of that passage from one world to the other would be. What I did sense was that her self-interest gave me an opportunity to negotiate.

"No problem. I shall be there. Just tell me when and where."

"Tomorrow morning in the Lab. At 9 am sharp. Please arrive 15 minutes early."

"Ok. I was thinking that perhaps you could just finish the paper work so that I can spend a few days on the outside." She nodded. "You know that the Governor gave me clearance. I just need you to set the dates and co-sign the document."

"You are taking advantage of me, Pamela." She tapped her fingers on the arm of the chair. "You know that I think that you should wait a while yet. But, ok. It's a deal. You bring me the dates and I shall approve them when I wake up." She bent over to plant a kiss on the top of my head. "See you tomorrow."

I was there as arranged at 8:45. Dr. Crawford was already seated and speaking to the engineer and another board member when I walked into the Lab. Dr. Gordon had not yet arrived.

"What are you doing here?" He asked with that hollow, piercing android voice.

"I was invited by Dr. Gordon. She will explain all that to you when she gets here;" I said casually as I took a seat.

"Impertinence, utter impertinence and disrespect for administrative procedures. That Dr. Gordon is going too far." He said it loud enough that his colleagues could hear.

Dr. Gordon rushed in before anyone could reply. She was enthusiastic. Her tunnel voice was more android than ever, even though she tried to cater to me. She greeted everyone and then explained why I was present. Dr. Crawford emitted a strange sound of disapproval but his colleagues waved their hands rejecting his pleas. She went to the examining booth and the engineer ordered her to shut down.

It is true that this had an effect on me, but not in the way she had expected. I was even more disgusted and embarrassed with myself for having had intimate sex with what looked to be a rubber doll. This made it difficult for me to concentrate on what was happening. In fact, 10 minutes had already passed before I truly realized that Dr. Gordon's circuitry was visible and that the engineer was testing her programming.

At this point, Dr. Crawford suggested that I leave if I found the situation unbearable. Maybe he suspected the real reason for my presence and was trying to get rid of me. The truth was I did not just want to leave, but to escape from the Center again. But, I had made a promise that was in my interest to keep and the mere fact that Dr. Crawford was making the suggestion was enough to raise the red flag to keep me in my seat.

I just shook my head and straightened myself up in my chair to show him that I was perfectly alright.

I paid close attention to the clock. The engineer examined the circuitry by passing a small scanning machine inside Dr. Gordon, and validated her programming. Five minutes were remaining on the clock when he closed her back up. Nobody moved. The next two minutes ticked by and Dr. Crawford got up to leave. "Don't bother to do anything now," he said. "Leave her like that until I come back." Was that an order?

My heart started beating rapidly and my hands were wet with perspiration. I was shaking with a mixture of trepidation, concern for this awesome rubber doll, and for my survival as well as that of the community. Dr. Crawford had moved to the door and had reached to open it when I dashed up to the examination chair. I stared in Dr. Gordon's face and opened my mouth to speak and then hesitated. I saw Dr. Crawford freeze in his tracks and bend his head towards me, which made me nervous and I momentarily forgot what I was supposed to say. Only one minute was left and I had to do something. If I said the wrong thing, I was the only one who would suffer. Dr. Gordon, you may now--You may now--why hadn't I paid more attention. What was that word---I could see that Dr. Crawford started to move in my direction. He had a crooked smile stretching his weird little face. My blood curdled at the same time, as the order came to me, "Dr. Gordon, you may now reactivate!" I screamed. I repeated the command over and over again just to be sure, but her reactivation was instantaneous and she had responded to my first command. She was back, holding my face between her hands and reassuring me that I had done the right thing.

Dr. Crawford hadn't budged; even the distorted smile was still smashed into his flat face. Dr. Gordon looked at him and nodded. The engineer assured her that all was well, but that Dr. Crawford had asked them to hold off the command until his return. Dr. Crawford, being their superior, they had no choice but to obey. Dr. Gordon took my hand and led me past Dr. Crawford and out of the room.

"Thank you, Pamela. I knew that I could count on you. Now, when would you like to leave?"

"As soon as possible." I was still trembling a bit. I didn't know for how long Dr. Gordon could continue to protect me.

"Is tomorrow too soon?"

Tomorrow could never be too soon I thought to myself as I nodded with satisfaction. My thoughts immediately shifted to how good it would feel to be with Peter and Frederic again after what seemed light years.

"I'll stop by to see you at the end of the day," I called out to her as she turned down the corridor leading to her office. I am not certain that she heard me. After what she just experienced, I imagined that she must have been a bit preoccupied with her new strategy to up seat Dr. Crawford; at least I would have been focused on that.

Light-hearted and beaming with happiness, I hurried to see Randolph. As I sped to his side, lusty ideas invaded my thinking; hurried thoughts of his holding me in his arms warmed my loins as I justified them by declaring under my breath what a waste of a beautiful hunk, taking those disgusting sexual inhibitors. I diverted my lascivious thinking to focus on other priorities rather than a complicated future involving more than one man and several children.

His personal android supervisor was present, monitoring his progress. She moved closer to Randolph when I entered the lab to send me the usual message that she did not appreciate my visits, which, as I understood, she saw as a waste of his precious time.

"How are you both doing?" Unfettered enthusiasm bubbled over as I spoke which Randolph immediately detected, making the corners of his mouth curve slightly upwards. He sensed I had something important to tell him and nodded.

"I am in the middle of a very complicated procedure, Pamela. So, I can't just sit around and gossip with you right now." He winked a couple times to let me know that he was just covering himself. "How about lunch in 30 minutes? I could meet you just outside of my lab and we could walk over together if that's ok?"

"Sounds Good." I had picked up some of the strange expressions from the 20th century over the last couple weeks. I liked the easy language of that period. What I read in the earlier centuries seemed to be a much more complicated, sometimes arduous, English. They also seemed to speak in ambiguities and addressed each other in a reserved and hypocritical way. They played a lot of word games at that time, but I preferred to be direct, "I have a few things to do right now, so I'll be back."

I went directly to see the Governor. He was already aware of my departure being scheduled for the next day. Apparently, Dr. Gordon contacted him and explained-complained-about the morning events. I was in the middle of thanking him for his original authorization when he changed the subject.

"What do you think Dr. Crawford wanted to do? Or, better yet, who did he want you to see?"

"I haven't been following the latest events in the on-going conflict between Dr. Gordon and Dr. Crawford. Anyway, Dr. Gordon decided that I should hang out with humans and try to find a kind of balance between my real and natural environment." I couldn't believe I was using 20th century words like "hang out" with the Governor, who in spite of this visibly slang expression, seemed to understand.

Even though Dr. Gordon had not exactly suggested this, it seemed appropriate and maybe even plausible at the time. But, his constant fidgeting and stares like he was closely analyzing me told me he was not convinced. So I started with the basic point by asking him if he knew that I was invited. He shook his head affirmatively.

"Ok, Governor, I didn't take Dr. Gordon that seriously last night when she asked me to be here for her deactivation today. And, for that reason, even though I heard her give me the reactivation order, I wasn't certain that I registered it." I sighed. "I don't like Dr. Crawford, even though he has always played everything by the books, at least with me. And, in spite of his threats, he did not impress me as the kind of person, android, who would take such a controversial position. I just couldn't imagine his putting Dr. Gordon out of commission."

He said nothing so I continued. "I was uncomfortable just being in the room and never imagined that my services would be necessary."

"What made you change your mind then?"

"Dr. Gordon had been very clear about the fact that I should reactivate her if no one did within the last 2 to 3 minutes. It was at that point that Dr. Crawford decided to leave the room and informed the others to await his return before taking any action. That triggered something inside of me, fear perhaps. I knew what I had to do and that I had act rapidly."

"How did Dr. Crawford react?"

I explained to him that Dr. Crawford seemed very pleased that I was struggling to remember the command and that he liked my agitated state; he was even. . . smiling.

"The expression that I read on his face reminded me of the urgency of what I was supposed to do and I gave the command. I then panicked and gave it over and over again. I didn't realize that Dr. Gordon had already reactivated."

"And the others?"

"They were just following orders. I didn't understand why they didn't question Dr. Crawford, though." And then I added, "'They didn't even seem to be disturbed. When I think about it maybe they had all colluded before."

"So, you would agree that Dr. Gordon would not have been reactivated in time if you hadn't been there."

"No question about that."

"Ok. Now let me ask you how you felt when she shut down."

"I knew why it was important to Dr. Gordon that I be present. She did not like the fact that her deactivation was being carried out in front of board members and not in private. She also indicated that she did not have confidence in Dr. Crawford to approve her reactivation. Thus, I was present to make certain that she would be reactivated. I have to admit, though, that I felt very uncomfortable with this assignment and worried about my own safety." His eyes were practically popping out of their sockets, so I continued. "However, while she was deactivated, I with great difficulty ruminated over the reality of her existence. Even though she had become a vital part of my life, my mind was telling me that humans must feel more comfortable with biological life forms, like other mammals." I hesitated. He was waiting with bated breath for the rest. But, should I tell him how I honestly felt. I decided to take the risk. "Quite frankly, during the first ten minutes of her deactivation, my mind was assailed by her being a machine with a human exterior, distorting that vision. Because of my promise to help her that repeated over and over again in my mind, I finally reacted and gave the command to reactivate her. I always knew that she was a machine, but I gave her a real body and soul. Maybe that is why it was so difficult for me."

"A soul? Where did you get that from?"

"I don't know; but it could be because I have read a bit about religion. I like the idea of transcendental passage. . ."

The Governor obviously fascinated, interrupted me. "Really. And, we androids don't have souls then?"

That struck me as so funny that I started to laugh until he cleared his throat and put an end to it. "I am waiting for an answer?"

That brought me back to reality, "Of course you don't. But you don't need a soul. You can live on forever. We need a soul to explain that we never terminate, or end, our existence. It gives us the feeling that we can exist in another form in perpetuity after our physical death. It is comforting; and, to a certain extent, it explains what happens to our energy and intellect, that they don't perish with our bodies."

"Oh! Oh!" He shook his head in regret. "No matter what period you live in, when your emotional patterns are assembled as a whole, you start to believe in something. The vast majority of you believed in a superior being; others believed in not believing. Everything revolved around the existence or nonexistence of a God. It makes me sad to think that you have fallen into that dark pit of controversy about such an empty thing."

I was insulted by his pretentious remark. But then after all he was an android without feelings.

I cleared my throat and said as emotionlessly as possible, "I came to see you to thank you for the general authorization to leave the Center for a week or so. Dr. Gordon has approved my departure date. I shall be leaving tomorrow morning."

"Yes. Yes. There is no problem. You must be excited about seeing your son?

"Very much so. I have been gone for a long time. He must have changed a great deal."

"Well, Pamela, I have so much paper work to take care of." He looked down at his crowded desktop and called out. "Enjoy your vacation."

The thirty minutes had run out and I found Randolph waiting for me outside his lab. We drifted off into a corner of the corridor that was always empty. Randolph said that there were no visual or listening devices in place and that I could speak freely. I told him about the morning and then my interview with the Governor. He laughed about all of it, even went so far as to call it a big farce. He seemed to think that it was all staged just to see if I felt anything for Dr. Gordon. My sense of fidelity and honor were in question and I had responded with a conditioned reflex, just like Pavlov's dog; an experiment that he had to explain to me.

"Who cares, Randolph?" I did in a way, but didn't want him to know. If it was just part of an experiment, I had fallen for the whole thing. But, then Randolph wasn't there and he didn't know Dr. Crawford like I did. And, as I am an experiment for the center, they will have something to study while I am on the outside.

"I wondered if there was anything that you would like me to tell John." I said in a melancholy tone. My humiliation saddened me.

He didn't react to the sadness in my voice but went straight to the point. "Yes, Stuart and I have broken the code for the land transport terminal. I shall give that to you. But, you should tell John that the base is under constant surveillance and that it would appear that each vehicle has its own activating code. This complicates things a bit, but I think that we shall be able to give him more details long before he is able to access the base."

"That should make him happy." I wondered how much progress the group had made with the tunneling.

"Randolph, I learned something recently about Stuart that surprised me."

"Oh—and what might that be?"

"He and Diana and a few others in this center" before I could say more, he spread his hand over my mouth. I didn't understand; if it was a secure area why did he do that. Maybe he lied.

He whispered in my ear, "It is safe here, but this subject is very top-secret." He opened one of the doors and we found ourselves in a kind of closet. "We should be more careful. Already I mentioned the code. Stupid! Sometimes I feel too free. "He was angry with himself. I waited until he calmed down and was ready to continue. "I know all about it, but he and Diana are all that is left of that special unit. When Diana got out of hand, they terminated the others." He saw in my eyes that I wanted to know more. "You are not going to like what I have to say, so don't tell anyone, especially Diana." I nodded. "Stuart was interviewed twice by Crawford. He told me that he fooled the old bastard, as he put it, but that he had to prove his loyalty. They sent him out to get the other three. He spoke to me and we both agreed that he had no choice. We needed him on the inside and the others were still under the programming. He brought them in to be terminated."

"That is horrible, cruel, revolting! Inexcusable!" I screamed in Randolph's face. I was disgusted that this Stuart could act so cold-bloodedly. He was no better than the emotionless androids!

Randolph was quick to defend Stuart's action and their mutual decision to put an end to the others. "He had no choice." He argued vehemently. "Stop and think, Pamela. If he hadn't done that we would have lost him as well. He and Diana work well together. They can lead an attack. It was a judgment call. The three others were definitely acting under orders from the androids; they were still programmed. They were more our enemies than our allies, or potential fighting force for our unit. He made the right choice. I don't see the horror." His voice sounded cold, but calm, in spite of the fact that he was clearly upset with me; anger spread over his tight face. There was tension in his lower lips and his lowered eyebrows hovered over his tense, straightened eyelids. Undoubtedly, he disapproved of what I said. I had never seen him like that before and stood speechless. "You too should be careful, Pamela. You know that you are under observation." And then, as if nothing had happened, he took me in his arms and surprised me by planting a friendly kiss on my forehead. I pushed him away and suggested that we get on with constructive business. We slithered out of the closet.

When we reached the end of the corridor, he grabbed my arm and said. "There is something else that I want to tell you. Your guardian angel, Dr. Gordon, knows that I bypassed my program. She confronted me with that just after you left."

"Are you going to have problems, Randolph? If so you must tell me because the Governor has a special interest in me; I could probably convince him to let you move outside the center."

"Your Dr. Gordon is quite pleased by the news." It was evident that he was trying to recall the essence of their conversation. "She promised not to reveal this to anyone. But----well, how much can one trust an android?"

"No, you can't trust her." Her interest in Randolph was certainly part of her new, warped strategy to study me. That could only spell danger for Randolph. "I recommend, Randolph that you leave with me."

"I can't. I need to finish my project. The results will be very helpful for us. I just can't walk away now. I shall have to take the risk." He stopped and rubbed his face vigorously. "I have to take the risk. If I move out now, we, the group, stand to lose too much. And believe me about this, my android assistant asked me to take her outside with me."

"What? Why would we want an android spy living amongst us?"

We rushed back down the same corridor and returned to the safety of the closet.

"That was exactly my initial reaction. And then she started to talk about a change in policy. She mentioned that there were androids amongst us who wanted things to return to another time. That they were ready to help us if ever we were able to revolt."

"Revolt? Randolph, be serious." What he told me sounded ludicrous. "We are in such a pitiful situation. Our pathetic community has been wasting away on the outside. We spent too much time learning how to submissively live together in a community. We are only now getting the energy and enthusiasm to train and design a strategy to fight. The idea of joining forces with a small android group, claiming to have a desire to reinstate humans to their previous time of glory-that is if it ever existed-is just impossible right now. Our best allies are Dr. Gordon and her team, along with the Governor. We don't need to associate with a bunch of loser androids."

"Just one minute, Pamela. My android is not a loser. She is a vital part of the scientific unit and has worked on major projects. No the danger is more in giving her the idea we're preparing to revolt, to take over. I have already told her that she is imagining things when she suggests that there are humans organizing a revolt. I even mentioned that her suggesting that any of us humans plan a revolt and join forces with her android allies would be considered treason, if the androids in control got wind of that." He gave me a sweet reassuring smile. "Maybe I can play the androids from another angle. For example, I can use her to learn more about how the center is equipped in the event of a revolt and how to penetrate the land vehicle base. But, then I have to be very careful. These androids are not used to curious humans and even if they dream of change, they're not going to want to share authority with humans and certainly not surrender authority to us. Come on!"

"Your lunch hour is running out. You don't want her to get suspicious. But, Randolph, don't let her gain your confidence. You will need to do a thorough background search of her first. And, even if she doesn't like certain people in authority, you don't know with whom she is associated. Be careful." Now there were so many reasons why I was worried about leaving him alone.

"No problem there. I already told her that I liked my life at the center and didn't want to become a full-fledged human, like you are. I also said I enjoyed working with her and appreciated her ideas and encouragement and I made it clear that the last thing that interested me was changing my comfortable situation." He laughed heartily. "You know, I told her that I wasn't the kind of human who would take those kinds of risks. I was happy just living out my lifetime in a no stress environment. She smirked like she expected a human to think that way and then seemed a bit disappointed, but let it drop."

"Ok, well you take care of yourself and Stuart. I shall bring John up-do-date on everything. One last thought, before joining a revolution, you might consider joining the human race and ask her to bring you untainted food!" I had to wink.

We smiled at each other when we reached the end of the corridor and parted company. I had one more stop--Dr. Gordon. Should I just ask her straight out if all this was planned?

She was sitting comfortably behind her desk, the door ajar. She seemed happy to see me and thanked me again for giving her the command. She carefully avoided my emotions by not asking me how I felt when she shutdown. But there was something different about her. Maybe the way she didn't act, as opposed to how she was acting. She had such an officious stand about her.

Maybe the shutdown had erased some of her memory. I sat observing her, trying to relive the scene. I tried to recall whether the engineer had taken something out of her or had he added something. By now, she should be approaching me and running her fingers up and down my spine.

I sat there for 20 minutes watching her work before she turned to me and asked me if I was happy to leave the Center for a week. She even asked me if I was scared to confront the group after all this time. I thought that she was joking so I laughed and said, "No." She scribbled something down in her notebook.

Finally I got up to leave. That was when she moved towards the door and clicked it shut. She put her finger to her mouth to indicate that I should say nothing. She took out a piece of paper and wrote SYL at YP (her code for see you later at your place). I looked at her and she said, "Goodbye, Pamela, have a nice vacation."

I was tired and didn't need any more news of any kind. I realized though that she was telling me that she would see me at my place. I didn't want that. I could never imagine myself now wrapping legs around this rubber doll. But I couldn't find the words to tell her that.

Well, I arrived and looked around the cubicle. I didn't have to pack. But, I did want to take my sweet smelling soap, perfume and shampoo. I was feeling nostalgic about returning to the outside and that brought to mind a conversation I had in passing with Dr. Gordon. In fact, I think it took place the evening that she caught me in the shower and I was bragging about the keen human sense of smell. My remark provoked an unexpected reaction from Dr. Gordon.

I sat back on my kitchen chair trying to recall all the details. Although the conversation was vague, I remembered the essence of it. She told me that the androids have a more developed olfactory sense than humans and are offended by the natural body odor of humans. She even mentioned that humans stink. Daily hygiene, as she called it, is the only way to deal with this offensive body odor; the reason why we are expected to take daily showers and brush our teeth at least three times a day. Of course, as she put it, the androids have no odor whatsoever, another reason why they are superior to humans.

She explained to me that the use of perfumes and sweet smelling soaps was a human invention, as humans were also offended by unpleasant natural body odor; which was more or less dramatic depending upon the period of human history. The androids adapt the perfume and soaps to each individual, just like they do the food and the sexual inhibitors. General hygiene is accorded to the outside community, because humans are used to it and the androids feel obliged to take care them; at least to keep them clean and smelling good. The beauty products that we use on our bodies are chosen to enhance individual organisms but the perfume odor is lighter, less heavy smelling; adapted to the human olfactory sense. Apparently the products we use in the center are fabricated to appease the androids' sense of smell.

I shook that horror story off, but did stuff my heavy scented beauty products into a small sack. My daydreaming was over ---time was passing quickly, so I went to shower and change, and when I was finished my meal was on the table. I ate without much interest even though I was hungry; this was my first meal of the day. And, then Dr. Gordon appeared out of nowhere.

"Sorry, Pamela. I have to be very careful for the moment. I don't know who I can trust, apart from the Governor and a few members of my team. If I didn't know better, I would say that I am feeling anxious and don't trust anyone; remember you explained that feeling to me awhile back." Dr. Gordon mumbled.

I decided to be direct, "Well, I feel about the same way. Although I would say that I don't think that I can trust anyone, not even you."

"That is normal, Pamela. Today was a very special day. I hope that you were not traumatized by it all."

"I can never look at you the same way." I said in a low voice, showing regret. That seemed to hurt her, but she nodded with understanding. "I noticed that everything went so well, even the timing was perfect. I have the distinct impression that I was part of a comedy routine; that everyone but me had a script. In fact, I was the only one who was not acting." I said emphatically. She sat silently so I went further to provoke a reaction. "What a farce! I'm embarrassed more than traumatized." Anger spilled uncontrollably.

She took her time to reply, but when she did, she appeared very sincere. She denied any complicity in the event and told me that she owed me her existence and that she would never forget that. She talked about the Crawford crowd as hypocrites who wanted to take over the direction of the center.

"Pamela, these are difficult times for us androids. We have been following a pre-determined course of action for a very long time only to finally realize that we may not be able to achieve our initial objectives. Everything was based upon human participation and that isn't happening." She rubbed her beautiful hands in a suggestive way and then sighed deeply as if she sincerely needed to take in a large dose of oxygen. "Your future like ours is in jeopardy. You will be called upon to choose your camp. Make the right choice for you. Don't let your emotions decide for you. I am what I am; an android that would like to better understand humans. I am an android who appreciates the complexity of human personalities. Nonetheless, I am not naive enough

221

to believe that humans should be allowed to develop their own emotional configuration to its maximum."

"Dr. Gordon, you are scaring me." I replied in disgust. "I had enough emotional shock for the day and I don't want to have to make any major decision now or in the near future. So please, if you came here to make me regret who and what I am and wish that I were not returning to my own community, then please just leave. I don't need to worry…"

She interrupted briskly, "You don't have a choice, Pamela. I, of course, wish you a nice vacation, but you cannot escape your destiny. You are my experiment and will be until the end. So, as I said, think before acting." She needed a few minutes to collect herself. "I shall not approach you sexually again. All of that was valuable for my study. That helped me to better understand the basic instinct of your species. But, you should know, that I am there if you need consolation. I shall not reject you, as you have me. We are different, very different."

"Wow!" I was completely shocked by her remark. I felt like she had smacked me in the face. "Do you realize what you just said to me?"

She looked me straight in the eyes and said. "No, I have no idea why you are reacting like this, but then it is very interesting for me to observe."

"Sex with me was for your experiment, is that it?" I asked showing my anger.

"Yes, and why would it have been for any other reason?" She asked complacently; completely oblivious to my feelings.

"Don't you remember telling me over and over again, I love you, Pamela?" I asked furious with what I now realized was manipulation.

"Oh! That. You didn't believe it, did you? How can I experience love?" She sat so erect in the chair with her hands folded on the table in front of her.

I started to laugh-at her, at myself. How much more hypocritical can someone be? I mused. But, when I answered, I took a neutral, disinterested tone, "You, are absolutely right, Dr. Gordon. How could a machine experience love? I knew that as much as you knew that I did not love you. So we were equal partners." I was now aware of something else, we were rivals, of sorts.

She stood up and brushed herself off as if she had picked up some invisible residue of my existence which would be better wafted away. "I am glad that we understand each other so well. Again, have a nice vacation. We shall have so much to talk about when you return. And, my dear Pamela, remember that I shall always be there for you."

I felt like an enormous weight had been lifted from me when she left. I just sat there staring into space and wondering why she decided to unload all of her problems on me. What did I care if she didn't want sex any more, as that was a relief for me; but what bothered me is the way she admitted that she never loved me. I was disgusted that I had given thought to my feelings for her in face of her declarations of love. I had feelings for her, nonetheless. She was more than a friend; she could have been a sister, or my aunt, or my mother. What a thought! But, I might have reacted too strongly and too quickly to what she said; she may have responded defensively. And, she did say that she would never reject me which might be as close to admitting love as her android mentality can reach.

Sadly, she has no one else. I am so lucky to have Peter and Frederic. That thought brought a big, wide smile to my face.

What a strange conversation; I was replaying another part of the scene in my mind. Why should I be choosing a camp? If the choice was Gordon or Crawford, there was no doubt in my mind where I would be aligning myself. But, what if Randolph's android had something better to offer. Ridiculous! I vitally needed to get some sleep, so I stood up to stretch a bit before going to bed when Randolph entered abruptly.

"Sorry, Pamela. I know that it is risky for me to be here but I had to give you the copy of the code." He handed me a piece of paper. "Keep this on you. I don't think that you will be searched when you leave. These androids think that they are too clever to be outwitted by us. But, don't lose it. If they get their hands on it, we're through."

"Thank you, Randolph. I shall hide it on my person and deliver it to John. I think that he is going to be surprised and pleased." I said as I smiled at him.

"I haven't eaten anything in 5 days, Pamela." That remark made him start to laugh.

"Are you insinuating something?" I felt a bit nervous now. Of course I had been teasing him about all this, but I wasn't expecting him to do anything so radical.

"I am embarrassed now." He must have noticed my wide-eyed startled expression.

"Forgive me for being so foolish. Look I shall just leave and start eating tomorrow. And, everything will go back to normal. I don't know what got in to me, what I was thinking about when I decided to starve myself." He was rambling incoherently. "But, you know that you are fabulous looking--very sensual and sexy. I didn't need to go on a hunger strike to see that. But, I suppose that I took your teasing remarks more seriously." He stuttered a bit between his laughter, as he continued. "I, I'm not saying all this very well. I just thought that perhaps it wouldn't be so horrible for us to enjoy each other from time to time. To have some fun, if that makes sense."

"Oh, Randolph, I don't think that I can deal with this right now." I saw his face go white. "I have had my share of problems and complications. I had a visit from Dr. Gordon, just before you arrived. Can we just take this up another time?"

"I didn't know that you would be leaving the center for a week before this morning. You can imagine how that shocked me. But...where is the harm in getting closer. You can still love Peter and cherish Frederic."

He was very close to me now and I could feel his arms move around me drawing me up against him. I wanted to resist, but I worried about how he would deal with rejection, after all I was more or less responsible for his taking that dangerous step forward--not eating. And, I needed his friendship. I knew that I could push him away, but I didn't want to hurt his feelings. I wanted to do or say something clever; but I did not know what. I found myself in a very awkward situation, where I was not experienced enough in life to know how to respond properly. How could I discourage him and flatter him at the same time? All of this was running through my mind when I heard him apologizing to me for his need to explore a world of sensations that he had not yet discovered.

"If tomorrow I am terminated, I want to experience that sexual pleasure and intimacy reserved to us humans." He pleaded. "And, you are my only hope. I am desperate; you'll be leaving tomorrow. One week is a long time for me now that Dr. Gordon is on my back."

Before I realized what was happening he was lifting me up in the air and placing me lightly, delicately on the bed. I thought that men would instinctively know how to excite a woman and that there was nothing to teach them. But, it was not the case. I was the experienced one, and I guided him as he struggled to understand what was happening to him and, to perhaps, give me pleasure.

He was still apologizing to me when he finally climaxed and collapsed on top of me; I could hardly breathe under his weight, but knew better than to push him aside. I caressed him gently and eased him off of me.

"I was no good, Pamela. I know it." He sounded disappointed in himself and embarrassed.

"Will you please stop apologizing, Randolph?" I was searching for the right way to console and encourage him. "The first time is like taking your first step or saying your first word. There is no energy lost in simply reaching the objective. And, a first time with someone you desire and want to please, no matter how experienced you are, is never perfect; too much energy is wasted on trying to please the other rather than trying to participate and reach a moment of sublime pleasure together." I was talking very softly. He was on his side, bracing himself with his elbow, looking down at me. "But, Randolph, you were not that bad at all." He laughed amusedly.

"Thank you for understanding. It was tonight or never for me, because I absolutely need to eat." This apology was so scientific and clinical. His innocence and uninhibited honesty made me laugh. He looked more relaxed with my laughter; I even saw a smile replacing his pouting mouth. "I am so sorry that I pushed myself on you. " Again, the truth, because he gave me no choice, but his confession made me laugh even more. "Listen to me, Pamela; please be serious. I felt obsessed with the need to know what I was missing, if I was missing anything." After which he joined me in laughter.

"And, what did you discover?" I was tired and confused with everything. I thought about how frightened I was when I first made love. Mathieu was gentle and kind. He made me feel beautiful and special. He even made me believe that I was exciting and fulfilling. And, then he went back to Isabelle and never came near me again. I longed for sex. Was that why everything seemed so perfect with Peter? Randolph was very attractive and I liked how he held and supported me throughout. I also liked his tenderness. I sensed something different in Randolph, than in Peter. Peter is a serious and committed person; Randolph is playful—fun loving—logically, he will probably be insincere in relationships. He could be the male version of Mathilda in a certain sense.

"I discovered that I like you more than I realized." He hesitated and then looked so serious. "I've always enjoyed seeing you, but wondered how much I could trust you. Strangely enough, now, after making a bit of a fool out of myself, fumbling through making love, I realize that you are a source of strength for me. I believe that you have given me the courage since the beginning to commit myself to our cause. I never took so much initiative and searched for so many solutions as I have since I ran into you. Maybe that is why I wanted to know more about men and women. Maybe that is why I felt so compelled to show you that I could cross back into our world full of many emotions and desires."

"You did that for me?" Surprising, he was able to express his attachment to me quite well. Or, he was also a convincing actor.

"Yes and No. I did it because of you---because you encouraged me. But, I did it for me, to show myself that I was not afraid to face an emotional commitment. I think that it is what I want to say. Making love, being intimate with someone else--another or the same sex, as one prefers---opens up a new world of feelings. I know that I shall know how it feels to be jealous, sad, rejected. But, I am ready to face that because I want to discover everything that made humans so different from the androids. It will explain to me why they hate us so much."

I liked his words. His words made it easier for me to believe that our single encounter would be our only one and it relieved my feeling of guilt. I would be seeing Peter tomorrow and I didn't want to feel guilty. Peter's arms were waiting to hold me. I knew he was faithful to me, to us and I felt secure in his love. But here I was, yearning to touch another man. If tonight was his last night, I owed him a second chance. I moved closer to Randolph and pulled his arms around me. I kissed him gently on his lips.

"I like slow sex," I whispered in his ear.

He gave me one of his sly, sexy smiles. "You mean like this?" He took his time. His kisses intensified and he let his hands move more confidently over my body in a sensual, rhythmic style, as he sought to give me pleasure and invite me to join in and encourage him. He held me gently as we changed into different erotic positions, as he searched for new sensations. We were breathing in unison and our moves were slow and stimulating. The moment lasted much longer, and, this time he was not the only one to experience heightened carnal pleasure.

Randolph collapsed next to me and, with a happy expression on his face, fell sound asleep. I guessed that starvation plus vibrant sex had drained him of his energy. I watched him sleep for quite a while before anxiety overcame me; he had to leave before the androids came to escort me to the outside. I had no idea what time it was, but I knew that I had to wake him up.

"You'll have to leave Randolph." I said several times, before his eyes opened. He was a bit groggy. "Your partner must be worried or confused. I hope that she hasn't reported your absence."

"No." He started to move. "She wouldn't do that. Often times I stay all night in the lab, so she's used to it and won't be worried. But, it is late and I have to sneak past the security up to my lab. I don't want you to have any problems."

"It is possible that the androids are watching my room. I hope not. Anyway, Dr. Gordon would not want anyone to have witnessed her exploits with me, so I assume that she did not authorize any video-surveillance. At least, I hope not." I bit down on my lower lip; I wasn't certain about anything anymore.

His eyes were wide-awake now. "Sorry, Pamela, what are trying to tell me? "

"You know that I had a sexual relationship with Dr. Gordon.

"No, I don't remember your telling me about that." He gulped, as if the knowledge of this was stuck in his throat.

"I know that all that is weird, but just don't think about it. "

"Yes"—he held up his hand. "I would have laughed about it before." And now that I have been baptized with sex, I find it even funnier. I can just imagine the two of you together. Oh yeah!"

"Well, it was not easy for me." I was being serious while his snickering had turned into a belly laugh as if he were imagining my protective angel and me entwined.

His laughing grated on my nerves so I grabbed and tried to shake him, "Look, I am her experiment, Randolph." He tried to stifle his laughter as he looked straight into my eyes. I started to push on him teasingly. He was just so nice to look at. And, then I got caught up in his mood and found myself laughing as well. "Yes," I admitted, "we probably did look a bit ridiculous, probably weird. But, then, believe me, she is a phenomenal partner."

His eyes took on a pensive allure. "But, Pamela, what isn't weird in this Center?" He either wanted me to feel better, or he was serious about what he said.

"Please, Randolph, let me finish what I started; it is important." I coaxed him. "You know that she was here tonight?" He nodded. "After seeing what I witnessed, seeing her as a machine, like a rubber doll, she told me that she knew that out sexual relationship was over." I was speaking fast. "My point is that she would not have come to see me tonight, risk being heard and viewed in my cubicle, if my cubicle was being monitored. That is the reason why I doubt that there is any video-surveillance equipment in my cubicle. You should be safe."

He jumped up and put on his robe, and then bent down and kissed me in a wonderfully inviting way. But I said, "Stop. We must stop now. It is late and you must leave. I guess that I am going to have to find a way for you to receive untainted food," I added laughingly.

That made his chuckle. "Be careful, Pamela. They are letting you visit the others, but they are not doing that to make you happy, it is part of their strategy. Don't give them any reason to question your sincerity to them." With a quick kiss on the tip of my nose, he was gone.

I slept very soundly. At 6AM, two android escorts woke me up and by 6:45 I was traveling down to the adjoining tunnel.

Chapter 30: Homecoming

The closer that I got to my destination the more anxious I became. I worried that they would not be so happy to see me. I was aware that I had been gone for a long time. I heard Dr. Gordon say 2 months, but it seemed like six; it could have been longer. At the center, the passage of time was unimportant, even irrelevant.

The androids have a life in perpetuity. For that reason, I believed that time had no importance for them. They didn't know what earth century we were in and it did not bother them in the least. Their indifference to time certainly affected us humans living within the center. And, admittedly, I lost track of days and weeks, let alone months since I have been back in the confines of the Center. Disturbing as it might be, one day in the Center could be one week, if we slept for days at a time. On the outside, our days are signaled by the rising and setting of the sun. We follow the lunar cycle that defines the months and helps us to calculate a year. The primitive method we used, markings on the cavern walls, gave us an idea of how long we were living in exile in that barren wasteland.

I had time to think during this long walk in the company of two android guides, and my thoughts, as always, were relatively dismal. For example, I agonized over my ignorance about life in general. I did not have any notion of how childhood progressed, at what age children walk, talk and become self-sufficient. Moreover, I wasn't certain about the accuracy of most of my childhood memories. My only clear memories of my childhood were those in front of a computer screen. Every day we put on a special helmet and reclined below our own computer terminal. The greater part of the day went by like that. I didn't remember playing sports; in fact, I didn't remember any kind of recreational activity. But I did remember jogging in place. I wasn't certain that group exercises qualified as playing. We never had any contact with the adult members. There was no need as the androids took care of us and our everyday needs. That was when we adopted the term "the bright ones" certainly at their insistence.

Oh well, I would soon find out at what age a child becomes independent.

I hoped that I would be able to relate to Frederic in spite of my absence these last few months.

"You can go outside. The door is open. Just wait by the food depot and the others will come to get you." I nodded.

The piece of paper from Randolph with the code numbers was hidden in my only under garment, a triangular piece of cloth that was knotted around my waist. I stood and watched the androids place the food boxes on the ledge outside the Center and leave.

I took the time to breathe deeply, to fill my lungs with the air on the outside and compare it with the sensation that I experienced when I took a deep breath in the Center. Yes, the air on the outside was clearly distinguishable from that in the Center. I noticed that it smelled differently, heavy with odors that were unidentifiable. I could taste particles of dust that floated up from the sandy surface. The air on the inside was purified, clean and completely odorless. Was that necessary for the health of the androids? That was an interesting thought. I wondered for how long they could stay on the outside without damaging their internal circuits, unless they had some built in filtering system. If that were the case, it was unfortunate for them, since it would be very easy for us to shut them off permanently by cutting off their filtered air supply. Too bad that I had not thought about that when the androids were outside with me. I could have studied their reaction.

In the distance, I vaguely saw two members of the community ambling towards me. It took me a few minutes to recognize Jonathan. It appeared, and I was right, that he was with Diana. As they approached I noticed that Jonathan was dragging his left foot.

Diana, screaming with excitement, rushed to throw her arms around me. She stepped aside as Jonathan approached. He gave me a big hug and kissed me affectionately on the side of my cheek.

"We didn't know that you would be spending time with us?" Jonathan spoke up.

"Only a week, but I have missed everyone so much and I have information to deliver, other than that which was hidden inside your clarinet case, with the clarinet." That brought a huge smile to his face.

"Of course, I want to know how you managed that, but I shall wait for your explanation later on." He quickly added. "It is wonderful being able to play the clarinet. And you, are you playing the piano?"

"Yes. It is the one thing that keeps me from going crazy living with all those androids."

The shower was next to the food depot, so both Jonathan and Diana came ready to suss up. While Jonathan showered, Diana and I sat under the high rocky ledge that provided privacy for showering and shade from the hot, dessert sun.

I looked at Diana. She was pulling nervously on her right thumb as if she would be able to remove it if she persisted in her effort long enough. I so desperately wanted to have all the news of my family and the rest of the members of our community, but as Diana is not very talkative, I focused on what she likes, by asking her how things were going with our combat unit. She burst out with enthusiasm as she told me how impressed she was with the group. She felt certain that the members could take down a major android advance in hand-to-hand combat. Her only concern was how they would protect themselves from the laser weapons. This was her next project—to get them ready to advance cautiously and to dodge the laser beams.

"Pamela, you must tell Stuart that I am counting on him to fire on the androids in order to give my group a chance to engage them in hand-to-hand combat." She sounded so motivated. "It is not easy to coordinate a real attack when certain vital people like, Stuart and Randolph, and the rest of the special force I used to work with, are not available to help plan an effective strategically designed attack." I was right, she certainly did like talking about this.

"Diana, I have some bad news?" I promised Randolph not to mention Stuart's role in the termination of these three other individuals, but I felt that it was important for Diana to know that she could no longer count on anyone other than Stuart to help.

"What? What do you mean?" She asked. I noticed that her eyes were bright and her nostrils flaring as if she was ready for a fight.

"I saw Randolph recently and I mentioned that you were with us. I told him that you were training some of us for combat. He was very pleased. He indicated that you were the best qualified to form a real fighting unit." She smiled at me. "But, Diana, he also told me that the other humans, except for Stuart, that you trained with in martial arts were terminated just before your arrival here."

She jumped up and looked at me with real hatred. "You told the androids about them and that is why they are gone." She came at me like a wild animal and we started to fight. I had kept fit in the Center and put up a reasonably good fight; but I was no match for her. She finally knocked me flat on my back and jumped on top of me. She grabbed my head in her hands and started pressing against my temples. My head felt like it was going to explode when Jonathan grabbed her from behind, forcing her to release her death grip on my head.

"What is going on?" he screamed.

"She is a traitor!" Diana was livid with rage. "She told those androids that members of our special forces were spying on them."

"Is it true, Pamela?"

"No!" I screamed back. "I didn't do anything. She didn't listen to me. Randolph told me that Stuart was the only martial arts expert left in the center. He told me that when Diana went mad the androids terminated everyone else except him and her."

Her anger turned to tears. "What are we going to do?"

Outraged by her violent irrational behavior, I sat at a distance watching Jonathan try to comfort her and calm her down. She was in a state of panic; hyperventilating and gagging. It took her a long time to gain control of herself, and finish with all that unnecessary hysteria.

I caught a glimpse of Jonathan, with his hand pressing up against his forehead and his mouth awry. He looked worried. He was obviously very much affected by her emotional reaction. It was not the warm homecoming welcome that I was expecting, but then I should not have mentioned the termination of her friends. I approached the two of them and reached out to take Diana in my arms. She didn't resist. I repeated over and over again that we would win; that nothing had changed. Our courage and determination would make up for our small number.

"I am sorry, Pamela, I should never have acted like that. I guess that I am still not completely in control of all my emotions." She said an apologetic tone. "You are right we shall win. We must win."

"Forget it. I am just fine. I can understand your pain and sorrow at the loss of your friends and allies." I was still holding her, so I squeezed her arm a bit and said. "But, I am no match for you in combat!" And, then started to laugh, breaking the tension.

She gave me a big smile when she got up to leave for her shower. She laughingly called out to me while on route. "I guess that you are going to train a bit with us this week."

I turned to Jonathan who didn't look well and that made me sad. "Are you ok?"

"Not really." He answered. His voice was low and listless.

"Do you want to talk about it?"

"It is strange, Pamela." He was shaking his head as if to clarify his remarks. I listened patiently as he went on to explain what had developed. "I noticed a stiffness in my shoulders. That would have been ok for me, but when the stiffness developed into a chronic, piercing pain in both my shoulders and my upper back, I began to suffer. This started a few months ago; and it has continued to increase in its intensity. Before that, and in spite of my physical deformities, I never felt in any way inhibited by them. In fact, under my programming, they didn't even exist, the reason why I was so horrified by my own reflection when I finally bypassed the program."

He stood up with difficulty to see if Diana was showering and then sat back down. "Every day is becoming more and more difficult for me. Walking has become a tedious and painful task. I am forcing myself to keep going to avoid becoming a burden on the community. Already my deformities are making it difficult for me to assist with the evacuation of the tunnel, so I can't refuse a simple task, like retrieving the food for the group. "

"I don't understand. When I left you were in the combat unit giving everyone a difficult time." I shook my head and asked in dismay. "What happened?"

He told me that he had thought about this over and over again and that he came up with two possible reasons.

"You know, Pamela, I was scheduled for termination?" I didn't know that, I was deep in thought. I surmised that if he had been scheduled for termination so was I. Everyone we knew lived in couples and I didn't know of anyone who changed partners. Of course, Sarah did tell me that her partner was terminated and that she was living alone. Where is the truth? Worse, the androids were telling us whatever they wanted; we were not seeing reality; so how could we honestly know if our partner had been replaced?

"How can you be so sure of that?" I wanted to know more.

"Dr. Gordon told me."

"She says lots of things to get reactions. And, Jonathan, if you were scheduled to be terminated, I was as well." I ventured this just to see his reaction.

He confirmed what I thought. So, I was nearing the end of my existence as well. "You know, Pamela, our replacement series are born already."

"Stop it!"

"It is true, I saw them. Pamela 14 was, I think, ten years old when I left." He seemed surprised that I didn't know. But, how could I since no one had ever invited me to the reproduction center. That would mean that my termination was to have taken place several years ago. How horrifying!

"Jonathan, I don't like this subject at all. You know that I live in the Center." I stopped to find my words. "This kind of information is sending chills up and down my spine. It frightens me. You're cruel to scare me like that. After all, I can be terminated more easily than you." He didn't seem to be affected in anyway by my fears, but did nod his head in agreement that it would be easy to terminate me.

"Ok, Jonathan, why are we still alive?"

"Because they need us for something. Our replacements are not old enough to provide them with the information or assistance, or who knows what they need."

"I don't want to think about this anymore; not now anyway while I am here with all of you. I shall find out more when I go back." I wanted to forget that for a while. "So your other theory?"

"Well, I didn't quite finish my first one. My termination was programmed and cancelled, which means that perhaps they want to see what kind of end I might have. How much I might suffer, for instance, and how, emotionally, I deal with that sufferance."

Unfortunately, that did not sound so farfetched. The androids could never relate or experience pain. I then recounted my witnessing the shutdown of Dr. Gordon without revealing the details of my sexual intimacy with her.

"I wondered if the whole scene was staged, whether they were testing my feelings for Dr. Gordon. I remained stoic during the procedure, however. I do not trust her, but I have no choice. Without her, I would be handed over to Dr. Crawford. My life expectancy would not be the same with him, that's for sure."

"So, do you agree with this assumption?" He waited a second before adding, "You are in the best position to answer. You live with them."

What could I say except that the androids were very unpredictable and utterly strange in their relationships even with other androids? "The problem with them is that they have no code of ethics, no sense of morality, so to speak. They don't feel guilty or malicious if they lie." I stopped to gather my thoughts. "Because of their cold, calculating android logic, your assumption seems very credible." I shook my head in disgust. "So...your second hypothesis?"

"Ok, it's simple. They gave me medication regularly so that I would be able to live with my deformities, in a painless state. That medication must have been in my food."

"Logically, they could have put anything in our food." I replied in agreement.

"Yes, but that brings me back to the same conclusion. If they are not putting it in my food now, then it must be because they want to study my reaction to pain and witness my natural death through natural causes, with horrible pain."

"I believe that Dr. Crawford would go to that extreme just to prove that Dr. Gordon's methods are risky for androids." I took his hands in mine. "I am only here for a week. When I return I shall defend your cause before Dr. Gordon and the Governor, who has been very nice to me. I promise you that I shall do something to help you through this even if I have to smuggle the medicine out to you. As an afterthought though, why do you suppose that it has taken more than a year for you to start suffering?"

"I asked myself that question many times and I don't have an answer."

"Maybe, Jonathan, you lifted or moved something that was too heavy for you. Even when I was here, you were letting the children jump all over you. You were digging big holes and lifting heavy piles of sand. Maybe, your pain is related to something you did here on the outside." I wasn't certain that I should make the next statement, but I took the risk. "You resemble your reflection in the visual receptor. You are very good looking now. Even your back is not that noticeable. I don't understand what happened exactly, but I would venture a guess that falling in love was curative. That is why I don't understand why you have so much pain."

His facial expression was very serious. "You are not the only one who has mentioned my transformation. I hear it every day. And, I am fed up with hearing about it! "His lips tightened as he paused. "I am ok, Pamela. Don't worry," he sighed. "Sarah told me that it was probably the dynamic surge of testosterone that brought about my physical transformation. Maybe it would have happened even if Diana and I had not gotten together; but certainly that relationship accelerated the changes."

He admitted that he was still sensitive about his former appearance and even compliments over his new found looks made him think about the past. He preferred that everyone would just stop reminding him of the past. I told him that I understood his feelings and promised never to bring up that topic again.

"I don't understand all my pain either, but you could be right that I hurt myself by lifting something, in the wrong way. And, when I think about it, all of this pain started when I was actively participating in the tunneling. I have always been very strong, which is why I didn't hesitate to transport heavy piles of stones." He smiled back at me. "And," He continued with a heightened enthusiasm, "I felt great with the combat exercises." His face brightened up. "Yes, Pamela, perhaps that is all it is, I pulled a muscle or pinched a nerve, you might just ask for some medicine for me. Thanks for helping me, thanks for caring."

"In the meantime, Jonathan, you should get off your feet for a week or so. Relax completely and see if the pain diminishes. It could just be minor, as I said, and you will know that better if you stop forcing yourself to walk." I twisted my mouth up in thought. "And, now that I am back, I can replace you and accompany Diana to get the food. And, you can play the clarinet for all of us and particularly for Frederic. I want to see if he appreciates music."

"Actually, I should have started with that. The clarinet does act like a placebo for me." His face was flushed. "Your positive thinking is already having an effect on me. And, you can be sure of one thing, I shall definitely play the clarinet for you.

It was much better for his recovery to focus on letting his body heal than on imagining a dismal destiny of cruel pain and suffering. I felt good that I had given him hope. Jonathan had given me information that was vital to all of us; our replacements were there. For some of us, John, Sarah and Ruth, their replacements may have come of age. What kind of diabolical plan did these androids have in mind? "Oh, Diana, you finished. That was a long shower." Jonathan was up and ready to go.

Diana reappeared, refreshed and calm; her exquisite Asian beauty, an ethnic group that my studies helped me to identify, was glowing. "I took my time because I thought that perhaps you two had some things that you would like to talk about. I was right, no?"

I smiled and picked up my share of the evening meal. Diana ran ahead to announce my unexpected arrival. I let Jonathan lean on me. He refused to give me more to carry even though he was visibly suffering. I hoped that I was right, that his pain was just temporary.

We were both lost in our own thoughts when Peter came running towards us with Frederic in his arms. Jonathan gave me a shove forward and I took off like the wind. Tears of joy streamed down my face as I ran to meet them.

Peter put Frederic down. He ran towards me, screaming at the top of his lungs, over and over again. "Mommy, you are home!" I grabbed him, picked him up and smothered him with kisses, as he squealed with joy. Peter arrived right behind and threw his arms around the two of us. He buried his head in my long, curly hair, as if breathing in my very essence and I heard him whisper—"Oh, my love, how good it is to have you back!"

We stayed like that for a long moment, before Frederic, trapped between us, pushed and shoved until we finally put him down. Frederic was still full of excitement as he danced about in front of us. This made me laugh with pleasure. I took his little hands in mine and then reached for Peter's hands; we turned in circles, kicking up our feet, as we danced together on the barren earth in the hot dessert sun.

I slowly became aware of their physical changes. Peter's hair was much longer and his beard, thicker and more prominent, but well groomed; this look accentuated his normally sexy features and radiated his virility. His upper body was more muscular and toned, from combat training. He sensed that I was observing him and for a slight instance our eyes met; long enough for both of us to feel that flaming passion, still alive inside of each of us. And, my son, my little Frederic, was now dancing and talking. Even though he was walking and running when I left, his movements were awkward. Today, he was no longer a baby, but a young child. How could that be?

Peter recognized my surprise. He put his arm around my shoulder as he called out to Frederic. "How old are you now, my big boy?"

"You know, Daddy, I am close to two year olds." He started laughing.

It was a good thing that Peter was holding on to me, because I would have fallen over.

"Close two years old?" I repeated.

"Yes, my love, you have been gone for one year." He waited a minute. "Time stands still in the Center." He said. So I was right about that. "We shall find out why when we overthrow the ruling class" He had a smile on his face as if imagining our victory.

Other members of the community followed like a curious herd of animals. Their surprise was warranted as no one expected my visit. I explained that I had been asking Dr. Gordon for leave to visit them for some time and then suddenly my request was granted, and 24 hours later, here I am. "Everything happened so fast." I began enthusiastically. "I thought that you would have gotten word last evening of my arrival today. Unfortunately, I have to return at the end of the week." I felt certain, though, that I would be able to get more opportunities to visit in the near future; but hesitated about mentioning that in case my optimism was not justified.

John pulled me aside and asked me to meet him later in a discrete part of the cavern. I understood why. He knew I was carrying that document and microchip with all the codes for the air transport unit.

We sat down to eat. I couldn't take my eyes off of my family. I marveled in the fact that Frederic was the product of Peter's and my love. He looked a bit like both of us. "He has his father's mysteriously captivating eyes." I mused. "He remembers me and he must love me to be climbing up on my lap and cuddling in my arms so often."

Here he comes again, I thought preparing myself for the arrival by standing up. This time he was running fast and jumped with all his force into my open arms. I wobbled, as I caught my balance. Laughing euphorically, I put him down on the floor and tickled him playfully, as he laughed and kicked his long legs. I caught a glimpse of Peter who was watching us with a big smile on his mouth. Frederic eventually disentangled himself from my grip. Free once again, he called out to me to follow him in what turned out to be a long round of chasing him as he dashed outside the cavern, running and jumping from one sand pile to another. I let him keep a lead.

Eventually, that was enough for me and I collapsed on the ground. He rushed towards me and gently curled up, like a kitten, on top of my belly.

What more could I ask for, I have everything, my son, my Peter, my friends… I mused. He lay still as I rubbed my hands through his thick curly, blond hair. I shut my eyes, totally relaxed and happy; we, all of us, have not just bypassed that android programming, but we have by-passed and overcome their denial of our natural right to reproduce." Wonderful thoughts ran through my mind.

Peter was tapping me lightly on my arm--"Are you awake, Pamela?"

"Just resting—I am not asleep." I answered softly.

"Stanislas suggested that everyone leave us alone because we have a lot of catching up to do."

"That was nice of him." I whispered in Peter's ear. "But I have a package to deliver to John. I won't be long. Can you just take Frederic in your arms, I think that he is asleep?"

"No problem." He said as he gently picked up Frederic and grabbed my arm. "Hurry Back."

I dashed back into the cavern and slipped out through the sidewall, where John was waiting for me. When we were a safe distance from all the surveillance equipment, I handed him the package.

"Thanks, Pamela. "We are all very happy with what you have been doing for us. I always had confidence in you to come through, but you have surpassed all my expectations."

"I did not think that you were someone who would resort to flattery." I was laughing and tapping him on the shoulder.

"Well, you better get back to Peter, before I forget that you already have a lover."

"No. He is more than a lover." I corrected John, spilling out my inner feelings for Peter. "He is even more than just the father of my son. I am more than just romantically and profoundly in love with him. I believe that he is part of me; that I am bound to him emotionally and spiritually; and that this extraordinary closeness that I have for him will endure throughout my entire life." I know that I had one of my naïve, silly smiles on my face when I said that, but John didn't laugh, he smiled back.

"Then get back there quick." He gave me a paternal slap on my bottom to get me moving. I walked away, looking back with a pretended frown on my face.

The pat on the rear from his informal gesture made me think that maybe he was beginning to finally trust me or at least accept me as one of them.

Chapter 31: Aspirations

If the first evening was any indication, I was certain that nothing but total bliss was in store for me with my little family. After I left John, I dashed back to spend time with Peter, who was lying awake waiting for me.

"That was quick! " He said, registering surprise and satisfaction.

I saw that Frederic was still asleep, so I sat down on the bed next to Peter and admired him with that same desire that I felt three years ago when I first made love to him. "Do you mind, Peter, if we talk for a few minutes because I need to catch up on life in this community; what has been happening for the last six months for me and more than a year for you…and, would like to know more about Frederic."

"Ok, but rapidly" He replied and then gave me a complete run down on Frederic and all about life in the community. "Our son is very curious and is learning fast. I believe that he has a quick mind but then that might be the Father in me speaking." He chuckled. "In any event, he sincerely enjoys listening to Jonathan play the clarinet. Jonathan has already taught him some of the basics in producing clear sounds, tones. Frederic told me how much he wants to play a tune for you tomorrow."

"Wow—that is impressive! He is only close to two and can already play tunes on the clarinet." I was very excited about that.

"I knew that you would be happy to hear that." He said with a broad smile. "So, what else is there… oh yes, Frederic spends most of his time playing with the other children. Diana knows a lot about games and she likes competitive sports; so she is the one to spearhead games in the community. You'll have chance to see what kinds of games they like to play. You are not going to believe this." He said with excitement, as he clapped his hands together, hoping to get a reaction from me. "The community now has a rudimentary ball that we use to play baseball, a team sport. We made it from a piece of rubber that we found." He pointed in the direction of the tunnel. "We broke a leg off of one of the empty beds in the only unoccupied cubicle to make a bat to hit the ball around; and we constructed a loop-rather primitive-from a piece of the old mattress wire, so that we could play basketball. Frederic is a bit young to participate but he likes watching us all play."

"I don't know anything about either sport. It all sounds like a dream. It is too good to be true, everyone playing competitive team sports." I was happy that they were having fun. "Maybe, I can participate a bit while I am with you?"

"Great idea!"

"And the tunneling, how is that going?" Before he could answer, I ventured. "Are there any new projects?"

"The equipment that arrived soon after you left us has been very useful." He went on to explain that he was cautious and sometimes worried about the project. He expressed trepidations that we were too small a group to launch a revolt against the powerful androids. He was to a certain extent right; he had witnessed how the androids perfectly orchestrated the elimination of the astronauts.

"I know that you will find what I have to say too optimistic, but I am going to pass it by you anyway. It seems that there are more people on the inside ready to help than you can imagine." He shook his head in disbelief. "Randolph knows a lot of people and thanks to him and his associates we now know the layout of the transport center. I just gave the building code to John tonight."

He wanted to know more about the group on the inside. Actually, I realized then that apart from Randolph and Stuart, I couldn't name anyone else, but that did not mean that there weren't others. His brow furrowed telling me he was not convinced.

He caught himself and said, "It's ok my love, we can count on each other. That's what matters the most. But, Pamela, remember that if you know others who are deprogrammed then you must be very careful. The androids are good at spying in the center. They might let a couple humans retrieve their emotions so long as they don't create problems, but, they will prevent a community of deprogrammed humans from increasing their numbers." He was right.

When I mentioned the fact that there were androids that were ready to overthrow the androids in charge of the center, the furrows of doubt returned to his forehead as he shook his head. He retorted that his experiences taught him that androids were incapable of confronting each other in a struggle for power. He warned me that there was every possibility that Randolph's assistant was more dangerous for us humans than for the androids.

The conversation returned to the transport vehicles. He showed his concern again. "I'm confused over how these vehicles will be useful. We need to be able to drive them and no one in our group has ever driven anything before."

"True, but before that even, we have to know how to turn on the machines." I regretted having to admit that. "But, Randolph is very optimistic. He is certain that we shall soon have the capacity to turn these machines into lethal weapons against the androids."

"If you like, Pamela, I'll just take your word for that for the moment, because I do have others things on my mind. For example, it has been a long time since I held you tightly in my arms. I missed you. I love you. I love..... you." He looked at me with his longing puppy eyes. Melting fast, I started to ease closer, drawn by his soft and sensual voice repeating over and over again his love for me. And then, I hesitated, pulled back for just an instance. I felt guilty and worried that he would notice that I was a different partner than before. Should I hide my sexual escapades or infidelity from him?

I didn't know what he thought; he said nothing. But, he didn't seem to be disturbed by my reaction; instead, he seemed to be more excited by what he took for a sign of sexual innocence, on my part; like I was worried that I had forgotten how to act and how to move.

He pulled himself up in a sitting position and wrapped his strong, comforting arms around me. He held me tightly letting me feel the heat of his body against mine; and my body started to relax, molding itself with his. He took his time, running his fingers through my hair and laying moist, lingering kisses along my neck and over my shoulders. I shuddered as an exquisite sensation of desire ignited inside of me. He gently turned me in his direction, holding my face in his hands; as he tenderly started his seductive descent of my body, kissing my forehead, my eyelids, my cheeks, until his warm lips were firmly pressing up against mine; my mouth opened so slightly; just enough to invite him to enter and he did. His tongue slid in and out of my mouth in a slow and sensual cadence, which gradually quickened and intensified.

When his mouth moved slowly down my throat and found my breasts, I gasped and gripped his shoulders with pleasure. We were breathing rapidly as we tore our robes off and threw them on the floor. And so we set out to enjoy each other with that same burning desire that first brought us together, as we unselfishly and unhurriedly savored the happiness reserved to those whose love is without limitation.

I didn't want to wait longer. I was so alive with a desire, a lustful hunger, a yearning; something unfathomable that only he could arouse inside of me and that only he could satisfy. I tried to ease him inside of me. He resisted my advances; he was not yet ready to abandon his seductive and sensual descent of my body. And so we continued unselfishly and unhurriedly savoring the happiness reserved only to those whose love knows no earthly limitation; our movements were like improvisations passing beyond the strict borders of reality.

He cuddled up against me and moved his hands up and over my naked body, before delicately spreading my legs wide enough that he could taste my moist warmth. I was breathing rapidly and uncontrollably exhaling cries of pleasure; seized by a rush of euphoric sensations. I wanted him inside of me as I turned and reached out to fondle, stroke him…seeking his exhilarating virile essence.

I was alive with a vibrant pleasure, when his gentle caresses started up again and continued until our mouths were back together. He lowered himself gently on top of me. Hardened and burning with a new unquenched desire, he glided deep inside me, responding naturally and eagerly to my every move as I encouraged him to continue his quest for ultimate physical and emotional union. And then, it came, in an overwhelming surge of spasms that engulfed us, as we trembled against each other, collapsing under the force of that violently fulfilling final expression of love. Rolling to his side, he brought me along with him breathing heavily as he sucked in my warmth. "If I am not in love—if this isn't love-- then no one, no one in all that long human history, ever was!" He said, breathlessly, as he fondled my hair and smothered me with more kisses, before closing his eyes and falling asleep.

I lay awake spellbound by that heightened pleasure that drained me of all my physical energy, and fulfilled my inner most desire to be loved beyond reason. With Peter, it is more than physical satisfaction; I am lifted high above this earthly universe, drawn outside the limits of my own body into a place of absolute ethereal pleasure. "He revives me." I mused. "With his odor- an aphrodisiacal blend of sweet and spicy vanilla, with his ambrosial taste, and with his gentle, sensual, seductive touches; and with his love, the same genuine devotion for me that I feel for him along with a fervor of adoration that I understand. I find it so natural to be lying next to him. I smile to myself and at him; with Peter I am making love; and I am making love to the one with whom I have the strongest emotional attachment. He is my other half, my one true love.

I laid my head against his chest to listen to that the strong, slow rhythm of his heart. I thought that I had memorized him in every detail and that there was nothing that I would not recall. I lost touch with him over time while I was in the center and I didn't want to do that again; even though I reveled in the rediscovery of him.

I was leaning over him crying when he opened his eyes. Frederic was still asleep and I didn't want to wake him.

"Well, Pamela, is that the best face you can put on for me this morning?" He looked confused with his eyebrows raised and mouth slightly open.

That brought a smile to my face, and I apologized at the same time for being so sentimental. "I am just so happy to be here, looking down at you." I forced a smile. "My tears are tears of joy."

Then the entire panoply of my past affairs returned to haunt me. I needed to turn the page on them and the best way was to come clean with Peter. I wanted to tell him how I vulgarized the idea of love with Dr. Gordon; but I was afraid to. There was a chance that he might find it as humorous as Randolph did, but Peter was so serious that my confession could hurt or at least seriously confuse him. I was certain that he would not approve of what had happened between Randolph and me. It was innocent; just as innocent as my adventure with Mathieu in the beginning. I didn't want him to be consumed by jealousy, even if it would overcome my, sometimes, warped insecurities regarding his feelings for me. Nonetheless, I decided not to bring up the subject.

I told him that I had missed him so much- that was true-and one week was not going to be long enough for me. "A lifetime with you, Peter, would not be long enough for me." I said with sadness in my voice. He grabbed me and held me so tight as if his intense physical force would make us forever inseparable. And then, gasping, when he finally released his grip, I actually felt as if I had received something more than a giant bear hug.

"Can I ask you something---a bit personal?" I was on a constant search for answers.

"I have a feeling that this is going to be serious---but, if you need to." There was an anxious tone in his voice. Was I going to put him ill at ease?

"How did you learn how to make love, so well?" I went straight to the point.

"That's what you want to know?" He sighed with relief and then laughed, as if he were reliving his experiences, before continuing. "We were all hypersexual after the first ten days of living together without contaminated food." He raised his eyebrows and puckered up his mouth. "This is all a bit embarrassing." he started to laugh as he let the scenes pass in his mind.

"Please, it is important for me to know." I pleaded; I kept a straight face, in spite of his silliness.

"We just started to jump randomly on each other; we didn't care which sex we were with." His laughter turned raucous. "It must have shocked our android observers." He said in a haughty tone of disdain. "The thing was that all that we wanted to do was to release our obsessive, driving sexual urge. There was nothing romantic in this."

"Go on!" I encouraged him.

"The only person who did not participate in this crazy display of emotions was Mathilda." He stopped. "She even hit me and others when we tried to approach her. Her resistance was quite violent." He stopped to regain his normal calm composure. "Actually, she was studying us. You know that she is a psychologist?" I nodded affirmatively. "After weeks of observing us, she introduced her program to educate us in the art of making love." He looked straight in my eyes as he announced. "We all passed by Mathilda!"

"Well, she is gorgeous and wreaks of sex." I commented, hiding my unfounded jealousy.

"She understood how to introduce foreplay---something that we were not using at all." That sent him off on a violent display of laughter. I sat looking at him, trying to imagine him jumping on others. I just couldn't picture him that way.

"Eventually, we introduced our own seductive moves; based principally on achieving personal sexual satisfaction. It took more time for each of us to become sensitive to our partner's, randomly selected at the time, personal needs." He was bright red with embarrassment. "Effectively, Pamela, we matured. We passed by a primitive bestial period on into an exploratory adolescent stage, as we matured and took on a more-hmmm- civilized approach." He creased his eyebrows, as he curled up one side of his mouth, before adding. "Of course, not everyone here is adept at making love." He chuckled. "But everyone has a better idea of how to do it."

"And forming couples? Did that happen automatically?"

"You don't want me to take you back in my arms and play around a bit?" He asked sheepishly.

"Yes." I was forcing myself to resist him, because I wanted answers. "But, I need to know."

"They formed naturally. Ruth and Sarah gravitated to John, their protector. Mathieu had no choice as Isabelle is very possessive; but he seems to like her possessiveness; at least, he never complained about that to me." He sighed. "Stanislas and Benjamin found their happiness together."

"And you, Peter, why didn't you form a couple with Mathilda?" I wanted an answer even though I was afraid of what he might say.

"Mathilda?" He laughed. "Pamela, she is a sexual predator. Anyone of us, at any time, can spin around with her." He said in a high voice.

"Oh, I didn't know that." He confirmed my worst thoughts.

He rubbed the top of my head teasingly. "Of course you did, but you wanted to hear it from me."

True, but I wanted to hear something else as well. I forced a laugh and went on with my questions. "When I arrived you were described as aloof, pretentious? Why was that?"

"I am serious, maybe pretentious, at least I am not hiding my intelligence, which might bother some people who are less secure about that. I calmed down, as others moved together in couples. No one attracted me so strongly in the beginning and playing around with Mathilda was perfect for me." He stopped and looked intensely in my eyes, annoyed that he let that remark slip, and hoping that he did not hurt my feelings. I acted like I hadn't heard it. "Right, do you remember the evening of our first encounter?" I shook my head. How I could ever forget that evening? "As I said then, I am obsessed with the heavens. Often times, watching the movement of the celestial bodies is calming and hypnotic enough to relax me and bring on sleep. Your arrival had a different effect on me. I started to feel something different when I was around you."

"So why didn't you accompany me on one of those exploratory trips? Why was I only with Mathieu?" I asked, bitter that my first experience was with Mathieu.

"He liked exploring the barren zone and you wanted to explore as well. Seemed logical that you should go off with him." He tried to read what was going on in my mind. "Sex is one thing; making love is something else. Stop complicating life by thinking too much and asking so many questions."

What he just said removed all my vestiges of guilt. I felt cleansed. He is right, making love involves emotions, deep emotions. Sex is on a different plain where pleasure is the ultimate goal. And, Randolph, in all his innocence, understood that when he said that we could play around together, without that changing my love for Peter. I breathed a deep sigh of relief. "Just one more question." He nodded. "And, Mathilda…" He didn't give me time to finish my question.

"Mathilda has other projects for the moment. Since the arrival of Diana she has been focusing more on psychological issues. She is studying Diana and her interaction with the children and the rest of us."

"One last question?" I kissed him lightly on his mouth.

"I thought that you just asked me your last question." I looked at him with pleading eyes. "Ok, but make it fast!" He was getting tired of this discussion and interested in doing something else.

"How did Mathilda bypass her programming?"

He started rolling with laughter as he choked out. "It is quite funny, actually."

"I gathered that." I said as I watched him roll about like a child.

"John fell on top of her in one of the crowded hallways." His laughter was contagious. "She didn't see him, his code was not functioning, and he was in such a hurry dodging curious androids that he didn't notice her until he fell on top of her." He could hardly speak with all his laughter. "He smashed her on the floor and even rolled over her. She was screaming; she did not realize what happened to her." I could just picture John, with his size and weight, rolling on top of Mathilda. "He quickly jumped up and took her in his arms. He ran off to the Governor's office and dropped her on the Governor's desk." He stopped for an instance to savor the humor of this situation. "We had just gotten our permission to leave, so the Governor was not surprised to see John, but he jumped away from the package that John laid on his desk." He was laughing so loud. "To make a long story short, Mathilda's wristband was in pieces, something that she noticed straight off, which increased her anxiety as she realized that she was able to see John, without a code, when he leaned over her." Peter was calmer now. "John explained that the Governor gave him permission to add her to our list. Our departure was scheduled for two weeks later, which gave Mathilda time to come to terms with her new situation."

"Wow. That is unbelievable!" I exclaimed.

"Actually, with the time warp in the Center, two weeks was more like two months, which is why she was capable of joining us as an active member when we finally left." He said as he retrieved his composure.

This time he didn't give me chance to pose another question. He reached up and grabbed me, pulling me down next to him, ready to show me how much he loved me, when we both heard the pitter-patter of Frederic's feet.

He was happily calling out to us. "Good morning, Mommy and Daddy!" Life stood still for me. I was finally where I wanted to be and where I should be. I saw the three of us running off hand-in-hand into that infinite barren wilderness.

"Why was I destined to be some sort of heroine for this group," I mused. And, why did that Dr. Gordon choose me instead of Sarah or Ruth or Isabelle or Diana." I shook off those thoughts after castigating myself for feeling sorry for myself again.

Everyone was already up and almost finished with breakfast when the three of us arrived. There was something nice about communal living. I had forgotten the pleasure of conversation first thing in the morning. Back at the Center, I always ate breakfast alone, I started my day alone and I finished it alone. I was determined to take advantage of company, especially the company of my family. And, then I had an eerie feeling that nothing ever happened according to plan. Shortly after we finished our breakfast, Frederic disappeared to play and John invited me to visit the tunnel.

The digging equipment, although rudimentary, had helped them make enormous progress, as Peter had mentioned to me. Before I could ask how they actually opened up an entire chamber, John explained that Jonathan had been incredibly effective in evacuating large amounts of sand and stone. We talked a bit about Jonathan's health and he, more or less, agreed with me that his physical efforts could have caused other problems related or unrelated to his deformities. He told me it would be great if I could get the Androids to give him medicine.

"And, if they want to examine him?" I said. "What should I say?" This time I wanted to anticipate problems. I had to be better prepared than I was the last time. I didn't want to have to make critical decisions on my own. "So why not take advantage of John who likes to give orders." I said convincing myself.

"Complicated." John replied." I doubt that they would invite him back inside. You are already a risk. But, they are very unpredictable these days. Do you think that you could keep him under your protection?" I nodded a definitive no. "In that case, we shall just have to hope that they will send out some medicine." He retorted. "And," he went on, "try to follow up on that."

He picked up the map that Randolph placed in the clarinet case. I was staring at the impressive result of their digging when John called me. "Come here and look, Pamela." I moved next to him as he pointed out on the map our emplacement and the transport building. "We are very close to the transport terminal building. This building is slightly outside the main building of the center, which makes it strategically interesting." He explained, "But, the transport vehicles are the most important booty. Even if we can't make a frontal attack on the center itself, we will be able to defend ourselves while being in a position to leave the area and look for new territory." I looked at him a bit confused. "We can pile into one or more transport vehicles and leave to find a new and better location for us."

"Excellent. That is incredible. But how are we going to drive them?" I asked, reminded of what Peter said about our ignorance in driving these machines.

"True. That is a problem." John was already aware of this problem, "But, we shall find a way around that. After all, we are used to solving technical problems of all sorts. But, what is more important for me is where to go once we get the transporters off the ground. Do you have any idea, yet, where that fertile land is?" The imploring sound of his voice reminded me of my vital role for this community.

"I'll tell you what I know." I explained the overreaction of Dr. Gordon every time I spoke about Jason. "She always referred to him as an old fool, reminding me that I would be better off forgetting what he said."

"Not good news, I am afraid." John jumped in. "Even though I had about the same impression of him as she does, I was hoping that I was wrong."

"Wait. You didn't let me finish." I thought for a minute about how to explain the shower because I couldn't let him in on my secret.

"Ok. I am waiting."

"Well, very recently, I confronted Dr. Gordon about the end of human history. Our history stops after the 21st century. So, I asked her if we were still in the 21st Century." I hesitated. "Actually, I believe that our story ends a long time after the 21st Century."

"Maybe. Go on." John coaxed me.

"She told me that human history stopped when android history began and that time was of no importance to the androids. So, I don't know what year it is now." I stopped to be sure that he was following me. "I brought up Jason again and this time she said, 'well, yes the earth was in a renewal phase. Perhaps the old fool had discovered a fertile area.' She mentioned that we were located in a dry zone, maybe a desert; I am not sure, but, Peter did tell me that the sandy surface, coupled with the hot days and cold nights, make him believe that we are living on a desert." John nodded, as I went on to add. "She just talked about wet and dry zones."

"Do you think that you can find out more about the wet zones?"

"I would have to find someone who is in geographical or geological studies." I was hoping that he would not ask me to look for someone in those fields and quickly diverted him by returning to what I learned from Dr. Gordon. "Yes, John, I got the impression from what Dr. Gordon said that the earth had gone through an enormous change and that it would be necessary to see very recent studies to know the earth's status today."

"Of course. The problem is that geographical and geological changes may not be of much interest to the androids. They live in the centers, so they don't care what is happening on the outside."

"Yes and No." And, then I told him about the conversation I had with Dr. Gordon about water and the source of water.

"Fascinating. Yes, the water sources are underground, like what we see from the high cavern ledge." He hesitated. "You remember Jason talking about lakes and waterfalls, the kinds of scenery that pass by in semi-blurs as we peer out windows of trains chugging in the mountains, not the desert. But, Jason lived it. Much as I hesitate about believing that eccentric old man, I might be wrong. I vacillate back and forth. Maybe he actually did discover a heaven on earth." John spurted out with excitement. "Maybe there's still hope for us, Pamela."

"I hope." I was less convinced now about the sanity of Jason than I was a year ago. I guess Dr. Gordon had brainwashed me a bit. "Let me just finish what I was saying, John." He looked at me intent to listen. "They need constant sources of water to keep us alive, John."

"Yes, of course. So, when their underground sources run dry, they will have to look elsewhere." He snapped his fingers. "That's it, Pamela, someone must be working on that problem. The androids must have assigned that problem to someone."

I didn't answer straight away because I was not certain that either Randolph or Stuart knew anyone in these fields. "John, I don't know many people in the Center. The ones that are under visual control are blasé. It is impossible to have a conversation with them." I sighed with disgust. It was true; they were like empty shells--empty, smiling shells. "You know, they don't even see me, unless I give them my code number, and that seems to confuse them a bit. They are not cooperative."

He ignored my last comment and went on with new instructions. "You shall have to find someone in that sector." He was looking straight into my eyes. "How many people are there in the center?"

"The adult population is not very big. We are only a few hundred. I saw that figure some place; I think it was on Dr. Gordon's desk. I am not certain of the accuracy. But, there are the children--our replacements."

"So there are about 400 humans there?" John replied.

"I shall try to confirm that." I thought that we were less than 400.

"The number is not what interests me the most. The humans are not a problem for us. The androids are. But, among those humans, how many are still under the effects of the visual receptor?

"I don't know. All I know is that Randolph gave me the impression that we are the only humans that are no longer under the programming. He does have his network on the inside, which was considerably reduced when the three other martial arts experts were terminated."

"Really, I didn't know that. I was counting on them." John shook his head in disgust. "Yes, Randolph, though, is excellent. The information he just sent me is vital to our cause. And, I have many questions to ask him."

I felt nervous again. I wanted to be happy for a week and now I realized that I was still on a mission. "How many humans do we need to destroy the androids?" I asked hoping that he would give me a low number.

"Pamela, we might not even be able to revolt. We may only be able to just leave the area, find our own food sources and become independent." He went on to say. "Well, now that they eliminated those three programmed ninjas, so to speak, the androids cannot count on any humans to help them against us; unless, of course, their replacements are ready for action. I hope not. You have to find out from Stuart." His mind was working fast and his list of orders was getting longer and longer. "No matter," he concluded, "we shall just have to fight the androids on our own. Hopefully we'll be able to defend our position and even overcome them." He took a long deep breath before adding. "Naturally, the more people we have on our side, the more chance for success."

I told him that Peter also believed that there were not many, if any, other deprogrammed humans. John replied that Peter was always pessimistic even though his pessimism was often right. I wanted to know how the people on the inside could help us if the transport center was independent from the Center. He clarified that saying that it was at the far end of the complex, but that there was a corridor that attached it to the Center.

"So it is not independent?" I asked.

"Yes and no, if that makes sense." He pulled out the map again. "You see the corridor is shut off at both ends with huge electronically controlled doors. When we access directly through the floor into the unit, the androids will probably not be able to detect our presence. Their sensory equipment is outdated and certainly focused on unauthorized access at the front end of the corridor."

"Ok, but I think that we should take over the center, not just steal the vehicles." I don't know why I said that.

"What? That is too risky?"

"True, but we need to have supplies. What if it takes us weeks to find fertile land? What are we going to eat and drink? And, how can we abandon all those other humans? And," I added, "We have an excellent fighting unit thanks to Diana."

"Ok; those are good points. But, then we will need you to cover us so that we can get into the center and shut down those android machines." He smiled maliciously. "Do you think that you can do that?"

I smiled reassuringly at him and said, "Why not? Stuart is with me and Randolph is in good shape. Stuart has access to the codes because of his part time activity and he knows how to get around." He started to talk but I cut him off, "Then, I should probably tell you something else. Randolph and I have both discovered in our own ways that there are different interest groups forming among the androids. There are not two opposing forces within the center, but rather various small groups of androids that have different views on specific issues. I felt the tension from the beginning but am now convinced that all the androids have taken a position, either for or against my presence and the nature of Dr. Gordon's study. For example, it is certain that Dr. Crawford and his group are diametrically opposed to Dr. Gordon's project and are even ready to sabotage it at every occasion." I stopped for a minute to collect my thoughts. "But, I think that there is a more serious opposition group, behind the scenes." I briefly described my experience with the primitive robot, Dr. Miller, at the library,

"Wait just a minute, Pamela. Are you telling me that there is jealousy among the androids; that is just impossible." John said firmly.

"No, not jealousy. They would deny that in any event. But, I think that there is a natural hierarchy among the androids. Certain androids occupy the same hierarchical position held by their creators. They even immortalize their creators by taking on their names and certain of their mannerisms. They exhibit the physical reincarnation of their creators, especially those who came into existence when android technology was at its highest point." I stopped again to digest what I had said and take a deep breath. "Their power is breathtaking. But, their numbers are limited."

"Wait just a second, I am getting very confused. You said that there were androids that wanted to revolt." I nodded yes. "Then you said that the androids in control are divided, or better, they disagree, over how to interact and study humans?" I nodded again. "So, then what are these creations? In which group are they, the ones in charge or the group seeking to revolt? And, do they show emotions?"

"You have met the creations, so you know that they are part of the ruling class." I replied. "Dr. Gordon, Dr. Crawford, the Governor, Dr. Miller, and maybe others, are the ruling class and they have taken on the distinct image of their creators and occupy positions of authority held by their creator. I have never witnessed emotional reactions-clearly emotional reactions-on their part." I wondered if I should I tell him more about my relationship with Dr. Gordon? I decided not to. "They always boast that they have no emotions and that they couldn't be jealous or competitive like lowly humans; it is impossible. They also like to remind me that they are superior beings because they don't need reassurance, like humans. They accept their situation, their appearance, because their priority is to function, not to look good or gain power."

"So, if I understand correctly, they took on the same profession of their creator?" He went on to answer his question. "Of course they did. I know that already. I only had contact with the Governor, but the androids that you just named now, were part of his team. Some things remain fuddled in my memory because I was in my early stages of deprogramming when I met with the Governor."

"It seems that you remember quite well. Only Dr. Miller is occupying a less important position than her Creator. She is the librarian." I went on to tell him about the explosion in the lab, the reason why she was working in the Library

"Pamela, I know that you want to relate to these creations like you do to humans." He smiled patronizingly. "I know that there is a pretense of infighting within the ruling class of creations. Don't forget that I dealt with the Governor. I don't know the others very well, but, importantly, they are not human. You have to keep that in mind every second that you are with them. Better to stay suspicious. I think that Peter is right when he says that the androids would never vie against each other for power. It is not part of their logic."

"Ok, I shall be careful; but living with them is like being put directly into the most complex conundrum imaginable while you are being asked to find your way out fast."

He snickered. "Even the lower echelon androids are not going to revolt. They are at the maximum level of their program so they can't move up." He smiled. "Well, we really better hurry back to the others. Your absence might be signaled and I don't want any problems for us. You have given me a lot of important information. I shall think about it for a while. All I know is the more we learn about them, the better prepared we shall be."

We walked silently back to the meeting room pondering what had just been said. My thoughts were on Dr. Gordon. Randolph found our tryst amusing, but would John? Would he suspect me again of collaborating with the enemy? Or, would he simply consider me incompetent for the mission? At least, thanks to Peter, I don't have feelings of guilt. And, my intimacy with Dr. Gordon was important for all of us because she confided in me. Her obsession with emotions is now clear to me and I wonder if androids actually need us.

The week went by very fast. I spent time with Frederic playing children's games, like hide and seek and, the one he liked the most, 'Try to catch me if you can." I got a lot of exercise running after him. He did not ask me any questions about where I went when I left and I did not broach the subject. He was happy to play a few simple songs that he liked-Twinkle, Twinkle, Little Star and Row Your Boat-on the clarinet for me. But, what strongly impressed me was when he played a short excerpt of Mozart's Clarinet Concerto A. Jonathan was working wonders with Frederic, inspiring his musical talent. I went around bragging that my son was a virtuoso and that he could be the incarnation of one of those classical child geniuses like Mozart.

Diana made certain that I attended the martial arts classes. My kickboxing in the Center was not enough to defend myself effectively, in the beginning, against Isabelle who had progressed impressively during my absence. By the end of the week, though, I was Isabelle's equal, something that was a big ego booster for me.

I participated in baseball and basket competitions. I was the handicap for whichever team got stuck with me. I did not like basketball very much, in spite of the fact that my height gave me an advantage over Sarah, Ruth and

Mathilda when it came to sinking the ball. I preferred baseball, especially when I was up to bat—I was not bad at all!

There were serious moments as well. At one point, I gave a brief presentation of our history to the whole group, explaining the evolutionary aspects of our race during the prehistoric period and concluding with the end of the 21st century, emphasizing the fact that I was certain that human history ended much later and that the androids, for whatever reason, did not want me to have access to anything that happened after that date. I mentioned that they know that we were all trained to retain information and even if we weren't human computers, we were all very accurate in exposing facts.

When I said, 'Our entire human history has been edited by the androids and went on to mention that certain "irrelevant" and unnecessary information had been deleted, there was an out roar of surprise.'

They were horrified that the androids would just wipe out parts of human history and wanted to know on what basis they made those decisions. I apologized for not knowing the reason or reasons behind this irrational behavior or irresponsible conduct, and reminded the group that I was fortunate to have this special hard fought access to our history. Ferdinand and I were the only humans who ever entered the sanctity of the library. By adding that, the intense rumbling simmered down.

"I am very proud of the inventions and talent of humans." I announced in a strong voice. "For that reason, my comments and suppositions may not be completely objective." No one was bothered by that so I went on to tell them that I thought that we were very curious and that our curiosity led us to make major discoveries. "We were a very versatile, competitive race that was inspired by challenges, even those that seemed insurmountable, and were not afraid to take risks, even major risks, to move forward scientifically. Nonetheless, something happened to give the androids a clear advantage over the human race. I hope to discover what that was and how these androids took control."

I expressed disappointment in our cruelty to each other and with other species of animals, including the use of torture. I added that wars and senseless killings were commonplace in our history. "The history of the human race is the story of Good versus Evil. For every good act there were at least a dozen bad acts. I had the impression, as well, that many leaders were cruel, and that they would stop at nothing to stay in power. I was surprised that there were more bad political regimes than good ones, even though historically, evil regimes were brought down as often as good ones were. It often took too many years and a lot of suffering before qualified people with egalitarian ideas gained control." I felt relieved sharing these truths with them; I would no longer be the only human haunted by the atrocities of past generation humans. I mentioned the general political regimes and the rivalry between countries based upon economic and political grounds.

Naturally, I presented controversial observations and theories that provoked discussion among the group. I even went so far as to suggest that, as absurd as this sounded, the Center qualified as a Utopia; in our programmed existences we were at peace with ourselves, our world, and beaming with happiness.

"There is something else that we have to be aware of, even now." I started off. "All of us have learned how to deal with strong emotions like frustration, jealousy, denial, hatred, anger, etc.; none of us have even done anything cruel or mean. We accept the existence of these negative emotions and simply factor them into our personality as they arise. But, some deprogrammed humans may not be able to control their negative emotions enough to resist violent actions."

Another issue I brought up was that we are developing a sense of hierarchy. For instance, John acted as our undisputed leader. We never decided officially on that, it just happened. As John himself admitted, he never sought it and found himself in charge of a group after he left the Center. He explained that his personality was more developed when he left the center simply because he had bypassed the effects of the visual receptor a long time before he was allowed to leave. But I pointed out that he must have had the basic profile for leadership and decision-making or it would not have happened.

There were many questions concerning the choice of parentage made by the androids. I realized again that I had not paid enough attention to that. I repeated what the governor told me that he knew my parents. He told me that he had to terminate the 12 other Pamelas because they all showed negative traits. He was happy to declare that he was the one who decided that I should study music, rather than science, because he wanted to see if that would be better suited to my genome or genetic makeup. I regretted not having access to those records which prevented me from comparing myself to my predecessors.

I understood immediately that that information made everyone a bit uncomfortable. We all knew that we were not the first series. What happened to our predecessors was disconcerting to all of us so, naturally, no one asked for more details about that.

Everyone had difficulty, though, understanding the concept of wealth. Money didn't exist in our society and we could not imagine money being so important. Arguably, we never needed to purchase anything as everything was provided for us. So we had no concept of materialism. During one of our usual discussions on the subject, Mathieu brought up the point that our musical instruments bore our names. But we had to admit that a clarinet was a clarinet and that it made no difference to Jonathan whether it was his or someone else's. And, I pointed out that the three available pianos did not have nameplates on them.

Money was a common subject of conversation. In fact, it went further than discussion. One morning Stanislas appeared at the breakfast table with 5 pebbles and pretended that his five pebbles entitled him to have two meals and he would thus pay for one. No one wanted his pebbles so in the end he ate only one meal. But, his idea took off as everyone clambered to find smooth, big, round pebbles, which were very difficult to find in our sandy soil. Those who had the most pebbles tried to negotiate with the poor ones to pay for a part of the evening meal. The exchanges were never serious, but we all found the game quite amusing. And, although it didn't have an impact upon anyone at that moment, I worried that it might evolve with time into recognition of wealth.

One evening when we gathered after hours in our secret cavern, the subject of religion came up. I was so fascinated with the subject myself that I was happy to share all the information I had absorbed at the Center. I had their total attention as I traced religion from its early stages with the worship of many Gods to the evolution of defined religions based upon a single God. Each religion with its practices and beliefs traced its existence back to a prophet. That person, I believed, was human, chosen by God to define morality and the proper way for humans to live together in a given religious community. Ethical principles like "thou shalt not steal" and "thou shalt not kill" were notions that we had not yet encountered and could not yet envisage. I told them that I was mesmerized by the idea of the existence of this superior being, or God. I recounted that prescribed rituals set forth in the different religions helped worshippers get the attention of the God.

"There was even an ideology based upon the denial of the existence of this God." I began. "There appeared in different periods of human history non-believers who all followed a formalized tradition of non-believing. If one were a believer, he or she would fervently defend their right to believe. If one did not believe, scientific evidence as well as the suffering of those deprived of family, food and shelter, were used to refute the existence of God."

"I am particularly opposed to violence of any kind and shutter, when I think about it. That is why I appreciate, as brilliant, the creative way in which some religions introduced the concept of sin to discourage violence." I was convinced that this idea was the most acute form of manipulation. "Religious leaders referred to crimes as heinous, and even defined other improper behavior towards others as sins; and the more sins you accumulated during your lifetime, the more your inner self, or what was referred to as your soul, would suffer after you were terminated or died." My audience gasped with surprise. "Then there were also religions that advocated that their practices purified the spirit, the soul, during one's lifetime. Thinking and speaking in a certain way, and controlling your negative emotions, allowed you to pass into a higher spiritual level after death."

"So, what is this soul," Benjamin asked.

"I do not know. The idea of a "spirit" or "soul", which I don't understand, is also something that I cannot even relate to, so I naturally I can't explain it. It was, however, the subject of many inspired discussions among clergy and others throughout all of human history." I realized that my answer was far too vague. "When I mentioned to the Governor we humans have souls, he told me that I was naïve and foolish to believe that religious nonsense. That is why I imagine this concept to be a pure invention to encourage human believers to live properly in society." I paused. "But then I am more inclined to believe in a superior being than a soul."

I reiterated to all who would listen that I pined for a meeting with this God. I even wistfully mentioned my fascination with religion to Dr. Gordon, hoping she would open up the channel of communication.

"When I raised the subject with Dr. Gordon, she laconically responded, "Religion is absurd." She then proceeded with a diatribe filled with skepticism, such as God was invented because humans desperately sought an explanation for the beginning of life. That led to beliefs that humans were made in the nebulous image of some superior being . . . essence of life. It became an obsession, driving humans to the brink. She haughtily added that Androids did not need to create an artificial being, because they all knew who their creator was. She maintained that such knowledge only confirmed the superiority of androids."

But I remained perplexed as to the number of wars provoked by religious conflict. Consequently, entire populations of non-believers were eradicated, massacred by so-called enlightened ones.

"It is difficult to believe, but each religion endeavored to be universal, the only true faith. That was incomprehensible to me since the main religions share many similar principles, even rituals, in particular, how they worship God. The spiritual leaders of the different religions, however, played a big role in inciting rivalry and conflict over the right to worship this God freely." I knew that I was summarizing complex philosophical, and maybe spiritual, beliefs in just a few words; but, it was my way of throwing out the subject for them. Hopefully they would have the opportunity to study it in more detail; that is if we successfully wage our campaign against the androids and overthrow them.

I tried to answer some of their questions. "For example, in some cases, I observed that humans from different parts of the world with different beliefs relentlessly pursued money and power, often inspired by ruthless greed and not by spiritual enlightenment. Each group wanted to control the others and in the end this forced people to fervently defend their right to believe differently."

"So, Pamela, why do you want to believe in this God?" Benjamin asked, and others joined in.

"I want to because I want someone to guide me and us to find a better world or, at least, a better place to live. The androids are devoid of feelings and translate everything into their own logic. It is easy to accept what they say simply because it is logical. The existence of a God attested to our need to use emotions and rely upon instinct. But both humans and androids make mistakes. A logical android decision, like termination, can be both cruel and inappropriate."

The consensus was that we needed to develop all of our human traits and attributes. They agreed with me that the androids did not have the right to deprive us of our right to exist as human beings. And, of course, we believed that we were certainly on the upper limit of the evolutionary chain. The use of violence, murder, and heinous acts should be controlled and punished. For whatever reason, the group in general felt that it was too dangerous to try to contact this superior being.

These discussions were tiring and almost frightening. They reminded me that we were heading towards an unpredictable world in which I was playing a vital role. I was afraid of what the future had in store.

Spending time with my family was curative, helping me to forget all those impending obligations and the unnatural lifestyle of the Center. Just thinking about Dr. Gordon made me nervous. Was she studying me as I interact with my family? Watching us like we were panthers in a cage? Should we be cringing from her empty vulgar stares? I certainly hoped not; but, if she were, perhaps she would be annoyed to see what makes humans happy. That visual receptor and those programmed careers and programmed exchanges gave us an artificial sense of pleasure; real happiness must come from within. Ridiculously, I wished that she could be jealous and would be jealous of my love for Peter and my Frederic. I wanted her to feel the emptiness inside of her. . .inside her chrome-lined body moving from an oily combination of moveable, metallic parts. It seemed natural that I should want to hurt her, because she was hurting me by making me the subject of her project, depriving me of being permanently with the ones that I love.

The evening before I left, I spent a few hours alone with John getting together all the questions that he had.

"Pamela, I am sorry; I know that it will be difficult, but I have to ask you to get into the reproduction section. I want you to find out more about the genetic profiles, the genome, used in procreation in the Center. I am also very interested in whether or not there were any real physical and/or intellectual differences between the various series. Test it. Take the basic genome of you, Pamela, for example, and find out whether there were any major differences— physically, intellectually, whatever-- between you, Pamela Series 13, and the other twelve?"

"I'll try, John, but can't promise anything." Actually this request interested me personally.

"Our education is another factor that preoccupies me. Like you, I have very little recollection of my early years. For example, I am not even certain that the memories I have of things like playing ball with other children are real or artificial. I also want Randolph and Stuart to find the codes to unlock and operate the various vehicles, including the aircraft, in the transport facility. What they sent me is not enough. And, remind Stuart that we should have weapons. He'll know how to get them."

"You want us to have weapons, John." I turned white and weak, leaning up against the wall to stabilize myself. I thought our offensive attack would be limited to hand-to-hand combat and, at the most, stunning the opposing forces, but not destroying them. "You want us to fight the androids; to destroy them."

"Pamela, be rational." He looked at me a bit askance. "You do not honestly think that the androids are going to let us break into the transport center and just leave with the flying machines, aircraft, and the rest." A few days ago, he had advocated seizing the aircraft and other transporters, but he said that we would be leaving as quickly as possible. I was the one who suggested we take over the Center, something that he found impossible. I stared at him in disbelief; as he clenched his teeth and fists. His eyes took on a glassy glare and he lunged forward swinging his clenched fists at invisible objects; as if he were striking down and destroying androids. I heard him scream. "Pamela, don't you remember what Peter said about how they coldly and calculatingly eliminated the humans in the spacecrafts?"

"Yes. I remember. The androids disintegrated them." I replied in a low sorrowful voice. "You were not so keen on having direct contact with the androids, let alone, destroying them just a few days ago."

"I agree, but I was testing you at that point." He smiled scornfully. "We test each other and, what do we discover? It is simple. Normally, we have the same position. You know as well as I do that they would not hesitate to do the same to us. "

"I don't know what to believe any more." I answered very sadly. Actually, I had not thought about all this as being a war. I read about wars, the horror and devastation that resulted; it made me cringe. "But, John, we don't know how to fight a war. Hand to hand combat and a couple of laser guns will not be enough to win." I tried to persuade him to change his mind.

"I know that. Why do you think, that I am trying to anticipate all the eventual problems that could arise to assure the success of our frontal attack?" He answered dryly. "Unlike you, Pamela, I want to believe that we have a winning chance." I looked at him skeptically.

"Are there weapons on the transporters?" I asked out of curiosity.

"I don't know." He shook his head. "The only thing we do know is that the androids launched a missile interceptor. I think that it was on the transporter, but . . . Do you realize that we don't even know how to launch the missile." He smiled for a minute and then said. "Yes, that is it. You must find someone who is working on missile launchers and other weapons. We must get that information directly." Now, he was enthusiastic. "You get Randolph and Stuart working on that. Maybe, someone in that sector has bypassed the programming."

"Ok. I shall do my best." I said unenthusiastically. "Nonetheless, we should be prepared for the androids to fire missiles back at us. We don't know how to turn on these machines, let alone get them off the ground. How are we going to maneuver them in combat?"

"True." This stopped him in his tracks. "Yes, that is a potential problem." And, then as if he received an invisible message of hope, he smiled at me and said. "We shall confront the obstacles and, I am certain, surmount them. In the meantime, you shall do more than your best. You are our link with that center." His voice was bellowing. "Listen to me and try to understand that our survival is becoming a delicate issue. We cannot survive forever in this little community. Our dependency on the center is delicate. The day that they no longer want to observe and study our mundane lifestyle, the day that they decide that we are a burden, a problem, for them they will cut off our lifeline. That means no more food or water. And maybe they'll come and collect our weak bodies and term. . ." His tremulous voice stopped; he couldn't say it.

He took a deep breath and pressed onwards, "You know that we have not found any suitable place to live within a fifty mile radius of this alcove. They set this place up for us, which means they can destroy it as well."

"Aren't you being just a bit dramatic, John?" He was going too far. "The Governor agreed to let you live here. Why should he change his mind?"

"Dramatic or not, I want to be sure that we shall survive and I'm not sure that our survival is their ultimate goal. You are in the position to secure information, to make contacts. You, Pamela, must do it; you must stay focused on our situation and stop caring about them!" His face was crimson and his body was trembling.

"Ok!" This time I was screaming, "But, John, maybe we don't have to destroy the androids. Maybe we can just force them to shut down." The idea of seeing Dr. Gordon going up in smoke revolted me. Even though I did not want to make love to her ever again, I could hardly imagine destroying her. She had been kind to me. She saved my life when she decided to study me.

I saw the tightness in his eyes and in his lopsided smile. I felt his contempt for me. I owed him an explanation. "John, I told you that I could not bear to see Dr. Gordon lifeless, the day that I witnessed her invasive examination. I know that it will sound strange to you but I felt lost and abandoned without her, even for that short thirty minutes. It was like losing a family member." Tears were filling my eyes, as I imagined never being able to speak to her again.

"Don't dramatize all this. She is after all a machine and, as you said so many times, she has no feelings. If you were terminated tomorrow she would replace you with someone else. So, try to keep a clear perspective. If you get emotionally involved with these machines, you will not only be risking your safety, but the safety of all of us." He seemed calmer. "But let's consider the idea of forcing them to shut down. I don't know how we could do that, but it is an interesting idea. If that is your choice, then you will have to find out how to shut them down. There must be a shut-down procedure."

"Yes, Dr. Gordon was ordered to shut down, but by her own kind. I don't know if androids are programmed to respond to a human order to shut down their systems." I thought about it for a second. "I don't think that we can do that otherwise they would not take the risk of having deprogrammed humans living around them."

"True," He said as he stroked his beard. "But, again, there may be someone in the computer section who is working on android capabilities who could help you. And, obviously, it will certainly not be possible for us to access their systems from far away. And, I doubt very much that we will ever have the opportunity to strap them to a chair and reach inside their bodies." He, paternally, took my hands in his. "You must not forget Peter, Frederic and the rest of us; we are the same race and should be your priority." He smiled warmly. "I know that all of this is not easy for you and that living with androids in the Center can be mind-boggling. If I have any advice to give now it is that our time is running out and surprise is our strongest tactical advantage. Do not reveal our objectives to anyone. Stay naive and inquisitive and gather all the information that you can. I have confidence in you, Pamela. So, don't let us down." Those words would ring in my head for the months to come.

I prepared for my return. I would carry with me that feeling that it was unfair that I had to leave my little family again. I tried harder this time to paint a lasting picture in my mind of Peter and Frederic. Would I be able to close my eyes and see them in front of me, something that I wasn't able to do for very long the last time I left them? Would I remember their smell, their laughter and their special mannerisms? One of the most painful consequences of the separation was the feeling of emptiness. I longed to be in the arms of Peter as much as I longed to hold Frederic in mine. That physical contact gave me courage, a sense of security and a reason and desire to live. If only that feeling of physical contact with them could accompany me, keeping me strong in the insensitive, bleak environment that I would soon be entering.

Like the first time my family, Peter and Frederic, walked me to the meeting place, I was not the champion I would have wanted to be. Every step I took felt heavier than the last. I languished in my own despair, insensitive to their pain. Peter and Frederic were on either side of me holding my hands. I knew that I needed to show more strength and say that they should not worry, that I would be fine and would be back soon. I finally brushed away the tears that were incessantly streaming down my face from my swollen, bloodshot eyes, and stopped our lugubrious procession.

I gave Frederic a big hug and kissed him tenderly on his cheek. "You are my little love. I want you to continue to learn, have fun, and practice your clarinet. I am expecting you to be even better than Jonathan when I get back." He giggled. I then stroked Peter's face and kissed him passionately. "I love you," I whispered in his ear. His hands clenched my body.

"I have to go, Peter."

"How I hate to see you leave!" he said as he released his grip.

I could see the android guards from the corner of my eye, so I forced a big smile before I waved goodbye. When I was far enough away from Peter and Frederic, I buried my face in my hands and started to cry again. "How many more times would I have to repeat this scene?" was the question that preoccupied me.

Chapter 32: Complicity

Iwas back in the center with its sterile walls and streams of programmed humans who seemed as much machines as the androids. I stood observing and eavesdropping on a small group. They were discussing their research. They were all delighted with the excellent results. I broke into their conversation and asked what kind of project they were working on. They didn't answer me so I repeated my question, emphasizing the fact that the purpose and reason for the project interested me. They ignored me.

A young woman with a very prominent chin and long nose asked the others if they heard a voice. They all agreed that they heard a voice but they couldn't see anyone. Finally, she asked me to identify myself. "If you are not a transmission, would you please give us your code number?" In a heavy monotone voice she continued. "You probably should report to the infirmary. You must have a problem." I stared back into her blank eyes and at that plastered smile on her face.

I had forgotten that I was invisible to her and all the others because my wristband was no longer functioning. Of course, she needed my code, and the rest of the group needed it to see me. I didn't know if I should laugh or lament my foolishness, my extreme recklessness. Dr. Gordon encouraged me to circulate and meet humans, but to make contact was a slap in my face. I was more than just the experiment for Dr. Gordon; I was also an informer. The androids could identify a deprogrammed human because we would have eye contact. I had to be more careful. Just spending a week with the outside community had made me too much at ease with humans. Fortunately, everyone in this group was still under programming. That was evident.

I lost interest in them an eased away ignoring those who were still calling out to me. I went off in the direction of Randolph's lab. He was alone when I dashed into the room. I turned in circles to be certain that I was not being followed. As always, a beautiful, genuine smile appeared on his face and I felt safe

"Well, you are back already?" He asked teasingly.

"Yes. I wish I weren't. I feel like I am living in a prison here." I sighed. "And, I already miss Peter and Frederic."

"Tell me about it." he asked nonchalantly.

I watched him as he started to arrange his things. "I just made a bit of a mistake. I forgot that the others cannot see us and I tried to enter into one of their conversations. How stupid?"

"Wait, Pamela, just a minute." He put his finger over his lips to hush me as he picked up a strange device and carried it as he swept the area like a minefield. When he finished, he started to talk. "I have been careful about who I speak to since I bypassed the programming. People who do talk to me are all in the same situation as I am." He took a long breath and went on. "I did make the link between seeing and not being seen. We talked about it. Remember?"

"Right, no reason to repeat the same things over and over again. What, by the way were you doing with that device?"

"Just checking to make sure that no one planted any listening devices in this room. Since you left, Dr. Gordon has been hanging around my lab a bit too much."

"Well, she is a real enigma." I commented. "Do you think that she used me to find others in our situation?"

"No doubt about that." His raspy sardonic laugh filled the air "Can you imagine how much fun she had with that. It is so diabolical that it stinks."

"You told me that your partner doesn't see you?"

"Yes. She started to. She was one of us. I didn't tell you because it wasn't necessary for me to do that. Her program imploded a long time ago now when she made her own shocking discovery about our world."

"I don't understand, why didn't you tell me?" I found that rather strange on his part, I thought that we were friends and confidants.

"You were so consumed with Dr. Gordon at the time that I didn't see the point." He hesitated." I didn't want to worry you."

I was too tired to argue over that so I embarked on my information-gathering mission.

"What does she do?"

"She was a geologist, strangely enough. Her projects have all revolved around another period in time. Quite by accident, she searched beyond the parameters of one her projects, into maybe a dark, undiscovered world. She never talked much about what she discovered, but I think that it is why they terminated her a few days ago."

"What? They terminated her?" I was horrified. I could see tears in his eyes.

"Also, after you left, Dr. Gordon ordered unlaced food for me. My partner was not that good looking but she had a seductive air about her. She didn't realize it though." His downturned lips and dropping eyebrows were enough for me to see that he was profoundly affected, and, even though it did him good to talk about this, I could see how difficult it was for him. "I started to imagine a real, full relationship with her. Can you picture that, Pamela?" I smiled. "I even talked to her about how I stopped eating the food and all my human urges surfaced. She followed my example for 24 hours and then she was gone. Terminated!"

He was emptying out all his pain. "Your Dr. Gordon came by and remarked, 'Too bad for you, Randolph.' I knew right away that she knew about us and our relationship got under Gordon's android outer shell. She did not want me to be having fun with my partner. I feel certain that she is the one who recommended my partner be terminated."

That carefree, always smiling Randolph was …hot and livid. This was the second time in only a couple days that I saw a man physically display outrage and anger. Randolph took on the same look as John did; his eyebrows were tight, his lips drawn back revealing his clenched teeth, and his eyes were lit up with that same icy folly that I saw in John's. Instead of flinging his clenched fists wildly in mid-air, Randolph started to throw his heavy equipment on the floor as he kicked the equipment and the lab table, violently. I was surprised that nothing collapsed. I froze, afraid of what he might do next. I don't know how much time passed before his display of uncontrollable anger subsided, but when it did, he took up the conversation as if nothing spectacular, strange or out of the ordinary had taken place. He stopped and stood in a visible calm and I started to tremble involuntarily, certainly in reaction to that dramatic scene. "That's why I am worried about being watched." He looked at me with disgust and then asked with audacity, "Did you know that Dr. Gordon was watching your every move when you were in your cubicle?"

"What? Oh, what horror, why did she do that?" I murmured. "No, I didn't know that. I was worried that Dr. Crawford may have ordered surveillance, but I never imagined that Dr. Gordon would go that far. I was so certain that she would not act so recklessly. She had a lot to lose if anyone else saw the love scenes." I sat down and covered my face. "How disgusting. She must have watched our love making over and over again hoping that the videos would help to incite human emotions in her!" I spit the words out with disgust. "But, worse than that, she saw the two of us. I understand why you suspected me." I was revolted. "She actually watched us having sex that famous night before I left and, she heard our discussions." I felt a wave of panic overcome me. How was I going to handle this?

I yearned to walk directly into her office and rip out her inner circuits. I was living a nightmare. I already dreaded returning to this Center, and now with all this bad news, a termination, video surveillance... I can't bare living another day in this environment.

"Of course, she saw our sexual encounter. That is why she has been strutting around in front of me. She changed her wig. She has hair like yours now." I screeched in horror. "I guess that she wanted me to fall into her arms." He hit the table hard with his hand and screamed, "Never. Do you hear me you wretched machine. Never!" He raised his voice in a loud, resounding tone.

"Ok, Randolph, please try to calm down." The more he continued with this unabashed, angry behavior, the better for her study of human emotions. "Does she know that you gave me the codes?" I was afraid to ask, but it was important to know. He raised his shoulders and flipped open his hands; he didn't know. "Maybe then the video equipment was only around the bed?" I was desperately hoping that that was the case. He didn't answer.

He was not ready to calm down and everything that I said was fueling his anger. If I was studying human emotions, I would have found that interesting. But, that was not the case. I sat down and started to breathe slowly and deeply; trying to relax and hoping that he would follow my example. It worked. I saw him, from the corner of my eye, repeat my moves as he sat down on the floor and took long, deep breaths.

We both needed time to approach this problem in a rational way. I was the one to speak up first. "Let's just try to get everything straight. If she has planted a non-detectable device in this lab and is watching and listening to you, we have everything to lose. She can just throw away her project and get rid of us. However, if she finds your anger interesting, I can assure you that her reaction to you is not at all what you are hoping for. Remember, she has no feelings. She is a good actress, so to speak, and, an excellent manipulator. But, the most that you can expect from her, concerning you, is an appendix to her study of human emotions, entitled the extent to which a human can mourn the loss of another human. So stop." I said without raising my voice. "Don't let her recognize our weaknesses. Pretend that a partner is a partner and nothing more. Please don't give her that satisfaction or anything to use against us."

I was calmly begging him. He was looking straight in my eyes, as he listened intently; so I continued. "Look at her as if she doesn't exist. Even the androids cannot accept that. They need to believe that they are important and that we feel humble in their presence. If you ignore her, she will use more excessive displays of interest and resort to ostentatious, flamboyant behavior, just to draw android attention to herself. I have seen her do that in that past. That kind of behavior interests Dr. Crawford and his allies who have been trying to put an end to her study of me for a long time. Remember, she has to defend her actions before the commission."

"Ok, Pamela. I know that you are right." Even though his mouth and fists were no longer clenched, his muscles looked tight. He was not yet relaxed. "But, I could kill her! In fact, I want to." He looked anxiously around the room in spite of having determined earlier that the room was not bugged.

I quickly retorted, "Who knows, you might have the opportunity to do that. But, now is not the right time." I followed him as my eyes circled the room in his rhythm until we were looking directly into the others' eyes. "Do you think that we are safe to talk here?"

"Yes." His voice was much calmer.

Relieved, I immediately released a stream of air I didn't even know I had held in. "The present research in the telecommunications department is so far behind what John and I discovered and adapted for our own use." He smiled now. "Of course, it is a bit humorous that they are using outdated surveillance equipment. Don't you think?"

"I am aware of that. John already explained that the video surveillance that they use on the outside is so dated." I was hoping that he would not flip over what I was going to say now, but I had to get on with information gathering, the ultimate objective of my mission. "I am very sorry that your partner was terminated. It may not have been because of Dr. Gordon's interest in me and you, but because of her discovery; and" I ventured further, "she would have been terminated regardless of the deprogramming."

He was sitting, leaning on his elbows. My remark seemed to interest him as he took his chin in his hand and stroked it pensively. That encouraged me to continue. "She was working in one of the areas that we need to investigate." He nodded. "John would like a reasonably detailed map of the planet." I murmured. "Randolph, Dr. Gordon spoke to me about dry and wet areas in a very vague and nonchalant manner. We need to find a zone that would allow us to develop our own community and survive."

"We can just take over the center. That is the most logical thing to do."

"John is not completely confident that we can defeat the androids. Only a small group of us are trained for combat and no one knows anything about military strategy." I was studying him. He moved from a violent, emotionally charged mood to an ultra-calm, neutral, indifferent mood, neither one of which represented the Randolph that I knew. I shook off my thoughts and laid out my most convincing argument. "Let's be rational. None of us know how to fire or use weapons."

"I do. I know how to fire a weapon."

If I hadn't been sitting, I would have fallen over. "What? You never told me that. It isn't even in your project area."

"True. But, I had training in weapon firing when I was growing up. For some unknown reason, I was selected to target shoot. As I was relatively good at it, I was given the opportunity to try laser weapons and explosives. Of course, I was under surveillance. Those creations were impressed with my accuracy. I fooled around with that for a long time before I was redirected to physics and chemistry as a profession."

"Great News!" I exclaimed. "But, even so, you cannot go it alone." I continued. "Do you want to know about the conversations on the outside?

"I don't have to go it alone, Stuart will be with me." He said so convincingly. "And, why not? –to answer your question. What is happening?"

"Well a lot of the same old things actually but, apart from what I just mentioned, genetic combinations was one of the highlights of the last conversation I had with John. He wants answers to a number of questions. For example, on what basis do they select the combination of male and female donors? We know that the sperm and the ovules are collected. I remember being held captive in a hospital zone long enough for them to extract ovules. The fertilization is done in vitro. You know that?"

"I am familiar with the idea, but I don't know exactly how the procedure works. But, John does have a point there. They must be mixing and matching genomes with combinations of superior genes to come up with individuals that will excel in certain areas." He stopped and rubbed his hands over the corners of his mouth. "That could explain why they don't consider our long term survival important, especially since our replacement is waiting for us, in vitro."

"Yes. That part is really bizarre, petrifying." It was horrifying even to imagine running into a manufactured version of... myself.

"Did you know that humans tried to clone themselves?" He lifted his eyebrows to emphasize the point.

"No, I don't even know what cloning is."

"It was a way to make an identical image of yourself. It took time before the method was perfected enough to accomplish this ultimate result. In the beginning, the clone was to be kept alive but in suspension, a kind of suspended animation in some refrigeration facility during the lives of the original donor. Their very existence was to provide body parts, organs that could be transplanted into the body of the donor, when needed. And the worst of it is the clone is a human being continually frozen and only thawed out and returned to life long enough to be operated on and robbed of another organ and then refrozen." I involuntarily heaved, a dry heave like I was going to vomit and then it stopped.

"Sounds horrible to grab organs; it's monstrous, perverse!" He nodded his head as I continued," So, where are they now, the clones?"

"Don't know. I have a friend who works in the field of genetics. He told me about clones a while ago. He just said that it was a dangerous idea. Cloning was abused by people in powerful positions who wanted to continue to exist beyond a normal human lifetime, but I don't know how long a normal human lifetime was at that period in our history." He told me everything that he knew. "You know, Pamela, we don't have access to all the information. Maybe you should look into that at the Library."

"Maybe your friend can give us some insight into the genetic selections."

"Probably. He is not easy to find; they isolate him a lot. Maybe he is working on projects that they consider top-secret." He paused. "So what would be top-secret for the androids?"

"Well, going back to your partner. Could you get access to her projects?"

"That is not possible. But, I do know someone who was working closely with her. She must be deprogrammed like us because they were always together. Let me see whether I can contact any of these people."

"Ok. One more question: Is Stuart still around?"

"Yes. We should try to meet him in a protected area. We don't want the androids to get the names of everyone needing to be replaced; do we?" He said sarcastically.

"I am off now. Will stop by later. Thanks Randolph. I feel better knowing that you're around." I smiled.

"Me too."

When I opened the door, Dr. Gordon was standing there. Randolph was not kidding, she had changed her look and, although she could not pass for my twin, she had my hair, a wig identical to my hair. I smiled and said hello.

"Hello, Pamela. I am so happy to run into you. You must stop by my office and tell me how things are going for your family and friends." She obviously was not aware of my meeting with Randolph or she would have reacted differently. "Perhaps you don't know that Randolph's partner was terminated. His emotional state is very interesting for my study. So, you will excuse me now. I want to talk to him. "

I knew exactly what she wanted to talk to him about, but pretended otherwise. I shook her hand and moved on. She was a walking paradox.

I decided to visit the library for the afternoon. I might find some information about cloning and maybe something concerning the geographic changes. Perhaps I could set up a better relationship with Dr. Miller. She might be willing to give me more pertinent information, if I ask the right kinds of questions.

Dr. Miller was behind the front desk when I arrived and was quick to ask me where I had been. I explained that I was outside with my family, something that seemed to interest her quite a bit. She found it amazing that humans could have that kind of emotional contact with another and with their offspring. "Of course," she added. "We don't reproduce so, naturally, we cannot identify with you." She acted as if our first, and only, encounter was amicable. Either she did not realize the negative energy that passed between us or she just wanted to start over again. Either reason was ok for me, as I saw her as a source of information.

"But, Dr. Miller," I began, "as has been pointed out to me on many occasions, you androids do not have an emotional configuration. So, of course, you cannot relate to us." And, then I logically followed that up with another question. "Did you have a special relationship with your creator?"

I was surprised with her response. "Strange that you should ask that, Pamela. We have often asked ourselves that same question. We all admit that we miss the presence of our creators." She stared at me for a minute before going on. "You know that with time and technological advancements, our creators created us in their own image. Some of us, Dr. Gordon and I, before my accident, were so much like our creators that we often were mistaken by others for the human version."

"Were you and Dr. Gordon good friends? And was she good friends with any humans?"

"No, not at all to both of your questions. The humans didn't like her because she was difficult to work with. And, she was competitive on every level with her human co-workers.

"Interesting. I thought being competitive was human." I noticed that her body started to jerk with that. "So, if I understand, that is why you don't like Dr. Gordon?" I asked as I started to walk over to the computer terminals.

"Pamela, you are mistaken. There is no rivalry between us."

"Not since your accident. But before?'

She started to turn in circles again. I wondered if that was her natural reflex when I touched on the truth of something; or otherwise brought up a sensitive subject. So, quickly, I added. "Just teasing! Something very human, so don't get all upset."

"I am not upset." Clearly, she was no longer upset because she was under control, gliding forward in a straight line. I smiled to myself, as I confirmed my suspicion. I liked having this kind of control over her.

"So what would you like to absorb today?" She broke into my thoughts.

"A bit about the planet earth, like the geography and the geology, how that evolved with time, if you don't mind?"

I sat impatiently for a good half hour before she returned with just a couple disks.

"Is that it?" I was disappointed. "I thought that I would have hours of reading."

"There is just not much on the subject." she explained.

"Why not?" I persisted.

"How can I say this?" She bit her beautiful android lips, a very human reflex that she must have gotten from the real Dr. Miller. "Geography and geology were not considered a priority because the earth has changed so much that it is useless to hold on to old information that has and would never have much relevance." And then, referring to what she had said before, she added that human history was carefully edited. Entire chapters were abridged, non-essential facts were omitted and irrelevant data deleted.

"And these disks, what are they all about?"

"The end, or just before the end of human history." She could have stopped there, but I think that she wanted to push the envelope on taboo subjects and, of course, that would certainly upset Dr. Gordon. "You see the climate was changing so rapidly. You do understand what climate is?" I felt insulted, but just nodded my head. "There were so many inaccurate predictions and even more inaccurate solutions, as history would confirm. But, humans were aware of the dramatic climate changes and tried to become more ecologically sensitive. They invested a great deal in cleaning up the environment, which they themselves had polluted." She saw my look of astonishment. "It doesn't matter, the earth continues to exist. It's just that humans need a myriad of toys, their machine games."

"Toys? What do you mean?" I remembered hearing Dr. Crawford's warning to Dr. Gordon when I was feigning unconsciousness in the hospital's pre-termination unit. He told her not to become a toy in my hands. I didn't know exactly what that meant, but it, nonetheless, sounded like a dreadful, perhaps, dangerous, situation for her to find herself in.

"Toys is a very broad word. Humans liked, from the very beginning of their history, to play with balls and sticks, I guess you called them "bats" and whatever else they could get their hands on. For example, the vacation center has all kinds of activities, balls like basketballs, footballs, and so forth. You have fun playing, don't you?"

"Yes, I never engaged in team sports until recently." I put out for comment. "But, we never called balls toys."

"No, of course not. Team sports are forbidden. You just learn how to put a ball in a loop or hit a ball with a bat, or other such activities, for your own pleasure, or amusement." She tried to pull herself to a very erect position of authority, an effort that highlighted her awkward appearance. I swallowed my laugh. "Some of us know, as you just mentioned, that you and your friends on the outside are engaging in team sports." I just stared at her. "Be careful to whom you mention that. Some people will not be happy with that news." I nodded that I understood. "Oh, well, toy is a very broad term. The word, toy, has been removed from the dictionary and no one uses that word today."

"But, toys were objects to play with and some were designed for children and other toys were designed for adults. Adults played with machines and transport vehicles and destructive objects, like guns, especially the men and boys. I even think they called them, 'boys' toys', although girls and women eventually took a liking to them." I wasn't following her very well, but I realized that it was better for me to pretend I understood so all of it flowed from her lips. And when she spied my smile, meaning I agreed, she'd continued like an open faucet.

"So, you see Pamela, some of their toys were destructive for the environment. Oh, humans were very clever as they invented so many things. Their curiosity about life and improvements was insatiable. So, they were, as I just said, very creative. But, not everything they created was harmless for them or the environment. So, the earth's climate changed radically bringing about many natural disasters. Their attempts to alleviate disasters often failed." I could not understand the connection between toys and environment, but I was pleased to hear her address this point. It could be useful for us.

"But," She continued at high speed; "it is not because humans could not have avoided natural destructions, it is just that their hypotheses and their conclusions were wrong. They did not properly identify or even anticipate the exact causes of the environmental changes and therefore did not introduce effective measures to prevent ultimate environmental destruction. In effect, the environment started collapsing on top of them. So their attempts were also too little, too late. " She shook her head as if she really regretted what happened.

"So, that is why there are now wet and dry areas?" I was trying to pull answers from her.

"Oh, that has taken a long time to develop. But, climatic changes did not bring an end to human history. They would have maybe had time to restudy and thwart radical climate changes before doomsday; if they had not destroyed themselves first."

"They destroyed themselves?" I asked with trepidation in my voice. I didn't believe for one minute that humans could have destroyed themselves. Why would they have done that? If they had, why were the androids still around? Our eye contact was intense at this point. I almost felt that I could reach another personality hidden inside of her, and then, just like that, she turned in circles and meandered back to her place. Her explanation left me more confused than ever about climate change and environmental destruction. I had the impression that she did not know much about the subject and her long-winded speech lacked credibility.

The computer disks she brought me were not that interesting. I already had an idea of continents, countries and climate before the end of human history. The only interesting point in these disks was the mention of climate warming. A great deal of attention was focused upon the melting of the Polar Regions. There seemed to be more natural disasters from the beginning of the 21st century. The discs that Dr. Miller gave me did not give me any idea of the topography of the earth today.

My thoughts started to move in other directions. Radical changes in the earth's temperature took place during the prehistoric period, if the information that I was given was accurate. The earth went through a glacial period, lasting for thousands of years, which I believe was followed by earthquakes and volcanic eruptions—a period of very high temperatures, again lasting thousands of years. Perhaps the radical changes in the earth's temperature near the end of human history were linked to the earth's internal clock. Perhaps, even assuming that humans miscalculated the causes of climate changes, they may not have been able to do anything to prevent or reverse the earth's natural programmed development. I sighed to myself. What did I know about that? I have absolutely no scientific training. I got up to leave.

I handed Dr. Miller the disks and told her that she was right. There was nothing very up-to-date in the file. "Don't look so disappointed, Pamela." She moved very close to me and then whispered in my ear that I should come back the following afternoon. "Maybe there will be something more interesting for you then." This time I could see beyond those android eyes. I felt like I was speaking to the real Dr. Miller. I just smiled and nodded because we understood each other.

I meandered back to the lab area to pop in to see Randolph. I found him slouching on his lab chair with his head between his hands. Taking a lock of hair between my fingers, I lifted his face gently. His downturned eyes and dropping lips gave me the impression that he was definitely depressed. I rightly surmised that his session with Dr. Gordon didn't turn out as he expected.

I went straight to the point. "So, she got what she wanted?"

"Not really. She is just not my type. I told her that I couldn't get interested sexually with a machine." Just getting that off his chest gave a slight glow to his cheeks, making him look a lot better. "She told me that she did not appreciate my uncooperative behavior." He shook his head in disgust. "You know, Pamela, you set a dangerous precedent for all of us. That android just cannot accept "No" for an answer. She is persistent. What I am worried about is that she won't stop."

"Well, I told you that I said "No" too in the beginning. Then she caught me off guard and things just flowed naturally." This time I was smiling because it was nice to know that I was not the only human to face this dilemma.

"Maybe you could talk to her for me?" He suggested.

"Randolph, she is not going to discuss this with me. And, it would be very dangerous for me to bring up the subject. She has her own agenda, but, like all the androids, she doesn't completely trust humans, and therefore her reactions are unpredictable." I was worried about getting involved and sincerely believed that Randolph was capable of dealing with this situation on his own. He had to. He just had to make up his mind.

He didn't answer, so I tried to persuade him, this time in a different way, by putting pressure. "You know, Randolph, there is no way that I am going to risk my life or the whole group to protect you." That got his attention. "I would recommend that you show some courage; prevent her from getting her way." Now he was sitting upright. "Ah, I know what you can do, slyly turn it into an educational experience for her by teaching her that rejection is a human emotion. That it is painful to be rejected, but it happens and humans learn to deal with it. She might find that interesting."

His eyes started to sparkle with interest; I paused for a second, to formulate an alternative.

"You know, she was a very good partner. She is curiously stimulating, and enjoys trying different positions, and her vibrating hands create new, sexually dynamic sensations. It might be easier to give up fighting, and go for sex. You won't fall in love with her, but you could have some real fun."

And then the absurdity of it hit me and I let out a belly laugh, jiggling and wrenching my innards until the pain tempered it. I sheepishly looked at Randolph whose pierced lips opened to show his teeth as he gasped, his body shaking as he belted out his own belly laugh until he placed his forefinger between his teeth, and stopped.

His lips pierced again to signal the end of our hysterical catharsis.

"She reminded me that I was living without a partner, which was forbidden at the center. When I asked why this was the case, she said that it was because she was protecting me. She insinuated that I was scheduled to be terminated at the same time as my partner and that she could only protect me for so long."

That was definitely bad news. It was clear that we could not afford to lose Randolph.

"Do you understand, Pamela? She is quite vicious for an android. She barred her teeth as she chomped down on the word, protection, like she was sucking me into her, reminding me that I owed her." He took a deep breath, exhaling vehemently before continuing. "For certain, she is responsible for the termination of my partner. She must have planned all this, to get my partner out of the way, to get her claws into me. And, now you recommend that I play the game?"

"It would appear that you don't have a choice. Your life hinges on cooperation. Of course this changes the strategy." I tried to imagine how we could control this android that was manipulating everyone in the center. "Yes, Randolph, play the game, but play it better than she could ever imagine. Make her crave our world of sensations, a world that she is incapable of crossing into. Create an inextricable dependency and need for you that we can exploit for our projects. Make her wish that she could fall in love, in some perverse androidian way. We humans can be very vicious as well. You don't have to feel anything but contempt and disgust, but go through the motions keeping your eye on the goal."

Randolph was hunched over and again holding his head in his hands. I reached over and stroked his hair.

"But, just pretend that she means something to you and make her fall completely under your charm. That is it. Make her feel that she can trust you. She has very powerful enemies who would revel in naming her a… traitor."

"And you, will I ever be able to be alone with you again, Pamela? You know what I mean. How can you ask me to replace you with her?"

"We are great friends Randolph. Just knowing that you are here with me in the Center gives me courage. There is a strong bond between us that means that we can express ourselves on any level. Your involvement with her does not affect our deep-rooted friendship; and could not prevent us from being close, even physically close." A slight smile reappeared on his face. I guess that I said that well. I could not be passionately in love with two people at the same time, it did not fit into my personality, I suppose. But, I had great affection for Randolph and would not refuse a playful spin with him, if the occasion presented itself.

"Because, we have no choice; we've got to win or die. And, she is, above all, a means to our success. Let's keep in mind that even though she was happy to be with me, she was not looking for love. With you, that could be different. You're a man and she might be hungry for a classical, typical human relationship, between a man and a woman, well a …"

I was searching for ideas to convince him that it was in all our interests he engage in a relationship with her. I knew, from what she said to me, that she could not experience emotions and as such love was certainly outside of her android capacities. But, I sensed that she could be possessive of someone. I am an object that she possesses; she can amuse herself with me. And, she will defend me if someone tries to take me away from her. That might be the closest to a love relationship that an android can ever have. But, that is not so reassuring, because the day that I am no longer of interest for her, she can just throw me away, without regret.

He interrupted my bantering, and my couple minutes of reflection, obviously trying to change the subject, "Well, I'll think about it."

By the way, did you find out anything about the geography and geological structure of the planet?"

"No." I then related Dr. Miller's offer.

"Do you think that she is against the controlling group at the center?"

"Don't know, but her creator and the creator of Dr. Gordon were not good friends. I wonder if the personalities rubbed off. If not, maybe there is something subtle in their programming that recalls personality traits. These androids seem to be at a critical stage in their history. I sense diversity in their group. Look at your supervisor, for example?"

"Talking about my supervisor, she told me today that she was going to inform Dr. Gordon that she had no authority in the lab. She didn't want her to show up in the lab when she was not on duty."

"You see. I am right." That news made me happy, even if his android was only vying for a better position in the hierarchy, and not an outright revolt. "Let them fight it out. We just go with the flow when the dust settles." Then I remembered that I would have to see Dr. Gordon about Jonathan's pain. I explained all that to Randolph and promised to keep him informed.

The hall clock read 5:30 PM. I could still see Dr. Gordon today if I hurried up a bit. I passed rapidly by the other humans who walked casually down the hallway. As I approached Dr. Gordon's office, I saw the Governor leaving. I recoiled into the shadows until he disappeared down the corridor and then stepped up and knocked on the door.

She stood up and asked me to sit down for a small chat, as she put it. She had a real flare for human small talk as it gave her the opportunity to identify and read different human emotions. She didn't have to introduce subjects, something that always put me ill at ease. I preferred small talk because I got to choose the subject. I mentioned Jonathan's problem and was confronted with her usual indifference.

"You are talking about pain, are you, Pamela?" But before I could answer she went on with what sounded like a prepared speech. "Pain, Pamela, is human. How can I understand that? We never have pain."

"Yes, you do." I was walking on sandy soil with that but wanted to confuse her. "Remember when you came to see me because you were worried about being shut down permanently?

"Yes, of course, but there was no pain."

"Well, there might have been if you hadn't been asked to shut down before the examination. Imagine if the technician were to open you up and pull out wires while you were awake."

"No, you don't understand." She shook her head. "We shut down because it is easier for a technician to verify our circuitry. There is no element of pain involved. Being awake, so to speak, would, of course, be a rather disagreeable way to examine an android only because we would recognize that certain functions were inoperable. But, pain? No, Pamela, we would not experience pain."

"How do you know? If I were to open the control panel and undo a wire, maybe you would have pain. Would you like me to try?"

"No, because you are not competent to replace the circuitry." Her expression was blank. "But, I assure you, that I would have no pain."

"If you like. But, I believe that you would have pain." She tapped her android fingers on the desktop to annoy me. "So, if you want to know how Jonathan feels, you should let me try to explain pain to you."

"I can see that your week with family and friends has made you very bold." She sat back in her chair and stared at me as if she were able to see through me. Finally, she nodded and said that she could at least understand and would accept that pain, a physical condition of humans, causes suffering, if that is what I wanted her to understand.

"Well, now I can speak more freely. Jonathan never had any pain when he was here in the center. It is only recently that he has started to suffer." She was fiddling with her fingers, pretending to be bored. I was not going to get discouraged. "Well, he can hardly walk now. He doesn't understand why he has so much pain and why he never had it before."

She sighed as if she had to deal with a moron and wasn't certain how to begin. "Did you take a good look at Jonathan?" I nodded. "He is deformed. He was scheduled to be terminated before his deformities became intolerable for him." She forced a kind of smile. "You see, Pamela, we care about you humans. We don't want you to suffer."

"That doesn't explain why he didn't have pain throughout his childhood and adult life. I've never heard of deformities deteriorating and becoming very painful later in life."

"Yes, yes, but…Oh, why do you come with such stories? I don't care about all of this." I just wanted her to get on with it. She seemed to purposely evade my questions, obscuring their importance. I wondered if she was hiding something or simply didn't care.

"Human anatomy and physiology is not my field." She resumed. "But, I can still explain this problem. The programming system has a blocker in it. There are many of you at the center who are deformed. So, to rectify that, a nerve blocking system prevents you from experiencing discomfort. In effect, the pain, as you put it, is there, you just don't feel it. With Jonathan, his nervous system had been dulled for so long that it took time for him to get back in touch with it."

"Then, you just lied to me when you told me that his termination was scheduled to avoid the discomfort of oncoming pain?" I dared to proceed even though I expected her wrathful indignation at my confronting her. But I may be dangerously pressing her limits. . .

The way she acted frightened me. She raised herself high in her chair; rubbing her hands together, as her eyes turned into two huge black holes, beckoning me to fall deep inside. I never saw her like that before. I grabbed the sides of my chair and moved my body closer to the edge, perched to jump up and run should she approach me. She spoke; her android body, stiff and menacing, in contrast to her calm, clear voice. "Pamela, androids cannot lie. We can't and we don't lie. You humans could misunderstand us, but we don't lie. Lying is human."

I wondered if I should stop; even though I savored the power of putting her on the defensive, I questioned whether I was pushing her, and maybe she'll go ballistic, over the top. She would then be dangerous.

I decided to back-peddle, "I misunderstood, if you prefer. But, then what can we do for him now?"

"Nothing, absolutely nothing. He wanted to leave the center." She looked more relaxed as she smirked and flipped her fingers in the air, as if by this gesture she was getting rid of Jonathan.

"Again, I misunderstood. I thought that you decided to send him on the outside." I played with my fingers and kept eye contact before adding. "That his arrival was part of your experiment with me."

"I don't know where you got that idea from. The decision to let him leave the center was made by the Governor."

"And you had nothing to do with it?" Now I was clearly treading on dangerous ground, but I intuited that if I pushed further, just a little bit. . .

"Well. I was not that much in favor of the decision." She pushed back her chair and stood up. She peered down at me with her glaring black eyes. "Disappointed, Pamela?" She sat back down and waited. Her furrowed brow and haunting eyes turned on me, waiting for a response. She was studying my body language and had been since the beginning. I realized that our entire exchange was an opportunity for her to visualize my emotional reactions through my unconscious body movements. I found that despicable. But, what if my body language signaled an imminent violent reaction on my part?

I was deep in thought, pretending to study her. I decided to disappoint her now, if she could experience disappointment. I changed my strategy. I was not going to give her any satisfaction; there would be no uncontrolled, emotional reaction from the bird in the glass cage. She was a machine, a machine devoid of emotions, but not a machine imbued with a heightened sense of morality. She was adept at twisting the facts and omitting information in order to back up her position. Yes, she could lie; I had no doubt about that. She knew now that I didn't believe her. That would have to be enough for the moment.

My voice was calm and clear when I said. "Whatever. But, what can be done for Jonathan now? He is suffering. There is nothing available to take away the pain except for the nerve blocker that was connected to the visual receptor, if I understood everything you said?"

"Oh, Pamela. Look around you. Everyone is in good health." She stopped for a minute; probably, to get my full attention. "Let me tell you a story. A long time ago, because it is a long time ago now, humans did have problems with their health. There were all kinds of illnesses, some of them fatal, others debilitating; and others, very mild. There were treatments for these illnesses. I use to think that humans enjoyed taking medications, little colored tablets and capsules. We androids found it interesting how dependent humans were on all these chemical blends. Then came the end to all of that chemical dependency. It happened so fast. There were no more tablets." She just stopped at that point and moved to stand up again. Her nonchalant behavior emboldened me again to pursue her.

"But, me, I was treated with chemicals. And, I saw Doctors. You are a doctor and you took care of me." Now, I was rambling. "I spent a long time on intravenous treatment. I lost my hair. I lost my sense of taste. I want some answers."

"Of course you do, Pamela. " She said so patronizingly, as she sat down again. "We all want answers. There just aren't any. As for your treatment, it is all that we have. One of our specialists worked on chemical therapy technology. We saw that in some cases chemical imbalances caused the visual receptor to shut down, so, we used a pre-fabricated blend of chemicals. In most cases, though, we were forced to terminate those who were unable to readapt because the chemical treatment didn't work. But, that is all we have." She looked into space as if she was returning in time.

"What do you mean, pre-fabricated chemicals?" I asked, as I twisted my mouth in disgust.

"That, Pamela, is none of your business. I have nothing more to say about that. But, I shall consult my memory banks on treatments for pain." I waited for her to do her thorough search, hoping that she would find something interesting to say.

"I found it." She announced. "In the past, there was medication for pain. Unfortunately, we have no record of what chemicals were used and in which proportions. And, even if we did, those chemicals may no longer be available. "

"That is it? That is all you have to say?" What a wretched creation she is.

"Others like your Jonathan have lived happy and comfortable lives. Everyone's termination date is randomly selected on the day of birth. Or, not really at birth as you know it now. No one here gives birth to a child like you did with Frederic." She looked at me with squinted eyes. "There is far too much discussion among you deprogrammed humans. I am certain that Sarah or Ruth explained to you in vitro fertilization." I nodded.

She raised her eyebrows and puckered her mouth. "But, as I was saying, there is a date when a baby is capable of living without life support, and we call that the birth date. Every human here is terminated before the age of 30. Some of you live to that date; others leave sooner. The time, year, month, day, hour and minute, even second, are set on the day of birth. The visual receptor protects those who are not physically perfect from realizing their deformities and suffering, as you put it. Jonathan bypassed the visual receptor and then left the center. What more can I say?"

"So, then, why don't you terminate deformed babies?"

"What a horrible idea? Very human, though. Yes, very human indeed." She repeated herself. "It is part of your history, even though it is an appalling solution. Everyone that is conceived has the right to live. And, here at the center, conception is so specifically realized that each creature has a function, a role to play; like we need the Jonathans to play clarinets. Each genetic composition is vital to the development of this center."

Did she disclose more than what she was authorized to do? She was not telling me everything. I wondered, but would she continue. I dangled the bait. . . "So, deformed Jonathans are necessary?"

"Not all Jonathans are deformed. Some are very attractive for human standards. In fact the Jonathan that you saw in your visual receptor was the prototype of a perfect Jonathan. But, like with everything, even mixing the same genetic composition can produce something different. Jonathan's replacement is close to what you saw." Now, she realized that she had gone too far.

"Well, if he had been terminated on schedule, he would not be suffering, as you call it, now." She continued. "The best that I can recommend is that

I check with the chemical division, pharmaceutical section, to see whether there is anything that can be done for him." She forced a kind of smile. "And, I shall do that. And now, Pamela, you shall do me a favor in return."

My heart stopped and I gulped. She stood up and moved around her desk until she was next to me. She took my face in her hands and caressed it. She pulled me closer and starting kissing me. I hated her for what she could do to me. But, she stopped and backed off and continued in a very business-like way. "You shall convince your dear friend, Randolph, that he should rather must accept a brief relationship with me. It is in both of your interests to cooperate with me. Do you understand, Pamela?"

There was now no longer any doubt about what she was offering. I nodded. But even though our lives were in her hands, I intuited an opening, somehow. I also realized that she needed us as much as we needed her. I stood up and grabbed her hands. She was not anticipating my move and she lost her balance. "I don't like to be threatened. Don't forget that I am a very important part of your professional life. If I go, so do you. Perhaps you should keep that in mind." I could see that she did not like what I was saying but I continued. "Get this into your head, Randolph is not a toy. He is a human with feelings. You say you want to learn about us. . ."

That hit a sensitive note as Dr. Gordon interrupted, "Did you use the word toy, Pamela."

"Yes." I regretted that. "I know that Dr. Miller mentioned that the word was taboo.

"And, so where did you see that word?"

"Actually I discovered it quite a while ago; I don't remember where. Maybe I didn't use it correctly." I knew that I wasn't good at lying and was worried that she would catch on, but she let it go.

"Oh well, be careful. That word has been removed from the vocabulary list because it represents dangerous objects. It is a word that is associated with a violent era in human history." And then she shifted to more important matters. "As for the favor I have asked you for, let's just say that you will do your best, won't you?" She moved back behind her desk and added that I should come to see her the following day at 1 PM. I didn't like leaving with her having the last word, but I was glad that our discussion was over.

I wasn't certain that I had accomplished anything for Jonathan, even though the conversation was very interesting and informative. Little by little I was starting to understand our lives at the center. Now, I understood from Dr. Gordon that the fertilization in vitro was genetically determined and that, apparently, the same donor ovules and donor sperms were inseminated to produce identical, or close to identical, prototypes of a given family tree. In my case, it was possible that I had a male version of me somewhere in the center.

Nonetheless, how was the original donor selection determined and why did they stick to the same genetic blend on the genome? Why didn't they vary genetic blends through genetic manipulation? Or, had they already done that and decided that the best blends should continue? How long have they been experimenting with genetic reproduction? As Dr. Gordon said, human history ended a very long time ago, which means that Androids certainly had time to fool around with that. There was one more thing, which Randolph would later confirm, that was worth investigating. Why were our genetic profiles so important for the Android community? I was convinced that the more information I obtained the more confused I became. Something was utterly immoral, wicked, but I didn't know why and a conspiracy had raised its ugly head, but I couldn't identify it. A musty air wafted my face, turning my head around as I looked up at the hall clock. It was late. I headed directly to my cubicle and as soon as I arrived, I envisaged burying myself deep in the covers and…as I walked I reflected upon the very demanding utterly exhausting day. However, sleep wasn't yet my priority as Randolph was waiting for me in my bed.

I stood in the doorway for a few minutes, just observing his every move. He was facing me and smiling mischievously. He was reclining comfortably on my bed. He was a superb specimen; that is what the androids would call him. He must have been the ultimate in physical beauty for that genetic blend. I could not imagine a better result than the one in front of me.

Randolph's appearance made me think about the Greek and Roman period. The Androids apparently liked Greek and Roman mythology, as there was an abundance of information on the subject at the library. I snickered as I imagined them identifying themselves with the superb force and beauty of those mythical Gods. I was also fascinated with the subject and, in particular, the specific traits of their mythical Gods.

My attention was back on Randolph. He was tapping on the bed, coaxing me to come over and sit down. I stared at him. His handsome young face, brown eyes and long curly blond hair reminded me of the computer image I saw of Apollo, the ultimate in physical masculine perfection. Randolph, very tall, robust, with large sculptured muscles in both his upper and lower body, is the embodiment of Herculean strength, force. With his exquisite body and quick intellect, I could understand why Dr. Gordon picked him as her next conquest. He was certainly considered by the androids to be the ultimate representative of a human male.

I was seeing different sides of Randolph since my return to the Center. I prefer the carefree, happy, optimistic one that I met first. His laughing eyes and enticing smile made me feel that he could conquer the world. That Randolph made me feel light-headed and happy. The Randolph of today is sober, sad and pensive. This Randolph could easily pull me into the depths of despair if I let down my guard for a few minutes. Peter was still too present in my mind for me to think about anyone else. Sex was about the last thing that I wanted. But, would Randolph understand that; that is if he was here for sex. I stood waiting for the offer that I was prepared to refuse. And, then he spoke.

"Pamela, I need to get out of the Center. Can you help me?"

I was in shock. Reclining on my bed in that seductive way and asking me to help him escape. Impossible! But instead of being relieved by the request, I was a bit disappointed; incredible how human psychology functions. You don't want something, but when someone deprives you of it, you want it more than anything else. Well, I cleared my mind of all that and replied without emotion, "I am sorry Randolph, but I don't know how to get you out of here."

"What? That's ridiculous. You have left the center so many times." He had pushed himself up into a sitting position.

"True, but never by the same route. And, I think that I do not have a good sense of orientation. But. . ." And, then I remembered being just at the orchestra pit when I arrived back the first time. "I don't know how much help this is, but I remember arriving directly into the orchestra pit when I accompanied Dr. Gordon into the center the first time."

"Alright. Can you meet me at the orchestra pit tomorrow?" He asked enthusiastically.

"Yes, but what good is that? If you escape, they shall come to get you. They allowed me to escape even though it was a terrifying experience for me. But, Randolph, Dr. Gordon will not let you out. I hate to tell you that, but she'll have you terminated before she will let you live outside the center."

"That bad!" He let himself fall backwards as if someone had thrown a hard punch.

"Yes, it is that bad." And then I told him about my conversation, her promise to me for Jonathan, and my favor to her. He shook his head sadly. I thought that he would start to cry, but instead he laughed heartily.

"Ok, so I'll go for it."

"You will have to. We need you on the inside, Randolph. You are the person with the most contacts. And, you can use her to get information. That's it, Negotiate. Yes, and you could get access to other information. For instance, get her to give you the names of geography experts. Try to find out what your partner had discovered. I noticed that she talks when she thinks that you are just her play thing, her experiment, as she likes to call me."

"True. She seems to have told you quite a bit today."

"That is the strange part. She didn't have to reveal all that. She went farther than was necessary, than probably was authorized. Maybe, she thinks that I already know all that. Maybe she is just feeding me information to study my behavior. Like, what my next step will be. And, she probably anticipates me going to the birth center tomorrow or the day after to learn their operations."

"And. . ."

"No. I won't go. I don't have time for that. I shall go and play the piano. I miss my instrument, my music. So, tomorrow morning I shall practice Mozart, Chopin, and Liszt… That will upset her. She does not like seeing that I am not doing what she expected me to do." And, then I remembered that she had a camera in my room. I pointed to the ceiling and his eyes brightened and his smile broadened.

"Anticipated. I tracked the system. She will see you in bed sleeping and, I shall be at my place, snoring away."

"And, if she is at your place."

"There is no chance. When she left, she gave me 48 hours to change my mind. She promised no pressure and no visits for at least two days. And, my android supervisor told me late this afternoon that she had informed the Governor that Dr. Gordon's frequent visits were disturbing me and the project was behind schedule now. I think that she will respect the 48- hour limit. It is in her interest. At least my supervisor gave me the impression that the Governor was her strongest supporter and the only person that she respected."

"Oh, so that explains why I saw the Governor leaving her office. So, that only gives you 48 hours. And then, what is your strategy?"

"I guess that I am just going to follow your best advice and fall helplessly into the seductive arms of an android with your hair. My sacrifice for the group." He was rolling around and laughing so hard.

"Is it ok with you if I stay here tonight, I just cannot bear to be alone in my cubicle? There are too many memories."

"No problem, but…" He finished it.

"No Sex tonight." He was lying peacefully on his back looking up at the ceiling, his eyelids heavy with sleep. I watched him doze off, and then, within minutes, awaken with laughter.

"What are you thinking about to make you laugh like that?" I asked groggily.

"My sacrifice for the group. Well… It might just be a little different." He fell back into a deep asleep. I looked over at him, wondering what he meant by that. He lay peacefully with a big grin on his face, something that was not there before. I closed my eyes and went to sleep.

Chapter 33: Openness

Randolph and I saw each other regularly over the next few weeks, but only to compare notes. He kept a real sense of humor about his relationship with Dr. Gordon. There was one thing that we both agreed upon; our Dr. Gordon knew how to satisfy someone. What I did not realize was that we were not talking about the same kind of sexual relationship; that we were not on the same wavelength. Finally, Randolph had enough of my sensual descriptions of sex with Dr. Gordon.

"I am not so sure that you are going to like what I have to say, but, I think that I should tell you before you find out from that sex-driven android." His brows were drawn tight and his eyes were piercing.

I was worried that something had gone wrong, that she was going to have Randolph terminated. "I'll protect you, Randolph." I blurted out.

"No. Just sit down and listen. This may come as a shock." I was too nervous to say anything.

"I am going to tell you a story, in detail, of my first sexual encounter with Dr. Gordon, because I just can't continue pretending that we know her the same way. Are you ready?"

"I guess. Anyway, I hope that I am." I was sitting stiffly, biting the end of my fingernails.

"I am going to tell you the story and act out the scenes. It will make it more believable. A bit of drama should appeal to you." I nodded.

"I was sitting, like this, at my lab table, when she sneaked up behind me and planted several kisses on the back of my neck. I spun around and grabbed her neck just underneath her chin with my right hand and lifted her android body several feet up in the air. She squirmed a bit as I let her down slowly. I pressed my body up against hers forcing her to move backward against my weight away from the lab table and up against the adjacent wall.

She made a mistake, she was no physical match for me. She underestimated me and hadn't turned her force up to maximum. I put my weight up against

283

her blocking her solidly against the wall and said—in a slow, low voice, "So you want sex do you? Is that what you want... sex?"

She nodded as she tried to regain control by moving her legs between mine and pushing up on me. I laughed, as I pulled off her wig, grabbed her android hands tightly in mine, and then forcefully raised her arms up over her head. She did not resist, when I tightly laced her arms together and secured them under the pressure of my right hand. "I'll give you sex," I said sadistically, my mouth twisted in a mocking smile, "I'll give you sex; but, sex like I fantasize having sex with one of you android creations. "

"I turned my sensory organs on to the maximum before I came into the lab; just for you, Randolph, so that I can give you real pleasure." She said seductively as she tapped into one of her sexy voice tones.

"Don't worry about me. I know what will give me pleasure." I smiled maliciously. "Do it for yourself." I said, as I slapped her expressionless face with my left hand and then squeezed her breasts, so hard that she clamored with Pain? Pleasure? I didn't know because she had lost control of her audio system and was sending off piercing sounds." He chuckled and I screeched.

"I didn't stop as I bit down on her permanently hard nipples. Her body was collapsing in even vibrating waves as I explored between her legs." I was letting all my anger out, letting her feel my physical force. She liked being dominated, I sensed that straight off; a stalker, she was always the dominant party and I was giving her something that she had never experienced."

"And, dominating her, excited me and inspired my wickedness. I was rough, brutal; I fought against a mounting urge to rip her insides out. But, strangely enough, her almost innocent acquiescence and feigned confidence in me prevented me from doing something rash or reckless."

"I knew that she could feel how hard and hot I was. I would have preferred to ejaculate on the floor, but I knew that that would show my weakness. So instead, with her hands still entangled above her head, I pulled her long body violently down on the floor and then I turned her swiftly onto her stomach. Her hands free, she tried to get up, as I jumped on her back and entered her from behind. I was not in the place she was expecting me to be and she tightened up as I forced my way in. In the midst of violent spasms—giving me the impression that her internal circuitry was crackling from electrical shocks---she screamed in what appeared to be an all- consuming climax, as she fell completely limp on the floor. Drained of all my force, I let myself collapse next to her."

"She didn't move for quite some time. I started to worry that I had shut her down permanently. I raised myself above her to be sure that she was still functioning. She forced a smile, grabbed me gently around my neck and kissed my open mouth. "Thank you, Randolph. I think that I finally understand why humans like sex. You have opened up a beautiful world of sensory pleasure for me." I looked at her with wide eyes. "Don't worry, Randolph, I won't let you get bored. I have finally found someone who cares about me. Next time, I shall bring you some interesting gadgets that will make our encounters even more memorable."

My eyes and mouth were wide-open. I didn't know that sex could take that form. I was seeing Randolph as a brutal beast and Dr. Gordon as a sexual pervert. Randolph was waiting for me to say something. He had a self-satisfied sneer on his face and I guessed that he wanted me to applaud. But, I couldn't. Instead, and I don't know why, I asked, "What did she mean by —interesting gadgets?"

"She likes rough sex, being tied, whipped or beaten. I couldn't have slow sex with her, like I did with you-I might have vomited-so this works out fine. She finds me to be absolutely sadistic and this seems to excite her more than if I were a perfectly receptive and obedient partner. And, now that my dominance has been confirmed, I am the one who decides when and how we shall play. All of this helps me release my stress and prepare me for combat. I am becoming more insensitive to these android creations!"

"Ok, but what are these interesting sexual gadgets?" I was more than curious. I was fixated on this point even though I was not certain that it was in my interest to know.

"Well—whips, chains, handcuffs, ropes---whatever that will prevent her from resisting me. The gadgets are over there in the box under the table, if you want to take a look." He pointed to the other side of the room. I changed my mind and listened to him. "Of course the game is that I have to catch her first. It is not always easy as she moves quickly, hand springing and flipping up in the air. I actually caught her a few times in one of her aerial flights, bringing her down hard. Sometimes she appears with her maximum force on and that means that I have to take a few punches before I get the wild animal under control."

"It all sounds horribly disgusting. If I started my sexual life like that I can assure you that I would have turned celibate. I am glad that you didn't approach me like that. I don't know how you can handle it with her." I was totally revolted by this kind of sexual encounter; just imagining myself in this situation gave me cold chills.

"If it helps, I have protected us both because I told her that I was keeping videos of all of our violent sex; that would be automatically released to the Board members if one of us were ever terminated."

"Do you have those videos? "

"Of course. She understood right off that I was not fooling around and there is no one at the Center competent to find my surveillance equipment and dismantle it."

"But, on another point, are you basically sadistic, Randolph? Is that the sex you prefer?" I needed to know if he was oriented in that direction. I would never want to be alone with him again if this was his sexual preference.

"No, I am not sadistic, and would not be with you, but then you are not an android creation." He smiled so sweetly and flashed his eyes at me. "Are you ok with what I told you?" He was concerned.

"I think so." I let out a deep breath. "I am glad that you told me. I feel terribly foolish about how I talked about Dr. Gordon." I needed to confess as well. "Actually, she gets into sex. Her sensory system is attune to our bodies and she knows where and how long to caress. She is always perfect with her moves. I was not much of a participant with her; I was principally on the receiving side. "

"Well, actually, there are moments when I forget that she is a machine." He said as he ran his tongue slowly over his lips as if savoring a moment. "One has to admit that she is perfect physically; a masterpiece in robotic craftsmanship. She is even quite sexy looking, especially when she dresses up in tight shorts and low cut, skimpy tops, wearing bracelets with spikes and long chains that curve sensually around her breasts, accentuating her cleavage." He stared intensely at me as if he were tapping into my inner thoughts, where I was imagining myself participating in this comedy with him. He let his mouth drop slightly open as his lips moved to form a devilish smile. "Recently, she changed her wig. She is wearing short black hair that forms sexy spikes around the top and sides of her head. She looks lethal, dangerous, as she stands with her long, sleek legs spread apart, slowly moving her hips round in provocative circles, as she then cracks out her long whip, sliding it back and forth between her legs; tempting me to respond. I have to admit, I find myself rising to the occasion." He broke out in one his belly laughs while I looked on in dismay.

"She dresses up?" I wondered how that could be possible.

"She told me that she has an assortment of special period costumes, but she prefers the gothic look." He rubbed his chin in thought. "Perhaps the Goths practiced sadistic and masochistic sex?"

"I don't know. All this sounds so weird!"

"Let's put it this way, Pamela, you had to live your sexual experience with her the best way you could and…" I interrupted him and finished his sentence, "and you, Randolph, have to live it the best way for you!" We smiled in our complicity.

"I am running late, must go." I chirped up. I gave him a big tap on his shoulder and a friendly kiss on his cheek and left in a flash.

I went straight to meet with Dr. Miller to get more information about the geography of the Earth. She showed me photos of the Earth after natural disasters and devastating wars that took place during the 21st century. I was aghast with what I saw. Watching dinosaurs being devoured by flaming volcanic eruptions had little impact upon me. But, seeing humans sucked up by the earth's insatiable appetite made me sick. I had nightmares for a long time afterwards.

What I understood from Dr. Miller was that humans, as an animal species, disappeared somewhere between the 21^s and 25th century. They left behind them a barren planet. Water sources were so polluted that there was nothing to support life. The oceans ravaged certain continents burying in its depths whatever vestiges of human life remained.

A limited number, she did not know exactly how many humans and android creations survived this doomsday phenomenon. They shut down their systems and slept for thousands of years; programmed to awaken at a randomly selected year in the far future. When they finally awakened, they found that the earth had started to rejuvenate and dry and wet zones became visible. The continents of the past were gone; eventually, new land mass surfaced. Water was plentiful and pure. And Human life was possible again. These android creations started to bring back human creatures.

When I told Randolph, he was less impressed with the story than I had been. He told me that it was too neat; too perfect. He couldn't believe that the androids were such nice creations. "Think about it, Pamela." He said shaking his head in disbelief. "It just doesn't make any sense that the first thing that the androids would want to do is to put humans back on this planet. If we had been so horrible, evil, destructive, and so forth, they should have forgotten about us. There was absolutely no reason why they would want to risk their existence and that of the planet for a second time."

I was slapped with the reality of what he said, which was more believable than what Dr. Miller told me. My face turned bright red with embarrassment. Was it my overall naivety or my lack of analytical skills that made me so susceptible to manipulation and, in this case, finding her story so touching? "Yes, you made an interesting point. But, when Dr. Miller described the return of human life and how the android creations constructed magnificent centers for humans to live in so that they could experience an idyllic life, she sounded so convincing." Randolph smiled at me patronizingly, as he raised his eyebrows, but I continued in spite of his haughtiness. "She told me that there were no animals, all were now extinct. They didn't want future generations of human creatures to discover that harsh reality. They wanted us human creatures to learn about other animal species inhabiting the earth at the time humans reigned; hence the reason for the zoo in the vacation center. Unfortunately, as she pointed out, none of the animals are real, but our imaginations, enhanced by our visual receptors, give us the impression that they are alive."

Randolph's expression had not changed. I did not convince him so I went one step further: "Maybe Randolph these android creations were designed to serve humans; the only reason why androids existed. That could be why they wanted to bring us back." I thought that I made a valid point

"I am sorry, Pamela, but all this sounds like android rubbish." I bit down on my lips to show that he offended me. "Look, where did they find the very first groups of sperms and ova to make us on this barren, unfriendly planet." He patted my brooding face teasingly. "No, Pamela something is missing in this story."

I went back to the Library every day for the next week, and, each time I brought up the second creation, trying to get more information and fill in the missing pieces. Each time, Dr. Miller turned nervously in all directions. At one point she admitted that she was putting herself in danger by giving me any information concerning the end of human history.

She did show me what she pretended were recent maps of the planet. She held them at a considerable distance from me, so that I could barely see the details let alone study them. She told me that we were in a very dry zone that spread out for miles and miles. Outside this hot, dry zone was indeed a tropical forest area. Plant life had returned and now I was certain that Jason had told me the truth. If only he had kept a better map, we would have been able to find this tropical zone a long time ago. Dry and Wet zones applied only to the land itself. The oceans occupied more of the earth's surface than they did in the past. All this information would be helpful for our group, but I needed copies of the maps to show to the others and Dr. Miller was not willing to give copies to me. Her refusal to give copies of the maps to me or even let me get close enough to the maps to make a rough drawing seemed too convenient. Eventually it all became clear and I understood that she was taking advantage of my credulity. I was so frustrated that I wanted to abandon the project and would have if Randolph hadn't given me the name of someone in the geology department, a certain Caroline.

I had a difficult time finding her and when I did, she was not very cooperative. My thoughts turned first to her physical attributes. She was one of those less attractive human creatures. She was very short, at least in reference to myself, and visibly overweight; something that surprised me, as

Dr. Gordon had recently bragged to me that all humans were given properly balanced diets that would assure good health. Her weight made no difference to me, but I did wonder whether being overweight was considered to be good health by the androids in certain cases? Her short straight, mousy brown hair, round face, with its low forehead, large, upturned nose, broad fleshy lips and popping eyes, set me back for an instant. I quickly pulled myself together remembering that physical appearances should not be that important and gave her my identification code. I knew that she could see me but giving my code would protect her if one of the androids were watching.

She was hostile, holding me responsible for the termination of Randolph's partner, Samantha. Whenever I tried to defend myself or deny her accusation, she put her hands over her big, flat ears, refusing to listen.

"Just being seen with you could have serious repercussions for me." She cried out hysterically. That I could not in all honesty deny. "Your being here could make them suspicious about my programming no longer functioning." she screamed as she rushed at me and tried to force me to leave. She was not very strong so it did not take much effort on my part to stop her attack. When I grabbed her, I could feel her body trembling with fear and my heart went out to her. I took her protectively in my arms and repeated over and over again, that I would assure her safety; that no one would hurt her. I asked her if her partner was still alive and she answered yes. "That is a good sign." I said, hoping that I was right to draw that conclusion. But, no matter, I had my objective and needed to use her, regardless of what might happen to her.

I looked for a safe place where we could speak. I noticed a closet at the end of the room and pointed to it. She left first and I sneaked in beside her a few minutes later, after having carried out my own quick search for audio-visual equipment.

By the time I squeezed into this closet, she had calmed down and was ready to speak. "Randolph's partner was a geologist like myself. We were studying the violent geological transformation of the earth's surface, due presumably to climate warming, near the end of the 21st century." She explained. "Randolph's partner…"

"Samantha," I interrupted her.

"Ok, Samantha discovered that in fact climate warming was not the cause of the earth's volcanic eruptions. She found that there was an unnatural and violent explosion in the core of the earth that precipitated the famous doomsday."

I asked her how her android supervisor reacted to Samantha's conclusions and she responded that he made a strange statement. "He said that he didn't realize that human intellect had evolved to such a level because the advanced level of human reasoning reflected in her conclusions was scheduled for a much later date in human development. He warned Samantha to immediately halt further studies in that area and concentrate exclusively on the assigned project." Caroline paused. "It is true that we did not have any solid proof to support her conclusion. I had the feeling that she was simply throwing it out for discussion when she added it to her report. The android supervisor must have informed his superiors of the discovery."

"Can you show me her conclusions and what she based them on?" I asked, hoping to get more details.

Caroline fidgeted, making the tiny closet space unbearable for me, before she told me more. "Samantha's conclusions represented no danger for the androids." I couldn't understand how she could say that; perhaps she needed to express her own reasoning on Samantha's termination. "It was not her discovery that precipitated her termination, but her relationship with Randolph and you." Her popping eyes were erupting with volcanic flashes as she continued. "Even if she didn't follow the instructions of her supervisor there would have been no reason to terminate her. She could have been transferred to another center. But, they discovered that she had bypassed her programming. And why? Because the androids were following Randolph very closely and noticed that Samantha was able to see him without his giving her his identification code." She said as she clenched her teeth in anger.

"So you hold Randolph and me responsible for what happened to your friend?"

"Exactly. And that is why my life is being compromised right now by you visit. I shall have to explain why you were here; that is, of course, if they were watching my lab before we hid in this closet." She answered bitterly.

"I don't understand, though, how this simple discovery could have created the kind of violent emotional response necessary to bypass the programming." I wanted to get her back on the subject.

She went on to explain further what happened when the report was produced. "The reaction of the android supervisor was excessive. He threw a pile of papers on the floor and ripped up our report. Both of us got into a hand to hand encounter with him, trying to retrieve the details and our conclusions. This must have been the reason for our bypassing the system, because when he eventually pushed us out of his way as he left the room, we both felt dizzy and confused. I think I was the first to say that I was able to see her. I was panic stricken." She breathed hard. "We encouraged each other with own hysteria to bypass the programming."

"How did you know that other humans could not see you?'"

"By accident, actually. I went to sit down at the table for lunch. Someone else sat down on top of me and started to complain about the seat itself. I quickly moved out of the cafeteria before a member of the kitchen staff started to ask questions. I realized that even when I pushed the person off of me and ran away, she didn't understand what had happened. The programmed humans could no longer see me. I rushed back to the lab to tell Samantha. We had to protect ourselves"

"So she must have told Randolph."

"She told me on many occasions over the years that Randolph was often working late into the night. She surprised me by telling me that she should have realized that Randolph was deprogrammed for a long time. He was always giving her his identification code. But, she never connected with that reality until she actually bypassed her programming. When he saw that they were both seeing clearly the environment they were living in, he explained to her that his frequent absences were to protect her from discovering his deprogrammed condition, and not, as she had suspected, to avoid being with her. In spite of his confessions and kindness, she told me that she didn't trust him enough to reveal her discovery to him. Randolph did not put pressure on her to tell him what had happened. Perhaps he thought that she would eventually open up. I do remember her expressing concern about your relationship with him. She thought that you were working for the androids."

"I sincerely appreciate your sharing all this information with me." I saw that she smiled sheepishly. "I should tell you that the week before she was terminated, she and Randolph got closer. She told him that she was working on a sensitive project, but she never had the opportunity to give him any real details about her discovery. Regrettably, her time ran out."

She felt inspired to say more. "Even if she told him that she discovered that a violent explosion in the center of the earth might have caused massive destruction of the earth's surface and existing life forms, he would not necessarily have accepted her conclusion as the truth. He would have probably wanted to test her reasoning on his on."

"I think that I am going to see this again with Randolph. But, for you, just deny that you ever saw me. If they were not watching or recording our conversation when I entered your lab, you are safe. You simply didn't see anyone in the work place."

"And, you will confirm that?"

"Of course." I smiled down at her as we climbed out of the closet.

I did bring up the subject with Randolph at our next meeting. He was apparently confused about a lot of things concerning Samantha because he was surprised to learn that Samantha was a geologist and not specialized in geography. He was surprised that Samantha had bypassed her programming long before he realized it. But, as he said so many times, he was protecting her. He was also so involved in his work and gathering information for the outside that he did not pay that much attention to her; and, he often returned late at night. He was very interested in Samantha's discovery and disagreed with Caroline's position that the androids would have ignored this kind of discovery and the conclusions that Samantha had drawn from it.

"If there was an unnatural and violent explosion coming from the center of the earth then perhaps the androids were responsible for that. But, then, it makes no sense. Logically, an explosion from the center of the earth would not be in their interest. They would have been as vulnerable as humans in the face of such an explosion. Unless. . ." He was thinking out loud. "Unless they were temporarily protected from…the fallout."

As always, he convinced me. I decided to raise another puzzling issue. "The androids still seem to worship their individual creators, carrying their names and occupying the same professional situations, so why would they have taken such a risk?"

Randolph sat there with a creased brow, thinking. I continued, "But, if you think about it, Randolph, they have not tried to recreate their creators; or have they? In fact, I am not sure. We don't know much about how they go about selecting the new generations of humans; and, how they went about recreating us." I back-tracked slightly. "We know that they have a genetic base, genomes, they draw from. But, I agree with you that they would not have risked their existence and that of their creators…and, yet…it is so frustrating. I am going to have to find a way to get more answers." He nodded.

"I would love to stay longer, but I have that meeting with Dr. Gordon." After all, I was still her project and a lot of time had lapsed since our last discussion.

My visits with her didn't last long. Our first meeting after my return was dedicated to Jonathan. She didn't seem to care much about how the community was doing. I saw her for a quick few minutes after that and I learned that she did consult the pharmaceutical section and gave me some medication that Jonathan could take. I had it sent out with his meal. She did that for Jonathan because she thought that I had convinced Randolph to engage in sex with her. I did convince him that it was in the interest of the group, but I had no idea that he was going to approach her in that sadistic way and hoped that she would not ask me about that.

No, she didn't mention the violence that passed between them. Instead, during our last session she asked me a lot of questions about love. What does it feel like to be in love? How do you know that you are in love? I didn't know how to answer those questions. I told her that it was very personal, that kind of feeling. I talked around the subject trying not to show her how nervous I was as I grappled to say something that made some sense. Her last words, still ringing in my mind, were. "I am very disappointed that you do not want to share this strong, human emotion with me and hope that you will be more cooperative the next time."

I took that as a warning and rushed straight off to the Library to find a good definition of love. I know that I am in love with Peter, but find it difficult to intellectualize feelings, describe it in a way that she can understand. There was very little about love in the Library and Dr. Miller was not cooperative. She found it "ludicrous"—that was the word she used --to read about love. The writings I found focused on the five senses as persuasive, at least in terms of rudimentary attraction.

After leaving Randolph, I took my time meandering around the corridors thinking about how to present this subject to her. Admittedly, I was preoccupied by the news about Samantha's discovery. Dr. Gordon's understanding love was not as important. I was not in a hurry to arrive for this session. I could easily enough use the five senses as a starting point as she told me that the androids have well-developed sensory organs. Touch, sight, smell, and hearing were evident, but I was not certain that they had the sense of taste. They wouldn't need this in any aspect of their lives; they never put anything in their mouths. I would just have to skip over taste as being relatively unimportant.

I was outside her office. It was time for me to confront the impossible. I tapped on the door and heard her call out to enter.

Odor was not that important to her because, as she explained to me a while ago, the android's were offended by natural human body odor and therefore provided special perfumed soaps, individual specific, to make humans smell nice. She expressed an affinity with the sensuality of the touch and warmth of the person next to her. Her sensory systems were acute to temperature variations; she found it mind-boggling how human skin grew warmer and warmer over the course of sexual relations. As she said she could appreciate the warmth of the human body in still another way; her body was naturally drawn closer to heat so cuddling up next to a warm human body stimulated her inner circuits. What an obnoxious statement that wiped out any semblance of romance in her relationship with me or with Randolph.

She was not impressed with my definition of love. "You have given me a clinical analysis of love." She protested. "I want to understand yearning for someone." She said, as she violently hit the top of her desk. "I have physical cravings and sexual satisfaction with Randolph and I want to know whether this is love." She came directly to the point.

I sat leaning back in my chair, keeping a blank expression on my face, hoping to hide my shock and disgust over what she said. I took a good look at Dr. Gordon, trying to imagine her participating in the kind of violent sex that Randolph described to me. She was sitting so patiently now waiting for my answer that I was certain that she didn't know that Randolph had confided in me. I squeezed my lips together in thought. It was part of her game, her vicious strategy.

Certainly she was just coaxing me, in her usual style, to tell her more so that she could more easily control and take advantage of Randolph. So, I tried to discourage her by reminding her that she could not experience this emotion reserved only for us humans.

"Come on Dr. Gordon, you are not made to fall in love. You even told me that you are incapable of loving." I stopped to evaluate the impact of that on her before continuing. "Whereas a human can be giddy and overdosed with affection for someone, you must not try to experience what you are not programmed to experience." I sounded convincing to myself and carried on. I reached across the desk and took her hand in mine, to reassure her. "You are lucky that you don't need love to exist; because love is a double-edged sword. When everything is good, it is wonderful to be in love. But, when things go badly, for whatever reason, lost love can be very painful. I think there's a blurred distinction between profound love and profound hate. Just be glad that you won't have to suffer like humans do." I was baiting her a bit and she took it.

"But, I do". She reeled from those words. "I know that Randolph has no feelings for me and I know that he has feelings for you. That bothers me. It is not logical for someone to reject someone who can offer him every advantage." She was staring very intensely at me. I didn't see any flicker of pain in her android eyes. What I saw was good acting. "You have everything you want, Pamela. Why? Why are you so special?"

I had to think fast. It was better for me to turn the discussion; to confuse her and put her on the defensive. I hit the ball back to her. "Maybe, but I didn't get you, Dr. Gordon. You showed no sincere compassion for me and never worried about whether the end of our relationship had any impact upon me. You simply told me that it was over and went off looking for someone else."

She reacted as I hoped. 'But, Pamela, I didn't know that you had feelings for me."

"No?" I had to be convincing. "You saved my life. You comforted me. You went even so far as to give me pleasure--real pleasure." Now my emotions had taken over and the walls of disguise collapsed in the truth of my words. "And, then, when I felt protected and needed and loved--yes, loved, in a way--you just said Goodbye. Why do you think that I spend hours in the Library and long nights on the piano? There is nothing here for me except that. You even took a real friend, Randolph, away from me. He made me laugh at myself. Now, he is no longer there for me because you spend every possible minute with him."

"So, I was right, you love him?" She was obsessed.

"No, I love Peter! I like Randolph!" I screamed, my voice vibrant with human emotions. "There is a big difference between the two feelings. Peter completes my life; Randolph listens to me and makes me laugh." I stood up now to leave. I didn't think that it was worth it to go on. She was not going to understand, at least that is what I thought. But, she grabbed me tenderly as I reached for the door and kissed me with a certain passion that she had never shown me before. And then she told me that I was her jewel, her most precious human, and that she was sorry that she hurt me.

"Trust me, Pamela, I am just trying to understand how human emotions function. I have not forgotten you and what we shared together."

We parted like that. But, if I had known what I know now, I would have reacted a lot differently.

Chapter 34: Discovery

Both Randolph and I received the news about the same time. Caroline was terminated. I felt guilty and Randolph, angry. To make things even more complicated, his android supervisor was called in for a revision and she never returned. We were wrong to believe that Dr. Gordon was at the mercy of the Governor. They must have been plotting together for a long time. Now more than ever Randolph and I were in danger and there was no immediate escape.

I felt sorry for myself and spent far too much time thinking and rethinking the past. I was more than certain that I had made too many mistakes. I miscalculated the capacity of the androids and imagined that I was clever enough to control the situation. Nonetheless, I boiled with frustration not knowing how I could have acted differently, done better . . .

I found consolation again, in music, in playing the piano. I avoided the library and Dr. Miller, who I now confirmed had been manipulating me as well. Dr. Gordon was so occupied with Randolph that she didn't notice what I was up to or how I was feeling. And, Randolph proved to be very much of a challenge for her and he kept the upper hand. I don't know how much time passed before I finally decided to fight back.

I realized that nothing would make any sense until I visited the birth center. I had to find out more about the second creation. Now both Dr. Gordon and the Governor probably considered me little threat to their operations. I chuckled to myself that they had underestimated me by giving me unlimited access to the center so I decided that I should get on with this visit before they changed their views.

I got lost easily; the last time was when I visited the late Caroline in her office. I found it complicated to find my way around. What was confusing for me was that there were so many corridors off the main circular path. Each corridor led to a new circle with its own independent corridors. I knew my way to the library, Randolph's lab, Dr. Gordon's office and the Governor's office because I kept a mental count of the number of corridors and circles that I had to pass through before turning into the office I wanted. As time when on,

I got use to the fact that every department had the same configuration so it was easier for me to find the rooms and the persons concerned.

During a conversation with Randolph, he insinuated at one point that I had no sense of direction which was why I was turning around and around many times before realizing that I should be taking a left rather than a right turn. I defended myself by pointing out that the center reflected the android sense of organization and planning which was not necessarily adapted to humans. He only laughed and said that, on that single point, he did not mind being compared to an android. But, he corrected me by mentioning that androids would not have chosen circular formations, as their systems are more adapted to linear, which implied that I was more android than him? Or that androids did not construct this Center?

With a great deal of concentration and effort, I found the birth center located in the fourth circle off the first major crossing. The android receptionist stood up as I entered, and asked me if she could help me. I gave her my name. "Oh, yes, I do believe that Dr. Flanders has been expecting your visit for quite a while." She ushered me into a small room where Dr. Flanders and his assistants were working.

I found Dr. Flanders quite good looking. His chiseled face and square jaw, prominent nose, dark brown oval eyes, and sensual mouth with a dominant lower lip gave him a rugged, masculine look. He was wearing a smock with the sleeves rolled up well up above his elbows and I noticed that he was flaunting muscles. How could this be? It didn't seem possible. I thought that androids could not have muscles, at least that was what Peter told me. But, in front of me, stood a tall, well-built, athletically charged male android; he made me think of a marathon runner. Whether he was the image of his creator or his creator wanted his android to be the envy of all of his colleagues, Dr. Flanders was a prizewinning android.

His assistant, however, who he referred to as Audry, was his opposite: round, with large limbs. There was nothing attractive about her shoddy features that gave me the impression that she was compiled of discarded android parts; or her creator had no sense of symmetry and beauty. I am very sensitive to proportionality, and she had none; legs too short, arms too long, cut-off neck, and large, long face. She might have been considered a plump, bulky human, except that she had no sagging skin. Her appearance was completed with small, beady eyes, a tiny nose and pursed lips.

"Pamela, we have been waiting a long time for your visit." Dr. Flanders took the first initiative.

I explained that I had been preoccupied with human history and that I didn't realize how much of my time was dedicated to that thereby excluding other research. And I nonchalantly slipped in that I was interested in learning more about the second human creation.

"The second human creation." He repeated the expression several times and then asked, "What was the first one?"

"I am not sure that I know." My breath stopped as I tried to squirm out of a trap, as it suddenly occurred to me I hadn't given much thought to the first one.

"Well, reading human history, whatever we kept of it, was probably not the best use of your time. Your search appears to have given you a blurred idea of creation." He stopped and tapped his fingers on his desktop in a very rhythmic way. I surmised it was probably a nervous twitch he picked up from his creator. I shook my head in disbelief that I was following the beat, even liking the way it calmed me.

I wrenched myself away from this hypnotic beat and refocused on Dr. Flanders, "Perhaps you could clarify things for me then." I stated, trying to get back on track.

"Quite frankly, then, human life evolved with time, starting in your prehistoric period." I had forgotten how strange the android voice could be. Dr. Gordon and her entourage all modified their tonality for my ears. Dr. Flanders' voice was more earsplitting than any android voice that I had heard before. And, my heart sank at his lack of expression in contrast with that beautifully carved face. I felt a hallow void, a sad emptiness like I had never felt before. So bizarre! When he turned to look at me he could have been a statute staring majestically from a prestigious pinnacle. Nonetheless, he perfunctorily continued his story, without either noticing me or my silent depression.

"There were two main schools of thought concerning the creation, 1) the belief in superior being capable of creating life and 2) the belief in evolution." He was boring me. "The believers in a superior being attempted to justify that with scientific evidence. Those who rejected the idea of a superior being focused on justifying the theory of evolution underlying the roots of mankind. Are you following me?"

"Yes, of course. " I was bored. "I studied all of that and have to admit that I was personally convinced more by the superior being because it was a nice story. And, it gave me a bit of hope for all of us humans if someone was really looking out for us."

He had no sense of humor, naturally, so he couldn't laugh. He just opened and shut his mouth several times as a sign of frustration, I suppose, and then commented briefly on what I had to say. "You should not feel ridiculous about your position, many humans believed like you during your history.

Nonetheless, I find it very lucid on your part to recognize that you were convinced only because it was a nice story. There is still hope for you."

"And, so the second creation?" I didn't want him to forget why I was there even though his android memory would never let that happen.

"I assume that you have come here well-informed. So, you know that the humans destroyed themselves, directly or indirectly, who cares and that we, the androids, gave them a second chance."

"Yes, that is how it has been explained to me. But, if that is the case, how did you recreate us? "He was leaning back in his seat observing me. He was so sure of himself just like the rest of the android community.

"That is easy to explain. One simply introduces a sperm into an ovum." He sat back up and tapped his fingers. "You must know by now that we take that from you when you are young and we freeze it, unfreeze it and let the fertilized egg develop in an artificial uterus until the baby is nine months old. "

Now I wanted to upset him, to push him off his seat; to pull him off his condescending cloud and bring him down to my level. Several notions rushed through my brain and I had to regroup, take a deep breath, so I could be calm enough to put them into intelligible, provocative thoughts to attack him with.

"Interesting. I know that I spent time in this unit when I was young. I was told that it was a medical examination that would take days. I don't remember much more than that but then you probably did something in this unit to erase chunks of my life from my memory."

"My compliments, Pamela. You do seem to be able to think rather logically and strategically for a human; or rather a human musician."

I ignored his comment and went on. "Nonetheless there are many humans with horrible deformities, so you must not be as adept as you would like me to think in selecting the right genetic blend, or in the effectiveness of your procedures used to fertilize the ovum with the sperm. Right?"

"Childish on your part. We are not looking for physical beauty, we are looking for intellectual capability." His voice slowly screeched out the last two words as his body quivered. His eyes turned red, as they bulged from their sockets. Audry rushed to his side and pressed down on the outside of his throat and that helped him to regain his composure.

He looked straight into my eyes as if he could read my thoughts and then apologized for his behavior explaining that he needed to have an overhaul of his circuitry.

That made it easy then for me to repeat what he had said. This time he had no reaction, but rather picked up the conversation. "Yes, well, you humans are so sensitive to appearances that we had to try to bypass that. So we inserted a kind of computer chip into your visual center to help you to deal with the reality of your lives and thus become less sensitive to appearances. Unfortunately for you, Pamela, bypassing your visual reception, meant that you have had to cope with the physical differences among humans, some of which are less pleasing to the eye. That cannot be easy for you."

"You are wrong." He sat straight up. "I like being human and I am very happy to be free of your programming. Yes, I had to adjust to the real world and now I am capable of going beyond physical appearances."

"Charming, she is charming, isn't she Audry?" Audry nodded and I thought to myself that his circuitry was in real danger.

"You have not answered my question, though. How did you find and decide upon the genetic blends for us humans." And," I added a point that was bothering me from the beginning, "where did the first sperm and ovum come from?" I didn't want to give him an opportunity to stop my momentum, so I added, "After all, humans were destroyed. Weren't they?"

"I know that you are entitled to have that information, but I don't think that you will like it very much. There are some things, Pamela, that you should just let go, things that should remain a mystery. This is one of them." He had, in the meantime, adjusted his voice, more like changed to a different program; it was softer and smoother now. "What I think is that you should know that we, the android population, have always liked living with humans. We missed them." He stopped as if he had some cerebral burst of nostalgia. "And, of course, you are like children; so naturally, we have to protect you and control you. You are here today because we like you. Yes, like you; and for that reason humans will continue to live so long as we are around."

"That is a cute story---but I don't believe it. You know that you need us. Why deny it? What is the harm in telling the truth?" He was shaking again as my voice rose to frenetic screams. "You need us; you are using us. Just tell me why you need us?

All those weeks of frustration gave out and I couldn't hold it in any longer. My shrill screams turned into short convulsive grunts. Finally, when I was able to reel in the screams and temper the convulsive grunting, I looked up and saw him frantically waving his hand. In my calm stupor, I was reminded that androids couldn't handle strong human emotions. At that moment, I knew that I had gotten to him; penetrated his stoic defenses; upset him. My whispered yes was stifled under the slap of a frantic Audry, who reached with the other hand to press on Dr. Flanders' throat again.

After he regained his composure, he calmly asked me to leave through a tight smile; his excuse was he had a very heavy schedule. I left despondent.

It was late so I returned to my cubicle for a long shower to rinse away my despair. Nonetheless, I had a restless night. I was confused and frustrated and I missed my family and friends. I was tired of going around in circles with little to show for my efforts, and I was in desperate need to see my loved ones. I stepped out of bed minutes before breakfast was delivered and side stepped the delivery person who couldn't see me.

I grabbed my special cookie and devoured it. I wondered about its composition. It was energetic and apparently adapted to my system and its special needs, but it was dry and tasteless. My mind drifted back to the day I first bit into this cookie. I shuddered as I remembered awakening in a creepy, unrealistic environment where I was fed with chemicals day in and day out. How I longed for something to eat that tasted good. Dr. Gordon brought me this same cookie that at that time I devoured with pleasure. How could I have euphorically enjoyed eating this cookie that today I know has no taste? I shook my head in disbelief, pulled on my white smock, combed my long, thick, curly hair and stepped out of my cubicle to run straight into Audry, Dr. Flanders' assistant.

I almost knocked Audry on the floor. I saw her wobble and sway before regaining control of her body. Her face remained expressionless, as if she gets knocked around every day. She perfunctorily gave me the following message. "Dr. Flanders asked me to accompany you to his office. He would like you to spend a day in the medical unit—no, the birth center." She quickly corrected her error.

She took a faster route to the birth center, by monorail. We entered the monorail and rode together in silence. The invitation-request-order was ambiguous and disturbing, but I wasn't in the mood to discuss anything with Audry, a very loyal and devoted servant who wouldn't be sensitive to my misgivings, my doubts and even more…my fears. For all intents and purposes, I didn't care if I was walking into a trap.

I wondered. "What real difference could it make? I had already done that so many times in the past. What could he actually do to me? He might consider me his prisoner, but for how long? Dr. Gordon would eventually come and get me at the end of the day, I was her project."

Those cogitations relaxed me. But not for long. . .

The android moved at high speed as soon as we exited the monorail. Most androids just seemed to float over the floor's surface like vampires even though they went through the artificial motions of walking; but Audry was strangely hopping, then jogging and then poured it out, almost running, in a very human way in spite of her strange built and excessive body weight. I could hardly keep up with her, but she never looked back, never noticed my gasping attempts to reach her. I caught my second wind, thanks to the residual effects of my energy charged cookie, and was finally able to jive with her rhythm.

Dr. Flanders was waiting patiently when I arrived. He had hair this time and when he said hello his voice was strong and mellow. He looked even better with hair. His wig fit his athletic style. Thick, straight brown hair that was long enough for him to pull back in a ponytail. It suited him and gave him an even more masculine presentation. My thoughts wandered. Did androids always wear wigs? Were their wigs the style of the day in the period they lived in? In other words, were humans wearing their hair in the same way? Was there a status symbol among androids, whereby only the important ones wore wigs? All these questions seemed relatively insignificant in face of my situation and that of my family and friends today.

I complemented him on his wig and he forced a twisted android smile back at me. It was obvious that he wanted to impress me with his wig; hoping that I would drool over his sexy style. So I pretended that it worked by telling him that he was a very sexy android. That made his stiff body relax. He liked seeing me in this new light.

"Pamela, I am so happy that you are able to spend the day with me and my staff." Apparently he didn't have enough training to be convincing. "We started off a bit badly, as you humans use to say. I wanted to make it up to you." He leaned back in his chair, rather naturally. "So should we start with a tour of the facility?"

I didn't have a choice. He was holding all the cards, and he knew it. I realized that I had to always adopt an opposing position, if I wanted the androids to do what I wanted. Easily acquiescing in their offers is what they expected. So I started in a different manner.

"Of course I appreciate your invitation. But I do believe that it is a bit more than I was expecting yesterday and can deal with today."

"Sorry. I don't understand."

"I had questions yesterday. I still have those same questions today." I stopped to look into his eyes. Like most androids, one never had the feeling that eye contact was of any real importance, not like humans who valued it. So, I continued. "I don't believe that a tour of your facility is going to give me answers to those questions. Which means that it is a waste of my time." I got up and started toward the door.

He arrived so fast behind me and grabbed my arm, gently, but firmly. "No, you don't want to run away. You must be just a bit curious about what goes on here."

I nodded and he took the initiative to open the door and usher me into the birthing corridor. I was confronted with an enormous laboratory full of microscopes, test tubes, computers, and embryos in different stages of development lining the countertops. As I turned in different directions to get a perspective of the room, my eyes fell upon a large freezer unit occupying the far wall, filled to capacity with vials marked with codes, the kind of code that would indicate our name and series. I screamed loud enough to attract the attention of all the lab technicians that looked in my direction. I felt dizzy, like I might faint, and leaned up against one of the many closed cupboards. An android pulled me rapidly away and warned me not to touch anything.

Dr. Flanders turned to me and dryly asked me to follow him closely. "This part of the birth center is of no interest for you. Don't touch anything, just follow me closely." He grabbed my hand and led me out of the lab into a long corridor. Windows opened up onto different theaters of human development. I couldn't understand why he was doing this to me. I felt like I might vomit. It was alarmingly revolting; but, I knew that I had to pay attention and try to understand, because I had to report back to the outside community.

Dr. Flanders was chatting about, explaining what was going on at different stages of human development. His carefree, insensitive manner was gritting on my nerves. How could he present the development of human life in such a callous, heartless manner?

I felt myself wanting to strike him down, as my hands formed solid fists. Nonetheless, I listened. As I passed by the first window, I progressively saw a more advanced stage of human development, tiny fetuses, in the second month after their conception, displayed in artificial wombs. I was fascinated by the beauty of these tiny, fragile beings and, yet horrified by the context. I thought of my son when he was in the early stage of development and how he must have struggled and vied for survival. But at least compared to those born inside the center, my child received more than just nourishment fed to him in tubes during their development. He was nourished by my human emotions, those positive vibrations touching and comforting him as he matured inside my nurturing, loving womb. This reality made me sad for all those little ones developing before my eyes who like me would never know their parents.

"Pamela, perhaps this is too much for you?"

So he finally took notice of me. Why should he care or pretend to care? What did he see in my eyes? "No," I answered softly. "Everything is ok. I am ready to continue."

"You, know, Pamela. . ." He stopped and turned his head to me, making certain he had my attention. "In human communities, not every baby that was conceived had their Mother's love. There were some Mothers who did not want the child. Sometimes they aborted the unwanted pregnancy or gave the child to someone else. And, sometimes they raised them in an environment without love."

It was like this revolting beast was reading my mind. Yet I knew that I was capable of confusing these android, not all the time, but that I developed or was developing, the capacity to hide my feelings ."You actually want me to believe that an artificial uterus is the best place for a fetus to grow." I said with a vicious smirk, revealing my contempt for him.

"Oh, but it was a very popular choice near the end of human history." He was certainly pleased in his android way to throw that point out. He continued. "Women, not all, but the majority-yes the majority-did not want to ruin their bodies through a pregnancy. So, in fact, the artificial uterus was an excellent solution."

"Let me just say that we don't see things the same way." His analysis was just too neat and simple for me. "Even though I do not know what the tendency was at the end of human history, I read enough to know that there must have been medical reasons why women chose this option." I didn't know how else to defend that choice. He had already made that remark about my being a "human musician" so I feared he would not treat my response as more than a musician's emotional reasoning. Without a valid scientific argument, just a feeling, this callous android would see my responses as a sign of weakness. Passing from emotional to logical was not that easy for me, but it was the only way for me to put myself close to their pure intellectual reasoning. "I just want to add something though." I said before he could scoff off my last remark as pure nonsense. "You don't understand love. Those women who aborted and those women who gave their children up for adoption probably made those decisions because of their love for the child. Not wanting a child to suffer psychologically can justify either choice. I am not saying that some women, a minority of women, I imagine, made that choice for strictly egocentric reasons. But, I don't believe that it is possible to place all those caring mothers in the same position of the few indifferent ones." I stopped and added. "I am saying your conclusions are too general."

"Interesting, without more." His lips begrudgingly opened into a starched smirk; or rather grotesque, forced grin. "You are naive and idealistic. But, then you cannot help that; it is in your nature. Should we continue?"

He was patronizing me; referring again to my musical background. "No. I still have something else to say." As I spoke, I grabbed his arm. It was a very human thing to do and quite unnecessary, as he hadn't started to move away. So, before he could say, yes, Pamela, what is it that you want to say, I spilled out the rest. "I believe that what you are doing at this birthing center is quite degrading and inhumane. You are reproducing human life in an environment devoid of love and affection. You are creating human robots, programmed to see and react to the information and the misinformation you are feeding them. You have destroyed human dignity more than any human would have ever imagined doing."

My intense frustration provoked by constant verbal intercourse with these humanoid machines evolved into shrill screaming, for a second time, this time directly into his angry face. His omnipresent blank eyes were focused on me; and, then, he withdrew his regard as if there was nothing of interest to him hidden in the corners of my mind.

As expected, my antics did not provoke a violent reaction on his part; he stayed under control. Nevertheless, I had to stop the sirens, get myself under control as I was losing sight of my ultimate mission, which was to find out as much as possible about our existence. So, I let go of him and bent over, letting the blood flow to my brain.

I then slowly lifted my head, took several long, deep breaths, to regain control before I feigned a smile. "Can we please continue, Dr. Flanders, this is all so very interesting?"

"Of course, Pamela." He complied with a bland smile, Android bland. He took my hand to lead me down the next corridor where he stopped abruptly. "I shall ask the librarian to let you see a more accurate representation of humans at the end of their history. In fact, I want you to view the tape before you see the rest of the birth center." His eyes were moving strangely in their sockets, as if he were excited or thrilled about his own suggestion. "You will come and discuss it with me afterwards. And, then, only then, will I decide whether you are ready to continue this visit."

He ushered me rapidly back to his office, dialed Dr. Miller and announced that she would receive me early in the morning. The tape would be in the system when I arrived.

"I shall inform Dr. Gordon of my decision which she will no doubt find excellent. You are too idyllic about humans." He was opening up to me. "I understand that they were an extraordinary species. Their creativity, curiosity and energy are to be admired. But, not everything that they did was nice, positive or in any way commendable."

I stopped him. "I know all of that already. There were wars, lots of cruelty. I read about torture and destruction. I don't need to see all of that again."

"No, I am talking about how humans viewed their history at the end. I am not referring to all of their bad behavior." He was no longer sitting behind his desk, but pacing back and forth like an animal in a cage. "We never judged humans. You must understand that. We are machines. We are fed information and we compute it. We worked alongside humans."

"So, why do you detest us so much?"

"Detest? No I wouldn't use that word. It infers emotions which we don't have. We draw conclusions and our conclusion is that humans never matured. They never developed beyond a primitive form of social consciousness." He wanted to impress me. "They repeated the same mistakes over and over again, as if they were unable to break the momentum pushing them to their ultimate doom; it was as if they sought their own extinction. They also never demonstrated what they put in us, pure intelligence. They let their emotions guide them and by doing so, they programmed their own destruction without realizing it."

"I don't understand your last remark?"

"You never will, Pamela. You are human. You can fight against injustice and cruelty. Many did that in the past. What you cannot fight against is a kind of fatality that your species succumbs to."

"And, you are part of that fatality?"

"We witnessed your fatality. We are not part of it. Our "raison d'être" is not the same as yours. And, we are neither obsessed with trying to understand why we exist nor what our purpose is. We are very different. You will see. And, you will certainly agree with me that our species is far superior to yours." He clapped his hands and told me to come back in two days to discuss the tape.

I was glad to leave. The androids don't understand how exhausted humans can feel after one-sided emotionally draining sessions with them. And, today was emotionally draining. What I saw was alarming, even terrifying. I didn't know if it would have been as shocking if I hadn't gone through a pregnancy. In spite of his remarks, I still believe that human love is the necessary ingredient for a healthy and productive child.

It was late afternoon when I arrived at my cubicle. I was surprised to see Dr. Gordon was there.

"I am tired. I am sorry but I am tired. I just don't have the energy to talk to you tonight." I pleaded, hoping that she would just leave.

"But, you are my project, Pamela. I haven't seen you for a while and today I discover that you are in the birthing center flirting with Dr. Flanders."

"Is that what he told you?" I sounded so disinterested. "Are you now jealous of him?" I knew how ridiculous it was to make that kind of statement even to Dr. Gordon.

"I wish that I could say Yes, Yes, Yes. But I can't. That must make you happy?"

"Not really. I have nothing against your joining the human race. In fact, I would just love it." I said with sincerity and a tone of regret. I wish that she was 100% on our side. She was so clever and I imagined that she could also be quite a brilliant General if she were human.

"Thank you. I do believe that you mean that as a complement and I appreciate your fidelity to me. But, if I couldn't fall in love with you, how could I fall in love with anyone else. You were the most stimulating and desirable of all my lovers. And, even though you are the only woman that I was ever intimate with, it's not the reason why I was attracted to you." She stopped to see if her confessions had any effect on me. I remained cold and unemotional. I was use to her game now and was not interested in pursuing a discussion. I pointed to the door, hoping that she would take the cue and just leave.

"I think that I should tell you a few things before you see the tape and return to see Flanders." She sounded serious, so I sat down on the other chair in the kitchen area, facing her. "You know that when humans ruled the earth they used some of us androids as sexual partners, in fact to replace themselves. They ordered them to carry on a normal sexual relationship with their partners so that they could be with their lovers." She stopped and apologized. She realized that what she said made no sense.

"Dr. Gordon, I don't care. I am not interested in hearing about sex." I said firmly and started to stand up. She grabbed my arm and pulled me back into my seat.

"I wasn't very clear." She paused. "I wanted to explain human relationships with each other; not sex, exactly." I conceded. What else could I do? "Humans liked to live in couples, like you do here at the Center. Marriage was the name given to a couple's public acknowledgement of fidelity to each other."

I sat in front of her playing with my hair, twisting it around my fingers and showing her how bored I was with this subject. She didn't seem to care; she was determined to continue. I listened half-heartedly, picking out key words here and there, which is why I am not certain that I understood everything. I just didn't care.

She rambled on about studies that proved that love between two persons in a marital context would not endure forever. I understood where she was going when she talked about children living through broken relations. I was no longer naïve about these androids and had the sneaking suspicion that she was with me at the request of Dr. Flanders. He wanted her to convince me that humans did not always prioritize the interests of their children.

"Children suffered from frequent ruptured relationships, divorces as they called them. Love turned to hatred and rapidly caused instability for everyone involved in the relationship; the children were the main victims. . . thrown out of the traditional family unit. New marriages, producing new children, created -how can I say -incoherent and often dysfunctional family units." She rubbed her eyes to pretend she was crying. "In any event, the government enacted laws which forced individuals to change partners every five years. And, after a certain age, I believe 25 years old, everyone had to follow this procedure. Those who were unable to find a partner were given one by the State, much like what happens here at the center. The difference was that these relationships had a limited life. As a result you never lived with the one you loved."

"Weird! What was the point of that?" I was a bit more interested now and had to bait her to continue unraveling history for me.

"The children, as I just explained. Divorces between those passionately in love often times ended in conflict. The pain of rejection by someone whose odor, touch, taste, appearance-basic elements of attraction as you explained it to me—that had incited profound desire to remain together later drove humans mad. And, humans had a tendency to tire of one another and imagine a better life with someone else; the ambiguity of marriage blurred the reality. Do you understand?"

"Yes and No." I didn't know what to say. I didn't understand marriage, so how could I understand divorce.

"Ok, think about yourself and Peter. He is back on the range raising Frederic and you are here at the Center being your promiscuous self." I shook my head in disgust; she dared comment on my intimate life, my trysts. But I had to let her continue. "How would you feel and act if Peter was being like you? Or, how would he feel if he knew what you were doing?"

"Wow, you do make me look like some kind of a sex fiend, maybe a monster. As you well know, I have not promised anything everlasting to Peter. Yes, I love him today. But, maybe I won't love him tomorrow. It won't be my fault, it will just be life."

"Well, what you are doing was not considered proper behavior when once you entered into a marital relationship. And, as marriage, a sincere promise to love someone, was forever, there was no tolerance of other relationships. Marriages broke up because one member of the couple was unfaithful."

I interjected, "And the betrayed one felt hurt and abandoned, even humiliated. So, as you say, love turned to hate." She nodded. "And for the children?" I started to focus more on her discourse.

"The children that were products of these intense love situations and were often traumatized by the intense sometimes irrational emotions surrounding the divorce. It invaded all aspects of their lives. So the law tried to remedy the problem and, even though the law recognized that humans were social creatures that need companionship and love, a new social order was created.

And, as was the nature of humans in society, everyone sought to get around the law or rebel against deprivation of their family rights. So, eventually, couples lived in fictional harmony with different legal partners in compliance with the law and had extramarital relationships with the ones they loved."

"And, the children, were they better off?"

"I don't know. There were studies underway, but human history did not survive long enough to validate the studies." She tightly puckered up her lips, like she was concentrating. Interesting reaction, I thought.

She finally picked up the conversation. "I would say that the cases I saw were quite encouraging. The children did not need to know who was there father because they knew who their Mother was. And, basically, no other children knew for certain who their father was. It was like that with humans. Not being able to identify the father became the norm. So no one seemed to be particularly concerned that the male figure's parental role had completely disappeared."

"That is very strange." I wondered whether it was true and, if so, whether it was the cause of the decline of human domination.

"I must confess, Pamela, I have not been completely honest."

"What? What do you mean?" I was annoyed, angry and embarrassed that I didn't just push her out of my cubicle in the beginning. I did not like being made to look like a fool.

"Rather, I did not tell you everything in the right order." She cleared her throat. "In fact, marriage and legitimacy of children had completely disappeared near the end of human history. What I told you concerned an intermediary period."

"So, you told me that to justify your relationship with Randolph, or to over rate maternal love and under rate paternal love, or to defend the birth center's policy of reproducing and educating children?" I asked, as I hit the table violently with my hand and moved to stand up.

"No." She replied firmly. "I told you that because it had a profound impact on the emotional and psychological stability of their children. Whereas, our system, in which children are not reared by their biological, rather human parents, offers real emotional and psychological security."

"Well, you did not convince me." I said with a slight smirk on my face as I sat back down in my chair. She leaned back in her chair, with her arms crossed on her lap and her eyes glaring back at me. She looked like a professor, who was very disappointed with the observations made by her student. Seeing her in that light made me feel more comfortable about asking more probing questions; one of which just slipped out. "What do you think, Dr. Gordon, of artificial uteri?" She raised her eyebrows, something that I didn't know she could do and that distracted me, as I wondered how much control these androids had over their outer shells. Perhaps I was just more conscious of her varied facial expressions; did she receive new programming? She was mimicking humans facial expressions a bit too much these days.

"You saw that part of the birth center." She paused. "It shocked you; I imagine. And, Flanders told you that artificial uteri were very much in demand?" I nodded. "From a scientific point of view, they are ingenious. It is easier to study the baby's development and to identify medical problems and potential abnormal developments. Yet, there is something ominous about them. They are in contradiction with life as humans experience it?"

"I found them monstrous! It is a way to strip a human of his or her emotional development from the date of conception."

"Now, don't exaggerate. There is music in the center and the nurses talk to the babies. They hear voices and pleasant sounds. There is no risk of permeating negative emotions, like rejection, being transmitted into the minds of these tiny beings."

"Do you think that I should see the disk?"

"What disk?"

"Dr. Flanders authorized the librarian to let me see a disk on what humans were like at the end of their history."

"Oh yes. That Famous disk. Flanders loves it. It is his justification for everything. But, I am warning you, what you will see in this film can be associated with reality; it was produced and directed by a very famous producer. It was quite popular and a strong counterculture devolved around it. Dr. Flanders is convinced that it is a true representation of the immaturity and cruelty of the human race. For him, it explains why human civilization and your history ended in such a cataclysmic way."

"Is it true?"

"True. Not exactly, but it is a prophecy of the imminent and close future. Humans were very critical of themselves and even though they were incapable of evolving beyond a certain intellectual level, they were always trying to achieve a perfect world. Idealist, idyllic, and dreamers..." She let out a deep breath. "They were destined to die off."

"But we haven't died off. We are still here."

"And so you are, thanks to us. What would you have done without us?" The discussion was over. I could feel it. She had another reason for her visit.

She grabbed me, pushed me up against the wall and blocked my arms above my head. Holding me in place with one arm, she slowly moved her free hand down over my breasts, squeezing and pinching me around the nipples. I was breathing heavily as her gently vibrating hands moved down over my stomach and around my hips. I could resist, and I must resist, even though my body screamed for more and more. . .

My body receptive, but my mind alert, I came to my senses. She was repeating what Randolph had done to her the very first time, but not with the same brutality. I had to stop her. I must stop her were the thoughts running forcefully through my mind. All that training with Diana paid off. I took her off guard as I drew my knee up and hit hard between her legs targeting her pelvic area. She wobbled back, startled, as I released myself from her grip moved rapidly to the other side of the room. I stood with my arms outstretched, beckoning her with my hands, to come closer. I wanted to put her flat on the floor. I saw the android machine side of her as she struggled to pass from one programmed action into another. It only took a split second, but that was all I needed to know that she was not invincible.

"Why did you do that, my Pamela, why did you do that to me? I thought that you felt something special for me." She was not speaking without reason; she was trying to manipulate me, as she slowly moved in my direction.

"No! No!" I screamed several times as I maintained my position. "I don't want sex with you. I want something greater than that. I want your friendship."

She stopped in her tracks. "Friendship. You want friendship, but I thought that you loved me? That must mean sex? Yes, sex goes with love." How foolish she sounded to me. It was not the first time and would not be the last time I threw reason to the wind; but, I saw that for once I was not making a mistake.

"I don't need sex, Dr. Gordon; but I need someone who I can trust and count on to be there for me."

"I promised you that many times. I thought that we were clear on that point." Her head was jerking from side to side. She did not want me to play mind games with her; she wanted to control the discussion, something that she had been doing up until now; in spite of the fact that I naively thought that I was sometimes the party in control. Today, I knew that I was in control.

"Yes, you have assured me of your protection. And I appreciate that." I was slightly confused. Her memory was not as acute as mine? Or she refused to access her memory bank? Because she told me years ago, when I first woke up in a deprogrammed world that she wanted to be my friend. So why was she offended now?

"So, no sex then, Pamela." She said dryly; she was regaining control. I nodded. "All the better," she said, "now we can be "friends", as you said. I am very interested in discovering the emotional links in friendship like those you have with Randolph so we shall talk about that soon."

"Not exactly like my relationship with Randolph." I corrected her. I recognized now that I should not have used the word friendship. She knew that my friendship with Randolph was broad; the problem was there. "I want only the most important part of friendship—the trust." I had maintained my distance from her, so she had only one option left, to leave. She smiled wickedly and waved goodbye. I felt slightly exacerbated by her exit, but pleased that I had shown her yet another side of me; a Pamela capable of physically defending herself.

As I woke up I felt bold, more sure of myself, nourished with a self-confidence that I had never known before. I thought that I was ready to tackle the next project, a film about human diabolical behavior before the end of human history. But, I was wrong. Just remembering the film, my renewed energy launching my day recoiled me and emptiness pervaded me, anticipating the depressive scenes of my kin, slithering like snakes, coiling and spitting venom before their end. I lay in bed trembling. It was like waking up after a nightmare, except I was too awake, too, too awake.

I dressed rapidly, mechanically downed some breakfast without even realizing what I ate and ran to catch the monorail. My trepidations were confirmed. I should have stayed in bed that day.

Chapter 35: Perverse Vision

Dr. Miller seemed delighted to have me back with her. She had already retrieved the film and had popped it into the terminal.

"Are you ready to see this piece of horror?"

"I hope so." Her concern seemed a bit misplaced. "I don't have a choice anyway, if I want to continue my tour of the birth center."

"If you can't handle it, press the small red button on the right. I promise that I won't tell anyone that you did not see it from beginning to end."

"I don't understand. It was a cult film and many people believed in it, right?"

"The people who believed in it were not exactly normal, if you understand what I mean. We kept the film because it was representative of the worst of human existence." She laid her robotic hand on mine. "Pamela, it is one thing to read about horrible things such as wars, exterminations and torture; it is another thing to see it. Trust me. In any event, I am here if you need me."

I pressed the start button. The title, "The End" was in bold letters framed in drops of blood, with Bach's, eerie and foreboding, "Toccata und Fuge in D-Moll" as intimidating background music. My heart started to beat rapidly and I felt very much on edge. I was definitely daunted, anticipating the crumbling, crashing down of my comfort zone, the bubble bursting for all time. As my breathing quickened, I clutched the arms of my chair with a deathlike grasp. I felt the waves of fear, starting to build and move inside of me, wrenching my stomach and tightening my throat, making it difficult to swallow. I knew that I was not ready for this film; and I knew I'd never be ready for this film but I was stuck. It was too late to leave. It was starting. This strange masterpiece of horror, a story without a beginning or an end, was flashing before my eyes. I saw the evil force within us that can drive humans to inflict the most heinous acts of barbarism on others. A seemingly interminable number of malicious, brutal, cruel, blood filled scenes of diabolicalness, by those motivated and driven by hatred, power, or an unfathomable desire to destroy; to commit horrific acts like those of serial killers, for whom murder is never enough to satisfy their lust for evil, and who resort to other forms of repugnance, including dismemberments and cannibalism. All these ghastly scenes made me want to vomit; instead I let my tears flow in raging torrents for those innocent victims.

Another long, tedious, and psychologically oppressive part of this film displayed the horror of families ignominiously being shoved into torture centers by non-human, supernatural creatures, like zombies, who sniggered uncontrollably as they prepared for their moment of sublime pleasure to arrive; waiting to be nourished; salivating as their appetites mounted with the sounds of human pain and suffering, those agonizing screams of tortured humans whose bodies were torn apart, amputated, brutalized, disfigured...

There were ghastly scenes with vampires and werewolves and other weird beasts performing horrifying human sacrifices. The sex scenes were disgustingly sick, sadistic, infinitely perverse, and filled with their own form of abominations committed in cold indifference...Flaming swords, phallic symbols of dominance, brutally forced into the womb of innocent young girls; a gigantic werewolf strangling then raping a young girl from behind; a vampire stalking, seeking orgasmic pleasure, as he violently drove his vulgar canines into his victim's throat, sucking out her blood, and depriving her of her right to mortality.

I was sickened by the horror of what I saw. I was mortified by the expression on the faces of those tortured, helpless victims, and their cries for mercy, knowing that death was their only escape, their only relief from the atrocities they were enduring. Incoherent with all the rest that proceeded, the film ended with a brilliant piece from Beethoven's fifth and an extraordinary explosion that wiped out human. . .life.

The film ended and my eyes were still on the screen. I felt like I was in a trance as I struggled to make some sense out of those three hours of grotesque horror scenes, one after the other, sometimes so disjointed and incomprehensible that they bordered on absurdity. I heard Dr. Miller and her android colleague asking if I was ok and felt their pushing and pulling on my shoulders to make sure that I was still alive; but I said nothing.

I was in deep concentration as I searched for explanations of what I saw. Murders, rapes, mutilations, and other despicable crimes appeared throughout human history. Wars seemed to be a haven of delight for those who liked and wanted to kill and for centuries there was no limit to how someone could kill or abuse their enemies. Did these ruthless people still exist when the human race became ...civilized? I didn't know.

Those creatures who tortured families and humans could be compared to those who sought to exterminate and destroy others races, simply because they needed to blame a group for their own misery and hardships; and witnessing these deaths fed their egos and made them feel superior.

The vampires, werewolves and other supernatural creatures were like those dictators, emperors, or leaders who, along with a selected group of faithful servants, enjoyed using their power to terrorize their population and perpetrate atrocities. They showed no mercy to those who opposed them; and took pleasure in randomly selecting innocent people to die as human sacrifices and to suffer perverse sexual abuse.

Yes, there was definitely an underlying message in this demented film, but it was not the one that the androids understood; it was not a film to denigrate the human race and call for its extinction, but to incite the human race to fight for a better world. I didn't see the date when the film was released, but I imagined that it was a time of turbulence, when many groups were forming, all promising a better world. This film was a warning to all humans to make the right choice in leadership; and to specific individuals and groups to protect themselves against impending dangers.

Certainly some of those creatures resembled in an innocuous way the evil and ruthless individuals in power or seeking power. I was not certain that I completely deciphered the visual messages which were directed to a class of intellectuals who were capable of saving the day; but I understood that this strong message of hope and call for action hidden deep within those ghastly, hideous visual images was essentially why it was referred to by humans as a cult film.

I pulled myself out of my thoughts and called out to Dr. Miller who was moving uncontrollably around in large circles. My voice calmed her and she rushed straight to me. She and the other technician were now staring at me.

"Are you alright, Pamela?" She asked.

"I think I am," I replied. I was rubbing my chin and looking at their inexpressive faces. I thought again about the real context of this film. I found it quite android to preserve a film like this; a film that they did not and could not understand. Humans would have eventually disposed of it to protect themselves, if they survived extermination. But, for these androids this film justified whatever they did to bring an end to human history and a beginning of android history.

It was at this point that I lost all reason. The excessive horror of the film, my interpretation of its meaning, the absurdity of the logical android analysis of human civilization, the insanity of my finding comfort in the arms of these two androids surrounding me, sent me off on a kind of hysterical laughter; it could have been tears and incessant sobbing, but it was laughter which brought my human fragility into play. Nothing made sense. My entire body roared with a frantic laughter, fueled by a fear, which turned into convulsive, gasping, lunges that shook my entire body. Dr. Miller reached out and laid her hand on my shoulder obviously trying to calm me, but it inspired more convulsions as I helplessly stared back at her.

The next thing that happened was Dr. Gordon pulled me out of my chair, and dragged me down the corridors to her office, where I sat pitifully gasping from the physical effects of my laughter over a sadistic horror film. Every time I tried to stop, I saw her disconcerted movements, and that ignited my folly.

Finally, she spoke. "What is the matter with you, my dear, sweet Pamela? Were you that frightened by the film?"

"What?" I was startled by the concern, almost maternal concern that came through in her voice. "Frightened by that?" I could feel my blood rushing to my face in embarrassment and I could hear a voice inside of me begging me to get back in control, but the emotionally charged side of me would not give way to reason, so as I said, "You told me that Dr. Flanders loves it?" I thought about the intensity Dr. Flanders summoned when watching this film. The humor was there. I wondered, who was the lunatic? I turned and faced Dr. Gordon.

"You weren't frightened?"

"No. And, I imagine that it had its following because it was one of the best sadistic comedies of its time." I retorted in a condescending way. At this point I was so weak from such intense, frenzied laughter that I felt limp; instead of collapsing, I was saved by a violent surge of serenity as my inner calm started to return.

"Did you see what was happening?"

"Did you ever see the film?" I asked, struggling to sound a bit more serious now.

"Yes, of course." She hesitated. "No, I did not find it an exceptional film like Dr. Flanders, but, I did not find it funny, either."

"But then, you have no sense of humor, do you?"

"Bravo! You hit the center of the target. But, just because I have no sense of humor doesn't mean that I am incapable of determining what a human might consider to be funny."

"Then you must understand why I was laughing?" I was glad that she did not realize the source of my laughter; it was better that she thought that I had a depraved sense of humor.

"Pamela, please, you are not yet calm enough. I think that you should return to your cubicle and think about how you are going to discuss this film with Dr. Flanders. It is important that you convince him that you share his convictions regarding the human race. He is very powerful here at the Center and you know there is a hierarchy here. I need to keep him on our side. So, be careful what you say." She was warning me.

"I am simply not going to discuss it with him. There is nothing to discuss." I was back in control of myself. I regretted losing control; it showed them that I was not emotionally strong. I felt an agonizing need to be with those I loved. I missed Peter and Frederic. It would be good for me to discuss all this with the others humans, to have their point of view, before I saw Dr. Flanders. I was ready to ask for leave to visit the outside, when I realized something even more important about what had just happened. Dr. Gordon was worried that I could insult Dr. Flanders. How could that be possible? He might not like my reaction; but he could not be insulted. And, even if my reaction were diametrically opposed to his, the worst that he could do would be to prevent my visiting the birth center. I decided to continue the discussion. "But I don't follow your logic. Why can't I have a different opinion from Dr. Flanders? You do. "

"Don't listen to me then. Do what you want, but, if things get difficult for you, don't come complaining to me."

"Ok. I admit that I am being a bit aggressive, but I don't feel comfortable lying about my feelings."

"No?" She interrupted me. "Isn't that what you are doing all the time telling lies about what you want, what you are doing, what you are thinking and what are your priorities?"

We were both looking into each other's eyes knowing that the truth was buried deep inside. I was not going to back off. It was better for me to keep that intensive eye contact hoping to put her on the defensive. Then unsettling invaded my mind: Did she know why I was in the center? Did she know that I had a mission? No, I was certain that she did not hold me in such high esteem that she might imagine that I would be plotting against her as she continued to underestimate me. She was bluffing.

"I have no idea what you are talking about." I replied. I was careful about my body language. She mentioned to me on several occasions that it was so easy to see through humans. One only had to observe the facial expressions and the rest of the body posture to determine the truth of someone's statement. I gave her a natural, friendly smile and used open hand gestures to show that I was relaxed with what I said. I was not certain that I used the best body language, but it worked because she surprised me and left that discussion drop and turned to a new idea.

"Pamela, I would like to feel protective of you; but I can't, even though, because of my work with you, I am starting to understand the power of emotions. So I am going to be logical and ask you to engage in the right strategy. Effectively, I have an excellent working relationship with Dr. Flanders who supports my projects. I don't want someone like Dr. Flanders to join Dr. Crawford's camp." She stopped for a few seconds before going into detail. "It is not a question of insulting Dr. Flanders. I believe that is what you are thinking. Am I right?" I nodded my head in agreement and then felt angry that she was reading my mind again.

"It is a question of following protocol. Dr. Flanders is the head of the birth center and makes all the decisions on human babies, their genetic make-up. He chooses the genetic composition of each fetus to avoid what he termed malignant genes for violence and cruelty."

"But, we are programmed." I jumped in to let her know that I wasn't going to let her dictate the conversation and to manipulate me.

"Yes, of course. You are right. The programming suppresses emotional development; but I am talking about weeding out malignant genes in humans." She noticed my indignation and returned to address my comment. "Of course, there are accidents, like yours and the others. The Governor follows the policy of other centers and lets you live outside the center. It is a risk; a very big risk." I was listening to her attentively.

"And," she continued, "It is for this reason, that Dr. Flanders' selective breeding process is so important. In fact, even if you discover the wide range of emotions that have set your species apart from ours, genetic modifications, Dr. Flanders believes, will result in your species natural inadvertence to violence, murder, brutality, hatred and other violent acts and emotions."

"Do you agree with him?" I was very curious of where she stood.

"I believe that humans are more productive and interesting when their complete emotional structure, with those positive and negative emotions, are in place. But, I have not been able to date to prove my hypothesis and therefore respect research projects in other areas, like that of Dr. Flanders. This is why I am asking you to show him respect. Even if you feel this film is ludicrous, you must give him the impression that you respect his contempt for the atrocities committed in the film. And, I do believe, Pamela, that your uncontrolled, hysterical laughter was in part based upon the psychological impact these diabolical images had on you." She forced a relatively convincing smile. "It does not matter whether you believe that all humans turned into heinous monsters in the end or not. Do you understand?"

"Yes, I understand." She was speaking easily so I did not want to stop her. It was the right moment for me to raise another question. "Do you remember Diana?" She answered affirmatively. "She was not calm."

"Yes, she is unstable. We all know it."

"So, why did you send her to us?"

"I didn't. I was opposed to the idea, but the others insisted. They expected your people to return to past savage behavior and even to terminate her, or for her to terminate one or all of you." I didn't know then that this was an outright lie and that she was the one who masterminded this charade.

"But, that didn't happen."

"Not yet, Pamela. But she is definitely unstable. There is still a risk that something dramatic could happen in the future. She has the kind of personality that can kill. In fact, she is the kind of person who would or could enjoy the horror of some of those scenes in the film. She should have been terminated in the center." She stopped to move more comfortably in her chair. "There were other humans like Diana, whose brain waves malfunctioned."

"I don't understand." I was a bit confused. I thought about the discussions I had with Mathilda, who studied psychology, even though she didn't work with patients in the center; but rather explained certain behavioral problems revealed in studies of past mental cases. Peter told me that Mathilda was fascinated with Diana's interaction with the children and was studying her behavior. I preferred to believe what Diana had told us. I had confidence in her. I had nothing to say so I sat waiting for Dr. Gordon to continue.

"I don't think that even humans specialized in the treatment of mental disorders were able to explain and resolve the vast majority of affected humans. In fact, at one point, they sent hardship cases I believe that was the term, to other planets. They got rid of them. It was a way to clean up society and avoid crimes. But. . well. . .there were still many perverted individuals who were not identified in time. And, there were groups, namely sects or cults appearing; that is what they called themselves."

"And why were there sects or cults?" Today was a day of real revelation and I did not want Dr. Gordon to stop.

"Oh, yes. Remember when you talked to me about a God?"

"Yes." She accused me of being obsessed with religion, and yet she brings up the subject quite often and is always defining religion as the source of all human problems.

"As you know, you have a vision of a merciful and kind superior being whose purpose is to save and protect his or her children." She hesitated. "I was never certain whether this generous God was male, female, or neuter. I don't suppose that it matters."

"Please, go on." I encouraged her because I was hoping that her discourse might be revelatory.

"In the physical sciences, every positive has a negative. So, it was with this God. There was the opposite; the antithesis. Some called it Satan, others the Devil; but there were many names. This individual demanded animal and human sacrifices. This Satan took on many different forms, sometimes eloquent and seductive, although he was more often portrayed as a red-hot creature with horns, or as a ravenous beast. But we, Androids concluded, based upon our observations and the information that we had easy access to, that the more torture, deaths by violence, etc., perpetrated in his name, the stronger this Satan became."

"Do you believe all of that?

"It is not about beliefs, it's about... a logical analysis of the human condition."

"So, the film for you portrays the decline of human history, human existence, because Evil has triumphed over Good."

"Yes and No. One would have to acknowledge the logical existence of those Good and Evil creatures to come to your conclusion." She glanced around surreptitiously, as if she was verifying the absence of a Good or Evil force present in the room. "We androids have not been able to identify scientifically the existence of a God or a Satan. But, the Satan had his rivals. There were many notions of the force of evil and who or what presided over it like Vampires, Werewolves, Zombies, and other supernatural creatures. The various sects and cults were constantly in conflict, never united, even though there were more humans that believed in Good. The religious people fervently disagreed with the rituals followed in giving praise to God. Those profound differences gave rise to a myriad of religious wars throughout the history of mankind."

I didn't know what to say. I had already read about the horrible wars that took place in the name of a good God. I had to agree that I didn't understand why it was so important among humans to exhort the superiority of one faith over another. I had merely concluded that the idea of a superior being was comforting. I was less familiar with the devil, because he was only alluded to in the literature that I read. I was discovering more about his nature and disguises right now from Dr. Gordon.

"Did you read about the decline of the Roman Empire?" She interrupted my musings.

"Yes. I was sad for the people living in the Empire. They had a very rich and interesting culture. But, they believed in too many Gods."

"Who cares about the many Gods?" She interrupted me. "There are no Gods at all, Pamela. There is not one God and certainly not many Gods. There is no good God and no evil God." She threw her arms up in the air in frustration, as I raised my brows and opened my mouth in surprise; after all she was the one who brought up the subject. "This is all propaganda to help humans live in society and accept the idea of their existence terminating; a termination will open up a beautiful, euphoric, immortality in some celestial universe. That simply does not exist." After denouncing Gods, she maintained that if humans had accepted that they evolved naturally on a planet without supernatural intervention by any creator, they would have been better off. She again shared with me her immutable position that androids had an advantage over humans because they knew who created them.

She was still talking and I was tired of listening. "Back to Rome. It became extremely decadent at the end of its history. Decadence destroyed that civilization as it eventually destroyed the human world. It is that simple and is why the film means so much to Dr. Flanders. It foresees the end of a world dominated by humans, until doomsday. Do you understand?"

"Yes." But I was not sure that I agreed with her.

"Do you think that you can discuss this with Dr. Flanders and give him the impression; if nothing else, that you owe your existence to him?"

"Yes; but, what about my laughing?" He might already be aware of my incessant, convulsive laughter after the film.

"I shall explain to him that your hysteria was brought on by shock. Laughter is a form of hysteria in humans, even Dr. Miller thought so. I shall tell him that it took me a long time to calm you down." She stood up. "Well, we did get into emotions today like your laughter so I'd like to continue this in a few days."

I got up with the intention of returning to my cubicle to relax. Instead, I walked slowly; wandering aimlessly through the corridors. Every time I thought that I was getting close to understanding what happened to bring about the end of human history, I saw, read, or heard something that raised doubts as to the accuracy of my conclusions. The androids saw everything in black and white and were loath to enter a grey area. The film, Dr. Gordon's strange interpretations of humans and their relationships, children, religions and Dr. Flanders' clinical approach to human procreation sickened me; it all left a bad taste in my mouth. I wanted to believe that those humans who created androids in their own image, were not psychologically disturbed; that they did not have a perverse view of others. They could not have been so decadent. I had to confide in and, maybe…brain storm, with Randolph.

I burst into his lab, and even though his android assistant was not there, he was not alone. He was in deep conversation with a stunning young man, standing next to him. Randolph turned and motioned me to join them. He introduced me to the mysterious Stuart who he reminded me was masterminding the theft of equipment, new technology for our outside community.

We stood there, our eyes met as they completed a mutual body scan. He was wearing his white smock tied up above his knees, with the sleeves rolled up high on his arms. His lean, muscular body was taller than that of Randolph and I pictured him moving easily in combat situations. His long, wavy chestnut brown hair, pulled back in a ponytail, enhanced his virility. His thin, high, cheek boned face and mellow velvet olive skin was a delicious contrast with my white, very white skin. His brow furrowed and his big, brown eyes fixed on me like radar, giving me the impression that he was penetrating deep inside of my consciousness. And then, as if I passed the screen test, his expression changed; he raised his eyebrows and gave me a friendly smile. He took my hand in his and thanked me for helping them in their fight against the insanity of this center. In spite of those words which I wholeheartedly resonated with, I still had to shake my thoughts away from his luscious physical side to be able to follow the discussion.

I learned that the tunnel was advancing at an alarming pace. Apparently, there was not much real excavation to contend with since this former, effective escape route had not been damaged as much as we all imagined. Once they dug through the enormous thick rock mass, they found another footpath that was wider than the thin, dangerously high ledge that they were accustomed to working on."

"Nonetheless," he said in a deep, masculine voice. "There is a problem. How serious a problem, I don't know." He informed us of obstacles on this path. "There are thick stone structures placed 20 meters apart. They were man-made. John has suggested that they are now digging through the remains of an ancient Egyptian pyramid."

"How do you and John know about Egyptian pyramids?" I interrupted him.

"From our research we know what they looked like, even though we don't know why they were constructed."

"How much time do we have before they arrive?" Randolph asked, changing the subject.

"Impossible to say." Stuart sucked in his lips as if that would make it easier to answer. "We must be ready for them whenever they arrive, which means that we have to train ourselves for the attack and identify possible allies." He was looking at me as he said those words.

"Possible allies." I repeated softly.

"There are two groups, Pamela, those humans who have bypassed the programming and have not yet been identified by the androids and those androids who are not happy with their situation and would be willing to work for us. And Pamela, you circulate freely and meet androids every day. You are the only one who can secure this information."

"You are not serious, Stuart." I protested. He was asking too much.

"Yes, I meet these androids all the time, but they are also programmed. They were programmed by their creators and reprogrammed after the disaster that took place; I don't know when. There is a hierarchy, but androids are not independent thinkers; they are not like revolutionaries." I already had this conversation with Randolph, Peter, and John and was now convinced that there could be an android uprising. "For example, there is the librarian whose creator gave her veritable beauty. She was the victim of a laboratory explosion that she insinuated was caused by Dr. Gordon. She pretends that her android head planted on top of a primitive, robotic body does not bother her in the slightest. It may bother her, though, but, in spite of that, I cannot imagine that she would ever revolt."

"Yes, you might be right; and yet, she is a potential prospect, but not your principal prospect. The key figures are Dr. Gordon and the Governor. They have been resisting the opposition for a long time, an opposition obviously led by Dr. Crawford." Stuart spoke as if I should have known this all along, Ironically, I just learned about it from Dr. Gordon today.

"Wait a minute. How do you know all this?"

"I have my ways."

"Your ways." I repeated. "Are they human ways or android ways? Are you one of us? Are you human, Stuart?" I did not like his sly, secret side and wanted to be aggressive to get answers. It worked. His eyes turned cold as ice and his posture stiffened. I continued, without giving him the chance to answer. "I know that Dr. Gordon asked me to protect her when she was forced to shut down to validate that she was still 100 percent android. But, after the scene, I had every reason to believe that everything that happened was staged to make me even more dependent upon her. I have never gotten the impression that Dr. Gordon is interested in bringing down her colleagues. I recognize that I am unable to relate to her cold, calculating android logic and am limited in what I can surmise. If you are not an android, then you cannot penetrate their consciousness. So are you or are you not an android?" My voice rose to a fever pitch as I glared in his eyes.

Without waiting for a response, I stammered, "Prove it. . ." Tears began to well inside as my voice trembled.

His beautiful face was taking on such a menacing appearance; even Randolph stepped away from him. And then, he replied. "And, what if I am? Where is the problem?"

Randolph reached for my hand and squeezed it slightly as if to reassure me that he was on my side.

"Are you going to answer, Pamela? I see no reason why I should be the one submitting to such offensive questioning."

I was not going to force him to back down. And why should he back down, he hadn't done anything wrong. The problem was with me. I had overdosed on stress; I was confused and depressed; and I needed to talk to Randolph, alone. Accusing one of us of being an imposture took me over the top. Randolph's calming arms were around me.

I apologized to Stuart for my behavior and for my irrational accusations. "I came here to see Randolph, because I needed to talk to him." I told them about the absurdity of the film, the stupidity of Dr. Flanders and the idiotic recommendations and explanations of Dr. Gordon. They listened intensely.

After I finished my long story, I explained, the best I could, why I reacted so foolishly. "I said what I felt, Stuart. I want to believe that someone will tell me the truth. I don't care whether you are an android or a human, I just don't want to join forces with someone I can't trust." I paused. "Why couldn't you have humored me? Why did you refuse to answer? After all, there is something unsettling in this. How and why can you penetrate the android consciousness so well?"

Randolph released his grip and moved towards Stuart. Their widened eyes honed in on me as if they were staring at a mad dog; then Stuart picked up the conversation.

"I apologize for frightening you, Pamela. " He spoke softly. "You have definitely lived through a traumatic week and I can understand why you might be seeing enemies everywhere. I need time to reflect on what you have told us. Nonetheless, and I hope that this will be encouraging for you, your reasoning is convincing. I would like to give it a bit more thought, though, and let you know later if I have any other observations that could be useful to you." His whole face lit up under the effect of his broad smile.

"Now for the rest. Admittedly, I did not appreciate your comparing me to an android, but," he quickly continued, "to set the record straight I am not an android and, if my words are not enough to convince you, I can just cut my skin and let some blood flow. We all know that androids can't bleed."

"No, don't do that." I laughed embarrassingly.

"Ok—well, I started my career here at the center following the Head Android Doctor; the one that ordered Dr. Gordon to shut down. I bypassed my programming when I reached puberty. I found it amusing to pretend that I was still one of their toys and to carry out their orders with enthusiasm. They have never realized that I could see them. My brief experience in the android treatment center was useful because I know how their circuitry is aligned. I understand them and, more importantly, how they function. The androids in charge of this center have---how can I say it?" He rubbed his chin and twisted his mouth in thought. "They pretend that they are at a higher level of technological advancement than staff androids. They have authorized changes, but nothing radical." He started chewing on his lower lip again. "In my estimation, what distinguishes them from the others is their organized meetings and discussions. They have a form of government and hierarchy in place. Only the Governor is authorized to make unilateral decisions. Actually, they meet to come to compromises; something that seems to be in conflict with pure android logic." He stopped, obviously hesitating to reveal more information.

After a long pause, he continued, "I think that you should know this, Pamela. No matter what they tell you or promise to do for you, they cannot change their basic program, whatever the parameters of that programming are. So, don't let them fool you, manipulate you, into believing that they have omnipotent power. And, they will try to do just that by revealing slight adjustments or modifications in, for example, their reactions like showing human facial expressions; all of which are compatible with and permissible within the limits of their strict programming." I nodded pleased to know that I was right not to put too much confidence in them. Then he changed gears, "Well, are you still willing to stick your neck out just a bit for the rest of us?" He was looking at me.

"Yes, of course, I promised to help in any way I could a long time ago." I cringed as I was being backed up against a wall and I didn't feel confident at all about android complicity. "I'm afraid of sabotaging the mission by doing or saying something foolish."

"But you're always doing or saying something foolish," Stuart said nonchalantly, maybe facetiously. But I was livid.

I couldn't believe he could he be so judgmental so I jumped up and headed for the door when he called out.

"Stop! That was not meant to be a criticism." I turned and looked at him. "You are either very sensitive or you lack a sense of humor. Am I right Randolph?"

Randolph, who hadn't said anything for a long time, spoke up. "No, actually, Stuart, she has a very good sense of humor. It is just that your humor, Stuart, is a bit too subtle for her, and even for me sometimes, to catch on to." I was delighted that Randolph took my side.

"Ok, my fault. But, I meant because the androids, Dr. Gordon and the Governor, are protective of you, Pamela, your mistakes are treated as delightfully interesting emotional reflexes. This is how they find excuses for you and are always turning your errors into discoveries useful for the success of their project. That satisfies their protective tendencies, so it's good. So, you have nothing to worry about. Am I clear?" He looked at me with a warm, inquisitive smile.

Later I would be angry with myself that I was not nicer to him, but, at this moment, Stuart annoyed me and I didn't know why. So, instead of humoring him, I made another provocative remark. "I know other things about you, too, Stuart."

"I am sure that you do." But, before I could recount my major discovery, he said that Diana was his training partner. He also mentioned that he was glad that I was aware of his skills and hoped that I would count on him in the future.

By this time, I could vaguely hear him, let alone concentrate on what he was saying. I needed to get away from mind-games and revolutionary talk. I had more than my dose of discovery for today. I looked at the both of them and imagined that they had other things to discuss and that my presence was no longer that important to them. "I'm a bit tired. I've had a rough few days. I wish we could meet at a different time, when I'm feeling more, alive." I smiled. "I'll do my best to weed out our allies and our enemies from among the group of humanoids. But," I forced myself to yawn, "I would like to get some sleep." Nobody objected when I opened the door and left.

I did not take the monorail back to my cubicle; instead I slipped over to the music center. I rushed to my piano and let my fingers spin over the complicated chords of Chopin's nocturnes… until sleep overcame me.

Chapter 36: Determination

I must have dozed with my head crunching the piano keys for several hours until I heard a door creek open. It must be the arrival of a group of musicians. Being invisible allowed me to slink around, a definite advantage; but I had to leave before the android instructor arrived, or I would have to explain my presence to the Governor. The androids, particularly the Governor, were strict in applying rules and I would have been obliged to give my code number to the instructor. I crept out the back door and rushed to grab the monorail back to my cubicle to take a shower and prepare emotionally for my meeting with Dr. Flanders.

However, it was unbelievable that the beginning of our meeting went so smoothly. I said that I was very much affected by the film. As Dr. Gordon had already contacted him describing my laughter as an extreme form of hysteria, he did not question me about the content. He simply comforted me by saying, "Oh, my child, you know now why we androids are so selective in human breeding." I made a grimace. What a revolting expression, breeding. He did not seem to notice my reproach as he nonchalantly stepped forward and opened the doors to the birth center to continue our tour.

This time I asked more probing questions. He had already explained that certain physical anomalies were not always manifested in the early stages of fetal development. My Jonathan, he confirmed what Dr. Gordon had told me, was the first of his series to present such extreme genetic deformities. Genetic deformities were not the most important criteria for terminating an individual in its infancy.

"You know, Pamela, that we are not that concerned about physical appearances." I nodded, that was evident. "As I mentioned before, your programming is in place principally to help you, as individuals, to go beyond the physical aspects, by ignoring them or by not seeing them." He was watching me very intensely. "I believe that Dr. Gordon has already explained to you that humans are visual creatures and first impressions of other humans are decisive. In fact, physical traits are the first criteria for rejection, followed by mental defects, mannerisms, and so forth. Logically, physical attributes should be very low on your pyramid, which is what the visual receptor has achieved. It's like you see the world through rose-colored lenses." He stopped and forced a weird cackling laugh that seemed out of place, because I did not see the humor in what he said. "But humans liked to see the world in rosy colors, namely, in peace and harmony."

He was odious in his arrogance and in his condescending belittlement of humans. I didn't want to know about the rosy color, something that I had the impression that he was hoping to explore with me. But why? Was his rosy colored world a euphemism; or was it a subtle allusion, an invitation for intimacy…with him? I felt my guard go up. I was on the defensive. He could have the rosy colored world; I wanted answers. "So what do you do when a child does not conform to your standards?"

"Our standards. How curious, for you to say that. They are not our standards but those for humans to guide them in their communities. We simply terminate the child or adolescent who is unable to interact properly and produce."

"To produce? What does that mean?"

"Every human has a role to play." He sounded like he had given this lecture many times before, but to whom? "We orient you towards the career that is the most adapted to your intellectual capacity. We expect you to contribute; produce something noteworthy, or of value, in your specialty. That is what humans always did, anyway. They had a career and they worked. They were rewarded with friends, vacations, sports, money and so forth. Isn't that what you did before your system shut down? Weren't you happier just living an easy and fulfilling life? Aren't you much more frustrated and unhappy today?"

"You have a lot of questions for someone who seems to have all the answers." I had a smirk on my face. "In any event, none of your questions are easy for me to answer." He thought that he understood human behavior and what was best for us. "You know Dr. Flanders there is something that makes no sense, does not seem logical." His eyes were straight on me. "How can you say that humans are happy when they don't know or understand that emotion?"

"You sound like Dr. Gordon!" He exclaimed, waving his hands in the air, like he was swatting away offensive particles. "She raised that question so many times that we all had to agree to let her go forward with her study. But, look what we have now. We have a young, beautiful and very talented musician who is confused, curious, emotionally unstable and unable to behave correctly in society. Would you say that you are better off than your colleagues in the music department who have a real purpose for living and developing their talents?"

"I may be all that you described; but, I have more. I'm alive. I can construct my life, dream about my future, create music different from what existed and what you know. I can even go beyond the projects and instructions that you give me. I am free to think, act..." I moved closer to him to make my last remark more impressive. "But, you did not answer my question."

"Of course I did not answer your question because it is impertinent." He said authoritatively. "But, what did you mean..." he asked aggressively.

"About what?" I interrupted him.

"What did you mean by go beyond the projects that we give you?"

"I don't know exactly; it just slipped out. But, in reality, I am no longer hampered by your programming so I can be all that is human having spontaneous notions as well as living life to the fullest with all its dichotomies, between the good and the bad, constructive and the non-constructive, etc. "

It was difficult to decipher his mumbling but eventually I understood that he was repeating over and over again the same thought. My thoughts turned to Dr. Gordon. She was right, human creativity is perhaps linked to emotional development, but how? When he realized that I was observing him, he stopped.

"Do you want to continue your visit?"

"Of course. I find it very informative and interesting." I furtively withheld the goal of my mission. We passed rapidly in front of the sectors that I had already visited until we arrived at the children's center. Many children sat behind their individual terminals; their little eyes moving rapidly backwards and forwards then up and down. This is where we stopped the last time.

"What do you do here?"

"Well, it is more complicated than it appears." He liked to give the impression that he was the genius in the center and was solely responsible for its successful operation, a human characteristic. Apparently his creator wanted his android to be a look-alike physically, with his creator's intellectual ability, as well as his creator's personality. As Stuart mentioned last evening, these androids can modify slightly their behavior within the fixed parameters of their programming. If that is true then Dr. Flanders' creator was also pretentious and overly self-confident and wanted his spirit preserved for posterity.

Dr. Flanders' voice was now ringing in my ears as he explained to me that humans are tested for their innate abilities or talents, at 2 years old. It was a policy set up at the end of human history. Once humans realized that it was possible to identify future talents or lack of talents, young children went through further rigorous testing. What was happening at the center was exactly what human progenitors were having done to their offspring. Dr. Flanders was just implementing procedure.

"Are you following me, Pamela?" I nodded, the cue he needed to continue. "The result," He stared off, "is that children are given the basics in language and mathematics through visual learning techniques. Each child is connected to a terminal, adapted automatically to a child's rhythm and learning capabilities. Everyone, including a slow learner, will be able to understand the fundamental elements of various subject areas. After that is achieved, children are oriented to the right form of education to ensure their productivity in the job market. No one will be working in an area that is inferior to or beneath, the individual's full mental capabilities." That did not surprise me at all. There were humans doing menial tasks at the center as well as those involved in high-level scientific and intellectual activities. Nonetheless, he was not clear as to whether he was addressing the existing or the future needs of the center in planning the child's eventual entry into the job market. I didn't bring that up because it was not the most important issue for me to explore at this moment.

"You know, Dr. Flanders, I had a conversation not too long ago with the Governor. He told me that I was the exception, that all Pamela's were directed towards scientific research. He also told me that he had made the decision to change my direction and orient me to a career in music, in the hope that I would not bypass my programming like my predecessors. Is that true?"

"Yes. We," he corrected me "the Governor and I meet regularly to discuss career orientation. He is also a brilliant geneticist. We made that decision because the Pamela series has always been a problem." He slightly advanced like he was floating down. Then he stopped, his face turned toward mine, "I thought that if your scientific ability was channeled to another creative sector like music, you would be able to live out your term without any problems. Obviously, I was wrong."

"Did you terminate the others?

"Of course. Just like I would have terminated you if that meddling Dr. Gordon hadn't intervened with her project to study emotional development." He then claimed that her study was completely useless.

"Oh. Strange, I thought that you were a supporter of Dr. Gordon?" I chimed up.

"Supporter, I don't know what you mean. But, if I have to align myself with someone, I would rather align myself with Dr. Gordon. After all, she has the Governor on her side."

"Going back to what you said before—the fact that you would have ordered my termination--are you disappointed that I am here with you today?"

"No, not at all; although I would not describe myself as being happy, either, as these are emotions that only humans succumb to. I just find it interesting to share information with a curious human whose termination is getting very close." With that remark, I felt my legs going limp and my stomach clench. He pretended not to notice and smiled his perfunctory android smile. "Do you want to continue?"

"Absolutely!" I snapped up energetically as I grappled to move forward on my wobbling legs.

We passed into the playground area. The androids were expelling enormous amounts of light that, even the decoder I was still using to cut off the blinding android light when I was circulating in the corridors, could not erase this luminous fallout. It became clear why we, as children, were so sensitive to them that our eyes squinted in their presence. Did the androids use this high-powered luminosity to subdue curiosity and eschew spontaneity in children? Another question to pursue at a later date.

The children were sitting in a circle passing a ball from one to the other. It was sad. They were not laughing or joking or speaking. They were simply carrying out a command. I stood perhaps too long watching this very depressing scene. I knew that Dr. Flanders was studying me. At one point he motioned me with his hand to approach him, but I ignored him. I was struggling to remember myself in that playground so long ago, obeying the androids but experiencing neither pleasure nor frustration. The children who caught the ball showed no satisfaction and those who missed their turn showed no frustration. How horribly contrived. A consoling thought entered my mind, fortunately the children living on the outside of this center know how to play. They compete with each other. They are happy when then win, and try to do better after a defeat. They are acting human.

"Pamela," he was calling me. "We must continue. It is getting late. But, look over there, your replacement Pamela 14 is sitting next to a playmate watching the ball."

I unwittingly moved toward the spot he was pointing to. I stood glued up against the window, not out of curiosity over Pamela 14, but to prevent myself from falling. A quick flashback of my waking up in the hospital bed overcome by ripping surges of violent emotions that I didn't understand but that I liked because they make me feel alive invaded my thoughts. I was afraid then and I am afraid now; afraid for my life. Dizzy, nauseous, light-headed, I struggled to keep my balance on my trembling legs; every organ in my body was over reacting to my charged anxiety. He noticed how I was betraying myself by losing my calm and showing fear. I could see his reflection in the window; his face lit up in pleasure. That was enough to turn my fear to anger;

as bursts of adrenaline flowed through my quaking body and palpitating heart, restoring my vigor and unleashing the right amount of energy and strength to rip Flanders' body into tiny pieces. Before I turned to face him with my clutched fists and bold, menacing eyes, I took a good look at that young girl marching in programmed style around the room. I was blind with anger; I had only contempt for her.

"She doesn't look it, but she is 14. Your sister, for lack of a better word, is scheduled to replace you very soon." He was rambling, but stopped in his tracks when my eyes met his.

He may have been baiting me along. And, maybe I was lucky that he did not call for reinforcement and have me terminated on the spot. But, nothing that happened next was what I anticipated. He backed up a bit and assumed a subservient manner; he bowed his head and looked down at his feet; he remained immobile, like someone ashamed to have defied authority. But, what authority? My authority? How ludicrous could I be to imagine that? He remained in that position long enough for me to gain control of myself, before he coughed and cleared his voice. "Well," he said as he approached the window. "Time is still on your side, Pamela." He shrugged his shoulders and backed away from the window.

"She could never replace you." He murmured.

I ignored his remark and followed him quietly down the remaining part of the corridor. As we neared the end, I spoke up. "I have another question, if you don't mind? I forgot to ask you earlier." I said politely to cut the tension.

"Ok, but I have a busy schedule this afternoon, so this will be the last question for the day."

"What happens then if a child is unable to master the fundamentals of various subject areas; I think that it is how you described it?"

"Oh, that is simple. They are terminated. We have no place here in the center for anyone who has severe learning disorders."

He tapped his foot as if to clear his mind. "Bravo, the phlegmatic stiff machine has learned another human trait." I whispered to myself. He continued; his arrogance had disappeared. "It is true that human society took great pains to integrate those whose learning capacity was obstructed. It is also true that these humans brought other beneficial contributions, non-intellectual; they were often capable of profound kindness and pure love and affection. But, as I said, we do not have enough room in the Center for those individuals who are not productive."

"So then your criterion for survival is intellectual capacity. In fact, you are focusing on an inner organ, the brain. The brain is your reference point." I was adding new suggestions, because he was not responding.

"Quite simply then you don't reject someone because of their physical traits, but rather their intellectual ability. Isn't that a blatant discrimination, android style?'

"It has nothing to do with discrimination. And, even if it is android-style discrimination –an incredulous idea- I want to remind you that we can only make logical decisions. Discrimination is a human response based on a wide range of factors most particularly, in my estimation, fear. The center must function and humans must work alongside androids to assure the proper functioning of the center."

"That is not true. You don't need humans to keep the center functioning. What's the real reason why you need humans?"

"No. I said only one more question." and then he added that tomorrow we would be visiting the maternity section. His devious, arrogant nature was back, evident in the sardonic smile on his face. "You might find that visit particularly interesting." He was obviously referring to the fact that I had already been a patient in that ward and had little memory of it.

I walked back in the direction of Dr. Gordon's office, hoping that she would not be around and that I could avoid another mind-boggling encounter with a machine; but her door was wide open and she quickly signaled me to enter. I did not want to go into any details, so I stuck to a simple thank you for arranging things with Dr. Flanders. "You see, Pamela, we can work for our own mutual interests. Isn't that what friends do for each other?"

My eyes were wide in their sockets. I had forgotten my stupid mistake. How could I have put friendship in her mind? "I guess you are right." I acknowledged disgruntling.

"Can you just give me a couple minutes to finish this note and then we can have one of our exhilarating discussion…about, emotions." She pointed to the chair.

I sat back and crossed my legs comfortably and studied her. Maybe Stuart was right that there were those androids that would join in our cause. The idea still seemed dubious. They had been the masters for too long. I could not see Dr. Gordon or the Governor compromising their position to help humans. But, then there was reason to believe that the androids did not all share the same ideas and that I was the catalyst for the division into two camps. I just couldn't figure out why Androids would team up with humans, like there was a key piece of the puzzle missing.

I didn't give her chance to bring up friendship. I took advantage of the lull in the schedule to ask for leave to visit my family. Dr. Gordon ignored my question, pretended not to hear it, by rummaging through papers piled on one corner of her desk. So, I repeated my request.

Patricia Lee Strunk

"Not now." I jumped as her hand came down hard on the top of her desk. "It is too soon."

"I have been inside for a long time."

"Not at all." She said adamantly. "You have only been here for two months. It is too soon for you to return. Besides you are not spending enough time with me. I have a report to make soon, and I need more details, more information…credible information," she said as she shook her finger in front of me. "There is another big meeting scheduled in two weeks." She grimaced. "No, I refuse to authorize your departure now."

She knew that that was not true; there was no meeting, she just did not want me to leave. "So what would you like to know? I have all afternoon to discuss emotions with you. But, have you already forgotten how much time I spent with you yesterday. You can always talk about hysterical laughter triggered by my reaction to decadent human behavior."

"Yes, yes, there is that. But, I am interested in hatred, rejection, resentment, vengeance, and so forth."

"For the moment, I don't hate anyone. That might come one day, but I can't describe an emotion that I have not yet felt. And, as for resentment and vengeance, I don't understand them."

"Then perhaps I can help you. I know things that might make you very angry."

"Like what, for example."

"Dr. Crawford has suggested that we should start to terminate some of the members of the outside group and bring the children into the center for a proper education." She was testing me? "I am very much in favor of ensuring proper education. Dr. Flanders discussed learning in the center with you today and you were no doubt impressed with the speed at which children learn and develop."

"You are going a bit too fast." I said. I needed time to think. "What is this termination of outside members?"

"Well, I suggested that we should put Jonathan out of his suffering. Even you told me that he has suffered much pain. There is nothing that we can do there."

"And the medicine that we sent out?" I thought that the medicine was working.

"That was just placebos." She sighed in annoyance. "A fruity biscuit. We have nothing else available."

There she sat in her android glory talking down to me. Shutting her down was less revolting than terminating Jonathan. My hands were clenching the sides of my chair and I felt my face muscles stiffening. "Really, that is what you think; that the children should be programmed and Jonathan terminated." She was in her favorite position now, leaning on her elbows with her hands in a steeple position; her android eyes blinking calmly back at me.

"That is all you have to say, Pamela?"

"No. You must be losing your memory. You have already threatened me with the idea of Frederic being brought into the center to be programmed for learning. And, well, quite frankly for your other threat, Dr. Gordon, even if I thought that your decisions were very radical, I have no authority in this Center to do anything. I am helpless. But you, I thought that you were in a stronger position than Dr. Crawford and would oppose these kinds of injustices. I guess I was wrong. That does not seem to be the case, does it?" I was trying hard to confuse her. If she were expecting me to be verbally angry, she would be searching her system for a new logic. That would be advantageous for me.

"So then you believe that these decisions are improper?"

"Certainly, but, as I said, there is no reason for me to get upset and angry when I can do nothing."

"And, what about Frederic? You don't care that he will be programmed?"

"He will at least, as you said, be educated."

"And, if I authorized your leave, would you warn everyone?"

I started to laugh, because now it was ridiculous. She undoubtedly wanted me to confirm that my allegiance was with the human community outside.

"You laugh very easily these days, Pamela."

And here my sarcasm took over. "Perhaps it is because I am beginning to realize just how absurd everything is around me." I left, still snickering.

Dr. Flanders' faithful servant, Audry, was waiting for me just outside the door of my cubicle. She asked me to follow her immediately. Within twenty minutes I was standing next to Dr. Flanders who miraculously had his afternoon free.

We went directly to the "maternity center." I recognized the center straight off. Of course I had been there during various times to provide for the continuous of my series. Did they save only one fertilized egg and throw all the others away?

"You did not realize at the time what was happening. You were told that you were in the hospital for treatment because you had problems. Weren't you?" I remembered quite well what had happened.

"Of course I did not know what was happening? I was still connected, rather programmed, at the time. But, I did dream about being there many times over the years."

"That is simply impossible. You can't dream. We can, however, induce dreams, and we do that regularly. And, even if you could dream on your own, you would never have remembered a dream. You are repeating nonsense just to try to minimize the importance of my work here."

I was surprised with his reaction. We were all conditioned to sleep on contact with the pillow. Our individual diets included sexual inhibitors. That was all part of our programming. Yet, I did dream and I did remember certain dreams. Why couldn't I have dreams? "Maybe my programming was not properly adapted or was not sufficient for me?" It seemed like a logical response.

"Maybe. Yes, maybe certain people need more surveillance. But, dreaming?"

"Why does that you bother you?"

"Because it means that other people might be dreaming as well. And, they may end up confusing their dream world with the real world."

"Dr. Flanders, they are never in a real world. Look at them; they are lifeless shells of humanity. Even the children don't laugh or argue anymore. It's like they've been drained of all material substance, replaced with sawdust. So, even if a few still have dreams, what difference does it make?"

"Well, I want you to discuss these dreams with Dr. Gordon." I nodded to get him off that subject.

We stood on the outside looking into small cubicles that were housing for men and women during the period of fertilization. He started explaining the procedure. "We follow your development in every aspect. When a young person has entered puberty, they are assigned to this center. A treatment is administered to help a young woman develop quality ova that are surgically removed. The sperm is extracted from the young men and a fertilization takes place in laboratory plates; or fertilization in vitro." He pointed to the back of the room where android personnel were involved in effectuating this procedure.

"The vast majority of young women undergo another routine operation to tie their tubes and a vasectomy to sterilize young men. For certain individuals, like yourself, whose genetic heritage is particularly interesting, we leave your reproductive organs in place; you are given sexual inhibitors. Do you have any questions?"

"You have gone a bit too fast, so I would like to backtrack on some points, that is, if you don't mind." I decided to manipulate him with a bit of politeness.

"No problem. I am listening."

"If I understand correctly, not every human living in the center is scheduled to reproduce." He nodded yes. "Only those whose genetic lineage interests you will produce the ovum and sperm for future generations." He nodded again. "The Pamela series always reproduces."

He stopped me here. "To the extent possible. As I explained to you before, your series has always created problems, so we have often had to terminate a, 'Pamela', before her reaching puberty, or very close thereto." His brows furrowed. "That simply means that we had to start with the frozen fertilized ovum of a previous series. The inconveniency being that we have to wait another 14 or 15 years before recuperating "fresh," unfrozen ovum."

"I understand what you said. But why then is the Pamela series a priority for you?"

"That is confidential information. I am sorry but I am not authorized to disclose more."

I sneered at him and went on. "The sexual inhibitors are only given to those humans who will be called into the maternity section regularly." He nodded. "Then why are other people eating foods sprinkled with sexual inhibitors?"

He raised his eyebrows in surprise. "The sexual inhibitors are necessary even when organs have been tampered with. You humans are sexual creatures; we inhibit your natural, perverted sexual instincts."

"Ok." I thought I understood. "Jonathan was taking sexual inhibitors. A vasectomy does not diminish sexual desire"

"No. It sterilizes a man just like tying tubes is a form of sterilization, but it does not prevent promiscuity."

"If the fertilization does not work, or rather, none of the fertilized eggs develop, can you reverse the operations on the young men and women?"

"Excellent question even though it is completely irrelevant." He shook his head in a dramatic way, took a deep breath and continued. "Your question is interesting in that this often happened in early years of fertilization in vitro. There was a risk that the Mother-the human Mother-would reject the fertilized egg. Once the artificial uterus was invented, this risk vanished. Today, the risk that a fertilized egg will not develop into a baby is one in a million.

"But your answer does not explain whether or not you can reverse a vasectomy or tying tubes?"

"Right. I see that I have to take things one at a time with you." He took my hand and looked me straight in my eyes. "Try not to be so insolent." He paused. "Yes, it is possible to reverse these operation, without provoking side-effects. Nonetheless, and perhaps I was not that clear. Those whose sperm or ovum is recuperated only once during their lifetimes, are not series of primary interest to us. Often times we have no real immediate need to replace their series; or we prefer to wait or to skip a generation; or we would just as soon resort to a frozen fertilized ovum." He stopped to ask if I understood and I nodded affirmatively.

He slowly picked up the discussion. "Often times, these individuals interest us for another reason; their unfertilized ovum and the sperm form the basis of our research. We try different combinations; trying to find better blends. We are a research facility as well as a maternity unit." His lips lifted in a condescending way and he marched forward.

I ran after him, calling out. "Do you always use the same genetic match?"

"Yes, if we are satisfied with the intellectual competence of the offspring. We have been working this system for a long time. In the beginning, we made some mistakes and had to terminate the offspring. We are now at the point where we feel certain that we have found the best combinations. But, as I said, we continue our research to achieve human perfection. It is something that is still outside our grasp, even though it is our ultimate objective."

"And, my series?" He turned with squinted eyes. "Is intellectual capacity genetically transmitted?"

"Yes, you have finally raised an interesting question." He scratched the back of his head, lifting and readjusting his wig. "We are close to proving that hypothesis. I believe that it is the case. For example, as the Governor told you, both of your parents were renowned scientists." And, then anticipating my next question, he added. "There are a few of you who are descendants of those who lived a long time ago. Their fertilized eggs were frozen." He changed the subject in mid-stream. "From a few excellent specimens we have developed an intellectually significant community at this center. Nonetheless, many things were destroyed and... I think that we shall stop here."

"But, who is the father of my fertilized eggs here in the Center; the father of my issue here at the Center?"

"You don't know? You can't even guess?"

"How could I guess? That is ridiculous." I couldn't believe that he would say such a thing. "You never showed me any of my descendants here at the center. I don't even know if there are any. You only showed me my replacement."

"That is true, but you should have an idea. It is the person with whom you are.... in love?"

"Peter?" I choked out in surprise. He nodded. "But those fertilized ovum, here at the Center, --

He interrupted me and finished the statement. "Have not yet been placed in an artificial uterus." He just grinned, waved goodbye and walked off in the direction of his office.

I exited the birth center in a passive, lethargic manner. I was under shock. Did they send me outside to reproduce with Peter? How could they know that I would be attracted to him? Was it a surprise for them, as well? These and many other questions were running through my mind and I was also worried that what was happening at the birth center was even more horrible and decadent than anything I saw in the film.

In the midst of all these oppressive thoughts, I ran into Randolph on his way back to his cubicle. I pretended that I didn't recognize him but that didn't work. He grabbed me from among the crowd and pulled me into a narrow corridor. "Are you ignoring me?"

"Yes and No." I said as I shook off his hands. "I was not that happy with the meeting the other night. I did not find Stuart, particularly, how can I say, friendly." Randolph smirked. "I mean, I was looking forward to meeting him for so long and then, because of the effects of the film and his rather serious, intense style, I went off an accused him of being an android." Randolph smiled teasingly. "It isn't funny, Randolph." I said, as I started to chuckle. "I looked so stupid. It made it so easy for him to remind me that even Dr. Gordon and the Governor find all my mistakes, refreshing."

"That is his style. He is just like that. He doesn't trust anyone, but then, can we blame him?" He looked intense. "After all, he was disconnected from the programmed humans when he was just a child and it took years before he discovered that there were others like him. And, I might add, he accepted to stay on at the center along with me to help the others, when John and his group left." He pinched my cheek playfully. "If it makes you feel better, he told me that he regretted being so critical of you even though he said that you are provocative. You will both have the chance to make up for that first encounter."

So that explained why he knew John. They were friends or colleagues. "So he was the one who notified the rest of you that I had bypassed my programming?"

"Absolutely. In fact you owe him a big thanks." He smiled slyly.

"Depends upon whether or not I am better off running around this crazy center because I am Dr. Gordon's special project or, I would have been better off terminated." That made us both laugh in a morbid way.

"He is in touch with Dr. Gordon?" I don't know why I asked that question. It just slipped out.

"Brilliant, Pamela. Yes, Brilliant! Now you are starting to understand things."

"She confides in him?" Randolph nodded. "That is why he is so sure that Dr. Gordon and company would be happy to join us in getting rid of some of the more anti-human members?"

"You got it. But, he does not have the same leverage with her that you do, and she trusts you." His teeth were sparkling behind his wide smile. "Maybe because of your, let's say, close relationship."

"You are one to talk. By the way, how is your 'tight' relationship going with her?"

"You know I think that she believes that she can pass from android to human and you know through what vehicle?" I voiced the word "sex" and frowned to play it up. "No, no, she's convinced that love is her transition to our world." Now it was my turn to laugh.

Randolph, undaunted, continued, "And she wants me to help her to feel that emotion, as if it is the catalyst for everything human. What do you think? After all, you are presumably in love with Peter?"

"As a matter of fact, she asked me to explain, more than describe, the feelings that I have for Peter. That is very difficult. I have told her many times that it is as if all the 5 senses explode at the same time, each with its proper ultimate, sublime satisfaction."

"I am sorry, Pamela, but I don't know what you are talking about either?"

"That is because you have never fallen in love." I regretted bringing up this subject. I was no expert on love. I was just in touch with my own feelings; which I did not want to render mundane by analyzing and talking them to death. But, I have fallen into another trap, this time with someone who is special for me; someone whose very presence is a sustaining force, giving me courage to confront my existence in this Center. He was not an inquisitive android exerting power over me. But, how could I explain love, a feeling that consumed me when I thought of Peter and enflamed me when I was in his presence?

I looked at Randolph whose curiosity beamed through his ardent eyes. I had to say something; I had to start somewhere so I started with the ABC's of love. "In my mind, that is the beginning, and hopefully that lasts throughout, and then people move to a higher level of consciousness where confidence, trust, closeness envelop and nourish that strong physical attraction, as it continues to grow; a harmony, balance, appears in their lives together, binding them in a way that their very existences, their destinies, become entwined. Love brings fulfillment, both physical and metaphysical, in sublime serenity." I stopped. "Did you understand?"

"I think. But, then I have the impression that love must be lived not defined and you are inspiring me to find it." He moved closer to me. "So, what about me. Which one of your five senses is not satisfied with me?" He looked very serious. "For my part, my five senses were very much alive with you."

"Oh, just forget it!" I exploded. "I am not an expert on this subject and have read nothing meaningful about it. I just came up with a theory that is apparently full of holes." I wanted to say something nice about him, but I did not know what to say.

He swept me up into his arms and planted a warm and enticing kiss in my steaming mouth. "Which place, yours or mine?" he asked. He let me down slowly and I took his hand and led him into the monorail going in the direction of my cubicle.

I was ready to satisfy my desires, to ignite my five senses, but he wanted to talk about his relationship with Dr. Gordon.

"Has anything changed since the last time we talked?" I asked just to get the conversation over with. I was in dire need of being held and fondled by him; reassured through his virile attention that I was still alive.

"A bit, actually. Things have calmed down slightly as she seeks to impose herself as the sexual predator."

"I don't understand."

"Apparently the kind of sexual relationship that I found stimulating because I was the one controlling everything was not bringing her the kind of personal results, whatever they are, that she was seeking."

I now sat down on the bed next to him and listened as he described her as a sexual predator. He told me that she showed him some films; porno films, is what she called them. He found them incredibly informative, educational and even admitted that he could not help feeling sexually aroused from time to time; although he could not understand why humans, in another period, needed to fuel their sexual desires in this way." I never saw one of these films, so I didn't know what to say

"It is all sick, though, Pamela." He went on. "She was studying my reactions to different scenes. I found it revolting. In fact, she replayed different scenes just to watch my reaction to what was taking place on the film." He chuckled. "I disappointed her, I know, because I understood her disgusting intentions and kept my expressions as neutral as possible." That confused her. "I think that she expected me to be so sexually aroused by the films; that I would reach out to her or even touch myself."

I giggled, something that made him a bit uncomfortable. "I can't help myself, Randolph. She never ceases to surprise me with how obsessed she is with sex as the starting block to an emotionally charged future for her." He teasingly snarled at me. "Come on; it is funny. She must have chosen the films that she, in her android deliria, wanted to experience with you; to feel the same movements and gestures with you. "

"Oh course she did! "He screamed at me. "That is what is disgusting about it. She showed me the films, noted my reactions, and then went about kissing or touching or sucking my body in the same ways to excite me." He clenched his teeth in rage.

"I am sorry, but I still find it funny. And, the main thing is, was it good sex?" I over blinked at him, full throttle on one eye, my lips crunching down in a crooked smirk. Then I burst, my convulsive laughing filled the room then stopped, holding my breath, as I noticed he was ruefully shaking his head. He stood up disgusted but I pulled him back down and motioned him to continue. I was stone sober now.

"It is worse than that. She doesn't care if I have good sex, apart from arousing me. She is the one who wants it! And, she never gets it because she can't."

"Oh, I see." Now I needed to stop as my senses were very enflamed, but he still needed to talk.

"She comes with creepy gadgets." My eyes opened wide. "Yes, gadgets, other than those we used before. The last time she had a phallic contraption which looked like …a penis extension." My eyes were certainly wide. "She wanted me to put it on so that I could reach as far as possible inside her android body to stimulate her circuits. And, she handed me a vibrator to pass over her body at the same time to ignite her electrical parts and temper any stimulation inhibitors. It was gross. . ."

"She must be desperate." I started to laugh but I jammed my forefinger between my teeth and looked at him with as serious, attentive eyes as I could conjure up. I did all I could to prevent myself from losing it totally as I've done in the past.

"Desperate, she wants me to continue to grab her hard and pinch her in presumably tender places; none of which she has. She even asked me to bite her harder. Repulsive! There is a limit to what I can do; how hard I can bite. After all she could be toxic. I don't know what she is made out of."

I knew that he was not trying to be funny, but it all came across that way; I was biting down hard on my lips to stifle a big laugh building up inside of me

"Dominating her meant that I could set the limits; keeping a sense of rationality in place. I did feel excited by her. I already told you all that. I had great sex with her then. Now, copying these porno films doesn't do much for me." He paused. "Now to get sexually aroused I have to think about someone else, like you, Pamela." I gulped and he snarled.

"The other day, just to please her in her sexual feeding frenzy, I reached over and tried to pinch her behind. I almost cracked a finger nail on her steel plating."

Admittedly, I hadn't thought about that. "Well, Randolph, sorry you've had to put up with all that. She never asked for anything like that from me. She was the one giving pleasure. Ok, we rolled around a bit and I made an effort to caress her, but I never focused on what she might want or need. I guess that she is frustrated with your manliness, liking to be dominated but needing to be the predator." I decided to confide in Randolph about my last almost sexual encounter with Gordon. "I refused her sexual advances recently. I even pushed her violently away from me." His eyes widened. "She came on to me the same way that you did the first time you were together; I recognized the scene. It bothered me that she was in a replay mode, this time she was the dominant."

"Bravo! What did she do?"

"She was surprised by my reaction and pretended to be hurt. We both know that she cannot experience that." I went on to tell him how I stood defiantly on the other side of the table. "In any event, I just couldn't go through with that; it was too experimental. She must have understood because she accepted my proposal of friendship as an intermediary choice for the moment."

"Well, that is interesting to know; perhaps the next time I shall throw her porno films in her face and remind her that I can be as strong physically as her." Now he laughed.

"You did exaggerate a bit, didn't you?" I asked teasingly.

"A tiny bit, to make it more entertaining. But, there is more truth than exaggeration."

He stared at me with a hungry, longing look on his face. "I am not made to spend my sexual life attached to a machine; whose electrical and sensory systems are either malfunctioning or over reacting with high voltage energy." I wasn't sure where he was going with this, so I tried to stay serious.

His eyes were penetrating, as he spoke in a soft, seductive voice. "I want to breath in your delicious ordure, Pamela, experience the warmth of your body as it rises and falls naturally against mine. I want to be captured in your seizing waves of orgasmic pleasure, pulsating up and around me, draining me. I want to listen to your heart beating up against mine, and be spellbound by your human cries of pleasure triggering mine…and more!" It didn't matter whether he had prepared this speech because he delivered so well; his voice was warm and tender, his words were titillating, and his eyes were ablaze with lustful passion. He felt my body sliding closer to him, melting under his charm, as he hung himself out to me, waiting for me to make the advance. "You know, Pamela, there is always a good side to everything. Apart from her sick ideas, I must admit that I have compiled a rather impressive list of exciting sexual positions…Interested?" He asked fervently.

He didn't give me a chance to answer. He stood up, dramatically tore off his gown, and pulled me up off the bed. When he enveloped me in his strong, protective arms, I was already so sexually aroused. I was his and he could do whatever he wanted to me. "Slow sex, isn't that what you said that you like." He whispered in my ear. I nodded even though I could have skipped the foreplay, just this time.

His hands travelled slowly over my entire body, caressing me, kneading my soft, voluptuous skin, until I stood naked in front of him. His eyes moved slowly up and down my body; and, for a brief instance, I was embarrassed, worried that I was no longer irresistible enough for him, now that all my five senses were ignited with lustfulness and a delirious ravenous sexual appetite was rushing upside of me.

He lifted me easily and delicately, cradling me against his muscular body, erasing that momentary inhibition--my seductiveness restored. His warm breath and rapid heart were against me. "Let me show you my vulnerability, your power over me. You beautiful, precious, enticing, sensual… his mouth sought mine. I leaned back in his arms, beckoning him to continue, his kisses intensifying, lingering, descending over my breasts, longing for his caresses and reveling in the sparkling sensations left behind.

And at last, he was inside of me, his hands lifting and moving me, as he plunged deeper and deeper arousing and drawing my energy, my vitality, towards him under his seductive rhythm. I dug my nails into his back as my excitement mounted and buried my head in his throat, savoring the marvelous sensations of his presence, until I met his expectations; draining him in my vibrant, pulsating orgasms and drowning him in human screams of pleasure as I incited his. I felt his legs weaken as he pulled me even tighter up against him to protect me; he stumbled backwards and crashed onto the bed.

"Phenomenal!" He screamed as he rolled onto his back; his legs and arms spread out in total bliss; his eyes dilated with that special orgasmic brightness.

I smiled down on him and contemplated our relationship. He is I thought for the second time, such as farceur, a real actor, but, it didn't matter. I needed to make love tonight, or simply to have sex to recapture my human side. I was relaxed, satisfied, and complete. He is definitely my friend and we are true friends. That is what we are and will always be. We are there to make each other laugh; and, how we do laugh, in face of austerity. We are there to give each other confidence to tackle those seemingly insurmountable obstacles. We are there sharing in each other's pain and suffering as we search for solutions; we are there to listen; and we are Playmates, having fun being human, playing adult games. Just like tonight, we both needed to have fun, to play, and to feel alive. And, we played just so well. I could see that in the big smile on his face and sense that in the smile beaming on mine.

He reached up to me and pulled me down next to him. I cuddled up in his arms and fell into a deep sleep listening to the comforting slow beat of his heart. I was in his arms all night. That was a bit bold and dangerous, but no one came looking for us in the morning. We woke up in a hustle and rushed out in different directions. As he hurried off, I realized, in the heat of the sumptuous night, I hadn't talked to him about the most startling information of all, that Peter and I were one of the center's planned breeders. I didn't know who else was pre-matched.

And, sitting there so dazed, even though the night seemed like years ago, I realized that the androids had forgotten about breakfast. "Oh No! No!" I screamed: all of a sudden it came to me. Breakfast wasn't delivered because Dr. Gordon knew... she knew about our steamy night.

I didn't see Randolph for almost a week after that famous evening. I spent my days with Dr. Flanders, in his office listening to his explanations of programmed, human reproduction. Much as I was horrified by what was happening at the birth center, I had to admit that everything was so well organized and even human sexual cycles were relentlessly and effectively monitored and controlled. They were meticulous in their planning. The choice of hormone therapy, who should be sterilized and whose ova will be used in vitro, were subject to the needs of the center; present or future needs? The center did not have enough space for accidental reproduction. Determining which fertilized eggs should be put into circulation-an expression that Dr. Flanders vaunted maliciously-was vital. Making a mistake, choosing the wrong eggs, could have major consequences on the future development and productivity of a human. This, he claimed, could interfere with the smooth operation of the center.

The subjects varied from one day to the next, as did the time I spent with him. He often had only a few hours to consecrate to me. On one occasion he explored a problem that fascinated him.

"You know, Pamela, that since your body was functioning normally, logically, so were your reproductive organs?" I shook my head to acknowledge all this. He had more or less explained that before. "We provide you with the proper sanitary support for that, just like we do now."

"Please Dr. Flanders let's not talk about that." I protested. I guess that I was not comfortable discussing female intimacy with this machine that enjoyed degrading humans whose bodies could not be regulated by tightening a screw.

"Why not? It is only natural. Isn't that what you want that humans should be aware of their own body, both physically and mentally?"

"Yes, but. . ."

He interrupted me. "You don't remember experiencing menstrual cycles?"

"No. Of course not. My body was on off!"

"Not at all. We wanted you to reproduce for us, when we were ready for

345

your eggs. When you entered the fertilization center, we simply gave you extra hormone therapy so that you would produce more and better quality eggs the time you were with us."

I was shaking my head. How could I have gone through a monthly cycle and not known anything about it.

"You don't remember, do you?" I shook my head. "Then our system functions perfectly." He gleamed at me. "Once a month you went for a medical examination, am I right?"

"Yes, I remember. But I didn't know that it was once a month."

"That is normal. Your programming interferes with passage of time." I had a feeling that he would have been very happy, if he were human, to have announced all of this to me. And, I am certain that he was delighted with my reaction when he told me that I would sleep the 5 to 7 days of my cycle.

"I think that I understand now." I frowned. "It is all a bit sick." He did not reply. "I didn't have sexual urges because of the sexual inhibitors and I was completely unaware of my menstrual cycle because I slept here in this fertility center during the menstrual flow." He nodded.

"So, why then didn't Jonathan say anything to me?"

"He was unaware of your absence because he was in the same deep sleep that you were during that period of time."

"But, the others, my colleagues?"

"If I could laugh now, I would, but I can't. You just don't understand the extent to which the programming controlled your every move. You don't need to be physically present for someone to see your presence."

"What, that is preposterous!" I screamed. I actually wanted to slap his face and to wipe off that android smile.

"I strongly disagree with you, Pamela; it is ingenious." He retorted. "Think about the brilliance of this. Your colleagues heard you playing the piano because your concerts were recorded and later played back to them through hidden speakers. And, they saw you playing the piano, because your code was activated in their visual receptors. And, just to demonstrate how organized we are, we made certain that, during your absence, the conductor only worked on orchestra pieces in which your piano part had been recorded." He glanced at me. "Just like your colleagues still see you today as a member of the orchestra or when one of your masterpieces of improvisation is requested by your android fans in the audience."

"You have absolutely gone too far, beyond reason. What you are doing is monstrous!" I shouted. "Peoples' lives have been created, shaped and adjusted, just so easily, like a submissive clay statue, like it means nothing? And that isn't enough for you." I said as I grabbed his arm an aggressively pinched down on it. "You have to go so far as to feign our presences…steal our identity. You are detestable…absolutely detestable!" I shouted at the top of my lungs.

He undid my squeezing hand with a quick jerk, letting out a disgruntled sound. "You have to learn how to control your emotions; your outbursts and your aggressive physical behavior will cost you your existence." He nodded his head in disgust. "Stop judging us. Just listen and learn." He smiled perfunctorily.

"Ok. I shall try." I was actually trying to stay composed, every time I was with him; but his remarks, revelations, and observations, provocative and hurtful, flowed in such numbers that I was unable to maintain control.

"We have to be very alert and follow everyone's life so closely. It is a lot of work for us to keep this center running so smoothly. And," his head stretched out like a rooster as he flaunted his power and bragged—"this center is regarded as the best among the others."

His macho behavior inspired me to shift gears; concentrate on putting the pieces of the puzzle back into place. It was clear that we were submissive dolls for androids to play with. Sarah and Ruth were right. We were drugged and manipulated at the center and worse, we were wound up like silly toy soldiers, pushed left and right, up and down, and if we didn't measure up, discarded like a wet rag. I had to bite my lip to pacify the anger raging through me. An idea came which added to temper my volatile emotions.

"By the way, I've already spoken to Sarah and Ruth about all of this, a long time ago now." I hoped to shock him.

"Oh, yes, the two of them were working on a research project together. What a disaster that was!" He slapped his hands together to emphasize his displeasure. "They were not discovering anything that had not already been discovered. It was so evident that, even though they had the intellectual ability, they were unable to apply it." He looked at me for an instance. "I suppose now you're going to tell me," he paused to snicker under his breath, "that it was when they were taken off the project that they bypassed their programming. We already knew that. We were aware of their relationship with John and the others. It was interesting to observe their reactions."

He bent his head back, like the images of all this were moving across the ceiling, and then turned back to me. "We found it particularly interesting to see how they formed a small group. Yes, Pamela, we have eyes and ears everywhere. Maximum surveillance was essential at the end of human history. I do believe it is a perfect system that can't possibly be improved upon." He tried to distort his face to look like a sneer, as his lips receded back to show perfect white teeth. It looked more like the teeth of a predator before sinking into its victim. I turned away as my body shivered, as my anger turned to trepidation and a feeling of total despair, like I was lost in a river whirlpool sucking me to the bottom, to the bottom. . .

My body trembled as I awakened to the truth, the pathetic lives my fellow humans and I were living under the thumb of these sterile indifferent robots. I took a deep breath.

I followed him lethargically and focused on a chance for immediate revenge; sweet revenge effused through my veins, renewing my strength under its prodigious glow, calming my tremulous body. I was able to turn and to face Dr. Flanders. My confidence crept back as I searched for a weakness in the android's manipulations. Of course, it was their antiquated surveillance equipment in the caverns. I started to divulge it and stopped myself. It would have been foolish to reveal something that the robots could fix, that had served our purposes.

The last lecture-style meeting in his office returned to the original discussion. It was now very clear that the real geniuses at the center were those descendants of humans; living just before the end of the human history. Their frozen fertilized eggs were coveted and treated with great respect. Those individuals born in the third generation, like my son Frederic, were not considered as having that extraordinary intellectual quality of their genetic grandparents. And, those coming from other sources of fertilized eggs were often steered toward menial tasks at the center. They were produced in greater numbers because they were terminated at their 18th year; their menial tasks were often physically demanding, causing premature physical aging and suffering, the reason why the androids terminated them at an early age.

"Moreover, it is rare to have one of the laborers bypass the programming." Dr. Flanders mentioned to me at one point. He then added that early termination could also be one of the reasons why this class of humans rarely escapes, bypasses programming. He told me that Diana was an exception and that her bypassing her programming must have been caused by her extreme paranoia. "Those rare cases of paranoia were terminated instantly." He said scornfully. "They were not clever enough to try to hide their transformation. "

I looked at him. I knew that he was lying like Dr. Gordon. Diana was an engineer and a martial arts expert. He knew all that as well. Did he think that she had forgotten what she did in the center? Did he think that Diana's paranoia wiped everything out of her mind? Or, was he lying just to see my reaction. He was obviously tempting me; it was a trap. I responded by ignoring his overtures.

The androids set up a human hierarchy based upon the intellectual capabilities of the genetic donors. "Admittedly, it makes sense and we have no intention of changing this policy. It is a logical method, actually too logical for humans to understand, for running a city, a state, a country or this center. Let me tell you, this policy evolved at different stages throughout human history. In fact, it was controversial at one point because it was considered discriminatory. Even you, Pamela, with your presumed innocence, would have to agree with me that everyone cannot have the same value within society. Certain people have to be dispensable in order to assure the survival of an intellectual elite. They are expendable for the common good."

"If I were you, Dr. Flanders, I'd watch what I say. One would have the impression that you are in awe of humans and that maybe, you are one." I paused to allow my sarcasm to sink in before continuing. "Presumed innocence, I don't know because I have no idea what you mean. You are wrong about my feelings towards other humans. For me, I don't like the idea of hierarchies among humans. I imagine that you must be opposed to a hierarchical order where androids are concerned."

I wanted to say more, but he stopped me. He stopped me rather violently by grabbing my arm and wrestling me to the floor. I lay next to his desk petrified with the thought that an emotionally empty android was furious? He didn't raise his voice and hurled in his hollow Android voice tones, like sounds that flowed from a long tube, which jarred the entire room. He rose, leaving me on the floor and turned, violently smashing the table and then turning to me, shaking his fists directly over me before collapsing on the floor next to me. I was too frightened to move and his system seemed to need time to readjust, so we lay next to each other looking pitifully into each other's eyes.

There was no one who came looking for us during this interminable pause. Dr. Flanders decided to receive me alone in his office, with the door tightly closed. I had not seen Audry at all that week; she was not hovering about to adjust his system so I had no choice but to wait. I don't know how much time passed before he spoke, but it seemed like hours.

"You are beautiful, Pamela, very beautiful for human standards; even for android standards of a perfect female specimen. It took 13 series before I recovered the beauty of your genetic mother. She was embarrassed because of the stares of admiration and those of contempt thrown by those less physically gifted females; she was almost angry to be so beautiful because she had to fight harder to be also recognized for more than that beauty, or for her intellectual ability. I remember her telling me once that her beauty stood between her and her extraordinary career." He stopped and his eyes glistened, but distant as if his mind had shifted to another time. "Would you like me to show you how she was? I can. Everything about her is in my memory banks." His face took on a bright, almost happy look as he spoke about her. "I can show you her beauty. You can see for yourself why people were in awe, mesmerized, by her physical appearance.

"Did you love her?" I asked, embarrassed to have gone so far. "How stupid; he'll have a snicker at that," I thought to myself. "He'll ignore me . . ." But his next move shocked me. He answered my question.

"As you must know, we cannot love; but we can appreciate beauty and intellect. She had both. I am the android I am today because of her."

What a weird thing for an android to say. I mused. But then, was he so completely android? Is it possible?

"Dr. Flanders, what were you working on together?"

"What you see today; that was the beginning of the new book of Genesis." He was speaking as if he were in another world. "Genetic selection. That is what she called it. Humans called it eugenics."

I raised my body in disbelief. How could I carry the genes of someone who was creating a super race; a genetically perfect human. He pushed me gently back down next to him.

"I regret having been violent with you. I wish that you had her fire and energy, her vision of a future." He sighed. "We could have made such a perfect team."

"You are forgetting that I am not a scientist, but a musician. My view of life and humans is based more on interpreting emotions, fed by passion and romantic notions."

"No, Pamela. You could be her. You have her genes. You could lead an army, if you wanted. It is just a question of desire." He raised himself on his elbow and looked down at me. "Do you mind if I kiss you?"

"What? Are you crazy?"

I expected a perfunctory kiss, cold and sepulchral. But it was deeply warm and tender. Then he reached out and helped me stand up. The contrast between the machine that threw me on the floor and the one that kissed me and gently held my hands was infinitely puzzling. I felt I was going mad especially when I realized that, at that very moment, he craved my biological mother and imagined, by some dark black magic, I would turn into her or he would become human. I wondered where the android logic was now. But he got to me as my eyes welled with moisture, while I was strangely empathizing with this circuited robot. My unbridled empathy for anyone suffering was instantly unleashed from forces greater than me. I actually felt sorry for him and wished that there were something that I could do to ease his pain. And then I realized that I could do a lot for him and all the others that were counting on me because I had her genes. I could have her determination and energy if I wanted it. I realized at last that I was the right person to lead my people out of slavery. Didn't he just say that I could win a war if I wanted to? Today was the beginning of a better tomorrow. But, there was still a lot that I needed to know about what happened before and what was happening now. I needed Dr. Flanders.

"I am sorry that I shoved you so violently. I realize that some of my circuitry needs a going over. That happens with us Androids. We need a kind of maintenance." He replied very civilly.

"I am glad that it happened." I spoke with a voice full of determination. "This was probably the most important moment of my life." I turned to leave and added that I would take him up on his offer to see the film of my biological mother very soon.

He ran towards me and whispered in my ear. "It must be tomorrow at the latest. I want you to see her and other things that may be useful for you. But, I was ordered a long time ago to erase all memories of her. I couldn't. I just couldn't. But if ever my defiance is discovered, you and I both will be in terrible danger. So, be here tomorrow and don't say a word to anyone. It is our secret for the moment as least. Now go. Run home and relax."

I hugged him and left to go home. That is what he said, to go home;

Chapter 37: Revelations

I was restless all through the night, turning over and over in my dreams until I awoke bathed in sweat. It was a steamy nightmare; a sick mixture of having sex with Dr. Flanders at the same time Dr. Gordon was kissing my back, a scene that turned even uglier when suddenly their artificial skin disappeared and was replaced by hard metal plates, pounding me into the bed like a jackhammer. All this time, Randolph danced naked around us; tossing his head, stomping his feet, throwing his arms up, wildly, savagely in the air, as he chanted Battle Cries. I shook off the haunting effects of this nightmare as I dragged myself out of bed.

I ate my breakfast slowly and pensively, as if the food would give me more insight into the present. I started to nibble on toast and then threw it on the floor. Randolph had told me when, in my nightmare, that the bread was laced with sexual inhibitors. I sincerely doubted that, even though I might be consuming birth control drugs; my promiscuity was underway again. I shook my head in disgust. Whatever they were dosing me with, I was taking no risks this morning so I threw my energy drink alongside the toast on the floor. I showered and grabbed my clean, white smock that hung, as always, just outside the bathroom door. Everything was, as Dr. Flanders reminded me, as if I needed to be reminded of that, programmed for the comfort of us humans.

I took a quick detour. I hadn't seen Randolph for a week and was worried about him. I saw him sitting at the lab table, working diligently. I sneaked up behind him and threw my hands over his eyes. "Hi, Pamela!" I was disappointed because he didn't even jump. He turned around and smiled. "Is everything ok for you?" I asked out of genuine concern.

"Nothing new for the moment."

"Listen, I can't talk right now; things are happening fast and I should have lots of things to tell you very soon." I kissed his cheek. "Take care of yourself and don't worry about me or anything." I dashed out of the laboratory and headed over to Dr. Flanders.

I smiled and rushed past Dr. Flanders' secretary who looked up from her desk and motioned to me to go in the direction of Dr. Flanders' office. That was the extent of her interest in me these days, as I was becoming a normal visitor to this part of the Center. He greeted me kindly and led me into a very small room at the back of his office. It was the first time I was in that room; it was dark and musty, like a vault. When the door shut behind me, resonating eerily, I felt trapped in an ancient Egyptian sepulcher. As if that was not enough, I noticed that we were in a padded room, my legs grew weak and I dropped down on the empty straight-backed chair next to me.

Dr. Flanders sat across from me. He bent over looking with concern directly in my eyes; it was surprisingly not contrived, it seemed real concern. "Don't be afraid. You are safe with me." He recognized my hesitation. "I needed a room that was sound proof and had no visual equipment. We need to be very careful, as I said. This room was set up for people like Diana, who had psychological difficulty adjusting to life. They won't hurt themselves when they go berserk and beat their heads, fists, whatever, up against the wall." he smiled; then the corners of his lips hooked downward as his eyes seemed to recede inwardly.

"Before we start with the clips, I must bring you up-to-date on some very important elements." He pretended to swallow. "I had your replacement, Pamela 14, terminated three days ago."

I gasped. "How could you do that? Why?" My response was politically correct; a natural reflex even though this news was the best news I could have received. Her very existence was a threat to mine; and my life meant more to me than hers. Yet, I did not want Dr. Flanders to see how much I appreciated his gesture.

"She was inferior to you physically and intellectually." He flipped into android mode answering impassively, as if he were counting from one to ten or brushing his metal teeth.

"What difference does that make? She was a living human." I enjoyed seeing him rattled, maybe confused. He didn't answer straight off

"Stop it!" He ordered and I complied. "We do not have time for this kind of useless, emotional drive. If I hadn't terminated her, your termination would be very close-too close for my comfort. And obviously too close for your comfort." He smiled sardonically.

"And, you are a complete duplicate of her. You must survive. Your presence is necessary for those of us who have been waiting for her return." He insisted.

"Ok," I said. I had regained my composure, which was expedited as I reflected on the importance of what he had just said. Why were they waiting for her return?

"That's better." He waited until he was certain that I was calm and ready for the next bit of information before continuing. "Your genetic mother, so to speak. I do not want to debate this aspect as we both know that an artificial uterus is not the mother's womb, but, she is your biological or genetic mother as we used one of her ovum, frozen for centuries, to reproduce you, Pamela. Your mother, as you will see with your own eyes, was ageless. There are those who claim that she was more than 250 years old. Records of her birth miraculously disappeared during her lifetime. But, she looks exactly like you and you are only 20 in human years." I finally found out how old I was. In fact, how young I was; far too young to be terminated, is what I thought to myself. And, far too young to be that great hero and visionary that she was.

He was still talking, making sure that I understood that humans showed their age; in time their body functions slowed and their skin wrinkled. I said under my under breath "Jason."

"Yes, Pamela, Jason. I know, and I am glad, that you met this man. He is admirable-an explorer, a pioneer, a dreamer of sorts." He blew out his breath "But, a complete idiot." He shook his head.

"Well, to get on with things. Even though humans lived longer during her generation and easily reached the age of 150 years, she was the star." He let out a rasping sound as if he were clearing his throat. "There was so much research and eventual progress made in treating diseases and malfunctioning human organs that it was normal that human life span increased. There was also a net disappearance of invasive, unfriendly bacteria and viruses; the residual effect of their destructive absence assured a stronger, more resistant race of humans. All of this did not prevent them from aging, even if aging was slower than that in earlier human history. For example, when they reached 150 years old, their aged bodies resembled that of earlier generations at 80 years old. One could say that they aged twice as slowly as previous generations. Are you following me?" I nodded.

"She was the only one who had no outside signs of age. You'll see." He took a deep android breath. "I told you that society globally was divided between the intellectually superior and inferior ones. And, I know that you find that upsetting." He stopped as if he was trying to access his memory bank. "Humans were unable to live as equals. There was always a division, a hierarchy based on something, if not money, power fueled by greed. There were wars, horrible wars, based upon those values as well as religious strife, trying to prove which was superior to all the others, whose God was the only omnipotent power, the other Gods being the devil. We've discussed that a bit and you entertained that topic several times with Dr. Gordon, right?" I glared at him.

My eyebrows raised and my eyes wide open, he recognized my surprise and had to explain. "Yes, she and I exchange information. We work very closely together." then he continued his story. "There were wars based upon race, nationality and ethnic origins. There were laws, unfair laws, giving more civil rights to individuals of a certain race or ethnic origin. How to determine superiority and inferiority in the human species seems to have been the paramount question in human history."

"Imagine, Pamela, that superiority was also based on how much money a person could accumulate." He quickly explained that owning material objects and living comfortably required wealth that was linked to some form of exchange. To have clothes you had to give the merchant something in exchange. This exchange was called money. You saw pictures of people living in poverty-no food, no proper clothes, no cubicle to sleep in."

I told him I understood money and why it was so important for humans; but found the focus on accumulating material objects and other things including money disgusting. "They are such superficial values." I twisted my mouth up in thought. "Perhaps that is the rational way for humans to live... I think that I shall have to look into the subject of wealth in more detail."

He shook his head and continued his speech. "I know that you already saw some of the records we have in the library that show a different standard of living. You understand what I am talking about. But, for now, you must trust me on that point. It is important that you understand that no matter what century of human history we observe, we find a division in society based upon some artificial standard, giving certain individuals more power and comfort than others."

"Why couldn't everyone be equal like we are here at the center?"

"Because we, the androids, have made you equal through programming." He shook his head. "It is just not human nature to be the same as everyone else. Equality! However, human history indicates there were some notions called communism, or socialism or something like that. It has no importance, because all such attempts to create equality were futile. All of them failed because basic human nature triumphed."

I tried to interrupt him but he ignored me. "But at the end of human history the most logical, as I said yesterday, form of discrimination, an anti-equality principle, evolved. Superior intellect assured power, respect, and comfort and so on. Inferior intellects only got the basics of life, nothing more."

"But, your favorite film is. . . The End?" He was confusing me. "That is far from an anti-equality principle."

"Yes, I know that you found the film ridiculous. Gordon actually told me the truth of what happened and I promised her to just forget about it." I choked over that. Dr. Gordon was capable, as I suspected many times, of lying; telling lies was somehow compatible with her logical android reasoning.

"I imagine that it is not easy for you to accept what happened with your species. We, the androids, were able to understand because of the underlying logic—the inevitability of human self-destruction. I should add that the intellectuals of the world were also sensitive to the problems of the intellectually deprived masses. At one point, they even decided that if the world population was divided in half, that the inferior individuals would have more comfort and be happier with their fate. They mutually subsidized the research and development of spacecraft that could transport people to other planets. They ran a campaign, as they called it, and published it in newspapers and broadcasted it over the air waves. You know what I am speaking about?"

"Ferdinand wrote articles for us to read about a subject like this." I surprised myself with what I said. Up-until-now, I had no recollection of his newspaper campaign. What else was hidden in a deep, dark section of my brain? "I remember seeing the titles." I replied unemotionally. "We were never allowed to read them."

"Yes, Ferdinand, we shall talk about him another time." He flicked his hand as if he were tossing away an annoying particle. "Please, Pamela, just listen. I must get on with the rest, because it is getting late." I nodded. He explained to me that the advertising campaigns asking for volunteers to build new lives on other planets were an amazing success. For the next 10 years spacecraft were being launched with hundreds, even thousands of people on board. The earth's population was reduced by almost 70 percent. The intellectual community was able to put in place a better system of housing, food supplies and clothing. And, they controlled the birth rate by imposing heavy fines." I must have looked perplexed. He looked at me and held up his hand as if to say, "I'll explain. . ."

"The inferior members of the community were overjoyed by the situation. And, then the truth leaked out. All those spaceships carrying the non-intellectuals were programmed to explode in deep space. Hundreds of thousands of humans lost their lives and those left on earth began to collude, revolt, and create problems." He sat with his head tilted to the side, rubbing his folded hands together and then he licked his lips and added. "You will understand and applaud the ingenuity of the decision to destroy these crazy, non-intellectual space voyagers, before their ideas and values contaminated other planets."

I had to stop him at this point, because of what Peter told me. "Were there any humans who actually founded colonies on other planets?"

His eyes lit up. "Yes. There were some humans from that period: the first group of space explorers did colonize other planets."

"I remember hearing about the success of their missions before the end of human history, although many of those ships were sent light years away and news from those groups would not have been forthcoming before the end of human history. In fact, some news should be arriving now, as should certain programmed return missions. But, Pamela, I have no knowledge of that. I am not working in the right sector to be privy to this information." Then he added. "The only group of astronauts, space voyagers, who would ever return were those selected from the superior intellectual group. They left on their own spacecraft with orders to explore and colonize."

I hesitated about repeating what Peter told me. I was still not certain whether I could trust Dr. Flanders, so I decided, to keep that information to myself. If I were convinced he could help save visitors from space, I would perhaps consult him in the future.

"Well, you should be ready now for the clips. The period you will be seeing is very close to the end of human civilization. The special interest groups and counter-culture groups, such as vampires, werewolves, etc., existed then. They were, of course, humans pretending to have supernatural powers. Interestingly, many of these non-intellectuals were imposingly tall, more than 8 feet in height, and had formidable muscles and body force. They dressed up like and played the ghastly roles of those horrifying creatures; and, I can assure you that they were convincingly demonic. The non-intellectuals were starting to join together and resist. It was a very difficult period. Your Mother was considered to be the "crème de la crème" of the intellectuals and had ultimate decision making authority globally."

He opened up his jacket and pressed a button. A screen slowly opened up in the middle of his android chest, the visual and sound track systems were so perfectly conceived that I had the impression that the person on the screen was standing in the room next to me or that I was passing into the screen; whichever, it was incredibly lifelike. The woman talking was my biological, genetic mother. It was as if I were looking at myself in the mirror. We were identical physically. We could have been twins. She was delivering a speech from a podium in a big auditorium overflowing with men and women. Everyone in the audience flaunted their own special style of hair and clothes; some of the colors were so bright and flashy, while others were sober blacks and browns. Their faces were painted in different colors to contrast or to match the colors of their clothes. I was shocked by some of the hairstyles, whether short or long, and of all the shades of color. As Dr. Flanders explained to me afterwards, the more extravagant the color or combination of colors and the higher the hair was plastered upwards, the higher up he or she was in the hierarchy.

My Mother looked young, vibrant, and elegant. She wore a long, black tightly fitting, very low cut dress that revealed her beautiful hour glassed shaped body and her firm, voluptuous breasts. She had curly, reddish-brown hair that she proudly wore loose, letting it fall to the middle of her back, just like me. Her green eyes, like mine, flashed in contrast. She was delivering a speech, exhuming charisma with her voice, rising and falling, in intensity and her gesticulations wilder and more vibrant as she advanced her arguments. Her eyes steadfast on the audience were bright with passion for her cause. The audience was shouting and applauding in approval. I had to listen closely to her words as she spoke with a strange accent; perhaps the original human accent and not the one we developed under android guidance. I understood that she was calling for action. "We must stop the rebellion at its source. We have infiltrated their units and we are able to identify the leaders. When this is over, we must find another way to maintain obedience, control their anger and make them think and feel happy. I am working on a method of programming, an adaption of the android system for humans." There were screams of approval and someone from the audience, started to applaud vigorously and chanted, Dr. Reinhart. The chanting was contagious. For a good five minutes, she stood smiling in satisfaction. "We shall overcome this problem like we have overcome the others!" she shouted and then the video ended.

"Do you want to see more, Pamela? "

"I have a question first?" He nodded. "I didn't see her android opposite. I thought that she had one, where was she?"

"Oh, I can show you what happened. I recorded this scene because she asked me to." He went on to explain what had happened. "I told you that your Mother created and used humans to test the programming system that we use today. She just needed the consent of the intellectual community to begin the human programming." He was stroking his chin now, as if he had a long beard. "As you understand by now, only what were identified as negative emotions were eliminated, or removed. The programming created the same responses in her test group as we reproduced here with you. Basically, if humans were happily programmed with their work and did not seek anything else, there would be no more uprisings and violence." He stared hard at me. "These programmed humans where given codes and visual receptors linked to a microchip in their brain that projected pleasant, wonderful images. They saw the world in rose…just like you did before you bypassed your programming. Her idea was ingenious. Yes, ingenious!

"I suppose that that made sense to her." I said even though I did not believe that stripping humans of their human nature was the best solution. I was much happier today, because I understood what being happy is. And, so that is the rosy-colored world, I mused.

"But. . ." he continued, "she was at the same time in the midst of modifying the basic programming for a small group of androids, to give them emotions."

"What? That doesn't make sense."

"Yes, it does." He protested. "We are the superior intellect and we can live forever. It was brilliant; just brilliant. She could continue her work infinitum by imprinting her total identity onto the android. It was so ingenious, and yet, so personally instructive, that she did not need to ask for permission from the other members of the community. She selected several androids and started to introduce a very primitive emotionally based program."

"You were one of them?" That accounts for their limited human mannerisms and corresponds to what Stuart told me about being able to adapt and modify their programming within limits.

"Of course, her research was extremely important in my case. I may have forgotten to tell you that my creator was poisoned. His death was a shock to the whole community, and, in particular, to your Mother. My creator's research was relevant for her project; and, they were very close friends."

The impression I had of my Mother did not at all match up with that. She came across strong and determined and the death of Flanders' creator seemed too convenient-- opportune. If anything, maybe she was responsible for his being poisoned; that is if she felt that she could work better with his android replacement than with him. I shook these thoughts out of my head. I was definitely freaking out. I just did not want Dr. Flanders to follow my thoughts. So I nodded in approval.

"I still have certain human mannerisms. And, as you noticed, I can have a violent temper. Even though, all the elements that she introduced were to have been erased, I was never able to completely return to my previous android programming."

"Why couldn't you erase them?" I didn't give him chance to answer. "It seems like it would be relatively simple to erase new programming." I persisted.

"We, those of us who received this primitive programming, tried. We would never have refused an order from Dr. Reinhart, we respected her too much." I smiled viciously at that.

"We have had to be very discrete over the years. Should any of my colleagues witness any form of emotions, we would immediately be shut down."

"So, if I am following your story. Her android counterpart was one of the androids who she selected for her experiment."

"Yes, of course. It was logical. Her android counterpart, after all, received the essence of your Mother-her full imprint and all the qualities emotionally, psychologically, intellectually, and others that made your Mother so exceptional."

"So what happened?"

"It was working out very well. Your Mother replaced or adjusted the programming several times before a true, accurate and complex emotional vigor and charisma was achieved." He stopped and shook his head, reminding me of his primitive human emotions. "Even after all my experience with androids and humans, I was still not sure if I was facing a human or an android. It was remarkable. You will see in an instance." He shook his head again.

"Her profile was too exact; to precise and immutable. Dr. Reinhart was an indescribably complex human and, the beginning of her life was so very different from her life before the end. Her android counterpart received her entire emotional profile, even to the point of acquiring feelings and sentiments that she herself had repressed over time. And, therein lay the error, which produced a disastrous result. "

"She didn't agree with my genetic Mother?" I questioned, not knowing any other theory to propose.

"Precisely! It was that. But not at first. It happened when her android counterpart was given the opportunity to think and reason independently from her programming." He started to stroke his chin. "Normally, her android creation would have been given orders and instructions-thinking and reasoning reserved to Dr. Reinhart. But, Dr. Reinhart was certainly so enthusiastic that she went too far when she removed backup systems and let her android develop." He huffed. "Dr. Reinhart made a mistake. Perhaps the only one she ever made, but she made a big mistake."

"And you?" I was very interested. "Do have independent thinking?"

"No, I never had that opportunity. Your genetic Mother realized her mistake and had us erase all those emotions; which, as I just told you, were in a very primitive stage under a limited, restricted programming."

"But it didn't work?"

"What? The removal of the emotional programming?

"Yes."

"No, in fact it was impossible to completely remove the primitive emotional programming because her order was in direct conflict with a priority command system in another program that she had downloaded into us a week before. She told us at that time that the new programming was for our protection." His brow furrowed. "Come to think about it, she never mentioned what it was protecting. But, as that programming had overlapping elements, we could not carry out her order to the letter. As you have witnessed, we, or I, have no developed emotional structure; we have only spasmodic jerks, or responses." He finally explained why they could not erase the primitive programming.

"I just explained to you that I could not speak for the others; although I have never seen them develop defined human emotions." He eyes moved rapidly around the room as if someone might be listening. "No, I couldn't do it, but I didn't tell her. Quite frankly, she should have realized that as she was the one who oversaw the android production project. She was capable of recognizing malfunctioning and in which zone that malfunction took place without even opening us up. She was one of the principal engineers in that area; the party responsible for android creation." He moved around in his chair, uncomfortable with the discussion? "The fact that she certainly knew that we were trapped with this frustrating primitive programming that would never develop into more and which didn't seem to bother her meant that she was still studying our behavior."

"So what happened between Dr. Reinhart and her android opposite?" I asked, not knowing what else to say.

"They argued. Her counterpart did not agree with human programming. She liked the non-intellectuals and wanted to give them more power. She pleaded with Dr. Reinhart to give them more rights so that they would prove their real value."

It was how I felt as well, but I didn't let him know.

"The video that you will see now will explain everything."

My Mother had her long hair tied behind her head in a ponytail, letting her hair in front fall in long curls that hung wildly around her face. I thought that she was even more beautiful now than in the last video. Her green eyes radiated energy. She was wearing a white lab coat and stood behind a laboratory table complete with high-tech machines, metal and plastic tubing, along with an assortment of chemicals in small bottles and vials. The white wall behind her was a tangle of mathematical problems and equations. Her eyes honed directly into the camera.

"Oh, you finally arrived. Where have you been?"

She was speaking to her android opposite that moved towards her and onto the film. "I have been thinking a great deal about your projects." She smiled slyly as she cocked her head in the direction of her creation.

"A bit too much, I would say." The android retorted sarcastically.

They both stood silently now looking at each other. The film continued with no action and then Dr. Elizabeth Reinhart picked up a heavy object and shook it in front of the android. "I should let myself go. I could break you apart. Or better, I could start to dismantle you."

"No! Not that! Please! Let me continue." The android screamed and begged her creator.

"You know that I am the best of your experiments. You have accomplished with me everything that you hoped for. I am a complete person." The android pleaded.

"No, a person?" she interrupted and let out a hideous laugh. "You are only an android, a programmed machine whose programming I can erase completely in a second..."

"You wouldn't do that? Would you?" The android reached out to touch her creator. Dr. Reinhart did not show tenderness instead she struck her with all her force sending her flying across the floor.

"Why? Why are you doing this?" The android asked with tears streaming down her face. "I love you. I respect you. I would never do anything to harm you!"

"Oh, is that how you see it. You would never harm me. Well, I'll tell you what you did even though you already know." She replied as she turned her back to the android. "I thought that I could trust you and that you would make me immortal. As such, I thought that I could transfer my very essence into your body so that together we would continue to live on to achieve the ultimate of human progress. I never thought that you would. . . betray me!" Her voice softened with deep emotion.

"But, I didn't betray you."

"No. You think that telling certain representatives of the non-intellectual class that their courageous space voyagers met with instant death in deep space was not a betrayal?"

"No." The android answered softly. "No, it was not a betrayal of the Dr. Reinhart that I am programmed to reproduce. What you did was very cruel. I didn't want any more people to die in deep space. The hopes and expectations of those space pioneers were real and they believed in a better future. They wanted to accomplish something more with their lives. They were even ready to face unknown dangers and difficulties to build a new world for their community. I can't believe that you have forgotten the importance of trust and sincerity to your species?"

"What? Are you playing mind games with me?"

"No. I am telling you the truth." Her head drooped and her arms went limp in dismay. "You asked me to study your profile, who you are, how you think, your emotions, beliefs."

"Stop! This is insane."

"You are different now than you were three years ago. You are bitter and full of hatred. Don't you want me to be the real you, the Dr. Reinhart who so brilliantly contributed to human development? Don't you want me to be the visionary who has so brilliantly led her race?"

"I don't want you to be anything for me. Your stupidity has cost me too much. In fact, I no longer want you to be a part of my life."

It all happened so fast. She turned and glared at her recalcitrant android. Her eyes were burning with rage. Her beautiful face quickly distorted as her lips stiffened, rolling over her sharp, white teeth.

"Self-destruct!" She growled.

The android pitifully crawled towards her and laid her head on Reinhart's feet. She begged for forgiveness and another chance. Dr. Reinhart stood her ground, unaffected; and, repeated her order. The android executed the command; the explosion that followed was so violent that Dr. Reinhart lost her balance, falling forward on her hands, as her laboratory table collapsed around her. She eventually pulled herself up, brushed off the dust, and violently kicked around the metal body parts of her android creation. She turned to Dr. Flanders, who, covered with dust and submerged in metal parts, trembling struggled to maintain his balance.

"You understand now, Dr. Flanders, why I wanted this recorded. I want all the androids to see their fate. We, their creators, control their very existence and they should never forget that."

The video went black. I understood why the androids would not challenge her authority. Dr. Flanders turned to me, amazingly with moisture, a slimy, oily liquid oozing from his metallic android eyes. I didn't know what to say. I felt so badly for him. "How could she have been so cruel," I mused.

But, when he spoke, it resonated pure admiration. "I am not crying for the loss of her android opposite, I am crying for the loss of this brilliant, courageous woman." He said.

I stood looking at Dr. Flanders, completely confused. "But, she was incredibly cruel." I stammered.

"She was a genius who understood that no one, nothing could stand in her way. Even her chance for immortality had to be sacrificed for the greater good."

I was getting used to having my human emotional responses shattered by cold android logic. "What happened after the android self-destructed?"

"I transmitted a copy of the video to each and every android. The androids were immediately informed of their fate should they defy their human creators."

"How did they respond?"

"The androids registered the message, as a command, as did those of us who had rudimentary emotional programming." For him, there was nothing special about circulating commands and having androids incorporate them immediately into their systems. "Don't forget, Pamela, that there were only a few of us who had any notion of human emotions; and, we were, as I said, in the very beginning stages of sensitive robotics. We had no reason to question her order and truly believed her actions were purely logical. We are not programmed to harm our human creators. We are programmed to protect them and obey them. How could we see things differently?"

I did not pursue that discussion even though I was not convinced that these androids would not harm humans, it looked to me like they had been doing just that for a long time. As he did not proceed with his analysis of android programming, I let it drop. But there was still something that was bothering me. I saw other people in the film who were like Jason. Their skin was wrinkled and their bodies were not fit. So Dr. Flanders was telling the truth when he mentioned that human aging was inevitable. How did Dr. Reinhart stay looking so young? I was certain that Dr. Flanders knew her secret and brought up the point again.

He denied having any knowledge of why she was ageless since humans are not ageless. "I was, and still am, as surprised by her eternal youth as you and the others. The only logical explanation was that she had found an anti-age remedy that she was not willing to share with anyone else." He stood up, ready to leave. "Her agelessness was a source of power for her. She used it to control others and to maintain her position. She pretended that she was chosen by God to save humanity and for that mission she was condemned to stay young. She mentioned, quite frequently, that her eternal youthfulness was more a burden than a gift. People expected the impossible simply because she was ageless. For certain groups of individuals, especially the very religious ones, she certainly looked like the chosen one. She could have been like… God."

"You are contradicting yourself, Dr. Flanders?"

"That is impossible. I am a machine and thus can't contradict myself."

"You told me earlier that she confessed to you that her beauty stood in the way of her career. And, now you are telling me that that beauty which never changed with age made her some sort of a God."

"Oh, it is not a contradiction. As I mentioned, early in her career she was not taken seriously because men were so mesmerized with her beauty that they treated her like an object and not someone to be contended with; they did not even listen to her and just wanted to be able to gaze into her seductive green eyes. With the passage of time, her eternal youth and beauty brought her fame and power. She was different than the others who were aging and terminating naturally."

"Ok, but what about her anger? Did she change as much as the android suggested?"

He sat back down and shook his head and sighed. "Yes. But, it was not a voluntary change. She and her partner, husband, were very close. They never had any children because procreation was not their priority. They were always involved in some critical, important and certainly time-consuming new research project." He reached over and took my hands in his. "She confided in me a lot near the end of her life. She apparently did not want children during her lifetime which is why she had her best ovum frozen." He tapped my hands as he withdrew his. "They were above all, scientists. And they worked in the same field. He was an ordinary looking man, short and a bit stumpy with age. I have no picture of him. When I knew him, he was already bald. Even though he was not handsome, he was so charming that women liked to be in his company. He had "style," as humans use to say." He stopped abruptly and started trembling as if he were losing power.

I panicked and screamed his name several times before he responded. "Are you alright? You frightened me." I was still shaking a bit.

He didn't seem to be alarmed at all. "Yes. Thank you for your concern. Actually, I don't understand what happened. I told you that I need an overhaul, but I am reluctant to shut down, as I'm afraid I won't come back. There is no one here in the Center competent enough in android technology to recreate parts. But, yes. Where was I? Oh, right. Then Dr. Robert Reinhart was kidnapped and assassinated, brutally murdered by non-intellectuals. Before that happened, Elisabeth was very sensitive to the needs of these individuals. She sincerely wanted to help them. In fact, she fought hard to raise the money to develop the spaceships, in the interest of helping these people to start new lives. And then, only one year before the ships were scheduled to leave, Robert was kidnapped by a group of these savages. They called themselves the army for the salvation of the non-intellectuals. They tortured her husband in horrible ways and then sent his body back to her in pieces. Organs were missing, presumably eaten by members of this savage army. She held all non-intellectuals accountable for the viscous death of her loved one, even though only a tiny minority had been involved. "

He stopped for an instance, his rapid eye movement giving the impression that he was reliving everything. "She pretended, publicly, to forgive the members of the army because they didn't understand the horror that had been committed in their names; in fact they were mentally incapable of understanding it or the consequences of what they did. Her forgiveness was demonstrable in her unremitting and dynamic campaign advocating rights and freedoms for this lower class. She used all her energy to motivate more and more individuals to embark on the spaceships. 'You have the right to start a new life on another planet,' she would say over and over again in her speeches."

He stopped, a big, wide smile on his face, showing his admiration. "Brilliant. She was brilliant. How well this charismatic woman manipulated that utterly useless mass of individuals. But then she snapped. She ordered them exterminated in outer space, millions of light years away from earth. She contended that they were all responsible for her husband's death and should be punished severely. She moreover claimed that they were a substantial threat to the survival of the intellectual community. She explained that each ship was equipped with a detonating device that was scheduled to explode when they had reached the outer sphere of our galaxy."

"She sounds so diabolical, even worse than those who tortured and murdered her husband. There were probably children among the voyagers." I twisted the corners of my mouth up in disgust.

"Sometimes, you are just too sensitive, Pamela, but you will learn to be rational with time. And, to continue, most of the council members had wanted to reduce the numbers of those "morons," as they called them, for years and now was their chance. As such, Elisabeth's plan was applauded especially since there would be no trace of their deaths. Henceforth, they all agreed that they could more easily govern the remaining 30 percent. The few who found her plan too diabolical for their taste eventually disappeared altogether from the intellectual society. Ironically, their views on that stigmatized them as non-intellectuals. Whether they died or joined the non-intellectuals became a non-issue for us."

"So the loss of her husband was the reason for her dramatic change of heart. She must have loved him very much to muster up the kind of hatred she would need to annihilate 70 percent of that population. Now I'm not so proud to be her successor." It was all too much. Yet, I could appreciate better why Dr. Flanders liked the film, "The End."

A long silence followed; I broke it with another question. "I guess that you don't have to worry about my addressing the last video publicly as she wanted it to be circulated." He nodded. "Well, are there any other videos?" I asked.

"Yes, I have two more, but we're out of time. Our absence has certainly been noticed and I think it is best for us to go on with this in a few days. I also have a very important meeting in a few minutes. I suggest that you go to the library now and view the disks dealing with non-intellectuals which will help you to understand the next few episodes."

He hugged me and opened the door for me to leave. I was surprised to see Dr. Gordon on the other side. She smiled and rushed past me. I learned later about the weekly meetings that took place between her and Dr. Flanders in this sound proof room. My imagination began to run…wild.

Chapter 38: Compromise

While I was in the library reading a pre-selected number of disks on wealth in human society, the benefits and the detriments and, how to eliminate non-intellectuals, the two of them were discussing my emotional development. Interestingly, the androids always recorded their meetings, whether board meetings, individual discussions, including discussions with me and so on. It was a reflex, certainly a programmed reflex which is why I found out about the content of this meeting and others later on.

Dr. Gordon started off the discussion. "I still see Pamela as a naïve and immature adolescent, driven by hormones. I don't believe that she has had enough opportunity to experience negative emotions, although she gives the impression that she is often frustrated and confused about who she was and why I am studying her."

Dr. Flanders did not share the same opinion. "I disagree. I find her very inquisitive." He said as he went on to compare me favorably to my genetic mother. "Pamela has the intellectual capacity but lacks motivation. We should be focusing on how to motivate her."

Dr. Flanders suggested that I be given the opportunity to return to the outside community, but not before he finished bringing me up to date with the last chapter of human history. He wanted me to be able to communicate all the information in a convincing way to the others.

"What is the point of all this?" Dr. Gordon objected. "What difference does it make what she says? We have been observing those people for so long now and they are as lethargic as they were the first day they arrived on the outside."

She went on to defend her position with more detail. "In fact, they have never done anything constructive. They are like nervous animals running in circles, kept in a zoo. The only real difference is that they come to the center doors every day to get their food and take a shower. We don't hose them down and throw their food into their cage. Do you realize that, in all these years, they have not wandered farther than the mile radius that Pamela and Mathieu explored a few years ago? They live in the cavern and are content to just. . .exist. That is what is so surprising; they are happy to do only that, eat, sleep, copulate, etc. etc. Apart from their active sexual life and consequent reproduction, they are doing nothing. Even that is done perfunctorily. They even give us a list of supplies, clothes and so forth that they need, like kids being sent off to summer camp. They are pathetic."

They stared intensely at each other. "I expected them to be a bit more curious. But, then, there were no life-threatening challenges for them; they never felt endangered. John negotiated their departure with the Governor and with us. I think that Dr. Miller and Dr. Crawford were suspicious of the project but agreed to provide them with food, clothing…everything that they needed to survive." He stopped to look around the room as if other solutions were hidden in the padded walls. "What were our alternatives? Terminate them? Force them to live longer at the center and try to inspire some negative emotions. Or, leave them on the outside to fend for themselves by refusing to supply basic life support." He shook her head.

"We made living in that cavern just too easy for them. Took away their fighting spirit." He pulled his lips up under, drawing them back inside his mouth. "I never understood why Jason's discoveries didn't arouse more interest and a desire to find a better place to live.

Dr. Gordon smacked her lips in disgust. "It is simple. The only negative emotion that they know well, and that has not outlived itself, is fear. They were afraid to wander too far away. I suppose though that they did believe that Jason had hallucinated. He is a strange character." Dr. Gordon interjected.

"We should not have awakened him. I am not even certain why we kept him in suspended animation all those years. He was one of Dr. Reinhart's experiments. She was testing the effects of suspended animation on humans. She carried out her experiments on the non-intellectuals. She liked to experiment on young children, like Jason. She wanted to see if he would age on awakening." Dr. Flanders was involved closely with Dr. Reinhart's perversion. "These experiments were necessary for the space program. Humans had to be transported light years away from the earth and suspended animation was a solution that was proposed hundreds of years before Dr. Reinhart was born. She just perfected it. So, naturally, we did not wake up a genius. As I understand, he thinks that he was programmed and bypassed the system. He even believes that he dramatically escaped from the center. To a certain extent, it is better that he doesn't know where he came from. The sad part is that he has no real communication skill. He doesn't fit the role that we wanted. Oh well, Dr. Gordon, it's not our fault he's insane."

"I didn't know all that about space programs and suspended animation. I have no such information in my memory banks." Her voice was agitated. She moved forward in her chair to show her irritation and the fact that she was not privy to this information

"I don't know everything either. But, you should have noted that we awakened him." He stared intensely into her eyes. "You do remember that he was in that state for centuries perhaps more, as we never were able to determine what earth year we are living in."

"Yes. I have information on Jason in my memory bank. But, neither you nor the Governor explained why he was in a tube. I assumed that he had been sick and that it was the right time to wake him up."

"Well, anyway," he continued. "I can't explain that point. Nonetheless putting someone in primitive life support systems, resembling the tubes that Dr. Reinhart used, was an archaic technique used by earlier generations of humans to keep people alive until medical cures were found to treat their illness." He stopped to scratch his head. "I have no information regarding the efficiency of these less-sophisticated methods of suspended animation; and, or the numbers of humans that benefited from this procedure." He stroked his chin. "No matter; as I was working closely with Dr. Reinhart, I was privy to a lot of information. Come to think of it, though, Pamela asked me today whether the intellectual space voyagers have returned to earth."

"What?" Dr. Gordon's mouth dropped open.

"Yes. There were a number of intellectuals that went up into space. They benefited from the experimentation on suspended animation. They were scheduled to wake up in the future." He sighed. "If my estimates are right, they should be sending representatives back to Earth soon."

"Does anyone else know?"

"I have no idea. I only tapped into that memory bank today when Pamela asked the question."

"This could be dangerous for all of us!" She moved impatiently in her chair. "Their return could upset everything."

"I don't know." He sighed again. "I was not working with that program and I do not know why I had any information and who could give us more information about that-that is if anyone else here knows."

"We are going to have to find out and fast." She said. "And how does Pamela know about these people? She must have gotten information from one of the others. We shall have to look into the activities of her friends." She let that subject drop and continued. "To return to our previous discussion, I think that Pamela believed Jason. She excused his inadequate verbal skills as a consequence of his age."

"True. When she mentioned him today, her voice showed compassion for him."

"So, how do you imagine that she will react to the rest of the story?"

"Well, I am not going to tell her the truth, regarding Jason's resurrection, being linked to experimentation with suspended animation for space voyage. I don't want her to think that he was a kind of "guinea pig." The story that I am going to tell her she should believe. She will probably feel grateful to us that some humans have survived. I can only see it as a plus for us."

"Bizarre. You are going to lie?" She commented. "That is not something that we androids can intentionally decide to do."

"No, I am not going to lie." He raised his voice in protest." I am just not going to add any superfluous information, the validity of which is uncertain for us. I don't see the need to go back on the space voyager question before it becomes clearer to us."

She tapped her fingers on the table that separated them and continued in different beats.

"Ok. I shall let you take care of explaining this. Of course, only if she brings the subject up again." Dr. Flanders nodded. "It could be a good thing, the return of space voyagers, because Crawford and his group are starting to react again. We could exploit this knowledge of space visitors to our advantage, showing them that we are much more capable of making critical decisions because we have more information about what is happening and, in particular, the potential outside menaces to our Center."

"Whatever you do Dr. Gordon," His voice was strong, "do not do anything to jeopardize my project. I do not want to lose my series 13. I have finally, by accident, certainly, come up with Elisabeth's identity. I have to make it work. This may be our only opportunity for hundreds of years."

"Well, we have the Governor on our side. He has a weakness for your series 13 as well." Dr. Gordon was quick to add.

"And, you? One could say that you have been having a good time with her!"

"Yes, that's right. But, I still believe that if we, the few of us that are caught between two worlds, could just fall in love we would be able to move beyond our primitive programming. But, I have been unable to conjure up this feeling even though she seemed to be very much satisfied by our sexual encounters, I was only pretending to have pleasure. I can't say that I had any pleasure at all with anyone. I even tried with Randolph."

"Did I hear you correctly? "

"Yes. Well, I thought that you knew. In any event, I thought that I needed a heterosexual relationship; oh, let's just forget it. And even worse, I don't even feel frustrated about not being able to feel any strong emotional ties. I suppose that that means that it is hopeless for me. And yourself?"

His eyes took on a dreamy look. "I think that I came close to loving Elisabeth. I was so attached to her and I felt empty after she was gone, if you know what I mean. But, I am not sure that it was the same type of love that humans experience. Pamela looks so much like Elisabeth that I even thought, like you, that hugging and kissing Pamela would be the catalyst for me. That I would become human. Apparently I have not evolved more than you have. It is clear that we need a program." He was so convinced. "I was so convinced that if she looked like her genetic Mother that she could be her."

"But, she is not a scientist."

"She can be; we just have to give her the schooling; it wouldn't take that much time. However, for it to work, she has to ask for the training. You'll see; soon she is going to show ambition. A stay on the outside may just be a way to ignite her interest in saving whatever is left of the human race."

"No, I am not sure. I think that she needs to be pressured in a different manner; she has to feel threatened. We tried to frighten the entire group with Diana, but that didn't work. I still don't understand what happened to change Diana."

"What then do you think would be an effective threat?" he asked.

"Well, I was thinking more in terms of bringing her son here to the center to be educated." She replied. "I already mentioned to her that Dr. Crawford was promoting that."

"Maybe you should not have mentioned Dr. Crawford, but what does it matter. In any event, you are right there. I suggested that he should be trained in the center." He replied and then added. "Now, we should tell her the decision has been made to bring her son here for training. And, to accomplish that education, he would have to undergo the classic form of programming—a visual receptor added. Ok, so agreed. Which one of us is going to tell her?"

"I mentioned the visual receptor too, and she did not seem to be upset. I will bring it up again, but not yet. I want to spend a few days in conversation with her after she sees all the videos. Is that ok with you?" She asked.

"That is fine with me. I need about a week more to work on her and then she is all yours. You'll let the Governor know?"

Dr. Gordon was planning on seeing him the following day to discuss the space voyager situation so she would also discuss this issue. "By the way," she started. "Pamela's question continues to disturb me."

"What question are you referring to?"

"The question about visitors from other planets."

"Oh, yes, that one. So what is bothering you?" He asked perfunctorily.

"Certainly she brought up the subject about space voyagers because someone mentioned that to her." Dr. Gordon was homing in on the suspicious nature of the question. "I know that she would not have come up with that kind of question on her own. She is clever and curious about issues that she has studied in the library or topics raised by other members of the outside group. Evidently, she knows when to bring these questions up with us. I am bothered by who could have suggested to Pamela that there were visitors from space? Her circulating around freely like she does makes it easy for her to meet other people."

"I have looked over the members of the outside community. None of them were working in this area. Peter wasn't associated with this area either. Randolph's partner worked in the geological area. Do you remember that we terminated her before her time because she got too curious about changes that were produced in the center of the earth?" Dr. Flanders replied.

"I do. It was an excellent decision. And yes, Pamela and Randolph spend a lot of time together. She needs to meet others like herself in the inside, so I don't pay much attention to their relationship. But, they both speak to Stuart, from time to time. He is a brilliant engineer assigned to the military transport section. We kept him in the center because he is very useful. I don't want to terminate him or even send him on the outside. He doesn't know that we know that he bypassed his programming. How strange?" They both engaged in violent android spasmodic jerks—a kind of laughter. "He takes us for real idiots. Like Randolph, though, they work very well and never cause us any problems." She stared into space for a few minutes and then added. "No, I believe that someone else in this center has said something to her."

"Well, until you speak to the Governor about it; we don't know how true it is." He stood up and shook her hand.

"You know Dr. Flanders, maybe we should be spending more time together. We think a lot the same and I find you quite appealing."

"Are you suggesting that we could develop complex emotions if we were to fall in love with each other?" He smiled.

"Something like that." She answered and opened the door. She was on a roll.

And with that Dr. Gordon was off. She went to see the Governor early in the morning. She detailed what was happening in the reproductive center and then raised the question of space visitors. The Governor didn't seem to know anything about it. There were the android drones that were programmed to protect the center. They were members of the militia. Each center had no more than 10 active drones. There was no need to activate the others.

"We do have vehicles that patrol the center. From time to time, they disintegrate space debris that has fallen onto the earth. It seems to happen once a month. I know that they have gone off on missions to destroy the debris." He was stroking his chin as he spoke.

"Don't you find that strange?" She asked.

"I didn't before now. In fact, I never even questioned the missions. Maybe I should have." He seemed uncertain. "The best I can do is call up one of the officers."

She was becoming sensitive to misinformation from her android colleagues, trapped like her in the rudimentary stage of emotions. Why should she feel so suspicious of her colleagues; she had no reason to believe that they were withholding information intentionally. Like them, she had gaps in her memory banks. Was she moving forward and starting to develop emotions, like suspicion; or were they farther along and could now tell human style lies? Or worse than that was lying a programmed reflex, an involuntary action, automatically executed under certain defined parameters? She shook off the idea and looked up at the Governor and replied that she thought that his suggestion was a good one. Commissioning these drones would be the best way to find out what kind of debris, if any, they were intercepting.

"You mentioned Stuart." He questioned.

"Yes. Stuart is that brilliant engineer. He is perhaps our best hope for human scientific advancement." She stated.

"By the way, is he one of the deprogrammed humans that you are studying?"

"No." She surprised herself. She just lied, but why? Why would she want to protect Stuart? She gathered together her logical android reasoning, defying her programming and explained herself. "Stuart interests me." The Governor grimaced expecting her to tell him that she had a sexual interest in him as well. Her sexual exploits were a source of gossip among the androids. "He is different. One can read this in his deep, serious, penetrating eyes; he has android eyes; and he is very mature and serious, less prone to foolish playfulness like the others. I have never gone so far as to make personal contact with him because of his enigmatic nature. I sense that he reads us and that intrigues me."

"Oh. Whatever, you can keep him alive." He stopped to observe her. "So then how do they see each other?"

She lied again when she said that Stuart knew how to decode his fellow humans. The Governor found it incredibly interesting, if not ridiculous, that humans would want to make contact with their programmed colleagues.

Uncomfortable with what she had just said, she changed the subject and asked for the Governor's approval on forcing Pamela's child to be programmed and educated in the center. He agreed reluctantly. He said that he did not want to hurt Pamela, but approved the idea if it was the only way to get her motivated.

Chapter 39: Frustration

I was reading about something that I found particularly boring: Accumulation of wealth, power based upon wealth, purchasing power, investments, and so forth and so on; it all made very little sense to me. I had been through all of this before although Dr. Miller, the robot with a beautiful android face, pampered me, by bringing more and more detailed discs on wealth. I saw pictures of extremely rich people with all their jewels, transport vehicles, enormous cubicles with vast gardens... I was revolted by the way in which these people worshipped government issued paper, called money and flaunted their wealth.

In a very brief meeting the following afternoon, Dr. Flanders confirmed for me that money was necessary to assure research and development. As a result, certain rich geographic zones were more advanced technologically than others. I had skimmed over the value of money in the early history of humans because I found it such a primitive notion that I was genuinely surprised that it had endured through the ages. Now I realized that money bought everything that one needed to survive. Without money, one could not even eat.

"Do our Centers use money to buy food and clothing?" I asked, exploring the question concerning monetary exchange in the world I was now living in and hoping that this discriminatory practice had been abandoned. I know that I had discussed this before with Dr. Gordon, but wanted confirmation.

"No." He gave a definitive No; I was satisfied. "Money is a human problem. We want nothing to do with that. Each center is relatively autonomous. We use and reuse the resources that we have here. We grow our own food in "green houses," facilities set up to provide the proper heat, light, water and soil to grow crops. We control production so as to avoid waste. And, other food sources discovered over time provide the protein and additional minerals that humans need to absorb for good health. All food, I might add, comes from plants. We do not believe in raising and killing animals to satisfy the carnivorous appetite of humans." He smiled, obviously pleased with the successfulness of this center. I grimaced at the idea of eating an animal. "Some centers do not have the advanced technology that we have in this center, but that does not make a difference. We, androids, are not programmed to compete on monetary levels. And, basically, we are not programmed to compete on any level. So, we share and assist and support each other."

I was surprised that he used the word compete. I saw it used in the section on money over and over again. Humans were very competitive among themselves. Did androids admire our competiveness or did they abhor it because it was an emulation of human achievement, a negatively inspired emotion that brought success? I decided to test him on that.

"Dr. Flanders, would you have preferred being programmed to compete?"

He brushed my question off as nonsense. "Complete nonsense, Pamela," is what he said. After which, he told me that he would contact me soon to meet again.

Days went by before he contacted me. I was starting to forget about the horrible things that I had read about and seen concerning wealth when his assistant appeared at the break of day in my cubicle. She told me that Dr. Flanders had time to continue our discussion, if I could get away. I had plenty of free time now, much of which I spent relaxing in the orchestra pit or in a small music room that Dr. Gordon had set aside for me. Playing the piano was my therapy. It helped me to retrieve my energy and think clearer; I was ready for the next session with Dr. Flanders.

She escorted me to the reproduction center and left me to return to the padded cell. Dr. Flanders rushed in and shut the door behind him. "Dr. Gordon is going to have Frederic brought into the center to be educated. You mustn't let her know that I told you." He stammered.

I felt my heart drop. Dr. Gordon had turned incredibly vicious since our sexual relationship ended. I had to stop her, but how? My face flushed and my palms grew moist as waves of total panic set in. Gasping for breath, like I was being strangled by his very words, I stuttered out. "I know; I know that I have been pretending…only pretending…only pretending that bringing Frederic here does not bother me." I grabbed the sleeves of Dr. Flanders' white smock, shaking him back and forth, as I screamed. "You all know that it does. Why would Dr. Gordon want to hurt me by bringing my child in here? Why don't you try to stop her?" I asked in disbelief, releasing him from my grip. Tears were streaming down my face. I was sobbing hysterically, cupping my hands over my face to hide my despair from him.

"Oh, she is like that." He started off, unaffected by my state of mind. "She gets an idea and can't let go. I can't say that she will have much support, not even from Dr. Crawford for that matter, but no one will try to stop her, because you are her experiment." He replied.

"He will, of course, have to be programmed." He added.

"Are you crazy? She told me that Dr. Crawford is the one pushing for this solution." I stopped to look at Dr. Flanders and wondered who, if anyone, was telling me the truth, and then continued. "Do you think that I shall just stand back looking on while you put microchips in his tiny brain?" I wanted to punch him hard, but he could be my only ally. So I lashed out at the padded wall, kicking and hitting, letting out all my anger and frustration, just like Diana must have done in the past, until I was so exhausted that I collapsed on the floor.

He stood with his arms folded and his legs apart in a relaxed position watching the scene. He waited until I was calm enough for him to approach me and offered me his hand. I took it cautiously and he drew me up in his arms. "Oh, my dear child," he said in a soft, paternal voice mode, "You must, as I have told you before, learn to calm down. These dramatic scenes are not going to help in any way. "

"Why does he have to be programmed to learn?" I asked in a voice weakened by my despair.

"Come, let's sit down and I shall explain." I followed him, taking the chair in front. "It is because the programming speeds up the learning process; one simply learns more rapidly."

"That is not true. I absorb information very rapidly and I am no longer programmed."

"Ok, you might be right, but he is a child. In his situation, it is best that he has contact with other children, even if that contact is rather artificial. You cannot bring him into the center and isolate him, especially after having been in contact with other children on the outside. It will not be good for his development. And, our method of education requires a child to be under the supervision of an instructor all day long." Dr. Flanders seemed focused on convincing himself.

"You know that that is not true either. On the outside, his contact with other children is real. He sees them and interacts with them in a human sense. Programming him now will be emotionally disturbing. No, I am opposed to Dr. Gordon's idea." I spoke as if I had decision-making authority in the Center. "Of course, I do agree that he should receive proper education. We do not have the ability to adequately educate the children on the outside."

"Well, that is a start." He stopped to stroke his chin. "Quite frankly, regardless of what you want to think, the programming does accelerate learning. There is no doubt about it. In fact, humans recognized how much easier it was to educate even the non-intellectuals, once they were programmed."

I just let him speak. "You were a productive and talented pianist when you were only 12 years old. Did you know that?"

Patricia Lee Strunk

"No, I didn't know that." I only just learned that I was 20 years old the other day.

"You were already performing and interacting with your colleagues at a very young age. You were already sharing space with Jonathan. As your life span is limited, it is better for you to complete your education rapidly; in other words, accelerated learning and productivity from the earliest possible age." I listened. "It is the same in every field. Even those experienced scientists started producing at 12 years old." His lips moved tightly into a self-satisfied smile.

I asked Dr. Flanders how old John was as he looks older than me and the rest of us. He replied that John had well outlived his programmed life span. He was not certain of his exact age, but put him at 40 years old. He took the opportunity to remind me that the outside community was one of many different experiments related to human behavior. He carefully explained that androids wanted to see if humans had evolved since the end of their history.

"Unfortunately, it is impossible to determine human evolutionary tendencies by studying small outside communities, because humans are only active participants within the center." He shook his head back and forth several times before proceeding. "You have no motivation, no creativity and no values. You lack all the human behavioral factors that are necessary for a real study of the evolution of your species. We have done our best to breed you!" He realized that he shocked me and quickly added, "so to speak. We have been careful with mixing genes and have made enormous progress, as you have seen. And, we have given you the level of education and training that corresponds to your natural ability. But something is wrong. You don't think or act like the humans we worked with at the end of your history. The only rational theory is that proposed by Dr. Gordon, who has been convinced for a long time that without a complete emotional reconfiguration, you humans are too complacent."

He stood in front of me dissecting me with his eyes. He turned his back to me and said in a low voice. "It is pitiful how your community vegetates. Your emotional configurations are intact and you are no more interesting for us than those programmed humans here at the center. I don't get it. "

I secretly knew how wrong he was and how clever we were. He turned and looked at me intently, waiting for a response. I looked back, and refused to take the bait.

That seemed to irritate him because he approached me saying in a mocking tone: "Don't you care? Don't you want to construct a new world for yourselves? What is wrong with you?"

I laughed nervously and shrugged my shoulders.

"Say something" he insisted.

So I said something completely ridiculous for my own ears, but hopefully reassuring for his. "It is quite simple, Dr. Flanders. Why would we want something different or something more, when you have given us such a perfect world to live in? Even deprogrammed, we admire what you have done for us."

"Hmmm!" He looked at me in ironic disbelief. "I want you to calm down. I shall try to stall your son's arrival as long as I can." The conversation ended on that note and he quite enthusiastically reminded me to come back the next day to see another video.

It was very early in the day when I walked out of the reproduction center and wandered down the various corridors. I was not paying any attention to those brushing up against me; everyone was in such a hurry in the morning. I was about to turn in the direction of the music room when someone grabbed my arm and covered my mouth with the other hand. The grip was very firm and it frightened me. Whoever it was started to drag me in another direction. It all happened so fast that I didn't even have the opportunity to be frightened until, at last, I found myself behind a door. He let me fall on the floor. I scrambled to my feet, and was finally able to turn and face my aggressor; my eyes swooned as they looked straight into the face of Dr. Crawford.

This man's killer eyes beamed into mine. I wondered how many times he had requested my termination. Being alone with this monster, far away from Dr. Gordon's protection, so petrified me that when I opened my mouth to scream, there was no sound. He bent down towards me, his cold, unyielding eyes and stern lips closing in on me and I was too helpless to respond. I closed my eyes and waited for him to terminate me.

It didn't happen; instead he grabbed my hand and pulled me to my feet. I nervously smiled back to him; it seemed to mellow his tense regard.

"Hello, Pamela." He said in a calm voice.

"Ah, hello Dr. Crawford." I said my voice trembling. "That's a weird way to greet someone!" I exclaimed as I adjusted my robe. He didn't answer so I went a bit further.

"Why didn't you just schedule a meeting instead of kidnapping me?"

"Let's be serious. It is not easy for me to get in touch with you beyond the typical channels as Dr. Gordon and her crew watch me very closely."

"I am confused. Aren't you the one spying on them?" My calm was back and I was able to think clearer.

"Of course, I am." He admitted. "I have good reasons to keep a close eye on what they are doing." He was wobbling from one leg to the other and chewing on his lower lip, in contrast to his earlier expression of death. "That Dr. Flanders is a strange character." He said brusquely.

"Dr. Crawford, forgive me for saying this, but you are all strange characters. Most of you don't realize that you are just programmed machines."

He sighed and looked away, then his glaring eyes honed back in on mine again. My body trembled involuntarily and I started coughing, a desperate smoke screen.

"Do I have to repeat myself over and over again with you? Let's be serious. Be assured that I am not that wicked, diabolical creation that Dr. Gordon wants you to believe I am. You know, I am sure that you do, that we are the embodiment of our creators. I am the Dr. Crawford who fought against the violation of human rights; the Dr. Crawford who at one time was a respected politician, statesman, and scientist."

"Interesting." I said with enthusiasm. In fact it was interesting. I never thought of Dr. Crawford as an ally for us humans. He never treated me with any degree of respect.

"In any event, that does not matter. I know that you are afraid of me, for various reasons…" He moved his index finger along an imaginary line as if he were ticking off a list of reasons why I was afraid of him. I watched attentively; curious about what he might say next. "You, Pamela, should never have interfered with Dr. Gordon when she was ordered to shut down. She is dangerous." He paused, his eyes still fixed on mine, "she thinks that she is human or can become human, or something along those lines, completely irrational. It is a veritable obsession with her and she will stop at nothing to achieve it if it's achievable. That makes her dangerous and unpredictable; her actions and reasoning are in conflict with android logic. Her system is overcharged, which means she needs to be shut down temporarily or permanently."

As he spoke, his eyes grew sullen, drooped downwards. He was worried. I pounced on the moment to take the offensive. "And, you? What do you want?"

"I don't want to help in the deprogramming of humans. It is the best thing for you." I made a grumbling sound and he corrected himself quickly. "Programming may not have been what my creator advocated. It is, however, what I, relying upon his deep concern and compassion for the human race, believe provides a blissful existence for humans." His last remark signaled danger and I prepared for a rapid escape by moving myself forward on the chair. "I am also not interested in crossing a barrier between two worlds or species. The consequences could be very serious." He stopped to study me for a minute. "I am not on her side, but a strong defender of the world as it is today. You have no idea," he said, "just how dangerous a world run by humans can be!"

"Perhaps not, Dr. Crawford." I said. I thought to myself that I had a very good idea how inhibiting, unnatural, and immoral a world run by androids could be.

"You would never have been anything but happy if you had just stopped listening to that Ferdinand."

"No, Dr. Crawford, you are wrong. I don't know how to explain to you how much humans need to be confronted with the good and bad. From that, they can make their own happiness. The happiness that you are giving us is what you, a machine, an object without emotions or dreams, a machine that thinks linearly, relying only on the logic of things, believes is the best. Living on the outside is, from my viewpoint, the best way for human beings to live even though we remain dependent upon this Center for all vital life support."

"Let me ask you how far along you are in understanding what brought about the end of human history."

A light went off in my head. He's been baiting me from the beginning and I've got to reel in my thoughts. The cold metallic trap had grated open.

"I have not been given much information about anything, much to my disappointment." I knew that I had to be careful, but not so careful that I sounded unconvincing.

"Evidently," I said calmly. "I do ask a lot of questions about certain subjects like religion, economy, education, and other basic areas that are part of human history. I have spent a great deal of time with the outside community learning how to deal with my newfound human emotions. And, as you know, I was pregnant and gave birth to my son, Frederic. I like being a mother." He shook his head complacently. "The library is open to me, but I do not select the information." I stopped again to evaluate my situation by closely observing him; his expression was neutral but he was nodding his head as if everything I said corresponded to his aspirations. "In any event, I am more focused on emotions, which I discuss regularly with Dr. Gordon. I would like to know more about the end of human history, Dr. Crawford, but all my efforts to learn more have been thwarted."

"Very well—very well indeed. We can leave it at that for the moment." He hesitated and added. "You should feel free to stop by to see me from time to time. I love music and always appreciated your skill as a pianist. We might have many more things in common. What do you think?"

"I think, Dr. Crawford, that it would be better for me to drop by to see you than for you to dramatically drag me into your office. Right?" He did not reply.

I got up and left wondering how informative this conversation was for me; and hoping that I had not passed onto him any vital information regarding my mission and our hopes for a better future. All that might be clearer to me with time. I was now certain that all the androids, including Dr. Crawford, knew that Dr. Gordon was committed to becoming human by discovering emotions. All the humans that I know believe that she is not going to make it. In any event, she is far from it.

I decided to drop by and see Randolph to let him know about this unexpected encounter with Dr. Crawford. Randolph was with his new assistant intent on carrying out a new experiment. He looked up when I rushed in and gave me a very reassuring smile. It made it easy to wait until he finished.

I sat watching him play with the different instruments as he produced parts that he inserted into an unfinished metal structure. He adjusted knobs and pushed buttons to secure them in place. The charts, graphic designs and complex mathematical formulae on the white board in front of him fascinated me. I was breathing slowly and calmly; my curiosity mounted.

I imagined myself working in a laboratory, surrounded by test tubes, machines, computers, and more, inspired by new mathematical formulae on a white board in front of me. I saw myself inventing, or reinventing, new machines and structures. My desire to participate in all of this scientific research amplified, only to be extinguished by the knowledge that it was too late for that. I sighed. No matter, I had other important things to do and I had too much responsibility at the moment to take on anything else. But, it was nice to dream and want to pretend to be in Randolph's world. I was so immersed in that dreamland that I didn't realize that his assistant had left for the day and that Randolph and I were. . . alone.

"Hi my favorite visitor." His arms were folded on the top of the table and he was leaning in my direction in that carefree, friendly manner of his. The way that he could see humor in life, making me laugh. I also imagined this seductive young man breaking lots of young girls' hearts in the future. "Are you ok?"

How could I answer that question? Of course, I wasn't ok. Yet, I wasn't sure how much of what was happening I wanted to share with him.

"Yes and no." His smile disappeared. "I don't know how to begin a discussion, Randolph." I said in a slow, soft voice. "So many things have happened that I don't know whether I am at the end or the beginning of something else."

"What can I do to help?" He asked in a voice agitated with concern.

"I don't know." I sighed, disheartened with the news I was going to announce. "I have been informed that a decision has been made to bring Frederic to the Center to be educated and that he will be have to be programmed; the visual receptor and the rest." Tears welled up in eyes for a second time today.

Randolph's body became tight with anger as his muscular arms bulged under the force of his serried fists. "I have had enough of their "android humor"—should we say?" He shouted. "It is time to finish with all of this."

"Dr. Flanders told me that Dr. Gordon was pushing for this, but that he would try to stall Frederic's arrival to the Center for several months." I stopped. "But, worse, not too long ago, Dr. Gordon told me that this idea was introduced by Dr. Crawford."

"We shall have to get organized; we are wasting precious time thinking instead of acting." He was definitely right.

"Brace yourself," I said to turn his attention off of dismantling androids. "Dr. Crawford grabbed me in the hallway, much like you did once; the whole scene with his hand over my mouth and a firm body grasp, his android force on maximum, and dragged me into his office."

"What did that wretched, beady-eyed, cantankerous bastard want?" He struck the lab table hard with his hand and then kicked over the empty lab chair, which made a loud, resounding sound when it fell, startling both of us.

"He was just curious about how much I had learned to date about the events bringing about the end of human history. That was the impression he gave me."

"No, he is a virtual snake, slithering around just waiting for the opportunity to swallow one of us. Watch out for him!" he warned me.

"I didn't tell him anything important; at least I don't think I did. He is, as you said, a slimy creation." I ran the conversation rapidly through my mind. "I think he wanted me to believe that he was my protector, not Dr. Gordon."

"Pamela," he took my face in his hands and looked intensely into my eyes. "None of these androids are your protector. You must keep that in mind all the time. You have to be on alert every time you meet one of them. Do you understand?"

"Yes, but. . ." His comforting arms were around me when I broke down in tears; choking and gagging under convulsive waves of anguish that spread through me. I don't know how long we stood like that, before we lowered ourselves onto the floor.

We both needed human contact, which is what drew us together. His flirtatiousness was simply innocent playfulness that made it so easy for me to seek sexual pleasure with him, something that only we humans could experience together. Just knowing that this world of physical sensations and lustful satisfaction was reserved for us humans, fully justified sex. I wondered sometimes if I was just promiscuous, or even a nymphomaniac, because I sought intimacy with Randolph, when I was in love with Peter. Did it make a difference? Peter drew a distinction between sex and making love; I have no other standard of morality to follow. And, Yes, Sex is my drug; a driving force that sustains me in this unrealistic environment. It elevates me, gives me an emotional high, energizes me and reminds me that I am human and alive. I made the first move this time when I ran my hands through Randolph's curly hair and drew his face up to mine.

"Are you sure, Pamela?" He asked, with a slight hesitation. I nodded. "Wait a minute. Just in case that miserable beast of a Gordon has found another way to observe me in my lab, I just want to send her a message. "Hey, Gordon, we are going to help you to break through your emotional barriers and feel jealous."

He cleared a space on his lab table and lifted me up. Just being in his arms for that brief moment before he laid me gently on that cold metal surface was all that I needed to feel that longing and desire for him. Was he putting on a show, a great show, for Dr. Gordon's benefit? The steamy caresses, sliding down my body that responded with molten gushes of pure emotion. . .was all that I could think about as we slowly unfolded our bodies and slid off that uncomfortable surface.

I would have told him that the risk, the danger of our adventure was our stimulus, but I couldn't because he was whispering how much he loves me; I know, though, that Randolph is a player, an actor, just like Mathilda.

We were about to pull off our robes when the door to the lab opened. In a split second, Stuart was facing us. I was embarrassed. "So what brings you to my lab this early in the day?" Randolph asked, irritation in his voice, as we both got back up on our feet and stood on either side of Stuart.

He was meticulously checking the lab for sound and video surveillance. Was he worried or angry? It wasn't that clear, because he always appeared very serious, calm and focused.

"We can't stay here any longer. It is too dangerous." He was speaking so softly.

We followed him out of the lab. He led us down unfamiliar corridors before we entered the transport wing. He opened the coded door to the vehicle terminal, the land and air transport unit of the Center, filled with big and small transport vehicles. For the first time, I saw a way out of this turbulent world we lived in. John was right, we can break in here and steal the transporters and look for a better place to live, far away from android surveillance. There were many varieties, big and heavy land vehicles alongside slim, single passenger vehicles floating in an anti-gravity state. Some of them had heavy weaponry attached to the outside, laser and missile projectors. Others looked quite harmless, appearing unarmed. I was to learn later on that the unarmed ones were the most rapid and dangerous, because the weaponry became visible when a target came in range.

"Do you know how to operate these machines?" The same question echoed from Randolph and me.

"Some of them." He was still stiff from fear. "You need keys. I sent some keys to the others. But, we have a problem!"

We sat on the floor hidden behind two huge armored vehicles and talked. Stuart wanted me to tell him everything I knew to date, what I had learned since the last time we met. I unraveled everything about what I saw in the birth center. He and Randolph sat comfortably, their legs drawn up under them and their arms relaxed, and they listened intently to what I had to say. I told them everything from A to Z.

I ended by revealing the identity of my biological mother; her agelessness, her power of manipulation, her brilliant discoveries, her programming the androids emotionally, the self-destruction of her android opposite and her order to erase the emotional programming from the other androids that worked closely with her. When I told them that Dr. Flanders ordered the termination of Pamela 14, my replacement, and wants me to see the last film he has of my biological mother, Dr. Elisabeth Reinhart, apparently a remarkable genius, they gasped in awe. Simultaneously, they asked, "What is Flanders' objective?"

"He mentioned that I could be her; that I could lead armies and win battles." They looked at me like I changed from Pamela to someone else before their eyes. "He even suggested that I could be a great scientist if I wanted to be. That he could help me to become Dr. Elisabeth Reinhart..."

"I don't know if I should keep his suggestion that I pursue a career in science a secret, or I should talk to the Governor about it." I was so excited about the idea that I could hear the enthusiasm in my own voice and in my dramatic gesticulations. I was convincing myself that I should go forward with this project. "I think that our group needs a new leader." I rambled on. "John was the chosen leader and has played that role effectively over the years. He forced the Governor to let our group leave the Center, an excellent move. I just think that the time has come for new leadership. If I could emulate my biological Mother, then I would be able to lead all us into a better future."

They sat speechless; their bodies rigid and their eyes glued on me.

"Dr. Flanders worships Reinhart; he is under her spell. I am certain that the Governor shares his admiration for this woman and, well, Dr. Gordon would follow them. I do believe that it is in my interest and in the interest of our group to pursue this option. I shall have to learn more from Dr. Flanders about how he wants to proceed." I paused. "I'll be seeing the cassette tomorrow. I can't wait. So what do you think?"

Just silence. "Hey!" I flung my hands in their faces. "Hey, Randolph, Stuart, I am still, Pamela."

"Incredible story." Stuart spoke, in a barely audible, raspy voice, "You do what you think is best. We," he looked at Randolph who nodded, "are behind you 100 percent and will be there if you need us. Yes, you'll have to do what you think is best, taking into account the personality of Dr. Reinhart and the maliciousness of the androids." He swallowed hard, as if some of what I had told him was stuck in his throat. "It is just, Pamela, that, from what you mentioned, and I am certain that there is more that you kept to yourself, this Dr. Reinhart appears to have been a very cold and calculating woman. We can protect you against the androids, but we can't protect you against her or against yourself. Do you understand?"

"Yes." I did understand now that he put it that way. "I shall be careful." Many thoughts passed rapidly through my mind. I was not as worried as Stuart. I did not see myself as frail and naïve. Their lack of enthusiasm bothered me. Is it because I am not a man, but a woman, that they doubt my ability? Or, is it because I give the impression, with my emotional highs and lows, that I am irrational, that they doubt my leadership ability? Perhaps Dr. Flanders is right, I have to learn how to control my emotions. I turned back to them and smiled pleasantly, to hide my disappointment.

"One more point," Stuart again broke the silence, "the problem I mentioned in the beginning, well, I am a bit worried about my situation. The androids have ignored me up until now to my advantage. Associating with you, in particular, Pamela, has put me in a risk situation." His eyes squinted and his lips tightened. "I noticed that I am being followed by android trackers. I know how to lose them. What bothers me is that there are a couple young humans who are accompanying these androids during maneuvers. They must be training for ninja style combat. I can take down the androids but taking down the humans at the same time may be more than I can handle." He stopped, his eyes penetrating mine. "I don't show my stress. I have learned over the years how to hide my emotions. But my insides are tied up in knots!"

"Perhaps I can reassure you about this. Dr. Gordon holds you in high esteem and considers you to be a brilliant mathematician and physicist; as well as accomplished in robotics. She would not let you be terminated." She mentioned Stuart to me before in a laudatory fashion. I felt safe with what I said.

"I think I need time to digest all of this. Will catch up with you both over the next week." Randolph finally said something, even though it was not what I was hoping for.

Stuart led us back through the labyrinth of corridors and we split up to go to our own cubicles. I had a strong feeling that my life was about to change, radically.

Chapter 40: Transformation

Returning to the outside community was not my priority, even though the knowing tremor of homesickness often attached me in the night and I would wake up missing Peter and Frederic. It was time that I followed my own instincts. It was time that I did things my own way, without having the approval of anyone else. While the atrocities that my Biological mother had committed were unpardonable, her scientific contributions were extraordinary. I had no doubt that my destiny was linked to her and I had to find out why.

Dr. Reinhart's faithful androids accomplished the unthinkable when they recreated her physical likeness in me. How did they imagine now that they could give me her intellectual superiority? How were they going to transform a brilliant pianist into a brilliant scientist destined to be a formidable leader? I was curious about what they were going to propose; and, hoped that I would remain rational and cautious and that I would not let myself be misled by their enthusiasm. Stuart said that I should do what I think is best, taking into account the personality of Dr. Reinhart and the maliciousness of the androids. In retrospect, that advice was the best advice that anyone could have given me. "Thank you, Stuart," I said out loud, "I shall do just that."

As I walked slowly into that tiny padded room to meet Dr. Flanders, I felt as if a heavy burden had been thrust upon me. He recognized the change in me and let me speak. And, I asked him to retrain me in the scientific field of my genetic mother. He surprised me and agreed. We chatted enthusiastically about how and when all this could be done. He wanted me to go back to my programming so that I could absorb the information more rapidly. Naturally, I refused. I didn't trust the android programmers as they could, during the process, terminate me and call it a terrible mistake. Thoughts of Crawford made me quail; my body began shaking involuntarily, again. Also, I wondered if I might end up a prisoner in my own mind.

"There is a serious risk that we will not be able to properly monitor the rapidity of the absorption process and stop any corrosive effect linked thereto.

The absorption of her knowledge could damage your mind if you reach undetectable levels of saturation."

I threw up my hands and yelled stop. "I don't understand anything."

"Ok, I'll try to simplify. Your mind might just collapse from absorbing too much information too fast but the programming system will signal absorption problems so that we can stop and start up again later on. The programming would buffer the impact of rapid absorption and assure real success. I strongly advise you to have the programming." I shook my head in a definitive "No."

He paced up and down the room scratching his android head. "Please, listen to me. We don't have any neurobiologists in this Center. We are not that knowledgeable about how the human memory functions in a non-programmed state. How, for example it decodes, registers and later retrieves information. The visual receptor has other programming capacity, one of which allows for cataloging of memory. By using our programming techniques, your own brain, its cerebral processes, do not have to catalog the vast amount of information in rapid sequence." I listened.

"If you are afraid that we will keep you programmed and use you for us; you are wrong. Once she, Dr. Reinhart, is present inside of you, you will be able to undo any harmful system. And, once she is present we will obey orders." I still nodded "No."

"And, Pamela, we need you to be a complete human, so we won't keep you programmed." He tried very hard to persuade me, but I refused; I wanted my mind to be unhampered, free of their programming, and no more microchips attaching my brain to a visual receptor. "One more point is that, without the programming, even if you had the capacity to retain or store the information, you might not be able to access the information let alone put that information to use and/or develop new applications. The programming would eliminate eventual problems."

"You raised good arguments, Dr. Flanders." I had to have things my way. "I don't want programming. I want to have a rescue button available to me if I find that the absorption is too rapid or that my mind is oversaturated. I shall signal the problem and then you, or whoever is there, will stop everything."

"I still think that programming would be better. I shall talk to the others about all of this." In the meantime, I want you to see the last two videos. "

As always, he opened up his jacket, exposing his android flesh and pushed down on his stomach region. The flesh opened up and exposed a small screen, on metal supports, that moved several inches away from the interior metal structure of his body. He tapped into his memory bank and uploaded the film onto the screen. He always stood during the replays of these scenes; I assumed that it was because he was more comfortable in that position.

Dr. Elisabeth Reinhart was sitting behind a large wooden desk. She had only a few papers in front of her. On either side stood the android, Dr. Flanders, and an android that looked very much like Dr. Crawford. In a flash, the desk turned into a huge podium placed in the middle of a circular auditorium. Dr. Flanders and Dr. Crawford were still on either side of her. She stood straight and proud behind the lectern with her hands firmly gripping its sides. She smiled radiantly at the audience, waiting for the shrill screaming and applauding to die down.

"Ladies and Gentlemen, friends and colleagues, members of the Global Community to Preserve the Human Race, we have a difficult task in front of us. The winds of war are felt everywhere. The lower intellectuals are fighting amongst themselves over who will wage the battle against us." She said calmly but sternly, articulating clearly every word. Her voice changed, as she sought to motivate the crowd, addressing them with her vibrant, charismatic energy. "We are not afraid!" "Their efforts are futile!"

She waited for the audience to calm down. "But, ladies and gentlemen, we do not have that same hatred towards them that they hold for us. We don't want to destroy them. We need these non-intellectual humans to free us from menial tasks; and we need them to serve our daily needs so that we can continue to use out intellectual capacity to achieve greatness." The audience was roaring and applauding with enthusiasm.

"We have evolved. We have gone beyond simple day-to-day chores of surviving and we have reached the horizons beyond our wildest of dreams. We have penetrated and now occupy that exclusive domain once reserved for the ominous, supreme being, God." The audience sat spellbound by her words.

Her voice changed becoming soft and foreboding. "We know that what happened in the past is happening today. We know that we can predict what will happen in the future. And, there, ladies and gentlemen lies our imminent problem..." She let her voice carry, revealing her frustration.

"We must prevent our," she breathed out, and her eyes glinted with emotion, "demise!" I could hear the gasping sounds from the audience.

"I have, as you all can witness, discovered the key to immortality." There were noises coming from the audience. "I am ready now to share this with all of you." She stopped until the rumbling calmed down. "But my offer of immortality has a price." There was total silence as they listened intently. "We have the burden of preserving the human race as it is today; a human race comprised both of superior and inferior intellect. We need to save our opposites. Your immortality is in your hands. You follow me in my campaign to find peace and harmony with the inferior class of humans and I shall give you immortality. If you refuse---then I alone shall continue to live on forever." There was clamor in the audience as some members started to move or stand up to leave. She continued with extraordinary energy in her voice. "Our destiny is upon us. Our existence is threatened. We must prevent our mutual annihilation."

"So if you think that we have to save those who threaten us to achieve some sort of perfect balance in nature, then what solution do you propose?" The camera did not capture the person speaking; her voice, however, was full of mockery and contempt. "And you try to buy our cooperation by promising immortality. How can we be sure that you will respect your part of the bargain?

"I give you my word!" There was laughter. Someone yelled out, "Prove it now! Take one of us and make that person immortal right before our eyes."

Her eyes grew stern and her mouth drew up in anger. "My word should be enough!" She screamed out in a high, piercing tone. "And now, for the rest, the solution resides on our generosity." Dr. Reinhart answered in a soft, sullen voice. "Compromise seems impossible. We cannot work side by side with those whose sense of justice, education, welfare, value, whose ideas of life will drag us back in time. We cannot return to the past and give them participation in government."

She looked out upon the audience her eyes searching for allies. "Our story is now, here today where we have achieved excellence. We are at the pinnacle of our existence. And, yet, we cannot survive without our opposites. They are like rebellious children. We must, therefore, calm them down by offering them more comfort. We can placate them so that they will want to survive and serve us." She had tears in her eyes and her throat was choked with sorrow. "How can we call ourselves superior, if we resort to something so treacherous and primitive like the annihilation of our less fortunate children?" I found her statement in total conflict with what she had actually done in the past, destroying all those space voyagers. Was she different now, more compassionate?

Someone in the audience screamed—"You may look young, Dr. Reinhart, but your ideas are old and are certainly not those of a leader." He then continued in a thundering voice. "There is an easy solution, send the androids out to kill them—wipe them out." Others agreed by shouting: "yes, send the androids. They can fight for us. And afterwards, they will serve us, perform menial tasks, just like the non-intellectuals today."

I saw Dr. Flanders' and Dr. Crawford's heads drop. They were being condemned without the opportunity to defend themselves.

"And, they will fight with what? "She screamed back.

"They will fight like in the past, with knives and guns. As the inferior humans do not have access to our technology, or our machines of total destruction, we will give them a chance. Our androids will fight on equal terms; our androids will fight with their hands just like the others. And, only if these androids lose will we disintegrate this inferior class of humans with our weaponry. Whatever happens, we will win!"

She held her own and got back the attention of the audience by pounding violently on the lectern. "This is a solution, if you want to resort to war. I was expecting something different from all of you. I was expecting that your intelligence had not stripped you of compassion for those less fortunate." An uneasy silence set in. "Intelligence, void of compassion, is revolting!"

"Who are you to speak of atrocities? You committed them." A soft, feminine voice interrupted her.

"You are right. I regret what I did." Dr. Reinhart was not ready to give in. "Because I made a horrible mistake does mean that we, all of us, should make that same mistake a second time." She paused. "No one should be fighting, neither us, nor these magnificent android creations. It would be a pity to destroy them and they are not programmed to fight. War is not the right decision. So I ask again, does anyone have another humanitarian solution to propose?"

"Yes, I do." Another male voice exploding. "Bring those inferior humans into the center and shut down the life support systems. We have the capacity to survive with proper equipment. We would protect ourselves and let them die." The audience was silent. "Even if this alternative sounds hideous, it would still be a gift to them…the end of their miserable lives."

Dr. Reinhart sighed and shook her head. "Oh, how treacherous we have grown." She was not ready to give up as she repeated one more time. "We need each other; we need earthly opposites because they play an important role in our lives. And, they assure a natural balance."

Another strong, male voice from the audience was heard, "Even though I don't agree at all with Dr. Reinhart's perverse reasoning, I believe that wars and battles are heinous. And, if we use our weapons, we could destroy our environment. These weapons are too powerful. They were developed to end all life." There was no response to him.

"I agree with shutting down life support long enough to exterminate the lower class." Someone else had the floor. "Let's just destroy the lower species of humans. We don't need them. You feel guilty, Reinhart, because of what you did in the past. We never criticized you. You convinced us that you did the right thing. The only question we have to answer today is: Do we want to survive?"

"I am embarrassed with your cold, inhuman suggestions. We must, as I said before, placate them. They will calm down and everything will return to normal."

"No, Dr. Reinhart, you are wrong on every point." For whatever reason the camera was focused on him. He was tall and robust, with long blond wavy hair, that fell naturally around his face; a slightly older version of Randolph. He was wearing a khaki-colored uniform and he had, what looked to be a laser gun slung over his right shoulder. He took long strides across the auditorium and stepped up on to the podium. He had one of those flirtatious smiles on his face that Randolph loved to flash at me as he approached Dr. Reinhart. "Hello Elisabeth."

"What are you doing here, Dr. Murdoc?"

He spoke softly, "Trying to save you from yourself. We need you as a leader, not the soft, pushover you are today." She lost control and rushed at him, pounding her fists into his chest, taking out her anger and frustration. When she tired, he grabbed her hands tightly in his, looked intensely into her eyes, and spoke to her between clenched teeth, in a voice too low for the audience to hear. "It is over, Elisabeth. I just came back from the bush, the outback. They are running wild. It is bloody dangerous out there. I am lucky that I got out of there alive. We have no choice now but to fight. And, I am not so certain that we shall win."

"But, the androids, those who embody the essence of former colleagues…" She didn't have chance to finish.

He turned to the audience and screamed. "We shall fight! We shall win!" His voice resonated in his call to arms. He continued under the uproars from the audience. "The solution was given to us. The androids, all the androids without exception, shall do the dirty work for us; and I shall reprogram them to kill!" He exclaimed.

The audience was screaming, applauding and asking for a vote. The vote was unanimously in favor of having the androids reprogrammed to fight. The members moved to leave, chanting, Dr. Murdoc, Dr. Murdoc, over and over again.

Dr. Reinhart made one last futile effort. The auditorium was practically empty when she urged them to return to their homes and reconsider their decision. "Members of the Global Community to Save the Human Race, you still have time to change your mind. We can meet in a few days to take another vote and anyone who has another solution can come to see me any time over the next few days."

And then her podium transformed back into her desk. The auditorium disappeared and she was alone with her two androids, Dr. Flanders and Dr. Crawford?

Dr. Flanders did not give me the opportunity to ask questions before the final disk started to run, picking up where the other ended.

"Did you hear what they said? All the androids; that means us as well." Dr. Crawford asked.

"Yes, I heard them but I am not ready to sacrifice you." She answered softly.

"I am what is left of him. I am the android creation of Dr. Crawford." His voice got screechy. "How can you send me to war? How can you let me be your servant?"

"The vote was taken in a very democratic way. I know that they are not going to change their minds." Tears were running down her face and her voice was choked up with emotion. "Unlike the two of you, though, I shall suffer."

"How will you suffer, Dr. Reinhart?" The Crawford android went on to ask.

"I will be humiliated every time I see, you and others, that through my genius housed the intellect of foregone friends and colleagues, treated like simple robotic machines. To see all that I worked for, all that I adored and coveted, either destroyed in battle or forced into servitude."

"Make android soldiers," he suggested.

"No! No! I cannot do that. There is no way to control those kinds of creations. It is, also, an offense to my intelligence to ask me to make toy soldiers, when I am able to create geniuses that resemble me."

"Then, is it more of an intellectual task to die?"

"It is intellectual to transcend this reality and capture another, if the immortality that I created here on earth has some form of transcendence."

"Then I shall help you to experience the better of the two worlds." And, with that he slipped around the back of her, slid his right arm over her shoulder and around her neck, and searing her neck tightly in the fold of his arm, he used his left hand to turn her head, swiftly and violently, cracking her neck in two.

The clip ended and Flanders was shaking his android head. I looked into his pathetic, blank eyes and screamed: "He killed her!"

"Yes. Yes, of course. It was the right and logical thing to do. As she said, she would suffer. We couldn't let that happen. She was our creator, our protector, we didn't want her to suffer."

"Was it the Dr. Crawford here at this Center who killed her?" I asked.

"Yes. The android community applauded his decision."

"And, what about her human intellectual colleagues? How did they react?" Hoping that he would tell me that they tried to vindicate her death.

"You will find out later what happened. It is not the right moment for me to disclose more." I reached out to strangle him when he grabbed my hands in a firm grip.

"I don't understand." I struggled to release his grip. "What he did was monstrous. He ended the life of someone who could have made many more marvelous contributions scientifically to humans, and even to you androids."

"True." He released me. "But, she would have suffered. He gave her what humans want, happiness in a new reality."

"You are a bunch of fools. The rudimentary emotional configuration she gave you was not enough to make you understand what she was saying." I grabbed his body and shook him violently back and forth. I wanted him to feel my anger. "How stupid could you be? Logical? She didn't want to die. Abominable, stupid, dumb bastard machine! You make me sick. You are revolting!"

I kept on like that for at least 5 minutes. He said nothing and when I finally sat down exhausted by my useless efforts to shake or talk sense to a machine, he commented.

"Pamela, believe me, her death was only a few hours or a few days premature, she would have died anyway; and she would have died a cruel death. Dr. Crawford gave her a quick and merciful one. This film was the beginning of a rapid end to human history." I did not know what to say. "Would you like to accompany me now to see the Governor to discuss your accessing Dr. Reinhart's memory banks?"

"Not yet," there was something else that was bothering me and I wanted him to clarify it. "When they spoke about moving the non-intellectuals into a Center and shutting down the life support system, what did they mean?"

"Oh!" He bit down on his android finger. "I don't think that any of us are competent to explain this structure well. So, my explanation is probably as good as anyone else's." He looked up at the ceiling for inspiration. "You saw this center when you were on the outside, so you know that we are living in a dome---a very high ceiling dome that gives the impression that we are in open space." He started to play with his fingers, moving them one at a time as if he were counting out the next series of explanations.

"The environment was unstable at the end of human history, and, effectively for a long time before. The intellectual community had a system in place that would maintain clean air, proper levels of oxygen, for example. The system was invisible to the naked eye. All the intellectual cities were built in a circle with the detection system encircling the outer limits. There was a protective screen, invisible to the naked eye that maintained proper air, temperature, humidity, and so forth, by emitting corrective beams to insure the maximum comfort for humans."

His brows furrowed and his lips grew tight. "The non-intellectuals were exposed to all the natural elements like heat, cold, storms and harmful pollutants. All those non-intellectuals who lived in the Center to serve the Intellectuals benefited from that invisible bubble of protection."

"Those living in the outback were not so lucky. They too worked for the intellectuals, growing food, working mines, clearing forests, and so forth. The Intellectual community provided them with proper shelter, clothing and food, but their standard of living was still inferior, because of the environment itself. That is why they revolted."

"That being the case, bringing them into the center to die, doesn't make sense?" I was definitely confused.

"Yes, it does. The intellectuals would have released massive doses of toxic waste and pollutants. The proposal was basically chemical warfare in a confined environment; a despicable, inhumane act." He shook his head violently, as he let out a long, tedious breath of air. "After they were dead, the life support system would have been reinstated to clean up any toxic wastes. During this period, the intellectuals, who were very sensitive to the caustic air outside the center, would have had to use air masks and to wear protective clothing to survive. Fortunately, this solution was not approved."

"And, the young man who came in from the outback, how did he survive out there?"

"He passed between the two zones regularly. There were others who did the same. Their systems tolerated the harsh environment and adjusted easily."

How could humans be so cruel? Maybe we should be programmed if this is what human emotions produce? My mouth had fallen open and my eyes were glazed with fear.

Maybe these android monsters were nicer and kinder than most humans. I had no desire now to move off this chair. What was the point of learning more, if in the end I would be one of those wretched creatures who had no respect for human life, who could be more of a cold-blooded monster than the android standing in front of me? He reached out to me and took my hand pulling me to my feet. "Are you ready now to accompany me to the Governor's office?"

He led me down the corridors to the Governor's office. The long walk helped me to recover from those horrifying stories. My desire to go forward with the Reinhart project was restored. We arrived and Dr. Gordon rushed in behind us. They started to talk among themselves. They might have been considered excited, as their faces were mechanically twitched to look like distorted, even forced, smiles that ended like self-satisfied smirks. They were better at mimicking human facial expressions; since their emotional configuration was so primitive, it was not clear what they wanted to communicate to me. I waited until they stopped chattering and turned to me for answers. It was the Governor who addressed me first.

"I wholly approve of your decision to undertake scientific training. But, you should follow Dr. Flanders' advice; let us reinstall your visual receptor as a protective measure. You don't want your mind to shut down, do you? Or, worse, you may not be able to deal with the retraining and that it might end… well your life."

"I know." I turned away disgusted. "I understand the risk. I want to be alert; and I refuse categorically reprogramming."

They did not bring it up again. I suppose that I should have shown some more concern for my own life, after all I had Peter and Frederic who loved me and wanted me back. But, I was only focused on discovering what Dr. Reinhart knew and having her…power. I had trouble connecting the dots!

"How can you give me this training when you never knew what she knew?"

"I shall explain this." The Governor looked at his colleagues who nodded in approval. "Generally, we use disks to transmit information to you humans, but disks were actually primitive forms of registering knowledge. The more advanced form, which required very little space for storage, was using empty DNA strands; a life form that is preserved in a liquid state in a test tube. Most of these DNA registrations were destroyed at the end of human history. But, we managed to salvage her DNA knowledge bank. Are you following me, Pamela?"

"As well as I can, please go on."

"She gave us her knowledge encoded in these data rich DNA strands, in a test tube, a few weeks before she died and asked me to keep it with me at all times. She left instructions on how to connect this live substance to a computer that would read and transmit her knowledge to you."

"Before you killed her," I interjected.

"Whatever pleases you, Pamela," Gordon said. "We are not here to discuss human ideas of morality. We are here to find solutions for the world today. And, if you can achieve her level of intellectual maturity, then perhaps we can all live better. You can save the world."

I was not yet certain that I was not being led into some kind of trap. "If you have her intellectual configuration, why haven't you used it yourselves? Couldn't you just manufacture someone who looks and thinks like her?"

"We are not human." They echoed each other.

So, Dr. Reinhart didn't trust these androids either, I thought to myself. But, she was not careful enough because she got herself killed. "So what do you, you androids, want?"

"We want a better life." They again echoed the same time. It was like they were wired together.

"A better life." I started laughing. "What more could you want. You rule the world and you control the human existence. You stopped recording our history and started writing your own. What more could you want?"

There was a long silence this time. Finally, Dr. Gordon spoke up. "We were on our way to joining you. She put an end to all of that, as you know, when she ordered us to erase the emotional programming. Those of us who were left with weak strands of this primitive emotional programming are like a hybrid, neither androids nor humans. We are a small number and ready to put all our energy and knowledge into helping humans recover their own history on the condition we can share in that history as part of the human race."

"How can you be certain that I will do that? That I won't be as vicious as she was? You are not worried that I might not order you to shut down. Could you resist that order?" I was testing them. They were so potentially diabolical that I could not even imagine what unpleasant or dangerous scheme they may have designed for me. Additionally, I needed to know that I would not be as cruel as she was. In spite of her good qualities and desire to be more compassionate with the non-intellectuals at the end of her life, she was cold-blooded. I did not want to receive her emotional configuration, just her knowledge.

They all tried to assure me that that would not happen. "It is only her knowledge that has been preserved in the DNA strands. And, she would have been different, kinder, more benevolent with the non-intellectuals, like she was earlier in her life, and, as you saw, just before she died, if her husband had not been brutally murdered and dismembered by the lower class. Your basic nature, Pamela, which is much kinder than hers ever was, would never allow you to become the person she was." The Governor reassured me.

It didn't matter that I wasn't completely convinced by what they said. I wanted her knowledge so badly that I was ready and willing to take the risk.

"Ok. I am ready to go forward. As I told Dr. Flanders, I want an emergency system available to me that allows me to signal someone if I recognize a 'mental overload.' And, I don't want Dr. Crawford to be around me at this time. I don't trust him. "

"Pamela," Dr. Gordon was speaking to me patronizingly as she took my hand in hers and patted it. "Dr. Crawford is not an easy android to interact with, but he was completely devoted to Dr. Reinhart. We all agreed that he made the right decision when he ended her life." She stared at me looking for an expression of approval that I was not going to give her. "Well, Dr. Crawford lives and relives that scene over and over again. He is just not convinced that his decision was purely logical and not based upon some, as he says, vial human emotion. He argues that if he had never received that primitive emotional configuration that he struggled to erase completely, and had a tiny taste of what he refers to as irrational, emotional human decision-making, he might never have ended her life. That is why he opposes my study of human emotions. He believes that human emotions are the source of all evil."

I wished that I could read their minds. Something was wrong again. I could hardly believe they were trying to convince me that Crawford was right in killing my Mother and that I should not be afraid of him, when he had just warned me recently about them. How vicious and manipulative they are. Something was missing in this puzzle. I loathed to consider it, but I may be required to contact Crawford to clarify what was going on.

"Alright. I am ready." Seeing Crawford can wait and, maybe I'll understand these androids better once I receive Reinhart's knowledge. "Just tell me how long all of this will take?"

"It should be rapid. We will keep track of your ability to absorb day by day. If we notice that your brain waves are irregular or if we receive a signal from you, we shall stop and restart the program at a later date. But, if all goes well, it should take less than a month. Meaning, mind tracing all day and all night." Dr. Flanders explained.

"And, you are certain that I have the capacity to absorb all the information and understand it."

"No doubt. You could have been in the science department." Answered the Governor. "I told you that we were unhappy with the other series because they bypassed the programming. It was Dr. Gordon here that convinced us that bypassing the programming was indeed what we needed from your series. We needed creativity and your species needs emotions to be creative. We shall see if Dr. Gordon was right."

"A month is a long time. How am I going to survive? "

"You'll be fed by intravenous." Dr. Flanders spoke up.

"Wait a minute." I held up my hands as blockage. "Not the same chemicals I received in the past."

"No!" Dr. Gordon replied energetically. "You will be receiving nutritional substances."

I was feeling nervous now. I should probably run directly out this center and not go forward with this project. Again, the urge to be as brilliant as her was so strong that I followed them to the educational center.

Within minutes I was in front of the terminal with an enormous cask planted on my head. I was focusing my attention on that screen and learning about mathematics and science. It was more difficult than during childhood when my mind was more open, less jaded. And other thoughts ran through my mind parallel to the Reinhart program that invaded my consciousness and made it difficult for me to concentrate. Streams of questions like: Would I still love Peter? Would I be able to interact with my friends? Would I still be a talented pianist? I was also distracted from the programming, by noises, movements, flashing lights on the screen, making it impossible for me to retain anything in the beginning. The androids were not discouraged and continued to download the same information several days in a row, until eventually, my mind retained it and my concentration became ultra-intense.

Learning was visual when I was awake and verbal when I slept. I had no real notion of time. I was aware that I was receiving continual information, even if I didn't have the time to fully digest and understand any of it. The androids never had to stop the flow of information as I was capable of absorbing it at a fast pace; and, eventually reached a level of saturation when I received all that she knew in the vast fields of mathematics and science.

For a brief instance, I was conscious of my surroundings, only to be distracted again by the sound of a voice that sent chills through my body. "You are one of my descendants. I know that because I verified your genetic code before authorizing the flow of information. You must not be afraid. We are being merged together on a purely intellectual level. What I have given to you is the entire bank of human scientific discovery, from the earliest point in our history until my time. I have not replaced you. You are still the same person that you were before. But, you have given me immortality, through you. Whether or not my personality will develop in you depends upon you and how you see yourself in the time and place you occupy now. Whether my essence is being sent to you and absorbed by you-- or you are directly entering my brain waves and absorbing that way--makes no difference. The main thing is that my secrets are so important that I hope you will use them for good and not evil.

Close your eyes now, my child, and listen. Listen very closely, as I explain the secret of life and the secret of my immortality."

Chapter 40: Power

Night had fallen and I slept. The buzzing from the machines cradled me like the sound of the train passing in the night. I don't know how long I slept and the androids were unable to tell me how long the programming had lasted. But, when I opened my eyes their faces were upon me and a fourth face hid in back of the group. It was Dr. Crawford.

"No, you are not all here. Dr. Miller is missing." I said. Something had radically changed from before the programming. Emotions swirled inside me, my heart palpitated as I automatically felt differently about the four standing over me. I had great affection for them, for these machines; an affection that I had never felt before, as if they were my children. The corners of my mouth seemed to involuntarily stretch into a wide smile. It disgusted me. "How, how?" I mused

Dr. Crawford spoke first. "You are back Elisabeth. I have missed you so much over all these years." He approached me, taking my hand in his and kissing it softly. "Dr. Miller will join us later."

I was still obnoxiously smiling, but resigned myself that I was no longer totally in control of my emotions. "No, I am not Elisabeth Reinhart. I am Pamela Series 13, but I understand you much better now. I realize that you embarked on a courageous mission; that you worked closely together to build a new world. And, I forgive you for all the terrible things that you have done. Yes, I forgive you for all the terrible things that you have done in the interest of saving humanity."

"What terrible things, Elisabeth?" Dr. Crawford asked. Before I could answer, he kneeled down on the floor and bowed his head. "I am so sorry Elisabeth. I should never have harmed you, killed you. I thought that I was protecting you from suffering. I have been unable to erase that terrible memory from my system. I am so sorry."

"I am not Elisabeth. I am Pamela." I repeated. "I forgive you for stripping humans of their dignity, by programming them. That and the humiliating consequences of your programming of humans, is what I forgive you for, because I sincerely believe that you didn't understand just how cruel you have been." Dr. Crawford stood up and moved close to his colleagues. They joined hands, showing me their solidarity, and stared at me.

I stood up and stretched, "I need to be alone. And, I want to take a shower and have something to eat." I noticed that they were whispering to each other. They were confused as to who I was and this worked to my advantage. They escorted me back to my cubicle and left, bowing to me as if I were someone important. I enjoyed it to the extent that I was finally treated with some kind of dignity and not the guinea pig in Dr. Gordon's experiments. I also realized that I could do whatever I wanted now. They believed that I was Reinhart, even when I told them that I wasn't. Maybe I should play it out. Yet, I was slightly confused myself as to who I was. My mind was cluttered with a massive amount of information; it was almost like my mind was carrying a heavy weight inside of it. I had no idea how to retrieve the information let alone use. What I definitely needed was to be with my family and friends to mentally put things in place.

I took a long shower and put on the clean, white smock that was hanging on the rack in my room. The table was laden with all the kinds of food that I liked and that were recommended for me so that I would stay slim and fit. I ate the crunchy colorful pieces of vegetables, carrots, celery, salad, radishes, cucumbers… and then devoured with pleasure the apples, bananas, oranges… after which I quickly rushed to catch the monorail to see Randolph.

He jumped up when he saw me and accused me of having let him down over the last month. When I questioned him about the length of my absence, he showed me a primitive wall calendar and the days that he had ticked off since he last saw me.

"I didn't know that you had a wall calendar?" was all that came to mind.

"I didn't until I realized that you were missing." He said, raising his masculine voice to a stronger level, to show me how concerned he was. "And, I didn't start ticking off the dates for more than a week after your disappearance, when I came up with this calendar. Do you realize that you have been gone for probably 6 weeks?"

"No. I didn't know that." I said as I frowned and bit down on my lip; my involuntary reflex when I was confronted with adversity. The androids said that they had no idea of how long my programming took. "Randolph, I am going to tell you a story that you are probably not going to believe. Please sit down and listen closely. Remember when I told you that Dr. Flanders told me that I could be my biological Mother?"

"What?" He moved nervously in his seat. "Pamela, you did not let those android creations play around with your mind? "He grabbed me by my shoulders. "Look into my eyes and tell me that you didn't do that?"

I turned away. "I decided to acquire all her knowledge."

Randolph took his head in his hands and pressed down on his temples. "Don't do that? I am fine." I retorted. "I did not let the androids reprogram me with the visual receptor. I stayed mentally alert during the more than six weeks of the absorption process. And, Randolph, my mind is now just bulging with information; I don't know whether it might explode."

His eyes were big and his mouth twisted in a strange expression, which I identified as disbelief. It took only a few seconds before he threw his head back in laughter. At least one of us had not changed.

"Oh, Pamela, those androids are simply crazy creations. You don't believe that they downloaded all of that woman's intelligence into your brain? They probably just put you in suspended animation for a whole month."

His laughter made me feel embarrassed about everything. "Please sit down and think about it." He went on. "The last time that we talked we were hoping that you would be able to learn more. Right?" I nodded. "Do you remember that Stuart and I were rather surprised by your confidence in these androids to make you a brilliant scientist? It just does not work like that."

"No, it doesn't work like that. Do you know about the use of DNA strands as the most efficient way of stocking or storing information?" I asked.

"Heard about it, but never used it." He answered. He was holding himself straight and leaning his head in patient attentiveness while flaunting an air of superiority.

I told him what they did and how I spent 24 hours a day for more than one month receiving all the information. I even went so far as to tell him that I wasted a bit of time in the beginning because I was not able to properly concentrate. When I finished I said. "Ok, Randolph, I told you what happened. Would you like me to prove it to you?"

Was it the tone of my voice or my facial expression that turned his grinning face into an angry scowl? "No!" He grabbed my arm rather brutally and I shook and slapped him away. He didn't move, as if he were testing me. I stood staring angrily back, trying to come to grasp with the situation. Where was my life heading? And, worse, who am I? Was I still Pamela or was I someone else? I didn't hear him at first, picking him up half way through.

"…You should have come and talked to me about their offer. I know that you mentioned the possibility of retraining, but, we, Stuart and I, never imagined that you would go through with it. In fact, we were both so worried; afraid that they had terminated you. No news from you for a month. And, to make it worse, we were being followed. We had to avoid each other. They must be onto us. And, now look at you! You gloat over being some superior being. So, go ahead, if you are such a brilliant scientist now, tell me what I should do next?"

He offended me and I felt nothing but bitterness and anger. For a brief instance, I imagined that he might be jealous of my capability. So I answered in simple terms "I not only can tell you what you should do next, Randolph. But, I can give you the ultimate design for the future." And, then, I proceeded to do just that, surprising myself to a certain extent, with just how much I knew. It was clear that he too was impressed, perhaps even mesmerized by how easily I laid out the formulas and intricate designs. It was clear that I had absorbed and understood all that information, and that Elisabeth Reinhart... had returned. But was I ready for that and what might happen?

He stammered: "But you have given me the perfect design and correct configuration of a robotic structure that does not even exist. You should never have been able to do that; at least, you could not have done that one month ago." He plopped down on the chair and shook his head and looked at me like he was looking at a freak, a mutant.

"I told you that I was retrained. I don't know how she accumulated all that knowledge. Her real age was never known. But, it is certain that she was involved in every important scientific discovery, indirectly or directly, and she understood and memorized all the technological advances, and then created her own. That is if she was not the only driving force in all this creativity, no one else is ever mentioned."

"And, you, do you feel different?" His worried eyes followed me as I walked around the room, checking the charts and graphs on the wall. I turned and assured him that I did not feel any different. I avoided mentioning that intense merging sensation I had just hours before, when I imagined myself being nourished by some strong, underlying force.

His unbridled enthusiasm about my new found capabilities spilled over into his research. He couldn't help but pelt me with series of questions. What was very clear though was that the center was far behind the high levels of expertise and dynamic discoveries engaged in by my Mother's generation. It made no sense that Randolph and others were engaged in research projects that dated back to another period and did not reflect the latest scientific evolution at the end of human history.

"Do they realize, Pamela, just how much information you have acquired?" He asked with excitement as he picked me up and swung me around until we were both dizzy.

"I'm not even sure what I know, Randolph. It's scary! And, I am not sure the androids realize how far behind research is today."

"No, something is very wrong. You are now the walking and talking image of a brilliant scientist whose life terminated shortly before the end of human history." He paused. "Diabolical! They are diabolical! Pamela, you say that you can't explain why the androids have us rediscovering things that were already developed. "

"I don't know. It is true; we all know that to be the case, you, Stuart, John and Peter, and others, recognized, after bypassing the emotional controls, that they were not doing something new. John told me that he had gone in more depth in electronics, more in depth than the androids realized. But, I did not receive anything other than data from Dr. Reinhart. The data I received contained nothing other than actual scientific accomplishment. I received no information concerning Reinhart's life or even the actual period, the years, in which she governed. The cassettes that I saw are my only insight into what the world looked like and how it operated; and those cassettes could have been altered by the androids."

"And, what do the androids want?" He interrupted.

"They want the complete emotional configuration. . .of humans, but, I don't understand why." I smiled to myself. "And, between the two of us that is just too evident to be their real objective. It is a part, but not all of what they want."

"Hmm—I don't know where you are heading with that. Can you do it, give them emotions?"

"I believe so. I have a clear picture of android structure and the programming that Reinhart introduced into her android opposite. But, I don't want them to know that I am capable of reproducing that program. At least not yet." I stopped to take a deep breath. "I don't trust them, Randolph. It is strange to have the four of them hovering over me. I can deal with Gordon, Flanders and the Governor, but, Crawford makes me uneasy. He killed Dr. Reinhardt without blinking his steel eyes. I just don't understand what their game is. Why did Crawford play the nasty, dangerous figure with me? Is this good cop, bad cop? And, now, he returns to complete the inner circle, just as it was when Reinhart was there, minus Dr. Miller. Actually, it is a Group of 5."

"I don't know why they masqueraded like that and I don't think that I care. The truth is our survival now depends on android assistance. We talked about it before. We overestimated the number of humans who bypassed the programming which does make a considerable difference for us. Regrettably, a large percentage of those humans are apathetic about their futures. They prefer to remain emotionally empty rather than to move forward and change things. It's the emotions that are the generating force, for change. Do you know why?" He was very interested.

"Those that are more inhibited must have been descendants of the lower class population, referred to as the non-intellectual group. Reinhart had developed and implanted programs in their ancestors and that must have activated to prevent evolution of solid traits for future generations. Remember that I told you that she developed a system of complacent servitude, which caused major political unrest among those who yearned to escape its cruel tentacles. Certainly, members of the lower intellectual community still had visions of a better life and strived to protect themselves and the others." I stopped to collect my thoughts. "You and I, Stuart, those in the outside community come from ancestors who never underwent genetic programming or emotional restructuring. We are descendants from Reinhart's small group of superior intellects."

"Well, regardless, I don't feel proud of that." I nodded in agreement. "So we are going to have to save this center on our own and those couple androids who are ready to assist, could help us to succeed."

"I believe that we have other means at our disposition, but I can't see the solution at the moment. What I want to do is return outside and visit my little family and talk to the others. I do have to bring them up-to-date. After all we want to leave the area and start new lives. We don't need to overthrow androids and change the center if it's not necessary. We just need to take what's essential to build a civilization on the outside and…leave."

"You don't want war?" He asked in a thick voice. "I was under a different impression. Even so, now that you have the knowledge that we need to catch up with the end of human domination, I think that we should not abandon the center. Don't you remember that staying in the center was your idea?" I nodded in agreement. "We should use all the equipment here to move rapidly into the final period of the human race. We should start from there. By the way, the vehicles in Stuart's section must have been used before the end."

"I agree with you; it makes sense to stay where we are. And, you are right, Randolph, those vehicles were around in her time." The engineering blueprints of those air, land and water transport vehicles were flashing through my mind. I realized that mentioning something did trigger my retrieval process. I did not want to mention that yet to Randolph. Instead I said, "I need some time to think. Do you agree that a week on the outside will help me a lot?"

"Of course, that would be good for you. Just don't stay away too long, it is getting creepy here. Like I said, Stuart and I are under constant surveillance."

"I'll make a quick visit. By the way, I just thought of something else that is very interesting. You know that earthlings colonized other planets. Now I know which ones. And, perhaps now is the time when members were to return. Peter told me that he witnessed an android destruction of a spacecraft and the person aboard."

"What did you say? You can't just say something as mind-boggling as that and not give me more information." Randolph waited with bated breath for an explanation.

"Well, Peter confided in me and recently I raised the idea of space voyagers to Dr. Flanders." I knew from Reinhart that it was the case. "The androids, of course, denied knowing anything about this. But, with Reinhart inside of me, I can confirm that there are colonies on other planets and their return ships are on their way."

"Great News. That is Fantastic! We won't be just a few renegade humans vying for power. We may be receiving reinforcements." His voice was charged with energy.

"Pamela," his voice was serious, tense now, "there is another reason why we can't abandon the center. We can't leave the center without knowing how to provide for ourselves. We need to explore the outside. But, we also need to control the center so that we can advance rapidly; we just agreed that we need the equipment here at the center to conduct research. If we are outside in a barren wilderness, even one with jungle plants, life will be easier if we have basic machinery with us to build structures to live in. For example. I believe that we have to stay in connection with the Center, at least in the beginning." He stopped and a broad smile illuminated his face. "I think that I am starting to feel optimistic."

He was close to me now and we smiled the kind of smile that comes only when the cards are in your hand. He pulled me closer to him. "And, now, Pamela, that you hold the keys to our futures, we can think about being free. I know that you love Peter, but we have something too. I can't let you walk away from me now without showing you just how much I care. This may be my last opportunity."

Randolph would always be more than a friend. . .always. . .The erotic pleasure, the playful intimacy, he gives me fills my heart in another place different from that reserved for the euphoric pleasure and unremitting sentiments of love reserved for Peter. So, I just let myself go.

We could have gone on for hours, if Stuart hadn't shown up. He didn't seem surprised to see our naked, entangled bodies on the lab floor. We both jumped up and screamed when he addressed us with a hardy, "Hi, it is time to do more serious things. "

It was not easy to slip back into our robes and be ready for discussion, like Stuart expected. We needed time to cool down. I was embarrassed and grabbed my robe to cover myself up, while Randolph struggled to his feet and threw some cold water on his face. I slipped out of sight behind the lab table to get dressed and ran my fingers through my disheveled hair, hoping to look more presentable. Neither Randolph nor I were completely emotionally detached, so we were not in the mood for answering questions, but Stuart was not going to leave either.

"Where the hell have you been, Pamela?" His voice modulated with pleasure and anger.

I quickly brought him up to date and then gave him vital information about how to operate the vehicles in his sector. He hid his surprise and said something like, "Of course, I should have realized all that." I know that what I was telling them now seemed so logical-almost simple, and yet, a major problem only 30 days ago. I began to like solving problems so easily thanks to my newly programmed memory banks.

"Randolph told me that you both are under heavy surveillance these days. Are you ok?"

"It is not that easy to circulate." He did hide his emotions very well. "As I said the last time we were together, my problem is with those young males being trained to fight like me." He shook his head. "I have been watching them closely, though, and their lack of experience is visible. I just hope that I don't have to confront that problem."

"I don't have any solution. I don't think that I should mention this to the androids. As I told Randolph, I don't trust them. I shall think about it. I am going to leave for a few days to see my family and our friends."

"Do you think that they will give you permission to leave?" Stuart asked.

I surprised both myself and them when I answered that I didn't need their permission.

"Oh, my dear friends, let me just say that I am now the person in command!"

We laughed heartily and a bit nervously over the truth of my statement. And, I gave them both a quick kiss and dashed out of the lab to find my 4, maybe 5, devoted androids that were patiently waiting for me in the Governor's office. As I walked into his office, all eyes turned towards me; they approached obsequiously as if waiting for instructions. Even the Governor slinked behind his desk.

I thought to myself, "Since they are waiting for instructions, it's time to take control and dish them out." And, that is what I did to a certain extent when I announced my decision.

"I've decided to spend a week with the outside community. I want to see Peter and my son; I think that you can understand." They nodded in approval. "When I return I want to see that everything is still in place and that my friends and colleagues are still around." They nodded obediently. I hoped that my orders would assure Stuart's and Randolph's protection. "Now, how many of you in the center have rudimentary emotional programming?"

"In addition to us, there are three more. Dr. Miller, you know her, she is part of our inner circle." I nodded. Of course, Dr. Miller, the librarian was one of them. "She is in terrible shape, except that she has all the programming. And then there is Randolph's assistant and another android you have never met who is assigned to the space retrieval division." The Governor confessed. "We had them both shut down recently because they were not cooperating properly." He added in a soft voice.

I knew that these five were the only ones who had the rudimentary emotional configuration because the Reinhart inside of me flashed me the info. Why would they have mentioned the two others? The only answer that came to mind was that they wanted to see if Dr. Reinhart would speak up. So, I ignored what they said and raised another issue.

"I think that Dr. Miller doesn't like any of you. And, I believe that she thinks that, you, Dr. Gordon," I pointed at her," were responsible for her accident, the fire in the laboratory that destroyed her android body. Is that the reason why she isn't here with you now?" I needed to be outspoken, or someone else needed to be.

"Yes, she says that. That was the story that she was told to give you when we were trying to understand how your mind was reacting to all the information you were receiving. But, in reality, she knows that she was the unfortunate victim of an accident." Dr. Gordon answered dryly. "And, she is in the library, if you want to stop by later to see her."

"Ok. And now are there androids in other centers who have emotional configurations?"

"I am afraid that Dr. Reinhart's experiment in emotional configurations was limited to a very small group. You will probably find that somewhere in your memory now. We, the five of us, were recruited by Dr. Reinhart because our human opposites had disappeared, rather died, and because their knowledge and capabilities were very useful." Dr. Flanders added.

"There are many things that I want to discuss with you, when the time comes." They were so docile, like children. Were they acting that way because they thought that I was Dr. Reinhart? Or, were they acting like that because they wanted to make me believe that I was Dr. Reinhart? Either way, it was evident that I could never trust them. I would rather have them shut down permanently than to join them with my forces to recover the center. Nevertheless, I was resigned to being required to either use them or work with them in the future.

Both their subservient attitude with me, and that tightly knit complicity that they displayed for me irritated me. I did not feel at ease with them as a group. Were they congratulating themselves and talking about the success of their mission? I needed to find a strategy. As I moved to leave, I reminded them that I would be back in a week.

I changed plans and didn't go directly outside, as they had expected. I decided at the last minute that I should see Dr. Miller. She was the only android-robot that did not seem to be hiding anything; and, I was not so sure that I believed the story Gordon gave me about the accident in the laboratory. It seemed too convenient. When I opened the library door, Dr. Miller was shuffling through cartons, looking for something. She was not ready for my visit; that was clear, by the way her body turned in circles when she saw me. I had an advantage.

"Pamela, what are you doing here; and, what can I do to be of help?"

"I just wanted to talk to you about the progress I have been making." She clumsily closed one of the bulky boxes and meandered out from behind her desk. "I was hoping that you would be able to fill in the blanks for me."

She didn't answer, so I continued. "Do you know that I absorbed all the scientific information left behind by my genetic mother?"

"Yes, we all know. We all knew Elisabeth Reinhart. And, we all missed her after her untimely death."

"It was Crawford who killed her. Did you know?"

"Yes, we all knew and we all agreed with his decision, even though we all had to face difficult times after her passing." She stared at the floor.

"But, taking someone's life is improper. You do know that?" I couldn't understand their attitude and I guess that I expected something more human from Dr. Miller.

"There were laws that made taking the life of someone subject to punishment. But, in reality, taking lives was a daily routine." She acted as if she were teaching a class. "Some lives were not worth perpetuating. Rational, logical decisions had to be made to provide housing and food for the humans who could make meaningful contributions."

"Dr. Miller, please tell me what happened."

She started to turn in circles, losing control of her robotic body. If she wasn't expressing basic emotions, she was at least very nervous. I watched and waited until she regained control. She had a beautiful face that was true. And, I knew now how to construct the rest of her body. Even though I wasn't certain that all the material I needed was available, I could use the promise to reconstruct her body as a bargaining chip.

"I can help you. I know how to make you a new body, Dr. Miller." I could see that I hit a sensitive point, as she recoiled in disbelief.

"How can I be sure?" She did not seem to be shocked with what I said because she was in complete control of her robotic body; she was standing still.

"You have to take a chance. Of course it is a risk."

"I can only tell you what I have in my memory banks, and, so it is probably not complete."

I nodded in agreement and she started. By her account, the earth had gone through a transformation somewhere at the end of the 21st century. Humans were warned that their misuse of the earth's natural resources including the severely polluted atmosphere would cause permanent atmospheric changes. But she indicated that the scientific community was so divided over the actual consequences of atmospheric and surface pollution that efforts to improve the quality of the earth's environment were too little, too late. Nonetheless, with time it was proven that the earth itself went through evolutionary changes. Apparently, even drastic measures would not have made that much difference. I personally believe," strange for an android to give a personal opinion, "that it was, of course, the timing that was off. They should have concentrated on effective measures to save the population hundreds of years before the cataclysmic events occurred; they were simply not prepared to resist the violent changes in the earth's atmosphere and the geological consequences or changes that followed."

I was not certain if she was just guessing or she had proof. It sounded convincing though.

"Many animals, fish, plants and other life forms, different from humans, became extinct. They were replaced by smaller life forms in mass numbers, including viruses and bacteria. Sadly, these highly intrusive microscopic bodies were responsible for reducing the human population by more than 50%. Making humans more resistant as such developing immunities became a priority. But, winning against microscopic enemies was only the beginning of their problems."

As humans entered into the 23rd century, they were also faced with shrinking surface space. The oceans overran much of the land surface and humans were forced to live in crowded spaces. Interestingly enough, this problem was foreseen in the 21st century and artificial structures were planted along sensitive coastlines to prevent the oceans from flooding over the land in the beginning of the 22nd century. These structures were ingenuous, but unfortunately inadequate. Even the platforms that were designed to elevate land surfaces, making floating cities, were not enough. The seas and oceans were ruthless, dangerous places to try to live and work. The volcanic activity below the surface and the constant storms made the sea treacherous. Many courageous adventurers never returned to brag about their exploits."

"Do you want me to continue," she asked and I nodded affirmatively. "The economic effects were alarming. The fishing industry suffered for different reasons, principally because humans were afraid to consume mutant fish, when available, and the personnel and vessels were often lost at sea. Deep seabed mining ended overnight, as the structures were ravaged and buried deep in the ocean bed. At that time, the nodules, the fruit of seabed mining were the major source of energy for heat, light and electricity. The population was agitated by the loss of proper heating and artificial light. All undersea laboratories and experimental living centers disappeared; leaving no trace of their existence or of their habitants."

"Many different theories were advanced to explain the punishment that the earth inflicted upon its inhabitants. Naturally, the vast majority of humans imaged that it was the anger of God who was disappointed with his/her earthly children. The scientific community contended that the earth itself had experienced a rapid and dramatic evolution; impossible to have predicted, and that humans were fortunate to have survived that change. Humans, as opposed to many life forms, escaped extinction."

She stopped here to comment that the humans were actually fortunate that their population had been reduced by 50% allowing them to live more comfortably on the remaining land mass. But she stipulated that since the androids had recorded this history, and that she did not exist during the 21st or 22nd centuries, she could not verify the authenticity of the information she gave me.

"To complicate matters, from the middle of the 21st to the middle of the 22nd centuries humans were constantly fighting wars. As such, much scientific research and development focused on weapons and machinery designed for combat."

"You asked me about religion, Pamela. I saw how interested you were in that subject, but religion never brought real peace and happiness to the humans. The fighting ended with an international agreement to outlaw all religions. It was decided that fighting for an invisible superior being was degrading and that until this cosmic spirit stepped up and identified itself, it was better to worship something else. Science then became the God for everyone and eventually Dr. Reinhart became God's emissary. Worshiping science was a motor for change. It encouraged humans to use their intellectual capacity to improve life on earth."

"I know, Dr. Miller, the inhabitants of the earth, living on whatever an inhabitable environment was left, were subject to a hierarchy based on their intellectual ability." I suggested.

"But, not right away, Pamela. It took time for this hierarchy to develop.

In the beginning, those few scientists in fragile power positions set out to increase their numbers, by finding others, children, adolescents or adults that exhibited superior intelligence." She stopped. "I know that this might be confusing, but imagine a new world, born from wars, natural disasters, political chaos and so forth, ready to change and become productive. After the wars, which lasted more than a 100 years, more than 80% of humans were living in poverty. The wealthy class was comprised of military leaders and a small group of scientists who were formerly working on perfecting military hardware. A true intellectual, a brilliant person, can be found anywhere in the social stratum. Which is why the search for geniuses took time. "

And Dr. Reinhart, when did she appear?"

"Somewhere in the beginning of the 23rdcentury. I don't have the exact date.

"So how did she rise to power?"

"Oh, she never sought fame; it just found her. She was different from other earthlings. There was talk at one time that she was not even from the planet earth, but that was never confirmed. Those were common theories often applied to the origins of exceptional humans. It was almost as if humans were in denial that such an intelligent being could be human. Many even raised the presumption that she was a cyber-human that is part human and part machine. Experiments were undertaken in that field a few centuries before Reinhart's time. Strangely enough, humans imagined that they would have to merge with computers to survive and compete with this form of artificial intelligence." She muffled a forced laugh, but it resonated like an echo in a lonely cave. Even though I had recoiled, she hadn't noticed and kept talking. "Humans were so interested in immortality that they desperately experimented with different methods."

"The first one, cloning, was a disaster because the legal rights of the clone were undetermined. In the beginning, the clone was not educated and often times slept in suspended animation. There was something diabolical for humans to create an identical version from their own genome whose only 'raison d'être' was to provide organs for its intellectually imbued counterpart."

"The idea of giving legal recognition to the clone was suggested and finally accepted by a majority. Unfortunately the clone was only physically identical to the original human. Educating the clone did not produce the expected results. The clone developed its own personality through education and interaction with others. This flew in the face of the underlying reason for cloning: to assure the immortality of the biological parent both physically and intellectually. In some cases, the clone was seen as being competitive with the original party. Eventually, cloning lost support and the clones that were in existence were terminated to avoid continued moral issues."

"The second solution was that of cyber merging. Computers gained enormous popularity at the end of the 20th and the 21st centuries. In the beginning, computer games were favorite pastimes. Then humans became so attached to the potential of these machines, allowing them access to games and to do their work in a cyber-world, without even leaving home. In the end, humans started to believe cyberspace was more comfortable, challenging and rewarding than the real world." She stopped and stared at the computer screen sitting on her desk in front of her.

"Naturally, it appeared that opting for a virtual world instead of a real world was a better way to live. As humans were destroying their own environment, it was safer to live in cyberspace than on the surface of the earth. Efforts to merge the real and the virtual world failed. After all, humans could not hide in cyber space to assure the immortality that they sought.

The third solution started with primitive robots. We, the androids became their best chance at immortality due to our technological complexity and vitality; and a few of us were created with the physical traits of our mentor/creator. Androids were the fruit of Reinhart's genius. During human lifetimes, we followed them, like assistants, and at their death, their knowledge was downloaded into us so that we could take their place."

What she gave me was a facetious commentary on the absurdity of human scientific development, research and accomplishments. I was shocked. In face of all the problems that humans encountered during the last 4 or 5 centuries of their domination, their persistence and courage to survive was laudable. I mentioned that I was more impressed than amused by the enormous scientific progress of humans.

"It is because, Pamela, you believe that these efforts were made because of curiosity. Instead, they were inspired by quests for immortality and then aborted because of fear. Humans destroyed the clones because they might have taken their place. Humans destroyed cyberspace because it was too dangerous for humanity. They feared that humans would become unproductive in the sense that people would immerse themselves in games in virtual space and make no contributions to real space. What the humans, who predicted or invented all these changes, seemed to forget was that they could always have mastered their various inventions. The clones could have served them. People could have chosen to live in virtual or real space; there was no problem. But, instead, humans were afraid of depriving clones of their human rights by imposing servitude. They were afraid that artificial intelligence and cyberspace would attract more people. And, they were afraid that robots, imbued with civil rights like us androids, would surpass humans and run the world.

These were errors in judgment. But, of course the real problem for humans was that no one at the time was capable of designing a program that would be full-proof and could not be broken down and/or ignored by the various forms and forces of artificial intelligence, from computers to robots to androids." She ended as her voice bellowed in this laudatory expression of praise and personal pride.

"You are not referring to the programming inside of you?" Elisabeth broke in. Dr. Miller was feeling so superior that she made a mistake; she forgot that Dr. Reinhart was part of me. Of course, the functioning of their android program, that was the key. "I must find out how it works," I thought to myself. But, with all the information stock piled in my mind, I need time to access it properly. Certainly, unlike Reinhart, I did not have rapid recall of everything. I came to realize that my recall was better once I had accessed the information for the first time.

Dr. Miller was starting to spin around again so I turned to something else to distract her, by questioning her about Reinhart's age. All the knowledge that I had just absorbed from that woman could not have been acquired in a short 200 years, which was considered a long life at that time. Dr. Reinhart's agelessness could be why the androids were so confused about the years, even centuries she lived in. What was clear was that androids could live in perpetuity, unless or until they were shut down; and, apparently, so could Reinhart.

"Dr. Reinhart had to have lived for hundreds of years in a non-aging body. So, we could be talking about how many centuries?" I asked sternly.

"Are you sure, Pamela, that with all the knowledge you received, you did not acquire a method to calculate the number of earth years that she lived? Or, if you did, you still don't know how she remained ageless. I am sorry for you that you did not receive all her information. It must be so frustrating."

"Well, it is true, the information that I received is purely scientific, even though it is so vast and spans many different areas and different centuries. I believe that she left all this information to help future generations. She must have been worried about her own destruction when she downloaded her entire scientific knowledge into the DNA strands. Nonetheless, the thing that was missing was the history of her time. What did that matter?"

"I'm afraid, in retrospect, that it was reasonable for her to want to preserve the knowledge especially since the end of human history arrived shortly after her death." She said, ignoring my repeated requests for the dates when Reinhart lived.

"In any event, I gather that the non-intellectual community took over by killing all the intellectuals. And, I would imagine that the android population remained pacifistic during the demise of the intellectual elites. Am I right?" I was hoping that she would correct me and fill in the details.

"Why not, your reasoning is as good as any other." She sounded so indifferent.

"Well, Dr. Miller, I think that our conversation has come to an end. I promised you a new body for information. I just want you to know that you did not follow through with your part of the bargain, so why should I?"

She started to turn in circles and mumble under her breath. When she finally stopped, she said that she could not give me any more details, because she was not privy to that information. I whispered to myself, "How could that be, and her being in charge of the library? How could she pretend to be ignorant?"

"You promised to give me information." I repeated. "If you refuse to give me more, at least you could play me the cassette or cassettes describing the period in which she lived. Humans need to situate themselves in time." I declared angrily. "I am not asking for a lot, just the dates she lived."

"No, you must leave now. We have been together too long and I don't want any trouble from anyone else. You will have to be satisfied with the history of your people up to their death. The rest is the beginning of the android history, and, it does not concern you." Her mouth distorted into a straight line and her lips barely cleared her teeth in what seemed to be an attempt to…smile.

"No, problem, Dr. Miller, for me. I have the capacity to govern and command. I even have the capability of making myself ageless. But, you— you are a pathetic looking thing who has been stripped of all real value for humans or androids, alike" I smiled, in my sly way and then added, "Too bad, I could have given you back your body and along with it your android pride."

She did not move and did not turn in circles. She stayed planted in the same place, as if, she had been unplugged by some higher force. As I turned to leave I wondered if she really had access to the information requested either in her memory banks or through library files or if she was programmed to keep it from me.

Chapter 41: Preparation

I didn't bother to pass by Randolph's lab before leaving the Center; that would have made my departure difficult. I needed to muster all my strength to leave this place and my friends behind. I started down the same long, dark corridor that I took with Mathieu almost five years ago now. That was the beginning of my long voyage from fear to self-confidence. My passing from one routine to another made time wiz by. I realized that a month became three months in a click of a finger. Or maybe I had become programmed to ignore time?

I stopped along the way to inspect the corridor in the Center that frightened me that day when I escaped with Mathieu. Nothing stood in my way to harm me; not this time. Was everything that happened to me from the moment my visual receptor failed, my escape on the outside, my falling in love and giving birth to Frederic, as well as my discovery of Randolph and Stuart and, my relationships with the various androids. . .planned?

I exited on the outside and took the path back to the community. The first person I ran into was Stanislas and he yelled out to the others to come quick. Even though I was soon surrounded by all of them, my attention went straight to Peter and Frederic. I pushed my way towards them and was met with open arms. As we stood entangled in each other's arms I wondered how I could ever have imagined that they could be replaced.

My thoughts were broken by the commanding voice of John who reminded everyone that we could not waste any time. We all drifted into the interior of the walls that were far from the android captors. It was evident that they had grown confident and determined during my absence, because no one worried any more about disappearing from the android's view. And, yet, they seemed a bit too self-confident; that worried me. I reminded them that it might be dangerous for all of us to be gathered together outside of android surveillance. Someone must stay in view and so Mathilda, Benjamin and Isabel left the group.

I told them everything that had happened to me. I also gave them all the basic information that I acquired through my persistent questioning. The part that surprised them the most was the last few months: Crawford's revelations and the siphoning of the information that my famous genetic mother had left behind into my system. Their silence and their deep regard with expressions of awe when I finished made me uneasy. I waited until smiles of satisfaction finally appeared on their faces.

John was the first to speak. "You will share everything with us, won't you, Pamela?"

I wasn't expecting that. I didn't know how much I wanted to reveal. But, it was delicate. I could not treat them like the androids, and, yet, I wasn't sure that I could trust all of them either.

"Of course, I shall share everything with you, to the extent it's possible." They looked at me, their smiles turned to frowns. I quickly reacted to their disappointed faces.

"What I mean is that, although my mind accepted everything, I need time to access the information."

"Ok, so we can count on you?" Sarah spoke up.

"You never had any reason not to count on me except your own paranoia. I came here to escape from what I thought was my eventual termination. I sought refuge. I can say today that I didn't know what they had planned for me. Every step that I took in the center was risky. I was always worried that one day they would lose interest in me and drag me away, like they did Ferdinand. I felt better after I met Randolph, mostly because of his sense of humor. Stuart, on the other hand, is so intense; he put pressure on Randolph and me to produce." I smiled. "You don't know how much I missed all of you and how much I longed to be insignificant in this campaign. I wanted more than anything to be a loving partner and a doting mother."

Everyone had teary eyes as they applauded and cheered my remarks. A mysterious form of energy suffused my entire being and I liked the feel of it. I thought that it was power. But if it was power, would I stay faithful to myself? Thoughts pounded my brain warning me not to allow this mysterious energy force to dominate me. Or was it Dr. Reinhart that I felt growing stronger inside of me? Was she producing that energy that threatened to take me over?

"So where do we go from here?" Peter asked.

The power surge was still inside me, pushing me and I didn't waste time. "We go inside. We take the transport machines. I think that I know where the weapons are. Reinhart knows how to use them, even though I am not at all certain that I can capitalize on her know-how to be able to fire them properly. In any event, Stuart has the keys for the vehicles. If they don't work, I can start the systems on my own."

"We leave the Androids and explore?" Mathieu asked. "What do you think, Pamela?"

"I still have lots of questions about what we will find on the outside. I don't know whether all the information that I received is exact. The androids refused or maybe they are unable, to confirm even the exact dates of our history. I know the earth's surface was very small at Dr. Reinhart's death. It all depends upon what happened since then and whether we will have a large land surface to exploit. They are certainly hiding information that we will have to force them to reveal or find out for ourselves. We must keep in mind they have an android approach to what is important. For example, the androids do not need to focus on life-support, food, clothing, and the like." I stopped, remembering my last conversation with Randolph. "Randolph and Stuart believe that if we can take over the Center, it might be better in the long run. We need the basics; again, food, clothing, and so forth. The Center also has the technology and material that we need to build shelters and to continue research to improve our lives."

We sat and discussed this for quite some time. We came to the same conclusion as before that it was not possible for humans to have a new start if we didn't know how, what, when and where we became extinct. And, moreover, we needed to know more about the condition of the earth today, identify potential dangers linked to the topography, climate, geography and the species of animals that might be harmful for us. There were certainly precautions that needed to be taken.

When questioned again about the effect of acquiring all that knowledge, I answered the best I could. "I acquired something foreign to most humans. . .pure intellect. I however lack certainly with respect to her inspirations and her personality. But, I've learned that we are so far behind Dr. Reinhart with respect to research and development. The main problem will be filling in the gaps. The main question remains, "Why didn't the androids accelerate the education of the new generations? And, the response is still another question, why are we reinventing what had already been invented and exploited?"

After long discussions, Jonathan returned to our previous discussion and argued strongly in favor of adopting Randolph's and Stuart's position that we could not leave the area without taking over the center. A position that John and I had also agreed to during my last visit to the outside community. I saw John nodding favorably; apparently he had never elucidated this with the others.

"I find that critical to our futures." Jonathan was still talking. "We will have the weapons and will attack by surprise. I don't think that they would resist."

"But, of course, that depends on whether or not they were programmed to fight by other intellectuals following the death of Reinhart." I interjected. "That was the proposition that was endorsed by the majority of the intellectuals at the last meeting over which Reinhart presided. If they were programmed for combat, we would have to fight them." Those of us who trained with Diana, would we be ready...

I observed Jonathan. The placebos that Dr. Gordon had sent out to mask his pain, didn't work. That was not surprising. Now it was clear that his pain was physical and not emotionally induced otherwise those silly pills would have had a curative effect. Thinking about painkillers did not trigger anything inside of me. Medicine did not seem to be one of Reinhart's concerns: not even enough so to have left a trace memory. I resigned myself to finding something else. Maybe one of her other inventions would improve his life. My throat tightened up and my eyes drooped seeing this man who was present in my life for such a long time suffer so much.

It was very late at night when our small group broke up to go to bed. Frederic had long since fallen asleep in my arms. I liked to feel that indescribable warmth and the relaxed weight of his little body, as he confidently curled up in my arms. I looked down at my son, curious about his changes. He was tall and thin. I played with his thick curly blond hair and smiled down at his boyish features as I tried to imagine him ten years from now; a younger version of his father. I liked his happy personality; and his bubbling laughter. He seemed to be very alert and curious; something that pleased me. He asked me to describe the inside of the Center and the physical appearance of the androids. I exaggerated by giving more pleasant descriptions of the Center and the androids, so that he would not be worried about me. I wanted to believe, as I looked at him, that he would become a strong leader, guiding his people into new lands, new environments, retrieving all that humans had at one time and then lost.

I would not let Peter take him from me. I wanted to be the one to lay him gently in his bed and tuck in him. Peter understood and let me take the initiative. I gave my little boy so many kisses and told him over and over again how much I loved him, missed him and was looking forward to our having time together.

Peter finally came to get me, as I sat next to my sleeping boy, pulling me close to him. He was sure of himself; something that I had not remembered.

The way that he lifted me in his arms and laid me on the bed raised no doubt as to his sincerity and dedication to me. As he often did, he drew my hair back behind my head and stared deeply into my eyes. This time I felt that he wanted to assure himself that I was in no way possessed by my ancestor.

He smiled down at me and kissed me. I could feel his love in that kiss and hoped he could feel mine. He rolled over and lay next to me looking up at the cavern ceiling. "I am so happy that you are back. I missed you." I heard him take a deep breath. "There are stories that reach us, not all of them are what we want to hear. But I feel proud that the woman I love and cherish is leading us out of this barren emptiness. That through your actions we will all have the possibility of living, and I mean living, not existing, but living!"

I stared up at the ceiling like him, as if it was our door to reason. I was neither embarrassed nor ashamed. He must have heard about my promiscuity. So, instead, I rolled over and looked down at him. "I am human. And, I am happy that I can say and know that I am human; that being human has a meaning. It is because I know that I am human that I can in all sincerity tell you that I love you. With you, I feel complete. You represent more than just someone in my life. You represent life to me." I choked up with emotion and my voice became shaky. "I don't know what you heard. And, Peter, I don't care. Please accept me for who I am, the woman, not infallible that I am."

"Of course, Pamela." And, then he laughed at his own clumsiness and pulled me close to him. "You misunderstood what I said. I said it badly, but it is difficult to express. It was not your relationships that bother me. Some people here have their doubts of your sincerity to the group and the projects. They are insecure by nature, and, I think you know who they are."

"Yes." Of course I knew that Sarah and Ruth did not trust me. "They doubt my sincerity because they are jealous," I thought to myself.

"What you shared with us tonight, gives us hope. We have a better understanding of our past; even though I am not sure that I like some of the ways in which humans functioned in society. I hope that we will act differently and that we will stay united."

"There are so many more things to be said, but can't we let that wait?" I raised myself on top of him and whispered. "I missed you! And you're always on my..." I had to stop as the warmth effused my thighs and he gently balanced me onto my back.

When morning arrived, I wanted nothing more than to rest firmly in his arms. But, Frederic was not going to let me ignore him. It was nice to have him jump on us and scream with delight, "My mommy's home!"

The days were filled with meetings, interweaving with heartfelt family moments. The group seemed more dynamic each day and discussions began to engender solutions, then decisions. One thing was unanimous: the desire to take over the center. Anyway, there was no way that we could survive on the outside without having continual access to the equipment and knowledge in the center.

If everything was going to work smoothly, I had to be on the inside when they arrived through the tunnel. I had to distract notably the 5 androids that might present a problem to the success of our invasion.

Our small group continued training, under the direction of Diana. Her savage discipline, dedication and combat techniques molded us into real fighters!

After one of these self-defense sessions, which left Jonathan screaming with pain, another idea surfaced; perhaps Dr. Reinhart's immortality was the key to finding a solution for his problem. She rejuvenated her life, but how? Could rejuvenation be therapeutic and not just a way to stay forever young? Unfortunately, it was clear to me that merely receiving all the equations did not make me a scientist. I feared I was merely a repository for information. It was obvious that I needed the rigorous analysis of a scientist to determine how to use the information stored inside me. So I grabbed Peter's hand one day and led him away from the cavern bed after gently kissing him. His lips caressed mine and told me what he wanted. He followed me closely, anticipating a sizzling consummation. As I spoke his desirous full lips drew tight with disappointment.

"Peter, I don't believe that I should share all the information I absorbed with everyone." He shook his head in agreement. "I believe that I can trust you to keep certain things to yourself."

"Pamela, if you want me to keep a secret. I can and I can make a promise to you to keep it." He hesitated. "Or at least, I can try to."

Even though his answer was anything but convincing, he was so adorable. He looked straight into my eyes, revealing his unfeigned sincerity, which overwhelmed my trepidations and I opened up to him totally. "Yes, of course, you don't know if you can, but you've got to, Ok?" I paused to let that sink in. "Can I talk to you, as a scientist. I am a depository of information, but I am not a scientist. I have never conducted experiments, tested hypotheses, or even begun to discover something. Only a scientist knows what to do with this information and working with a scientist might trigger scientific reasoning in me."

He said nothing so I continued. "Jonathan has terrible pain. I discovered that the pharmaceutical division gave medication to Gordon that was presumably passed onto Jonathan. Asking for medication was like asking for an authorization to commit a crime. The treatment they used on me and on others was apparently used a long time before Dr. Reinhart arrived on the scene. According to Gordon, medication eventually became obsolete, either because humans were more resistant to diseases and so forth or because illness led automatically to termination. I know that the pharmaceutical section did not give medication to treat Jonathan's pain. Gordon told me recently that the medication that she gave me to send out to Jonathan was nothing but placebos, kinds of fruity tasting bits. Perhaps she was being honest when she told me that the chemicals used to make medication no longer existed; and that this placebo was the best that could be offered." I stopped to collect my thoughts. "In retrospect, I should have been more cautious. Maybe the medication destined for Jonathan was poison, to terminate him; I was lucky that that was not the case." Peter's eyes grew wide when I said that. "Additionally, Gordon told me that if Jonathan had maintained his programming, he would have lived better. And, as he was to have been terminated years ago, he would never have suffered."

Peter interrupted. "There is probably some scientific proof in that. But, even imagining that he saw himself as you did, a very good looking and well-built man, it is certain that he would have experienced pain. And the pain would have broken down his programming. So, the real question is why do they continue to produce mentally and physically deformed humans?"

"Yes, probably you are right to ask the question, but I would like to leave it alone for the moment. After all, we like Jonathan and he fits in well with our group."

He took me in his arms and stroked my hair. "I am ready to just listen now."

I explained to him that Reinhart had conducted many experiments before she found the right method to recreate her youthful genetic composition. I affirmed that by the time she arrived, cloning had become a dead issue. "Suspended animation was used for space travel, but, once the person reached his or her destination, they started to age. Longevity through genetic selection was used at her time, but even that did not guarantee life beyond 150 years. What she invented and, I believed this to be the case, for herself alone, was a way to gain respect and power. It was a kind of transporter that she used to transport herself back in time to retrieve a genetic structure minus aging factors. I could direct you on the construction of the machine, but I am not even certain that the materials and technology we have today, will permit that."

"Transporters were used in space travel. They were even used on the earth to go from one place to another. I remember studying that, quite briefly. It was nothing new."

"Yes, what was new in her case was the interim stage between break-down and rebuilding. She captured the physical characteristics of youth; and, early on, she erased certain hereditary traits that could cause illness."

"You could give me the technique?" His voice was alive with energy. I nodded; "I would like to work on that kind of project."

"I am certain that everyone here would. But, we have more important things to do for the moment." I realized that I was wasting my time. "No, it is ok, I was just thinking that if we had a system in place then we could give Jonathan a body without deformities."

"Yes, that sounds reasonable, yet unattainable today." He took a deep breath and let the air out slowly, as if that would help him to think. "She was the only one who had access to this?"

"I told you that I think she was the only one who used this technique." I sighed. "And she would never have died if that monster, Crawford, hadn't killed her."

"I know that you don't like him. I don't know him. But, Pamela, she was also cruel. She had lost compassion for everyone around her, including her group of androids." He pulled me tighter, as if he were protecting me from what he was about to say, or of who was inside of me. "We know now the kind of world we live in. We know how the androids have deprived us of our rights to live like humans. We know how unfair their visual receptors were. We also know, that she invented those visual receptors; and, they were used to control a large sector of the human population. Maybe, we were better off under the direction of those androids than we would have been under her tyranny."

I tried to push him away and he resisted. I didn't like his description of Reinhart, even if it may have been true. "She was brilliant, extraordinarily brilliant, Peter. You just don't kill someone like that on an impulse." I started to cry, big tears running down my face. He let me go and I ran off to calm myself down. I heard him call out to me, "Does being brilliant justify power for power's sake?"

But something stirred inside me, amplifying my sadness and I wondered if I was crying. . .alone?

Chapter 42: The Return

Icalmed down after pacing back and forth in the long common room. When I returned to our cubicle, Peter was there playing with Frederic who was awakened by my shouting. They were laughing as they chased each other around the mattress. I apologized and told him that there was a lot of truth in what he said. I also told him that, in spite of the fact that she was power hungry and cruel, she was still human. That made a big difference for me. One cannot reason with androids along human lines; and even if the group of five endeavored to develop human emotions, they would still function like machines. Whether it was true or not, I wanted to think that if she had lived she would have been more sensitive to the needs of humans and made concessions.

Sometimes I wondered if I was thinking and saying those things or a little voice inside of me was doing it. But I had to keep this to myself and maybe the time would come…

I spent the rest of my week discussing the strategy for taking over the center. Randolph, Stuart and I were the key figures. One of my roles was to keep the group of five occupied, maybe distracted. I also had to explain how to turn on the vehicles and fire the weapons. Peter promised to put the children in a safe place inside or outside the center and to explain to them that it was important for them to cooperate with the androids, if all the humans were terminated.

I used my time to create better relationships with Ruth and Sarah. I spent time with Stanislas and Benjamin, both of whom had been so supportive of me during my pregnancy and kind to Frederic. I realized that Mathieu and Isabel were true friends, and that John was very pleased with the information that I was passing on to them. I still felt relaxed and confident with Mathilda. Diana was so much more open with me and the group because of her relationship with Jonathan. Our commonalities brought us together; all these people, like myself, were risking their lives to make a better place for all human beings.

I left with a heavy heart. I hugged and kissed the two most important people in my life over and over again. I was afraid that this would be the last time that I would know happiness, love, friendship and complicity in a purely human way. Something was tugging inside me. . .

I returned to my cubicle on the inside using the same path I had taken to leave the premises. I collapsed on my bed and dreamed about loved ones. I knew that we had a very short week to get everything together in the center. So, in the morning, I rushed to shower and eat, so that I could talk to Randolph. But, he wasn't there. The lab was empty and all the equipment neatly arranged in the cabinets.

I felt like I did when I first woke up in that hospital room. My heart started to beat rapidly and my hands were wet and sticky. I felt weak and scared. I couldn't just close my eyes as I had done before and pretend to be unconscious. I had to act this time, and I had to act fast and intelligently. There was no turning back.

His assistant appeared out of nowhere. "You are late." She said. "They took him to be terminated." I stood frozen, as if her very words rendered me lifeless, helpless and defenseless in face of this horrifying reality. How could they have taken Randolph? How was I going to survive here without him? I was ready to burst into tears, when something inside me gave me the courage to act. So, without more thought, I dashed out of the lab and moved rapidly amongst the crowd in the direction of the termination center.

My fear turned to anger and then to determination. As I rounded the last corridor, I saw the androids carrying Randolph on a stretcher moving towards the door of the death chamber. It had to be that, where else would they be taking him and his assistant just told me... My thoughts stopped; their eyes were on me and they had dropped the stretcher.

I rushed at them and using all my bodily force knocked one of them helpless on the floor. Diana did not mention that under their tough-skinned bodies, lay heavy, hard metal structures. My body was still vibrating from my contact with the first one, and my hand was limp with pain, when the second android started to move slowly from the other side of the stretcher in my direction. From panic or anger, I let out a series of excruciating screams that resonated in the corridor, as my body, charged with adrenaline, leaped high in the air and came down hard on the second. He stumbled and fell in a heap next to the first.

It was not that easy to dispose of them. Their size, weight and tough interior compensated for their lack of hand-to-hand combat skills. I felt drained as I returned to Randolph who was lying on the floor unconscious.

Was he was drugged? How was I going to revive him? I pulled his heavy body with all my force some 3 feet in the opposite direction. I could hear sirens blasting. They knew what had happened. He wouldn't wake up. I stood slapping him with all my force but he didn't respond. I heard the other androids arriving. We had to move.

I looked up for a second and saw 8 androids, maybe more, less than 20 feet away, and they were carrying laser guns. I looked down at Randolph; how was I going to save him. And then Stuart was there. He yelled. "I'll take care of them! Move out of my way!"

The first thing that flashed through my mind was, "he is dressed for combat." There he was in long trousers and a t-shirt, his hair pulled back in a ponytail. He was moving fast. As he approached the androids, he leaped high in the air, forming and moving in a semi-circle as he hit them straight on, one after the other. I saw them fall like dominos on the floor.

He backed up cautiously, reassuring me with his words. "It is ok, Pamela. I won't let anything happen to either one of you." My short breathe of relief was premature. More of those android monsters were arriving.

I saw flashes of light. They were using their lasers. "Protect yourself, the guns are on death rays!" Stuart screamed. My heart was racing as I looked on.

This time Stuart moved in zigzags, to avoid the rays that were being aimed directly at him. Rapidly dogging them, as he moved up and under them, advancing in his efforts towards the enemy. He used his legs and feet like the last time to take them down, as he hit them in the face or in the lower body, whichever was the most open. Their bodies were strewn on the floor. He turned to me and said, "We've got to move fast now", when a human voice called out. "Where are you, you coward? Show yourself!"

Stuart stopped in his tracks. "Calm yourself. I am not your enemy. You are one of us. Let me help you."

"They warned me that you might say that! Show yourself to me so that I can see for myself what you are." Stuart did not have time to reply. One of the androids, immobile on the ground, called out Stuart's visual code; I heard the numbers: 19202501182006.

The young man was so tall that he towered over Stuart. He turned in Stuart's direction. His muscles, bulging as if inflated with air, gave him a menacing, superhuman appearance. I sat breathless as he raced towards Stuart and picked him high up in the air, swirled him around, and threw him several feet in my direction. Stuart lay stunned on the floor.

I had to do something he was coming after Stuart, but what? I was no match for that young oversized human. I used the only advantage that I had, my invisibility. I sneaked up behind him and grabbed his long ponytail that hung in the middle of his back. It was a ridiculous scene for someone looking on. He flipped his head forward, as I straddled his back, clinging with all my force to his ponytail. He shook his head and reached behind. I avoided his

Pamela Series 13

moves and held on like I was riding a wild stallion. I was starting to tire when I saw Stuart moving. I stayed my place long enough for Stuart to get back up on his feet. "But, can he handle this human?" I thought, as I let myself slide off his back onto the floor, opening up the fight to Stuart.

I crawled in Randolph's direction and turned back to watch a triumphant victory. Stuart was more rapid, his moves cleaner and his punches more direct and effective. The young man was down on the ground, groaning. I saw his swollen eyes and bleeding face when he looked up at Stuart. "He is deprogrammed, Pamela, we can take him with us." Once again, our efforts were thwarted. Before Stuart could do anything, one of those half-witted androids, recovering from its shock, fired on the human, exploding his head and body in front of our eyes.

"No!" Stuart screamed, as he jumped and smashed in the android's face.

I watched streams of human blood mixing with android parts, as my body wrenched until I vomited violently. Stuart dropped a pile of laser guns on top of Randolph's outstretched body and then took me comfortingly in his arms and whispered, "You, We, are going to be fine, but we have got to get out of here!" I nodded.

We grabbed Randolph and carried him and the weapons the best we could; he was so heavy. At one point I pressed against the center wall to balance myself under the weight I was bearing. What happened next was miraculous, the wall gave way. Was this our opportunity for survival or a trap? I thought that I heard Reinhart's voice inside me, repeating, "Go ahead; step in, step in…" That was what we did; Stuart, Randolph and I passed into a new space that opened and closed so rapidly behind us, sealing us in what at first glance appeared to be a control room.

Stuart looked at me, with squinting eyes and furrowed brows, "How did you know that this room was here?"

"I didn't, Stuart. I think it just happened by accident, unless, and, of course she, Reinhart, guided me?"

"Do you realize, Pamela?" I could see his body grow limp with relief. "She saved us!"

That brought beaming smiles and happy tears to both of our faces.

"What is this place?" Both Stuart and I were overwhelmed and stood in awe of its towering ceiling. We laid Randolph on the floor to explore the large, auditorium-sized, circular room. There was so much equipment neatly arranged along the interior, circular walls. The equipment, certainly coming from Reinhart's time, did not resemble anything I had already seen in Randolph's lab or even in the birth center. Stuart confirmed that it was more sophisticated than what he or Randolph were using. I could see that Stuart was fascinated by the various machines, computers, and... He lingered in front of certain machines, studying the control panels.

The middle of the room was filled with several long tables divided by low panels into smaller working areas. I could almost see the scientists, technicians, or others from another period, sitting on the large, comfortably padded chairs in their defined space working diligently on the computers in front of them. In the back of the room was a wall sized video surveillance system, presenting images of the inside of the Center. An imposing control panel was several feet in front of it. A glass dome, with panels that opened and closed to let in the natural light, formed the ceiling.

"Wow!" Stuart said in a loud, excited voice. "This room alone is wonderland. I can't wait to work in here!"

We were next to Randolph when he opened his eyes and let out a shrill sound. Why? Was it because he was alive or relieved to see the two of us looking down at him? "They came for me. They must know about our plans." He was rambling, still a bit groggy. "I am worried. They are ready for us. If so, we don't have a chance and you won't be able to go outside again to warn the others." He was not the smiling, laughing Randolph, but a beaten man, shaking in despair.

His eyes closed again and we waited alongside of him until he fully recovered. In the meantime, Stuart and I reassured each other that we would win; we've got to. I surmised that the drugs made Randolph look and sound so negative or depressed. Once he started to stretch his legs, he recovered his optimism. "Where are we?" he asked smiling his goofy smile.

"We are in a room in the inner portion of this complex." Stuart replied so matter-of-factly that Randolph pushed himself straight up into a sitting position. He went on to explain. "You were lucky. Pamela saved you from the two android terminators before I arrived on the scene. "Randolph turned wide-eyed in my direction.

"How do you feel, Randolph?" I asked.

"A bit dizzy. Those treacherous creations arrived out of nowhere. I need some time to put the pieces together." He paused, "so this is an inner circle? But, what inner circle? Where?" He asked pressing for an explanation.

"We are in an inner circle inside the Center. And, Randolph, of course," Stuart continued, "that explains a lot. Whenever I tried to make the design of this complex, I was baffled by what appeared to be a middle section. The space we used was only half the real distance. I assumed the life-support systems were in this middle section. I never imagined that we would have access to all of this. But, we don't know how to use it."

"I do." I answered as if that should have been evident. "The androids don't know that this part exists. They were never privy to the construction of these complexes. Reinhart designed them." I too was surprised; part of me anyway. I could see some things more clearly. Perhaps I had absorbed more than scientific information. "They needed to create facilities with life support systems in the event of a war. This idea, of a bomb shelter, was old-fashioned, and, usually turned out to be a useless effort. Nonetheless, hostilities were so strong, at the end of human domination, that at least one center was built on every independent piece of territory on the planet earth." I explained.

"Is that you, Pamela, speaking? You are not acting the same; you are spooking me out." Randolph replied in a menacing tone.

I ignored what I considered to be a rude remark. After all he was confused about what was going on. "It's ok, Randolph." I answered soothingly. "I am Pamela with a lot of Reinhart information flowing through my body. Somehow my mind is piecing things together. What I learned about the various periods in human history at the library and what I have absorbed scientifically from Reinhart can be interpreted in the way I just gave you. Of course, some of it is just conjecture. But, we are safe here." I added. "I would like to change the subject a bit, they must be looking all over the place for us." I was clicking my fingernails nervously on the table. "Actually, I am not cut out for all this violence." They nodded in agreement. "Even though they won't be able to enter into this space," Reinhart's assertion, "it doesn't mean that they won't try; and it doesn't mean that they might not go so far as to attack the outside community to get us to surrender to them."

"Talking about not being able to take care of yourself, well, I think that you acted rapidly taking out the android orderlies, protecting Randolph, before I caught up with you." Stuart never compliments so I knew it meant something.

"I trained with Diana. She is a demanding person and we all were stiff and sore after her long day sessions. But, I never imagined that I had learned anything." I replied partially not wanting to startle them any more with revelations of the possible return of Dr. Reinhart who may be haunting my body. "But, by the way, what were you doing in the area?"

"I am not proud of myself, because I didn't try to prevent anything. I arrived behind the androids in Randolph's office. I had stopped by to see you," he looked at Randolph, "before going to the gym. Actually, I hid in one of the cabinets." He stopped to collect his thoughts.

Now I know why he was dressed for combat, I mused. "We have all taken advantage of those cabinets, or closets for one reason or another." I laughingly commented.

"I don't understand why they didn't notice me." Stuart continued, ignoring my remark. "I was so nervous that I made noise when I opened the closet door. I guess that I acted a bit like a coward; just thinking about myself. But I never encountered a life/death situation where I was to save a human life and I was not up to par. Anyway, I waited until they left and then took a short cut around to the termination center. I saw you, Pamela; you were far ahead of me. By the time I arrived, you had taken care of those androids. It was amazing! I heard sirens as you started to drag Randolph and then, well … the rest."

"Randolph, you should have seen Stuart. He was lethal, a virtual killing machine. He jumped, sprinted, flipped, kicked…his moves fast and effective as he took down the android forces." I looked at Stuart. "Seeing you arrive gave me hope. Seeing you put those wretched machines on the floor made me proud and gave me confidence; it doesn't matter that you panicked at first— who wouldn't have? "I looked at Randolph and he nodded. "What matters is that you saved me and Randolph in a spectacular display of courage." He threw me a sheepish smile.

"By the way, Randolph, they gave you an injection. I believe that it was a strong sedative because you collapsed only seconds after they hit you with the syringe." Stuart added.

"Bastards! Cowards! Sneaking up behind me and driving a syringe into my body; I am starting to detest all of them!" He yelled and then punched the leg of the chair in front of him. He pulled himself up on his feet. "Now, what do we do?" He asked, fully recovered.

"Our friends will be here in a week's time, but I don't think that we need them." I went in the direction of one of those sophisticated machines and started pressing buttons. I activated everything in this middle region. Their mouths dropped about a foot open.

"In less than an hour the majority of the androids will be neutralized." I stopped again to retrieve information. "Reinhart died before the androids took power. They did not want to be programmed to fight; but maybe they were. The neutralizing program over there may not be as effective as I am hoping, so we must be careful. And, then our real problem is going to be with the humans whose visual receptors turn off, abruptly." I explained.

"Wait, Pamela," Randolph screamed, "can't you keep the humans under programming until we have help? Those humans might be hysterical and we can't deal with militant robots and hysterical humans at the same time."

He was right. "Good point. In that case, I'll wait until you have brought the other members of our community into the center. And we can group the humans in a large room together and deactivate their systems simultaneously." I suggested.

"Well, now we have a few days to ourselves before acting. Can you give us a visual on what is happening?" Randolph asked.

"I think so. Anyway I shall try."

I pressed another button and we had a panoramic view of the center. Things were not as I hoped. Only a small number of androids were shutdown. The others were scrambling about, in a kind of panic. To my real surprise, I saw a group of androids marching with weapons in their hands. They were acting as if they were accustomed to combat. I turned and looked at the other two, whose faces had turned white.

"Apparently, there are soldiers trained for combat." I said calmly. "So, we should start to prepare another strategy."

"Your Reinhart was not so smart." Randolph blurted out.

"Don't forget that she was dead when the last vestiges of human civilization were destroyed." I took a deep breath, as I searched for something more encouraging to say but what? The only idea that came to mind was that I needed to get back in contact with the Group of 5. "What do you think if I give myself up?" I wasn't interested about whether they agreed or not. I had a new strategy in mind. I told them that there was a way out of this middle section that would get them close to the transport terminal, or close enough that they could run to cover. They should hide out and wait for the others to arrive.

"Why don't you come with us then?" Stuart spilled out as he paced up and down the room; like Randolph, he didn't seem to be particularly impressed with my plan. "If you know where the exit is, why are we sitting here? Why haven't we left already?"

I calmly explained to them that pieces of information just came to me. The configuration of this center was a real mystery to me up until an hour ago. I told them that Mathieu and I had explored the outside of the center when we were looking for a better place to live. "I know now that we can pass through the center and that is what you and the group must do when you charge the androids. In fact, you should round up the humans and put them in an isolated area before attacking."

They were looking at me in disbelief. Pathetic, I thought to myself, but I focused on the fact that neither Randolph, nor Stuart, were better military strategists than I was. So, I commented that they should discuss this with the others when they arrived. "In any event," I added, "we have a week to reconsider my plan. I just want you to know that I shall go straight to the Group of 5 and negotiate with them."

We sat back on the comfortable chairs and watched the androids turn in circles looking for us and picking up the dead androids. They were banging and knocking the wall at the place where we exited. It would have been incongruous if the android fighting forces weren't present on the screen. In spite of my inner feeling that the wall was impenetrable, I trembled thinking about their actually breaking through the wall and grabbing us; ripping us to pieces. Fortunately, we had laser guns with us if we needed them. There was no doubt they were programmed killers and the screen showed their numbers growing fast. They were flowing from somewhere, out of the woodwork? But, where? I closed my eyes and tried to focus.

"Did Reinhart program them to kill?" Randolph asked.

"I thought that I told you that her death was a consequence of her refusal to program the androids to kill."

"Right. Then who programmed them to kill?"

"Interesting." I didn't know if I wanted to tell him. Oh, what the h__! "I don't know if you are going to like what I am going to say, Randolph. In the last Reinhart cassette, I saw a man, with your physical built and facial features, slightly older and more rugged than yours, dressed in military clothes and carrying a laser rifle slung over his shoulder." Randolph sat straight up his eyes intense. "Anyway, he pushed his way onto the podium next to Reinhart. He called her by her first name, Elisabeth, and she answered with a formal, Dr. Murdoc. He told her that he was there to save her from herself and that the end of the world was unavoidable. Then he addressed the crowd and told them that he would reprogram all the androids, without exception, to fight."

"Are you saying that I am him, his descendant? That I could be as crazy?" He shook his head in disbelief. "Come on, Pamela, I wouldn't do something like that!"

"No. But, maybe you are one of his descendants; the resemblance between the two of you is extraordinary." I stopped to think. "Reinhart died so I do not know what happened. If he reprogrammed the androids to kill, then how did the Group of 5 escape and avoid being reprogrammed, and why did they bring you back?" They looked at me, their brows raised and eyes popping. "Probably your genetic ancestor, and therefore his line, has the intelligence to fill in certain research gaps that are important for the androids." They nodded. "The next question is why would they want to terminate you, Randolph, now?"

"Because they hold me responsible for whatever happened and they don't want me to interfere again with their projects." Randolph spit out

"Sounds logical" Stuart and I said simultaneously.

"What are they made of?" Stuart asked breaking the tension.

"What are you talking about, Stuart?" I asked.

"The androids—what are they made out of? Do you know? Or, does she know? Or, did she make them? Because, if we know what they are made out of perhaps we might be able to rip them apart."

Rip them apart didn't seem to be the right action. Blow them apart was what I said to myself. "Their exterior is a plant." They looked at me as if I had lost my mind. "Yes, a plant. I know it seems strange, but Reinhart discovered it and its elasticity. Do you want to know more about it?" They shook their heads in agreement. What else was there to do anyway; we were stuck here for a while.

I reminded them that the earth's atmosphere and land surface changed dramatically in a relatively short period of time. The natural vegetation and animal life evolved as did the environment. Species disappeared and new ones were born, but there were less varieties of species than in the past. Some of the animals that we saw through our visual receptors in the zoo no longer existed during the Reinhart period.

"Interestingly enough, the plant was found in tropical waters." I felt inspired by the subject. "Apparently, it didn't correspond to the major needs of the time, in other words, it was not edible and had no medicinal purposes. They were the priorities of Reinhart's early expeditions."

"There was not enough food?" Stuart asked in surprise.

"No, the earth's surface had diminished so much that it was impossible to cultivate enough of the food sources that humans had become dependent upon. And, for that reason, Reinhart participated in expeditions on land and on water trying to find new sources of nourishment." They seemed satisfied with that explanation, even though I was not myself convinced with what I said. Then something from within shook me. The little voice continued, "In any event, she came across an enormous low water plantation filled with these strange plants. The plant was tested and quickly discarded for its lack of nutritional value. Nonetheless, she recognized that it had a certain elasticity that might be used in the construction of dwelling places. When it was heated, it could be smoothed over a given surface to form a protective seal. Reinhart compared it to human skin, in texture and appearance. And, she imagined its use in covering the hideous robots that humans were using to carry out mundane tasks."

"So, she covered her metallic creations with human skin." Randolph spurted out contemptuously.

"Stop and try to listen. It was actually ingenious on her part. But, from what I can feel and understand, she was ahead of her time." I turned away from them for a minute and added that unfortunately their skin was impenetrable.

"Another problem." Stuart said in a low and lifeless voice.

"Not really; we can still succeed. But, that is why I must get back to the Group of 5. They are the key to our future; we cannot start doubting our ability now. We have come so. . ."

"You could spit out all the blueprints to help us to catch up with our past." Randolph sounded serious.

I went on to explain that I had all the blueprints from her life, but I did not know whether or not it would be possible to fill in the gaps overnight. And, even if I imagined that it was feasible if I could connect long enough with her intellectually, I was not certain that it would be easy for me to do that. They nodded. .

"And, the earth's surface today, Pamela?" Again, it was Stuart pushing for answers.

"We are located in a hot, dry region. At least that is what it appears to be. I did not wander off very far, but far enough to know that there was nothing worth exploring near our cavern. I can only guess at what the rest of the earth's surface might look like." For a brief instance, I had the impression that I knew approximately what the ratio of land to water would be. And, then I remembered why. "Yes, I looked into that with Dr. Miller. You must remember that Randolph, I believe that I discussed it with you." He nodded.

"And, Dr. Gordon admitted that the earth's surface had recovered." I clicked my fingers together, as if that was enough to put everything in place. "Of course, there must have been a war. That explains why the earth's atmosphere was so contaminated that all life forms disappeared and why the surface was destroyed; and, yes," I was groping for answers. "The androids must have exterminated the human race."

"How horrifying! And, you want us to work with them?" Stuart screamed.

"Yes, it is horrifying, but we have no choice."

"But, if they won, why do they need us?" Stuart asked in dismay. "They could have inhabited the planet. They would not even have needed these oxygenized structures." He started to laugh, "Are they absolutely stupid or what?"

It was as if I was somewhere else looking out at a future that I never thought I'd know. Somehow I...could know. Something, anxiety, I didn't know, swelled in me. Then I could almost hear voices warning me about my total disregard for the life of future generations. I paced in front of them and then collapsed on one of the wonderfully comfortable chairs in this isolated unit. I saw that they were watching me intensely. My behavior was certainly bizarre. I could hear their thoughts the same way that I could hear their spoken words. I knew that they were worried. They were afraid that I had lost all concern for them and the others whose footsteps were coming closer. If I was no longer Pamela, then I must be Reinhart. The truth was, I didn't know who

I was. I was maybe. . .lost. I seemed to be passing from one to the other in my thoughts. Maybe the bridge was built and receiving traffic as I now had the capacity to transcend my reality, to move from one time and one space to another. "I was the God of the past." I mused out loud. I saw their worried eyes flash. Now their fear invaded the place. Their fear was suffocating me driving me to crave clean air.

But I was stymied, divided in two. One part of me was the emotionally intense Pamela and the other part, the cold and logical Reinhart. She told me that we would be merged together on an intellectual level and that I would determine to what extent her personality would become part of mine. I was aware, very aware, of my constant search for her knowledge and worse for her rational evaluation of the environment around us. I had to be careful not to underestimate Pamela's value and thereby lose my true personality.

I sat staring into space, ignoring both Stuart and Randolph. They were off exploring the equipment in the room. They called out to me frequently to join them but I didn't move; I was deep in thought. I eventually fell into a kind of trance, where Pamela and Reinhart used a form of seduction to draw me into one or the other's total consciousness. I recoiled from both of them, as if I were a third person who had the choice of who I wanted to be and could effectively reject them both. This game lasted for a long time, until I shook myself violently out of its dangerous clutches with a long, tedious scream. I jarred myself back into reality, bringing my two friends rushing back to my side.

"What happened?" They were yelling at the same time.

"Just tired, I think and worried about the future. Screaming just helped me to decompress." I smiled.

"Don't know what to say." Stuart shrugged his shoulders. "Actually, I think that we better check on those androids again." Stuart said through clenched teeth.

The screen beamed in on them. They had moved their forces and equipment farther down the wall. Perhaps they imagined that they miscalculated our precise point of entry into this inner circle.

"They believe that they are going to find us. Doesn't that seem strange?" Randolph asked as he scratched the top of his head.

"Yeah! It doesn't make sense. They don't know that there is an inside, so where do they think we went?" Stuart retorted.

"Look over here." I pointed out. "There is a group trying to drill through the wall on the opposite side. They might think that we passed through the wall to the adjacent corridor?" I suggested.

"Possibly!" Stuart exclaimed. "Weird, though! Are you sure Pamela that they did not know anything about this inner circle?" He asked dubiously.

His question triggered something else. It came to me: A decision made thousands of years ago, by a true genius, whose talent and creativity won her respect and provoked envy and hatred. A decision that my genetic mother made and a program that she created saved humanity. It made it possible for us to be born in a new world. "It worked!" I screamed with satisfaction and admiration of my mother's talent. "There were those who claimed that she had lost contact with the real world. They laughed at her project and ridiculed her for claiming that she discovered a way to control the intellectual development of the androids. But, it worked and she accomplished her objective."

"What worked?" they asked at the same time.

"The program; the program worked." I smiled with satisfaction and pride.

"Pamela," Randolph had now approached me and taken me into his arms as if I were hysterical or under shock.

"No, you don't understand," I said as I pushed him away. "She had the androids download a program just after she realized that her android opposite was developing her own personality. She, actually, put a bug in their system, a kind of virus, a blocker". I stopped for a minute to organize my thoughts. "As you must have suspected, their intellectual capacity should have been greater than ours. Creating the androids with pure intellect was a risk. They were capable of accumulating knowledge, tapping into each other's systems and reaching extraordinary capacities. That would have reduced humans to a kind of inferior race in a short period of time. Androids could have made us extinct. For that reason, androids were seen as a menace to human existence, by a large part of the scientific community. But, Reinhart had the answer. Near the end of her life, she made their creativity, their ability to progress, dependent upon humans, by ordering them to download a program that she pretended would reinforce their optimum performance and intellectual capacity. Even though she was most interested in the Group of 5, other androids could also present a danger, so she ordered the Group of 5 to automatically transfer this program, through their networking system, to all existing androids."

I wanted to laugh with pleasure, but it was time to explain. "Just to back-track a bit, she ordered her android opposite to shut down because she defied Reinhart's way of governing. She had to accept that command. But, without that command coming from the creator, she feared that the other creations would be free to develop beyond our capacities." I took a deep breath. "Even though she knew that the Group of 5 was very loyal to her, she also realized just how dangerous they could become and she anticipated the consequences by making it impossible for them to be more than a recipient of knowledge.

As I just mentioned, she destroyed the android's independent creative ability and then needed to destroy any existing emotional configurations, which she had recklessly given to members of the Group of 5 that could inspire them to develop human traits. Before the Group of 5 had the opportunity to realize the consequence of this virus on their creative ability, she ordered them to erase the emotional configurations. So even if they believed that they could accomplish everything, it would be impossible."

I took a deep breath and exhaled slowly. Randolph broke the silence and said he understood nothing that I said. So, I simplified it. "They want more progress but they are stuck with what was communicated to them or only what they directly participated in, nothing else. And in effect, I am only talking about the Group of 5, because they learned certain techniques, while, as I said, being denied access to the creative side, even the problem solving efforts behind the projects. Reinhart, and her other brilliant colleagues, refused to make them privy to all that information. In effect, they did not even receive the entire knowledge bank of their creators. The scientific community stayed on the alert, destroying or shutting down other androids, outside of this group, that showed any signs of creative thinking. In any event, all that I propose is verifiable. For instance, Dr. Miller's old robotic body was all that they could give her. They had no idea of how Reinhart created human looking machines. That is why they are giving us projects to develop new techniques. And, if my guess is right they are reaching the end of their knowledge of how to produce. Their projects are coming to an end. They are even unable to understand the equipment in this inner circle. Of course, they don't even know that this area exists. . .the reason why they are now focusing on a tunnel system in the wall. Do you understand?" I asked rhetorically. "They need to stimulate humans to want to go further. Her program worked. They can do nothing without us!"

"And, I might add, that they were frustrated by the fact that humans were complacent and happy. They had no competitive spirit and were not at all interested in developing new techniques. And, that was precisely why they allowed a small, select group of us to develop normal human emotional configurations." I added.

"It must be very alarming to observe that we are more obsessed with sexual pleasures and love, than creativity. But that is all they see. We have deceived them. We are even more interested in acquiring real freedom than they can imagine, which we have fortunately kept a secret." I said proudly.

"I am still a bit confused." Randolph replied. "Why didn't she install this debilitating program earlier?"

"Reinhart followed the cautious procedure of her colleagues in the beginning, principally because she hesitated about sharing her discoveries with them. Her visionary techniques were often scoffed at and her genius ridiculed. At best the scientific community found her naïve and overly self-confident. They wanted androids to have only rudimentary capacities and did not have confidence in the new group of android creations, or the Group of 5. But, at one point and in spite of her colleagues' warnings and objections, she wanted to use her elite androids like other members of the scientific community to participate in discoveries and even replace their defunct creators. She was so convinced that her program, when installed, it would ultimately inhibit independent thinking and creativity, while blocking their access to relevant information, as well as deleting other highly sensitive scientific information. She never felt obliged to demonstrate the credibility of her project to the other scientists. She was, moreover, so confident that she had anticipated all the various and complex ways in which these machines could override the program or by-pass the system, after once it was installed, that she decided that she didn't need to get the approval of the other scientists for how she wanted to interact with these machines. She simply ignored protocol." I stared at them trying to read their minds, before continuing. "She developed her blocking programs years before she even created this exceptional group of androids. She probably should have installed the blocking systems from the outset." I stopped to look for an answer. "I can only surmise now that she was so fascinated by her creations that she wanted to study and observe them; and they appeared to be in awe of her genius and completely obedient to her. Fortunately, her android opposite rebelled. So, even as she finally installed the various viruses and other blocking systems, near the end of her life, she never had the opportunity to see how well they worked. She was certainly reckless, but also extraordinarily brilliant." I sighed in complete admiration of her. "And today, we know the secret. The Group of 5 needs us to advance. All androids are completely dependent upon us. They can do nothing without us."

I was speaking so loudly that I could hear my voice resounding in the room. My two, should-be admirers, showed no emotion. I couldn't understand their reaction. "I know that we have always suspected them of needing us, but now I can absolutely confirm it. So, what do you think?"

They were both in shock or disbelief of what I had just said because they did not reply right away. For certain, they both suspected me of being delusional. Who wouldn't? And, I must have given them the impression that I was suffering from a kind of schizophrenia; I was switching from Pamela to Reinhart. I couldn't blame them for being suspicious of what I just said. I knew that what I said would become evident with time and their skepticism would disappear. No need to belabor it right now.

Randolph let out a heavy sigh, just as Stuart took up the discussion.

"What you say makes sense to a certain extent; but, it is only conjecture, isn't it." Was he just being diplomatic? I mused. "We have been playing with that idea for a long time now and they still continue to channel us towards other projects. So, even if it is true, I believe that there is a lot of catching up to do, unless…they were, for whatever reason, unable to save the data."

"Yes, but there is no other rational way to explain what has happened." I turned away from them for a moment to give myself time to think. How could I explain all of this? "Think about it. You, the scientists are given projects. The projects that you handle during your lifetime give the androids the proper method to instruct the next generation about the most recent techniques. That generation's accomplishments will be transmitted to the next, and so forth and so on."

"But, all the techniques up until now were known by the androids. Why didn't they just start where they left off?" Randolph asked.

"Some of those techniques were presumably made redundant by the blocking program, assuming that it worked. Otherwise I can offer you different reasons, if you want?" They nodded in agreement. "To completely understand what happened, we must ask them. But, there are some factors that I should point out. First, the androids knew how to perform different complex techniques where their assistance was needed. There were many things like Reinhart's ability to stay young, which she never shared with any of them. They were not as I mentioned privy to all the research and development. The gaps in their knowledge might explain why they could not pick up where humans left off." They did not respond so I continued with the monologue.

"Secondly, the androids served humans. They did not mingle with each other and even though the Group of 5 knew each other, they were not working or functioning independently from humans. There was no android networking, so to speak. It must have been difficult for them to find themselves in a totally android world, if that is what happened after the end. They may have just needed humans to justify their existence." They were listening intently.

"And lastly, perhaps vital information and computer banks were destroyed at the end of human history. The androids were probably not competent enough to put together a human educational program and needed to rely upon human progress and discovery to educate the next generation."

"Your final argument is the most convincing for me." Stuart replied. "What do you think, Randolph? "

"I am inclined to agree with you, Stuart, and go with the third suggestion. They are so deceptive. The first two arguments assume that the androids either admired humans or respected them. That doesn't hold water. If they admired humans in the past, they would never have bred us like they are doing now.

439

And, with respect to the second reason, they would have found ways around the procedure in place and compared notes with each other and then tapped into other programs and procedures underway to download progress. That is why the third possibility sounds the most convincing. They effectively put themselves in a bad situation because they lost information that they never had the opportunity to steal beforehand. And, Reinhart's blocking program made it impossible for them to fill in the gaps on their own and start from where Reinhart's research left off."

"But, why did they program us?" Stuart broke in.

"Because it was the method that Reinhart used to keep humans happy and under control. The androids simply used her visual blocker for everyone since they believed that what they referred to as negative emotions were responsible for all the in-fighting, prejudice, discrimination, etcetera that destroyed human society." All three of us saw the stupidity of the android reasoning.

"They thought that this programming would prevent conflicts and wars. They did not understand the complexity of human emotions and the need to have emotional opposites in place to have normally functioning humans. The problem was that androids needed the intellectual community to progress scientifically and technologically. But, without a real emotional structure in place, we humans were happy just to be happy. We didn't need more." I gave them a broad, happy smile, just thinking about how problematic the situation was for the Group of 5.

"I don't understand why they produced musicians and artists. It seems strange why they would need to be surrounded by culture." Randolph had a sardonic grin on his face. "Can you imagine them relating to music? Is it some sort of pathetic farce? The androids, as we know them now, sitting through a concert or seeing an exposition appears surrealistic!" That triggered some laughter, which seemed a better choice than tears.

I tried in vain to give some rational reasons why the androids might have needed or wanted to passively participate in human pleasures. The fact that some of them have sophisticated sensory systems that might have been stimulated by the musical chords or a beautiful painting seemed to be too farfetched. Even suggesting that some of them may have needed to recreate the harmony that music and art brought to humans, caused heavy snickering. But, Reinhart's logic was telling me, that it was a way for them to study the extent to which the intellectual elite could have natural ability or talent in many different areas depending upon which one of them was accessible. Stuart and Randolph nodded.

"That does explain," I went on to say, "why the Governor mentioned to me that I was the first in the Pamela series to go into music." Thinking back, I understood just how significant that conversation was. "The 12 others before me were terminated early simply because they had bypassed the visual receptor. But, as they were all trained in a branch of science, the androids must have been more concerned about prolonging their existence. They did not feel threatened by me in the beginning because I was pianist. How could a pianist be problem? And, I was lucky that Gordon, along with others, was convinced that humans needed a complete emotional structure to be productive. "

We sat in silence for a while, each of us wondering how we would each be contributing to the creation of a new world. I was particularly worried that I was becoming far too rational. I was haunted by the question of whether we should awaken all the other humans regardless of their missions, allowing them to feel emotionally free. My thoughts were on my mistakes and my reluctance to make critical decisions. Perhaps Reinhart had difficulty making decisions, as well, I thought. Maybe it was not so easy for her to decide to separate humans on the basis of intellectual capacity.

As always, I was plagued with a list of interminable questions that had no immediate answers. How could one determine intellectual capacity anyway? What kind of people would we be once we gained control of our destiny? If we didn't divide society by intellectual standards, would we divide society by other means? Would we fall into the human weaknesses that were imbued with violent acts? Was our history edited to show the worst of human practices? Vying for power at any price clearly permeated our history. Forms of discrimination transformed with the times, just as wars were fought to wipe out the bad. Engaging in war was based on the premise that their convictions and beliefs were better than the enemy's. And, now, were we, that small number of humans who bypassed the programming and were allowed to live, the good element of our society? And, if we were, did we have unfettered freedom to decide the future for the other humans in this center and elsewhere? Or, should we force every other human to deprogram? Was there a limit? Thinking about how we learned to deal with our full emotional network, made me tremble when I thought of how dangerous and even hideous it could be to reveal to the masses the complexity of human consciousness at the same time? It did not seem rational. And yet, I did not venture to raise the subject for fear that my opinion might not be considered neutral. After all, my consciousness was in constant transition and I was still not sure who I was. So, I sat next to my friends and allies…and waited.

So much time passed before Randolph brought up this very disturbing problem from another aspect. "How are we going to maintain control once all the humans are deprogrammed?"

I could hear the same thought racing through my mind. "Where is Pamela in all this?" Expressing my dissatisfaction, I twisted my mouth into a wrinkled ball. "Do you want me to introduce the Reinhart strategy of deprogramming only those whose intellectual capacity is equivalent or superior to ours? Or, do you want to introduce the strategy of Pamela, which is to wait and see?"

"What does that mean, wait and see?" Two great minds speaking at the same time with the same notion, I thought to myself.

"My wait and see strategy is not status quo. It means that we should group the humans to protect them while we deactivate the android army, after our victory," I spoke with bold optimism, "and decide in which order we should deprogram a group or groups of individuals. We need to be certain that these deprogrammed humans will have immediate psychological support. We don't know how many androids apart from the Group of 5 could be useful for us. Those whose talents can be used to help humans deal with their newfound emotional freedom should be identified. We shall need support groups and surveillance. I told you about how dangerous Diana was in the beginning. There might be others like her. They could be dangerous and must be monitored."

"So far so good. I think I might like the Pamela strategy. But, who gets to be deprogrammed first?" Stuart commented.

"I am not sure. We shall see that when a decision is imminent. For the sake of discussion, however, we might focus on age. That is to say, deprogram the children first and work up in age groups. And, we must identify everyone who has bypassed their programming before focusing on anyone else."

"You think that there are a lot more like us?" Randolph was smiling.

"It is possible," Stuart broke in. "I have been suspicious about different people. But, a number of my contacts in the center were terminated. Mathieu had worked with an informer in the medical unit where you were for a while, Pamela." I nodded. "She was terminated shortly after you left. If you, Pamela, hadn't gotten to us through John, we would still be playing our game, pretending to be programmed."

"True, but it wasn't that easy as the programmed humans were unable to see us. We were just like the bright ones –the old androids—to them. I was very uneasy in public places because the androids did watch us and the humans were often times walking into me or even sitting on me," Randolph said. We could all identify with that.

"Well, in any event, I vote for the Pamela plan." Stuart replied. "But, I might suggest that we deprogram a fixed number at a time to give us the opportunity to study their individual profiles; remembering that we won't be deprogramming anyone until we are definitely in control of the Center. And, Pamela, we are going to have to set aside the physically deformed humans and integrate them slowly into society. Remember how shocked you were when you first saw Jonathan?" I nodded. "The babies, by the way, will be easy. We remove the implant."

We sat in silence for a few minutes before the discussion resumed. "I have one small problem with the Pamela strategy. It is perfect if all those humans are off the battle field, in a room where they are nice and safe." Stuart clicked his tongue to be sure he had my attention. "What about those humans who find themselves deprogrammed on the battle field, like today?" He looked at me. "Do we ignore them and risk our lives to save them?"

"Wow! That is a real life situation that you are talking about, Stuart." Randolph broke in.

"I don't know." I replied. "I forgot about that possibility. A true battle field can have innocent victims."

"Well," Stuart went on in a strong, determined voice. "I am for letting them fend for themselves once we have called their attention to their state of mind."

"Ok, by me." Randolph and Stuart often held the same positions.

"I believe that we have to attain our objective; take over the Center. Everything else is secondary." I added.

"Wait, once we are in control we have to take care of the babies, so we will certainly have to determine who among the androids we can use." Then I realized something else. "If I give you a new configurations for the androids to assure their compliance with our instructions, can either one of you make the adjustments?"

"Of course, any of us scientists can do that. I don't understand though why you can't do it yourself?" Randolph added ironically.

"I probably could, but I have never manipulated anything scientifically. I don't feel comfortable with the idea; that is all." They huffed over that answer. "Ok, I'll explain. Reinhart used her hands. Knowing the technique requires manual practice as well. When you studied in your areas of specialization, you had practical laboratory training alongside. You learned how to manipulate chemicals, equipment, and so forth. I have only used my hands in a technical sense to play the piano. Knowing how to write the musical score does not mean that one knows how to play the notes on every instrument; the same goes with lab work. I have the knowledge but I lack the practical skills."

"Ok, I agree." Stuart said waving his hand to stop me from saying more. "But, you are going to have to try to manipulate equipment. You are going to have to develop the practical skills." I nodded. "For the moment, until you get over your insecurity, we shall carry out your directives. Won't we Randolph?

Randolph nodded complacently.

I then stood up and told them that I wanted to explore a bit more. Actually, I wanted to know if the rejuvenation machine was intact. "But, before we move out of this control room we better check again on those androids." I didn't want any bad surprises.

"They are still in the same position. Banging against the wall." There was laughter in Randolph's voice.

"And the Group of 5? Let me try to locate them." I gently pushed him out of my way. They were all in their private offices looking over paper work. "Get over here and look at this," I called out to them. "What do you two think?"

"Weird. In all cases though, they are definitely studying files." Stuart commented.

We watched them until we were convinced that they were actually in their offices and that we were not seeing a film.

"Ok, let's leave." I suggested. They followed me as we went into well-equipped laboratories. Both Randolph and Stuart were very excited about what was available. There were project designs on the walls in all the different rooms. And, we found a 300 square meter room that was filled with dehydrated food products. We used a rehydrating machine to make our lunch; or was it dinner? There was another area that was used to recycle water.

"I don't understand why the androids don't know about this area, after all they provide water for us. If something goes wrong, they must be able to repair it?"

"I have no information about that, Stuart. Gordon told me that natural water sources existed today and that the natural sources were providing for our needs. Why would she say that if it weren't true?"

"Who knows? What do you think Randolph, your partner was a geologist?"

"Really? We never discussed that. She never revealed anything to me about her work. I didn't even know that she was a geologist. Pamela, you told me what her colleague told you about an artificial explosion in the center of the earth. Remember?"

"Oh" I was sitting up now. "Oh, oh, your partner must have been brilliant. I wonder how she discovered that." I wanted to have something to drink, I felt so thirsty, but it was not the right moment to start looking for a bottle. "Yes, that's it; an explosion in the center of the earth."

I could see from their expressions that they realized that I had somehow sorted through all that mind-boggling information that had been fed into my brain and was now ready to explain it. "Without being able to understand all the data, it would appear that we are all lucky to exist."

And then slapping my hands in frustration I added in a loud voice as if the stupid androids could hear me. "And, those androids, are lucky that they are still around. How could they have been so reckless? That system was never to be used for anything other than total destruction. Doomsday; that is what they called it, the End of the world! I think that there was a security system in place. That's it a decision that had to be made by a group and it took three different people holding separate keys to activate the system. And, if you can believe this, those individuals were scanned and identified before being allowed to enter the control center." I know I was shaking my head at this point because what I had to say didn't make any sense. "Reinhart was one of the people entrusted with this duty and this happened after her death." I hesitated before saying, "That is why I must be troubled because it was not coherent with the information I now have."

"Oh, it is so disgusting." I was definitely back in control. "They must have kept her body intact but for how long? The Group of 5 has a lot of explaining to do."

"They planted a nuclear device near the earth's core?"

"Yes, Randolph but that device was planted in the center of the earth, not by the androids but by Reinhart and her team. The androids participated in the implementation of the project, not in the creation of the device."

"I am worried about you though, Pamela." Stuart spoke. "Those androids gave you more than just her knowledge; they gave you her reasoning or even some of her personality. It is not normal that you should be going back and forth like this. It is, nonetheless, reassuring to know that she would not have taken extreme action like the androids did. But why?"

"The war, probably, Stuart, the war that was imposed upon them. After Reinhart's death they no longer had a mentor and they tried to second-guess what she would have done. Of course, as they are operating on pure logic, they never factored any sense of morality into their decisions. But, I can just imagine, that your partner's discovery was not on her project list. She must have been wired and when she communicated that information to her colleague they saw her as a danger."

"Can you reprogram the Group of 5?" Randolph asked.

"No, Randolph, they would not cooperate. They have an auto-defense system to resist certain kinds of degenerative reprogramming. Could they have been reprogrammed to kill? As we discussed earlier, I have a feeling that Dr. Murdoc was privy to most of Reinhart's discoveries, including the intricacies of android fabrication and programming. Perhaps, we could bypass their auto-defense system by pretending that we were going to give them part of what they want-a real emotional profile. In any event, we have time for all that." As I started to stand up, I turned slightly to the right and then I saw it; it was there—her famous machine. "Look, over there. The rejuvenation machine, it's there." I was pointing at it. I was so excited that I forgot how weak I still felt and I stumbled forward on wobbly feet. "She must have had more than one or she had it moved in here."

"How does it work?" Stuart was already checking out the interior. So many buttons and levers.

"Don't touch anything." I had this incredible desire to keep the machine for me. How selfish; how could I feel like that. "It is dangerous to play around with it. At this moment, I have only a vague idea of how it works."

"Well, tell us. You are not planning on keeping this for yourself, are you?"

"Actually, Randolph, the idea is quite attractive." I said teasingly. "Look, it functions like a transporter." They just looked at me. "You know about this form of time travel. Oh it was something that they used in the 22nd century to travel. The system was developed to protect the environment. Unfortunately, the environment was already in bad shape. It took a long time for the humans to develop the technique and install terminals. But, in fact, you entered a terminal and entered the code for another location and your body was transported through a kind of spatial tunnel." I stopped. "You both told me that you were aware of this kind of device." They nodded.

"That is how she stayed young. She transported herself a lot."

"You can't be serious, Stuart." I said laughingly. "Of course not, everyone would have stayed young."

"The genetic code, the genome, of humans was their identity card. All humans knew their potential physical and mental problems. In fact, it was a source of contention, because it formed another basis upon which humans could discriminate against each other." It was a good time for comic relief. "Imagine, Randolph, that you met a gorgeous human."

"Like you?" he interrupted.

"Better, if one can be found." We both smiled. "She would want to know your genome before committing herself to you or having children with you. Perfect matches were sought after, and those who had too many bad chromosomes were on the "unwanted list, like a wall -flower at a dance."

"So... what about the young side?"

"Ok, Stuart, this is about all that I can say. She experimented for a long time before finding the right solution. But, in effect, she transported herself back into a former genetic time frame to recuperate her youth. It was complicated because in her experiments certain subjects came back young in all aspects, including loosing what was precious for her, all that they had learned during their adult years. She finally solved that problem." I paused while the Reinhart inside of me flaunted her genius. "She ultimately identified those aspects of her genetic code that should not be altered and that which should be reinforced and those, like potential for illnesses or senility that should be deleted during the round trips. So, she remained physically young with a great deal of energy, vitality and was mentally active and creative, with her memory intact."

"And, this machine can do that?" Stuart was very much interested.

"Yes, but we need the proper genetic code, which I am not certain that the androids have paid all that much attention to." Of course, I was hoping the contrary. "I spoke to Peter about this machine because I thought that I might be able to use it to help Jonathan. Peter told me that if I had the details he could construct the machine. But I didn't know that it existed." I stopped to take a deep breath. "I realize now that it would not be useful for Jonathan. He never had a genetic code that was minus all his deformities. And even if I were to cancel the deformities, it would not mean that Jonathan would be physically normal."

"Too bad. Is there anything else that you can do?" Randolph was definitely interested.

"Now that I am here in the inner circle I know that there is what humans referred to as an "operating room." Doctors, surgeons, were trained to operate on the human body to correct an anomaly. It is possible that we could straighten his back using invasive, or non-invasive surgical means. If not, we could remove the twisted vertebrae and add bionic parts." I shook my head. "This is not my field. I would have to find someone whose training could be used for surgical procedures."

"Then there is hope?" Randolph asked.

"There is always hope, Randolph." I smiled. "By the way, I am dying of thirst." They related to that.

The dehydrated food we had eaten must have been the source of our acute thirst. We were next to the water purification system that gave us no direct access to the water. We started opening cabinets in search of bottled water. I let out a hideous scream when I came face to face with a huge reptile with a flat head and enormous teeth floating in a large jar. We grabbed doors after doors of cabinets that were home to a vast assortment of reptiles, fish, plants and other aquatic life forms arranged in alphabetical order in large jars. Whether these creatures represented extinct species or existing life forms for that time period made no real difference. Their presence was more horrifying than reassuring.

"I found something over here." Stuart screamed with excitement. "It looks like a large jar of water and it has a label on it. It reads 'for human consumption.' What do you think?"

We were upon him in a split second. "I'll take the risk. Just help me to get that jar out and open it." I didn't care my thirst was overcoming me. They didn't object and I swallowed a huge mouthful of what tasted like the water that we drank every day. They were not convinced; waited a couple minutes to be sure that I was alright, and then downed big gulps themselves.

We started laughing, giddy with relief that we were still alive. It was time to move on so we took the jar of water along with us. We passed through an area filled with models of transport vehicles; blueprints lined the walls. It was so fascinating that for a second I forgot the urgency of our rapid departure. The operating room we stumbled across was quite impressive. The shelves were packed with training manuals and computer disks…hope for Jonathan. And, finally we came upon a room filled with tables, armchairs, and long sofas; it was divided into small spaces for dining, relaxing, having a drink, or even sleeping. We moved in the direction of the cubicles with beds. We had our choice of bedroom style and bed size. The beds had wonderfully soft quilts in vibrant colors, unlike the stiff covers issued to us. I chose one in the big bed cubicle with a luscious green and blue cover.

My friends went off in their own directions. I wanted to fall into a sound sleep but lay staring at the ceiling and wondering how everything was going to end. I thought about Peter who was preparing to leave for the transport center. That worried me. We had lost track of time in this inner circle. I started agonizing over the thought that we could be late; and if they had already arrived they would be unceremoniously escorted to the termination center because we weren't there to help. We absolutely had to return to the control center as soon as possible.

Then I saw Randolph and Stuart looking down at me. Randolph put his finger up to his mouth to warn me to keep quiet. He whispered in my ear that they heard voices coming from the lounge area. "Strangers have joined us in the inner circle." Stuart's stern voice confirmed the possible danger that was awaiting us.

"How could the androids have gotten into this inner circle?" I asked in a quivering voice.

"Shh!" Stuart put his hand over my mouth. "We don't know if we are facing androids or another life form." He said softly, as he released his grip. Whatever the case, this is not good news, I thought.

"They are moving closer and closer." Randolph said, his pupils dilated.

I heard the voices now. My heart was pounding my chest. I looked at Stuart, standing ready to pounce on anything that entered this room. I jumped out of the bed and stood next to Stuart, pushing Randolph off behind me. I was not certain that Randolph knew anything about physical combat; or rather self-defense. His being there behind me, though, was comforting; I imagined that just his physical built and size would give him an advantage, or discourage an opponent. But, then… I remembered what happened to Stuart earlier today when he underestimated the young human. It was a good thing that I was there to help out.

Stuart and I positioned ourselves on either side of the door hoping to take them by surprise. We could hear their shuffling getting closer and closer, as they came through the doorway at the same time. I quickly surmised before I struck that it would be easier for us to knock them on the floor and take control.

I floored one and Stuart cornered the other and held out his hand to stop me from crushing my victim. "Wait! What are they?" Stuart was screaming.

"We are the same as you—human," one of them answered.

We instinctively relaxed our grip and moved away giving them the opportunity to recover. "They can't be human. Look at them, they are all grey and wrinkled with white hair, and smell very bad." Stuart screamed, wiping his hand on his trouser, while Randolph stepped back from the two figures on the floor, as if they might contaminate him.

"They are human," I interrupted." I could relate to the reaction of Randolph and Stuart. I had acted the same way when I first met Jason. "Age, is hard on humans. And, sadly, this will happen to us." I said quietly and then turned to look at them. "What happened?"

"I escaped. In fact, I escaped when I was escorted into the termination center. I can see that you don't believe me, but it is true. The androids left me, just for a couple minutes, when my friend here appeared out of nowhere to pull me into this 6th dimension; where we are today."

"And how did you know about this inner circle?" I asked the friend.

"I was lucky, Pamela. Your spectacular performance after I was ushered away by those guards gave me the opportunity to break away from the androids. I ran like a fool and stumbled over so many humans in the labyrinth of corridors. My body was bruised all over and, when I finally stopped for a breath, I leaned up against the wall which opened up to this place." He shook his head.

"Ferdinand, it's you?" I threw my arms around him. Even though I thought that I was deprogrammed much later, it didn't matter whether Ferdinand's reasoning or mine was more accurate. "Stuart, Randolph," I screamed, "he was my friend when I was programmed. I thought you were terminated?" Tears of joy were streaming down my face; my mentor was alive and well.

"They never told you I disappeared?" I shook my head. "I should explain. After they dragged me out of the orchestra pit, they locked me in a padded room. Gordon came to see me every day. She pretended that they kidnapped me because they liked me and wanted me to continue to exist. I knew better. She asked me too many questions about you, Pamela. I saw through her game and understood their wicked conspiracy. Believe it or not, I was still under the programming when the androids came for me. They knew that we were close and that you would be strongly affected by my disappearance. You actually witnessed my deprogramming which I surmised was to have been the catalyst for yours. As you did not deprogram straight away, they kept me around to use at a later date; to shock you into reality." He sighed. "To finish with this, two androids came to escort me to the termination center the day you finally deprogrammed. But as your deprogramming got so much attention, they got distracted and I had time to flee. The rest you know now."

"Wow." I shook my head. "They planned everything down to the finest detail. How diabolical!"

Ferdinand broke the silence. "Anyway, I discovered that there were other passages into this center, but I think that it's either our body weight or our body heat that creates an opening. In any event, I saved "Ralph," that is what I call him, a while ago now. It was just luck."

"That's clever…body heat. I should have realized that straight away." I quickly brought him up-to-date, especially concerning my newly found talents and capacities. We would have time later on to talk about other things. "Are you willing to help us?"

"Are you kidding? I have wanted to overthrow these androids for years. Whatever I can do, I am ready. "

"Just tell me one thing, because my friends here," I pointed to Stuart and Randolph, "are focused on your physical appearance; how old are you?"

"I am not young, but I am not certain of my birth date either. I do know that the androids gave me more time than I was destined to have. I believe that I am probably in my 60's. But, their crummy food made me look worse." He laughed maliciously. "I have an uncompromising loathing for those androids!"

"So do I." I could understand his hatred. "Your age doesn't matter. But, now they know why my genetic mother created that rejuvenation machine." I looked at Stuart and Randolph.

"She could have just covered herself with the same plant to have youthful android skin." I applauded Randolph's, albeit feeble attempt, to joke at a time like this.

"They lived a lot longer during her life time. The aging process had already been slowed down with hormone treatments. These hormones don't exist today; in fact, because there is no real medication on hand. That makes termination the best option for the androids to employ. It keeps infections from spreading." Ferdinand was enjoying himself and muffled an upcoming belly laugh he miraculously succeeded in stifling.

"You won't be surprised to know they kept me alive because I was a bit of their court jester. That was why they also let me use the library. I played the role of the village idiot, saying simple, illogical things. They earmarked me as totally harmless. They changed and considered me dangerous when I began my fruitless campaign to educate humans about their servitude. We'll have to compare notes someday, Pamela."

"Right. I would like to know more about what you discovered, but not now. At this moment, unfortunately, I am so tired that I would like to sleep. I am afraid that we're behind schedule." I was starting to yawn and had trouble concentrating.

"The inner circle gives you the impression that time stops, but I assure you that your human clock is accurate. Get some sleep. That is what Ralph and I are going to do as well."

We parted for our chosen cubicles and I slipped underneath the covers to discover that I was not alone. 'Randolph, what are you doing here? "

"Not what you think. I just didn't want to leave you alone. We are lucky that these visitors are friends." His face looked drawn. "I won't be able to sleep just worrying about you. "

"Of course, I am glad that you are here. I think that I shall sleep better as well. We have a long day ahead of us." I curled up next to him and fell into a sound sleep.

Stuart woke us up early in a fury, shouting that Ferdinand and Ralph had gone off to get food and that we should meet them in the control center. Randolph and I jumped up. "Did you see a bathroom around here?" I asked.

"Yes, there are several and there is everything that you need to shower and brush your teeth, and so forth." He pointed us in the right direction.

As I showered, I wondered why Ferdinand and Ralph were not clean. Did they prefer to be natural? Another conundrum to resolve. I shook my head.

There were no short cuts in this inner circle so it took us a while to get to the control center. Ferdinand and Ralph arrived a good 30 minutes after us laden with all kinds of rehydrated food to go with our water. We had already scanned the center and the outskirts and were about to focus on the transport center, our meeting place. We were looking for any kind of movement. And, then we saw her, Diana, appeared out of nowhere. "It must be the tunnel," Stuart was saying, "that forced them to burrow upwards. In any event, they have arrived and we have to get started."

"Wait, we are still 2 days ahead of schedule." My voice was high and screechy.

"It doesn't matter, Pamela. Stuart's right we have to get started." Randolph looked at Ferdinand now. "Do you know where we should exit this inner circle so that we are close to the transport building?"

"I am not very good at directional games."

"Ok, where were you when you popped into the termination center?"

"Oh, that's easy. I was near the bar in the comfort lounge."

"Ok, so we should pass through the middle of the back wall in the water recycling section." Randolph looked so serious now, a huge contrast from the clown who makes me laugh. He had leadership ability and was ready for action. "Even if we miss the straight line to the transport building, we will be next to my lab and from there we can shortcut to the rendezvous site. What do you think?" No answer. "Are you ready then?" Heads were nodding. "Let's move it!" He looked at me. "And you, Pamela, do you still think that you should meet with the Group of 5?"

"Yes, but I need some help, like Ferdinand, on where I should exit."

"That depends upon who you think that you should see first, doesn't it?" I was relieved he had taken charge.

"Flanders, I think?" I replied, but without conviction as I wasn't quite sure. "He is the one who likes to organize meetings and there is that special padded room where no one else can hear us."

"So to the birthing center. Not easy." His forehead wrinkled as he squinted his eyes, studying the problem. He didn't disagree with me though. I took that for a good sign. "Ok, for me, you should slip through the far right, that is when you are standing facing the hydrated food section side of the wall." His pointed fingers showed us the way. "But, you know, you are going to have to move fast, they are probably looking for us and you will be alone. Are you going to be alright on your own?" Now, he looked concerned. I had seen more sides of Randolph in just a couple minutes than I had seen the past few years.

"I should be. In any event, I have to distract them away from you. We shall be passing near them about the same time and so it's better they focus on me."

"We are all going to have to be ready for action. We might have to fight." With a faint smile at the corners of his mouth, he nodded at Pamela and Stuart, "You'll take the lead there, Pamela, as dealing with the Group of 5 is not my strong point. We are going to have to stay together and protect each other." Randolph was still giving orders. Everyone nodded this time.

"Listen, Randolph, we are old now and not prepared for all of this. You remember how easily we fell over last night; we're not what you would call an experienced military unit." We all laughed at that one. "But, Ralph and I are ready to do whatever we have to for the success of this operation even if it means rolling around the floor to trip up those crazy machines."

"Well said!" Then Stuart gave Ferdinand a friendly tap on the shoulder. This turned into a series of friendly back slaps and laughter among them. This must be a man bonding thing, I thought. A low chuckle cracked my throat.

"We have to take these laser guns with us." Stuart said, passing them out. "You too Pamela. The extras will be for the others."

"But I don't know how to shoot them." I protested.

"You should. She must know." Stuart insisted.

"It's ok, I'll show her." Randolph, the notorious sharp shooter, gave me a quick demonstration of how to hold the gun and fire it. It looked easy enough.

"But to focus…Just fire it randomly and hope that some of them fall." He yelled.

"Well, I'm off." I announced in a less enthusiastic voice. "I am going to let Reinhart's logic and weaponry skill guide me through."

"Good Luck." They chimed in as I started off in the direction of the dehydrated food reserve. And then I heard Randolph running after me. He grabbed me and gave me one of those passionate goodbye kisses. "How will we keep in touch? How will I know that you are ok?"

"We can't, not right away. But, if my plan works, the Group of 5 will put an end to the offensive and we shall all work together." I looked up into his big, brown eyes and then shoved him lightly away. "Don't worry, I won't say or do anything reckless. Keep your fingers crossed," I yelled over my shoulder.

"Ok, whatever that means?" Of course, he didn't understand that. He never heard about human superstitions.

I was running fast, feeling ready to carry out my mission. With each footstep I was coming closer and closer to realizing our dream. I felt more and more certain of myself as if I finally accepted the decisive role I was to play. I knew that I had to succeed for Peter, Frederic and all my friends inside and outside the center. It had to be the right moment for humans to take back the dominant role that always belonged to them. Those who did replace us for a time would have to bow down to us now. I wondered if that was Reinhart speaking inside me.

Our destiny, their destiny was upon us, were my last thoughts as I leaned heavily into the back wall of the hydrated food reserve, letting my body heat suck me through to the other side.

I was alone and very close to the birthing center. I knew the route well and took off directly for Flanders' office. I was surprised to see that no one was there. I breathed deeply to overcome the fear and anger that was erupting inside of me. And, then as if submerged in a more positive sensation, I marched confidently down the corridor where I had witnessed the different stages of human fetal development. I thought that everything was still in place and that the androids had not made any radical changes so they were not worried about the latest crisis. But something was wrong. . .It seemed contrived. . .

No one was near so I decided to snoop around. There was something that I never understood and that the Reinhart in me could not explain: Why were there deformed, in some cases, hideously deformed humans? If they were using a system of selection that was already in place at the time of Reinhart's disappearance, then the humans should all be perfect, or close to perfect, physically.

I tried entering the room where artificial uteruses were the embryo's maternal womb; the door was locked. I tried station after station to find the same problem before finally deciding to go back to Flanders' office. He was there waiting for me.

"You enjoyed your tour of the unit?" he tried to laugh. "You are a bit early for the meeting that we scheduled for you, so that gives us some time to talk." It seemed I was stuck in a time warp, as if the events of the past 48 hours were imagined. . .

I took a seat and stared at him. I had no intention of talking to him until the others arrived. There was no point in it. He didn't like my silence and started to play mind games with me, insinuating that my form of schizophrenia would soon disappear along with Pamela, to allow Reinhart to take over. He talked on and on about what he referred to as their ingenious project to bring back their mentor. He moved from behind his desk at one point to stand in front of me, to let his body language accentuate his words.

"You might as well let go now, Pamela" he said. "Even though your body is identical to that of Elisabeth, it is her mind that counts the most for all of us." I didn't react. Instead I focused on whether or not he would be useful for us in the future; that loosened my tongue.

"So, Dr. Flanders," I started off in a cold, calculating tone that brought him to quick attention. "Would you mind explaining to me why there are humans in this center who have physical deformities?"

"Who is asking?" he queried.

"Who do you think?" I answered dryly, definitely not in the mood for his games.

"Well, I know that the physical deformities bother you, Pamela," He emphasized my name, "but they are not important."

"It is during Reinhart's time that humans were physically perfect. It was the requirement, wasn't it?"

"Yes, ok, there is an explanation, but it is slightly embarrassing for us." He reminded me of a child for a second, playing with his android fingers and looking down at his feet. He was fidgeting about wasting time probably in hopes that the others would arrive and change the subject.

"I am waiting"

"Ok. We did everything that we could as the fighting continued. The android military, programmed to kill, was weak and ineffective against an angry human population. We, the five of us, realized that we had to escape and hide some place until the fighting ended. We stayed together and protected ourselves to avoid being programmed to kill by that despicable Dr. Murdoc. We contacted others who Elisabeth respected, relied upon and agreed with to decide which ones would occupy the various centers." He stopped for a minute to ask me whether I had received information about the centers. I nodded yes. "The land surface was very small at that time and there were only 4 centers operating. One of those centers was destroyed, leaving three. We have the most equipment and brain power here." I looked at him askance and he quickly corrected his statement indicating that the creators of the androids in this center were considered to be among the most brilliant in the world at that time.

"As for the deformities?"

"It is simple. We wanted to take with us the sperm and ovum of the best of the world. There were even frozen fertilized eggs that we took. The problem was that in the haste, we mixed the good with the bad." He stopped as if I should have understood.

"What are you talking about? What happened to android logic?" I was starting to get annoyed with his evading the issue.

"Dr. Reinhart would certainly remember. She started everything a long time ago when she got involved in producing genetically mutated specimens of humans capable of living on a changing planet. The land surface was small and Dr. Reinhart contended that the possibility of eventual evolutionary mutations in humans was inevitable if humans were to survive. So why not provoke the mutations artificially? She had no legitimate support from geneticists and even her other friends and admirers rejected her theory. The majority believed that the land surface would reappear and with it proper life supporting atmosphere and food sources. There was evidence to show that this was what was happening. In any event, she decided to accelerate this artificial mutation of humans by adjusting chromosomal configurations or even adding new combinations of chromosomes in laboratory experiments. In fact, there were a vast number of mutated sperms or ovum in the in vitro center. We accidentally picked up these genetically modified organisms and when we mixed them with the normal genes, we ended up with physically unattractive humans, rather unattractive for human standards." He was still rubbing his android fingers.

"Idiot! Complete Idiot." He didn't respond. "Everything was always properly labeled, and when you discovered your mistake why didn't you destroy the mutants?"

"Because their mental capacities were in place and often superior to the physically normal humans. Some of them were quite brilliant. So, we just relied upon the visual receptor's capacity to pass a better image on to other programmed humans. This gave us time to strive for human mental or intellectual perfection, without wasting time improving the physical aspects."

"This was certainly rational from the android's point of view. But, the morality of it is shocking." I said calmly but firmly. "And, these deformed humans who suffer from their deformities; that didn't mean anything to you?"

"I know that you are referring to Jonathan, but he was to have been terminated years ago. Terminating prevented ultimate suffering and we had replacements ready to move in. From all standpoints it was the best method to use." His unalterable stern eyes were peering at mine.

"Terminating?" I raised my voice, showing disgust and anger.

"It was Dr. Reinhart's idea anyway. She did it regularly. Termination was a way to rid society of, what she referred to as the worst human developmental mistakes. So, I don't understand why you are not pleased with what we did."

"Because I am not Dr. Reinhart; I am not Dr. Reinhart with her cold, calculating attitude. I am Pamela, your series 13. Dr. Reinhart was building a world based upon her idea of humans. She had decided what kinds of people should and should not constitute the human race. And worst of all, she had lost all her principles as she showed no compassion for those who were what she called, "inferior beings.""

"No, I don't agree. She was willing to have physically mutated humans, even in a grotesque form, live and work in society, so long as they were intellectually productive. And, she was kind to those with an inferior intellect because she added, when she could, the visual receptor that helped them to be happy in life."

"Flanders, we don't see things the same way. She was cruel and inhumane. Humans do not need visual receptors to accept differences and to be happy with their lives. I just don't agree."

"Well, Pamela, you will see the true nature of humans. The world that you are part of today is controlled." He stopped as if to swallow. "You will see, Pamela; one day, you will tell me that Dr. Reinhart and her protégés were right."

"Bah!" That was about all that I could add. I had a better impression of humans. Certainly, we were capable of living together and striving for the benefit of all. But, I couldn't stop there. "All the Jonathan series are not deformed. There are normal looking Jonathan's that you told me about a short time ago."

"It depends on how you look at it." He started off cautiously. "Yes, well, they all have deformities but not always as many as your Jonathan had."

I left it there because I heard the others arriving. They took their place behind the table with Flanders, as if they were still in control.

"There is fighting, Pamela." Gordon took the stage. "Humans will not die in hand-to- hand combat, because our android guards are not programmed to kill offensively, only defensively. But, your humans have found weapons; and, our android guards will not hesitate to fire back, even if that means killing a human." She saw me smile with that. It must have been Ferdinand who showed them where the weapons were. "You think that what you are doing is best for humans, I would imagine?" The rhetorical question wasn't worth a response.

"Before replying, I have a question for you, Gordon." I intentionally dropped the Doctor part to see if she would be bothered. She didn't budge at all. "This haunting question has been bothering me for a long time. Why did you treat me with chemicals? I know that it is not a treatment from Reinhart's period. Where did they come from?"

"Oh, how curious, but very human to dwell on something like that and especially at this very moment when other kinds of decisions must be made." She sighed. "Actually, the clean-up crew we left behind found them when they struggled to dig out the remains of an old building. From what they told us, they found the old structure quite fascinating which was why they wasted time digging it up."

She must have noticed that I was not interested in all her commentary. But it didn't bother her so she perfunctorily continued. "They found thousands and thousands of sacks of chemicals with instructions for use to save humans. I believe that they were used in the 20th and 21st centuries to destroy invasive cells, something like that." She turned to the others and asked if anyone knew more about this treatment. They shook their heads no. "In any event, we have no other medications. As the earth went through major changes, so did humans especially concerning their health. They became very resistant to viruses, bacteria, and germs." She coughed; to clear her throat? "As I said, humans were very resistant and the invasive microscopic organisms that were life-threatening in the past mutated and did not have the same effect during Dr. Reinhart's reign." She saw that my mouth was twisted in disbelief, so she went further. "These microscopic organisms lived in perfect symbiosis with humans."

The Governor picked up the discussion from there. "The only real treatments administered to humans were those necessary to repair injuries and that was easy with non-invasive surgery. Invasive surgery still existed, but was exceptional. In any event, we believed, that a chemical imbalance in the programmed human was the principle cause of their bypassing the visual receptor. We decided to use these chemicals to establish a prior chemical balance in these humans. It worked in many cases, including yours."

"You took an enormous risk!" I virtually screamed, as I threw my hands wildly up in the air. "You didn't correct any chemical imbalance in me. I was never connected to the visual receptor again. I didn't need that treatment at all. These drugs could have been contaminated. We all could have died." The use of these chemicals was both irresponsible and appalling. I wondered whether I would have problems in the future.

"Oh, Pamela, your hysteria should be directed towards what is happening right now." Gordon tried to grab my hand and I backed off. "In any event, if the chemicals didn't work, the subject was terminated. The chemicals gave them the chance to live longer if their systems readjusted. I don't see why you are so angry with that, you survived."

"This is too disgusting for words." I folded my arms and legs to send them a message. There was no reaction, so I continued. "I gather that you were being honest when you told me that there is no pharmacy here either." Even though my question was directed to Gordon, Flanders spoke up. The Group of 5 was taking turns answering, probably to confuse me.

"Well, we do have biologists studying diseases that existed in the past." Flanders huffed a bit. "But, we do not have the chemicals to make pharmaceutical products. Many of the chemical components used in drugs disappeared. And, as Dr. Gordon and the Governor pointed out, humans had become more resistant so drug production was neither a priority nor a necessity during Dr. Reinhart's time."

"So, what did you give Jonathan?" I asked Gordon and this time she answered.

"Exactly what I told you I gave him. I just gave him a fruit pill." She responded stiffly.

So she didn't lie; at least not that time, I thought to myself.

I turned my attention to Crawford. "So you killed Dr. Reinhart and this is the world you created." I shook my head and snickered as close as possible to his indifferent, removed eyes.

"We created the world that she wanted." Crawford added with contrived detachment as he looked away, feigning boredom.

"You created the world you needed. You know that you need us to invent, to create and to develop superiority in science." I repeated. "When did you discover that you needed us?"

"You want the truth, Pamela, but it is not always easy to accept the truth. As you are so sure of yourself, I'll tell you," Dr. Gordon replied. "We realized that there were overriding programs that prevented us from making independent decisions, even in face of world disaster. You can imagine how alarming that was."

"So what did you do?"

Dr. Crawford took the initiative to explain. "We acted logically and went to the chief android engineer, Dr. Drager and asked him to suppress those programs so that the android community could take charge. The humans on the board and those who participated in the General Assemblies in the legislative Branch were unable to take control. The lower class was determined to destroy everyone and everything in their path to win. In addition, our android army was inadequate." He took a deep breath. "The humans needed a leader. But no one among them was willing to replace Dr. Reinhart, not even those who had opposed her at the last and fatal meeting, like Dr. Murdoc. Those who lived in other districts returned home and left the capital a nightmare. Dead bodies were everywhere. Members of the lower class were in a killing frenzy, destroying everything in their paths…other humans, buildings, monuments, homes and bridges, and the list goes on and on."

"So what did the chief engineer Dr. Drager do?"

"He refused to cancel the programs by emphasizing and warning that if he tried to suppress the programs we would shut down permanently. We didn't agree. As a result, his sincerity has always been considered. . .dubious. "

I interrupted to tell Crawford that Drager was right. The program did not allow for any adaption. Reinhart was very cautious. She believed that machines, no matter how sophisticated, remained a potential threat to humans. "You should have trusted him." I said remembering that famous shut down session that I attended. "Is that why you wanted me to be present when you went through a routine overhaul of Gordon?"

"It is improper to call that an overhaul. I am not just any piece of machinery. I am the embodiment of a brilliant woman." Dr. Gordon interjected contemptuously.

I sighed showing just how much I believed that while she went on to explain that it was necessary for her to go through that session because the rest of the group believed that she had become far too attached to me. I interrupted her and mentioned that I understood the theatrics of that moment. She and the others were obviously testing my loyalty.

Dr. Gordon placed her hands on the table, her eyes flashing shades of red. "We, the Group of 5, as you refer to us, were acting together; and, yes, we were hoping for the return of Dr. Reinhart." She forced a smile and added. "And, we have done just that!"

I ignored her remarks, left her to retreat from me, as she moved back into a position of attention, and I returned to the previous discussion. "Well, anyway, what did you do after the engineer refused?" I asked, desperately searching for more answers before the others arrived.

"We gathered up the fertilized eggs, the sperm and the eggs of the most brilliant scientists and left for this center. We gave instructions to the android army leaders to join us as soon as the situation was under control." Dr. Flanders was back on the scene.

"That is not true, you did something first; you know you did." I stopped, imagining the whole gory scene. "You all, Jarod, Fleming, Crawford, Gordon, Miller, Flanders and Venderkof, met as a group to find a way to set off the bomb. Yes, admit it; it was a bomb that Reinhart had planted in the Earth's core that destroyed the world."

Before I could say more, Dr. Miller jumped in. "We killed them! We had too! We did not intend to kill them, at least not in the beginning, but it happened, because of their insolence. We explained to frightened intellectuals, cowering in the confines of their homes, that we should all, meaning the elite intellectuals and us, the superior android creations, go to this and other centers. That was our only way to survive and fight against anarchy. There was no way to calm the anger of the lower class and there was no way to win an armed conflict. The risk of having a world ruled by intellectual misfits would be catastrophic for everyone regardless of their social status. The intellectuals would end up their slaves and we, the androids, would be forced to perform menial tasks, to serve them. However, those in power were reluctant and paralyzed with fear at the same time as they were caught up with a sense of irrational morality. They adopted far too late the proposal on which Dr. Reinhart had called for a vote. They wanted to negotiate with the rebels and help them to live better lives. It was absurd since they were already living in a better situation than they had ever lived in before."

"So, you killed Landau and Firste and then used their body parts, like you did Reinhart's, to press the button." I finished this sad story.

"We had to transport the intellectual android elites before the explosion." Miller avoided answering my last assertion. "It was difficult. We had many items that we could not leave behind. You cannot imagine how difficult this was for us. Pressure was mounting and we were focused on the difficult burden we bore to save the human race." She insisted.

At this point, the other humans, who had been waiting and listening behind the door, barged in. "We should shut them down forever, explode them in pieces." I recognized Peter's voice.

"I wish that we could, but we can't." I answered sadly.

"Do you see, Pamela, they are all here. We are complete." Gordon interrupted.

"What are you talking about?" I screamed at Gordon who was getting on my nerves. I didn't know exactly why my admiration and confidence in her was breaking down so fast.

"All your team, we have given them back to you." I looked at her in awe and she started to read off the list:

Dr. Stuart Rever, Aeronautical engineer and expert in Martial arts.

Dr. Randolph Murdoc, Nuclear Physicist

Dr. John Gunther, Telecommunications and Computer Engineer

Dr. Sarah Brown and Dr. Ruth Fielding, Geneticists.

Dr. Mathieu Le Clerc, Mining and Civil Engineer

Dr. Isabel Radcliff, Engineer specialized in Military Defense systems and weaponry.

Dr. Mathilda Vernon, Psychiatrist

Dr. Benjamin Davis and Dr. Stanislas Borsky, Bio-chemical and bio-technical engineers

Dr. Diana Ming, Engineer in Air, land and sea transporters and Marine Biologist

And, last but not least, Dr. Peter Feragan, Engineer specialized in bio-chemistry and bio-physics, with a sub-specialization in human surgical practices and astro-physics."

She continued unabashed, "Not to mention, that we, the group of 5, are capable of assisting you, as did our human counterparts: Dr. Victoria Gordon, Dr. Edward Flanders, Dr. Rudolph Crawford, Dr. Agnes Miller and Dr. Eugene Venderkof (the Governor)."

I had to flash a reluctant smile, pushed by something inside me; but it was true that all those with whom Reinhart had confidence, whose ability and creativity were beyond reproach, were present.

"And, Jonathan?"

"Yes, Jonathan Craig, Musician, Actor, Composer."

Of course, Jonathan was one of my closest friends. How could I have forgotten that? I wondered.

"Ferdinand?"

461

The Governor spoke up. "Yes, Ferdinand Hakim, that strange man, driven by a pathetic dream to create equality among humans, is an Historian and Politician." He stopped a moment. "But Ralph, the man Ferdinand pulled out of the termination center, I never heard of him." He looked at the other members of the group who knew nothing about him either.

I stood dumbstruck, because of the Reinhart inside of me, by these revelations. I could feel her strong attachment to the entire group.

"We can help you," Crawford said enthusiastically, as he broke into my thoughts, "if you help us, Pamela."

I turned away from them and looked at our shabby group. They were war torn and I wanted to help them before anything else. "What is happening?"

"The android soldiers are inactive, some of them in pieces, like those over there should be." John was pointing in the direction of the Group of 5.

"The other humans?" I asked.

"Some of them bypassed their receptors during the conflict. We don't know where all of them are. Others were in sound proof rooms and they have no idea that there is a change of the guard here."

"Did you and Stuart have time to explain our concerns about how and when to override their programming?" I was speaking to Randolph.

"No! We had no time to talk. Everything happened so fast. The others were waiting for us when we arrived in the transport terminal. Ferdinand knew where the weapons were stored and it was not difficult for us to operate them. Laser beams and ninja giants that Diana and Stuart got off on. They were our inspiration and guiding force to take down our enemies. I had fun firing." Randolph went on to explain enthusiastically, obviously impressed with their combat skills.

"However, Sarah and Ruth are now reminding us over and over again about the need to protect the programmed humans." John added.

"Diana can you keep an eye on those 5 androids while I bring the others up-to-date on what I have learned? We shall fill you in later, ok?" There was no question that Diana was a trooper and would never let me down.

"I have no problem with that," she said smiling. "One move and I shall be happy to blast them all to bits."

"You heard that?" I asked the Group of 5 and they nodded.

I turned to leave when Gordon called out to me. "I am sorry to tell you this, but it is important anyway. Before we came into this meeting we turned off the artificial uteruses and emitted a toxic gas in the children's section. The only humans alive now are adults." I turned and raised my hand, ready to charge. I wanted to crush her. I was certain that she could see my anger exploding inside of me, but she didn't stop. "We also terminated everyone over the age of 21 before you started your attack. We informed the leaders of the other 2 centers who preferred more drastic procedure. They terminated all life forms under their control both inside and outside the centers. All androids, except Jarod and Fleming, shut down." She turned her back to me and added, "You should take this information into account in defining your next strategy."

Peter grabbed my arm and pulled me out of the room. How many people are left was the question running through my mind. I envisaged no more babies, no more children, just a small group of young adults, some of whom have already gone mad with deprogramming. Moisture flooded my eyes in disbelief. I felt so helpless and guilty. I didn't stop them from this senseless slaughter, not to mention we needed those humans.

"Don't let them touch anything, Diana and if they as much as move a finger. . ." I screamed as Peter closed door.

I heard at least part of her reply before the door closed, "No problem. I can't think of anything I'd rather do than…"

We went into another room where we put together a rapid short-term strategy. They were worried, like me, about the consequences for the deformed humans. Jonathan promised to intervene to ameliorate the impact of their situation on them and others. It was agreed that Sarah and Ruth were the most competent to deal with the psychological problems and that Jonathan and Stanislas should accompany them to the sound proof room. Benjamin, Peter and Randolph agreed to track down the humans who bypassed the visual receptors and take them to the infirmary.

"Don't worry, Pamela, we shall reproduce like humans should reproduce." Peter whispered in my ear before embracing me passionately and then rushing off with the others.

"Mathieu and I can organize a clean-up committee." Isabel suggested and I heard Ferdinand and Ralph offer their support.

Mathilda offered to go back and check on our children. The children were hidden in the transport center. Frederic, already close to 3 years old, and Samuel 6 and Rebecca 8 were the only children left.

John, Stuart and I were now alone. We agreed, as others did later, that we could not destroy the Group of 5. They were useful. They could also help us to reactivate the other centers.

"We need to explore this planet?" Stuart said enthusiastically. "There are others out there. I know, you told me, Pamela, about Jason. He met other groups." He started to laugh and slap his legs. "We will find them!"

"Yes, of course, we shall continue to look; but you heard what they said. Apart from our outside communities all the others have been destroyed. "Bastards, I said to myself; a word that meant nothing to me, even though I mimicked Randolph and used it often. I noticed though that it certainly meant something to the Dr. Reinhart deep inside me. "I still need more information. I need to know some other things about what the androids did."

"Will they tell you?" John asked.

"Only one way to find out." I said as I headed for the door. The androids had not moved an inch since we left. Diana continued to stand guard as I started my questioning.

They were quite cooperative; of course they had no choice with the savage Diana salivating in their face. When I asked them what year it was, they told me that they were not certain themselves what year it was.

Dr. Gordon responded. "We understood that the earth was devastated by the explosion. A clean-up crew of androids was sent out to disintegrate any remaining life forms and everything that was constructed by humans. The earth was cleansed of all life forms and structures, as they put it. Nonetheless, these androids did collect and store in the center objects, like books, art work, music, clothes that, by their programming were important to have for future generations." I mused, "That accounted for the fact that we dressed up elegantly for the concerts we gave using real instruments."

"And?" I insisted.

Dr. Gordon continued, "When the land was bare and the horizons barren, the clean-up groups returned to the centers they came from. They were to test the air regularly and release cleansing gases every 6 months to improve its quality."

The Governor took up from there. "We, the Group of 5 and our support staff shut down voluntarily awaiting a wake-up call from the clean-up staff the moment the air was able to support human life. So, the earth was starting to recover when we woke up. No one cared about the time continuum. There was no real need to calculate the number of years that might have gone by. Human history had ended and android history was beginning. Androids, unlike humans, have no effective relationship with time and could not even give a reasonable guess. The decision to recreate human life was agreed to by the direction of the various centers, as well as the decision to keep humans living inside. There were many generations of humans before you and they left behind them the formulas, the research, the art and music and other discoveries that corresponded to a given period in human history. We patiently trained and educated humans waiting for them to catch up to where Dr. Reinhart left off." I let him continue this long monologue.

"The major problem was the apathy of all the humans." Dr. Gordon picked up the dialogue.

"Different solutions were recommended and followed; all of which were focused on stimulating creative thinking in humans. It didn't change anything. Humans remained happy and cooperative, but completely disinterested and incapable of independent thought. They were like happy machines who carried out their assignments and nothing more." Dr. Gordon said she was the one who focused on emotions as an incentive to creativity and was severely criticized for a long time. She added that when Ferdinand, who expelled a certain inquisitiveness even before bypassing his programming, and reminded us of his progenitor, her theory seemed more credible.

I asked her, and looked at the others for confirmation regarding why they decided to terminate Ferdinand. She and the others scoffed at the question.

Dr. Miller then continued the discussion, explaining that Ferdinand, in his younger years, was an exact replica, not physically but intellectually, of Elisabeth's husband, the one whose body was mutilated and sent back in boxes. "Strangely enough, Ferdinand was equally obsessed with equality among humans and went about trying to inform all humans of their real life situation. As you were programmed, you did not understand anything that he was telling you; something that must have profoundly frustrated him. He was preaching revolutionary principles, trying to incite riots and revolt. Surprisingly, his programing was still functioning up until the moment when he was carried out of the orchestra pit. We were astounded by this revelation, which, of course, did not change our position regarding his living amongst other humans. We Androids found him to be a real threat to the security of the center and so we decided to get rid of him." It was evident that they were not happy to see that he had survived. "In the meantime, we wondered if the programming, the visual receptors were well adapted to the last few generations of humans. Bypassing the visual receptor was happening more often." She paused, her robotic body in motion. "John was appreciated by the androids so they were willing to let him take his little group outside to see how humans would react on their own."

I asked if they knew anything about the tunneling. No, they had no idea that humans were burrowing through walls and opening a tunnel into the center. No, they never imagined that the humans were doing anything other than sitting, looking out on a barren land.

Yes, they were enthusiastic when they saw groups of humans exploring the outskirts of the center. Yes, they were confused to see that no one tried to leave the area definitively. Yes, they were interested in Jason's visit, but then they reminded me that he was one of the humans who participated in the experimental project on suspended animation. The Reinhart in me appreciated the absurdity of the situation, while my Pamela side found it utterly depressing.

No, they were not convinced that humans were able to return to productive, creative lives.

They confirmed that when I bypassed my programming, Gordon convinced the others that my genetic make-up might be the key to turning humans around. I showed more emotions than any of the others; even those on the outside, who seemed austere and empty. I was to be the catalyst. The result was visibly disastrous as my presence made no apparent change in the routine lives of the outside community.

They then explained to me that Stuart and I had the same parentage. Flanders was happy to say, "Dr. Reinhart was also Stuart's biological mother and a certain, Cameron Davis, a human that died before the Reinhart era but whose sperm had been frozen for future use was his and your biological father. We found this genetic combination promising, as both Cameron and Elisabeth were the most renowned intellectuals of all the time."

That information left me a bit speechless. Stuart and I were like brother and sister because we had a natural kind of sibling rivalry. "Why didn't you download Reinhart's programming into Stuart?"

Flanders answered. "It was impossible, because Reinhart had given strict instructions. Stuart, we believed was still under the programming. And, even if he wasn't, which we now have to admit was the case, Dr. Reinhart only wanted her programming to be given to a woman. That was why you were the logical choice."

Gordon spoke up. "I knew that Stuart had bypassed his programming for years and more or less confirmed that with the Governor," who nodded, "several months ago now." She smiled as she watched Flanders' eyes flash colors of red in reaction to her derogatory remark.

"Why then didn't you give him Reinhart, as his last name?" I asked, out of curiosity.

"Oh," Flanders spoke up. "We reserved the last name, Reinhart, for her female descendant...You. Of course, we could have called him Dr. Stuart Davis; and maybe we should have done that. Nonetheless, as you must have sensed, the name Stuart Rever did not disturb Dr. Reinhart." He gave me the time to mull that over before continuing. "Elisabeth admired the achievements of Dr. Stuart Rever and often times referred back to some of his ideas. He died before her time, but his genius lived on."

"Yes," I replied pensively, "she likes having Stuart Rever living amongst us, even if it is only in name." I sighed and then continued with my questioning.

"Why did you keep me a prisoner in this Center?"

"To more closely study your emotional development. That should be evident." Flanders replied. "By the way we were aware of your intimate relationship with Dr. Gordon." He then went on to explain that even though Dr. Gordon was convinced that she could build a more complex emotional structure by interacting with me, they all knew that logically this was impossible.

"Why then did you download Reinhart in me and not one of the other Pamela series?" I had an idea, but was not yet certain.

"It didn't work for us, as we had anticipated." Flanders' words showed his disdain.

The Governor who sat listening attentively broke in. "You, Pamela, are the closest we have ever come to bringing back Elisabeth. You might not understand how important it is for us to find her. She understood us and respected us and would have helped us to achieve our objective."

"What objective?" I asked. They did not answer, so I gave them some time to consider cooperating with me, while I pondered the situation. "I was very curious about what they ultimately wanted. I thought that what they needed was for us to be productive. We were now emotionally complete and those negative emotions that they wanted to suppress, like competitiveness, jealousy, envy, rage, anger, and so forth were back in place. I understood that our being happy all the time led to intellectual inertia. Humans needed the good and bad sides of their emotional structure to be creative. So, their first objective, to stimulate research and catch up with the Reinhart era, was assured. Their second objective, trying to cajole Dr. Reinhart to reinstall a complete emotional configuration was not going to be easy. And yet, they seemed confident that she would do that. I now realized that getting back a complete emotional structure was the necessary last step to attaining their ultimate objective; whatever that was."

The fact that they refused to answer meant that I would have to discover that myself. I still had one card to play but I needed to verify something first. I turned to Diana and asked her to continue to stand guard while we went off to explore the inner circle.

I dashed out of that office and at the first possible occasion slipped through the wall entering the inner circle. I knew where to look. It was there, everything that I needed, with well-defined instructions that any competent robotic engineer could easily follow.

Diana was surprised to see me reappear so fast. It was evident that she enjoyed keeping the androids under control and that she would have liked to have had a bit more time alone with them.

I smiled at Diana and mentioned that her services were not over. I asked Dr. Miller to follow me and we entered into the small padded cell where Flanders had received me on many occasions.

"Do you want a body?" I didn't think that hedging words would be productive, as I had already offered that before. This time she nodded approvingly and then added that unfortunately it was impossible.

"No, everything that I need to give you back your graceful android form is available." I smiled, as if that would affect her. It didn't arouse a reaction. She just stood staring at me. That made me uncomfortable, so I continued. "I located the substance, a plant; the material is well preserved and ready for use, to cover your robotic body. And, I also have all the robotic parts. But, I want something from you first."

"What do you want?" she asked.

"I want you to tell me what the true objective of your group is?"

"I am not programmed to do that. You will have to ask one of the others." She was spinning around so I knew that she was not being honest. I had no doubts now that they could lie. But, she seemed to be more bothered by it. I would have to look into her programming at one point. Perhaps she was given a more complex emotional configuration than I thought. She interrupted my thoughts by mentioning that she would be willing to be our guinea pig for our robotic engineer and for studies in android anatomy.

I didn't have time to negotiate with her as I had other matters to attend to. I decided to hedge my words or my feelings. "I have made you an offer; an offer which I have no intention of repeating at some later date. Did you give me your final decision?"

"I can't tell you what you want to know. You should be able to deduce it." She stopped and stood her ground, as if she wanted me to know just how much in control she could be. "The group, myself included, and whether you believe it or not, have enough of an emotional structure to be frustrated and annoyed. We don't like playing people games."

"What are you suggesting?"

"I am telling you that we developed emotionally beyond the limits of our programed parameters."

I knew that that was impossible but saw no reason why I should get into a discussion over that. They obviously needed to believe that they were getting close to passing over into another world. "So…" I put my hand up to my mouth and drew it down toward my chin, a gesture that I developed very recently. The time it took for my hand to draw my lips together and relax its grip near my chin seemed to be the time that I needed to collect my thoughts. I imagined that it must have been something that Reinhart did. I understood too well what the objective was. I stared viciously into her squinting android eyes to confirm my convictions. I laughed a Reinhart laugh, which I noticed jolted her a bit, and then let a radiant smile appear on my face, before I bit down on my lower lip and said. "See you in surgery tomorrow. I have an engineer who I have confidence in." I was thinking about Peter. I turned to walk away and then added, "You are lucky that we understand each other and I won't change any of your programming."

I left the room and wandered off to where about 30 young humans were waiting to be deprogrammed. I could see that at least half of the group came from the wrong sperm and egg bank combination. I looked at Ruth, Sarah, Jonathan and Stanislas who were unable to interact with the group. The young ones didn't even sense their presence. They would soon be hungry and we would have to feed them and send them back to their cubicles. We didn't even know who they were. "We shall have to get their codes down soon. We have to continue the daily routine." I was saying all of this as if it made sense.

"But, can't you just ask the Group of 5 for help on this?"

"It is not so easy, Jonathan. I don't know that we want to work or even if we can work with them." I said in a low, unanimated voice. "Giving our codes to these programmed humans might simplify things for the moment. They will see us and follow us into the dining room. But, their codes for the food boxes?"

"There must be a reader somewhere. The androids would not have bothered to download everything." Ruth suggested.

"Of course, just a minute I'll try to find it." The four of us seemed to be thinking the same thing. Before I could take a step, I knew where it was. Reinhart was getting stronger and stronger. It was so obvious. "Grab that control on the wall."

"What? That black stick?" Jonathan already had it in his hand.

"We need to mark the names and activity."

"We don't need to record anything, I have a photographic memory, Pamela." Sarah came forward. "We can handle this now. Once we have the code we will get the food that goes with their numbers."

"You know how that works?" I asked excitedly.

"No, but Diana does. You'll have to send her back."

"And, leave the group alone." I shook my head. "It's ok, I'll get Peter to replace her.

I left the hospital center. Randolph, Peter and Benjamin were there. They had 5 young men under control.

"That's it. The others didn't make it." Randolph said.

I didn't comment on that. It was depressing. "Did you see Mathieu and Isabel? They left with Ralph to clean things up."

"They have a lot of work." Peter started up. "A lot of androids shut down, permanently, I hope. And, unfortunately there are a lot of bodies to dispose of. We were going to bring the bodies to the termination center." He looked at me with surprise and disgust.

"What is the matter?"

"Well, quite frankly, do you know what happens in that termination center?"

I did, but I was not ready to comment. So I shook my head with a firm no. "Peter or Randolph, I need one of you to stand guard over the androids. The others need Diana to get the food distributed to the programmed group."

"I'll go, Pamela." Randolph moved forward. "Why don't you take a couple minutes to check on the children, you and Peter?"

"Thank you, Randolph." I grabbed Peter's hand and we left for the transport unit. "Did you see John and Stuart?"

"We ran into them. I think that they were looking for you. Stuart told me that he was going to let John into the inner circle to see the equipment."

My heart stopped with that news. I didn't understand why. It was normal for John to see the equipment. "Did they mention which part of the inner circle?"

"Are you worried?" Peter seemed surprised.

"No." I insisted. "Just curious."

"You don't trust John?"

"Of course I trust him. After all he negotiated the departure of his group with the Governor, and he arranged for comfortable living conditions for everyone over the years. And, today, he led his group back inside to bring down android control." When I finished I knew where my doubt was coming from and why. It was Reinhart; future leadership seemed to be her problem.

"But, he is one of us." Peter seemed sure of himself.

"You are right." I smiled in agreement. "I will still have to watch him closely," I mused privately…

Then I saw little Frederic running towards us. I grabbed Frederic and swung him around.

"We are free now, my little love. We are free to be human. And, you can learn and play like a child should." He was laughing and clapping his hands. I knew that he didn't understand, but he would one day.

I showed Peter and Mathilda how they could get into the inner circle. I knew that the children were hungry and thirsty. I tenderly kissed my little family and told them that I would be back soon.

I had one more thing to say to that Group of 5. When I arrived Randolph told me that they were as gentle as children. I knew better.

The first thing I asked them to do was to move to the other side of the table. I took my place in the high backed chair with Randolph by my side and looked at them. I knew that they understood that I was the one in control.

"Dr. Miller will soon join your ranks with a real android body." I announced and to my satisfaction I saw that Gordon did not applaud the news along with the others.

"We are going to need your services with the 35 young people in our care." I started off. "They are still programmed and our intention is to deprogram them one at a time." They nodded in agreement as if that made any difference to me. "But, as you have been caring for us, your participation in this would be very helpful."

"You have our full cooperation." The Governor spoke for the group.

"I would like to set up a meeting over the next few days with the androids from the other two centers."

"No problem. But, only Fleming and Jarod are still active. Do you want us to order the reactivation of the others?" The Governor spoke again.

"No way; in fact, I might have to order some of the androids here at this center be shutdown. Nonetheless, Fleming and Jarod could be useful." They sat without moving, with android patience. "By the way, I'm going to suggest to our group that we name Ferdinand as our political leader. His job will be to set up a government. He has studied our history, culture and system of governance and has a real sense of justice. I believe that he understands the need for humans to work together in a democratic environment. In that regard, Dr. Venderkof, you are hereby officially relieved of your position as Governor of this center. You can also forget about your high commission as well."

"Agreed." He said and then mumbled under his breath that there never was a high commission.

"Another lie?"

"No. We all met, but only to discuss Gordon's experiment."

I took a deep breath and shook my head. It was not going to be easy at all to reclaim our history; but, it was ridiculous to believe that we could do it completely on our own terms. We needed their help and they knew it. I also realized that I had trusted Gordon a bit too much and that she had made a fool out of me. Now, I wanted to know just how much of a fool I had been so that I would be more alert, more cautious, when dealing with these androids in the future.

"Dr. Gordon, did you enjoy studying me?" I threw out this question. She seemed surprised but nodded emphatically, her android head bobbing up and down.

"Is it true then the first act of your theatrical production opened the moment you and Crawford visited me in the hospital?" She looked at Crawford who looked at me.

"You were our group project, Pamela." Crawford began. "Yes, we wrote the script, if you like, but, you modified it a bit too often." He stopped to collect his thoughts. "Why don't we just say that we're where we are today thanks to our mutual cooperation?"

I started to laugh. "Well then let's say that we must continue our mutual cooperation based upon honesty, this time, at least for a while." I turned to Randolph and said: "We can all start now. I think that we can trust them to help us." His face showed hesitation, but he relaxed his grip on the gun and set it on the top of the table.

"You all agree the war is over?" I slowly looked around a room full of nods.

"The war is over, I gather." Randolph said and heads bobbed again.

Randolph left the room first, which was what I was hoping for. That gave me the opportunity to make one last remark, which I thought would assure the complete cooperation and dedication of those androids to the human community. But, when I stated confidently, "By the way, it was easy to deduce. I know what your ultimate objective is." They did not give me the response I was expecting.

Instead, they said in perfect harmony. "We are so glad to have you back...................
DR. ELISABETH REINHART."

THE END

Patricia Lee Strunk

Ms. Strunk grew up in a poor, working class neighbourhood, in a small town in Pennsylvania where she dreamed about becoming an astronaut. Instead, Ms. Strunk became a lawyer. She holds an LL.M. Degree in « International Business Law » from the "London School of Economics," a Master Degree in "Comparative Law" from "L'Institut de Droit Comparé, Paris" and a "Juris Doctor Degree" from "Duquesne University School of Law." She is also a member of the California and Pennsylvania Bars. Patricia spent the greater part of her legal career in academia and had the privilege of being a Lecturer in Law with distinguished French Law Faculties like, "L'Université de Paris Ouest-La Défense, Nanterre," "L'Université de Paris 1, Sorbonne," among others and many institutes of – education, like "L'institut de Droit Comparé" and "L'Institut d'Etudes Politiques" (Science Po, Paris). Ms. Strunk never completely forgot childhood ambitions and fascination with science. **Pamela Series 13** reflects her academic interest in Bio-Ethical and Environmental Law, as well as her overwhelming support and advocacy of Scientific Research at all levels.